THULSA'S GATE

ROBERT SCHULTZ

Schultz, Robert, 1961-
Thulsa's Gate: a novel/ by Robert Schultz – 1st edition
RJS Publishing

ISBN-13: 978-0-9960448-0-6
Cover by Anina Laird Swallow
Titling by Kathryn Leslie Stone

Summary: Members of a salvage company get more than they bargained for when they search for a World War II bomber that went down in 1945 during a freak storm over the Teton Mountains in Wyoming and Idaho. Having stumbled through an inter-dimensional portal, they must fight their way back home to their own planet and time before the storm that brought them to the alien world, is gone.

A note from the Author

This story was actually written back in the summer of 1982. Sophomoric and very sarcastic, it was poorly written. Character development was next to non-existent and descriptions were like a quick conversation in passing. But it did have a good plot idea. While this is a work of fiction, the two main characters are designed around two very real people. How they are portrayed is how I remembered them, especially the heroine.

Actually, I've done this before. I was 17 when I did it, but it has been done before. While this adventure isn't my first work of novel writing, it is the first one that I have seriously tried to push to print. I am so grateful for the modern tools of computers used to publish this work. The internet has made this affordable.

After I originally wrote this story, I buried it and it was never supposed to see the light of day. It had remained hidden, packed away in a box of other writing projects for 30 years until my grown up sons were going through the box and found it. I read it to them, as it was only about 35 pages long hand written. They got a kick out of it, and then it promptly went back in the box. But as it did so, I told my youngest son that someday it needed to be transcribed into digital format for safe keeping. Little did I know the chain of events that statement would set in motion.

Unbeknownst' to me, my son retrieved the manuscript and attempted to do the transcribing himself so that he could present it as a Christmas present. With the help of his two sisters, it was transcribed, printed and presented as a gift for Christmas, 2011. What a wonderful thoughtful act on his part. After reading through it again the following January, thoughts began to flood my head about how I could really make this a wonderful story. Several of the "big" important scenes played out in my head over and over until I realized that I had to write it all down, and so in mid-February 2012, I began.

This has been a wonderful ride for me and even after it was completed and I have laughed and cried with the characters, I find that I miss them. I miss being with them in this adventure and experiencing every thought and emotion as they have. I did not think it possible to think this way about characters in a book. The wonder of a book is that you can go back through and experience it again and again, whenever you want. I might just have to write another one just so I can spend time with them again, through another adventure.

Scientific theories vary from one person to the next. If you've opened this story hoping for facts and get all caught up in the science which isn't there, then you've missed the point and the story won't be much fun for you. The idea here is to spark the reader's imagination and let them draw their own conclusions, whether it's factual or not. After all it is a work of fiction! Don't ruin it by trying to argue facts into it. Just enjoy the ride.

One other thing, for all you airplane nuts, specifically, war bird experts. I realize there might be some errors. I will apologize for them now and encourage you to see how it could be done instead of how it really was. I tried my best to describe WWII bombers and how things were back in 1945. The B-25 J Mitchell bomber is my favorite and I have tried to get it as accurate as I could with the information I had available to me. I didn't want to get too detailed as the majority of the readers will never have the chance to see or know of such detail, and most of them couldn't care less. Now, get in there and have at it!

Preface

Idaho 1940

"Dad?" Catrina Dallas hedged a bit. "Mom said you're going off to war."

"Yes sweetie, I am. Do you know what war is?"

"Yes, mom explained it to me. Why do you have to go?"

"Well, I don't exactly have to go, I want to go."

"But why? Why not stay home with mom and me?"

Tony had to think a while on this one. How do you put this so a five year old can understand it? Because of his age, he wasn't eligible for the draft and in the opening years of the war, many older men were volunteering because of their principles. But he wanted to be there, fighting for the freedoms of those who could not fight. Ultimately, this would transpose to the protection of himself and his family. Perhaps someday, others would have to fight for him and his family, so he needed to pay it forward. His age and flying abilities would keep him clear of direct combat, but assigned to underlying cargo flights; the engine that kept the fighting force operational.

"Because I want to protect you and your mother from the bad men that are trying to take away the freedoms of others."

"You'll be gone for a long time, won't you?"

"Yes, but I'll be able to come home and visit every so often, and I'll get to write letters. I better be for getting letters from you young lady. I know you can write pretty good."

"Can I write every day?" Tony let a soft chuckle go.

"Let's just try for every week, ok?"

"Ok."

"Enough talk about all this war stuff," Tony said, trying to redirect his daughter's attention skyward. "How 'bout Orion tonight? Sure is bright, eh?"

Looking up into the midnight Idaho sky, Catrina let her eyes dance from one star cluster to another as her father pointed to yet another constellation. Snuggling in a little closer to him, she lay in her warm sleeping bag looking out the front of their canvas tent. Directly next to them was her dad's airplane. They had flown into Johnson Creek, Idaho earlier that afternoon to camp and fish. She could still smell the smoldering camp fire occasionally popping, though the flames had died out some time ago. She followed the milky band of clustered stars from horizon to horizon, trying to imagine the earth's positioning relative to the band in the sky.

"So how would you know if you're right side up or upside down?" she asked, still trying to figure it all out. Her father let out a syllabled chuckle and focused on what his daughter was looking at.

"You really can't know for sure. I guess only God knows for sure." Tony turned his head a little bit to try and match the angle that Cat was using and where she was looking.

"Well, why can't we know?"

"Well, we sort of know for the most part, we're either upside down or right side up when it comes to looking at our own galaxy. But think about it this way. If we were down at the farthest tip of South America, would we be upside down or right side up?"

Cat thought a moment; her dad could almost hear the wheels turning in her head.

"Depends on the seasons."

Now how did she come up with that answer? She is five years old for crying out loud! Tony grinned broadly and turned on his side, watching his little girl gaze up at the infinance of space. She was so smart that sometimes it was hard to stay ahead of her. He was going to have to go back to college just to remain the parent and he'd have to drag her mother with him. Amanda hadn't even had the chance to attend college. He had sort of derailed those plans when they got married, but he had always maintained that someday, when they could afford it, he'd see that she got a college education.

"Oh you think you're so smart," Tony yawned, watching her eyes in the darkness. Even on a moonless night such as this, you could see so many things once your eyes got used to the light of the stars. He could actually see the star band of the Milky Way in the reflections of Catrina's shiny eyes.

"It just makes sense, doesn't it?"

"Yes, it does make sense, but it's always a little more complicated than that."

"What's complicated?" she fumbled through the word a little. She had heard it before a couple of times, but never got around to having her parents explain it to her.

"Means hard to solve, or something has more than one piece to it."

"So what's complicated about the stars?"

Tony started to answer her, but then stopped. He understood that she was smarter than your average 5 year old, but maybe he was trying to complicate things too much to match her. Actually, in her sharp little mind, her train of thought was running along a completely different course to that of her father. He was thinking that she wanted to know how it all worked. She was always asking how it all worked, forever curious and craving the knowledge of how and why. This time, nothing could be further from the truth. She wasn't after how the stars were made, what they were and how far away they were. At this point in her little mind, she wanted to know something entirely different.

"Aren't they just other planets?"

"Well, pick one," Tony directed, scanning the skies. Catrina passed a glance at her dad, then pointed at a bright spec in the sky.

"Jupiter, you know that," he nudged her. Cat giggled and then fell silent, letting her head sweep from horizon to horizon again. Finally, she stopped, zeroing in on her target.

"That one," she jabbed her finger up like an English Pointer directing a hunter at a hiding quail.

"Sweetheart, you're pointing at a patch of about a billion. Be a little more specific?" Tony instructed grinning.

"Those bunch there that look like a horse's head. Three really bright ones and then the little tiny one, where its eyes should be." Catrina held steadfast to her directions with her finger, locking her eyes on the faint spec of light among the molty array.

Tony tried lining his head up with Cat's, scooting close enough to touch heads together and sight up her arm. He was no astronomer and had no idea. He knew most of the major constellations, but beyond that, he was clueless, but for this particular discussion, he figured that it didn't really matter.

"That one is probably just another star, but it could be a planet. It's hard to tell just by looking at them."

"Do you think that we'll ever know how to tell the difference?"

"With people like you coming into this world, I have no doubt that someday we will."

"I wonder what it's like up there. What's happening on other planets right now?" Catrina's mind whirled up to speed just thinking about it. Was someone on that tiny little spec, lying out under a brilliant night sky looking up, pointing and asking the same questions?

"Wouldn't it be something to be able to go to one of those places to visit?"

Tony thought about it for a while, his eye lids growing heavy and starting to sting a little. Amazing these kids can out last their parents. It was all part of their master plan to take over the galaxy. Run the parents down, lull them to sleep and then take over.

"It would certainly be something," he yawned again, pulling his sleeping bag up around his neck and then closing his side of the tent. "Time for sleeping little one."

Catrina snuggled down in her sleeping bag but held her gaze skyward, steadfast on the faint spec still locked in her vision. Her imagination swept her from reality, her eyes lids dropping closed. She finally pulled her side of the tent closed and buried her face next to her dad. As sleep carried her away, she imagined that somewhere on one of those distant specs in the endless cosmos, another little girl was doing the same thing.

For Maria

THULSA'S GATE

Thulsa's Gate

Tony and Amanda

1934

Anthony "Tony" Dallas flew cargo and mail mainly in the northwest region of the United States. He especially loved flying the back country of the mountains, from southern Utah all the way up to the most northern reaches of Alaska and Canada. He loved the art of flying, and learning to fly anything he deemed as airworthy. He was no daredevil by any means, but he liked his share of thrills, mostly the challenge of flight itself. He viewed every flight he undertook as a challenge and an adventure.

At 25, he was an accomplished pilot and loved to fly just about anywhere. Any day in the air was a good day, well, most of the time. He was methodical about doing things by the book and did them so often they became second nature. He would prep his plane, call ahead and see what the weather was like at the location he was headed to, then take off and hope for the best. Many times he would have to divert to other places, set down at a safe airport or even soldier on through a storm or some sort of bad weather.

One such time he had a head wind so strong that it appeared that he wasn't moving at all, but holding right in place where he was, even with the engine turning at full power. Trying to change altitude to get out of the winds, he dropped lower and lower, inching down next to a two lane highway that had several cars moving along it. One of them was actually going faster than he was. The other was running at about the same speed. This was silly and after finding that there was no way out of the wind, he used up all his fuel reaching a suitable field. He landed alongside the highway near a town and tied it down behind a barn.

He would be stuck here until the wind passed. Where else but in Idaho would you find wind like this? While he was grounded, he made his way into town and found a diner where he could wait out the storm and sat down completely exhausted. It was here that the young pilot's life would change its course forever. Amanda Alice Gardner worked part time at the diner and just happened to be there when Tony stumbled in and plopped down at one of the empty window booths.

"Can anyone tell me what town this is?" he asked loudly, pulling his jacket off and looking around at the mostly empty diner.

He dusted off his short, dark, wavy hair and rubbed the dust from his granite jaw. He was a bit tall and a little wiry, but that was mostly because he was on his own and didn't eat like he should. He was always on the move, going from one cargo job to the next, sometimes camping beside or in his plane more than he did at home in Helena, Montana. He pulled his flight map out and started trying to pinpoint where he was.

"Dubois, Idaho," came the calm reply from a pretty waitress setting a glass of water down on the table in front of him. "What can I get you?" she asked, placing some utensils and a napkin in front of him.

Tony didn't even look up at her, grabbing the glass he started gulping.   The wind had parched him and the cold water was not only welcome, but very soothing.

"Geez-Louise there Texas," Amanda chuckled. "Best slow down there or you'll start leaking from places you didn't know you had."

Tony looked up and froze. He was instantly pulled into her big, beautiful, deep, brown eyes. What in the heck was he looking at? This was like nothing he had ever seen before, or experienced. This woman's big, soft brown eyes just seemed to melt and absorb him right into her.

Amanda was a big girl. She was tall, standing at 6 foot with broad shoulders. A big boned girl to be sure, not overweight, just a big girl. She was chewing gum and holding onto her little note pad wondering if this guy had gotten hit in the head or something before he had come in from the wind.

"Helloooooooo?" she asked smiling. "You ok? You look a little confused." *Yeah, that was an understatement for sure.*

Tony tried to make a sound, but nothing came out and he couldn't take his eyes off hers. Thankfully, there was no waiting going on in the diner, so Amanda just shifted her weight a little and started to enjoy the unintentional attention. Tony finally shook his head a little bit when the clamor of a cardboard box, blowing by in the wind outside, broke the trance those brown eyes had put him under.

"Oh, yes, I'm sorry," he fumbled stupidly, realizing that he must look like a complete idiot. "Yes, ah, you can get me, a little confused...." Tony stammered. "I mean, I'd like to order your burger special."

"Anything to drink with that," Amanda grinned happily. "Maybe try a Coke, coffee or something other than water?"

"Coke would be fine," he replied carefully, scooting the empty water glass back towards the statuesque waitress. "Do you have a place I could wash up a bit?"

Amanda motioned to the restroom doors towards the back of the diner and gave the young pilot a big grin, then turned and headed behind the counter to the order window. Tony carefully got up and made a beeline for the men's restroom, trying desperately not to look back at the waitress. Before he got to the door, he couldn't resist passing her a glance, hoping that he could just look at her for a couple of moments, without feeling like he was leering at her. To his utter embarrassment, she was looking right at him and he quickly ducked behind the restroom door.

Once inside he washed up as best he could and then just stood at the door, afraid to go out. *Who was this woman? She was a vision! The most wonderful thing he had ever seen before. He had dated girls, even kissed them, but one had never had this kind of an effect on him. Holy cow! Her eyes held him absolutely prisoner. That's not to say that the rest of her wasn't pretty, on the contrary. She was amazing in every way. Her eyes, yes definitely the eyes, the mouth, the short dark brown hair, her height. Everything about her was perfect!*

He finally took a deep breath, stepped back out into the diner and took his seat in the front next to the window, this time, without looking in her direction. He kept a close watch for her out of the corner of his eye, and when he knew she wasn't looking, he gazed at her every move, then would strategically look away when he sensed she was about to turn in his direction. Finally, he had no choice but to meet eyes with her when she brought him his order. The food smelled heavenly and the only thing that would have made it perfect was if she were to sit down across from him and talk while he ate. How perfect would that have been? However, she set his order down, emptying the carry platter and then turned back to her work.

"Nuts", he thought to himself watching her disappear back into the kitchen. He pulled the lid off the ketchup bottle and started letting gravity do its work. Watching it slowly run down the bottle opening and out into a pile on his plate next to the fries, he began to think that while he enjoyed life and what he was doing with it, he was in fact, lonely. A sudden longing to share his life with someone, anyone, filled him. The thought had occurred to him that after he was done eating, maybe he ought to go ask that waitress out on a date or something. It appeared that he had plenty of time. The problem there was what do you do in a tumbleweed town like....where was he? Oh yea, somewhere in Idaho.

He looked over as a figure emerged out of the kitchen. To his dismay, it was an older woman. She could have been his mother; she was that old. What happened to the young vision of beauty that had served him? Now he felt really bad. Not only did he not know who she was or where she went, he wouldn't get to give her a tip.

Turning his attention back to his slow moving ketchup, he just sat watching it slowly drip out onto his plate. He was a little weirded out when the waitress came up to the table and sat down across from him. *Ok, this is a little peculiar. Why is an old waitress woman sitting down at my table?* He didn't even look up. He was expecting to get some motherly pep talk about why he was alone and where's home and why was he so far from it. What he got came as a complete shock.

"Someday, they'll make those bottles out of plastic and you'll be able to squeeze the ketchup out."

Tony froze, then slowly looked up into the smiling face of the young waitress that had served him his meal. Completely dumbafied, he carefully looked around the diner at the other few occupants there, none of which seemed to be paying him or his guest any attention at all. Looking back at the waitress, he noticed that she had removed her apron and was just sitting there in her uniform.

"I imagine they'll do that with mustard and a lot of other things as well," she continued, a big grin on her face.

Tony set the bottle of ketchup down and picked up a French fry, dipping it in. He wasn't quite sure what to say or do; he had never experienced this before. Not that she was necessarily being bold, well, she was, but that's not what had taken him so completely off guard. The fact that she was so beautiful and he was so in love with her already had him completely outwitted.

"Is it any good?" she asked, watching him take another bite. "Cause I know the cook, and he'll be perfectly happy to get you some more if that batch isn't any good."

It smelled wonderful, and tasted even better, though he hardly noticed. He finally came alive, it registering that she was not at the wrong table. She was actually sitting right here in front of him and it didn't seem to him like she had any plans to go anywhere else.

"No, no, it's just fine. It's really good. Some of the best I have ever tasted," he said, taking a bunch of fries and dipping them, then taking a bite.

He finally got up enough courage to look directly at her. He hadn't wanted to before, for a number of reasons. One of which was to keep from being held hostage again. However, the thought had occurred to him in the back of his mind that maybe she was every bit as enamored with him as he was with her, so he looked up and engaged her head on. After he had swallowed what he had clumsily stuffed into his mouth, he smiled and made his introductions.

"Tony Dallas, I'm from Helena, Montana, and you are?" he asked, picking up his glass and taking a drink.

"Amanda Gardner, I'm from right here, Dubois."

"Is that where I am?" He grinned broadly, putting down his glass and picking up his hamburger. "Does this have everything on it?" he asked, looking under the bun. "I'm not big on tomatoes."

"You like ketchup don't you?" Amanda came back quickly. "They're made out of tomatoes." Tony pulled the tomato out of his burger and set it on the plate next to his fries.

"That's different." He said, putting the bun back on his burger and taking a big bite out of it.

"Wait, how is that different?"

"Just is," he said with a mouth full. "You don't have any seeds or that awful pulpy tomato texture and they put seasoning in it so it tastes a lot better. That's how it's different."

"Ok, whatever you say. So Mr. Dallas, what brings you through our little town and into Joe's Bar and Grill?"

"Well, to be quite honest," he said, looking around for the bar part of the place. "The wind."

"Okay," Amanda chuckled a bit. "If that's the case, you should be a regular here because that's what we're known for around these parts, wind, oh, and sheep. We have plenty of both."

She let her chin rest comfortably on her hands in front of her settling into the conversation.

"I'm a pilot. I'm on my way to Logan, Utah, from Helena, Montana. Carrying some light cargo for a couple of dairy farms, a cheese factory and some airplane mechanics."

Amanda was now sliding, ever so gracefully right into full focus with Tony. She got so wrapped up in what he was saying that she completely lost track of what was happening around them. As Tony finished his meal, she continued to listen to his talk of flying. They completely lost track of time, allowing the dinner hour to pass and it wasn't until the older waitress came to their table, reminding them it was closing time, did they realized that most of the evening had passed them by while they had just talked and talked.

"Guess I better figure out a place to bed down for the evening," he said, looking out at the empty, windblown streets.

The thought had occurred to Amanda that he could just spend the night at her parent's house, but thoughts of propriety, especially in a small town such as this, quickly knocked that idea out of contention.

"Across the street there's a pretty good hotel and it don't cost too much, if there's a room. Usually is though, and they have a phone there if you need to call someone and let them know you're all right."

Amanda didn't want to let him go, but it wasn't like they could just go out for a walk on the town in the dark. The wind was blowing harder now than when it was daylight.

"Thanks," Tony got up and held out his hand to help her out of her seat. She wasn't sure if it was just a ploy for her to let him hold her hand or just good manners. She didn't care which one it was, and gladly took his hand graciously.

"I need to go check on my plane first."

"I have a car," she jumped in for any chance to prolong their contact together. "I'll drive you out and back."

"That would be great," he smiled appreciatively, both for her kindness and the opportunity to prolong their association.

"Will I see you tomorrow?"

"If the town is still here," she came back, quickly starting for the door, "I'll still be here."

*　　*　　*　　*　　*

The next two days found them inseparable. The wind was still howling, so they were either in the diner, the movie house, or her house, visiting with her folks. Her parents quickly grew fond of Tony and were nervous at the prospect of losing such a wonderful individual. It was obvious to her parents that Tony and Amanda were inseparable, holding hands constantly and barely spending time apart. There were several times that Amanda's father had gotten Tony alone for a couple of minutes to do this or that and had a chance to try and get a feel for the young man's plans for the future. He dropped several hints, each more bold than the previous, that he should marry Amanda and take her with him. Each time, her father was met with silence, as if the young pilot had no idea how to answer or even address the question, if he had even gotten the hint to begin with.

*　　*　　*　　*　　*

On the morning of the third day, Tony awoke to the sound of a rooster somewhere outside, not the sound of the wind rattling his hotel window. The wind storm was gone and Dubois had an eerie stillness to the morning. Finally, he could continue his journey.

Heading for the diner, the morning was clear and quiet; a little disconcerting as wind was all he had ever known of this little town. Finding Amanda waiting for him inside, they ate breakfast together, but things were different now, knowing it was time for him to leave. Something was bothering him though and Amanda could see that he was really struggling with it. Try as she might, she couldn't get it out of him and now it was time for him to get going.

Amanda made arrangements with her parents to have some gas brought out to where Tony's plane was parked. After filling the tanks, Tony carefully checked his airplane before takeoff, Amanda and her parents watching nervously. Finally he turned to them to thank them for their kindness and pay them for their trouble. Of course Amanda's father wasn't one to take pay for a good deed. He was quite religious and felt like the payment he got in the hereafter was much more

6

important than what he could ever get in this life. Then Tony stepped over to Amanda and took her by the hands.

"You," he fumbled nervously, "are an amazing woman." He opened his mouth to speak the next sentence, but he couldn't get anything to come out.

Amanda sort of leaned a little forward, hoping it might help him spit out what he wanted to say, but nothing seemed to help.

"Thank you so much. The last three days have been so nice. I hope to see you again." He turned and stepped quickly towards his plane and climbed in.

Amanda just stood there, dumbfounded. *Nice? Was that it? Nice?* She looked over at her parents who were equally shocked. They still lived in a day and age when love at first site was not uncommon and they knew it when they saw it. With the engine starting to crank over, her mother motioned for her to do something, anything! Amanda's female impulse took command and she ran to the other side of the plane where Tony could see her and watched him as the engine sputtered to life. She carefully stepped under the wing, toward the cockpit window as he checked his instruments, the engine running a little faster and smoother.

She stepped up to the fuselage and stood right next to his window, the prop wash blowing at her as she knocked on the window. He was a bit startled when he looked up and saw her right outside, motioning for him to open the window. He throttled back so the engine was just ticking over and opened the window.

"I have to know something," she spoke loudly over the noise, sticking her head inside the cockpit as far as she could reach on her tippy toes.

"What?" he answered back.

She slid her arms around his neck and planted the grandest kiss she thought she could ever deliver. It took only a moment for Tony to get over the surprise of the embrace and start returning what he had wanted to do before he had even gotten into the airplane, but hadn't had the nerve to say or do anything about.

The kiss didn't end, and wasn't about to. Tony found himself losing all frame of mind and situational awareness. He finally pulled the engine mixture back out and the engine promptly died, but the kiss really got going. Finally, she had to break free. The way she was reaching through the window was starting to hurt. When she finally pulled away, she looked into his eyes.

"I had to know what it was like." She then stepped away from the airplane.

Tony looked out at her, watching her turn to rejoin her parents on the other side of the plane.

"Oh no you don't," he mumbled under his breath, crawling clumsily back out of the plane. His foot got caught in his harnesses, trying to deplane and he ended up flat on his face in the grass. He rolled quickly and started kicking at the harness to get it loose.

"How utterly stupid," he thought to himself. *"I must look like a complete moron!"*

He finally got free, got himself up and straightened out. Even though he had totally embarrassed himself in front of everyone, he reasoned that he would be even more embarrassed if he didn't keep moving forward, so he mustered what was left of his dignity and stepped back over to where the three of them were now standing.

Amanda stood straight faced, her arms folded tightly across her chest. Her mother had a frightened look on her face and her father was grinning from ear to ear.

"You're permission sir?" he asked, carefully looking over at Amanda's smiling father.

"Certainly," he answered, chuckling while rubbing his unshaven chin.

"Ma'am," he gestured to Amanda's mother who only nodded nervously.

"You, young lady," directing his comments solely at Amanda now. "I can't be without you. I need to take you with me."

That was his expert approach to this problem and he cringed a little after he realized what he had said and how he had said it. *What the heck kind of a stupid line was that? Come on! Make it sound pretty. Sweep the girl off her feet for heck sakes!*

"I'm sorry, I can't go with you," she answered, straight and emotionless.

A look of total rejection suddenly enveloped Tony's face. This wasn't good, not good at all.

"Why not?"

"Because."

"Because why?"

"Because I ain't married to you."

Well, that was a heck of a note! Tony sort of thought he was being rather romantic in his own little way and figured that it was a fore gone conclusion what he was trying to do.

"Well, I need to leave here pretty quick. Any chance you would want to marry me right now so we can go?" He made it as plain and simple as he could. *Now that's romantic, isn't it? Way to sweep her off her feet buddy!*

"I think we can make that happen."

Remaining emotionless, she turned to her father, who jumped for the car.

"Be right back," he called out, driving off to find a preacher or the sheriff.

"So is this how men ask women to marry in Montana?" Amanda asked, not letting him off the hook just yet. She stood unmoved from her original position and expression.

"I'm sure most men are far more eloquent. Afraid I'm not very good with these things. I don't even have a ring to give you," he said, a little bit of disappointment, his voice shaking slightly.

Amanda's mother started fumbling with something, then stepped forward and pushed something into his gloved hand.

"Here," she said with a quivering smile. "Give her mine."

Tony looked down in his hand at the time worn wedding band that still glistened in the sunlight. Pulling his gloves off, he carefully examined it. There were initials engraved on the inside of the ring, probably belonging to her parents.

He suddenly became very uncomfortable with this idea and opened his mouth to object, but one look at the woman's tear filled eyes and quivering lower lip, told him that to object to the gift would be a monumental mistake. Her whole demeanor suggested that she had worked alongside her husband most of her life and while it had been a hard life, it had been a good one. From what he had observed for the past three days of this family, the parents gave freely of their sustenance to their family and friends alike. It was obvious that she loved her husband deeply and that she didn't need a ring to prove that to anyone.

"Now," Amanda's mother spoke up trying to straighten her dignity. "Do it proper like and get down on one knee and ask this girl of mine to marry you the way you're supposed to. I don't care how they do it in Helena, this is the way you're gonna do it here in Dubois."

Tony only smiled and slowly sank to one knee, raising the ring towards Amanda.

"Amanda, I can't live without you and I won't leave without you." This was a little too serious for him and he had to interject some kind of humor in here somewhere.

"But I gotta get these pieces parts down to Logan and I want you to come with me. Will you marry me now, so we can go?"

"Oh goodness," Amanda's mother gave a disgusted snort.

"Sssssshhhhhhhh," Amanda motioned her mother back, a huge grin on her face and putting both her hands around his and the ring.

"Yes, of course yes!"

Tony was quick to his feet and they were repeating the same scene they had started at the plane. This time there was no airplane window to get in the way and everything was as comfortable as it could be. Their kisses were like nothing either had ever experienced before. It seemed like it took forever for Amanda's father to return with a Mormon bishop and a couple of suitcases.

Tony eyed the bags suspiciously as her father loaded them in the back of the plane. It was obvious that Amanda had more faith in him than he did. It wasn't too long before the basic vows were exchanged, the ring placed and the pronouncement of man and wife made, then another long kiss, congratulations and a bunch of parting tears were shed as they climbed in to leave.

"Ever been up in a plane before?" Tony asked, restarting the engine and prepping for takeoff.

Amanda was busy trying to figure out how to work the seat belt on her side.

"Nope, never," came her cool reply, turning to Tony with a confident look of accomplishment on her face at having figured out the complex harness. He looked her over real good, checking her harness. A bit surprised that his new bride had indeed figured it out all on her own, gave him a little reassurance that maybe she'd be just fine with flying. Most first timers got sick. Maybe Amanda was going to be different.

"Ok, here we go," he said, pushing the throttle all the way in.

Amanda turned and waved to her parents who were returning the farewells. She could see that her mother was still emotional. It wasn't that Amanda wasn't emotional about the parting, but she was just so excited that she had found her man and that they embarking out on their lives together in a grand way. Not many brides got to go on their honeymoon in an airplane.

Catrina Amanda

Tony and Amanda became inseparable. They did everything and went everywhere together. Whether it was by car or airplane, you could be sure that if one of them was there, the other one wasn't very far away. They became a complete team, an extension of the other, perfectly complimented one to another. They had made their home in Helena, but also had plans to build a wonderful cabin site called "High Mountain Heaven", back in the high mountains of western Montana on a piece of property he inherited from one of his uncles. It would be accessible only by several days of hiking with pack animals or by Tony's airplane. It would require them to pack in and spend weeks clearing and building a suitable landing strip, then fly equipment and supplies in necessary to build the cabin. The plan was to be able to live indefinitely there if need be, even during the long winter months. They relished the thoughts of being able to live in relative comfort off supplies and the land. To them, flying was the greatest mode of transportation invented. You could go just about anywhere whenever you wanted to. Traveling to distant places, they would stop in the grassy field next to that little town of Dubois to visit family and friends as often as they could. However, all these grand plans often hit a bump in the road and attention to completing the task they had always dreamed of was put on hold.

It wasn't long before Amanda could no longer follow Tony around wherever he went as she became pregnant. She soldiered on as long as she could reasonably do so, but soon she was grounded and stuck at the airport office as her time drew near. Even that became a stretch for her and she remained at home. It wasn't long before Tony returned home to find Amanda holding their little one, Catrina Amanda Dallas. Tony and Amanda's love and affection for one another never wavered, but only grew stronger after the birth of Catrina.

This little girl wasn't just any child though. She became everything to them, finding out just how much of a miracle child Catrina really was. Amanda could have no more children, this was it and while they had fully expected to fill a house, they became content to raise this child the best they could, with all the love they would have given a houseful of children. She quickly became daddy's little girl and there was nothing wrong with that. Amanda had her all day and even nights when Tony was away on a flight that didn't allow him to return home on the same day.

The more Catrina grew, the more it was apparent that she was no ordinary child. She had just about every one of her mother's physical traits, which pleased Tony to no end. Looking at two Amandas was a wonder, but more interesting was the child's ability to discern things that usually only age could provide to the mind. She began to walk, speak and problem solve much earlier than the other children in their neighborhood.

As a toddler, she was interested in communicating with her parents and listening to the stories her father would tell when he returned from a trip. She was held spell bound by whatever his adventures provided her fertile little mind. She did like playing with toys and normal things that little girls liked and was very friendly with any of the other small children around her. She often asked her mother about every little thing that happened around her, from bugs crawling on tree leaves, to why the clouds stayed in the sky.

Amanda often looked at Catrina and was somewhat surprised at how much they looked alike. She saw little to nothing of Tony in her, but what she didn't have from her father in looks, she made up for in her personality. Catrina was no carbon copy of her parents. While she looked almost exactly like her mother did at her age and displayed many of the same personality traits of her father, she was her own person. She had a very curious, methodical nature about her. Even as she grew out of being a toddler and into a little girl, she displayed a certain grace and elegance that seemed almost eerie for a small child. Was this girl for real? How did they manage to teach this child to act the way she acted? Her curiosity was almost insatiable and her problem solving skills were unmatched for any child at her age of four.

By the time her fifth birthday rolled around in 1939, war had broken out in Europe and while her father wasn't drafted, he did enlist. Because of his age, he wasn't assigned a front line position, at least not at first. He did see plenty of action in the Army Air Force flying DC3 cargo planes for the first half of the war, but then moved to medium range bombers, taking command of a flight group of B-25 Mitchells that flew missions over Italy, Belgium and Germany. While never shot down, he did loose several crew to interceptor attack and substantial damage to three different planes, including his own issued B-25J aircraft he had named after his beloved wife, Amanda.

When first issued in the summer of 1944, the B-25J was a drab looking aircraft, sporting the standard camo paint scheme. Because of his rank and position as flight commander, and the fact that he always brought his ship and his boys home, Tony was able to get her special attention. Over time he was able to fit "The Amanda" with the latest modifications and dress up the exterior. As the war dragged on, and the allies completely dominated the skies over Europe, the air force abandoned the camo paint scheme and went with the shiny silver polished skin. Tony was quick to have "The Amanda's" paint removed and her aluminum skin polished with new nose art expertly painted on.

In 1945, as the war drew to its close in the European theater, many of the flight groups were sent back to the states, including their planes.

Tony was assigned the logistical task of getting those flights back across the Atlantic, where the planes were dispersed across the United States to various locations for further use and training purposes. He actually led about eight of these flights himself before he was finally given his own release papers and told to ferry his own plane, "The Amanda," back to the states. Again, because of his rank and standing with his superiors, he was able to choose where he would disperse his plane to. Of course he chose East Base, in Great Falls, Montana. A hop, skip and a jump from Helena.

It was time to go home and bring the ship that had taken him through the war with him. While it was certainly Government Issue, the military viewed this plane as a bit of a show piece. Considering the amount of action it had seen, it had survived very well and was in very good condition. Its crew, while nowhere close to original, would never be as famous as the B-17 crew of the "Memphis Belle". The "Belle" had flown 25 missions without any incidents. The crew of "The Amanda" would still be considered a spokesman for their time overseas and fighting against the tyranny of the Nazi war machine.

*   *   *   *   *

The morning finally arrived for Captain Dallas to return, Amanda and Catrina waiting anxiously at East Base military airport. They were wearing matching blue dresses with white waist bows and dainty white gloves. Cat had on a pair of shiny black shoes and a light colored Barrette in her hair. Amanda was wearing heels and Cloche hat. Arriving at the scheduled time, they wouldn't have to wait very long.

Catrina heard the sound of the big Wright Cyclone R-2600 radial engines first, the beautiful aluminum polished B-25J Mitchell circling the field and making its approach. She ran to the window of the military lounge to identify the aircraft then turned to her anxious mother.

"It's him all right, it's daddy!" she announced excitedly. She was sure of it. There were plenty of other aircraft in the pattern, but somehow she just knew this was her dad. She darted out the door and into the cool of the autumn morning to watch him land. Her mother couldn't help but follow. She didn't have to tell Catrina that she couldn't go very far outside. Normally, civilian personnel weren't even allowed in the base control building let alone out on the tarmac, but because this was a home coming and a somewhat famous airplane, exceptions were made.

Both of them watched the plane lit gently down on its rear wheels first, then gingerly onto its nose wheel and carefully braking to make the turn off to the taxiway.

"He's so amazing," Catrina beamed. Not necessarily to her mother, but more to herself and to the world. "He's the best pilot ever." She said with a marveled look on her face.

She could hardly contain herself. Her daddy was home and she couldn't wait to have him holding her and her mother in his arms. She watched the thundering 25 rolling closer to their location down the taxiway and then turning towards the building.

"I see him! I see him!" she called out to her mother, the big plane pulling up in front of the building and braking. Amanda's emotions bubbled out when she could see her man at the controls of the powerful twin engine machine, he and his crew securing the aircraft for shut down.

*　　*　　*　　*　　*

"Looks like you have a couple of very excited fans out there," Tony's copilot Chuck Nibbly said, looking out at the two females standing out in front.

"Yeah skipper," came a call from the radio intercom, "And I'd say if you don't get out there pretty quick, you're gonna have that girl in here before we even get this thing all the way shut down."

Tony grinned broadly at the true comments from his crew as he looked out at his two girls.

"Sure are sights for sore eyes gentlemen."

"Go ahead Captain, get out there and show us how to do a homecoming the right way."

"You guys don't mind?" he asked, as Chuck worked the controls of the big plane, waiting for the engines to cool a little more before shutting them off.

"Go man, go!" was the resounding reply.

Passing a second glance at his copilot, he pulled his headphones from his head, wormed his way out of the pilot's seat and worked the belly hatch open. Chuck cut the power on the left engine and the prop ground to a halt. Tony slid down the ladder to the ground and turned to his waiting family, who could no longer be held back by any kind of rules or regulations of the military. Catrina, half crying half giggling, reached her daddy first and leapt into his waiting arms with a bear hug that nearly knocked him to the ground. He spun her around twice, her tear filled eyes buried in his shoulder and neck, and then he set her down. She instinctively knew she had to share the moment with her mother, spinning away just in time for a crying Amanda to remind him of one of the many reasons he married her in the first place. They could kiss like no other couple. Catrina wiped her face with her lady's handkerchief, smiling broadly at them, returning one another's affections.

14

Inside the bomber, Chuck shut down the other engine and the crew watched the touching home coming unfold before them. There were a couple of chuckles over the radio intercom.

"And that's how it's done boys!" The copilot announced loudly, shutting the rest of the aircraft systems off and started stowing equipment for disembarking.

While Catrina enjoyed watching her parents show their affection for one another, she was getting a little impatient for a little more herself and started tugging on her mother's dress and her dad's flight jacket. She cleared her throat a couple of times while she tugged to get some attention.

"Come on you two," she finally blurted out loud. "You can get a room when you get home. I know how it all works. I get to sleep over at Amy's house so you two can have the house all to yourselves."

That got their attention. A little bit shocked, her father broke free from Amanda's embrace and turned to his daughter while her mother straightened herself up.

"And you are how old now?" he asked, using a little confused tone in his voice.

"Come on dad, you know I'm ten," she said grinning broadly.

If he had any intensions of correcting her, he was quickly disarmed by her deep brown eyes that gazed lovingly at him. She was so like her mother, it was almost scary at times.

"All right young lady, your mother and I know how it all works as well. You get to sleep over at Amy's house tonight, like I know you have already asked your mother and she said no, but you know I'll give in and let you because it's homecoming."

Tony gave his wife a quick glance. It was actually all part of the plan. Amanda had already told her daughter no, knowing that she would ask her dad when he got back. She knew that he would cave in and let his little girl sleep at her friend's house, giving Tony and Amanda the night alone together, which is exactly what they wanted in the first place. However, you have to let the kids think they run the place. Her mother had to really stay on her toes in order to stay a step ahead or at least even with the budding young woman. Catrina snuggled into her father's arms again and hugged her favorite man, then turned to his airplane.

"Show us your plane daddy, can you?" she asked as his crew began to disembark from the rear.

The bomb bay had been opened while some of the crew worked to unload gear. Tony took Amanda's hand and stepped over to the left side of the big plane next to the nose.

"What do you think?" he asked turning to his beloved wife. Amanda was a bit taken back at the lavish nose art on the left side of the aircraft's front fuselage.

"Oh my goodness," she gasped, a bit embarrassed. Tony's expression suddenly changed to concern and pulled Amanda close to him.

"It's what got me through this war. A symbol of everything that I hold dear. It's there to remind me that you were always with me and that you would help keep me safe."

"I know, but," she stammered, stepping away from the plane for a better look. "It's so big………….and a bit revealing……don't you think?"

"Perhaps a little bit," Tony stepped over next to her and took her hand. "But there isn't a lie in any of the brush strokes it took to put it on there."

"Wow! Mom, it's you!" Catrina exclaimed, looking at the wonderfully detailed nose art painting of her mother on the silvery finish of the aircraft's fuselage.

She was depicted in a pinup pose, but with a lot more clothes on than most of them. She was wearing a very pretty, yet modest yellow dress that was shown in a blowing fashion, which in turn, showed off her figure and the curves the good Lord had blessed her with. It certainly wasn't tawdry or even degrading in any way. Beneath the woman's image were the letters of her name spelled out in bold beautiful cursive, "The Amanda".

"Why is she holding a sword?" Catrina asked, looking at what seemed a bit out of place.

She also noticed the scabbard strapped about the hips of the painting of her mother and that it was on the wrong side for the hand she was holding the sword in. It was just an odd pose, and the more you looked at it, the odder it became.

"Honey, Cat's right," Amanda said, looking at the painting. "What does it mean? It really starts to look kind of weird when you notice it and try to figure it out." Tony smiled broadly.

"Leave it to my two girls to notice a coded picture. The Germans never even noticed it, except that it was art and they were a bit apprehensive to attack the group when this ship was leading it, because of reputation. My boys rarely missed."

"But what's the sword got to do with anything?"

"It's a symbol of beauty and strength. Your image is the symbol of my everlasting love for you and for country. The sword is the symbol of the strength of country and honor. The scabbard is on this side of the hip to show its symbolism and coat of arms engraved on it. If I had put it on the other side, no one would have been able to see it. Does that make sense?" he asked, stepping away from the plane so they could look it over some more.

Amanda stood gazing at it, trying to put all the puzzle pieces together in her mind while her daughter simply shrugged her shoulders and started for the open bomb bay.

"Makes perfect sense to me," Catrina said, poking her head through the open doors, then peered up inside the open hatchway.

She could hear someone moving around up inside, so she climbed up to investigate. She wasn't bold or intrepidatious because of her father; she was because she was.

"Well," a pleased voice called out from the cockpit up front. "You must be the famous Catrina Dallas." Chuck said, looking back at her from his seat up front. "Get on up here and let's have a good look at you. Tired of hearing all about you from your dad and having to look at the same old picture every time we fly."

Chuck had a hard chiseled face with blonde curly hair that turned out from under his military cap. His voice was a bit gruff, but he inflected it in such a way as to not frighten the young girl. He was pleased as punch to finally meet Tony's daughter. None of the other men had any children or were even married. So they got to listen to Tony go on and on and on about how Amanda was like this and Catrina would do that, endlessly, but they really didn't mind so much. It reminded them of home and helped to pass the time during long missions to and from enemy targets.

"What do you mean, every time you fly?" Cat asked, making her way carefully forward.

Chuck pointed at two small pictures, one of Catrina and her dad, the other of Amanda, which was stuck to the instrument panel between two instruments, right about in the middle. She looked closely at them then started examining everything else in the cockpit.

"Your dad was always going on about Cat did this and Cat did that and she's growing up so fast and how wonderful you are. I was beginning to think I was going to have to come home and marry you myself," he said with a good chuckle.

Cat stopped looking for a moment, and gave the copilot a quick once over, smiled and went back to her examination of all the instruments in the cockpit.

"You can sit down in your dad's seat if you want," he said, pulling his stuff out of the seat and motioning for the young girl to climb in, which she did, ever so carefully.

She was in a dress and was trying her best to remain as ladylike as possible in such close quarters. Once modestly situated, she looked out the window at her talking parents who were still admiring the nose art on the side of the aircraft.

"What do you think dad?" she called out, waving her arm out the open window. Both parents looked up at their daughter, Tony with a little surprise mixed with admiration. Amanda was a bit horrified and motioned for her daughter to get out.

"Think you better get out of there before you get us all into some trouble."

"No," Tony cut in reassuring everyone, "it's ok."

"It's no problem skipper," Chuck called out from the other side. "We have everything well in hand up here."

The reassurance from the copilot seemed to pacify Cat's parents just fine and she sat back to continue her surveillance of the cockpit.

"Ok," she finally said, sitting forward and pointing at one of the instruments.

"What does this do?"

For the next 15 minutes, Chuck was busily engaged explaining what every single instrument and switch and gauge and lever and button and knob did. She understood most of what was being explained because she had flown many times with her father. Chuck would start to explain something to her and she would cut him off by finishing the explanation for him. He was completely amazed at her knowledge and ability to figure it all out. She was a little confused about why there were duplicate controls on each side, for shooting guns, and dropping bombs. Chuck explained that the plane was full of many redundant systems that were there for the crews safety, and the completion of the mission should someone onboard not be able to do their job for one reason or another. She understood what that meant.

She carefully climbed out of her dad's seat and made her way back into the top gun turret. Again, paying particular attention to her own modesty and after situated, asked questions of the gunner who had perched himself behind the turret over the bomb bay compartment. He told her all about the positions the crew manned in the bomber.

Normally, there were only six crewmen manning a B-25J, but this one had seven. The standard crew compliment was six men, "The Amanda" had been testing a seventh. There had been constant conversation about having two waist gunners in a B-25, much like its bigger cousins, the B-17 and B-24. The problem was available space. The 25's fuselage was a bit more cramped than the 17 and 24 was, thus the positions sort of got in the way of each other. The designers had staggered the positions to minimize that, but it was still being tried in a number of ships, this being one of them.

There were the pilot and copilot, the top turret gunner/engineer, the bombardier/navigator who sat in the nose, the left waist gunner/radio operator, the right waist gunner in the back and the tail gunner. Thomas Walker was from Billings, Montana, so he wasn't too far from home. Not sure how he got assigned to a ship going so close to home. All these men were enlisted men except for Captain Dallas and Lt. Nibbly. "Tommy," as he was affectionately referred to, was a stout guy with straight brown hair. His face was a little chubby, but there wasn't much fat on him. He smiled at the curiosity of his Captain's daughter. Half the stuff he was showing her, she already knew what it did.

"How do you know all this stuff?" he finally asked, exhausting all his knowledge of the workings of a gun turret.

"It just makes sense," she said, looking around outside and waving at her parents who had been walking around the outside of the plane. "Help me down please," she said, holding her arms out to Chuck, who had joined the tour at the turret before he disembarked himself.

He happily took her and gently set her down at the hatchway and she carefully stepped down and out of the plane. Chuck and Tommy looked at the other, grabbing their stuff.

"That is some girl," Chuck finally said, dropping his stuff to the ground through the open hatchway.

"There was no exaggerating on Tony's part when he described her to us all this time. I may just have to wait 10 years and come back and marry her. She's a peach."

"Take a number there Tommy boy, take a number." With that, the two men disembarked from the aircraft and joined their other crew members; Terrance Lieder, a short thin kid not more than 18 was the bombardier/navigator. Carl Lott, a tall muscular man from Murtaugh, Idaho was the right waist gunner.   Tim Hansen, left waist gunner/radio operator was about as toe headed as you could be and his hair was as straight as it could be, but it was kept cut within regulations. He was of medium build and from San Jose, California. Finally, bringing up the rear from Portland, Oregon, was Dale Parkinson, tail gunner. Another tall wirery guy with jet black hair and a lot of pock marks on his face from acne as a teen.

They all met around in front of the plane and waited for their commander, who presently showed up with wife and daughter in tow. Everyone stood at attention and Captain Dallas saluted his men, and then smiled.

"See you gentlemen in two weeks." With that they all grabbed their bags and headed for the military lounge, but Tony stopped them.

"Oh, and guys," he paused turning and facing the bunch of them. "Thanks," he said smiling, then turned back to his wife and daughter. Putting his arms around both of them, they made their way through the lounge to the parking lot. Once they were almost home, Cat leaned forward over the front seat from the back and looked at her mom and dad.

"So, what's in two weeks?" she asked.

"Well, that's a bit of a surprise that you just don't need to worry about right now young lady," her father grinned widely.

"AAAAHHHHWWWW," Cat whined a bit as they made their way down their neighborhood street. "Not much fun being a kid these days," she moaned as the car pulled into their driveway.

Her dismay didn't last very long as her playmates were out in their front yards playing. She quickly got out of the car, opened her father's door and waited for him to get out.

"Hey everyone!" she called out to her friends. "This is my dad, Captain Tony Dallas, United States Army Air Force!"

Every child within the sound of her voice stopped what they were doing and came running. Catrina had talked her father up to almost "Godhood" status and every kid on the block wanted to see and be associated with a living legend, if for no other reason than they lived in the same neighborhood. The kids that lived on either side of their modest little house counted themselves as extra special because they would be considered practically family because of their proximity.

Tony quickly found himself drowning in a sea of children wanting to touch his jacket and asking him all sorts of questions. He had hoped for a quiet homecoming and was looking around a bit bewildered wondering if the rest of the neighborhood would materialize. He glanced across the top of the car with a look of *"Help me get out of this"*, as Amanda stepped out and looked back at him with a big grin on her face. She couldn't help but be proud of her man and touched by their daughter's pride for her dad. It wouldn't have mattered if he had been a war hero or the garbage man, Catrina would have been just as proud and idolized her dad equally. He was about to make good on an escape when a firm hand squeezed his own and he looked down into the deep brown eyes and wonderful bright face of his daughter.

"Tell them a story dad," she beamed with wondrous pride. "Tell them about how you always brought your airplane and crew home, tell them," she almost pleaded.

Tony was a little embarrassed, but the quiet hush that fell on the crowd of children and their anxious eyes, gave him license to relent and he stepped over onto the still green lawn that was half covered in autumn leaves and sat down with all the kids forming a crowded half circle in front of him.

Catrina snuggled right up next to her father, clinging to his arm as he began to relay a couple of airplane war stories that he felt weren't too graphic or exciting. He was painfully aware of what the toll of the war was and how it had taken so many young lives before they ever had a chance to experience the wonder he had experienced. He spoke of the fight for the skies over Germany, pitting man and machine against opposing forces. Stories of the heroics of crewman saving lives in perilous circumstances and against all odds, held the children's imaginations spellbound. He certainly didn't want to set any precedence with storytelling or anything like it, especially when you consider the audience in front of him. Tell them too much and they go home scared out of their little minds and then they tell their parents, who get a slightly different version of actual events, then things start to spin out of control.

He told two fairly benign events, that shouldn't create too much hullabaloo, all the while, Amanda stood leaning against the car listening and watching her husband tell the stories to a completely captivated crowd. Catrina hung on his every word, even how he was presenting it. It almost looked as though she were watching his lips move as he spoke. She would often rest her head against him, holding onto him while he conveyed his story. Finally, he finished his two stories and Amanda decided it was rescue time, the kids all pleading for him to tell them another one.

"Ok kids," she called out above the clamor of little pleading voices. "Time for Captain Dallas and Cat to have some lunch and-." She was met with a flurry of objections and had to raise her voice a little bit to be heard. "And," she repeated a little louder. "I'm sure it's lunch time for the rest of you as well. Now come on everyone," she ordered. "Off you go and you can come back over and play after lunch."

Tony and Catrina got up and stepped over to the car by Amanda.

"My savior," he said, kissing her.

"Get a room," Catrina said with a smile, leaning against the car the way her mother had.

"Oh, get a room huh?" Tony said suddenly, the tone of voice indicating that a tickle session was about to ensue. "I'll show you get a room!"

Catrina let out a delightful squeal and bolted around the back side of the car, towards the middle of the front yard with her dad in hot pursuit. It was now a game of "dodge the dad", the two racing all around the front yard. Catrina, trying not to get caught but glad when she was; Tony, trying to not to catch her too easily.

"Come on you two," Amanda called out, heading into the house to fix lunch for her family.

She smiled pleasantly as the two raced past her, Catrina squealing loudly and Tony growling menacingly as they ran into the house and disappeared. Life was so good and she felt so content with it. Things were heaven on earth and she couldn't even imagine how life could possibly get any better than this. She had thought the same thing when she was rumbling down the grass field on takeoff from her hometown right after she had married Tony. There is always something wonderful just around the corner, but some things, maybe not so wonderful.

Tour of Duty

Two weeks went by fairly quickly. There was lots of talk around the dinner table, the living room, and in the evenings at bedtime, about what was to happen at the end of the time frame mentioned at the airbase. Catrina was constantly trying to collect clues about what was going to happen. Tony and Amanda had become experts at speaking in code around their daughter. She was just too observant and smart for her own good, at least when it came to surprises. Try as she might, she was never able to get either of them to slip up and let go of a good hint. Their cleverly conceived code talk they used whenever she was around their discussions had her baffled and frustrated.

Finally, the appointed day had arrived and Amanda had instructed Catrina to pack herself a suitcase of things that she would need for an extended trip. Finishing her necessary preparations and her mother having inspected her work, making sure Cat had everything from proper clothing to the right toiletries, she handed her a package wrapped in a plain brown wrapping held together with string. There was a label attached to the package that had a strange number on it, followed by, "Property of the USAAF".

"What is it mother?" Catrina asked inquisitively, examining the plain wrapping. Her mother handed her a small shoe box.

"Here, these go with it. Put them on now. You have to be wearing this when you leave," her mother directed, then turned and left her daughter to accomplish her assigned task.

Cat quickly opened up the package and held up a woman's Air Force dress uniform, in her size. The box contained the matching shoes. She was quick to put the whole thing together and had it all on in nothing flat. The blouse had an Air Force insignia on the shoulder and a name plate on the front with her first initial and her last name. She adjusted the dark skirt and slipped the shoes on, then grabbed the little chevron hat and set it on her head. She had seen plenty of pictures of women in uniform, enough to know how it was all supposed to look and be worn.

She was thrilled to death when she came down the stairs in uniform, suitcase in hand, and stepped in the front room where her parents were waiting. Her father was dressed up in his dress uniform as well and had his military duffle bag sitting on the floor next to where he stood with Amanda in his arms. Both parents turned and looked at their daughter who stood beaming proudly that she could be just like her dad.

"Ok, I'm ready. Now will you two please tell me where we're going?" she announced bringing them to attention.   Her dad stepped over and gave her the once over.

"You sure look all grown up in that getup," he said smiling. "You and I," he said, grabbing his own bag, "are going on a little trip."

"Oh, I like trips," Catrina spoke up a little excitedly.

"My crew and I have received orders to show off "The Amanda" on a short tour around the northwest states. We fly into big airports and people come to see the airplane and we show it off and tell stories about it and what we did in the war over Germany."

"You mean just like my friends wanted to hear all about what you did in the war, other people want or need to hear all about it as well."

"Exactly," her dad agreed, knowing she was following the conversation very well.

"Well, I arranged to have you fly with me as far as Salt Lake City in Utah. You'll go wherever I go and do whatever I do."

Catrina's eyes lit up and she jumped slightly up and down for a moment, and then suddenly stopped.

"Well," she turned to her mother. "What about mom?"

"Oh goodness," her mother cut in quickly. "Don't worry about me. I have a bunch of stuff I need to get done here and then I'm riding the train down to Utah and we'll all ride back together."

"In the plane?"

"No, the train."

"Well, what's going to happen to "The Amanda"?" Tony glanced at Amanda then dropped to one knee in front of Cat.

"Honey, I love that plane and we've been through a lot together, but she doesn't really belong to me, she belongs to the military, and they want it back so they can let someone else learn to fly her and help protect the country."

"Doesn't seem right that you should learn to fly her and go through all the things that you went through with her only to have to give her back." Catrina responded despairingly.

"I know what you mean." Tony chuckled softly. "I'd dearly love to keep her, but I can't be selfish about it. Someone else needs her now, so we're going to take her to a bunch of different places and show her off and then give her back to the military so someone else can learn to fly her too. Are you ready?"

Catrina thought hard for a moment, then stood at attention and saluted smartly.

"Yes sir!" She said firmly.

"Then we better get to it," her father said, standing up and grabbing his own bag following his daughter out the front door and to the car. Amanda quickly brought up the rear with a slight look of glee painted on her beautiful face.

                        *   *   *   *   *

Arriving at the East Base military lounge where they had met Tony two weeks earlier, the Dallas family created quite a stir among the base personnel. Tony and Catrina marched into the lounge in full dress uniform; their bags in hand with Amanda dressed to the licks in a beautiful yellow dress, heels and a pretty brim hat that was open on the top. The three of them were met in the main lobby by the base Commander and Captain Dallas's crew. Both parties saluted, and then all attention was drawn to Catrina.

"So, young lady, you look pretty official," the Base Commander said, looking her over. "Everything but these," he said, pulling something out of his pocket and pinning it to her uniform. Catrina looked down at a shiny set of Air Force wings.

"Now, you're ready to go," he smiled looking back at Tony and Amanda.

"I really appreciate you letting us have him for just a little while longer Mrs. Dallas. I promise this will be his last tour and then he's all yours. Hate to lose a great officer, pilot, and a good man." He finished softly, shaking Captain Dallas' hand. "Good luck Captain."

With that, he stepped aside to let the group move into the lounge area where there was a gathering of base personnel and a small contingent of newspaper reporters, who were all anxious to get pictures of everyone and "The Amanda." After pictures and fielding questions while standing inside, the reporters asked to have some more pictures outside next to "The Amanda".

To Catrina's delight, she was treated like just another member of the crew. Oh, certainly there was a little more interest paid her, beings she was a girl.   She was tall enough that she really didn't stick out too much. The top of her head came up even with her dad's ears. For a ten year old, that was pretty tall. Standing next to the plane and her dad, was the most fun part of the picture taking, but even that got monotonous after a while. How many different poses do you need for a newspaper? Perhaps more curious was the crew that was filming them. Military of course, but she was going to be in the movies, although she missed the director calling out "Lights, camera, action." Finally, it was just her and her dad getting a picture taken, and then she followed Chuck and Tommy, back into the building to get dressed in flight gear while her dad continued with the photo op with her mother and the airplane.

The flight suits were curious. Catrina thought they were sewn together like sleeper pajamas, except without the feet. The boots were kind of heavy to wear, but she didn't mind so much. When she picked up her suitcase, Tommy started going on and on about how he had the same suitcase at home and wanted to bring it, but because he was still in the military, he was required to use only military issue duffle bags for all his gear.

Chuck and Tommy stowed their gear, then helped Catrina with hers.   She was to sit in the back part of the plane, where the waist and tail gunners were for takeoff and landing. At least in the flight suit, she would be free to move about the airplane without having to worry about the problems associated with a dress.

While Carl was situating his gear next to the forward bulkhead at the rear of the plane, he watched Catrina looking at the odd plugs coming out of her jumpsuit. Just as she started to hold it up to ask him what it was for, he pulled a coiled cable from a compartment with a plug on the end and plugged it into the corresponding plug on her suit. Catrina looked curiously at it, then started to feel the suit where the wires entered, running her fingers along the wires in her suit. These were not regulation issued flight suits that crews normally wore, but test suits they had been assigned to try to see how well they worked. At altitude, a bomber wasn't the warmest place to be and while there were heaters onboard, they usually weren't enough to protect the men from the biting cold. Even oxygen masks could freeze up at high altitudes.

"Do you understand what this is for?" he asked, sounding a bit gruffly.

While he found Catrina completely adorable and irresistible as did the other crew members, he was a little bit bothered by having to babysit a 10 year old and a girl to boot. Military aircraft was no place for a woman and the only reason he wasn't vocalizing his objections were because they weren't flying into any enemy action. This was a publicity tour, pretty much just a joy ride for all of them. The real work was when they got on the ground and had to meet and greet the public. Catrina looked over at the box he had pulled the cord from and the controls that were in it.

"It looks like there's a heater in my suit for when you get really cold. Am I right?" she asked, sensing Carl's mood.

Carl unplugged her suit and put the coil away.

"That's exactly what it's for little girl."

Catrina watched him work for a moment; putting stuff away and situating everything so they could either sit comfortably or sleep and still have room to move around the cabin without stepping on each other or their own stuff.

"Are you mad at me?" she finally blurted out.

Her frankness stopped Carl short and he just knelt where he was, frozen for a few seconds, and then turned to Catrina.

"I think the world of your parents, especially your father. He has saved my life at least a dozen times. I think you are the prettiest little thing to come along and the boys are going to be fighting over you when you're older. You get your looks from your mother, but this airplane is no place for a girl. Having said that, it's my job to make sure you're comfortable back here and you don't get into anything you're not supposed to."

"Carl, lighten up on her will ya?" The other waist gunner said, as a duffle bag came up the rear hatch and Tim Hansen poked his head up inside.

"You never mind old sour puss over there and stick close to me," he said, climbing inside to stow his own gear.

"He's still in a bad mood from yesterday when we went fishing and I caught the bigger fish."

"Yeah, but I caught more," Carl came back quickly.

"More guppies don't make a bigger fish," Tim chuckled.

"Just means you have to cook more of them to get a mouth full," Dale said, tossing his stuff inside as well and climbing up the ladder. "Cat, you're wanted outside, time to say goodbye to your mom." He said, pulling himself up inside and helping her down and out of the plane.

Once back on the ground, she made her way under one of the wings and forward where she found her parents.

"Come on! We're burning daylight," she announced like she was an old hand at this flying stuff and was just one of the boys. "Let's get these blades to turning."

Her mother turned her attention to her daughter as her father worked to get the last of his gear onboard in preparations for departure.

"Ok, you have everything, right?"

"Mom!" Cat objected.

"Now hush girl. Let your mother be parental for a couple of minutes here. I know you can conquer the world all on your own, but I need to feel like I still have a place in it."

"Ok, I'm sorry, please continue," she said, almost disgusted that her mother was repeating something she had already committed to memory.

"Mind your elders. Be respectful, even when they don't deserve it," Amanda said, with a smile and so that no one else could hear that but Catrina. "Always remember that you are a lady and that you have certain responsibilities as such."

"Yes ma'am."

"Mind your manners, as I know you do," again she leaned a little closer and spoke a little softer so that only Catrina could hear that last part. "Have fun and I will see you in 2 weeks in Salt Lake, okay?"

The two just looked at each other for a long moment then Catrina threw her arms around her mother and the two embraced. This was the first time that these two had ever been apart for this length of time. Oh sure, Catrina had spent the night at friends or camping with her dad, but that didn't count as her mom was usually with them or she was home from friends first thing in the morning.

"I will miss you terribly," Amanda said, choking up a little bit.

"I'll miss you more," Catrina replied, from her mother's bosom.

"We're going to miss our departure time if you don't get on board so we can get this bird cranked up," Tony said, hugging both of them and sending Catrina back to climb on board.

He turned and gave Amanda a kiss for her to remember, for which he received the same in return, then pulled away and disappeared up the forward hatchway, closing the door behind him. Amanda stepped carefully and slowly back, hearing the electrical system in the bomber come on and Chuck starting to work the controls for startup. Before she could even see Tony in his seat, Chuck was cranking on the right engine.

The massive Hamilton Standard three bladed prop slowly turned with a whine of the starter and after about five or six turns, the engine coughed and began to bellow white puffs of smoke, then several cylinders began to fire, caught, and the engine rumbled to life. By now Tony was in his seat and Amanda could see the rear hatchway closing up. She stepped even further back watching her husband put on his headphones. He looked out at the left engine, repeating the same procedure as the first, until it began to fire, caught, and roared to life. A big cloud of white/blue smoke floated away from behind the rumbling airplane. It remained locked in place while the two pilots worked with her controls. Up front in the nose, Terry was getting all their navigation information set for after takeoff.

Tony looked out his cockpit window and saluted his commanding officer who stood just outside the doorway of the military lounge, just behind Amanda, and then looked directly at his wife, who waved bravely. He smiled and blew her a kiss, then mouthed the words, *"I love you"*, turning back to his controls and releasing the brakes. The big plane gently inched forward, reluctantly at first, and then began to roll freely. Turning its profile towards Amanda, Catrina waved wildly from the waist gunner's window, a huge grin on her face. Her mother waved madly back at her, blowing her a kiss, then the plane turned away, prop wash blowing right at the lounge. Everyone but Amanda quickly ducked inside, but she remained standing in the wind, watching until the plane turned onto the taxi way and rumbled away.

Takeoff was unremarkable for one of these planes. Multi engine radial operations happened all day, every day at East Base, but this takeoff seemed to really burn into Amanda this time. She had watched Tony depart many times before, but this time, something was very different. Watching the medium bomber roar into the sky and slowly out of sight, she felt strangely uneasy, but at ease at the same time. Turning to go back into the lounge, an autumn chill gave her a quick shiver.

"This is going to be a long two weeks."

One of the crew

Catrina had been flying many times with her dad in his small private plane. Her dad had already taught her all the basics of flight, and having such a curious nature, she had asked questions and learned more every time they went up together. So while "The Amanda" was a whole new place to explore, the novelty of flight really wasn't novel, except to compare how fast the ground was moving beneath them and how high they could go.

Criss crossing their way from one major town in the northwest to another, she was able to explore the airplane and get to know every inch of it. After only a short time, she was given several duties to perform every time they would take off and land or even while in flight. On the ground, she was the expert about the airplane to all the children. So as to not bother the grownups with a bunch of kids trailing through asking questions all the time, Catrina would pick them out of the crowd and sort of corral them together, giving them a prep briefing before they were allowed to approach the plane. She got so good at it and became so knowledgeable, that her father decided to just let her do all the youth tours. When word of this got out, it seemed to draw the crowds in even more. Everyone wanted to see and hear the young girl and the plane.

The whole crew just loved having her with them and doted over her all the time, being careful not to under estimate her understanding and capabilities, everyone but Carl. While he knew that she understood and was capable, he still had the hang up that this was no place for a girl. He was never rude, but wasn't warm to her either, a fact that didn't go unnoticed by her or her father. Tony was well aware of Carl's attitude long before Catrina was ever invited to come along, but something told him that she would win his heart, and he kept silent, watching to see if Catrina's irresistible charm would prevail.

Their tour took them all over the northwest, the last half in Montana. From Billings, to Glasgow, Great Falls, Kalispell, Missoula, Butte and Bozeman. Then they were to sweep down into Idaho and Utah, stopping in Jackson, Wyoming, then over to Idaho Falls, Twin Falls and down to Logan, Ogden and finally Salt Lake City. From there, "The Amanda" was to be turned over to the Air Force squadron at Dugway and another crew would fly it to its new home west of Salt Lake.

Somewhere between Butte and Bozeman, they hit rough weather and everyone had been ordered back to their positions to strap in.

Being mid to late autumn and somewhat cold, by the time she had made her way from the nose of the plane, her favorite spot, over the bomb bay to her spot in the back, she was a bit frazzled, becoming confused and having a hard time getting into her seat harness. She looked to Dale and Tim, who had fallen asleep, then over at Carl, who had been watching her struggle. As their eyes met, he pulled a bit of a bothered look, unstrapped himself and crawled over to help her with her harness. Just what he needed, more of a reason to believe he was right about her being onboard. Amid the turbulence, some of which was quite heavy, he was able to get her untangled from the bulky harness and strapped in quite securely.

The turbulence continued, becoming quite heavy, pitching the aircraft violently side to side. Several up/down drafts and Carl was thrown off balance. Without his harness to hold him securely in place, he was pitched about the cabin like a rag doll. Hitting a sweeping down draft, he found himself actually floating right in front of Catrina. Frantically thrashing about trying to get a hold of anything to pull himself down, he began to spin. It seemed like minutes that they were in a dream-state where time tries to stand still. Catrina reached out, grabbing the waist gunner by the heater cords and pulling as hard as she could, Carl spinning and landing right in her lap.

A moment of calm passed and Carl lifted himself up from off Catrina's lap. They looked at each other wide eyed, but then another sudden down draft, and he was catapulted into the ceiling of the airplane, knocking him unconscious. Catrina let out a startled squeal, the aircraft continuing to buffet violently. Carl continued to be thrown about the cabin until Catrina was able to grab him again, pulling him to her. This time she grabbed some loose cords and wrapped them around his waist, tying them into her own harness as quickly as conditions would allow. It wasn't terribly pretty, but it worked.

Both Tim and Dale had been awaken by the entire ruckus and had watched the whole event unfold in front of them. They had tried to grab Carl, but were too far away from him to reach. Even though the turbulence was still heavy, Carl was no longer being thrown about and they were now concerned that he wasn't moving at all and had Catrina check him.

"It looks and feels like he's still breathing," she called out over the noise of the airplane and the turbulent air.

Tim was getting his headphones put back on and trying to find where his microphone had gone in the mess that had been created, while Catrina ran her hands along his arms and sides, then up his back, neck and head checking Carl for injuries. Most of the turbulence was subsiding now but he was heavy. Lifting her hand from his head, she felt something odd. She set her hand back down on his head, feeling something warm and kind of wet. Looking back at her hand, it was covered in blood. She instantly planted her hand back down over the head wound and pressed hard.

"Dale," she called out. "He's hurt! I need the first aid kit, can you get it to me?" she hollered over the noise and the buffeting.

Dale carefully unbuckled his harness and moved towards a storage box bolted to the side of the fuselage as Tim pulled one of the headphone muffs from an ear.

"Captain says we're still about 15 minutes out of Bozeman. No place else to land though, so we'll have to wait it out," he yelled over the noise.

Dale moved very carefully, freezing at every bounce, trying to get the box over to Catrina. Once close by, he handed the kit to her, then strapped himself into Carl's harness right next to Catrina's, and proceeded to help render first aid to the waist gunner.

"Is he going to be all right?" Catrina asked, holding a large bandage firmly on the head wound. Dale wrapped a long bandage around his head to hold the compress firmly in place while still applying pressure to stop the bleeding. He smiled at her concern and reassured her.

"Oh, he's going to be just fine I'm sure. I wouldn't worry too much about him. I've seen him take shrapnel from flak and a couple of 20mm fragments before and he was back on board flying the following week. I think he can survive a little head bumping."

Dale passed a look over at Tim, who piped up quickly to assist in reassuring Catrina.

"It's the ribbing he's going to get from us when he hears who probably saved his life," he said with a good laugh, thinking about how that first conversation was going to go down. Tim pulled his headphones back over his ears and turned away from the conversation to listen. Dale passed Catrina a towel to wipe the blood from her hands.

"So what happened back there?" she asked, starting to get a little bit uncomfortable with the full weight of the waist gunner draped over her legs.

"Weather forecast was for moderate turbulence associated with thunderstorm activity along our route," Dale informed her. "We must have passed by a real nasty one. That's one of the worst I've ever been in. Gotta get use to those. Sometimes, they're no trouble at all and other times, you'd almost wished that you were flying into a swarm of German fighters or flake batteries."

"But I don't remember there being any rain or snow and it was sunny the entire time."

"You don't need to see the clouds in order to be affected by them. I've seen your dad fly through hail storms in the clear of day, from a thunderstorm about 40 miles down range," Dale informed her. "It just depends on what the storm is doing to the winds aloft, and what the air is doing coming up from the ground." Dale looked out the window, feeling the airplane starting its descent into Bozeman. "Are you going to be all right with sleeping beauty on your lap there?"

Catrina looked Carl over a little and decided that she could take the weight until they got safely on the ground.

"Yes, I think it would be best to wait until we're on the ground to move him. I'll be all right," she reassured him.

"Captain reports he'll taxi away from the main hangar to an alternate and they'll have a medical team standing by. We'll unload him hot and then proceed to the main hangar for the exhibition." Tim called out, pulling off his phones and setting down the mic. "Meantime, prep for landing," he said turning to get the gear around him back in order, as did Dale and Catrina. Well, as best she could with the waist gunner still in her lap.

Everything went off as planned on the ground. They offloaded the now conscious waist gunner into a military ambulance at a nearby hangar, then proceeded to the main area and shut everything down to disembark and greet the crowds of people who had been waiting. Before Tony exited his aircraft, he crawled over the bomb bay into the back of the plane to see how Catrina was doing.

"You all right?" he asked, sitting next to her as she prepared to disembark.

"Yes dad, sure got bumpy up there."

"Yeah, sorry about that. If only we can see the air we're flying through. Might make it easier to avoid the potholes up there huh?" he said good-naturedly. "Tim told me everything that happened. You did a great thing back here keeping your head and helping Carl like you did. I know he appreciates it and I couldn't be more proud of you." There was a big grin on her dad's face.

"I hope he's all right. I don't think he likes me so much," Catrina said, her head bowed.

"Oh, he likes you. He just has a really hard time showing it sometimes, but I think you'll find his attitude start to change a little now."

"I hope so," she said kind of quietly.

She seemed a little rattled by the whole experience, and why wouldn't she be? She was only 10 years old and just watched a grown man get tossed around like a rag doll.

"Ready to go to work?" her dad asked, holding her chin up.

"We're burning daylight," she said, getting up and starting down the rear hatchway, onto the tarmac with her father close behind.

*　*　*　*　*

The day went by quickly and soon evening and cooling temperatures thinned the crowds and finally everyone was sent home, leaving the crew to secure everything for the night. They had two full days here in Bozeman before they were to take off for Jackson Hole, Wyoming. Tony was just locking up the forward hatch on "The Amanda" when he spotted his daughter emerging from the hangar and trotting over to him.

"Where's your coat young lady?"

"They have dinner for us inside and a car waiting to take us to billeting quarters. My coat is in the back of the plane." She headed past him towards the back of the plane.

"Ok, see you inside," Tony called after her. "Don't forget to lock it."

"Dad," Catrina whined back in disgust. She quickly made her way inside and fumbled around in the fading light for some stuff that she had left behind, when she heard a noise at the hatch and turned to see who it was.

"You need a light on if you're going be working in here with it so dark."

"Carl!" she exclaimed, excited to see his head poking up inside the airplane. The head bandage was gone and he looked pretty good. "You're ok!" She was so happy to see that he was indeed all right.

"Thanks to you," Carl grinned broadly, pulling a flashlight out to help Catrina see in the dim light. She made her way back to the hatch and carefully climbed out, closing and locking the door behind her.

"May I see?" she asked, once they got out from under the airplane.

He handed her the flashlight and bent down while she examined the wound and the stitches. Carl was a little more anxious to talk as he really did have something he wanted to say to this girl.

"Ended up with ten stitches and a mild concussion, but it could have been a lot worse. I've been in flak storms that have tossed us around harder than that, but I've always been belted in."

"I'm sorry I couldn't get belted in faster than I did. It's my fault." Catrina said, handing him back the flashlight.

"It is what it is. It's nobody's fault really. I'm just glad that you were able to get a hold of me and tie me down. You probably saved my life up there."

Catrina smiled softly as they started for the hangar and their awaiting dinner.

"It's what I do," she finally said, with an even bigger smile. "I'm just glad you're ok."

"How'd you get to be so smart?" Carl asked good-naturedly. He really wasn't expecting an answer, but got one anyway. One that only Catrina would have come up with. She looked at him as they entered the brightly lit hangar.

"Excuse me; have you ever met my parents?"

Carl got a good laugh out of the comment as they headed for a banquet table and Catrina's waiting father. He sort of knew what had gone on at the airplane and by the expressions and body language of the two as they entered the hangar, things between them would obviously improve.

"So," Captain Dallas spoke quietly, but excitedly, next to his daughter. She picked up a plate to start dishing her dinner. "Looks like you've tamed the savage beast."

"Dad," she nudged him away. "He just thanked me for helping him, that's all."

"Oh really," her father chided.

Catrina was silent for a couple of moments, moving down the line dishing her plate.

"And for saving his life. Besides, he's not a beast, more of a Tom cat."

*　　*　　*　　*　　*

The next day was spent cleaning and doing maintenance. Catrina was basically exempt from most of that, but she wanted to help wherever she could. When she couldn't help, she got comfortable in her favorite spot in the nose of the airplane to read a book that she had brought along for just such occasions. For the rest of the crew, part of the day was spent just lazing around, until Captain Dallas came back from several meetings that he had attended and announced that they were taking on some unusual cargo for the rest of the tour.

Catrina popped open the top hatch of the bombardier's bubble and stood up through the opening to listen to the briefing in the cool late afternoon autumn air.

"We need to cargo some munitions to SLC."

"We're going to do what?" Tommy exclaimed.

"I thought they were supposed to truck that stuff to wherever they wanted it put?" Chuck piped up, a little bit irritated.

"They are," Tony agreed, "but they didn't have enough room in their last truck and needed to get it down to SLC on our arrival date. Normally I would have just told them to put it on another plane somewhere or a train or something, but it's our good friend Harley. Guys, remember Harley? Always had the right ammo for us whenever we needed it and as much as we needed? Remember Harley?" Tony said trying to convince them instead of ordering them. They all moaned a little bit and then agreed.

"Since it's Harley," Carl agreed, a little more upbeat. "How much is there?"

Tony scratched his head a little bit. "A couple of pallets."

"A couple?" they all collectively cried. "How we supposed to get that much ammo onboard skipper?" Tommy asked very concerned. "This ain't a cargo plane, it's a bomber!"

Chuck started running the figures in his head for weight and balance.

"There's hardly room in this thing with all the personal stuff we're carrying," Tommy continued. "You gonna put Cat on your lap to make room for all of it?"

Tony knew what he was asking and that it would be a squeeze to get it all in there.   The aircraft could certainly handle the weight. They had taken off on missions overloaded with bombs and fuel before, that wasn't the issue.

"Well, we won't be overweight," Chuck announced, "but there ain't no way you're gonna get all of it in the back of the plane. Even if you move everyone else up front, that stuff weighs a ton and a half. That'll put us tail heavy on takeoff and flying backwards by the time we get halfway to Jackson."

Catrina listened very intently to the discussion about the problem. She knew all about weight and balance from flying with her dad in his private plane. If the weight wasn't distributed properly throughout the airplane, it would either be front or back heavy to begin with and be totally uncontrollable, or become uncontrollable as the engines burned off fuel. The trick was to place the bulk of the weight as close to the center of the airplane as possible. In cargo planes, that wasn't a problem as it was just one great big flying storage closet, but this was a bomber. The only storage closet it had was the bomb bay and it was for dropping things, not storing them. An idea quickly formed in her head. This would certainly be a trick. Have a seasoned bomber crew listen to a wild idea from a 10 year old girl.

"I have an idea," she piped up confidently.

Everyone turned and looked up at Catrina standing in the open bombardier hatch. Better get it out now while they were quiet.

"We still have guns in all positions on this plane, right?" she asked, looking around at them. A few of them nodded, getting a little interested, not even noticing her gender or age.

"Why not treat this like a bombing mission? Load as much of the ammo into your guns as you can and maybe a little extra, then load the rest of the pallets into the bomb bay?"

Carl and Chuck remained silent, taking serious thought to what she had just proposed while the others started haggling over why it wouldn't work.   It seemed like a perfectly simple, obvious solution. Not sure why they hadn't thought of it to begin with. Regulations required that no live ammo be in the guns unless on an actual mission. Technically they were on a mission and they did have guns.

Finally, Carl and Chuck spoke up in agreement with Catrina.

"Why wouldn't we be able to do it that way?" Carl asked sternly. "There are no regs that say we can't hold or carry live ammo cross country in noncombat situations, only prior approval of the wing commander, which the Captain already has."

"What about how to get and stabilize two pallets in the bomb bay?" Tommy asked, being one of the guys in charge of the bomb-bay.

Terry shared Tom's concern, as he was usually the one that did the bomb arming and shared the payload responsibilities.

"The bomb racks have already been removed," Terry pointed out. "We had to lose them for the extra fuel bladder when we left Scotland. If you can secure all of the ammo cans and mortar packs onto one pallet, Tommy and I will figure out a way to secure the whole thing in the bomb bay."

"We will?" Tommy asked, giving Terry a surprised look.

"On two conditions," Captain Dallas said turning to Chuck and Terry. "We have to be able to safely drop the load if something goes wrong and no loaded gun belts in the chambers. Safeties all on no matter what, got it?" He finished looking at everyone, who agreed readily.

Sounded like they were all onboard with the idea. Never mind that it came from a 10 year old girl. Everyone scrambled to prep their areas for the extra load, while Catrina just grinned broadly. She rested her chin on her hands as her dad turned back to her, a big grin on his face.

"You are amazing," he said chuckling a little, trotting off to the LO's office.

*　*　*　*　*

It wasn't long before a big green truck pulled up to the bomber and unloaded two large pallets of army green ammunition boxes. Their ammunition supply guy from the war, Harley, was endlessly grateful for their willingness to get him out of a jam by getting these last pallets of ammunition down to Salt Lake City. Normally, he would have dispatched a cargo plane to take care of this, even put it on a train, but there weren't any trucks or planes available right now to get it to where it needed to go.

After reassuring them that he owed them big time for the favor, he was off, leaving the crew to start working. Catrina had already gotten the practical version of how to load, operate and care for a .50 caliber machine gun, and not surprising, she understood it very well, though the crew always marveled at how well she comprehended things. Now she was getting a new lesson on loading the guns. Normally, this was done by a loading ground crew and not the actual flight crew. The flight crews were taught how to do it as well; having to reload their weapons in flight after expending whatever ammo was loaded in their guns on the ground.

Chuck was running the calculations on the new weights being loaded in each position and where they fell in the airplane's envelope of center of gravity. There was added weight in the nose gun, the twin fifties in the top turret, the twin fifties on each side of the fuselage of the cockpit, the fifties on each side at the waist positions and the twin fifties in the tail. This also took into account the extra ammo that would be stored at each position just like a combat mission. By the time they had all their locations fitted and filled with ammo, a single loaded pallet had been secured inside the bomb bay and the doors were ready to close.

"We're ready to leave," Tommy announced, activating the doors, watching them swung shut.

Catrina looked through the viewing hole behind the top turret, into the bomb bay as the doors closed. She was tickled that her idea had worked. Even more exciting was feeling like she was of value to the crew. She understood who and what she was, but it was nice to know that these men were of the caliber that they would be able to seriously listen to her and consider what she was thinking.

"Get the weather for tomorrow morning. We'll leave at first light." Captain Dallas announced, taking his daughter's hand and making their way to billeting.

The next day would be another long one. Stop in Jackson Hole, Wyoming late in the morning, then head to Idaho Falls, Pocatello and Twin Falls, Idaho in the afternoon. Spend the night, then on to various locations in Utah.   Logan, Ogden, Hill field and their final destination, Salt Lake City. The trip was almost over and while they weren't exactly tired of it all, it was starting to wear on them.

Catrina was still having the time of her life and hadn't even really thought about being back home playing with her friends. She was thrilled to death to be, what she thought, a part of something big and important. To be doing it with her father, whom she idolized, made it all the better.

The Storm

The next morning brought partly cloudy skies and cooler temperatures. Though it was swinging towards mid-autumn, there was some thunder storm and heavy snow squall activity around the northwest regions and Captain Dallas wanted to get across the larger mountains before it had a chance to build up and cause a problem. He knew the weather around this mountain range could be quite unpredictable, having "thunder snow" on rare occasions. Tony had been in a couple of those hum dingers before and certainly didn't want to repeat any of those experiences. Tim had already reported that early snow storms had come through the Teton mountain range in the last several weeks, leaving a heavy blanket of deep snow all across the mountains.

The ride over to Jackson over the Yellowstone park area wasn't long at all and was quite uneventful. The airplane handled a lot differently with all the added weight, but it was just like flying a bombing run and there was little to no adjustment for the pilots. Tony and Chuck carefully eyed the buildups forming around the Teton mountain range to the southwest and had Tim call in to get the latest weather. Once on the ground, he excused Tim from his normal tour duties, to go to the operations building and continue to monitor the weather by radio and telephone as best he could. Thankfully during the whole time they were scheduled to be on the ground, there were no indications of anything significant to the west, other than a dry cold front. While winter had come early to this region, there was little to no snow on the ground here in Jackson. On the other hand, the Tetons looked magnificent with the white snow contrasted against the stark grays of the granite towers.

After talking to some of the locals about the behavior of the weather and their experiences flying in the Teton mountain range, Tony decided to make the short flight over the Tetons and to at least Idaho Falls, perhaps all the way to Pocatello, if the weather cooperated. Once everyone was loaded back up, he gave the crowds one last show, letting the engines roar on takeoff and circling the field a couple of times, gaining altitude, then heading off towards the north end of the valley before turning south west again towards the abruptness of the rising Teton mountains.

Starting their cut diagonally across the first range, the air started to get rough. This was expected. What wasn't expected, the speed at which the air became rough and the clouds materializing all around them. Every minute, things deteriorated tenfold. So much so that it took both Tony and Chuck completely by surprise. Even with all the flying Tony had done here in the northwest, he had never seen anything like this before. It was like it had just rushed out of nowhere and his options were quickly waning.

"Not liking what I'm seeing here," Tony complained, constantly moving his eyesight in every direction outside. "I'd feel a whole lot better if we could see some cloud definition here."

"We're going to be in ice here pretty quick if we can't get these conditions changed really fast." Chuck reached for the twin carb heat controls as per operating instructions. This shifted the outside air intake for the engines to air that was drawn directly across the exhaust manifolds, thus providing hot air to melt any ice that should try to build up inside the carburetors as moisture was drawn in with the air.

"Let's try this another day," Tony announced, trying to turn back around, but by the time he had his aircraft pointed in the other direction, the clouds had closed off their escape. He had flown IFR (Instrument Flight Rules), all the time, but as soon as he would enter a cloud, the turbulence went from bad to almost unmanageable.

"Ok, so that isn't going to work," he grunted frustrated. His only recourse was to maneuver his ship back to the west and try and fight his way through it. Even as he did so, the turbulence went from moderate to heavy.

"Not liking the ride back here," the complaint voice of the radio operator crackled over the headphones.

Catrina's eyes widened, lightning flashing constantly all around them and a pelting rain pummeling the aircraft, then hail, then heavy snow! Temperatures plummeting, Tony ordered everyone to tie any and everything down, including themselves while Chuck worked to get the de-icing equipment operating. The operational indicators came on for only a moment, but then went back off. Ok, this was not good in the least bit. Tommy checked the breakers on the main electrical panel near his location. Horror pierced through his chest as he pushed the breakers in, only to have them pop right back out. The de-icing equipment was dead. *Not good at all!*

Catrina tried to sit quietly next to Carl watching out the window, the sky darkening to almost black, then back to a dark grey. She was as tense as she could be; her teeth clinched tightly together, her hands and fingers white, holding a death grip on the bottom edge of her small seat and pushing back as hard as she possibly could. This wasn't fun anymore and she honestly felt as though they were going to break apart in midair. Nearly petrified, she clung to the hope that her dad would get them through this terrifying situation. Carl calmly leaned closer to her and began telling stories about flying through flak storms over Germany and how this wasn't even a shadow to what those were like. Of course, Dale and Tim had experienced those same flak storms and knew he was lying through his teeth, just to keep the young girl calm. They even embellished on the lies a little bit to help reassure her. In truth, the entire crew was nearly petrified with fear, but the last three to five years of their lives, dealing with the possibility of death every time they flew, had conditioned them to control that fear. Now, with Catrina onboard, it was just a little bit easier to spin their yarns, not for themselves, but for her.

Up front, Tony drew on all his skill as both a bush and military pilot to keep his ship airborne and in one piece. Finally, almost as suddenly as it had started, the turbulence dropped off to almost nothing, the lightning becoming more frequent and the snow thickening. Sticking heavily to the nose, cockpit windshield and top turret dome, the conditions went from bad to worse. With the de-icing system on the fritz, there was no way to keep the snow and ice from building up on the leading edges of the wings and tail. Chuck glanced to his right at the leading edge of the wing and the engine cowls. The snow was really starting to pack on to them. Get too much and the lift characteristics of the wing change for the worse and you start going down. If it was building up front, it was certainly building up on the tail section, and hearing the occasional banging of ice flipping off the propeller blades and striking the fuselage was quite unnerving.

Carl gave Catrina a quick glance. Even with the aircrafts heating system operating at full capacity, the inside air temperature dropped sharply. The tension, combined with the intense cold enveloping the fuselage, sent shivers firing through her body, making her heart pound harder and reinforcing that they were in trouble.

"Time to put these dandy heated flight suits the air corps has been raving about, to the test," Tim announced, struggling out of his harness and to one of the equipment boxes nearby. Carl and Dale carefully worked to pull the heater cords out and get everyone plugged in and warming up.

"This will have you fixed up in no time," Carl added, turning her temperature controls up.

"Thank you Carl." Catrina was certainly grateful for the warmth the suit provided, and leaned back in her chair as far as she could, trying to relax. She was sure that if anyone could get them through this terrifying hell, it was her dad. She just wished he could get it done a little sooner. It was all she could do to keep from bursting into tears. Yeah, that's all these guys needed was a sobbing 10 year old girl on their hands. Thoughts of her mother flashed through her mind and she knew she just had to figure out a way to keep it together until they got through this. At least the turbulence had subsided for the moment.

Tim turned on a flashlight and tried to look out each of the waist gun windows at the tails. His flashlight unable to penetrate the darkness, he made his way to the very back and looked up through the tail gunner's position at the twin tail fins of the bomber. Things weren't looking very good back there so he quickly made his way forward and grabbed for the intercom mic.

"Skipper, you've got a lot of snow and ice packing on the tail and stab back here."

"Can you give us a guess on the thickness?" Chucked asked, keeping his eyes on the right wing and engine nacelles.

"Still mainly on just the leading edges, but I'm starting to see layers forming at the rudders and elevators."

Tony and Chuck listened to Tim's report on the tail section. Based on what they were seeing and hearing, they were going to be falling out of the sky pretty quick if they didn't do something fast.

Chuck gave the altimeter a glance while trying to look at a small aviation chart he had strapped to his right thigh. Poking his finger at it with one hand and squinting to see in the dim cockpit lighting, he tried to give Tony as much information as he could.

"Those Tetons must still be on our left at just under 14,000 feet. We're at 11,500 feet, still plenty high above all these ridgelines down here at 9000 feet."

Terry pushed up between the two pilots with a small compass for Chuck to use, even trying to help direct him on how to use it to point the airplane in the right direction. It was tough to do as the aircraft was constantly buffeted in every direction. Tony gave the ADF a glance, hoping that it would help give them confirmation of the needed heading. Nothing, its needle just spun aimlessly counterclockwise.

"Running out of options here gentlemen," Tony grunted, noticing that the gap between control and out of control was thinning. Reaching forward, he bumped the throttles up a little more and adjusted the manifold pressure, trying to keep their airspeed up. "I need a direction." He was running out of options as the snow got thicker and the buildup on the aircraft grew heavier. Chuck and Terry supplied him a compass heading for Idaho Falls, but it didn't take Captain Dallas long to figure out that they weren't going to make it that far. He had to get his plane out of this storm, loose the snow and ice buildup or lighten his load.

Taking a bit of a gamble, he pulled the engine power back just a bit, allowing the aircraft to lose altitude. Air currents varied at different flight levels and since there was no way he was going to go up, down at another altitude was his only option. Holding his heading, he allowed their speed to drop closer to the indicated flap speed and had Chuck drop in a notch of flaps to provide some added lift. To their dismay, they found the flap control, inoperative. The reduction in power only served to pull the airplane down even faster and other options had to be considered at this point.

"We're just about to drop through 10,000 feet," Tony pointed out to his copilot. "Better dump our load. Hopefully we can lose enough weight; we can climb back out of this soup."

"Terry, you'll execute the drop," Chuck called out coming alive. "Tommy, need you to confirm."

Tommy clamored into position, watching through the bomb bay window for the doors to open, but it never happened.

"I can't get a confirmation that the doors are opening," Terry called out from his position.

"I can't see anything opening up back here skipper," Tommy confirmed excitedly.

Chuck tried using his control, but was met with the same results. There had to be a malfunction associated with the hydraulics of that system.

The dark, dull grey color of the blizzard began to lighten and then they could see sunlight. There was a momentary glow on every surface inside the plane, then the snow was gone and they were in clear air, but confronted with a giant wall of angry, dark clouds turning in a clock-wise direction in front of them. It was like they had just flown into a large cylinder of clear sky and all around them was swirling masses of snow and angry clouds. Straight up was clear sky and sunlight. Below them, they could see the mountainous terrain reaching up at them. They were down to almost 9000 ft. now, which would surely put them even, if not below the highest ridges within this part of the range.

Tony banked his sluggish, ice covered airplane to the right towards the defined wall of swirling clouds. Even with his vast experience as a bush pilot, he had never seen anything like this before. It was more than a mile across, but holding constant, almost like the eye of a hurricane. Chuck gave the outside temperature gauge a quick glance and looked the ice buildup over some more. This was not good in any circumstance. Even with the clear skies, there wasn't enough heat to melt this much ice off fast enough.

Tony turned the plane along the wall of clouds and swirling snow as they continued to drop. He pushed the throttles all the way forward, but held them just at standard full throttle. There was a pressure band that he could push them through, but that was only in case of extreme emergency, any prolonged operations past full power could damage the engines quickly. The powerful Wright Cyclone radial engines responded with a resounding roar that rose in pitch, slowing their descent towards the terrain below. The ground became more distinct as they circled within the towering cylinder of clouds and wind. One thing he had learned early on, while he had never crash landed any airplane in his life, he knew that a crash landing under control was better than losing control and stalling or winging into the ground.

It was quite clear now that there was no way they were going to get back up high enough to get above the ridges and safely to the west, and even if they did, they would still have to contend with whatever this monster storm was that had come out of nowhere and put them here. It looked as though they were between two ridge lines, but up in a high bowl shaped valley with three sloping sides that curved up almost vertically at the top on one side.

"Hey Chuck?" Tony asked, looking curiously out his window at the terrain below them. "What do you make of that?"

"Make of what?" His copilot strained in his seat to see out his Captain's window. "What in the name of Sam Hill?" He rubbed his eyes a couple of times and blinked. Both pilot and copilot strained to process what they were seeing. "Is this what snow blindness is like?"

There was something quite odd about the floor of the valley. Continuing to circle, just skirting the cloud walls, Tony and Chuck blinked repeatedly, straining to focus in on the objects covering the valley floor. One moment, they looked like small buildings on bare earth all over the place, then it would look like large rocks and trees covered in several feet of snow, then it would look like both at the same time. They could see a long wall of some kind that stretched across the valley, blurring and fading in and out of sight, blending with the actual snowy terrain.   Whatever it was down there, they were going to come in on top of it. Whether it was snow covered rocks or buildings, the resulting crash would be the same. Not good odds at all, and even if they got the plane on the ground with them in one piece, their cargo wasn't likely to fair so well; the whole plane would likely explode with it. Mortar ordinance didn't take too kindly to sudden stops. After all, it was designed to work that way.

Tony chose his spot and his method of landing. Normally, he would have just set it down on flat level ground, but because what was perceived as flat and level kept changing, he felt like his odds were better if he slid his plane in on the sloping sides of the bowl. That would give them more sliding room, less obstacles to hit and break up the plane, and there appeared to be lots of unchanging snow surface. The changing floor of the valley had to be some sort of crazy optical illusion, but he wasn't taking any chances. He set up his approach to follow the curve of the bowl for maximum sliding distance. This would be very tricky, having to continue to run full power right up to touch down and then implementing emergency shutdown procedures.

"Ok everyone. I'm sorry, but we're going to have to set her down here. Prepare for crash landing," Captain Dallas ordered. "Carl, can you make sure Cat is belted in good?"

"No problem skipper. We'll all take good care of her. She'll be fine," Carl responded. He could hear the deep concern in his Captain's voice, but knew he was concerned for everyone onboard.

Terry abandoned his position in the nose and started his crawl back to where Tommy was strapped in at the engineer's position. Making his way through the crawl space under the pilot and copilot's bulkhead, his foot contacted the bomb bay controls, unintentionally kicking the bay door controls.

"Something's wrong," Tony announced feeling an instant change in the flight characteristics of the plane.

"Yeah something's wrong," Chuck agreed, feeling it to. He looked back at Terry as he emerged from his exit tunnel. "Do you feel that?"

Terry looked around, looking for the source of the trouble. Tony and Chuck noted their airspeed dropping dramatically. Something was terribly wrong now and they weren't going to make their intended approach to land like this.

"The doors are open!" Tommy exclaimed, excitedly announcing that the bay doors had opened and indeed, the door lights on the console between the pilots had come on.

"Drop it!" Tony shouted.

Chuck hit his yoke control, the plane lurching a bit, both pilots feeling a change in their descent. Tommy scrambled with his controls at the bomb bay to close the doors as the pallet of ammunition dropped away from the plane and crashed into the deep snow against the bowl wall directly behind them.

They circled just above the trees, but Tony knew they were already too low and turning to head back up the bowl shaped valley wasn't going to improve their hopeless situation. He glanced over at the picture of his wife and daughter clipped to the console between two dials, and then pushed his throttles through the emergency tabs for full power. The needles on the RPM gauges climbed into the red, the big radial engines thundering. He lined up for his final turn on the wall as the bomb bay doors swung closed.

Chuck had hoped the loss in weight would have saved them, and had they been high enough, or even able to fly straight ahead down the valley, it would have. The problem wasn't weight, it was the lifting capability of an iced up air foil. Tony judged his turn and held the bank right into the touchdown, holding the airplane at the same angle as the steeply sloping wall of the valley. He could sense the props striking the snow covered ground, throwing up a huge spray of white. A moment later he felt them touch.

"Mixture off! Mags off! Fuel cut off! Throttles off! Master off!"

Both pilots were barely able to accomplish their tasks, the ride instantly turning quite violent. The spinning propellers sent up plumes of snow in all directions as the aircraft slid along what had once been its flight path. Finally, the propellers stopped turning, the blades bending over from the weight of the plane on the ground. Even though the snow was very deep, the plane started turning down toward the base of the valley wall as their speed slowed. Everything seemed to be going as planned. Sliding a bit like a heavy bobsled, the aircraft felt as though it were still flying until the left wing caught the ground, spinning the plane violently counter clockwise, hitting some trees and shearing off one of the wings and the tail. Then, everything went silent.

"I think we're still in one piece," Chuck commented, looking over at his Captain in a bit of a daze.

"Avalanche!" Tim yelled through the broken fuselage from the back of the plane.

No sooner did he get the warning out, than there was snow billowing everywhere and they could feel themselves moving again. Since they were pointed downhill already, there was no tumbling. They were covered in tons of snow as it started to go dark, and they could feel several violent jerks on the plane, like they were being hit, or rather they were hitting something. Everything went black for several seconds, then breaking out of the bury, they found themselves sliding through the mouth of a cave where the plane finally came to a stop with snow cascading over the entrance to their rear. The ensuing avalanche continued until the cave entrance had been completely covered.   Darkness was once again, the only condition they knew.

First order of business was to secure the aircraft and its condition. Didn't matter what condition the crew was in. If the airplane was about to explode, it wouldn't matter if one of them was bleeding or had broken bones. Chuck shut off the electrical master switches while Tommy and Terry pulled all the resettable breakers. Once secured, Tommy poked his head up into the top turret for a look around with his flashlight while Tony and Chuck did the same with their side windows. The crash had sheared off the left wing for sure and Chuck announced that the right wing was gone as well, probably torn off in the avalanche somehow. Right about then, as Tony relaxed somewhat from the whole ordeal, he remembered his daughter in the back of the plane.

A wave of panic suddenly streaked through him and she became Tony's number one priority when he heard the muffled voices of Dale and Carl calling her name from the back. He quickly scampered past Terry and Tommy and scooted over the bomb bay bulkhead towards the back, where he found the rest of his crew mostly buried in snow and other debris. No Catrina! Tony was down in an instant to join Carl, who was madly digging with his bare hands in the location where her seat should be and finally found the top of her head. A hand and arm burst from out of the snow and a moment later, her red, wet face appeared, gasping for air and shivering. After reassuring her that she was going to be just fine, they all quickly dug her out and unbuckled the harness.   Father and daughter held one another for several minutes. Catrina wasn't sure she wasn't consoling her father more than he was consoling her. Tony looked towards the back of the plane as Tim and Dale held flashlights towards a wall of snow. Looking out the window, they could easily make out the walls of the cave they had slid into. Time to salvage what they could, and get out to assess their situation.

The floor of the cave was smooth clay. No rocks or gravel of any kind, just hard packed clay. After surveying their situation and seeing no immediate dangers of explosion, fire or further avalanche, they started setting up a sort of camp against the pilot's side of the fuselage. Carl and Chuck began to survey the cave ahead of them, but were ordered back by Tony to have a bit of a crew situational awareness briefing. After some talk of what to do, it was decided that they should all try and get some rest first, then set out to try and find a way out.

With that, they all got comfortable, taking time, which they now had plenty of, to try to rest, even sleep. That wouldn't be hard for most of them. The stress and excitement had everyone completely worn out. Catrina cuddled up close to her father, who worked to wrap them in a couple of wool blankets, and then they drifted off to sleep. Several hours later, they were all awakened with a start, to the sounds of big men with bright torches giving loud orders in a language that no one understood. Catrina peered out from behind her blankets, up at several large men holding fiery torches and big swords. As if they weren't in enough trouble already.

WACS

21st Century

A blast of bubbles erupted at the surface of the ocean as two scuba divers surfaced next to a small chartered yacht off the east coast of Brazil. Working as part of a salvage team, WACS, Water & Aircraft Salvage recovering wrecks specializing in aircraft, these two divers had been doing salvage recovery since they were young teenagers.

Britten was older than Bryan by two years at 25. He was a little above average in build with sandy blonde hair. Bryan was shorter, not as husky and didn't share any of his older brother's likeness, having straight, dark brown hair, kept cut much like a 60s era mop top.

Their father had gotten them into salvage work at a young age, taking them out to rescue antique vehicles from farmers in the area and then restoring them. This branched out into recovering aircraft wreckage, cannibalizing them for good working parts. Both men served tours in the military, Bryan notably becoming a highly accomplished marksman in both rifle and pistol shooting. Returning home, they turned the salvage business into a lucrative enterprise and found themselves branching out into maritime ventures and from there it blossomed. Much of the work they found themselves doing was international and their travels took them all over the world.

While Brit and Bryan were not the only owners of WACS, they were the primary salvage operators. They had gone on salvage missions all over the world finding not just sunken treasure, but ships of every kind and age. Some salvaged for their cargo, some raised for reuse. Others were purposely sunk to provide for marine life in certain areas where habitat had become scarce. They had been to Russia, locating military tanks that had sunk in rivers and lakes, bringing them back out for the military or private individuals willing to pay for their services. They had been to the Arctic Circle and Greenland to help with salvage of numerous aircraft. Their favorites were military aircraft and even more favored were World War II aircraft. They had located and salvaged vintage Corsairs, Bearcats, Hellcats, P-38 Lightings, P-51 Mustangs, P-40 Warhawks, B-29s, B-26s, B-17s, B-24s, B-25s, and a host of other planes too diverse to mention.

They had just finished their last dive on a Brasilia turbo prop that had gone down in a storm off the coast of Cabo de Santo Auguostinho, Brazil, carrying some precious stone artifacts from some ancient South American ruins. The country's museums were glad to pay the price of salvage to get their property back. On this dive, it wasn't to bring the plane back to the surface, only retrieve the cargo, which turned out to be a routine operation. The WACS CEO had assigned his best men to this mission because the client was emphatic that there were no mistakes with the retrieval of this cargo.

Once safely onboard and heading for port, Brit and Bryan retired to their respective cabins for rest. Undoubtedly they would get to see if they were to have a couple of days in the wonderful March summer of Brazil before heading back to the frozen, snow covered country of the United States, specifically, Driggs, Idaho. Still a somewhat quiet little town nestled in the Teton basin, not as sleepy as it used to be years ago, but still obscure enough to provide solitude from the bustle of the world.

Unfortunately for at least one of them, it wasn't going to happen. Brit had just finished showering and stepped into Bryan's cabin, leaning against the doorway still in a towel and drying his hair, watching his brother read an email that their boss, Uncle Calvin, had sent them while they were out in the water.

"So, who gets to go?" Brit asked, with a sigh.

He was tired and ready for bed as his lids drooped half shut over his hazel eyes. He had already read through the same email Bryan was poring over.

"Did you look at the attachment?" Bryan asked his impetuous older brother.

Bryan was tired as well, but kept his focus on the images in front of him on the large computer screens. He had a bit of an overbite which allowed his upper front teeth to show a little while he was concentrating. Brit had a puzzled look on his face and stepped a little closer to the computer screen.

"Didn't see that part." He mumbled good-naturedly.

"I keep telling you that you need to read and look through the whole thing and not just the," Bryan held his fingers up in the quotations signs, "The good parts."

"Nag, Nag, Nag," Brit came back with a smile. "So, let me get this straight. See if I have all the facts here," he said, plopping down on Bryan's bed. "Cal wants to send us up the mountain, our own mountain mind you, to look for a plane wreck that he thinks he sees from a photograph taken about six months ago. That's what I got out of it."

Bryan remained silent, reading the entire contents of the email, and then clicking on the attachment which brought up a picture. It was very grainy and not in good focus, nor was it zoomed in very well, but it was taken of an area of the mountains that both men were familiar with. They had never seen anything there before and it seemed peculiar for there to be a plane wreck in an area that they frequented often, not only in the summer, but winter as well. Brit sat up, instantly recognizing the grainy form of the metal reflection in the photo.

"Skype!" he called out wide awake and very serious now.

Bryan scrambled to open up the program application, clicking on the right icon to make the call to their headquarters in Idaho. As the call started through, Brit stared closely at the photo trying to get his eyes to focus in on the image. Finally, the call was answered by an older gentleman, in his 50s, silver hair. His voice was gruff, but that was the voice, not the man.

"Ah, the Garrett boys; I knew I'd be getting a call from you two. Just wished you had waited another couple of hours. I'm not even in my rem cycle yet," he said, a little bleary eyed. "I suspect you have some questions," he said yawning.

"Ya think?" Brit piped up, settling down in the chair next to his brother.

"Well, I assume that you guys have finished with the Brasilia."

"Yeah, their rocks are stashed just down the hall from where we are right now." Bryan said quickly. "We're on our way back to Cabo right now.   Should make landfall sometime tomorrow morning."

"Good, I assume you've read our latest find then. Would you rather I send Luke and Derek on this one? They are a little closer and I know how hard you guys have been working and you are down there where it's summer and…….."

"Yeah, yeah, blah, blah, blah," Brit cut in quickly, knowing that Cal wouldn't have sent them the information had he wanted someone else on the job. "Get to the part, get to the part."

"Part? " Cal came back acting surprised. "And what part would that be?"

"That's a twin tail in that picture, which by the way is a terrible picture."

"I have an App. for that," Bryan cut in quickly.

Brit passed him a quick glance, then back to the computer screen.

"We know you're just playing with us. Come on, there aren't very many planes out there that have twin tails."

"Maybe an even better question would be what's a twin tail doing in that location?" Bryan asked. "We've been in that area a hundred times and there has never been any sign of anything. If a twin tail had crashed up there, we'd know about it."

"I agree completely, but there's more complexity here, than you know," Cal agreed, working with something on his desk. "I'm sending you the rest of the satellite photos I was able to get my hands on. Good to know friends in high places that owe you favors. These photos were taken about six months ago after a big storm passed through the area."

"Satellite command eh?" Brit piped up. "'Bout time Rhonda ponied up considering all the help we've given her for the past couple of years finding all of her crap. What took so long to send them out?"

"Rhonda said something about them getting set aside, and then declassified. They have been trying to track some odd weather patterns up there for years, but can't get anything definitive. She thought we might like to have a look see, since it's in our own back yard. You should be getting them any moment now." Both men looked over at their second screen as Bryan pulled up the email and started opening the attachments.

"The first one shows a debris field that has been uncovered by a snow slide or avalanche. You can see part of a wing and some of the twin tail."

"Wait! A snow slide?" Bryan adjusted the zoom on the picture while Brit cocked his head, as if looking at it differently would explain a snow slide at the height of autumn in these mountains. "How could there be a snow slide up there that time a year?"

"The second is a zoom in on the wing portion," Cal continued. "It doesn't really show much other than it's military and looks like a medium range aircraft. The third one is the kicker boys. It holds all the marbles. The tail," Cal finished, knowing that the expert would now be taking over the conversation.

Brit looked closely at the exposed tail and recognized it immediately.

"It's a 25," he announced.

Bryan studied it carefully in silence.

"Holy Hanna, what's a Mitchell doing up in Lake Valley?" Brit asked, completely astonished at what he was seeing.

"Most important to this photo is, we have the serial number on the tail, plain as day," Cal announced, pulling up more information and sending it along to them. "This plane went down in September, 1945 in a freak snowstorm. All hands were lost." Bryan studied not what the overall pictures showed, but the closer detail. The images appeared to be half exposures on top of other pictures. You could see through the images of the wreckage, as if they were ghostly apparitions, very odd.

"Another knot head maneuver by an idiot pilot who thought he was cool or something, just like that B-23 Dragon up north of McCall," Brit commented disdainfully.

"Not likely bro," Bryan interjected. "This one is way different. The Dragon at McCall ran out of gas, this one went down due to heavy turbulence and icing. If you'd read the attachment."

"Nag, Nag, Nag."

Britten's attitude deflated a little bit. He felt like most crashes were pilot error and could have been avoided had other decisions been made. That may well be true, unless you're the one sitting in the left seat making those decisions.

"Makes little difference right now. There are a couple of things we would like to know." Cal interjected. There was no need for speculation now, plenty of time for all that later.

"Ok, so what's the plan here?" Britten came back, staring at the tail in the photo.

"I've booked you both on separate flights home as soon as you make landfall. Bryan, I'm bringing you straight back here to head up all the ground preparations. If the weather cooperates, which it never does, you should be ready for your brother when he gets back from Montana."

Cal smiled with a yawn and he looked like he was getting ready to head back off to bed. Cal's time zone was several hours behind where Britten and Bryan were, but wait! There were still a whole bunch of unanswered questions here and more that hadn't even been thought of.

"Wait," Brit spoke up, bringing Cal back to his seat. "Whoa, Montana? Why am I going to Montana?"

"The pilot's widow still lives there. I'm sending you everything that I could dig up on her. She lives in Helena."

"What good is visiting her going to do? You have all the Intel you need on the crash, don't you?"

"I have intel from the military's point of view way back in '45', but not what we really need to know about him or his plane. The personal stuff will help us not only find it, but make positive identification. This one is a little strange I know, but that's the way we're going to work this one. Find out what you can from her and then get yourself back here to Driggs and up the mountain. Get it, got it, good." He said, getting up from his desk and shutting the connection off.

Britten spoke up to object, but the connection was already closed. The printer next to Bryan came alive, printing information and photos. Britten pulled the first sheet on his trip to Montana.

"Oh goodie, she's almost 90 for heck sakes, but holy smokes!" he exclaimed, picking up the next page that had a couple of her pictures on it. One was a black and white portrait of the woman when she was in her early twenties. Britten stared at the picture. He couldn't seem to keep his eyes off of it.

"Get a load of this girl," he said, shoving one of the pictures at his brother.

Bryan looked at it for a moment, passed it back to him and went back to what he was doing.

"She's pretty," he said almost at a mumble.

"You're kidding, right?" Brit said, flabbergasted at his brother's response.

Bryan looked up, a stupid look on his face.

"I'm sorry," he paused for dramatic emphasis. "She's not pretty?"

Brit stared at him like he was some kind of an idiot.

"Yes she's pretty!" He finally blurted out loudly. "She's amazing! Look at the eyes, the hair! Everything about her is a vision!" he exclaimed, voicing his thoughts to himself now, seeing that his brother didn't really share his enthusiasm. "You're such an idiot," he mumbled, staring at the image in the photo.

Even though it was just a black & white photo, his mind could almost transpose all the color into it. He just knew those dark alluring eyes were deep brown. The age and era of the picture couldn't reproduce those facts, but he knew they were there. She was indeed very pretty and he was absolutely captivated by her image.

"As soon as you're done drooling over Mrs. Dallas there," Bryan said, handing him a stack of papers he had just pulled from the printer next to the desk. "Here's the rest of the information you're going to need. Enjoy," he said with a smile.

Brit took the papers, keeping his eyes glued on the image of the Dallas woman as she appeared back in the late 1930s. Turning without a word, he stepped slowly out into the hall and down to his own room. There wasn't a whole lot of sleep for him as their ship made its way back to its Brazilian port. He had lost all interest in sleep when he received the information on the B-25 and the picture of Mrs. Dallas. He pored over the information on the accident and what the military was able to piece together, which wasn't very much, at least not much documented. It was a little hard for Brit to understand how a decorated WWII hero and crew could have gotten themselves into such a situation in the first place.

There were some odd notations and references made in a couple of the statements. The military personnel putting the sketchy information together probably didn't know what to do with some of the details. There were one or two references of a 10 year old girl onboard, the daughter of the bomber's pilot. No name given for the daughter. What the heck was his daughter doing with him on a military plane on a military flight? He and Bryan had spent a couple of years in the service themselves and there was no way anything like that would have been tolerated in today's military. It must have been different back 1945.

This was an early production model B-25J aircraft, but had been modified with all the latest field upgrades included through the end of the aircraft's production run. This particular model aircraft had been test fitted with some test systems not found on any other model Js, including a third set of auxiliary batteries located in the fuselage directly behind the upper ball turret. The records of the upgrades were meticulous. It was almost as if it's pilot and crew didn't want to let go of the original aircraft. Of course he was well aware of the affection many of the bomber crews had for their ships. While most of the nose art that adorned many of the bomber aircraft were generally pornographic in nature, many of them had special significance, such as a girlfriend, wife or even a mother. Lots of times it had to do with some sort of strength. There was no mention or photographs in the official reports, but there was a crew photo by the front of the plane and you could see that there was something painted on the side of the fuselage, but that was all. There wasn't enough in the picture to tell what it might have been.

There was almost nothing in any of the reports, military or civilian, in his hands about the pilot's widow. Only her name, Amanda Alice Dallas, an address and phone number in Helena, Montana. He'd actually been to Helena before, but only passing through on a connecting flight to northern Canada some time back on another salvage job. It was located on the very southwestern part of the great wide open plains of the state that was known as Big Sky. He looked at the information at least four or five more times on the flight back to the states, many times referring back to Amanda's photo to admire her beauty.

Bryan had his own work cut out for him. He was organizing the supplies they were going to need for the expedition up the mountain. Even though it was local, he wasn't going to take any chances. They would have what they needed with them, but have plenty of back up available at their command base located on the Driggs airport. He was even able to get several Sky Crane helicopters on standby in Jackson, Wyoming. There would be no way for them to get any wreckage out of that area otherwise. Since the weather is so unpredictable in those mountains, they would need to be close by to get in and out as quickly as possible, should a window of opportunity open up.

Much of the stuff they already had on hand; snowmachines, snow cat, basic camping, climbing, and winter gear, but he wanted to make sure they had plenty of extra muscle available. By that, he meant, a couple of other minds along for the ride. People who could help problem solve, but knew the mountain like they did. Their other two coworkers were going to be busy on other jobs, but he had just the pair in mind, a couple of boyhood friends, who had been and done everything with them. Daniel Niker and Gerald Gunn loved adventure, but their interests ran in other directions from the two Garrett boys. They preferred staying at home and doing the river rafting trips, local back country mountain skiing and snowmachining for high paying tourists. While they liked the water, they much preferred being on top of it, instead of under it, where the Garrett boys spent most of their time in the discovery and recovery of wrecks.

Bryan had already sent the invites ahead and pretty well knew that they would be all "gung-ho" for the adventure. While winter time was busy for them, he knew they would clear their schedules for this. They would most likely be waiting for him in front of the staging hangar at the Driggs airport, his final destination.

Amanda Alice Dallas

Britten stepped from his rental car, looking at the small house that lay silent before him. He was tired. The long sleepless night on the plane from Brazil had him a little wobbly. Add in the near frightful flight on the regional turbo prop into the Helena airport and all he wanted to do was find his hotel bed and slip into a coma. Unfortunately for him, his uncle Cal had put him and Bryan on a schedule, so sleep wasn't about to happen until he got this interview over and done with. The place had several trees in the front and side yards, but they weren't very big and were completely void of life. Even though it was still winter in the northwest, there wasn't much snow here in Helena, maybe a couple of inches. Somehow, even though he had lived in Driggs all his life and within spitting distance of the Tetons, it still seemed far colder here.

Stepping up the sidewalk towards the house, he checked the address again to make sure he was in the right place. Tired as he was, he almost didn't want to see this woman, being quite nervous. He had interviewed individuals before about their connections to wrecks they were working salvage on, but this one seemed far different somehow. A feeling of foreboding continually nagged at the back of his mind. Something was off, but he couldn't identify it. Approaching the house, the image in his head of what Mrs. Dallas looked like from her early photo ran in a continuous loop; he was in love with that. However, meeting her in person was certain to change all of that.

He stepped up onto the small, but neatly kept wooden porch and rang the doorbell, glancing over at a porch swing. There was barely enough room for it there. It didn't look neglected at all, rather well used as a matter a fact, even for it being winter. At length, he could hear someone on the other side of the door and stepping back a little bit, the screen door swung open and a figure stepped into the doorway. Ok, so this isn't what he had envisioned at all for a 90 year old woman. He expected silver white hair, if she had any at all; saggy baggy face with age spots all over, thick glasses, short and bent over from osteoporosis. This woman was still standing up straight, she did wear glasses, but she didn't look like she was in her 90s at all. Her hair was white and somewhat short, similar in length to her early photo. There was little to no change in what he had seen before and what he saw now in her eyes. They were still as deeply brown and alluring as he had imagined they were. Color pictures of that era where rare, but it wasn't necessary for him to see one in color now

that he had met her in person. Seeing her eyes now, made him a
believer in what he had imagined was true in the photograph.

"Hello," she greeted him warmly. "You must be Mr. Garrett." She
opened the screen door and welcomed him inside.

"Please call me Brit ma'am," he responded, moving inside and out
of the way so she could close the door. Stepping through the entry
hall, Brit thought he saw a shadow move across a far doorway at the
end of the hall, but it was just out of the corner of his eye. When he
looked straight at the door, there was nothing there.

"I'll be glad to call you Brit if you'll call me Amanda," she said,
grinning as she led him into the front room.

The place looked and smelled like the 1940s. This wasn't
necessarily a bad thing. Brit had been in far worse. She kept it very
tidy, but it didn't appear that she was a clean freak. He could see
some dirty dishes in the sink, a couple of suitcases in the main
hallway, but nothing was a mess. The furniture looked old as well, but
it wasn't all worn out like you would think old war era furniture would
be. In fact, the entire house looked as though it might have been
caught in a time capsule, as everything looked oddly pristine and
original. There were lots of knickknacks placed around the room and
lots of pictures.

She invited him to sit down and offered him something to drink,
but he refused. He first noticed the large picture of her husband in
uniform, on a small round table next to the chair that he came to rest
in and gestured for a closer look.

"You didn't say very much on the phone about what you wanted to
know about my husband," she motioned for him to go ahead and look
at the picture.

"Is this for some article for a book or magazine or something?"
Her voice was still quite strong and clear.

"No, I didn't and I'm sorry about that." Brit said, setting the picture
down and looking at another smaller one behind it. "The information I
wanted to discuss with you, I didn't want to do over the phone." He
gave the second picture a double take. It was a photo of Captain
Dallas with his 10 year old daughter sitting on his lap.

"Is this...?"

"That would be our only child, our daughter Catrina Amanda. We
called her Cat for short. She was daddy's little girl and went
everywhere with him." Amanda fell silent for a moment, playing with
a long golden necklace that hung around her neck. There was
something attached to it, but it was hidden beneath her blouse. She
perked back up, trying to get to the point.

"So what can I tell you about my husband?"

Brit gazed endlessly at the picture, noting how similar the girl in
the photo was to the early picture of Amanda. He felt like he might
well be looking at time travel right in front of him, in either direction.

Looking at the picture, he felt like a conceptual artist could have easily aged Catrina 10 to 15 years and come up with the black and white portrait of her mother at the same age. Conversely, it would take little to no effort at all to reverse the process. It was hard to believe that they were two different people.   Finally, Brit put the photo back and opened his brief case, noticing a couple of pictures on the mantle over a modest fireplace and stopped to take a closer look at them.

There was more here in this front room than just an old lady whose husband flew a bomber in World War II. He set his case aside for a moment and got up, looking at the pictures. They were fascinating and certainly worth closer examination. He picked up the first photo, gazing at it carefully. It was a picture of Amanda standing next to her husband's small private plane. She was sporting a pilot's outfit and holding onto a pilot's log book.

"A couple of years after my husband disappeared, I decided to get my pilots license. We both loved to fly and it seemed a shame to let his plane just sit in the hangar locked away. Best way to kill an airplane is to not fly it," Amanda said, grinning broadly. It was obvious now that she had had a long career of flying. He looked at several other pictures taken of her and her airplane in various places around the western mountains.

"This looks like a Stinson," Brit commented, doing the guy thing, looking at the airplane and not so much at anything else.

"You know your aircraft," Amanda commented, smiling as she watched him examine the photos.

"SR-10, very nice," Brit said, lost in the subject of airplanes, especially the old ones. There had been nothing in Amanda's file about her being a pilot and flying all the aircraft pictured here.

"Is this your husband's airplane?" Brit asked, pulling a smaller picture from the back.

"Yes," Amanda responded, standing up and taking the picture from Britten. She gazed at it with a far off look in her eyes. "He loved this one. It was his first plane; spankin' new Cessna 165. He got rid of it though; replaced it with the Stinson. I have loved it."

"What are all these other planes here?" he asked, looking at the different ones.

"My husband ran a successful airfreight service before the war. After I got my certificates, I restarted it and continued what he had started." Brit looked at another one that was hung on the wall next to a book shelf. It was much larger than the others and showed much more than just her standing next to her airplane. It looked like it was taken at a backcountry strip next to a cabin.

"And this one?" Brit asked, pointing to it.

"Still the Stinson," she replied readily.

"Where was it taken?" he asked, trying to picture where it might be.

"It's a place called High Mountain Heaven," she answered, moving next to him for a better look. "Tony inherited the land from his uncle Max back in 1932. Max had always planned to build a cabin up there. When we got married we always planned to carry through with it. We got the airfield built, but then he went into the war and well, there never was time after that." She paused a moment, thinking of something, then continued. "After the war, I used Tony's pension and profits from the freight company to finish it. I spend most of my summers there. I love the solitude," she trailed off, thinking of something distant, but always very close to her.

"How do you run a successful freight company and spend so much time there?" Brit asked, looking around for more pictures. Sadly, there were no more readily available. Amanda popped a smile and turned to sit back down.

"Being the owner has its perks. Simply hire other pilots to do all the work for you. You know, Dallas Freight," she said, with a gleam in her eye. Brit turned back and sat down.

"I have the official military report here on the disappearance of your husband's plane back in '45'. It's a little sketchy. Can you tell me anything other than what is here?"

"What's this all about? Why ask about the disappearance?" she inquired curiously.

"Please bear with me, Amanda. Anything would be helpful."

"Ok,"

She explained his war history and went through the publicity tour, everything that she could recall. Brit could tell that she was reliving it all over again, but braved on through her story. She recalled getting off the train in Salt Lake City, to several somber faced military people who whisked her quickly off to the air command control center. There, she got the news that her husband's plane had disappeared in a freak snowstorm over the Teton mountain range. She explained in detail how their radio man was able to relay information about the severe icing conditions they were enduring in the air. Completely iced up, they made it out of that horrible storm, and into a clear cylinder of air surrounded by the swirling mass of storm, over a valley on the west side of the mountains.

Preparing to crash land, they could see the ground changing and blurring beneath them, then there was nothing. The last part of this was documented in a separate report as it sounded too strange and there was so much garble in the transmission that it wasn't clear enough to include, sounding too bizarre for standard reports.

The report did include a record of a search and rescue, but no sign of the aircraft was ever found in the reported area. She had personally spoken to one of the local guides that had been involved in the search. He had described odd tales of that area and similar stories of other people who had encountered similar conditions. Unfortunately nothing could ever be substantiated and she could remember no detail of them. Only the name of one of the local guides she had conversed with.

"His name was Bill Kifey. I don't know if he is still alive or not, but you might try talking to him if you can."

"Yes, he's still alive." Brit knew Mr. Kifey. "I know him very well. Funny, he's never mentioned any of this ever."

"No, I don't expect he would. Would you repeat any of this craziness? The military threatened me to never speak of this either. This is the first time I have ever spoken of it to anyone else in all this time. I figured that I was protecting my husband's name by doing so. Changing ground isn't the reason they went down, it was icing. I'm sure they made the same threats to Bill."

"Tell me more about it sounding so bizarre. The ground was changing, how?"

"Not much more was ever said, just that it was changing. One moment it looked like buildings and a long wall, and then next it was just snow and trees, bizarre."

Brit pulled out the satellite photos of the crash site.

"Amanda, my brother and I spend a lot of time riding snowmachines in that very area. We have camped and hiked in this very same location for many years. I gotta say, we know that place like the back of our hands and we have never seen anything up there, winter or summer. Not a scrap of anything." He handed her the first blurry photo. "We only received these about three days ago. They were taken about six months ago."

Amanda examined the photo carefully, and then took the next photo as Brit handed it to her.

"These were taken by high power satellite. It clearly shows debris in a snow slide. This last one, shows part of a wing and part of the tail with the serial numbers exposed."

Amanda gazed at the last photo in utter shock. She held her hand to her mouth to keep her bottom lip from quivering. The serial number had been forever etched into her memory as she read it, recognizing it immediately.

"It's his plane," she gasped quietly, just staring at it. "It's "The Amanda"."

A noise came from the back room, diverting their attention momentarily, Amanda glancing quickly away, but then turning back to Brit.

"Stupid cat," she said quickly.

"Can you tell me anything more about his plane? Any other markings on it?"

"Why?" she inquired.

Brit cleared his throat.

"Amanda, I work for a company called WACS, it's a salvage company. We locate wrecks and recover them for historical, government or private purposes. We have salvage rights to this aircraft, if it's even really there, and we want to make a positive identification on it and, if there are any remains," he paused, looking at the pain in her brown eyes. "Bring them home to their loved ones to be laid to rest properly."

Brit thought she was going to burst into tears, her eyes welling up a bit, but she was able to hold her composure and gaze back down at the photo.

"He named the plane after me. I was a little upset with him when he showed me what he had done. He had an artist paint a picture of me on the side of the airplane. I hated being grouped in with all the other pinup girls on the sides of other planes. They were mostly naked, but this painting was done very special."

Amanda knew that Britten was going to need all the detail she could provide. She got up and pulled a couple of small photo albums from one of the shelves in the room and started going through them.

"The picture was of me in shoulder length brown hair, maybe a little shorter, but not as short as it is now and certainly brown, not what I have now," she chuckled softly.

Britten grinned broadly, making them both feel a little more comfortable with the conversation. Finally, she stopped at a page and pulled a picture from its sleeve and handed it to him. It was a broad picture of the B-25J Mitchell and its crew, standing on the left side in front of the lavishly painted nose art of Amanda and her name.

"The painting was of me in a pretty yellow dress holding a sword. I was standing modestly, not stretched out or bent over or on my back or standing on my head. Ridiculous poses for any self-respecting woman, but most nose art was pretty much pornographic. There were a number of bombs and enemy aircraft painted on it under the pilot's window, but I can't remember anything about all that."

They conversed for a while longer about the details of his departure and then Brit got up to leave. Again, he thought he saw a shadow of movement towards the rear of the house, but didn't want to seem rude by trying to look any more than just a passing glance.

Showing him to the door, Amanda turned to him and gently took his hand. She was still a very poised woman and her touch was quite soft and warm.

"If you find him," she teared up again. "Bring him back home to me."

Brit smiled and gently put his hand on hers.

"I will," he said, starting to pull away from him, but she held on tightly to him and gazed directly into his eyes.

"Our little girl, Catrina was with him. She was only 10 years old." She could barely choke the words out.

"Please, bring her home."

Brit started to tear up himself, the sudden urge to get the heck out of there as fast as he could, swelling. He was about as uncomfortable as he could be.

"I will. I promise." It was all he could muster and he gently pulled free from her and stepped back outside.

Amanda watched from the front window as Brit got in his car and drove off. She let her eyes drop back down at the table with the pictures, looking past the large one of her husband, at the smaller one of Tony and Catrina. She picked it up and held it softly to her bosom and let the tears of heartache flood over her.

Lake Valley

Normally, WACS would be driving in a small caravan of semi-trucks with gear trailers in tow for a salvage, or just lease the stuff on site if they weren't close to it, but this mission was in their own back yard. Everyone just had to show up at the command center at the Driggs airports with their stuff.

The hangar was well outfitted for year round operations. Well heated in the winter and air conditioned in the summer. They had everything imaginable. A full metal and wood shop and a nice large automotive repair bay, complete with adjustable machine lift for raising things as small as a snowmachine to their full sized snow cat. There was plenty of room for staging heavy equipment and vehicles inside and still hangar a couple of aircraft they used for travel, or recon. In this instance, they were staging three vehicles for the trip. Two snowmachines outfitted for high mountain powder riding and a Hagglunds STS199 Sno-Cat with cargo/camping coach. The Sno-Cat by itself would be plenty enough room for all of them, but with the added coach, that gave them twice the room, so they weren't camping in tents and since they had a road up to where they were going, it just seemed to make sense.

While people were not allowed to live on airport property, Cal might as well have. He lost his wife years ago and didn't really like being at home too much. His work was his life now and so he spent most of his time at the command center on the airport. Stepping out of the office and around a fully restored 1979 Kawasaki Invader snowmachine sitting silently next to the other mountain sleds, Cal worked on setting up all their equipment and getting it loaded in the brightly colored, red and white snow-cat. Everyone had arrived, including Brit and Bryan's two friends, Jerry Gunn and Danny Niker, who were catching up in the briefing room.

Jerry was a rather tall thin looking guy, a little older than the rest, with curly brown hair. Danny always seemed to be more like the comic relief of the bunch and was substantially shorter than the other three. His jet black hair was long, coming down over his ears. Brit had pulled the other three into their conference/command center room for a final briefing. Each had been given a file folder with all the information of this salvage, including satellite photos, technical information and photos of the Dallas family.

While filling them in on all the information he had gotten from Captain Dallas's widow, an old man, still quite stout and moving well under his own power, shuffled in. Dressed for outdoor weather, he had a walking stick and a small pack.

"Ah, good," Brit motioned for the old gentleman to come in and have a seat.

"You guys remember Mr. Kifey don't you?"

The other three looked at the old man in stunned horror, the thoughts of all the stuff they had done to his property over the years coming back to haunt them. Yikes! They were going to get an ear full and probably deserve it!

"I found out from Mrs. Dallas, that Mr. Kifey here was part of the local rescue group hired by the Air Force to help with the search when "The Amanda" went down."

"Who knew," Bryan mumbled under his breath. He kept his gaze down at the tablet he was twiddling with.

"Dang small world," Jerry fired back.

Danny kept quiet because he was usually the one that got caught doing something he shouldn't be doing on Mr. Kifey's place.

"Anyway," Brit said, a little slowly to keep everyone's attention. "He'll be joining us for a day or so on the mountain. Anything you'd like to say to my boys here before we head out?" Brit asked, looking at the old man.

Bill only grinned because he knew what was going through their minds.

"I'm sure there will be plenty of time for us all to get reacquainted once we're up on top."

Brit's big grin kind of melted a little bit when he realized that he wouldn't be exempt from whatever talking to they were most assuredly to get.

"Ok, Danny and I are on the sleds and the rest of you are in the Cat. We're taking the upper trail to Spring Creek, cut over to Lake Valley ridge and drop down in on the southeast inlet. Bryan will drive the cat up Green ridge road to the Chicken hump and then cut straight up the Lake Valley west face to the rim and make camp. We'll be in contact from the upper trail meadows and then the summit trail, then on to the southern Lake Valley ridge before we drop down in. Then we'll use the GPS coordinates on our trackers to zero in on the site, even though we all pretty well know exactly where it is, based on the photos. Any questions?"

Brit was about to turn everyone loose, but Jerry slowly raised his hand.

"I have a question," he said sheepishly, everyone turning to hear his inquiry.

"Who's cooking tonight? Cause I ain't going if Danny is."

The whole room erupted into a chaotic volley of funny insults fired back and forth at everyone. Mr. Kifey was the only one not making his voice heard. He was unaware of what the problem was here. Must be an inside running joke or something.

They all finally headed out of the room, still passing good-natured insults at one another as they dispersed, their vehicles being made ready just inside the large hangar doors. Bryan and Cal helped Mr. Kifey into the back seat of the quad cab pickup hitched to a large trailer carrying both the Sno-Cat and the coach, while Jerry jumped into the front. Brit and Danny piled into another pickup hitched to a trailer with two mountain snowmachines on it. Cal leaned against the big quad cab driver's side door as Bryan prepared to depart.

"I'll have Lewis, Dan and Mark on standby over in Jackson if you guys hit pay dirt. Chances are you won't have much of a window to extricate when and if you find it."

"All three choppers?"

"All three," Cal confirmed.

Bryan nodded, starting the motor and closing the window while Cal opened the hangar doors and the group headed carefully out. The Sno-Cat trailer was quite long. They might have been better off using a semi to haul it, but since they were only going 5 miles from their current location to offload, it just didn't seem to be a big deal. Cal watched them departing from the airport staging area, and then went back to his desk. He had a business to run and this salvage wasn't the only one WACS was working on at the moment.

*　*　*　*　*

It took only an hour to off load the Sno-Cat and snowmachines and get them on the road. Once Britten had gotten the signal that Bryan was on his way up the mountain, he and Danny started up the upper trail to Spring Creek. There hadn't been snow for a week, so the trail had been worn down a little bit and had a lot of washboard humps in it. This slowed the two sleds way down, until they reached the midway point, where the trail broke through the tree-line and opened into a wide meadow on the side of the mountain and as previously decided, the two stopped to make radio contact with the Sno-Cat.

After checking in, they continued up the mountain to the top of Spring Creek to the cornice ridge, down the razor back ridge to Lake Valley saddle and up to the south ridge of Lake Valley itself. This was now wilderness area, but with special salvage permits, they could go in legally. Riders often went across the line anyway, because the riding was so good in Lake Valley and the Pinnacle face on the east side.

Lake Valley was a gorgeous place, very bowl shaped except on the north end where it emptied out into the lower ranges directly north of Grand Targhee ski resort. Devil's staircase was directly to the east, just north of Pinnacle Peak. There were treed forests spotting around the bottom of the large bowl with lots of wide open clear areas. In the summer time, the bottom was spotted with several small lakes, hence the name Lake Valley.

Brit checked in again with Bryan who indicated that they were about a mile or so from reaching the west rim. Brit and Danny decided they would proceed into the bowl and make their way to the photo'd wreck site to check it out. When Bryan got there, he could use the onboard GPS tracking system they had with Livewire Sat tracking to pinpoint the coordinates given from the satellite telemetry.

"This sure is a hard life," Brit joked to himself, as he and Danny throttled down the shallow side of the south ridgeline and into the bottom of the bowl. The snow on these gentle slopes was deep, the prevailing southerly winds leaving heavy deposits on these north facing hills. They took aim at one or two spots on the bowl faces to climb part way up, but they knew better than to try and go too high. This was prime avalanche country, and going too high here, would most certainly bury you at the bottom.

Finally, after a little more playing around, they arrived at what they thought was the right location. At the same time, the Sno-Cat ground to a halt on the west ridge of Lake Valley and it wasn't long before Brit and Bryan were on the radio, using the latest and greatest technology to pinpoint the location. Brit sat on his sled talking to Bryan on the radio from the ridge above as Danny walked around the area with an avalanche probe trying to find anything that would resemble or even hint that there was a wreck where they were.

For more than an hour, they searched, but found nothing, not even a trace of anything. Nothing seemed to be disturbed in the area until they had gotten there and then it was just the snow they had tracked up. Continuing the search, Bryan finally made a call down to the command center and requested Cal do a fly over on the same flight path the picture was taken and compare the views. An hour or so passed and finally, the company Aviat Husky flew over to the north of their position. It made several passes along the same trajectory, then flew directly overhead for about ten minutes, then headed back down to the airport. Bryan called for Brit and Danny to make their way back out and to their position on the west rim. By the time the two snowmachines reached the Sno-Cat, it was growing dark and evening was coming on.

Sitting around the camp fire discussing the day's events, they all ate a hearty meal prepared by none other than Mr. Kifey. Brit hadn't brought him along to be the cook, but he seemed insistent to contribute and nearly kicked Jerry and Bryan out of the way as they started putting things together for dinner. Bill did an amazing job at cooking, amazing the young men at how well he got around and how he was able to do all the things he could still do at his age. Bryan pulled out his tablet and started fiddling with it, as they all settled into conversation.

Somehow, the subject turned to girls and all the relationship conquests everyone had ever had. Certainly these young men were not the crude selfish cads one might think of them, though there was an inappropriate comment here and there. All in all, the conversation was quite healthy and true to the heart. Young men don't normally go around pouring their emotional baggage out to the rest of their group, but the conversation seemed to meander in that direction. Bill was listening to everything these guys were laying down while cleaning up after eating his own dinner. Finally, he had to speak.

"You know, I just don't get your generation," he spoke up, heading over to the circle around the fire next to the Cat. "Back in the 70s and 80s, people griped all over the place about this huge generation gap. I never could see it, but this 21st century generation, I can certainly see some big differences."

The boys all froze in their conversation, watching him sit down on a fold up stool and rubbing the stubble on his wrinkled chin.

"Ok," Bryan finally said, looking at the others for backup. "What are the differences you see?"

"Well, let's start with how old you guys are," Bill stated more as a question.

They all looked around at each other to see who would blurt their age out first.

"I think Jerry's the oldest, 27," Danny spoke up finally. "Brit here is 25 aren't you?" he asked, looking at the Garrett brother. "Same age as me, and then Bryan is 24."

"Well see, that's just it," Bill said, smiling. "Up till around 2000 or something close to that, you guys would have been married with kids by now. But look at you, all you're talking about is how it didn't work out with this girl, or you weren't feeling it with this girl, or she had this problem or this or that or whatever."

"Well, that's how it is these days," Bryan spoke up in defense. "So many girls these days have so many issues. They're all screwed up. You don't want to be with someone that has problems, let alone marry someone that has them."

All the boys agreed with Bryan's general statement of the male condition.

"Girls are screwed up and have issues," Bill repeated, chuckling.

"It's very different today compared to your era when you had a match maker come to town and pick you out the ugliest girl in the county and you only get to meet her the night of your wedding," Jerry biffed with a bit of sarcasm. The others laughed out loud at the little bit of ridicule and disrespect they were unaware of presenting. Bill smiled good-naturedly at the ribbing.

"I've been in this world a long time guys and have noted that the girls of today really aren't much different than the girls of my era and really, neither are you guys. Granted, you have very different circumstances in this day and age of computers and cell phones. But what's the matter with the lot of ya?" He glanced around the circle at blank faces.

"I know people who fell in love the moment they saw one another."

All four men shifted uncomfortably in their camp chairs and Danny started tuning up to speak, but Bill continued.

"Have you seriously never met a woman that just blew your socks off when you first met her?"

"Well yeah," Danny agreed stupidly. "But you have to get to know someone before you can just haul off and ask them."

"Why?" Bill shot back quickly. "What for? If you know something is right, why wait to jump in?"

"Cause, you have to get to know each other first to see if you're even compatible, otherwise you'll have a disaster on your hands."

All the boys agreed with Danny on that one. In this day's culture, you had to know that things are going to work or at least have a good chance of success, otherwise, what's the point? Why even bother with it? This all seemed perfectly logical and was certainly how the world operated in this day and age, but Bill knew that they had completely missed the point. He grinned broadly and slowly shook his head. A bunch of misguided dumb kids, all of them, and he wasn't just picking on the male culture. The girls had similar attitudes, though it seemed they really wanted to get married far more than the guys did, and this really didn't make any sense to him at all. Men are ruled by their testosterone and the strong human desire to mate, with anyone! The trick for human kind is to control that drive and channel it directly at the right person at the right time. Somewhere in all the growth of civilization, that had been lost and the adage of self had taken control. Why buy the cow when you can get the milk free? Thus, the loose morals of the day.

"What is it that you guys really want?"

They all looked at each other, not really understanding the question.

"You want everything your parents have don't you?"

"And what's wrong with that?" Brit asked.

"There's nothing wrong with it," Bill replied quietly. "When I raised my kids, I wanted them to have everything that I didn't get as a child and did my best to provide for them, but I didn't just give it to them. I made them work for it."

"There," Bryan pointed out that they finally agreed on something. "That's all we want too."

"But you guys want it all right now and don't want to have to do any of the work to make it happen." Bill glanced around the circle. "All of you have this attitude of entitlement. You want the fancy car that it took mom and dad near 30 years to get. You want the nice house that they had to dig and claw and scratch and starve for, right now. You want marital happiness that it takes a life time to cultivate, right now. You want it to be just right before you make any kind of a commitment. You don't want to work for it. You don't seem to want to get into a fight with her, to cry with her, to laugh with her, to suffer with her, to grow with her and ultimately, to die with her."

Brit was starting to see what he was talking about. He thought back to his visit with Amanda Dallas and he could start to see how she might feel and how things might be with her and her late husband. Bill got up and started poking at the fire with a stick as he walked around the pit.

"Every one of you wants to have something for nothing." He looked over at Jerry. "You, you're 27, a menace to society. You're all good looking men, and I know you've been out with women before cause that's what's gotten this conversation started in the first place."

"Yeah, but you have to find the right one," Bryan pointed out, still holding onto his tablet.

Bill reached over and smacked him upside the head.

"There's no, what do you call it? There's no App for that. Pick a number, go with it and work to make it the right number. No one owes you guys a thing; get to it for heck sakes!"

With that, Bill started towards the back of the Cat to make sure he hadn't forgotten anything to be put away. He was tired and really wasn't certain why he was here in the first place, but he promised he would help anyway he could. He hadn't figured on being insulted by these four young men and the attitude of entitlement that young people had in this day and age, just pissed him off big time. He guessed he must have let it get the better of him and he felt sort of bad about the things he had said now. He knew these boys. He remembered their innocent vandalisms at his farm. It was all fairly harmless. Well, the runaway tractor that went through his neighbor's barn and hay stack, ending up in the pond, wasn't all that harmless, but it was just a fun joke that got a little out of control. He wasn't so old that he didn't remember ever doing any of that himself in his younger years. After several minutes of shuffling around, Bill reappeared on the front side of the Cat, facing the west rim of Lake Valley.

"Bill," Brit said, trudging through the snow next to the old man. The moon was riding high through a crystal clear sky and you could clearly see a light fog bank forming in the bowl below, the dew points beginning to converge in the valley.

"I'd like to apologize for all that back there. I'm sorry we weren't more respectful."

"No, it's me that should be apologizing to you four. It's hard enough for your generation growing up in this culture without a foolish old man ragging on you."

"No, I suspect what you've said is all very true, just hard for the young and dumb to comprehend and implement. I appreciate what you've said and the first looker I see next will certainly have my attention."

"I'll hold you to that," Bill said, smiling. "Just make sure that you treat her with the respect of a queen and the dignity she deserves."

"Nag, Nag, Nag," Brit mumbled, smiling and watching with the old man as the fog began to build, moving back and forth slowly across the bowl under the moonlight.

It almost seemed daylight with the full moon; everything was so clear and visible. In Brit's younger years, he and his friends would be up here riding sleds hard all night if they had a stash of gas somewhere close they could just refill from.

"Wonder if you could come back to the fire and tell us what you know about the search you did with the Air Force after the plane was reported missing up here? Then we better turn in for the night."

"Glad to," Bill said, following the Garrett brother back to the fire and the other three young men still seated there, staring at the flames.

After about 15 minutes of experience telling and pretty much following the same event line as the Air Force report, Bryan spoke up for more information.

"We appreciate the recount of the report on the crash and the search and rescue attempt, but tell us what you really know about it. What you really think happened. What are some of the other things you have heard about this place?"

"All we have ever known," Jerry piped up, "is that it's a great place to ride sleds in the winter and good camping and hiking in the summer, even a descent place to hunt. We've heard some boogerman stories about this place, but they're all made up, aren't they?"

Bill looked at the lot of them, trying to decide whether to tell them something they just shouldn't hear.

"Mrs. Dallas indicated to me that you told her stories of really weird things happening up here," Brit interjected. "It's not like we're going to get attacked by a couple of Jabberwockies and get thrown over the ridge or anything. None of us believe in the boogerman."

Bill finally sat back down and proceeded to rattle off everything he could remember about this place. Most of the time it was a wonderful place to be. There were many days not so long ago, that he himself would set out first thing in the morning on foot, for these ridges. He would come up to spend all day just hiking around the rims, sitting and enjoying the mountain air and sunlight. However, there had been some unexplained phenomena happen here from time to time, but none of it made any sense or followed any kind of a pattern. Most notably were the freak storms that occurred here, usually twice a year, just like the one that took down "The Amanda".

"I seen that storm come in a couple of times. Like nothing I've ever seen before in my life. Clear day and then the clouds started forming to the south west coming over the Victor area, spreading like wildfire and growing just as fast. Clouds like that tell you that something bad is about to happen and when it starts blowing wind, rain and hail, then snow and blow like you would never believe was even possible, it's time to duck under anything. I've only seen it snow and blow like that a couple of times in my life and those were storms that you just didn't want to be out in. The times I've seen this storm blow in, it would blast against the range here and just sit and you could see the whole thing, the size of the whole range, just swirling and blowing wind and rain and hail and sleet and snow and thunder and lighting. It was like no other storm we I'd ever seen before."

"Were you ever up here when one of those storms came through?" Jerry asked, hypnotized by Bill's story.

The old man thought a moment, and then shook his head fervently. Brit had to wonder if he wasn't holding something back. Something he didn't want them to hear.

"No, those aren't the kind of storms you want to be out in and if you were, you didn't stand much of a chance of surviving." He wasn't trying to scare any of them, not that they would have believed him anyway. He was just trying to tell it like it was. Everyone fell silent and just stared into the dying fire. Danny finally sat forward and clasped his hands.

"Well, how about a nice cup of hot chocolate?" he asked, a stupid look on his face. Jerry slowly turned his head to his friend and gave him "The Look."

"You are dumb. You are really dumb."

Danny looked around at everyone starting to get up to get ready for bed.

"What? I'm thirsty." He got up and stepping over to the pot on the cook stove, started making himself a hot drink.

Bryan closed his tablet and stepped over next to his brother who had moved off next to the rim of Lake Valley.

"Remember taking those 'piece of crap' old snowmachines down in there, way back when?" Brit smiled as Bryan continued. "We could have died on that trip."

"HHMMM, made it all the way to the other side and to the top of Pinnacle Peak," Brit chuckled.

"Then we got to walk 10 miles down the mountain to catch the last riders on the hill to get home before they called out a search party on us. That was a long day. Then we had to spend the whole next day getting those sleds back up out of here."

"Don't have that kind of problem much anymore," Brit commented, looking over at the snowmachines they had with them now. Both remained silent for a couple of moments, watching the fog move slowly around the valley in front of them.

"You think it's really here?" Bryan asked.

Brit thought a moment longer, and then turned to his brother.

"It's here all right. I can feel it," he said, still entranced by the fog. "We just have to look at the right time. We'll find it." With that he turned and headed for the snowcoach and a warm comfortable night's sleep.

The Wreck

Morning sunrise was crisp and cold; there wasn't a cloud in the sky. Brit looked out the window at the Basin valley to the west of them and the town of Driggs far below. Still in the morning shadow of the mountains, it lay pretty much in the center of the valley. Eight miles to the south was the smaller town of Victor and some miles just to the north of Driggs, was Tetonia, even smaller than Victor. There used to be a train line that snaked up the center of the valley all the way to Victor, through Driggs, Tetonia and Felt and all the way out to Ashton, where it joined up to the main line running back down the upper valley to places like Saint Anthony, Sugar City, Rexburg and Idaho Falls. The tracks were long gone now, but the rail bed was still there, having been converted to a walking, running, hiking, and bike path.

He looked back through the windows of the trailer to the east at Lake Valley. The fog was gone and the sun was working its way up the back side of Pinnacle, striking their location with brilliance. The places where the snow was untouched glistened and sparkled in the new sun. The moisture on the windows told him that it was fairly cold, although he knew that it would be far colder down in the valley because of an inversion. Inside, it was quite warm, the coach being out-fitted with many winter time amenities, the least of which was a very nice gas furnace.

He carefully stepped to the rear of the coach to a small table and console, turning some controls. Just outside the corner where he sat, an antenna came up out of a small compartment in the roof. A weather vane, complete with wind meter, direction vane, temperature sensor and some other sensors were already erected near the antenna. Brit looked carefully at the readouts in front of him. Barometric pressure was solid in the high category and the winds were almost nonexistent, and the temperature was a balmy 20 degrees. Looked like perfect late March snowmachine riding weather to him. He looked over at the other guys who were still sound asleep.   Bill was awake and rolled over, facing Britten.

"Do you always travel this way?" he asked, still groggy.

Brit looked around the cabin, then back at the snug old man.

"Most of the time. There are times when we have to rough it somewhat and actually sleep on the ground or in a tent, but those instances are so few and far between any more. I figure that the more comfortable I can be on trips, the longer I'll be able to do them. Sleeping on the ground all the time can really wear a guy out."

"Doesn't this seem a bit like cheating or something?"

"How do you mean?"

"Well, camping, you're supposed to be in sleeping bags," Bill said, pulling his very comfortable sheets and comforter up around himself. "Supposed to be on the ground with a couple of rocks or maybe a tree root sticking in your back, no matter how you lay," he continued, squirming in his bed on a very comfortable mattress. "There should be the thick smell of canvas, or better yet, military canvas and the only light you should get is from a crappy old flash light with half dead D cell batteries. Getting up in the middle of the night to take a leak should be paramount to torture because you're either stepping on twigs and sharp rocks bare footed or freezing your wee-wee off in the cold. This just isn't how it's done," he said, looking around at the inside of the coach cabin.

Brit looked with him at what their work had afforded them. They were well paid for what they did, but they worked hard for it too. They actually worked for it...

"I think it's a pretty good life," he said, relaxing a little bit. "Tell me Bill, some of the people you talked about and their wild stories. Were there any of them that you thought were, believable?"

Bill thought a moment, and then sat up.

"Only one," he spoke quietly, to not disturb the others.

"It was about 1960 or there about, can't remember for sure."

Jerry was snoring and Bryan was just breathing loud, while Danny looked like he had passed away sometime during the night, but every so often he'd stir and twitch, indicating he was still with the living.

"Never seen this guy before and never heard from him since. Don't know who he was. It's been so long ago, I don't remember exactly what he said or how he put it. This guy said he came through the same bad storm and was walking around this ridge trying to find somewhere he could hunker down instead of right out in the open. The storm had already been going on for a couple of days when I ran into him and it only lasted a little bit longer after he left, then it broke apart and cleared right up."

"What happened to him?" Brit asked, very interested in the story.

"Never saw him again to ask. He seemed kind of disoriented and left the area before anyone else could talk to him. It's just the way he talked, the look of him. He was wearing something like the winter clothes you guys have. Hard to remember, been so long." Bill looked out the window at the bright, almost blinding snow, the sun rising higher and higher.

"That was back in 1960 or there about, I think. When you get as old as I am, time starts running together. What are you guys really doing up here? There's no airplane out here."

"Oh, it's here," Brit said assuredly. "I think we're just going to have to wait and be ready for it when we do find it."

That was weird, but the look on Brit's face told Bill the young man was resolved in his convictions and it was doubtful that any amount of arguing on his part was going to change that. From the way they were outfitted, they could afford to be up here a very long time.

*   *   *   *   *

The day went by fairly quickly. Bryan stayed in the coach for most of it working with some satellite imagery and taking weather readings. Danny and Jerry were assigned to ride down into Lake Valley on the snowmachines to gather samples of the snow and the rocks at the GPS location of the wreck, but everything he looked at showed no signs that anything was ever there. At the base station down at the airport, Cal was confirming the same things and giving his version of the weather reports. Extreme clear for the next three days. There was nothing on satellite or radar. Of course the team would make the call whether or not to remain on the mountain longer. The rest of the week looked like it would hold out just fine and they had plenty of fuel and provisions for that long.

Bryan checked outside at Danny and Jerry tooling around in Lake Valley and noted Britten and Bill snowshoeing back up the ridge towards them from the south. He was about to turn back to his computer screen when he noticed a change in the light. Not the lights in the coach, but coming from the outside. He continued to look outside for whatever it might be. Perhaps a plane or a bird had just flown over or something. Bryan scanned the skies carefully for anything, the light continuing to change, like it would during an eclipse. He stepped over to a stash box on the other side of the coach and pulled out a small telescope about the size of a piccolo and checked the sun filter it was fitted with, then stepped outside and pointed it up at the sun for a look. No eclipse or anything, but the light continued to change shading and color. He glanced down the ridge at Bill and Brit. They too were looking around at something that just didn't seem right. He turned and started looking in all directions. An odd odor just came out of nowhere. No longer the scent of pine, it was almost a musty burnt wood smell. Then he glanced to the southwest.

Through the trees he could see something dark and building in the sky, moving fast in their direction. Perhaps it was a hot air balloon or maybe even a blimp? Up here, at this time of year? Not likely. Whatever it was, it started to elongate and grow exponentially with every passing moment. Bryan scampered back into the back of the coach to his computer and radio. No sooner had he sat down, than Cal was on the radio, excitedly informing him of action in the sky. Bryan glanced back out for a view, noticing the trees near them starting to move with a breeze coming up from the same direction as the mysterious clouds forming to the southwest. He reached for the hand radio, keeping his eyes glued on the clouds that were billowing up at a frightening pace right before his eyes. He grabbed the radio mic and pressed down hard on the key.

"Brit, Danny, come in!"

He was trying to keep his voice controlled as his eyes were widening at the pace the clouds were coming towards them. It was like a volcanic pyroclastic explosion coming right at them, but there was some weird organization to it. It seemed to be swirling as it built.

"Yeah Bryan," Danny called back over the radio. "We see it. We're on our way back right now."

Bryan eyed the storm. They were never going to make it if they went to the usual ridge entryway on the southeast side.

"Danny, point that thing straight and up bury the throttle! You guys will never make it if you go around. I have no idea what's inside that thing, whatever it is. Git out of there now!"

"Bryan!" Brit cut in. "What is it?"

"I think we're about to experience what our bomber crew did. Better get Bill back here as quick as you can!"

At that moment, Jerry came flying over the ridge, catching quite a bit of air and landing his sled some distance from the Cat. Bryan swirled back to the south to see Brit and Bill moving as quickly as they could through the snow in the direction of the Cat coach. The wind was really starting to whip up now and it wasn't just a hard blow, but rising to gale force. The surface snow suddenly became airborne moving horizontal, the winds racing towards hurricane force. Jerry stumbled inside in time to look back and see Danny's sled come flying up over the ridge and land right next to the coach. Bryan turned, looking outside just as a wall of pelting rain suddenly slammed the south side of the coach, followed a minute later by driving hail and snow pellets. Both Jerry and Bryan strained to see Brit and Bill still struggling to reach the coach from down the ridge still some hundred yards.

Now the sun was completely blotted out, the weather monster continuing to pick up strength. Jerry could see the form of Danny doing something on the back side of the coach, and then start off against the wind and weather towards Brit and Bill, still struggling in the snow. Bryan glanced back at the back door window. There was a rope tied to the handle, the other end wrapped around Danny's waist. They could no longer see Brit and Bill for the huge driving snowflakes. Bryan glanced down at the weather station readouts. The temperature was plummeting and the wind speeds continued to rise towards Category 1 hurricane force speed, certainly bad enough. He could actually see the barometric pressure needle falling.

Now, they could see neither Danny nor the other two. The rope was pretty long, but neither Jerry nor Bryan thought it was long enough. He might have been better off using the snowmachine to go and get them. Bryan melted back into the chair in front of his instruments, grabbed the command radio mic to call Cal and ask for some help, but then Jerry banged on the window he was pressed against.

"Oh yes! He made it!" he exclaimed, rushing to the back door, swinging it open to help bring the three back towards the coach.

Bryan looked out to see Danny helping a weather weary Bill towards the coach and Jerry struggling in the blinding snow to help Brit. Finally, after some further struggle at the back door, Jerry was helping Bill back up into the relative safety of the coach, while Danny and Brit clamored inside, closed the door and collapsed completely exhausted, either on the floor or the closest bunk.

"This thing isn't going to blow away is it?" Danny puffed, referring to the Cat and the coach, wiping the snow out of his face.

"No," Brit puffed, "This thing weighs too much for this wind. It'll take way more than this to move it. Bryan, what the heck is going on out there?"

"It's the storm," Bill rasped amidst his shivering.

Brit gave the old man a hard look, and then looked outside at the complete white out and the hurricane force winds driving it. Bryan was madly working with his computer.

"Can you see anything?" Brit asked, getting up and stumbling over Danny and Jerry to get to his brother.

Bryan gazed steadfast at the screen in front of him as Brit settled next to him. The radio was whistling and screaming static at them now, so Brit just turned it off.

"Yes," Bryan said, firmly entrenched with his eyes glued to the images coming into view before him.

"Based on what I'm seeing and what Bill has provided for us last night, I'd say this might be what we're looking for."

"What we're looking for?" Jerry blurted excitedly. "I thought we were looking for an airplane?"

"Yeah, is there something here you guys forgot to mention?" Danny puffed.

Bryan and Brit gazed in disbelief at the images in front of them. It was the actual satellite imagery, in real time, as it was happening, right on top of them. The image was zoomed way in, almost to the point where if the storm were not present, they could easily see themselves from orbit. It looked like a hurricane in miniature, complete with a very distinct eye. Bryan changed the image to infrared, and then zoomed in even farther.

"Wow," Danny exclaimed, getting up and looking at the image. "The toys you guys have are amazing!"

"It's the storm," Bill repeated, trying to sit up for a better look outside. The noise from the wind and even the snow striking the side of the coach continued to rise.

"What are we looking for?" Jerry asked, helping Bill up and trying to look around outside as well.

"There!" Bryan said, pointing to the screen.

The defined eye of the storm was overlaid over the top of the topographical map drawn out on the computer. If the information was accurate, the edge of the eye should be almost on top of them. Brit looked down at Bryan and then outside. He reached for his face mask that he used for extreme snowmachine riding. It kept all elements out of his face and the snow suit he was wearing was the finest that technology could produce.

"We might not be able to hear you over the radio with this storm, so use the tug method," Bryan called after him, as his brother headed for the back door.

Danny turned with a stupefied look on his face.

"Tug method? What tug method? What's going on? You're not seriously considering going out in that? You're out of your mind!"

"What the nipnard is happening here?" Jerry exclaimed. "What are you two really after up here? You're not going outside until we get some answers," he insisted, blocking Brit's exit.

Bryan turned quickly, the howl of the wind and the snow rising further.

"We're looking for an airplane that disappeared in 1945 at this location."

"Yes we all know that, what's this all about?" Danny retorted.

"There was never any accounting of how the plane went down from the military. Only that the plane encountered a freak storm that iced them up and brought them down. The navigator and pilots reported seeing the ground changing beneath them as they circled before they crashed. The storm was said to have had a huge rise of clouds first, followed by massive sheets of rain, freezing rain, hail, and sleet, then blinding snow, thunder and lightning. At the center of the storm was a calm cylindrical eye, about a mile in diameter that moved over Lake Valley, this Lake Valley, where they crashed their plane at the coordinates given from the GPS telemetry. We haven't found anything at that location, but maybe the storm has something to do with it."

"And you want to go out in it?" Jerry came back quickly, as Brit grabbed the end of the rope that had been tied around Danny.

Bryan noted the worried looks on their friends' faces and tried to reassure them.

"Bill told us that people have gone into the eye before and have seen things unlike anything that's supposed to be in Lake Valley. The eye wall is passing not more than 20 yards in front of the Cat right now and starting to settle."

"Settle?" Danny asked, looking outside and to the front of the vehicle.

"Slowing down," Bryan confirmed.

"I suspect that it will stop directly over Lake Valley and we'll find our answers in the eye."

"Don't you have a robot or something in all this gadgetry that you could send out there instead?"

Bryan checked the wind speed readouts in front of him.

"Sustained winds are almost 80 miles an hour. We're lucky there's any snow left on this ridge. The only reason the sleds are still out there is because they are on the lee side of the coach. For safety reasons, we really should be turning this Cat into the wind so there's less of a profile to blow against, but I don't want to chance it in this storm. We're heavy enough we'll be ok."

"I'll be fine," Brit indicated, securing the rope around him.

"But just to be sure," he said, looking at Jerry. "Hang on tight."

With that he pulled his mask down over his face and secured his winter hood over his head, slipped his gloves back on and opened the door, or tried to. The force of the wind didn't lend itself too much to let that happen. It took quite a bit of force for him to get outside. Jerry carefully let the rope out as Brit made his way along the lea side of the coach and along the Cat tractor. The wind was doing a wonderful job of clearing the snow from the ridge. There was already bare rock out in front of the Cat as Brit tried to step out in front of the vehicle, only to get torn at by the full force of the wind. He tried several times to hold his footing, but it was just too much. Finally, he got down on his hands and knees and started to crawl forward. Even this was a bit problematic, and he ended up on his stomach, scooting along the ground. He couldn't see anything but grey white horizontal snow. He could tell he was close as the snow deepened and started to slope, so he carefully lifted himself up onto his hands and knees to try and look over the edge of the ridge. While it was lighter, the wind and the snow still blasted at him, nearly lifting him right up off the ground.

Then with a mighty blast, the wind toppled him and he found himself looking straight up at the sun. He carefully rolled and looked over the edge of the rim at the valley floor below. Wiping the snow from his mask and blinking several times, he couldn't believe what he was seeing. The valley floor was blurring and changing. One moment there was a long rock wall stretching the length of the valley with houses beyond it and the next it was a blur, then the trees and rocks of Lake Valley. He pulled himself closer to the edge so that he could see the entire floor and then pulled himself completely clear of the storm wall and out into the eye. He looked back at his feet that still lay just outside the wall. He couldn't even see them.

The wall was so defined. It was perfectly cylindrical and the storm mass swirled madly around the eye. Energy bolted across the eye and into the walls in random fashion, leaving spidered plasma fingers fanning out from their points of impact. He turned back to the floor of the valley, more specifically; to the place they had been concentrating their search for the bomber. There it was, sticking up out of the snow, one of the twin tails of the B-25 bomber, just as pictured. It was there!

He pulled his face shield off and grabbed his radio. The noise from the swirling storm walls above was almost deafening, but he did manage to get through to the Cat, only 30 yards away. The plan was to leave Bill in the Cat to wait out the storm. They knew that it was going to burn out eventually and he would be fine there. That way when the storm cleared, he could call down to Cal and communicate with them down at the crash site. Bill was certainly fine with that. He was still completely exhausted from the mad dash with Brit on snowshoes earlier, trying to outrun the fast moving weather phenomenon.

One by one, the other three made their way along the rope with several packs of gear, to the ridge edge and out into the calm of the eye. Jerry and Danny were in total amazement, standing at the ridge's edge looking up through the eye at the swirling mass that hovered over the small valley in the mountains. Bryan was fascinated with all his surroundings and stepping closer to the storm walls, pushed his hand back into it. He could feel the roaring wind tugging at it and the driving snow on his glove, but right where he was standing it was perfectly calm. Even in the calm of the eye, the sound of the roaring wind was deafening.

Brit was already sliding down the face of the ridge slope towards the debris field and the wreckage. The sun was stark against the dark, grey walls of the storm. Occasional energy strikes still boomed in their ears as Danny and Jerry followed Brit down to the first few pieces of aircraft sticking out of the snow. After talking to Bill and reassuring him that everything was all right, Bryan took his turn heading down the steep slope to where the others were examining the wreckage.

After some preliminary examination and discovery, it was decided that they needed to have a quick way out if something unexpected happened with the storm, so Brit put Danny and Jerry to work carving out some good snow ladders and steps back up the wall they had come down. A couple of good deep snow caves were also ordered in case things started happening way too fast for them to make any escape up the wall. If the storm moved from its present position, the amount of precipitation it was producing would surely bury them or the wind would sweep them away. Really, they had no idea how long the storm would remain stationary. It could move off as quickly as it came or just collapse in on the whole valley.

With Jerry and Danny occupied, Brit and Bryan were able to concentrate fully on the wreck and the work they had to do to make positive identification and survey any salvage possibilities. While Bryan was digging around one of the wings and engine nacelles, Brit managed to crawl inside the tail section. It didn't take long to figure out that the plane had broken up when it went in, but there was no sign of the main fuselage. After some further searching, Bryan pulled some gadgets out of his pack and started working with his equipment. He had brought a portable range finder, GPS mapper, a ground radar apparatus, some infrared seeker sensors and his tablet. All used for locating metal, rubber, glass, and most importantly, petroleum products. He checked his gear against the known quantities in the engines and one of the wing fuel tanks.

Everything seemed to be working perfectly, so they started hunting along the top of the snow in the general direction that the rest of the airplane would have logically slid, given the terrain and the slope of the valley wall. Finally, they came to a halt in an area of snow right against a huge rock formation. Both men looked closely at all the readouts with dismay. It appeared that the rest of the wreckage was buried under several meters of snow, either against the base of these rocks or an overhang. In any case, there was no way they could make any further discoveries for more identification unless they were able to get some heavy equipment in here to dig it out.

"Nuts," Brit cursed in frustration. "Got an app for this?" he asked looking around.

Bryan kept his eyes glued to his equipment as something caught Brit's eye to his right and he trudged off to investigate. He made his way around the large rock formations and some distance beyond. It looked like some kind of a man made wall and getting closer, he could see it was quite tall and there were a set of large wooden doors smothered in the rock. Standing at the doors, he gazed up at the fifteen foot high stone walls, looking in either direction. Interesting that this was here, he never remembered seeing a wall in Lake Valley. This wall stretched for quite a distance, disappearing into the valley walls one way and curving out of sight in the other.

He studied the deeply inset doors carefully. There was a great deal of workmanship used to construct them. They were massive and had intricate scroll work designs all over. Huge planks, almost railroad tie sized, were bound together by large metal bands the color of silver with delicate designs etched into the metal that almost glistened in the sunlight. There was no visible means of attachment from any edge, top, side or bottom to the huge stone walls surrounding the giant doors. There were definitely two doors here though. They were held shut, or sealed, by several horizontal metal bands that were much thinner than the others. He examined the bands carefully for a means of removal. He supposed that they could always climb over the wall, but why go to all that work if they could just open the doors? Besides, they were a good fifteen feet tall.

"Well, what do we have here?" Bryan called out over the noise of the storm above, setting his stuff down and stepping up next to his brother.

"You tell me," Brit answered loudly.

"Looks like a door or a gate or something?" Bryan surmised, rubbing his chin. Brit slowly turned to his brother, giving him one of many disgusted looks to come.

"Really? I think I got that part," he said sharply.

"And how come there isn't very much snow here?" Bryan asked, kicking at what little there was.

Beneath it looked like tough dry grass, almost like tundra from northern Canada or the Arctic Circle.

"Can we see what's on the other side of this door? What gadgets do you have in your bag of tricks there that might avail us a peek?"

Bryan bent down to his bag and began going through it.

"Come on," Brit was a little impatient. "You've got to have some kind of magic gadget in there that allows us to see through walls," he said, feeling the immense door.

The horizontal bands had no visible means of securing the door shut. They only looked like steel bands glued to the surface.

"Come on, we're burning daylight here," Brit hollered frustratedly.

About that time, a small hatchet sunk into the wood with a "thunk" that could be heard over the noise of the storm. Brit glared at it with a disgusted looked, that turned to a smile while he rolled his eyes towards his younger brother.

"What, no double bladed axe?"

"Not in this pack," Bryan came back, not realizing the sarcasm.

"No machete either I guess." Brit shot back instantly.

"No," Bryan said in defense. "They're both back in the Cat."

"Better get on the radio and get Danny and Jerry down here. I suspect we're going to need them for these doors."

"Are you sure it's such a good idea to open this thing up?" Bryan asked, looking the doors over. "I would think it's sealed for a reason," he said, looking closely at some odd writing on the scrollwork of the metal holding bands.

"Well, we're here to explore. We need to try and find another way to get to that aircraft and since you can't seem to look through these doors with what you have in your bag of tricks there, we'll just have a look see the old fashioned way."

"I have a fiber-optic gooseneck camera. We could run it under the doors and have a look that way," Bryan spoke up.

"Oh, good," Brit said, pulling the hatchet out of the door and standing back so Bryan could go to work.

Both men just stood there and looked at the door, Brit waiting for Bryan and Bryan waiting to decide what to do next. Brit glanced over at Bryan a couple of times, and then finally blurted out his impatience.

"Well?" he exclaimed.

Bryan looked at him stupidly.

"Well what?"

Exasperated, Brit put the hatchet back into the door and turned to his brother.

"The camera, where is the camera? Let's get it out and get to work."

"Oh, yeah, the camera. Well, it's not in this bag," he fumbled. "It's in my other bag in the ......Cat," he finished.

Brit closed his eyes, trying to control himself.

"I'm sorry. I didn't think we were going to need something like that here," Bryan cried in defense. "Besides, we were lucky to get what we have here through the storm."

Brit grabbed the hatchet again and started hacking through the locking bands on the door.

"Get those other two down here."

It didn't take long for Danny and Jerry to make their way down to the gateway the other two were working on. About the time Jerry came puffing up behind Danny, Brit had hacked the last band from the door and started trying to pull it open using the two uselessly small hand ring mounted to the door. Danny joined in on the operation followed by Jerry and the three of them pulled and tugged with all their might for several minutes while Bryan looked on. Maybe they were just for show, because what they were doing wasn't producing any useful results. Brit glanced back to see his brother just standing there looking at them.

"Comfortable grandpa?" he gasped, both frustrated and quoting a line from a movie. Bryan rubbed his chin and smiled.

"Certainly," he paused. "Did it ever occur to you guys that maybe the doors open the other way? After all, there are no real handles on this side. If the doors were banded from the outside and there are no means to do anything with the doors from the outside, then doesn't it make sense to have them open from the inside?"

The other three stopped what they were doing and stood away from the doors, Brit sarcastically motioning for Bryan to take his turn at it.

"Please grace us, oh wise one," he said loudly.

Bryan grinned and stepped carefully forward, put his hands on the doors and started applying pressure. Nothing happened at first, but after really giving it some effort, the giant doors creaked inward.

Irritated and not wanting to give credit where credit was due, Brit leaned on the doors and pushed as well. Giving the credit would indicate that Brit was weak, even though it really didn't. Bryan was smug enough with so many other things as it was, his older brother wanted to have something he was a little better at. This wasn't it. All four men leaning into the doors, they reluctantly yielded to their combined efforts. Once the doors got moving, they continued to open all on their own so the four stepped through, then stood and stared.

There was no snow on the other side of the six foot thick wall. In fact, there was no cold either and curiously, no noise. Bryan and Brit looked back through the open gate. Lake Valley was still there and they could still hear the roar of the storm, lightning and wind raging around the perimeter. However, it was all coming through the open doors and not over the fifteen foot high stone wall. This seemed illogical, locking Brit deep in thought trying to figure it out. Inside the wall, the sun was still shining, but it was a different sunlight and when looking up from within the wall, he could see no storm at all. There were two suns, and three moons, one of them close enough to take up a fair portion of the sky. Brit looked back through the open gate again at Lake Valley and the storm. He took a couple of steps away from the gate and tried to look beyond the wall, but could only see strange colored sky. It was certain that they weren't in Kansas anymore. Jerry and Danny stepped past the two brothers onto a well-trodden path winding its way around great mounds of precious jewels and golden treasures, up between two large boulders, disappearing into a grove of trees beyond.

"Well I'll be dipped," Danny blurted out, gazing at the sparkling display of light that danced wildly around the reflective corners of the shiny bullion.

"Yeah," Jerry hypnotically repeated what Danny had just said. "Dipped."

Brit stepped over to one of the piles of sparkling gold and jewels, picking up what appeared to be a grail or cup made of solid gold, studded with red jewels.

"Looks and feels real enough," he said, weighing the mug in his hands.

Bryan finally stepped over to another pile and began running his fingers through a large pile of shimmering diamonds.

"There's enough treasure here to pay off the national debt and buy off all the politicians to put good honest people in their places. I bet this pile alone could buy off Fort Knox." Danny exclaimed excitedly, while dipping his hands into the nearest pile and running his fingers through probably millions and millions of dollars.

Queen of Thulsa

Brit watched his brother and two friends toying with more wealth than they had ever seen in their lifetime. Somehow, he seemed to be the only one to have his feet still planted securely on the ground here. While this was all neat and fine, the chances of them actually getting any of this out of here and back home seemed rather remote to him. Finding the pot of gold at the end of the rainbow was certainly exciting, but there was something nagging at him and he held his excitement in restraint for now. He had an uneasy feeling that something just wasn't right. He was always the one that was usually pressing forward without thinking things through very clearly, and now, he was being the cautious one. Maybe it came from the adage that you never get something for nothing. There was always a price to pay somehow.

The look of the sky had him spooked and while it was really cool looking, it had the appearance of something right out of a science fiction movie. His generation had been brought up with all the scientific and electronic gadgets that seemed normal for everyday life. Super special effects in the movies, just about anything the mind could imagine, could be brought to life in front of them. However, it was always known that it was artificial, an illusion. There was always an explanation for what was, and with his generation it was almost a requirement, but the scene before him now? He had nothing! He knew where he was supposed to be and he knew there was no IMAX theatre up here in Lake Valley. He wasn't aware of anything that could produce this kind of an illusion; even 3D movies couldn't come close to this. What really had him concerned, and that no one else seemed to be paying attention to, was the fact that judging from the sky, they were on a different planet now, but how can you step through a door and be somewhere else? How is it even possible to bridge that kind of distance? His mind couldn't fathom that you could just step from one planet to another. That was completely off the chart of reality. Laws of physics and relativity aside and more to the point here, there was a very large wall and wooden doors that appeared to act as the divider between the two worlds. These were man made and obviously put here for a reason. Perhaps his brother was right about opening the door in the first place. It had been sealed for a reason. Then, what about all this wealth just lying around in piles everywhere? It looked like some kind of an open treasury? If that wasn't enough to ponder, what about this well-worn path? He'd feel a whole lot better about things if there was some grass growing in the path, indicating that no one had walked on it recently, but this path was well used.

Scanning carefully around the area, his attention was drawn by an altar of some kind off to the left of the gate, away from everything else. It was somewhat hidden back towards a natural rock wall that intersected the manmade stone wall. Not everything here was just gold and jewels. There were statues of people and odd looking bat-like creatures, caches of weapons, strange looking gadgets and large objects that he had no idea what they were. Brit noted his companions were busy examining such a wonderful find, so he turned aside to have a closer look at the altar and some of the other items surrounding it.

Drawing closer, he looked back a couple of times through the open doors at Lake Valley and the storm beyond, trying to make sure he didn't lose sight of it. He had it in his head that if he lost sight of the exit back, it might disappear, leaving them trapped. Finally his curiosity turned to utter fascination and he forgot the doors when he caught site of two glowing objects floating above the altar, slightly beneath two intersecting arches. Stepping closer, slowly circling the altar, he recognized the two objects as hand swords. These were smaller swords than the conventional type that a medieval knight might use. Not big and bulky or huge and weighty, but much shorter, sleek and quite elegant. The two glowing swords radiated a mid-blue color and while they were floating about a foot and a half above the odd looking altar, they were not stationary, but gently moving slowly about a fixed area, but always the same distance from the other.

There was nothing truly remarkable about the swords themselves, other than the fact they were glowing and floating. He examined the altar and several other objects around it to make sure the light wasn't coming from another source. Once he was satisfied that it was indeed the swords that were creating their own light, he moved right up on them to examine them without touching them. There was some writing on the top of the altar beneath the levitating swords, but he could not make out what it was. The swords themselves had much thinner blades than what he was used to seeing and they were shaped a little differently. Instead of a straight edge all the way from hilt to tip, they were both tapered just above the hand guard and then widened towards the tip, finally the razor edges curved back to each other to form the almost needle point. The hilts were unadorned, just simple handles designed for maximum gripping power of the wielder's hand. Brit took note of the sheaths, or scabbards, hanging on the sides of the altar, one on each side. These were adorned with beautiful scroll work and design, but he was far more interested in the swords themselves. He fancied himself a little bit of an enthusiast. Not a pro or anything like that, but he had a small collection that he had acquired over the years. He had even learned to fight in mock tournaments with Medieval, Samurai and Ninja swords, even staff fighting techniques. He had been in a few competitions, was even pretty good with the staff, but not enough to be a master. These swords were like nothing he had ever seen.

Now the ideas sliding around in his head seemed to be a bit more realistic than what his brother and two friends were probably thinking of. They would try and haul all this loot out, through the snow on the outside and back up to the Cat. Something, which under their present situation would be quite impossible. However, a couple of small, lightweight swords would be doable. As they were all about salvage, they could always come back later and get the rest of this with the proper equipment. He lifted his hand to take hold of one of them but then caught movement on the far side, up the path leading out of the treasury into what appeared to be a forest. He looked hard as several torches approached quickly and as they drew nearer, he could make out many very large figures.

"What is this? The land of the giants?" he mumbled to himself.

A real knot started to form in his stomach as the torches drew close to the two boulders at the top of the path. Why were men holding torches in broad daylight? He tried to get Bryan's attention, but he was totally engrossed in examining a rather large gem he had discovered amongst the large piles of jewels and gold bars. Brit continued to try and get someone's attention while ducking back behind the altar. Then two huge figures holding the torches, appeared from behind the two large boulders at the top of the path. Four more figures appeared stepping between the two torch bearers, now standing guard at the top of the path so there was no entry beyond from where they had come. Two of the figures were shorter than the warrior looking men and wore full length cloaks with hoods draped over their heads far enough that you couldn't see their faces. Brit was now fully convinced that they were somehow on another planet and he was sure that Bryan would have come to that conclusion far before him had he not been so taken with the shiny rocks he was studying.

"Good night Ned," Brit mumbled to himself. "Them boys are huge."

He watched as three of the very large muscle coated men stepped up to each of the three intruders. Because of their size, there was very little struggle that his brother and two friends could put up. They were grabbed rather unceremoniously and dragged to a large flat open area within the treasury, away from the loot itself.

These men were enormous with thick, long hair, heavy, dark beards and big hands. Brit wasn't even sure big hands, was the right term. More the size of bear paws. They were almost giants, standing at well over six and a half feet tall with very broad shoulders and big arms. Their legs were covered with a mix of metal and leather armor. Thick animal skin wrapped boots that were well laced, melting into their trousers being made from a similar material. One or two of them were wearing a combination of chainmail and metal armor plates strapped around their hips and across their chests. All of them were wearing helmets of different varieties. Only one of them had horns sticking out the sides. Brit thought he had seen those horns on a goat before. If this was the treasury Gestapo, they dressed well for the part. They were armed to the teeth. Each had a very large sword strapped to them in various configurations. Across their chest, or waist, even their backs. There were also large daggers sheathed in scabbards against their armored hip plates. All had animal skins wrapped about their shoulders. Their armor was tinted the same color of medium Aqua pearl. Probably something to help identify their own clansman or soldiers in battle. They all wore various arm bands with different designs carved into them, presumably a symbol of their individual ancestry. They looked like Vikings, or something similar.

He continued to watch his brother and friends being held tightly by three of the brawny figures, facing the other two cloaked figures. They all just stood quiet for a moment.   Finally, the shorter cloaked figure stepped down towards the piles of treasure, slowly scanning the area, then carefully pulled the hood back.   Shock enveloping him, Brit's heart skipped a beat, trying to process the image of the person standing in front of him. He had an overwhelming urge to just run out to her, but somehow remained calm, crouched down and out of sight. Carefully keeping an eye on her as she scanned the area, he was completely mesmerized by her face, recognizing her instantly. How was this even possible? She looked exactly as she did in her photograph.

Brit pulled the photo from his shirt pocket, studying it carefully then looked back at the woman standing in the middle of the treasury. Why he still had the photos in his pocket, he couldn't remember. At the moment, he could barely remember his name. His only focus was her. Sure it appeared that they were on another planet, the extra objects in the Indigo colored sky made that obvious, but how in the heck did she get here? Was it possible that they had not only walked through some kind of a portal to another world, but that world was some kind of an alternate reality? Somehow, time was different here, or moving backwards, or standing still. These questions only sparked a myriad of others. How did she appear now as she had as a twenty-five year old? It was Amanda Dallas, as she appeared in the mid-1930s. Not only was he in shock that it was her, he was completely drawn into her beauty. He had never felt like this before. He wasn't even sure what it was he was feeling. His heart pounded uncontrollably, watching her turn and remove her cloak, revealing her full body armor. He was relieved to see she wasn't dressed like the Warrior Princess.

This wasn't sissy girly armor either. This was the real deal. If you were going to go into battle for real, this is the stuff you would want to be wearing. While it was truly beautiful and elegant to look at, it was absolutely fully functional and quite robust. This armor was designed along similar lines to the men in the group, but with a very feminine, sophisticated flare. Not fancy or decorative, very functional, extremely light weight which, made it very comfortable to wear. She wore a heavy white woolen cloak that was round stitched around all the edges. Two eyelet holes with an elegant golden crest clasp held it gently around her collar. There was a hemp neck choker with a simple ruby stone mounted on the front around her beautiful neck. She had shoulder armor over her left side to about halfway around her back. Beneath the cloak was a grey light weight chainmail that reached clear to her knees and was tipped with ringlets, spaced every foot and a half all the way around the chainmail covering. Normal chainmail of this set would be quite heavy and difficult to move around in, but she seemed to be having no trouble at all. This was because the material used to make the chainmail was extremely light weight. Not like the heavy steel rings used in traditional chainmail made in the era of the knights of Europe. A thin armor half vest protected her sides and under her arms. It was lined with some kind of thin animal skin. There was hip armor attached to a front and back armor plate and a band that covered her stomach and lower back with another band that hung down, but did not interfere with walking or moving. She wore two belts over the top of the hip armor, both sporting medium sized daggers in scabbards, with a pouch on the left hip. Her pants were similar to those the men with her were wearing. Shin armor was strapped around her lower legs and covered all the way to the top of the foot. A sword was strapped to her lower back under the cloak and a big round stick about two feet long on a hip holster. She also had forearm armor that covered to the elbow with bicep bands. All this armor was gilded in the same aqua pearl color with distinctive markings that he couldn't make out from his distance.

He kept his eyes fixed on her face. He couldn't take them off her. Her hair was worn the same way she had it in the photo, short and well groomed. There was a beret of some kind on top of her head with an Aqua blue stone adorning it. Her eyes caught him and held him prisoner. They were big deep pools of flowing brown, but at the same time, they were stern and meant business. Her lips had a pouty look to them, but not big or fat. She was a woman of large stature, but stood with poise and dignity, moving with sophistication and grace.

She looked long and hard at their attire, especially at the WACS insignias and USA flags on the shoulder of each of their coats. The woman reached over her shoulder and pulled her sword from its sheath, carefully pointing it at each of the three captives muttering something foreign. The language was completely unrecognizable. Brit was sure it wasn't Klingon. She looked quite formidable, stepping closer to the three intruders. They didn't dare move. The way their captors had a hold of them, they could easily just snap their necks with a simple effortless twist. Approaching them carefully, the other hooded figure pulled back his hood then removed the cloak. Something seemed kind of familiar about this middle aged man. He wasn't gruff and bearded like the big warriors. He was clean shaven and not built like the others at all. He was tall, but not as muscular as the others. He had grey streaks running through his sideburns. Brit wasn't sure who he might be or where he had seen him before. What was he even thinking, seen him before? How could he have possibly seen him somewhere before? He looked up at the three moons and two suns in the sky. Oh wait, yeah, it was possible. This had to be an alternate reality or something. That was the only reasonable explanation. Amanda was standing right there. Nope, none of this made any sense. The woman was most certainly Amanda; there could be no doubt.

He peered around the base of the sword altar and looked hard at the other figure, a man, dressed in similar type armor, still looking the three very nervous captives over. He too seemed particularly interested in the patches on their coats. Brit stared back down at the photo. He just couldn't place where he had seen the other man before. He didn't look like he came from this strange new place. The only thing Brit wanted to do right now was crawl back out the open gate and home. This whole episode, or whatever you would call it, was entirely too weird for him and he wanted no part of it. Only problem was, his brother and two friends had a very sharp sword pointed at them. Amanda stepped over next to the man examining their winter gear with her blade still pointed at the three men. Her blade glistened in the strange sunlight. Danny started to squirm as she stepped close to him.

"Hold still ya hose head," Brit muttered to himself. *You don't provoke an enemy or someone who was about to slice and dice you like a Juliann fry. You hold perfectly still.* Amanda barked out something in the weird language they were speaking and Danny's head was instantly pulled back to reveal his bare throat. She held the blade right up to his throat and barely touched his skin.

"Be still," she commanded softly in English.

With the cold steel on his throat, he didn't need any other reason to hold perfectly still. Danny instantly froze while looking fearfully down the long glimmering blade and into the soft brown eyes of the woman before him. The chainmail chinked and gently rattled as she lowered her sword and turned to the other two. She looked them over very carefully, taking special notice of the insignias on their parkas. Maybe they thought these men had taken some of this treasure, or were mistaken for someone who had.

"Where do you come from? Why are you here?" She demanded, her commanding voice seemed tempered by a certain elegance.

No one spoke a word or even tried to. Fear had them almost petrified. Jerry swung his eyes towards Bryan hoping that he would say something that would pacify these guys, but Bryan was quite uncomfortable was sure the others were too. The woman had a familiar look to Bryan, but he wasn't sure and the name that came to mind was completely out of the realm of reality. Even the older man looked a little familiar. She turned and raised her blade to Jerry's throat, loudly commanding the man holding him in the unfamiliar language. Things were heating up and not just because of the stress. Jerry gulped as his head was pulled back and she laid the blade flat against his sweating throat. Not only was this situation quite stressful, but winter conditions did not exist on this side of the wall and they were still wearing all their winter gear. It was getting a little warmer than they were normally comfortable with.

"Do you not understand where you are and what you have done?" she asked loudly, lowering her blade again. She was hoping that someone would speak up.

Silence continued as she stepped over to Bryan who eyed her carefully. She didn't even call for his captor to hold his head back this time. She just stuck her sword up under his chin until she could feel a little resistance. Bryan was frightened out of his mind, but stood resolute. He didn't care who she looked like right now, none of them did. He was far more concerned with the sharp pokey thingy pressed against his neck, which by the way, was causing a considerable amount of pain. He finally reasoned that if he was going to get skewered, he wanted a little bit of dignity and to be known that he went down looking like he wasn't scared, even though he was near to peeing his pants. Amanda turned away again, much to Bryan's relief and looked over the treasury they were standing in.

"Do you know what this place is?" She looked back at them figuring that they had no idea, which was true of course.

"This is called the Winner's Spoil," she spoke up, "It is a very sacred place where we pay tribute to our gods for the bounty and wealth they have bestowed upon our people."

Amanda turned and looked at the others in her group, including the older man standing there with her. She spoke several sentences in her strange language again and then held up her sword. This brought an instant jeering response from all of the warriors present and she leaned close to the other three.

"By the way, the punishment for desecrating the winner's spoil is death. I was telling them that we could either splay your guts out on the stone table up on Mount Tera, or feed you to the Jabbaway. They really liked that last idea."

Amanda turned and looked at her comrades. They all started to chuckle, reading the frightened looks on Bryan and his friend's faces.

"Cutting their throats right here and now is good too."

The older man cleared his throat and shifted his stance.

Amanda shifted her eyes back towards him and thought a moment, then turned back to the others.

"No," she paused for dramatic emphasis. "Better not, but the law is quite clear."

She suddenly turned to the two warriors standing at the top of the pathway with the torches and held up her sword, then started shouting again in the other language. The two big men pulled their own swords and responded in kind with the same thunderous language and enthusiasm. With that, Bryan, Jerry and Danny were pushed up the pathway towards the boulders and disappeared down the trail to parts unknown. Brit watched silently as Amanda stepped carefully down the path towards the open gate but stopped some distance from it. She was close enough that she could still see through it and could hear the faint noise coming from the other side.

She detected the older gentleman stepping up behind her, looking with her through the gate at the world on the other side. He too could hear the noise of the swirling storm. They understood what had happened, for they had heard and seen it before. Many times, the storm had come to this world. Sometimes it brought people from other places and sometimes, it took them. Keeping the doors banded shut had helped to lessen the frequency of the incidences to this world. Nevertheless, it couldn't stop the storm from coming as it always had. A gentle hand came down on Amanda's shoulders as she gazed outside.

"Did you see how they were dressed? Did you see what it was made of? Did you see the insignias and patches on their packs?" Amanda asked, sounding strangely emotional now.

"Yes, I saw them," he responded quietly.

"How can we stop the storms from coming? What do we have to do to keep this from happening over and over again?"

"We do what we have the power to do. That's all we can hope for."

"I so wished that-," she stopped short of finishing her sentence and glanced back at him. He could see the emotion within her starting to percolate into her eyes. He knew exactly what she was thinking and that going over it again would only bring more pain.

"How will we protect them from the law?" she finally choked out in dismay.

"We do what we can and hope for the best."

The two stood frozen, watching and listening to the raging storm outside, longing to go home, seeing it, maybe even reaching for it, but never able to get there. No way back. They finally turned, looking up at the two suns and the three moons in orbit, then over at the two remaining warriors remaining as escort. Amanda motioned to them, speaking the language of their clan, ordering them to see to the gate.

Brit suddenly remembered where he had seen the older gentleman and pulled the other picture out of his pocket, holding it up to compare to the man standing with Amanda. It was Captain Dallas! An older version of him, or, wait! How can there be an older version of Captain Dallas and a younger version of Amanda Dallas? Ok, so now he was exploring the furthest reaches of the twightlight zone. He shoved the photos back into his pocket and tried to shift to the other side of the altar, but in doing so, his boots came in contact with a rack full of spears and they all started to cascade down all around him.

The loud clamor in the direction of the sword altar brought Tony and Amanda to immediate attention with swords drawn. The two warriors at the boulders responded instantly, flying down the path towards the altar, Amanda stepping back, allowing them to do their jobs. The two stopped short of reaching the altar as Brit materialized with a big spear and sword in his hands. Amanda eyed him carefully as he tried to look as tough as he could. Brit had seen enough puffer fish in his days of diving that he knew if he could make himself look as big and as bad as possible, it might help any predator think twice about attacking. Problem here was his predators seemed like they were whale sized to his puffer fish and looked infinitely stronger. Brit counted himself kind of buff. He was no weight lifter or body builder, but he was stronger than most. He also felt like he was far more agile than these big guys were. He wasn't sure what his plan really was, but after giving away his position, he was making it up as he went along. He only knew that he had to find a way to retrieve his brother and friends.

"So there's another that I've overlooked," Amanda said, lowering her sword and putting her arm on Tony's shoulder. "It's hopeful that we can get a little better information out of you than your three friends," she said graciously.

"One of those guys is my brother," Brit spoke up, trying to use conversation to keep her two body guards from advancing on him. The fact that he had pretty fair position and a good supply of weapons behind him, made him feel rather confident about his situation.

"I see. And you are?" Amanda asked, looking him over carefully.

She cocked her head slightly, looking back at him through his drawn weapons. She put the point of her blade onto a log next to her and let her hand rest on the hilt. She really liked what she saw, watching him for a long moment. There certainly seemed to be something quite different about him.

She would rather have just ordered the guards to back off and leave them, but there was protocol to be followed here. She and Tony held status in this land and really weren't supposed to be doing any of the fighting unless it was in actual battle with another clan army. This was the work of the royal guards, who had now placed themselves firmly between the stranger, Amanda and Tony.

"Britten Garrett," he said reaffirming his grip.

He wished he'd picked up something other than a spear. These were good for throwing and charging, but he wasn't about to do any charging and he was too close for throwing. He wasn't out to kill anyone really. Maybe take a hostage and bargain for his brother and friends.

Amanda motioned for Tony to leave after the other group to make sure that something bad didn't happen to them in the hands of the clan. The mentalities of the people from this planet were somewhat primitive and superstitious in nature, being quick to judge and act rashly.

Tony could see that she had everything well in hand, as she always did, so he turned with a smile, pulling his cloak back around his shoulders and headed off up the path, disappearing between the two huge boulders and the trees beyond. Amanda replaced her sword back in its scabbard on her back and sat down on one of the chests of treasure. Her chainmail jingled softly as she situated herself very elegantly and set her outfit just right, so it lay correctly.

"So your brother is?"

"Bryan Garrett."

"I assumed the Garrett part beings how you said he was your brother. What about the other two?"

"I'm thinking I need a little information here first," Brit said, starting to get a little nervous. He swayed his weapons a little bit just so the two in front of him knew he was still loose and ready for a fight if it came to that.

"I really don't have time for this," she said, looking up at the two suns above.

"Look, we didn't come here to steal any of your treasure, although you pick a funny way to store it. We came here on an expedition to find something else. Please turn my friends loose and we'll leave, back the way we came."

Amanda gave him another good long look while she fiddled with one of the rings at the end of her elegant chainmail. She really liked what she saw in this man with every passing moment. She raised her right eyebrow, as Brit tried to step towards the open gate, but her guards responded to counter his every move, holding him in place.

"Were a law broken in your world, you would have to punish the offender," she said carefully. She was actually trying to get him to somehow give himself up. He stood a better chance of survival than if he were to fight the guards or do something else stupid.

"Lady, you're so far away from my world, you couldn't get to it to break a law," Brit said, with a smile of attraction to her. Amanda smiled as well, but for different reasons. She knew exactly where she was and where she had come from.

"We're here quite by accident, apparently transgressing an ancient lost civilization's laws," he said, looking around at all the piles of gold.

"Entering the Spoil isn't just any crime, intentional or accidental," the woman said, shifting her position on the chest. "The gates were sealed shut, banded on the outside with no handles. Seems to me like the smart thing to do was to have turned around and gone back to where you came from. Now, I have little choice here," she said, sitting up straight and commanding the guards in the clan language, her guards immediately advancing on Brit.

"Would have helped a little bit if you had put the warning on the door in a language we could have understood."

"It's considered universal."

"I can barely speak my own language, let alone some lost language."

He hadn't counted on this at all. He was really hoping to talk his way out of this or at least maneuver himself into position so he could take her hostage. That would have worked out perfectly. At least it always did in the movies. He threw a warning jab at the closest guard coming at him; only to have the spear shaft hacked in two with a simple swing of his sword. Ok, so that didn't work at all. He knew he had made the wrong choice with the spear in the first place. It was just the closest thing he could grab.

The sword in his other hand was a bit of a poor choice too. It was a little too heavy for him to wield properly. He swung it awkwardly with one hand, but it seemed to do the trick anyway. The two large guards chuckled, dodging the wild swing and started talking to each another in their own language. They laughed loudly as Brit swung again, this time holding the sword with both hands. He wasn't following any of his medieval sword training and all the swords that he had ever fought with didn't weigh half this much. They moved on him again so he swung hard again with both hands, this time his sword met with one of theirs with a loud clang. The shock of the blow nearly popped the hilt right out of his hands, cringing with the pain in his wrists and fingers.

"Life's wonderful," he mumbled, working through the pain and trying to maneuver backwards around a pile of jewels.

"You know, you have a much better chance of living if you'll just lay that thing down before you really hurt yourself," she said, resting her chin on her hand. "Personally I would much rather you chose to stay alive than lying on the ground in a couple of pieces."

Brit steadied himself and brought his sword back up to bare, pointed at his assailants. Both men had dropped their grins and decided it was time to put this one away. Nothing would be worse for them if they had let this go on for very long and then have it get out to their fellow warriors that it took two of them a long time to bring down a simple stranger, especially one that obviously didn't know how to even swing a sword properly.

"There, see? I knew I liked you. We share a mutual opinion."

He swung at another advance and the blow was met with a clang that threw him back and spun him. Unwittingly, he let the energy of the blow finish the spin and he brought his blade back up to meet with the second guard's sword. Again, he nearly dropped the sword while trying to reaffirm his grip, but it was struck again and again until he couldn't hold it any longer and let it drop with a clamor.

"Ah, now we're done," Amanda clapping once or twice and grinning broadly, until Brit scampered back behind the sword altar. "Uhm," she edged forward a bit. "It would be unwise to get too close to the altar."

Brit looked at the blades suspended beneath the dual arches spanning the altar.

"Why?" Brit asked, reaching for one of the floating weapons, but before he could touch it he received a sharp jolt of energy that knocked him right back on his rear end in a most unceremonious way. Thankfully, the winter clothing he was still wearing absorbed most of the impact and he was quickly back to his feet, only to find his enemies laughing hysterically. Embarrassed and angry now, he stepped back to the altar.

"Please don't," Amanda gasped through her own laughter. "'Twould be foolish."

Brit looked at both blades floating in front of him and forming a very determined look, deliberately shoved both hands at the hilts. The energy protecting the swords blasted at him and he was again sent sprawling backwards.

"Please stop," she said, still chuckling. "You're going to really hurt yourself."

The guards were still laughing hard. All of them had been witness to this before as others had tried and failed.

"I usually have to call in someone from one of the other clans for this kind of entertainment and have to pay for it with a sheep or something. At least consider joining me for dinner just for the entertainment value."

Brit wasn't amused at all. He got up and approached the altar again, but this time, gazing down at the writing engraven on the altar beneath the floating blades.   There was writing all over this altar, much of it between square holes on each side.   Much of the writing was accompanied by odd looking pictorials, showing examples of different things he had no time at the moment to really study to discover their purpose. He took special notice of the two narrow slots about eight to ten inches long, on each side of the top of the altar beneath the two intersecting arches.   Again, more drawings and writing.

"What the heck is it with this thing?" he asked frustrated. "Is there a remote for this, something to turn off the anti-thief device?"

Amanda stood up and stepped slowly in his direction with her hands clasped behind her back.

"They're called the Twins. They have always been here and no one has ever wielded them. They protect the Winner's Spoil."

"Apparently they haven't been doing a very good job," Brit said, looking over at Amanda.

"Sure they have."

"We made it in here." Brit pointed out.

"But have you made it back out?"

"How do these swords have anything to do with that? Your two goons here are stopping me from leaving, not these things."

"Well, yes they are, but technically I don't need them to hold you here," she said smiling, stopping behind the guards who had paused their advance for the conversation.

"Oh, you think you're that good."

"Oh, I know I am," she shot back instantly with a straight face. "Now, for the last time, please come quietly."

"Nag, nag, nag!" he snorted, taking a couple of steps backwards, the guards moving at him. He turned and jumped onto a nearby chest, then up onto a rock next to a cache of spears leaning on a rack several feet from the altar. Pulling a spear from the rack, he planted it into the ground between himself and the altar.

"Not the spear thing again," she moaned impatiently.

Brit braced himself then vaulted right onto the sword altar and stood looking right at Amanda, a big grin on his face. Carefully leaning down, he reached between the arches and took a hold of the Twin sword hilts, pulling them out and holding them up. The two guards were astonished and backed away a little bit as Brit gazed at both blades he was now holding in front of his face. Amanda stared in utter disbelief, surprised at what he had just done and what he was now doing. This was something she had never seen before and she was trying to figure out how he had made it happen. She knew of no one that had ever touched them.

Brit was transfixed by the glow of the blades. They seemed to purr in his hands, while looking them over and admiring his great accomplishment. Turning his gaze down at the three still standing in front of him, he decided that he was now in control. Holding the blades out, he took an offensive attack stance with both blades pointed at his adversaries.

"This being the Winner's Spoil, I guess this means I win. Now, I'll have your name missy," he said, looking right at Amanda. He knew who she was, he was sure of it, he just wanted positive proof. He wanted to hear her say it.

Amanda knew he had secured his own safety for now. Her guards were compelled to give him leave and provide him special protection, so she bowed gracefully, turning her big brown eyes back up at Britten and smiling with the elegance befitting her station in the clan.
"Catrina Amanda Dallas, Queen of Thulsa."
"Wait," he paused surprised. "Who?"

Thulsa

The city of Thulsa appeared to grow right out of a forest. A well-used road of clay burrowed through the thick foliage forming a tunnel-like enclosure that pretty well obscured the sky. Structures suddenly jumped out of nowhere until there were more buildings than trees.

As more of the city materialized, it appeared to have been built by several cultures. One culture building the original, then was conquered or died out and other cultures taking over, repeatedly. It held the resemblance of the ancient cities of South America mixed with the simple townships and coastal villages of Scandinavia. The city portion was built up with great blocks of stone hewn out of solid rock and placed together in as perfect magnificence as any great civilization would build. Enormous city walls flanked by towers, with buildings climbing many stories high, rose up above the forest canopy. Giant pillars, decorated in beautiful ornate carvings blended with gold and silver trim, supported huge vaulted overhangs on many of the central buildings. However, the city wasn't just stone structures and streets made of rock and brick. There were tracts of forest throughout and beautiful trees of different varieties everywhere. There were mostly pine trees in the western part of town, but there were other types present to. Some of the these species grew three and four times the height of normal pine trees, with big leaves the size of an elephant's ears and different colors of blue, purple and pinks mixed with the green of the pines. From the look of all the different colored foliage, it had the appearance of autumn in this land.

Bryan, Danny, and Jerry had been bound and brought into the city in a large wagon drawn by a four horse team, followed by several of the warriors on horseback. All three had expressions of confusion mixed with bewilderment, looking around while entering the more populated part of the city. This isn't exactly what they had expected from looking at their captors. A mental picture had formed of what a warrior's life style might be. Just by looking at them they had gotten the idea that these kinds of people lived in a stick hut with a grass roof or something similar.

As the group entered the main part of the city, horns began to sound. Not high pitched blaring horns, but a low throbbing horn. This was the kind of noise that penetrated right through your skull, clear through your bones. The sensation from the horns reminded them of being followed by a car with a thumper sound system installed and all you could hear is the bass turned up so loud, it would not only make the car hop, but the windows vibrate, the welds break and cause you to feel as though your internal organs might rupture.

Modes of transportation were by carts and wagons pulled by horse or oxen. The city's neighborhoods were well planned and laid out incorporating ancient architecture. There were numerous examples of technology in many different forms, much of which were unseen by the casual observer. This was advanced engineering that, based on the observed culture, really shouldn't be here. There were gas street lights and sewer systems, plumbing and running water. In most instances, lighting was provided by gas being well incorporated into their homes, work and the city streets lamps. The whole civilization for this part of their world was far advanced beyond any the surrounding regions. They had infrastructure and services. Construction workers, firefighters, plumbers and other repair workers kept this civilization industrious.

People here were dressed in the same manner as the warriors who had taken the men captive, excluding the armor and weaponry. Their clothing was well kept and while the styles were similar, differing colors and combinations permeated the whole culture.

There were no buildings at the square, only a square plot of land in the middle of several intersecting streets. It had the appearance of a park, with a grass like growth covering the ground and several trees strewn about. In the center was a raised platform of stone, surrounded by several fountains. Off to the side of the platform were a couple of ghastly apparatuses. A wooden gallows structure, which sat next to a set of stocks and another smaller platform with a single raised U shaped stone on it. Did they really need to leave this stuff out in plain view? None of them were of the frame of mind to see this and they certainly didn't want to stop for a closer look. Nevertheless, that appeared to be exactly where they were headed as the wagon creaked to a halt on one of the sides of the square.

"This is not good," Danny mumbled lowly, leaning against Jerry. He stared at the smaller platform and the U shaped stone.

It had been made clear to them that they were not to speak to anyone, including each other, so any communication had to be kept on the down low. Jerry looked around at the masses that were gathering around the square. It looked more like these people had come to see a show, not to look at the strange people who were dressed in strange clothes, especially the big winter coats that were getting more uncomfortable by the minute.

"Great! A meet and greet," Jerry said quietly back to his friend, who was getting quite excited about the events that were starting to unfold before them. "Got an app for this?" he asked, leaning towards Bryan who still had a dazed and bewildered look etched on his face.

Bryan was just getting his wits about him, kicking himself for getting so carried away with the treasure in the Winner's Spoil. Now he was trying to figure out what he could do to defuse this situation or at least slow it down so he could get some control of it. An app would be good right now, if they had such a thing. How to get out of a nutsy situation with the ancient natives?

He glanced back at the cloaked figure getting off his horse right behind the wagon and tried to make some kind of silent gesture to him about their comfort level in the coats. Tony obviously got the message. Removing his own cloak, he ordered the warriors to untie them and remove their coats. The three were then paraded to the center stone table and perched together for everyone to have a good look at them.

Meanwhile, Tony examined their coats closely, more to find out if they had anything that might be used against them in this township's version of a public trial, at least that's how it appeared to Bryan. The crowds really weren't making a lot of noise and he couldn't see anyone with stones or rotten food in baskets ready to pummel them senseless. After Tony had thoroughly gone through each man's coat, he turned to the three on the stone platform and stepped through several clusters of people to stand before them. He glanced around at the crowd that was still gathering. Many of them he knew personally. These men were warrior soldiers under his command and while not armed, they all certainly looked a bit menacing.

Tony paced in front of the three men slowly, looking them over carefully. He was trying to slow down what had to happen in order to formulate a plan that might be useful as a defense for these men, though he knew that their situation was dire. They had trespassed into an area of their kingdom that no one was allowed to enter without specific reason and escort. Many times had visitors come to their city and brought strange customs, even strange weapons and other things that didn't always make sense. These visits always seem to end badly. They used to just try and send them back the way they came, but that never seemed to work out well either. The culture's spiritual leaders made vague references to their gods forbidding the people from having any contact with the strange folk that came in this manner and when this would happen they would need to purge themselves of the infectious outside influence.

Whether good things could happen or not, it was better not to take any chances and just not have them here, but if they did come, they must be dealt with appropriately.

The law for trespassing the Winner's Spoil was straightforward. If you are caught in the Winner's Spoil, it meant the death sentence. The Spoil was not only a sacred place with access reserved for only clan hierarchy, but also the monetary depository of the clan. It was kept against the western wall because of tradition and security. All executions were done here in the public square, by whatever form the crowd chose from the three apparatus constructed here. The only other option was to take their chances in the warrior's arena, but that was by appointment of the clan high council and very few ever made it out of the arena alive. Generally, it was just easier to do the public execution thing, faster and much less painful.

"My people, we have visitors," Tony announced loudly, turning to the crowd in a presenting tone. "They have come to us from beyond the western wall." This statement seemed to draw quite a murmur throughout the crowd. The idea here was to create a positive spin on their introduction so the people would be a little more accepting.

"We have been visited many times by folk from the west. Many have been welcome," he paused a moment, looking around hedging, kicking at the ground. "Some were not." He turned and looked at his guards, then the people again. "These men have come to us through Gareth, the locked gates in the Winner's Spoil, from the same land that your beloved queen and I came from."

The murmur in the crowd ramped up at this announcement. Several of the larger men stepped forward, and a few outspoken women. They all knew the law and that there could be no deviation from it, regardless of where they were from. To do so would not only bring bad karma upon the community, but more importantly, possible consequences from their deity.

"Captain Dallas," one of the men said, stepping up to him flanked by the others.

Normally, they would be speaking in their native clan language, but because the Captain had addressed them in English, their second language, they addressed him in the same manner. Apparently it had something to do with these three strange men.

"It does not matter where they have come from. You know the laws and what must be done. Why do you delay?"

Certainly, rocks and clubs would be flying by now, but Tony was Thulsa's warrior Captain. He was highly respected, even revered somewhat by all. He held almost hero status among his warriors. Many times he had led them into battle against rival clans trying to take their beloved city. Each time, he had led them to brilliant victories, repelling these attacks on their sovereignty, even countering these attacks enabling them to capture valuable assets and more spoils to appease their gods. Hence, the existence of the Winner's Spoil, payment to their Deity for keeping them safe.

Captain Dallas had hoped that by aligning these men as having come from the same place he and his daughter, that their adopted clan would be more tolerant of their transgression. From the looks of things, he would have to call on every bit of his station as Captain of the guard to try and keep these men from being killed where they stood. The Queen was the only person in Thulsa that had the power to overrule law without question. Somehow, he would have to try and stall the situation until she arrived on the scene. Tony paused a moment, then turned his attention to the ever growing crowd.

"I present them to you for your consideration my people. They have come as peaceful explorers seeking our knowledge, wisdom and offering wisdom of their own, from their own culture and land. Will we not hear them first and see what they can provide for us?" Tony called out loudly to the entire crowd. He had to turn quickly while he spoke so that everyone could hear him.

The crowd's murmurings continued and some started calling for the strangers to be killed. Danny looked nervously over at Jerry who glanced back at him with a look that did nothing to reassure his friend.

"I'm sorry Captain, but the law is clear. We cannot presume to out think the gods or the laws made in this land. We must preserve ourselves for the sake of Thulsa."

With that, the guards were obliged to grab the three men and, with the help of some of the others, drag them kicking and squirming, up onto different platforms for execution. Danny got the gallows, while Jerry went to the stocks and Bryan was pulled up onto the chopping block.

Bryan was not happy about being forced to his knees and having his head positioned in the u shaped stone. He looked over at Jerry who was being loaded into the stocks and Danny who was struggling hard to keep from getting the noose around his neck, but ultimately there was little he could do. Bryan and Danny had their hands tied behind their backs again and set in position for their fates. Jerry figured he was the only one that was going to get out of it somehow, being locked into the stocks. He was not very excited about having to watch two of his friends die before him. He figured that they just didn't have enough room for more than two at a time. He turned his head to one side as a large man stepped up and picked up a rather large steel hammer, swinging it a couple of times at some rocks nearby. Ok, so this didn't do anything for his state or wellbeing and he felt like he was getting a headache now. So Bryan was going to get his head lopped off, Danny was to get his neck stretched and Jerry was going to get his head bashed in with a hammer. What a wonderful way to spend your time before getting any lunch.

Tony frustratedly stepped out of the way. He was helpless in this situation now. He had hoped that his people would be a little more friendly and curious. Actually, they were very much so, long ago, when he first came to this land and began to teach them new things. To intervene now would mean that he would forfeit his own life in only one of the stranger's places.

The axe man appeared at the stone platform with Bryan while Danny was readied for his plunge through the gallows platform. Tony stepped over next to the gallows, hoping he could somehow prevent this from happening, but the lever was pulled and Danny plunged through the trap door, dangling at the end of the rope. The fall didn't break his neck, so he was going to have to hang there until he choked to death.

The moment he dropped, there was a loud blaring horn and a call from the same direction that the strangers had been brought in from the forest. It was the Queen's party approaching. As everyone in the crowd turned to see the Queen of Thulsa approach, Tony dashed to the dangling and kicking Danny, grabbing him by the ankles and holding him up. Dismounting her horse, the Queen called out with the great authority of her office, in clan language first, and then English.

"Release them, immediately!" she commanded loudly.

Several men ran to Tony's aide to hold Danny up while the rope was detached from its holding and he was set to the ground coughing and choking, but very much alive. Bryan was brought back up onto his feet and Jerry was released.

"We were only following the law my queen," one of the men who had challenged Captain Dallas and incited the action in the first place, informed her respectfully.

"I understand," she replied sternly, jumping onto the main platform and addressing the crowd. "These men are far different than any that we have encountered before."

"Captain Dallas said they had defiled the Winner's Spoil. The law is clear to us," another of the inciters spoke up carefully. "Why do you counter the law?"

Catrina smiled slightly, scanning the entire crowd. It was quite apparent that they revered her even more than they did Captain Dallas and in truth, she revered her people above all and they knew it. They were all focused solely on her, as she was their ultimate leader in all matters that could not be resolved clearly.

"I counter the clear law because the Twins have been freed by these men," she announced, gesturing towards a figure on one of the horses that had arrived with her. Britten Garrett sat up in the saddle between her two royal guards as all eyes turned to him. He had removed his winter coat and had donned the two scabbards across each shoulder and around in front, like two gun belts. In them were the hilts of the swords.

A low commotion started rolling through the crowd as they waited to actually see them. Few had ever seen them in their floating place at the altar, let alone out of the Winner's Spoil and in the hands of anyone. Bryan was never so overjoyed to see his brother, but held his position right where he was as did the others. Their fate wasn't yet decided, at least as far as they were concerned. When they were safely out of this crowd and in a closed room, then he'd feel a little more secure. Britten looked blankly at Catrina as she gestured for him to show everyone the swords. He finally got the hint and rose in his saddle crossing his arms to pull the swords from their resting places.

He held them up over his head and turned in both directions so that everyone could see the glowing blue blades clearly.

The crowd really started to buzz when the two glowing blades were revealed. Tony motioned for the guards to escort the other three back into the wagon and depart for Stronghold Manor as quickly as possible before something else stupid happened. The queen was in full command here, but he wasn't taking any chances. Once the wagon was away, he pulled his cloak from his own horse and motioned for the queen to break everything up and get the other one out of there as soon as possible.

"What of the law?" some of the crowd still inquired.

While the Queen had the ultimate authority here, in the past whenever she had countermanded a law, she always gave good reasons or at least put the issue up for discussion with the Thulsa elders. War was brewing in their land as rival clans continued to make moves on this hugely successful and rich civilization. Suspensions ran high and the clan folk were understandably nervous and skeptical about anyone strange.

"I believe that these men would be our allies." Catrina stepped around the main platform, looking at her nervous people. "Send a representative from your varied clusters and I will convene a council of the elders in the grand hall this afternoon. For now, they are under my protection." Stepping quickly from the platform and to her horse, she motioned for her guards and Britten to follow after the wagon headed for Stronghold manor.

Stronghold Manor

Bryan and his two friends stepped down out of the open wagon that had stopped inside a large ornate gate behind large wooden doors. They were all gazing up at the huge entryway to Stronghold Manor as the other four came trotting up and dismounted. Bryan was again overjoyed to see his brother and quickly embraced him, as did the other two. They were glad to just stand and visit about what had happened to them thus far, each giving their version of what might have happened to them had Catrina and Brit not come along when they did. Jerry was trying to play his executioner up bigger than any of the others, holding the big sledge hammer and all, but Danny was quick to point out that he had actually been executed.

"Ok, so let's get the facts straight here 'les someone get the wrong idea about who was really in the most peril back there," Danny said, having the other three's attention. "The guy had pulled the lever and the door had opened. I'd been dead right now had the idiots not placed the rope around my neck wrong, a blessing I would like to acknowledge here and now before everyone and my maker," he said, rubbing his throat where the rope had pulled tight with his weight. "I was dangling guys! Dangling! It really hurt."

Bryan stepped closer for a better look at the red marks around his neck, while Jerry continued to try to make light of the attempted hanging.

"Just a little rope burn," he said snidely. "Captain Dallas here more than saved the day for you."

Tony wasn't content to be just inside the gates. They all needed to be settled inside the manor out of sight. Information gathering could happen after they were secure inside. Then they could try and work out the best strategy for keeping them safe.

"Gentlemen," Tony gestured towards the door. "Please, inside we'll have some food and then we really need to talk."

Catrina stepped off her horse without a word, pacing quickly through everyone and inside, while her guards gathered up the four men's packs and followed everyone in, closing the large entryway doors behind them.

"It really hurt Jerr-," Danny repeated, a little upset at his friend, the doors closing with a loud boom.

*   *   *   *   *

The hill fort had a large expanse, but not overly done. Its ceilings were hidden above brightly lit halls. Being well illuminated by overhead gas light, it didn't have that dark, dank feel to it. The connecting halls were not lavishly decorated. In fact, it was hard to find anything in the whole place that was there just for decoration. There were nice things that were sort of stored in such a way as to be presented to a guest or company, but they were all very functional and could be picked right up and used, whatever they were.

After guiding the group through several of these hallways, they were brought into a smaller room with several small tables and chairs. Food and drink had already been made ready and set in place around a couple of tables and after some odd maneuvering as to who should be sitting next to who, they were all seated and instructed to eat. During this entire process, Tony and Catrina had split off from the rest of the group, but reappeared a little later, having removed all their weaponry and armor. Both were still wearing the base clothing that was under their armor, boots, trousers and simple shirt.

Brit hardly took his eyes off Catrina when she reentered the room. He watched the way she walked, the way she held herself, the way she turned her head and the way her hair furled as she did so. He studied her hands as she ate and drank, even how she held herself as she sat. His study of her person couldn't go unnoticed. He was doing it so intently that it was painfully obvious to her. She could feel his gaze on her, but she had an image to maintain. They had to gain whatever knowledge they could glean from these men in order to have any kind of a prayer of defending them before the elders and the clan clusters. Brit could hardly help it though. While he had no idea what political or military issues they were having right at the moment, he knew he had a lot of knowledge about these two already and what the world had become since they had disappeared. One thing he was certainly relieved about was that this was not Amanda Dallas, but her daughter. The fact that Catrina, or her father for that matter, hadn't aged in proportion to what their own time and world had, did not even cross his mind, yet. He was too enamored with her to even do the math. Information on both worlds was about to come together as she finally returned his gaze. Her lovely brown eyes bumped with his hazel color, but neither would look away, as if trying to stare the other down.

Finally, woman's discretion took hold and she eloquently lowered her sight to something she was eating. None of this had gone unnoticed by Tony. At first he was observing it with a look of, *"What the heck is going on here?"* Then, he nearly slapped himself upside the head. How could he be so blind as to not see it? It happened to him in a little diner in Dubois, Idaho. That was such a lifetime ago and light years away; a life he would never know again. He had fallen for the most beautiful woman ever to walk the earth, and she with him. It had happened in an instant. He thought back to the Winner's Spoil, confronting Britten for the first time in front of the altar. Not only the way he looked at his daughter, but also the way she looked back at him. It was like a light just came on in his head. How could he have missed it? Of course, now was not the time to bring this up, but it was quite obvious that they were both taken with one another. He smiled to himself thinking of all the men who had approached Catrina for courtship and tried so hard to win her affections, but she had never looked at them the way she looked now, at Britten. Strange that it was an outsider who had caught her fancy. Not just any outsider, the ironic thing was that it was an outsider from their own world, Earth.

Finally, most had finished up what had been provided to eat and there was just the quiet buzz of talk around the tables, until Catrina stood up, motioning for her guards to leave the room. After the doors were closed tight and the six of them were quite alone, Catrina and Tony looked straightway across at Britten and Bryan. Jerry and Danny pulled their chairs a little closer to the table where the other four were sitting. Even as Catrina looked at both of them, holding at Britten, Tony stood up quickly next to her to speak in her stead.

"Gentlemen, you are in great danger here and not just from this people and laws that govern Thulsa. You have come here at a time when we're seeing war."

"Not just war," Catrina interjected quite firmly. "Thulsa has become quite large and industrious. It has grown rich in everything about it. Clans from without our borders have long looked to our wealth with envy. We have had skirmishes from three different clans off and on for many years now. Each time, our armies have exacted crushing defeats against them, but I have long sensed that these were only testing skirmishes. Not only to test the strength of Thulsa, but to also allow for diversions to bigger things. We have caught many spies entering the city to map out routes, fortifications and armories."

"Our spies have also found that the clans have joined forces and are massing their strength against us from beyond our borders to the east," Captain Dallas interjected. "We expect them to attack this city within days."

"So you understand the extreme caution of the people here," Catrina said, leaning further forward. "Now, please," she toned down and looked at both the Garrett men. "You must tell us where you are from and what you are doing here."

Brit only gave her a strange look and glanced over at Bryan and the others. None of them expected any of this. Well, none of them expected to be where they were, so the surprise department was starting to run out of inventory.

Catrina became frustrated and stepped over to one of their packs and threw it up onto the table in front of them pointing at the WACS patch on Bryan's gadget pack. Bryan carefully glanced over at his brother, and Brit finally spoke up.

"It stands for Water and Aircraft Salvage," Brit said, opening the bag. "Our company goes all over our world salvaging wrecks for various things, people and property." Brit saw both of their expressions change instantly. He started pulling things out of the bag. Most of what was in this bag was monitoring gear, range finders, deep detection devices, some tools and other various gadgets, including Bryan's tablet.

"Where exactly do you come from?" Tony asked, already suspecting what the answer to the question was. Brit wasn't exactly sure how he wanted to respond to that and hesitated, so Bryan cut in, having started to put the puzzle pieces together.

"21st century Earth," he stated straight way. "All four of us live in Driggs, Idaho. It's a providence located on our planet." Brit grinned a bit at his brother. He had most of the puzzle assembled, but was still missing a couple of key pieces.

Tony dropped to his seat, astonished. He hadn't dared even hope that it was possible that the doorway had opened up again to their home. It had opened many times before since they had been brought here by the mammoth storm, but seldom to their own world, and when it did and they had tried to return, they were stopped by its fury. Catrina looked down at her father, then back to Brit.

"So what were you looking for that brought you here?"

"Satellite photographs showed the wreckage of an aircraft in what's called Lake Valley, Wyoming. We're here to survey and if possible recover the wreckage along with any remains."

"What is satellite photography?" Catrina asked inquisitively.

"Pictures taken from space, high above our planet," Bryan replied.

"From space?"

"Yes, we have-," he paused a moment with a sudden thought. It dawned on Bryan that these two might not have any idea of what they were talking about. "We have small communication stations in orbit around our earth. Some of them can take very detailed pictures of the ground."

"Where are these satellite photographs?"

Bryan fumbled through the stuff on the table around his bag. Brit only sat back and watched his brother work, keeping the big grin and waiting patiently for everyone to catch up with him.

"Oh boy," Danny said with a little grin. "I think he has an app for that."

"Nuts," Bryan said, a little sarcastically, starting to swipe through the contents of his tablet. "No Wi-Fi here; can't check my email or Facebook. Good thing I have everything stored in this thing's memory."

Catrina had a puzzled look on her face and looked over at her father who was equally perplexed and shrugged.

Indeed, Bryan did have something that he could show them. He quickly pulled up the pictures they had of the wreckage and turned it so Catrina and Tony could see the screen.

"This aircraft, did you locate it before you came through the gates?" Tony asked, studying the pictures.

"Yes," Brit said with a smile. "We have identified it using the serial numbers on the tail. The main fuselage of the aircraft," Brit continued, looking down at Tony who remained transfixed by the information pouring out at them, but his eyes remained down at the floor. "We think we have located it buried under an avalanche in a cave of some kind. We had hoped to make final confirmation on it, but we'll have to bring in heavy equipment to dig it out. But we're fairly sure it's the same B-25 bomber that went down in 1945 in a freak storm over the Teton mountain range."

"Do you have identification of the crew?" Catrina looked over at her father, who remained unmoved.

"We haven't found any remains. We hadn't gotten that far. We were looking for another way of getting to the main part of the wreck when I found the gate." Brit finished, holding his gaze at Tony.

"It's ok," Captain Dallas finally said quietly. He turned his gaze back up at his daughter. There was a distant look in his eyes. "They are the real thing Cat. They have come from home." He looked over at Brit. "You know who I am."

"I have known for some time now Captain," Brit answered, pulling the photos from his shirt pocket and dropping them down on the table in front of him.

Tony glanced down at them, while Cat picked up the first one of her mother. She looked at it strangely, then at her father.

"This is me. How is it he as a picture of me?"

"No honey." Tony smiled, slightly shaking his head. "It's not you." His own mind flashed back to the diner in Dubois, when he looked up into the eyes of Amanda, then as he knelt in front of her with her mother's ring, to greeting him on the tarmac after the war. As she looked up from her hospital bed with an infant Catrina in her arms. He had his own little time machine in his head, not only rolling back the pristine images of his beloved Amanda, but also every emotion that was created and associated with her. Time could not dim or erase the intense emotion he still harbored for his wife. He had learned to live with the emptiness that had been left by her absence. Now, some of that emotion was billowing up and out. He began to choke up. "It's your mother."

Catrina gazed at the photo in shock and wonder as her father continued.

"You look just like her in every way. It has been the only way I have been able to stand the loneliness after all this time, because I have her right here, in you." He turned back to Brit. His eyes were misty and it was obvious that he was fighting hard to keep them from filling up and spilling out.

"It is "The Amanda" that's buried in the cave, but I suspect you already knew that too."

Brit only nodded in agreement.

"How did you come by these photos and know this was the plane?"

Brit's smile broadened. There was no way Tony would even be able to guess how he came by them and Brit was so thrilled to be the one to get to tell him. It was at this point, that he was blessing his uncle Cal for sending him to Montana to make the visit with Amanda Dallas.

"I had a little help," he said, leaning forward, his eyes beaming. "From a wonderful woman from Helena, Montana," he continued, a big cheesy grin indicating how thrilled he was to tell him who it was. Brit chuckled at his perceived cleverness. "I have never seen such devotion in a person before as this woman has for you, though she's still a little mad at you for painting her picture on the side of your airplane. Let's see," he said, acting like he had to think about it. "What did she call herself? Oh yes, Amanda Alice Dallas."

Tony lost the fight, his eyes overflowing and the tear dam bursting. These were tears of joy, sadness and loneliness all rolled into one. He had operated on faith for so long that actually hearing it from someone else was an overwhelming relief. Her feelings for him were still as powerful now as they had ever been and the thought that she remained faithful to his memory was of great comfort.

Amanda's image was in such sharp focus in his head now. He had been separated from her for what seemed like a lifetime. Actually, it had been. The knowledge of all the wonders of life together as husband and wife, blasted in vivid color into his head knowing that it was something that only a man and a woman can share together. Tony grinned broadly through tear filled eyes at his daughter, for it was true. He could see Amanda standing before him, in his daughter. He had both of them with him always, even though he and Amanda had been separated for all these years by time and space.

"Amanda," he whispered through emotion.

Brit nodded with a grin as Catrina set the photo of her mother down and looked at her father, then back over at Brit.   Danny and Jerry leaned in a little closer for a better look at the pictures that Brit had set on the table. These had been in their information packets they had gotten before they left Driggs, so they had already seen them. The pictures reaffirmed the notion that they had seen Catrina and Tony before.

Memories of her mother and the life they all had together when she was a child flooded into Catrina's mind. It had been a lifetime for her as well. While she had always been daddy's little girl, she had equal love and adoration for her mother and had missed her, but found other ways to fill the voids. She felt her own bosom start to swell a little seeing her father shedding tears. Her strong personality had concealed the empty spaces left by an absent parent and somewhere throughout all the time they had been in Thulsa, she had forgotten her. No, not forgotten, covered over to insulate her from the pain of the loss of a loved one.

All of the questions that had flooded her were suddenly being worked out in her head. Brit could see the wheels were turning in her head and it wasn't until Tony had wiped his eyes that many of the revelations swirling in her mind started to gel.

"What is it?" her father asked, as she turned from the table and paced slowly back and forth for a moment. At length, she stopped and looked over her shoulder at the group behind her.

"The gate is still open," she said, almost as a question. She turned and stepped back over to the table. "It's still open." She was thinking Brit, Bryan and his friends were now able to do so because of the advancements of the 21st century. Perhaps now, they could indeed pass back through the gate, back to their own world. With the gate still open to Earth, maybe they could all go back through now, back home. Certainly this was a bit of a knee jerk reaction to the possibilities, but at the same time, other questions were created with the advent of this new information. These men might hold the key to making that happen. Then the thoughts of their station and the love they harbored for their adopted clans people collided. How could you leave a people you have lived with and loved for so long? Nevertheless, how could you not want to go home to family? These revelations were filling her mind with all kinds of mixed emotions. They had created a life here with this people. Tony had proven himself a cunning Thulsa warrior, ultimately rising to commander of all the clan armies, certainly respected by all who served under him. The previous aged monarch, who had taken them in as a part of his royal family, was without an heir. He had come to love the young Catrina as his own granddaughter and before his death, asked Catrina to take on the mantle of Queen of Thulsa. He trusted her intellect and leadership abilities and knew he was leaving the good people of Thulsa in very capable hands. How do you just turn and leave them as lightly as walking back through a door? What of the impending war that they knew was only days away?

"What are you getting at Cat?" Tony was a bit bewildered. "Yes, it's still open. We both saw and heard it."

Brit got a confused look on his face. He didn't understand what the big deal was. He had made an assumption from the get go that once they had cleared up all the confusion with the Winner's Spoil mess that they could gather their things and walk back out the same way they had come in, up the valley wall and back through the storm.

"But you know we can't leave," Tony finished stating what they had always known.

"Wait, what? What do you mean you can't leave? Why can't you leave?" Bryan asked, a bit panicked.

"We've never been able to leave," Tony said, continuing to look at her with questions in his eyes. She had something in her head.

Bryan looked over at his brother, having no idea what the problem was.

"Why not? What, did you take an oath or something? Pinkie promised someone or something? What?"

"The storm has always been too much for anyone to get through. We have tried to send people through the storm when it has appeared, even right after they arrived and they were killed," Tony said, looking down.

"What do you mean, killed?" Jerry asked, setting the pictures down.

"I'm pretty sure he means dead Jerr," Danny interjected, sarcastically. "As in, you're no longer living, as in without life, as in dead!"

"The storm sweeps you up," Tony said. "It takes anything that enters it and if you aren't torn to pieces, it will throw you out the top, to your death." Danny turned a painful face and put his hand to his throat where his rope burn was still hurting him.

"Yeah, but that doesn't make any sense," Bryan said, looking over at Brit. "We went right through it."

"Are you sure it isn't that we have better equipment than any of you guys did?" Brit asked, looking at all their stuff on the table. "That storm is pretty nasty to go through. We had to slide along the ground on our stomachs with safety ropes to get through it."

"You came through the storm, but did you try to go back out?"

"No, but I did put my hand back out into it when I came through and nothing happened," Brit informed him.

"Not sure what that's all about," Tony said, a bit perplexed. "It may be that you didn't have enough of your body in it to create any kind of interference. From what we observed, when someone tried to exit back through, the storm became even more violent. Very hard for either one of us to describe because we weren't the ones that actually experienced it, just what we observed. The storm will remain in place for about three days, and then break apart, moving on. We have never kept a schedule as to when it will come, how often or where its gate opens to, but it always stops in the same place and always dies out after about three days or so. It's been said that before we came here, it didn't stop, it always just blew right through."

"Three days," Brit repeated, thinking of Bill still in the coach. That would be a long time for him to sit in there waiting out a vicious storm like that.

"What's wrong?" Tony asked, reading Brit's concerned expression.

"We have an older gentleman still up on the rim in our vehicles. He's safe as long as he stays in the vehicle, but that's a long time to wait in a storm like that."

"Especially if you don't know how long it will last," Jerry finished.

"He's waiting for our signal."

"Signal for what?"

"When we found the plane, we were to contact him and he would relay the information down to our command center in Driggs to have a crew come in and extract it from the area, if it was intact. Something we still don't really know about."

"Oh, it's still intact," Tony reassured them all. "That's something odd in and of itself. It really shouldn't be."

"What do you mean?"

"Didn't you notice anything odd about the wreckage that you found on the surface?" Tony asked, causing them to think back.

Both Bryan and Brit looked oddly at Tony and Catrina, then back at each other. Brit got a strange look on his face, thinking a moment about when he had climbed inside the tail section of the wreck. Everything was still mainly all in its place and how everything was as it should be, not just as a wreck, but as it had been when it had actually wrecked. The more he thought about it the more he felt like the plane could have been wrecked the day before they found it. The two brothers looked back at Captain Dallas.

"Uhuh," Tony nodded grinning. "We figured it out a long time ago, and it might explain why we look the way we do to you. We seemed to have aged at a much different rate as earth has. We look pretty good for our age, eh?"

"Ooo-oo!" Bryan cut in excitedly, lifting his hand up like an over eager second grader. "Pick me! Pick me! I know this!"

"Oh, you do?" Brit piped back, a little surprised, but very skeptical as well. "And how do you think you've solved the mysteries of the universe Einstein?"

Bryan shot his brother a simple disgusted glance, then started out.

"I have an app for that!"

"An app," Brit repeated very skeptical. "You have an app for time travel."

"Yes," Bryan repeated defensively, working his tablet again. "An app. May I have the floor?"

"By all means Professor, please enlighten us with your vast data base of knowledge."

There was a lot of sarcasm in Brit's voice, waving his hand airily across the room to make way for the flood of intellect that was about to ensue. Catrina and Tony both got a good chuckle out of it.

"Oh, this is nothing," Danny cut in, trying to fuel the fire. "You ought to be around when they are talking about who can dive the deepest."

"Yes," Jerry agreed. "We can sell tickets and make a fortune."

Bryan didn't care. He had seen this explained to him through a 5 part series on the PBS channel. "The nature of the Universe" and while there were still plenty of holes in what they were trying to lay out and much of it still theoretical, it made a lot of sense to him. The current circumstances seemed to fit close. It all had to do with String theory, quantum mechanics, time and space, all being related to the other.

"For the sake of time, which we have precious little of right now, please give us the nursery rhyme version," Cat said, giving the four of them a good grin and turning to Bryan.

Bryan was a little dejected, but undeterred. He looked through the electronic pages of his touch device until he found what he was looking for.

"It's not exactly an app for time travel, but in a *nut* shell," he laid strong emphasis on the word "*nut*" while looking at his big brother. Brit shifted his weight and rolled his eyes. "What happens on one side of the universe can directly correspond with what is happening on the other side and where they are in relationship to one another in time, and space. Meaning, both time lines can be moving in tandem with the other, but as they move and change distance from the other, the time line speeds up or slows down in relationship to the other. It may have been that earth fell behind Thulsa at several points in the last however many years they are arguing about how old the earth and the universe is this week. Apparently, this week we are back ahead of this place."

"So the wreck hasn't aged much either," Tony said, sitting forward.

"I would think that's because it's basically caught between two worlds where time is either moving so slowly that it doesn't seem like anything ages, or it's frozen altogether." Bryan said, confident in his hypothesis.

"That would be why the snow never seems to melt in the valley. It explains a lot of things," Tony said, thinking outside the box. "In fact, her auxiliary batteries are still up to full power and we can still smell avgas towards the back where the wings have obviously been leaking."

"Wait," Brit cut him off. "What do you mean her batteries are up? You can still smell avgas? You mean you can reach her in the cave?"

"Well, sure," Tony said rather matter-a-factly. "Stronghold is built into the rock bluffs here and there's an entrance through the Manor cellars to a tunnel that takes you right to it."

Brit and Bryan were nearly out of their seats, but Cat held them back.

"Hang on a minute here," she spoke up. "We have some other serious things we have to get figured out first. You guys may be out of the frying pan, but we still have the fire to contend with and if we don't have some kind of a good reason for keeping you alive, it's quite likely that you'll be in the arena."

"The arena?" Brit repeated, dropping back down to his seat. "What is the arena?" He wasn't sure he wanted to know. They had already been introduced to Thulsa's version of quick justice in the town square. The arena didn't have a very good sound to it, at least the way Catrina said it.

"It's a chance for the accused to either redeem or prove themselves. In your case it would be to prove yourselves worthy of life," she said, sitting down. "Each of you would be required to enter the arena and fight a warrior of the council's choosing, whether it's one of our warriors or an enemy prisoner, to the death. In your brother and friends case, as they were captured together first, they would fight together against whom ever was assigned to them. They would have a little better chance because they would all three be fighting at once."

Bryan and the other two weren't all that fired up about having to fight together in the arena, but things were only going to get worse.

"In Brit's case, he would have to fight one on one," she finished, a little hesitantly. Her fondness for him was rapidly growing the more they learned about the other. Catrina and her father were committed to seeing that none of this happened. It was clear that there was quite a lot at stake, even the possibility that they could all go home together.

"How did you manage to pull the Twins?" Cat asked, looking back over at Brit.

"Yeah," Bryan said, looking down at the two swords still in their sheaths leaning against the wall behind his brother. "Mind if I have a look-see at those?" he asked, taking them from his brother who had grabbed them, and was setting them on the table in front of them.

"My superior skills," he said, straight faced that brought a snicker from Danny and Jerry.

"He probably knocked them over," Danny chuckled, giving his friend Jerry the rib with his elbow. Cat smiled knowing that at the moment, it really wasn't important. She was just glad that he did. They wouldn't be standing here talking if he hadn't.

Bryan looked one of the swords over carefully as Danny and Jerry looked at the other one still sitting on the table in front of them. The scrollwork on the scabbard was amazing. The workmanship and attention to detail was unsurpassed. There was nothing on the hilts that really set it apart from any other sword other than it was a bit smaller and seemed to fit in the hand much more comfortably than most swords that he and his brother had studied. These had simple horizontal hand guards with wooden handles over the hilts. There were slender metal interlacing's inlayed into the wooden handles, presumably to provide stability to the wooden handle and to provide better gripping power. There was something rather small engraved on each sword at the hand guard. It was in a language that Bryan could not understand, so he handed it to Tony, who then turned it over to Catrina.

She studied it carefully. She had never held the twins before. She had seen them at the altar, even stood at the altar, but she had never studied it or the swords before. She had been taught since she had arrived here long ago not to touch or even approach the altar except when performing the ancient Thulsa gratitude rite, when they would deposit a portion of the treasure they had looted from other clans who had attacked their lands and been defeated. However, she did understand the words that were engraven in Thulsian across the hand guards.

"Knowledge is power," she said carefully. "Did you see anything else at the altar?" she asked, quickly looking back at Brit. Brit only shrugged.

"There was writing like that all over it."

"What else?" she asked, settling a little closer to him. "Anything else would be helpful."

"Like I said, there was this writing all over the altar. On the sides, front and the top under those little arches where the swords were floating, there were two slots on either side of the altar about a half an inch wide and about ten inches long"

Bryan pulled one of the swords from its sheath, revealing its glowing blue blade. Everyone in the room could feel it humming. They couldn't hear it, but they could feel it.

"On the back of the altar was a larger empty slot, like a shelf for keeping papers and scrolls organized or storing a closed book."

"A book?" Tony sat up. "What kind of a book?"

"I don't know," Brit came back, feeling like he was doing a terrible job of describing what he hadn't really paid a whole lot of attention to. Apparently no one else had ever noticed the slot either. "I didn't see a book anywhere, just a place you could have put a big book."

"The Signet," Catrina and Tony said at the same time with a smile.

"Huh?" Brit asked stupidly, as Bryan studied the glowing blade carefully. He pulled out some of his gadgets and started running some tests on it.

"The Signet is a large book of instruction that's said to hold great knowledge," Catrina informed him, watching Bryan do what he was doing with the sword. "It's supposed to give instruction on how to control the storm, but it disappeared long before we arrived here. The

clan elders speak of it from time to time, but none of them have ever
seen it, they just passed the story along from one to the other. If this
book even still exists, it's the only ticket you have for getting home,
but we would have to find it first. It's rumored to be hidden in the
lands of the Kenlar clan."

"Ruled by your favorite," Tony stated coldly.

"Yes, my favorite," Cat echoed disdainfully.

"Nice guy, close personal friend or just a kissing cousin?" Brit
asked, as the gadget Bryan was fiddling with started to make a quiet
whining sound.

"Not even," Tony grumbled unhappily.

"The animal's animal is Ivan Rubella," Cat spat completely revolted
by the thought.

"Sounds like some kind of a disease," Brit commented, smirking.

"Believe me, disease fits pretty well, he's a diseased animal."

"Tried to have himself married to Cat so he could take over Thulsa
without a fight," Tony said. "He would have succeeded had Carl not
challenged him."

"Carl?" Brit asked.

"One of my crew," Tony responded in almost a trance, thinking
about his fellow crewman and friend. Catrina sat down quietly and
stared at the wall with a certain reverence etched on her face as Tony
continued.

"Carl Lott, my waist gunner, looked after Cat when I was away
with the Thulsa armies. He was her personal body guard and
defended her many times with his own life. He was completely
committed to her protection and seeing that she was kept safe. He
drove Ivan from the city several times. The last time, he beat Ivan in
a very public and humiliating way in the arena. Ivan was branded a
coward then banished from Thulsa only to have Carl assassinated a
few days later on a hunting trip. He was stabbed in the back. Carl
made it back into the city as far as the gates to the Stronghold Manor.
He died in Cat's arms."

Tony looked over at his still mourning daughter. She had loved
Carl like a second father and he had loved her like she had been his
own daughter.

"I'd given anything to have spared her of that, but I was away
fighting. Seems like my whole life as a father has been away fighting
instead of at home with my family." Tony was sounding like he was
having big regrets about decisions he had made in his life.

"It wasn't your fault dad," Catrina returned softly, turning to her
father. Her eyes had welled up with emotion for her fallen friend and
for her father. "It is what it is and we do what we have to do to
survive. Carl knew that and we loved him for it. He was a good man."

Brit wasn't sure if he should say anything else or not. It was a bit
of an awkward moment for him. This was certainly a private and

solemn moment for father and daughter. Sort of like how he felt when he was trying to leave Amanda's house in Helena.

"The book," Brit started again on the conversation. "Is there any way to find out if it's really out there?"

"No one here has ever seen it or read from its pages. It's said that it's written in the language of another world. We have one account of someone seeing it, but we haven't heard from them for many years now," Cat said, trying to veer her attention from sorrow.

"What do you mean you haven't heard from them?"

"When we crashed here and found that we could not escape back to our own world, we assimilated into the Thulsa society. There seemed to be no sense in staying together. We thought it better to spread out. Perhaps we could do the clans more good by learning different ways and teaching others of our ways. We taught everyone English as a second language. This was a very primitive people, mostly fighting with the other clans for survival instead of relying on themselves. Dale and Chuck were killed trying to escape through the storm a couple of years after we got here. Terry lives near the base of Mount Boris on the north eastern borders between Thulsa and Kenlar. It's somewhat remote, but if Ivan's raiding parties haven't run him out, he may still be there. It's been a while since we've been there or seen him. Tom went into the northern countries of the Gaylens. We haven't heard from him since we lost Chuck and Dale to the storm. Tim married a Kenlar woman right after we got here and moved to Crosslake with their clan. Last we heard from him, he said that he had uncovered a large book called the Signet, among the items in Ivan's treasury and started translating parts of it. He seemed very excited about it at the time, but it's been years since anyone has heard from him."

"If this book is what you say it is," Brit said, taking a deep breath, "why wouldn't Ivan have used it by now? If it has all that information in it, wouldn't he just use it for himself?"

"If the idiot could read, or even had half a clue of what the book contained, he certainly would," Cat said, a contemptuous tone in her voice.

"We assume that Tim discovered the importance of the book and has somehow kept its secrets safe from Ivan," Tony said, starting to take notice of Bryan and what he was doing with the sword.

"Then it sounds like we're going to need to find it and fast." Brit turned his attention back to his brother. "What are you finding there, Sonny-Jim?"

"It's truly remarkable," he responded, still looking at his equipment carefully. "This metal alloy is like nothing I've ever seen before."

"Not that you're an expert or anything," Brit chided him good-naturedly. Bryan actually was very good at identifying metals, compounds and different "scientific technical stuff", as Brit often called it. Much of his college schooling was focused in this area of expertise and it had severed him well in his chosen professional field.

"It has some steel compounds in it, but there's something else there as well that I have never seen before. It's similar to a carbon fiber material, but it's harder than diamond. It also has Tritium blended with it. That's what the glow is. They used to use that stuff for the backlights in your LCD watches. Cool stuff actually. This is only a guess here, but I think that's why it seems to hum when you have it out of its scabbard, some kind of a reaction with the metal and the Tritium in the blade. The scabbard probably mutes it when you put it in. I'm betting with this other alloy that these blades never have to be sharpened and that might explain why it's so light weight. It would be like fighting with a small stick. You could swing and swing and swing with this thing and never get tired, amazing," he said looking up from the sword.

Catrina gestured to Brit for the other sword, which he gladly handed to her. She pulled the blade and stepped to the middle of the room, away from the others. Starting with a warrior stance, she gently swung it back and forth in front of her. Gracefully arching it over her head, around behind her, and spinning it back around in front of her. Twirling it in a fluid movement, she changed hands, swinging it back into and attack stance.

"It's probably similar to the material we use to make our chainmail," she said, hefting it in her hand. "This isn't a ladies sword, but I could certainly do some serious damage with it," she offered grinning. "But it's meant to be used with its twin," she gestured for the other sword.

Once both were in hand, she hefted them to test their true weight. Brit looked back over at Tony who had been watching him, watch her. He grinned broadly at Brit and shifted his eyes back to Cat. Brit watched her, becoming poetry in motion. Gracefully arching the swords in front of her in a slow methodical pattern, she stepped carefully around the room, turning with the elegance of a queen, but spinning the swords together with the precision of an expert warrior swordsman. She froze for a moment, slowly swung the swords out in front of her, then above her head and back down in front of her. She instantly spun on one heel while twirling the swords against the other like propellers on an airplane, but never striking the other. She stepped carefully towards the group with the blades spinning madly in front of her until she was standing right in front of Brit. He had quite the impressed look on his face, but was ignoring the blades spinning in front of him, gazing right through them, into Catrina's eyes. Her face was emotionless, gazing right back at him, speaking to one another through their eyes. Then in an instant, the twins sank into the table in front of him with a thud. Neither Brit nor Cat flinched or took their eyes off the other. Tony's grin turned to a little chuckle as Bryan and the other two were flabbergasted with her expert swordsmanship.

"That's how they were meant to be used," she said unflinchingly, her gaze locked on his hazel eyes. There was an awkward silence for a long moment as they continued to stare at the other. The other four looked at each other, then back over at the two infatuates.

"Are you two having a moment? Would you like to be alone?" Danny finally blurted out with a smirk. Jerry and Bryan snickered stupidly, but the comment didn't seem to deter either Cat or Brit.

"Sort of thought we were," Brit finally commented, breaking away from Cat's adoring gaze. Catrina turned her head a bit and looked down at the swords still wobbling in the wood, then over at her father who still had a musing smile on his face.

Now she was a bit embarrassed. *That was not the way a woman of her status should have acted.* Having thought that of herself, she realized that while a queen shouldn't really act that way in court or council, it was certainly all right for a woman to do so and she felt so much like a woman when she was in the presence of Brit. It was a feeling that she really hadn't experienced before. She only met this man this morning. How could she possibly feel this way towards him? She felt like she didn't want to be anywhere else but with him, wherever he was. She had certainly had plenty of suitors over the years but none had ever made her feel this way. Ivan of the Kenlars, her most recent suitor, definitely brought out very strong feelings, but those feelings were quite the opposite of what she was feeling now. There was nothing about that horrible excuse of a Neanderthal that came close to attracting her to him. He might be good looking if he weren't covered with hair, but how would anyone ever know? No, there was nothing about Ivan that was remotely attractive. He would have used and abused her, if he could, and then done away with her. She was no piece of meat to be chewed on for a moment and then thrown to the wolves. She was a woman and a prize certainly worth the treatment of royalty. That became secondary, as a summons at the door drew Catrina away from the table, only to return a moment later.

"That was fast. The Elder council and the city clusters are assembling in the grand hall," she said, a little bit worried. "We must get you to a safe place for now while the council convenes to decide your fate."

"Don't they want to hear from us?" Bryan asked, packing his gear back into his pack while the others grabbed their stuff.

"There's no need," Tony said, helping them gather their stuff. "They have heard everything they need to hear from the Cluster representatives. The royal guards will fill in their reports and then we'll address the council."

"This kind of sounds like taxation without representation," Jerry commented, following Tony to the door with Danny and Bryan hot on their heels. Brit pulled the straps of the scabbards over his head and into place as Catrina pulled the twins from the table and carefully handed them back to him.

"Are you going to be ok?" he asked, pushing the blades back into their place.

"Please," she stepped closer to him. The tone in her voice was that of a very confident monarch, but held the tenderness of a woman more worried for Brit's welfare. "I'm in charge here. I'm just being nice by letting them talk. I'll have all this worked out in plenty of time." Perhaps this sounded a little overconfident on her part, but she had dealt with the council of elders enough to know how it all worked and what kind of influence she had in such meetings. Besides, she felt like she needed to reassure him in some way.

Brit finished securing the swords and grabbed his bag. Looking up again, Catrina had stepped even closer. Now she was indeed inside his personal space, but he didn't mind, as he had been looking for an excuse to get into her space. He desperately wanted to touch her hand. He knew they were strong hands, but delicate at the same time. They just stood looking at each other. Brit found his hand reaching out towards hers, but their progress was stopped by some coughs and throat clearings coming from the door.

"We really can give you two a moment if you'd like," Danny whispered loudly.

There really wasn't any time for this kind of thing. Not here, not now. The want and the will were certainly there, but they had to get these men to a safe place before they were discovered. It would be the will of the council to cross examine these strangers if convenient to do so. It would be better to hide them in a good place that no one but Tony and Cat had immediate knowledge of. To protect her own royal guards from any chance of cross examination from the council, Tony would lead them to the secret tunnel in the Stronghold's cellars and let them hide back in the cave where "The Amanda" had come to rest.

Brit hesitated a couple of times with his hand still part way extended. Though Cat couldn't see it, she could sense him hesitating and held back, seeing if he would make the effort to carry through. Finally, the urgency of the situation tugged hard enough at him that he pulled back from her and turned to follow the others. Leaving the room, he turned back to look at her once more, but she was already heading for the other door to ready herself for her entrance to the grand hall. She was Queen of Thulsa and must dress appropriately for council procedures.

"The Amanda"

Tony carefully turned the valve on a mounted gas lamp in the tunnel entrance and stepped through a cleverly hidden door waiting for the other four to follow with their gear.

"You'll be quite safe down here until we come to get you. Just follow the path. There are no rocks down here. Couldn't tell you why, but all the same, you'll want light. I installed gas lamps all the way down to "The Amanda". She is pretty well lit and you guys can look her over real good if you have flash lights. Just hit the strikers on the lamp bases. You'll be fine. We'll be back as soon as the council breaks and a decision reached." With that Tony stepped back out and quietly shut the door behind him then made his way back up to his own chambers to dress for the meeting that was probably already in progress.

Brit and Bryan stepped carefully down the passage despite Tony's assurances that there was nothing to trip on. Every ten feet or so, there was another lamp mounted to the rock wall fed by a pipe that made a continuous route down the tunnel. After 20 minutes of walking from one lamp to the next, Bryan nudged Brit on the shoulder. Brit turned to his two friends, but found them looking straight in front of them. He turned back around, seeing the flicker of the lamp flame reflecting off a slumbering giant. Danny and Jerry caught the faint scent of avgas as they stepped closer to the nose of the bomber resting on its belly, on the clay floor of the cave. Brit and Bryan worked their way around the cavern, lighting the rest of the gas lamps that Tony had installed long ago. As the last of the lamps lit up, it was almost as bright in the cave as it would be if they were at home in the staging hangar.

Brit turned back to the left side of the fuselage and pulled out the picture that Amanda had given him for positive identification of the aircraft, should they find it. He gazed down at the nose art image of "The Amanda" in the photo, and then looked back up at the colorfully painted image on the side of the airplane. There was no doubt about it. With the exception of three crew members, they had found and accounted for everything associated with this wreck.

He stepped up next to the fuselage and put his hand up to the painting, but did not touch it. He loved old war birds, but especially the B-25 Mitchell. There was just something about this airplane that made it his favorite above all the others. The Mitchell was always loved by every pilot privileged to fly her. It was a rugged, sturdy and versatile aircraft, yet it flew like a dream. Only the B-17 could boast more battle damage to return ratio, but that was mainly due to there being more of them out there. The 25 had several companions in its class, but none of them had endeared themselves to their pilots like the B-25 did to theirs. It was truly a pleasure to fly and look at.

Brit could almost feel "The Amanda" still breathing, still living, waiting wounded for someone to come and rescue her from this prison she had slid into. He let his hand glide softly across the painting. He could hear something in his head as he held his hand to the metal skin of the old plane, but he couldn't distinguish what it was. It sounded like someone speaking at high speed and in a different language. He looked back at Danny who was looking inside the left waist gunner's window and then turned to Jerry as he peered inside the nose of the bomber.

"I assume the wooden stools were put here so someone could get in and out of her if they needed to." Jerry stepped back and motioned for Brit to have at the stool. "This is your salvage."

Smiling, Brit handed the twins to Jerry, pulled off his coat and producing a small flashlight, he climbed up and through the nose hatchway. Once inside, the odor of avgas mixed with the smell of military canvas was almost over powering. He looked around at the bombardier's position and examined the .50 caliber machine gun still loaded with ammunition. He thought it odd that it was loaded with live rounds, but was pleased that it was still in pristine condition. The entire ship appeared to be suspended in time from the elements. It was amazing! If it weren't for the fact that the wings had clearly been sheared off by the crash, he would have thought that there was nothing wrong with this plane at all.

He turned and crawled up the crawlway tunnel to the main compartment and up to the cockpit. It looked as though nothing had been disturbed after the crew had left her. Brit looked over everything with gleeful amazement. He was sitting in a time capsule to 1945. There was no dust, no cobwebs, not rust, no deterioration of any kind anywhere. The aircraft was just being held there, suspended in time.

He had noticed something rather odd when he had entered the ship. He couldn't hear it, but he could feel it. There was a humming surrounding him as he crawled around inside the cockpit and then back to the top gunner's position. It felt identical to the humming that his twins created when out of their scabbards. How odd it was. He wondered if Jerry could feel it sensing his friend following him into the aircraft.

Stepping partway down to the hatchway, Brit could see the electrical panel for the aircraft. All the electrical breakers were pulled out to their open position and the switches were off. He glanced up at the auxiliary batteries stowed over the bomb bay on the right side of the plane, behind the Top turret. Looking carefully down at the electrical panel, Brit started pushing the breakers back in. After moving the switches back into their "on" positions, he stepped past Jerry, to the front and flipped the master switches to on. There was an instant whisper of instruments energizing and several control panel lights came on. Brit passed his friend a wicked expression, stepping back to the top turret and climbing up onto the seat. Reaching over and activating the maneuvering controls, he tipped the twin guns up sharply, then turned the control hard to the left. The turret's power drive units responded instantly, spinning the whole gun assembly effortlessly to the left at lightning speed. *Hot dang he loved this part!* It was a real rush to be sitting in that top gun turret and able to turn 360 degrees in either direction at high speed. These guns had to be fast in order to take aim at incoming enemy aircraft that usually attacked from every direction.

Smiling broadly, he checked the operation of the turret. Everything seemed to be working perfectly. He checked the guns themselves. Like the guns up front, these too were loaded and in perfect working condition. He so wanted to pull the triggers on the big twin 50s and see what they'd do, but it was certain that they would bring part of the cave down on them if he did.

Stepping back up to shut off the master switches on the console between the pilot and copilot's position, he caught sight of two small photographs stuck to the instrument panel. He carefully pulled them from their clips and examined them. One was an old photo of a young looking Captain Dallas and a 5 year old girl sitting in one of Tony's private planes. Britten recognized a young Catrina, even though the photo was black and white and a bit faded, there was no mistaking the sassy short brown hair and the eyes. The other picture was a small duplicate of the larger one he had of Amanda. After looking at the pictures for some time, he carefully placed them back on their clips on the instrument panel. Shutting the master switches off, he returned to the electrical panels, instructing Jerry to shut everything off again. They then climbed over the bomb bay bulkhead and into the rear compartment. Both rear windows were open and as he stepped down, his brother poked his head inside as Jerry climbed out.

"This thing is amazing," Bryan exclaimed excitedly. "I have never seen a wreck like this before!"

"It's hardly even a wreck bro," Brit exclaimed. "Everything in here is operational. Nothing has aged or deteriorated, nothing. It's unbelievable!"

"And have a gander at this," Bryan said enthusiastically, stepping to the rear of the fuselage, still partly buried in snow. He grabbed a handful and tried to pack it in his hand, but it was like dry powder.

"What the-," Brit mumbled, climbing through the open window and back to the wall of snow. He grabbed a fist full in each hand, but it would not pack at all. "Ok, this is really weird."

"What's really weird?" Danny asked, stepping up behind the two with Jerry in tow.

"Here," Brit said, handing him some snow. "Snowball fight." Both Danny and Jerry tried to pack the snow, but it wouldn't unless they let it melt a little bit, much like powder snow that had fallen through subzero air and remained in a frozen state even after being on the ground for a long period. Both of them looked at it curiously, then at the snow wall blocking the entrance of the cave.

"I don't get it," Danny said, wiping the melting snow off his hands and stepping right up to the wall. "If this was an avalanche, this snow should be at the very least as hard as a rock."

"This whole wall should be an ice block," Bryan commented, gazing at the whole wall. "It would take dynamite and about a week to try and clear all this out. It should be glacier ice. And," Bryan added, pulling one of his gizmos out of his pocket. "Take a look see at this."

"What are we looking at?" Brit asked, stepping a little closer with his other two friends. Bryan messed around with the little gadget for a moment, and then turned to the others so they could look at the readout on the display. Brit looked up at Bryan a couple of times. "Where is this coming from?"

"The Amanda," he motioned back to the wreck.

"Not possible," Brit said, not believing what he was seeing. "It's an airplane. It can't possibly be producing that."

"Ah," Danny held up his hand. "Teacher, can I ask a question?" Jerry was quick to do the same.

"Oh, oooo, pick me, pick me!" Jerry puffed, raising his hand too and pushing himself in front of Danny, who wasn't going to give him any leave, struggling to stay in front of him.

Bryan turned a disgusted face at the two because he knew they had no idea of what they were looking at. He knew they were mocking him from earlier when they were examining the swords. Brit stepped back over to the gunner's window and climbed back inside. Instantly, he could feel the hum, almost a vibration existing only in his head, and then turned back to the open window, poking his head out.

"Jerry, hand me the twins."

Jerry stepped over to the window and gave Brit his two swords, then returned to Bryan and Danny for some kind of an explanation of what they was looking at.

"This is a," Bryan hesitated giving the real title of the box he was letting them look at. Probably best give them the layman's explanation. "A gadget that measures a couple of different things. Electromagnetic waves, alpha waves and some other stuff."

"All in one box?" Danny asked, looking at the small hand held box. "How convenient."

"Totes!" Jerry agreed, knowing they were bugging the heck out of Bryan. "Gotta get me one of these."

"If Abbott and Costello are finished here, we'll continue with preschool," Bryan snapped, a little miffed. Jerry and Danny passed glances, a look of playful fear popped up while raising a hand to their mouths.

"The electromagnetic waves are coming from somewhere above us. The only thing I can figure would produce something like that is the storm. The alpha waves are coming from "The Amanda". Somehow this airplane is reacting to the storm, and, as near as I can tell, the storm is reacting to the plane."

"So how is that possible?" Brit asked from inside. Bryan stepped over to the plane, leaving the other two holding the test box.

"What, you think I'm Spock or something? I have no idea. My best guess would be when Captain Dallas flew into the storm, it created some kind of electromagnetic charge that reacted with the plane's metal or structure or something."

"Ok, so explain the alpha waves," Brit said, strapping the swords over his shoulders. "They are measured only in living things, like us. Are you trying to tell me that "The Amanda" is producing alpha waves?"

"I'm not trying to tell you anything," Bryan responded defensively. "I'm just telling you what the box says and what my best guess is. What are you doing?"

"Get in here."

Bryan climbed inside and stood there a moment, then looked at his brother with an odd look that made Brit smile.

"Ah, I see you are having the same experience," he said, grabbing both hilts of the swords and pulling the blades from their resting places. The glowing blades instantly reacted to the presence of the aircraft and tripled their normal light output, beginning to sparkle wildly. The hum that was normally in their heads instantly became completely audible.

"Sounds like a light saber."

"Or a particle foil." Bryan stepped over to the wall of the aircraft and put his hand on the bare metal wall.

"Get a load of this," a smile melting onto his face. Brit handed him one of the swords and placed his own bare hand on the inner skin of the aircraft. It was almost like the old airplane was trying to speak right into their heads. It sounded like high speed gibberish at first, then it began to slow and there was some enunciation starting to form. The brothers gazed at one another wide eyed, hearing words beginning to form within their own minds.

Pulling their hands from the metal, Brit quickly sheathed the swords while Bryan scrambled out followed by his brother.

"Ok, so that was spooky," Bryan said, looking back at the airplane.

"It's haunted!" Brit exclaimed, stepping away from the wreck.

The four men explored everything about the wreck for an hour or so, and then three of them sat down on the stools used to gain entry. Bryan continued to examine things towards the rear of the plane with his little hand held analyzers. They had no idea how long the council proceedings were going to last and it had already been a very busy day for them. Danny and Jerry were recapping what their activities for the day had been so far and while it was all very exciting, this was a little more adventure than they had bargained for. They just chocked it up to standard operating procedure with the Garrett boys. More often than not, every time they did something with Brit and Bryan, there was always high adventure to be had. Not that the brothers were jinxed, they just seemed to really push the envelope, intentional or not.

As Brit sat waiting, he listened to his two friends recap the day's events from their own perspective, continuing to add embellishments to the same story. Leaning back against the fuselage of "The Amanda", he closed his eyes. He too was a bit tired and there was a lot to process. As the back of his head touched the skin of the aircraft behind him, he felt the hum melt into him and sounds started coming into his head. This time, they were different somehow. Not as high speed or jumbled as before when he and Bryan had felt them. There was a sense of calm this time and he relaxed a bit to let the sounds permeate through him. His mind seemed to blend into the sounds and he began to see images opening to his mind like a movie theatre.

He was there at the conception of this aircraft, in the factory as she was being assembled. He went through all the steps of the assembly line until she was rolled out and flown for the first time, all of the training flights, the maintenance work, the ferry time to Europe and then the introduction to Captain Dallas. She showed him what it was like to have Captain Dallas and his crew, touch her for the first time and how they all grew to love the other. He could actually feel how much it had hurt to go through combat and not only take battle damage from enemy aircraft and flak, but to see one of her crew get wounded or worse, killed. She would sit on the flight line after a mission and mourn the loss of a crew member. He could tell how overjoyed she was when one that was wounded would come back to active duty.

Slowly, Brit recognized that the sounds had become a narrative as she spoke most fondly of Tony. When he would talk to her and treat her so well. She loved him and did anything that he would ask of her. She had been a little worried by the painting of Amanda on her side, but after meeting his wife and knowing that he was in such good hands with her, she was proud to carry him wherever he needed to go. She especially loved his daughter. Catrina was the most wonderful girl she had ever seen and she was so excited to have her onboard for the post war tour.

Every piece of their journey was detailed, everything that happened, right up to the storm. She was so scared, as were the rest of the crew. Her biggest concern was for Catrina, who was so young and "The Amanda" was deathly afraid of the young girl getting hurt, or worse. She painfully detailed their ordeal inside the storm and how she gave her all to stay airborne, even after they came out of it. Nevertheless, Tony knew what to do for their best chances of survival and she gave her all to maximize those efforts. "The Amanda" understood that she might have to sacrifice herself in order to save them. She had seen so many of her brothers and sisters die in action and she knew going in that this would be her last mission and was prepared to do whatever had to be done to protect her crew. Like all the others, she expected to die violently, a plane's honorable demise, but in the mountains. However, here, that didn't happen. Something had happened to her in the storm, and now she was attracting and holding the storm. It had to be stopped, changed somehow.

"Can you hear me?" Brit asked in his mind.

"Yes, of course, as you can hear me."

"I don't understand this. How is this possible?"

"I'm an airplane, not a scientist, but there's a lot of truth in the beliefs and attitudes that most men have about their machines. We all have a life force of our own, albeit far different than what you have. We have feelings and aspirations just like you do. There has always been communication of sorts; we just have to learn to speak the same language. Most pilots and crew figure it out without having to actually speak."

"I know what you're talking about now. I've felt it before with other things, but we usually just dismiss it as a sentimental attachment we have with it. I have to say, that this is very cool."

"It's very nice to have someone to talk to after so long down here."

"I can't see you though, can I?"

"You're leaning against me. How much more do you need to see? You have seen my memories of flight."

"True that, just easier to focus if there's a face to go along with the voice."

"I shall work on that. For now, just imagine me as you see me depicted in the picture you're leaning against."

"That works. Are you in pain now?'

"No, not really. The crash only hurt a little bit. My pain comes from deeper than my broken structure. I've seen mechanics repair worse than me. My pain comes from the storm outside and it's attraction to me."

"I don't understand."

"The storm has always come. It has always followed the same path, never deviating, through this time and space. But it wasn't until I passed through it and crashed here, that it would stop directly over me, spinning until it would have to move on, to recharge itself."

"Why does that cause you pain?"

"The storm searches for me each time it passes over, taking a small part of my being each time.   It's attracted to me, but somehow, I remain hidden from it, like the snow and ice somehow keeps me hidden. But it knows I'm here because parts of me lay exposed on the surface.   I feel it searching for me, trying to find me so it can take back what it inadvertently passed into me when we flew through it."

"Do you communicate with it?"

"How do you communicate with a hurricane?"

"Good point."

"I only know that it seems angry, very angry and every time someone tries to pass through it, it becomes even angrier." The Amanda shuddered filling Brit with a flood of heartbreak.

"I felt it take Chuck, Dale and other unfortunate souls, and tear them to pieces. So much anger contained in it. It cannot be allowed to keep doing this. It must be stopped!"

"How? How do we stop it?"

"It's attracted to me. If I were not here, it would never stop and no one would be caught in it.   The storm would travel as it always has, never stopping, never taking anyone. No one would ever know of it again because it would never stop."

"So exactly what are you suggesting?

"Remove me from this place and you should remove the lightning rod. I know of only one way to remove me from this place and while painful for me, it would be the only way.

"You're talking about destroying yourself."

"Yes, it's the only way to stop it."

"No, there has to be another way."

"There is no other way. You must destroy me and every piece scattered, so that my energy can be released and dissipate back to where it came. Then and only then will the storm be satisfied."

Brit was already feeling an emotional attachment to The Amanda. It was difficult not to. He loved the B-25 as an airplane and after all they had gone through to reach this point, he had developed an even greater attachment to this one. Learning so much about the Dallas family, what they had gone through and what they meant to each other, not to mention how he was already starting to feel about this particular airplane. She had so much emotion and passion.   He couldn't even fathom doing what she was proposing. There had to be another way. Brit let his mind wander for a few moments, and then heard The Amanda again.

"How are Tony and Catrina? They rarely come here anymore. I haven't seen Catrina since shortly after she left here the first time the Thulsa warriors came and took them. It has been so long since I've seen anyone."

"They seem to be fine. Captain Dallas is commander of the Thulsa armies and Catrina is Queen of Thulsa."

"I really have no idea where I am or what has been going on around me. I mostly sleep and dream, unless the storm is here."

There was silence again in Brit's head, his thoughts turning to Catrina. He could think about her all day, not caring about anything that was going on around him. She was so beautiful and he found himself starting to list off all the things that he liked about her and what he wished he had done in a particular situation, instead of what turned out to be a silly, clumsy attempt at something good. Everything that he thought of brought him right back to her. Her hair, her lips, her nose, her eyes.

"What does she look like now?" The Amanda asked him carefully. "By the way, you're thinking really loudly right now. Remember that we're in here together."

"Crap," Brit was a little embarrassed now. He had no idea that this exchange in his mind was going to be a bit tricky. Think the wrong thing and you could really get yourself in a lot of trouble. At least while you're touching her.

"Sorry," he thought carefully. "What does Catrina look like?"
"Yes."
"Your painting is exactly what she looks like."
"That painting is of her mother."
"Exactly, she looks just like her mother did."
"Wow, no wonder you are so taken with her. You feel the same way about Catrina as Tony and Amanda felt about each other."
"I've never heard their story before."
"I have. Tony has told it many times. It's wonderful and so romantic. May I?"
"Please, I have nothing better to do here, but try and ignore what are supposed to be my own thoughts. I'm very new to this kind of communication and since Amanda and Catrina look so much alike, I'm liable to get lost in your story."
"Agreed."

Introductions

Brit suddenly sprang forward, releasing himself from the connection with The Amanda. He blinked wide eyed, looking up at his brother who was working with his pack.

"I've pretty well finished all the tests there are to run here on this thing. She sure is a beaut, I gotta tell ya. Most of the time we get to a wreck and it's in a million or so pieces or Mother Nature has done her work on it and there isn't much left over. This one," he paused looking at the nose art. "This one is amazing. The damage here is certainly fixable, but we could get more out of it with the condition of the parts than if it were actually flying. If Cal has all the paperwork intact from the surplus salvage, and we can get this thing out of here, we should be sitting really pretty with this one. She's worth a fortune just in parts. I bet WACS air restore could have this thing stripped down and sold off in nothing flat."

"No."

"No what?"

"No, we're not going to scrap her," Brit stated emphatically, coming back to reality. He had only heard about half of what his brother had said, but the last part was enough. "We've got to get her out of here."

"Ok, ok," Bryan said, trying to figure out what Brit was going for here. He was always the one who was looking for the most "bang" for the buck. Parting an airplane out was certainly a fast way to recover costs and if things were in good condition, you could really make your bottom line look very appealing.

"No problem with that. We can certainly make that happen if we can get back out on top and get a hold of Bill." Bryan set his pack down and sat down next to his brother. Something was certainly bothering him.

"What's wrong?"

Brit remained silent for a long moment, very deep in thought, and then looked back at the avalanche wall. He got up and looked around at the cavern that surrounded The Amanda.

"What's going on here bro?" Bryan asked, watching him carefully. Brit was completely preoccupied with a thought process of some kind.

"Ah, he's got that look on his face," Jerry said, watching him carefully.

"Yeah," Danny agreed. "It's never a good thing when he starts thinking like that."

Everyone watched carefully as Brit paced up and down the cave a couple of times, stopping once or twice at the avalanche wall and moving his hands about as if he were orchestrating some kind of a procedure or something. He finally stepped back up to his three companions.

"Yeah, this will work," he told himself, reassured.

"Want to let us in on your little enterprise there turbo?" Danny asked stepping closer.

Brit looked at the three of them carefully for a moment, trying to decide if they were going to get it or not, then finally decided that it might be better if he had a little backup on his side. He turned to the airplane nose art.

"Need your help for this one Amanda," he spoke up, looking back at Danny and Jerry. "Now, I need you guys to just relax and go with this. It really doesn't require a whole lot of brain power for this, so in your case Danny, that won't be too much of a stretch."

"And you're talking to the airplane."

"Just go with me on this," Brit reassured them, positioning them next to the fuselage.

Bryan gave his brother a worried look as he stepped over next to his friends.

"Uh, the last time you and I did this,-"

"Trust me," Brit smiled. "All you have to do is touch her and say hi." The three of them slowly raised their hands and touched the skin of the aircraft.

"Hello?" Danny blurted out. Both he and Jerry suddenly jump back with a yelp. "What the heck was that?"

Bryan held his hand firmly against the aircraft with his eyes closed, a smile slowly creeping across his face. Brit coaxed the other two back to the airplane.

"Just trust me. She won't bite. Talk to her. Ask her anything you want." After he got the two to hold still with their hands firmly placed on the aircraft skin, he stepped away and let The Amanda do the rest.

For the next 10 minutes, they listened intently, sometimes smiling, other times breaking out into laughter, shaking their heads or nodding. Finally, Jerry opened his eyes and let go, turning to his friend. Brit could see that he had been changed. Danny followed closely, but Bryan remained frozen.

"I could stand there all day and listen to her talk," Danny grinned.

"Awesome," was all Jerry could mutter, sitting down on a stool to soak in everything he had just experienced with The Amanda.

"She's pretty amazing isn't she?" Brit said smiling.

"Amazing doesn't even come close to covering it," Jerry said, still a bit under the airplane's spell.

"Hey dude," Danny was serious now, sitting down next to Brit. "We've got to figure out a way to get her out of here."

"Piece by piece if we have to," Jerry agreed.

"No," came the calm reply from Bryan, sitting down across from Brit. "She's coming out in one piece. There's no other way."

The brothers locked eye contact for a moment, confirming everything to the other. It had been a profoundly moving experience for Bryan and while he was still somewhat under her spell, he had gained a greater understanding of what was going on around them and the great danger that they were in. Not from whatever the council would decide for them, but from what the storm was capable of.

"What would you estimate is the height of the storm's eye?"

"You didn't ask her?" Brit asked, with a little bit of a smirk. Bryan was always the one who thought about the details, but he understood why he may not have asked. There was a lot to take in and surely details might get skipped somewhere along the line.

"Sorta missed that part," Bryan said, a little sheepishly.

"We estimated that it topped out at between 15 to 18 thousand feet," a voice said from behind.

Everyone turned to see Tony and Catrina step up to them from the lit tunnel. Brit instantly focused on the Queen of Thulsa. He just couldn't help it. She was wearing her throne attire which consisted of a simple turquoise and brown gown that came down to her mid shins. The full sleeves had elegant ruffles around each wrist. The neckline rose to her collar bones on the front of the gown with a matching ruffle lining the neckline around to the back, which had lacing from the waist to the back of her neck. She wore a neck choker of dark red with a turquoise jewel mounted on it. A small barrette clipped into her hair in the center of her head, donned a turquoise jewel. She still wore calve high animal skin wrapped boots, as it just wasn't practical to wear anything else in the Thulsa environment. Tony remained in his previous outfit, minus the armor.

"What are you thinking?" Tony asked, stopping in front of the men.

Catrina remained a step behind her father, trying to not look at Brit. She appeared a bit uncomfortable about something. Even with her apparent discomfort, she couldn't help but pass glances back at him. There were bigger things afoot now and it would require them to put their attraction on the back burner.

"We've discovered that The Amanda is acting as a lightning rod, attracting and holding the storm in place. It's a wee bit complicated to explain how, but,-"

"Try me," Tony replied, becoming very interested. He was going to need as much of this information as he could gather as it could have a direct bearing on the information that he and Catrina had.

Bryan passed Brit a nervous glance, and then pulled out the hand held spectrum analyzer he had been using for the past hour or so.

"This analyzer measures the entire range of atomic waves that are known, well, to earth anyway. Such as gamma, micro, radio, light, radiation, you know all that jazz. Our happy little storm above us is producing a massive amount of electromagnetic waves. When you flew through it, it reacted with the storm and the electromagnetic discharge created alpha waves in the plane. The storm is attracted to these alpha waves, but the molecular make-up of the snow and ice has a dampening effect on the storm's ability to locate her. It knows she's here, but can't find her. Every time the storm comes through, it anchors itself right above The Amanda trying to find and recoup that lost energy, but it burns itself out after three days because it must remain in continual motion. During that time, the eye itself remains locked in place and two worlds coexist during that time, hence the gateway to another place and time. I haven't figured out if this is random or if something else controls it or can control it. The point here is, The Amanda is the lightning rod for the storm and unless we can get her out of here, it will keep coming back again and again, bringing other people from other worlds here and killing those who try to escape."

"So how do you propose we get her out of here, and even if we can, how are you going to get her out of this valley in less than three days?"

"That will be the trick," Brit said, stepping forward. "We're going to need a lot of people to dig this snow out of here, or at least out from behind the fuselage and then winch it back out onto the surface. It and all the other parts that are on the surface will need to be staged in the center of the valley in order for our other guys to come in and haul her out. We need to gain access to the outside wall to get to the storm wall. We need to call our friend and let him know to send in the choppers as quickly as possible to get her out of here."

"Choppers?" Tony repeated, not understanding what that term meant.

Brit realized after he said it that neither Tony nor Catrina would know what he was really talking about. The helicopter had been invented during World War II, but not widely used and mostly only in the Pacific theatre. The Korean conflict saw wide use of the helicopter mainly as an emergency personnel transport for the wounded and then Vietnam was where the helicopter really came into its own.

"Difficult to explain, but it's an aircraft that can lift vertically. We have three of them on standby at the Jackson airport. In the 21st century, we have large ones that can lift whole airplanes and carry them to other locations." Brit read the expression of confusion on Tony's face, but there wasn't time to try and explain it any clearer than that. "So that's our news, now, what news from the council. How soon do we get out of here?" he asked, looking around Tony at Catrina who hedged nervously.

"Well, that's a bit tricky," Tony said grimly. "You are to remain here as a hostage while I take your brother and two friends here to the Kenlar regions to retrieve the Signet and bring it back for use in resolving the issue with the storm. If we do not return, you are to fight in the arena," Tony paused, looking at their faces. "To the death."

Brit was stunned. *Had he missed something? What happened to wielding ultimate power in Thulsa? He thought that Catrina had the final say on anything that came into dispute?* He looked past Tony, but his eyes only met with the top of her head, her eyes stuck to the floor. *Did she decide that she wasn't interested in him after all?* There were a myriad of different questions racing wildly through his head as he waited for her to respond to the outcome.

Tony stepped over to Bryan and his two friends, leaving Brit standing straightway in front of Catrina searching for answers. He was understandably a little concerned about having to fight someone to the death. The worst he had done in a fight was bloody someone's nose and break a couple of fingers and that had all been done during a mock amateur sword fight last summer at a Medieval Knights Expo down in Ririe, Idaho.

"What happened to having all the power?"

"Brit, please" she pleaded in a whisper, finally raising her eyes from the floor to his. "You must understand the position I'm in here."

Brit looked at her for a moment trying to hold his tongue. He had a sudden spike of frustration that could easily spring into anger and he didn't want that to surface. Not here, not now. He needed to hear her out.

"I want to understand," he finally said, in a controlled tone. Catrina pulled him away from the others so they could talk a little more privately.

"I rule here so well because I give these people the power to rule their own destinies and what they can understand as fair in their society. Yes, I could have stepped into the council and just told them how it was going to be, but that would have been wrong and I want to be fair to the people, not just to me. I don't want to see you in the arena any more than you do, but it was the only way to help the people understand and trust you guys. We need the Signet anyway and having my father, your brother and two friends go after it was a fair way of proving the trust they will place in you."

"What if they don't make it back in time?"

"Then you will fight," she said, keeping eye contact with him. "But I will teach you to fight." She reassured him, putting her hands on the scabbard belts across his chest.

Brit looked into her eyes again, but this time not to swim in their deep pools of ebony, but to find the reassurance she offered him from within her soul. It took him only a moment to realize that she was his best hope of making it through this and that she would do any and everything she could to make sure he would be all right.

"Ok," he said, after a couple of moments of seeing the reassurance in her face and eyes. "I trust you." He brought his hands up to hers and grasped them in his.

Neither of them was prepared for the energy that instantly melted into them. The warmth of her hands in his was intoxicating, waves of excitement rolling through him. Having already been somewhat prepped by his conversation with The Amanda, he felt a swell of warmth flood through his soul and he couldn't help but smile with the feeling. He certainly was not alone with what he was feeling. Catrina had the same response sweep through her being and she was almost tempted to close her eyes and lean against him, but her father brought them back to reality after conversing with Bryan and the other two.

"We have to leave within the hour," he informed them, turning and facing the others. "It will take us a half day's journey by horseback to reach the Kenlar frontiers of Mount Boris."

"You hope to find Terry there," Catrina affirmed.

"Yes, I hope he will guide us through the Kenlar regions to Ivan's stronghold, Crosslake." Tony turned to Bryan and his friends. "We'll have to travel light and fast. I'm having horses prepared with only the gear we'll need for a three day's journey. Please leave your things here with The Amanda.   It will be safe."

"Captain Dallas," Brit said, reading the expression on his brother's worried face.

Tony turned back and faced him. Brit wasn't exactly sure how to word what he needed to say. Everything they had done so far today was beyond bizarre.   What he was about to try and lay out required careful thought and explanation and there just wasn't any time now to do so, at least so Tony or Catrina would believe it.

"We have to get The Amanda out of here."

"When we have the Signet and your boys back safely," he responded in haste.

The more time they wasted talking the less time they had for their search. They were already racing against the clock and they hadn't even left yet.

"No, you don't understand," Brit reaffirmed insistently. "We have to get her out of here now."

"You're right," Tony agreed. "I don't understand and we have no time for you to explain it to me. Whatever needs to be done, you and Cat will have to deal with it. We must leave now." He looked back at the others who were peeling their stuff off down to their street clothes.

"There will be a change of clothes for you up in the Manor. Please, we must hurry."

He stepped to his daughter giving her a reassuring look, then turned to Brit.

"Don't worry; I'll have them back within the time allotted."

With that, he turned, making sure the other three were in front of him heading up the passage. He gave his daughter a quick look, then took off after the others, leaving Britten and Catrina alone with The Amanda. Cat finally turned to Brit and took his hand. Now they were finally alone and free to actually show some affection.

"Ok, so what's this all about? Why the urgency to get her out of here?"

A smile passed across Brit's lips, looking back at the airplane and remembering his conversation with The Amanda and all the things she had described to him about Catrina. He stepped a bit closer and squeezed her hand a little more.

"Now it's your turn to trust me."

Cat gave him an uncertain look. She did not give trust easily to anyone, but these new feelings she was experiencing seemed to set much of that aside, at least where Brit was concerned. For a moment she hesitated, but then smiled at his reassuring looks.

"Ok," she said, almost a little shy, another new experience for her. He stepped towards the airplane, holding her hand. She wasn't exactly sure what he was doing and didn't really want to move closer. She couldn't see what this was all about, but he tugged a little harder and she finally stepped with him next to the fuselage. He turned and looked at the nose art of her mother, then back at her spitting image.

"Cat, meet Amanda, Amanda, meet Catrina."

"Uhm," Cat hedged. She smiled broadly, looking up the passage and then back towards the rear of the fuselage. She was starting to think he was off his rocker. She was kind of falling fairly quickly for him, but this little episode of his was starting to worry her. Maybe she needed to get to know him a little better before she flung her heart wide open to this *weirdsmobile*.

"I've actually known this plane a lot longer than you've been alive," she finally said, still going with him on this.

"Yes, all three of us are aware of that," Brit said with a chuckle. He was very excited for this and just knew this was going to blow her mind. "This will work better if you close your eyes and relax," he instructed, holding her hand up to the airplane's skin.

She resisted a bit. This was pretty unusual to say the least, but she reasoned that there was nothing twisted going to happen to her. There was nobody around for her to get embarrassed, so she closed her eyes and felt his hand press hers against the airplane. Her head was instantly filled with the same humming she had felt several hours previous when she had held the swords for the first time and she could hear a jumble of noises racing through her head. Brit watched her facial expression change from bewilderment to astonishment. She suddenly opened her eyes and jumped back. Britten held on to her

and reassured her that everything was just fine. Just having his arm
around her was thrilling.

"Who said that?" she gasped astonished, Brit letting her go. She
now had to decide on her own whether or not to continue with this
very strange phenomenon. She looked at Brit in utter shock and
raised a hand to her mouth.

"How did you do that?" she asked, looking around for the source of
the voice she had just heard inside her own head. Brit laughed and
tried to reassure her.

"It's ok, I promise," he reassured her, reaching out for her hand.
"She's been waiting a long time to be able to talk with you. You're her
favorite."

"And just who is she?" Cat asked, looking around. She continued
slowly raising her hand back up to his. He simply turned to the
painting and pointed at the figure in yellow.

Catrina looked at Brit quite skeptically. Her curiosity started to
crawl back out, trying to process what was happening. Looking over
at the painting of her mother, she started to think to herself.

*"Good looking guy likes me. He seems really nice, feels the same
way about me as I feel about him, but he has me talking to an
airplane. Oh, by the way, the airplane is talking back. So maybe I'm
just as nuts as he is. Well, if that's all, it must be all right then."*

Smiling weakly, she stepped back to the plane next to the painting
and reached her hand back out to the skin, letting her fingers carefully
rest on the surface. She could feel energy flow through her finger tips
and the voice of The Amanda was right back in her head. Brit watched
her carefully press one hand firmly to the surface, then the other, until
she was almost leaning against it. Her expression quickly changing
from caution, to pleasure, to a broad grin, and then to bursts of
laughter. For what seemed like an hour, she remained at the side of
the airplane with ever changing expressions continually sweeping over
her face until she finally let go of the plane, sniffling and wiping her
eyes and nose. It took her several moments to compose herself
enough to turn and face Brit.

"I'm so sorry," she said, through sniffles and a wet nose. "Sorry I
didn't trust you and," she started to choke up again. She looked back
at The Amanda. "I'm so sorry for what she has gone through. You're
right!" she agreed, regaining her composure again and forming up to
who she was. "We have to get her out of here as quickly as we can."

Brit took her hand and quickly led her to the rear of the fuselage to
the wall of snow.

"It's amazing that this snow can shield her from the storm. Here,"
he said, showing her the condition of the snow. "This snow should be
easy to move, there's just lots of it. We only need to tunnel enough of
it out behind her to pull her back to the surface. Do you think your
people can do it?"

"Better to dig from the surface, isn't it?"

"Got nowhere to put the snow down here. I'm guessing there are four or five meters of the stuff, maybe more. It's got to be from the outside."

"I think I have just the right people to do this. Might take a little convincing of the council, but I think they should come around."

"Even with the storm outside?"

"Yes," she said, making a quick survey of the wall of snow that entombed the fuselage. "I have just the gentleman in mind. He is one of the best engineers in all of Thulsa and I believe he'll help get her back to the surface."

"What about your war preparations? Don't you need every man for that?"

"No," Cat responded, quickly turning for the front of the plane. "We have people who help with those preparations. We'll draw from some of our back line warriors, but most of the workers can be found in what we call the private sector of the clan. They do all the construction and repairs around the city."

"When will you have time to train me?" Brit asked, starting back through the passage to the lower cellars.

"We must get this project started and going. We'll train, as there's the time to do so. Once things get rolling, we should have plenty of time for training."

"You think you can make me a master swordsman in two days?" Brit asked, making their way up the stairs and out of the cellars.

"Nope," she answered bluntly. She wasn't going to beat around the bush with him. She meant to tell it like it is, with no sugar coating, but she was also quite confident in her own abilities to teach him what he needed to know to survive. The rest would have to be left up to luck and his own natural skill and prowess as an athlete.

"It takes many years to become a master swordsman, but I think I can teach you a few tricks that even a seasoned warrior doesn't know. First things first," she said, leading him through the fort manor.

"We've got to get you out of those clothes and into something better suited for what you're going to have to go through in the next two days.

"What's wrong with my clothes?" Brit asked, having to trot a bit just to keep up with her.

"Nothing," she stated abruptly, "but, too many people will be gawking at you in those 21st century clothes. We won't be able to get anything done with the crowds you're liable to attract. It's going to be hard enough to keep everyone on task as it is."

"But I like what I have on. My coat is best thing made. There's nothing better. These are comfortable clothes." Brit stopped behind her as she opened a closet in a side room that was full of all kinds of clothes. She and Tony had made these clothes ready for them directly after the council had adjourned.

"No complaining. We're all making sacrifices here. Now get to it," she said, tossing him a bundle of clothes and boots, and then heading for the door so he could change. "And don't forget to grab a different coat." She stopped at the door and looked back at him.

"Nag, Nag, Nag," he said, looking at the stuff she had given him.

She smiled in a rather dainty fashion and then slipped out the door, closing it behind her, then pressing herself against the door, leaning her head back against the wood. Her heart was racing and she felt weak in the knees, shaky in the legs, almost like she needed to sit down and rest, nervous, but so excited. It was so hard to describe it, even to herself. She fingered the stone on the choker around her neck, thinking about the man behind the door. If this was what it was like to be in love, then she was in trouble. How in the world can you effectively rule a clan, direct an aircraft rescue operation and teach a man sword play when you're feeling like this? How in the world would she possibly be able to focus? Now, a better question might be, how do you even walk down the hallway without looking like you're drunk or about to pass out? The only focal point she could see right now was Brit. Her thoughts once again turned to the prospect of leaving this world to go with him. She found herself wanting to be with him all the time and if he left, how would she be able to choose between him and her beloved Thulsa? The turmoil swirling in her mind was nearly unbearable and she felt herself start to sweep towards an emotional outburst.   She had to shift her focus for the moment and to the tasks at hand. Catrina finally straightened up, furled her hair good and stepped out into the main hall of the residence portion of the Manor, barking out for the house servants to summon her guards.

Vespa Cull

One thing was for sure, the Thulsa plain was flat, which made its indistinct rolling hills perfect for growing crops nearly year round. There were plenty of forestland and long grass plains, but no mountains where the band from Thulsa was riding. This suited one of the riders just fine. Bryan had little to no equestrian skills, barely knowing his way around a saddle and reins.   On the other hand, Jerry and Danny rode horses all the time, partnering guided tours of all kinds. Tony had worried that putting novice riders on spirited horses might be a problem. Couple that with having to ride hard to reach the foot of Mount Boris before dark had him looking over his shoulder to make sure his group was still with him. Thankfully, he had brought several of his most trusted warriors with him on this journey. To send just him with the other three inexperienced strangers, well, they would have been better off just walking back to the town square and going for the public executions. At least having his best warriors with him, they stood a good chance of success.

Since there seemed to be no way for the aircrew to return to their world and time, it didn't make any sense to just sit around thinking about it. Their lives had to continue where they were. The only ones that had any ties to home were Tony and Catrina. It had been decided the best thing for each of them to do was to spread out a bit, trying to keep an eye on each other, and build some kind of normal lives among the people of Argyle. The real wild card here was whether his friend and former crew member was still alive and if so, would he be willing to help. Living on the border with Thulsa and the Kenlars was always a precarious prospect. Terry had taken a wife and was up to about 10 kids.

Terry wanted to be a grocer when he was discharged from the military. Here, he ended up moving his wife out on the borders to setup a trading post and travel inn. Tony knew he had done very well in his endeavors, having frequented the Inn and trading post often during his own travels. With all the kids Terry and Caroline were having, they would have no trouble expanding and perhaps making a settlement of their own at the base of Boris.

After several hours of hard riding and watching the Boris mountain range creep closer, Bryan was about to the point where he was ready to let the horse ride him. His rear end hurt so bad and he thought his thighs were going to tear in half. There was no slowing down though.

Two of Tony's warriors had even spurred their horses far ahead of the others, likely to make way for their coming. In this land with strained relations between rival clans and the location they were in between two clans, it was a good idea for an advanced party to approach a settlement with caution so as not to surprise anyone and provoke an unintentional skirmish with a friend.

Finally, in the distance, the band could see a few smoke pillars rising into the evening sky. On a clear night, darkness here was nothing like Bryan and his friends were used to back home. Yes, back home on earth, the moon could really light up the landscape at night, especially when there was snow on the ground. Here, on this planet, the suns would set and the moons would continue their close orbits, illuminating this world with half the intensity of the day time suns.

Spurring their horses on, Vespa Cull came into view. This place was built into the side of one of the first foothills of the Boris range. Actually, there really weren't any foothills at all. The range just sprang up out of the flat plains of long grass and rose sharply up, towering high above, reaching to the three moons of Argyle. This was more of a roll or fold in the base of the mountain. The plains long grass grew right up to the base of the Boris range, and then the trees took command of the land. Everything around Vespa Cull was clearly visible in the evening light.

Vespa Cull was the name for this Inn/trading post complex that Terry and Caroline had built together. Its focus was the high fashioned log lodge similar to what one would find in the mountains of planet Earth. It had several stories with a steeply pitched roof. Its logs were hewn out of giant tree trunks that looked like they would have taken a crane to lift into place. Each huge log was deeply grooved so that they fit together tightly. This was about as luxurious as it could get, even on earth, although it might be more in the classic rustic category. This planet just didn't have the ability to produce the type of materials and amenities in their current technology era, to reproduce what 21st century earth was capable of. The architecture certainly didn't come from the prevailing clan societies, not on its own anyway.

Vespa Cull stood alone in its own little corner on the borders of Thulsa and Kenlar. Few others dared to live this far away from the protection of either of the Thulsa or Kenlar clans. Somehow, this outpost was able to maintain a delicate balance from all directions. Kenlar and Thulsa were not the only clans in the area. The Gaylens and the Omar were also major players.

*   *   *   *   *

Terry was the first one out the huge dual wooden doors to greet Tony as he dismounted his puffing horse. The two hadn't seen the other for many years and it was good to see them and know that they were still quite well.

"Captain Dallas!" Terry greeted his commanding officer and good friend with a hardy hug.

"Tony," Captain Dallas affirmed. "You know better than to call me Captain," Tony said, with a huge grin, just as grateful to see his friend. Terry looked around at all the riders searching their ranks for someone specific.

"Where's Cat?"

"It's complicated Terry," Tony responded, toning down instantly. "Can we bed down tonight? We need to talk."

Terry zeroed in on the men that looked out of place from the rest of the warriors accompanying Captain Dallas.

"These three are friends Terry. They came looking for The Amanda."

"Oh boy," Terry mumbled, rubbing his chin and giving Tony a worried look. He instantly had a picture in his mind of what all of this could mean. He had no idea what he was really in for, but what Tony was laying down here was a bit of code for the benefit of his men. The less detail they had, the better off they were right now. Finally remembering himself, Terry scrambled over the shock of knowing he had three more men from earth in front of him. One looking quite uncomfortable.

"Yes, yes of course. I'm sorry, please, you must all be terribly tired," he beckoned them down from their mounts and turned to the big doors of the giant lodge. "Caroline! It's ok, it's Captain Dallas and his men. They will be staying the night."

A short skinny woman appeared in the doorway. There didn't appear to be much to her at first, but once she pulled her hip long jet black hair back and tied it neatly on top of her head, her face shone brightly, recognizing Terry's friend coming up the steps to greet her.

"Tony Dallas," she exclaimed in an accent of some kind. "You've finally come back," she said, throwing her arms around him and letting him pick her up and give her a bear hug.

Bryan tried to smile as he started the dismounting procedure he was going to have to use to get off the horse. It certainly wasn't going to be easy or graceful. His muscles were screaming with every movement. His poor rear end was exceptionally sore and trying to swing his leg over the horse to dismount was rough. Danny and Jerry didn't seem to have too much trouble and got a little bit of a chuckle out of Bryan's discomfort, but, they too were tired and so they tried to stay focused on the business before them.

Bryan swung his aching leg over the back of the saddle just in time to see a hoard of children gush from the lodge. They ranged from ages 5 through 18. The older kids brought up the rear, staying to embrace their Uncle Tony. After it appeared that all of them had exited the lodge, a tiny little figure emerged from behind everyone else. She couldn't have been more than 2.

Bryan started counting the smaller ones running right past Tony and Caroline and down the path to the waiting group of weary travelers. A few stopped and embraced their father, a few went to the other warriors, but several went directly to Danny and Jerry who were forced to scoop them up as they flung themselves at them. Bryan was still trying to get down off his horse as the mob of noisy children took turns swarming everyone with cheerful greetings. By the time he had gotten down and straightened himself up enough to turn around, the bulk of the kids had run off, something he was quite grateful for. He would have probably fallen over in utter agony had he been attacked in the same manner as his two friends.

Turning around, Bryan found that he wasn't entirely off the hook. Standing before him was the cutest little 2 year old red headed girl with her arms stretched out to him and the look on her face could have coaxed a stone statue to pick her up. Bryan looked at her for a moment, then around at the others who were busy doing whatever they were doing. He thought about just side stepping around her, but the look on her little face finally melted him. His soreness seemed to fade a bit as he bent down, carefully picking the child up to ask how she was doing.

A little shy, she grinned, throwing her arms around him and giving him a huge hug. He was a bit taken back at her vigor and affection, then just went with it, enjoying the toddler's affectionate demeanor. Feeling her little body fill his with warmth, he opened his eyes to see Terry standing in front of him, Tony and Caroline were still at the doorway to the lodge and Bryan's two friends were standing with their arms folded, watching him. All of them had soft touched smiles drifting across their faces. Jerry and Danny could see the little girl patting Bryan on the back of the shoulders as if she knew he was sore from his ride and she was trying to comfort him. Her tiny little feet flexed alternately as he held her. He was a little embarrassed and assumed that her father had come to fetch her, but she didn't want to let go of him.

"You are a special man sir," Terry said, stepping up to him and pulling the little girl from him. The Innkeeper looked at the little girl curling up in her daddy's arms with her arms around his neck. "She does not take to anyone but her mother and I. Even her brothers and sisters have a difficult time with her."

"She is a beautiful little girl," Bryan commented, still looking at her and gently poking her, giving her cause to giggle and squirm. "What's her name?"

"Anna," Terry replied, looking at her as she continued to smile.

"Pleased to meet you Anna," Bryan smiled and touched her little cheek. Her smile broadened and she turned an abashed face, burying it deep into her father's shoulder.

"I'm Bryan Garrett; this is Danny Niker and Jerry Gunn, my friends." He gestured to his two friends.

"Your little herd of a family has gotten a bit bigger," Tony exclaimed from behind them as he walked down the pathway with an arm around Caroline. Terry turned to his friend and handed Anna to Caroline.

"Well, when you're in love with a beautiful woman," he threw a pleasing look over at his little wife, who grinned happily while looking the other riders over.

"Speaking of beautiful women, where is that daughter of yours? You know how all the kids just love her."

"Attending urgent affairs in Thulsa," Tony answered, starting to settle towards some serious matters, but outside was not the place to be discussing such things. This was the frontier of Thulsa and there were many spies from Kenlar and Omar that made this place a regular stop. Terry and Caroline ran a thriving business here and didn't turn anyone away unless they had provocation to do so. For all they knew, it was likely they were boarding a few prying eyes right now.

"Let's get you guys situated, we'll have a good meal and you'll all feel better." With that, he called to several of his boys who came trotting up to gather the horses and led them off to a stable tucked back behind the lodge in a wooded area.

Several of the other children, including a couple of the girls, helped the men with their gear as they all headed inside. Upon entering, Caroline started barking out orders in a strange language. It wasn't the language that Tony and Catrina had used. There was an immediate answer from most of the girls who dashed into the kitchen from a rear door and started preparing for a meal. It was well after the dinner hour and they had already cleaned up. Normally, any visitor that came through at this late hour would have had to wait till morning to get anything to eat. However, this was different. It wasn't often that Uncle Tony came for a visit, and so everyone was anxious to help make their special company comfortable and welcome.

As Bryan and his friends had gotten their gear situated in their rooms, the welcome aroma of food swelling up the loft stairs compelled them to follow it to its source. The large table had been cleaned off when they had come in from outside, but now, coming back down to the main dining area, it was all set, everything in its place. There was an army of kids working together to get everything set just right and get out of the way for their guests. It was all well-choreographed and as they sat down, the younger kids melted back into other rooms, away from the dining area while the older kids served. It was a wonderful meal of vegetables, wild boar served cold, round bread with butter, milk, and ale for those who wanted any. Afterwards, the children quickly cleaned up while Tony and his group sat around the table catching up.

As the children worked quickly and quietly to get their duties finished off, Bryan felt little hands pulling at his thigh. He looked down into the smiling face of Anna who was trying to climb up into his lap. He carefully scooted his chair back and helped her up. She was a doll. Putting her arms around him, she kissed his cheek, then curled up in his lap and just sat there as if this was her appointed place.

Caroline worked to help the rest of the kids finish cleaning up while Tony's men excused themselves to turn in. They knew that things would be discussed that were best kept from them. If they were to be captured by the Kenlars or the Omars, they could be tortured into revealing information that was best kept quiet. It was better to know only what you need to know so you can live to fight another day. At least that was the idea.

Soon, the children were headed off to bed, with the exception of Anna who was still planted firmly in Bryan's lap chewing on a wooden spoon he had given her. Finally, Terry turned to Bryan with a big grin.

"So Master Garrett, what is it about you that my little Anna just loves so much?" Bryan looked down at the toddler chewing on the spoon.

"You tell me," she looked up at him and grinned with the spoon still in her mouth. "Do I, like, smell funny or something?"

"Well that would have been our first guess," Danny piped up, chuckling.

"Usually, that's what chases them off," Jerry added with the same type of laugh.

"Whatever it is Master Garrett," Caroline observed, stepping up and holding her hands out to the young child. "You are definitely her favorite today."

Anna didn't really want to move, but finally dropped the spoon and went to her mother who turned to put her to bed. Bryan watched after her as she peered around her mother's head and waved with a tired twinkle in her eyes. He waved back with a cheesy grin, then turned and sat back in his chair, feeling quite good about this little relationship. He had never thought that this is what it might feel like to have a child. It was certainly a new experience for him.

Danny and Jerry were ever the comedians though and were determined to add one last jab, both giving him a good ribbing.

"AAAWWWW, so tender," they joked at the same time, but now the time for joking was over and Tony went right to the business at hand.

"We need your help my friend."

"So I assumed and of course you know I'll help anyway I can. It's a small price to pay for how many times you've saved my life."

"Good," Tony said reassuredly. "Afraid this one is going to call in all my markers."

"What's he got you into this time?" Caroline asked, reappearing without Anna. "Where is Catrina, really?" She sat down next to her husband to listen.

Tony took another drink, and then began to tell the tale of the day's events, all the way through to the council's decisions, preparations for war, then what Cat and Brit had to deal with while Tony's group was away.

However, that was only part of the story. Bryan filled in the rest, with the exception of the events in the cave with The Amanda. That part was sort of skimmed over as something that Brit and Catrina would take care of in their absence. There was no sense in adding information to an equation that would only serve to confuse the issues they needed to concentrate on. Nevertheless, the information about having to get the airplane out and away before the storm moved on was made abundantly clear.

Terry seemed to be somewhat familiar with Tim's knowledge of the Signet and how it could help. He didn't know any specifics, but remembered there was supposed to be information contained in its pages about the use of the altar and the significance of the twin swords.

"Getting your hands on the book might be the greatest challenge that we'll all face in this whole mess," Terry said.

"Last Intel we had was that Tim had it, but that has been many years ago," Tony commented.

"Oh, he has it all right, but Ivan has him, and Ivan doesn't let him out of his sight."

"Where does he keep the book?"

"In the Kenlar spoil at Crosslake, but that spoil is a cave, not an open pit mine like Thulsa's."

"How is it that Ivan is so attached to Tim? What does he have that Ivan likes so much?" Danny asked, a bit perplexed about the whole book thing.

"Knowledge," Terry came back readily. "Ivan can't read what's in the book, mainly because he can't read, but it's in a different language than any clan around here. Tim figured out the language and when Ivan found out, he forced Tim to use the information in the book for Ivan's own purposes. He has long looked at Thulsa as a prize to be had because of the riches we all brought to it. Now he holds Tim prisoner for the information he can deliver."

"How do you force someone to reveal information?" Jerry asked quietly, not really to the group, more thinking out loud.

"You don't want to know my friend," Terry reaffirmed. "Ivan is ruthless. He holds no regard for life. If it suits his purpose, he will kill anyone and anything that gets in the way of what he wants. If Tim doesn't do exactly what Ivan wants, he has no qualms about killing an innocent person or worse, a child."

"No way!" Danny exclaimed outraged. "You mean to tell me that if Ivan wanted to know what time of day it was and Tim refused to answer he'd knock a kid off in order to get what he wanted?" Terry nodded somberly.

"Oh," Danny was incensed. "This guy has got to go!"

"That, will be quite difficult my friend," Tony informed him, trying to calm Danny down a bit. It was best to keep their voices in lower tones so they were not so easily heard by prying ears. "Ivan isn't just a stupid lunk head. He's big, he's strong and he's good with a sword. His weakness is that he uses strength as his ace instead of any kind of skill. Better to overpower your opponent than out fight or out think them. His right hand man and head assassin is called Talon Thalar. Now that guy can fight. He is an excellent swordsman and maneuvers extremely well on his feet. He can out think you, pick you apart and then defeat you. Smart guy that Talon. Ivan's armies are quite large and he knows how to keep them happy. They get what they want so they stay with him. As long as they know that he will deliver to them, they will stay with him and follow his orders."

"Hasn't anyone ever challenged this knot head?" Danny asked, looking for some information to use against this guy.

"Yes," Tony answered, unmoving. He fell into a bit of a hypnotic stance, thinking of his friend and Catrina's protector. "Carl was the only one. He really put the coward in his place."

The group was silent for a moment, showing Carl respect for his bravery, and then Bryan sat forward.

"Ok, so, what's the hope here? How do we get our hands on the Signet?"

"Tim is the key. Get Tim and you get the book. Without Tim, the book is useless because no one but him can read it and even if you could figure it out, it wouldn't be in time." Terry glanced back at Caroline. She looked over at Tony, who looked back at Terry.

"Uhm, not going to happen," she objected. "You're not going to Crosslake. That's suicide!" she demanded in a loud whisper.

"Caroline," Tony pleaded. "I need him to get me to Ivan's strong hold. He's the only one who knows where to find Tim. You know what's at stake here."

"Come on Carol," Terry complained. "You know I have to do this. This is a chance to get these boys back through the gate and close it forever."

"What about you Tony?" Caroline asked bluntly. "Are you and Catrina ready to leave with them, back to your own world? Just drop everything and leave? Turn your back on everything and everyone you have come to know and love here in Thulsa? Is that what you want? You would leave Thulsa now, when war comes to your borders?"

"Caroline," Terry cautioned. She was being very blunt, but the fact that Catrina and Tony could actually leave Argyle had farther reaching consequences than just these men going home, or even Tony and Catrina.

"We have always looked for a way to get home. If I don't help them, they will lose the chance and the storm will keep coming."

"And what about you?" she asked quietly. "What about me? What about the kids? If the door is open for Tony and Cat to get through it and go home, what's to stop you from doing the same?"

"No," Terry said smiling, changing the whole demeanor of the conversation. "There's no need for me to leave this place to go home. I am already home." He looked around the room, at the whole building really. "My home is here now, because of you and the children. You are my home."

Caroline was stunned. She knew he loved her. That was never in doubt, but she had also heard everything about the world that he had come from and everything there. She knew how much further along earth was in their planetary evolution. It was indeed a wondrous place. In her mind, it was a place to aspire to live someday, a place that was to be envied and fought hard to return to. It was why his friends had risked and lost their lives trying to get back to it, and why these men now asked him to risk his own life, so that they could return home to their own world.

However, Terry had just acknowledged that he had given that up long ago, for her. He was from the planet Argyle now, not from Earth and he stayed here because he loved her more than he loved Earth. Was there a better way for him to proclaim his love and devotion to her? When they came to this place, there was nothing here. Nevertheless, together, they made a commitment to the other and to building this place. Here is where they had built their lives together and had become as one.

Looking at him now, she couldn't help but love him more. Neither was perfect or liked some things about the other. Even with all his faults and all the stupid things that he still did, she couldn't help but love him. It was certainly true that they had grown in love; becoming such a part of the other that leaving wasn't even in the realm of possibility. She gazed at him, not needing to use any words to express how she felt. They both understood he was going to help his friends by doing whatever was needed. She wouldn't expect anything different of him.

"Ok," she finally said. "But you better be home before the next second night or I'm coming to find you."

"Before second night?" Terry repeated. "Seriously woman, you can be so trying at times," he said, reaching over and planting a big kiss on her.

"So, I can get you as far as Crosslake, but from there, I'm flying blind. I have no idea where his spoil is other than in a cave, although I doubt that it can be that tough to figure out. Ivan is about as complicated as a two piece jigsaw puzzle. He doesn't spread anything of importance out, he corrals it in close, and then lets his people live wherever they want or can find space."

"Are we going to have a hard time getting through Crosslake to the cave without being noticed?" Bryan asked.

"No," Tony responded quickly. "As long as we stick to sides streets and don't draw attention to ourselves, we should be fine. For now, I think we'd better get some sleep. We'll leave at second sunup."

"Yeah, that's a weird way of saying sunrise," Danny commented, as the group got up from the table to head for their accommodations.

"How else would you put it?" Jerry asked. "There are two suns here. You can't just say sunup because you wouldn't know which one you'd be talking about. You have to choose which one you're talking about. Either first sunup or second sunup, like the man said."

"Really, Jerr? Really? Thank you, oh astute one," Danny shot back, trying to be hushed about it.

"Are these two like this all the time?" Tony asked Bryan, following the two quietly bickering friends.

"You have no idea," Bryan mumbled, heading to bed while Jerry and Danny continued to bicker.

*　　*　　*　　*　　*

Bryan had never slept in a more comfortable bed. When he got into it several hours before, he had been a little skeptical. It was a log pole bed frame with a pile of animal skins on it for the mattress and blankets. Getting into it, he was sure he was going to get scratched to death by animal hair or worse, get the bugs that lived on the animal all over him. To his utter amazement, he found it to be almost as soft as cashmere, if he even knew what that felt like. It sure was soft and he was having a hard time getting out of it after Tony had awakened him. The comfort of the furry skins and the stiff soreness from riding the horse for hours without stopping didn't help bolster his will to roll out and onto the floor, but he finally spilled out from under the covers and rolled up into the animal skin rug on the floor.

"Walk it off," Jerry said, putting his boots on and offered to help him up. Bryan only raised a hand indicating that he was tough enough to deal with it. Danny was slow just because he wasn't a morning person and it just didn't seem like it was morning yet. The light coming in the window was a deep purple, and it just didn't seem like they had been asleep nearly long enough. Working his way up onto his hands and knees, Bryan was suddenly aware of two tiny little feet right in front of him and he looked up into the bright, smiling face of

150

Anna. She looked him over for a moment, then stepped up and put both her hands on his bleary face, muttering some kind of gibberish, then patted him on the head and turned, running out of the room. He could hear the pitter patter of her tiny little feet on the wooden floor all the way down the hallway, squealing quietly as she went.

"See?" Danny said, slowly putting on his boots. "You've been blessed by the little Argyle goddess. You're ready for bear!"

"Yeah, just wished I didn't feel like a bear," Bryan responded, raising himself to the bed and working on getting his clothes on so he could join the rest of the group. By the time he got down stairs, everyone else was already eating, including Tony's men. Bryan glanced outside, seeing Terry's older boys saddling their horses, making ready for their departure. Caroline and her older girls were busy putting their gear together, while the others were serving breakfast.

"Come on Master Garrett," Caroline said, walking quickly past him. "You need to eat to keep your strength up and do so quickly. You must leave very soon if you're to beat the Jabba flocks."

Bryan sat down at an empty spot wondering what she was talking about. Before he had even gotten situated, a plate of food and a cup of drink were placed in front of him by a couple of younger girls. He looked after them, watching their speedy maneuvers around the table and back towards the kitchen, picking up empty cups and dirty plates from the warriors already finished and making ready to grab their stuff and head out to their mounts.

"Quickly Bryan," Tony encouraged him. "Caroline wasn't kidding."

"I don't even know what a Jabba is."

"You remember yesterday morning when you and your friends were taken in the Winner's Spoil," Tony said, gulping down a mouth full of food. "Catrina told you guys that they might feed you to the Jabbaway?"

"Yeah," Bryan admitted, starting to eat. "We hear those silly boogieman stories all the time back on Earth."

"Well, on Earth they are silly boogieman stories, but here they are the real deal."

"The Jabba is about the meanest concoction of fur, claws and fangs ever to be on the wing," Terry cut in, walking past with his own gear, ready for departure.

"Does that, uhm, pad thingy of yours have any pictures of Gargoyles?" Tony asked, and then swallowed down the last of his drink.

"Sure," Bryan responded, working to get his food down and catch up with everyone else who were getting their stuff picked up and out the door. He was sure the movies he had seen, depicted gargoyles quite a bit different than what Tony and Terry might have been used to.

"These things aren't anything like that. They have the temperament of a pissed off badger and a wolverine rolled into one. Twice the size, with arms and razor claws, and they can fly. Seen them take small children before, but it takes two to do it and they can't go far like that. But they don't need to. They can disembowel a man and have him parted out in less than a minute. It's best that we avoid them if we can." Tony finished grimly, picking up his stuff and heading for the door.

"So, where will we see these Jabba and what are you supposed to do if we encounter them?"

"They fly in flocks from tree top to tree top to open glades and meadows, but roost in the forest at night. If you see one, kill it. If you see a bunch of them together, steer away and get out of there fast." Terry instructed, grabbing his stuff and heading out the door. "Anyway you can," Tony said, finishing the thought, following Terry out the door.

Bryan finished his food and gulped down his drink. Whatever was in the cup smelled and tasted terrible, like it was spoilt. Somebody left a cup out too long and it went bad. It turned his stomach a bit and he pulled a repulsed face, sticking out his tongue several times hoping the air would somehow carry the taste away.

"What's the matter Master Garrett?" Caroline asked, sweeping by him. "Do you not drink the ale man?" she asked, poking her head back out the kitchen door she was about to go through.

Is that what that horrible concoction was?" Bryan thought to himself. *"For heaven's sake how can people possibly stand to drink stuff like that?"*

"I hear it's like beer from your own world," she said, rebounding back through the doors, picking up an arm load of dishes and heading back around the table towards the kitchen.

"I don't drink beer," Bryan admitted, still yucking out about the taste. "Especially at breakfast. Are you kidding me?" He couldn't stand the taste. "I don't see how anyone can drink it with what it tastes like. This reinforces why I don't drink." He grabbed his gear. "Tastes like horse piss would, if I knew what that actually tasted like."

He ran out the door where he found most of the group already mounted. Terry's family had surrounded their father embracing him goodbye. It made up quite the crowd. Bryan stopped next to his horse, attaching his gear to his mount and finding that he had a much different saddle now. He looked at it for a moment then touched the very soft furry seat. It was lined and well-padded in all the places where he was still sore. It made the prospect of getting back up on the horse actually inviting. He gave it a good looking over, smiling with profound satisfaction that, yes, maybe he could handle this adventure. He positioned himself to mount his steed, grabbing the saddle horn, but then stopped short for a tug at his pant leg. He turned and looked down at a smiling Anna.

"There you are young lady," he said, scooping the little wad of cuteness up and spinning her around. She giggled wildly as he tickled her lightly. "You've come to say good bye?"

"Bye," she muttered, in a coy little voice, putting her arms around his neck and hugging him.

Bryan suddenly felt very strange. Anna didn't move, but held onto him tightly. It was as if she sensed that he was not coming back. He felt like she had become a part of his very being, like she was his own. Is this what it felt like to have a child of your own? He could feel her little hands patting him on the back as she had yesterday. He closed his eyes letting her tiny little body melt into him again until he was brought back to the present by the snort of his horse and the feel of her mother's hands pulling her from him.

"Come on baby-boo," Caroline said, taking the child and holding her so she could see Bryan clearly. "It's time for Bryan to get going."

Anna started to wave as Bryan smiled and stroked her little check with his finger, then turned and climbed up into the saddle. Caroline stepped close to the horse with Anna still waving and smiling broadly.

"She loves you very much Master Garrett."

"Can't figure out why," he said, a bit perplexed.

"We can't either," Danny spoke up with a big grin. "Master Bryan," he finished teasing him.

Bryan grabbed the reins of his horse.

"This one knows people," Caroline said, looking at her own child. "You are special somehow. I hope we'll see you again Bryan. Be careful."

"I will," he said, turning his horse in the direction of the others who were departing. "Bye, bye my little Anna," he said, waving while riding off.

He looked back only once. Anna was still waving from Vespa Cull as it receded into the distance.

What a wonderful little girl," he thought, riding alongside his two friends behind Tony and Terry. Riding along with the rest of them, his saddle sore body seemed to relax a bit and he found himself thinking about how wonderful it would be to have a child of his own. He was a bit loath to think the lecture they had gotten from Bill was true. If all the work of being together with a woman can produce something as marvelous as a little Anna, then maybe he'd better figure it out and get on with it. A smile seemed forever stuck on his face as they rode along the Thulsa border for some distance before they turned into the regions of Kenlar.

Sargon

It didn't take long for the men of Thulsa to uncover some of the main pieces of The Amanda. This included the tail, which was mostly exposed to begin with. The left wing and engine were also easy enough to uncover. The right wing and engine were a bit of a trick, buried under several meters of snow and ice.

It had taken a bit of explanation on Catrina's part to convince the Council of Elders to allow the Winner's spoil to be used as a corridor through to the outer gate and into the realm beyond. With a little explaining from Brit about the importance of being able to remove The Amanda in order to allow the storm to move on, they had finally relented, but not without condition. Because of the sacred nature of the Spoil, guards were placed all along the pathway through the spoil to the gate. The pathway would be the only access through and if there was any deviation from that path, well, the law would take effect.

The Elders were also wary about their Queen heading up such a project herself, despite reassurances from Britten that he meant them and her no harm. He would be there helping to direct the operation. This seemed to work for the council, knowing that not only was Brit somewhat of a hostage here, but his brother and friends were as well. Brit wasn't going anywhere without Bryan, Danny and Jerry and vice-versa. The book would be retrieved and one way or the other, Thulsa would be rid of this swirling monster once and for all, or at least that was their fervent hope. Word was quickly dispersed throughout the city that Brit would remain at Catrina's side to help direct the aircraft operation and to see that he didn't go anywhere. Her royal guard would see to that.

Stepping out through the gates, you were indeed in another place, but not. Two worlds trying to exist in the same place at the same time; a flux plain between two worlds. A place where the light of two worlds blended and their realities mixed, meandering about, trying to comprehend the existence of the other.

Here, the wreckage of The Amanda had been frozen in space and time, waiting for rescue from both her icy prison and from the awful monster that searched for her when it came through. Now, it would take every bit of Brit's knowledge and know how to extricate her from this place. He was going to have to have as much help from Catrina as she could rally. Thankfully, for Cat and Brit, Thulsa had the best engineers of all the clans.

The lead engineer, Sargon had already cut his teeth with the improvements made to the City with infrastructure and architecture. Now, the Queen called on him to draw upon his knowledge and expertise to help pull the heavy pieces of the airplane out of the ice and snow. Brit requested that they be pulled into position towards the middle part of the valley so that when the time came, the Sky Crane helicopters would be able to just come in, hook up and get out through the eye of the storm, as quickly as possible. There was no way that a helicopter could navigate through such a storm and there was no telling what the storm was going to afford them.

This whole process would require thinking and problem solving skills heretofore unknown to the people of Argyle. Building city buildings of stone and wood was certainly a complex undertaking. Lifting heavy aircraft pieces out of the snow and moving them, without damaging them, would require uncommon skill. Especially considering what they had to work with. There were no heavy lifting cranes, backhoes or bulldozers here. Only manpower and the primitive lifting machines they had learned to make for the building of their city.

Stepping to the open gates, Brit and Catrina could again hear the noise of the storm outside. Reaching for his hand, she hesitated going through, looking carefully outside. She had never been this close before, not with the door open anyway. She held tightly to Brit's hand, looking around at the colors in the swirling mass surrounding the entire valley that lay before them. She had seen the valley when the storm wasn't present, but this was completely different. Brit tried to walk her forward through the gates, but she held him there at the threshold, not wanting to leave. In reality, this was fairly close to the truth.

Before her, at least in part, lay the world she had come from. Behind her, the world that she had grown to know and love. Surrounding her, the monster that she had grown to fear and hate over her time here, the storm that had brought her to this place. Britten finally took a step forward, still holding Cat's hand, trying to reassure her that it was ok. Finally, she bravely stepped forward and out into the snow. Her guards were even less sure about this, but wherever their Queen went, so too, would they go.

Snow was not anything new to the people of Argyle, but this snow was different somehow. It was new and pristine powder. A lite, dry snow that falls during a frozen, cold, day. It did not pack well at all, because there had been no melting. Everything here was suspended, as if time did not move, or even exist.

While the men of Thulsa continued the labor of digging, Brit and Catrina headed for the west valley ridge, her personal guard in tow. Climbing to the west ridge, they labored past the snow caves that had been carved into the icy wall of the west ridge face by Danny and Jerry. A nice set of steps had been hacked into the snow and ice leading all the way up to the top of the ridge where they had originally entered the valley from the storm. Working their way up these stairs was much easier than having to trudge through unpacked snow up the side of the valley wall.   It was nearly vertical towards the top. Once there, he found the handheld radio that had been secured there in a safe place on the ridge, just inside the storm wall.

His first order of business was to try and communicate with Bill. Catrina and her guard cautioned him several times to not try and pass back through the storm, as this is what killed Chuck and Dale when they tried to leave through the storm so many years ago. Brit made sure they understood that he had no intensions of leaving, at least not without The Amanda or his brother and friends. Once the aircraft was safely transported out by Sky Crane, then he'd worry about getting everyone back through the storm and home.

The storm's deafening volume made it nearly impossible for Britten to hear anything on the radio as he and Catrina huddled closely together just at the top of the snow stairs. With the walkie talkie tucked under the hood of the animal skin winter coat, he had to lay down on the ridge right next to the storm wall and try to raise Bill. He could barely make out the audio from the radio because the noise was so great, but if he tried to move away from the storm wall to a place that might shelter him somewhat from the noise, the transmission would not go through. He finally had Catrina's guards kneel over the top of his upper half and cover him with their own winter coverings. It was a bit awkward, but at least he was able to hear and be heard.

Scientifically speaking, this might seem extraordinary. Had this been a scientific expedition trying to discover the intricacies of space/time travel, someone would be up for the Nobel Prize for some category they hadn't thought up yet. Brit was just grateful that he could communicate with Bill. To Brit, Bill was only 20 yards away, not the other side of the galaxy.

Bill had started to get a little worried, not only for the status of his four companions, but for his own safety. The storm had not waned at all since it had arrived and while the wind had pretty well kept the ridge neutral in snow depth, the rim edge was swept entirely bare. The ground on the lee side, of the Cat and coach were covered in massive curl-back drifts that had buried the snowmachines and the entire north facing side of the coach.

Brit reassured the concerned old man that he would be fine there and that the storm would blow over in a couple more days. Bill agreed, but was a little unnerved by the fact that about the only thing he could see all day and night long was horizontal snow. At least he could communicate with Cal at operations. Even Cal had begun to get a little worried. From his vantage point down in the Teton Valley below, he could see the entire mountain range in heavy cloud cover. Even with the storm stationary, the associated cloud mass continuously moved about the mountain, or at least the outside of it seemed to. Bill had told him several times not to try and attempt to come up and get him. He was sure that everything would be just fine and for the moment, he was in no immediate peril.

In his solitude, he had plenty of time to figure out how to not only work and read the weather instruments in the coach, but also work Bryan's computer equipment. Learning how to surf the internet, Bill had set himself up and email account and had created a profile on a social media site. How's that for teaching an old dog new tricks? He was able to relay storm information not only to Cal down in the valley, but gave Brit storm information as well. He was relieved to hear that everyone was all right so far and that they had made a positive identification on The Amanda.

Brit gave him further instructions about the pickup zone that had been prepared on the valley floor and the status of getting the fuselage dug out and to the pickup zone. He left final instructions with Bill to hold off calling in the sky cranes until they signaled that they had the main portion of the fuselage in position with the rest of the wreckage. It was very hard for Bill and Brit to hear each other, so trying to discuss details any further was far more work than it was worth. Brit figured that Bill had plenty to relay to Cal down at operations in Driggs.

After securing the radio on the ridge, he and Catrina were about to make their way back down the ridge face to where, it seemed, half the city of Thulsa had come to help excavate the pieces of the airplane, but Cat stopped him for a moment, looking back at the storm wall. The last time she was this close, she was flying through it in The Amanda. It snarled angrily at her, taunting her. Brit was a bit bewildered at her apparent fascination with this mad killer. She gazed at it, almost taunting it right back. Determined to face her demons and fighting her fear, she resolved to overcome them here and now. She realized how close she really was to earth at this moment. The guards weren't sure what to do. They sensed an enormous amount of danger here, even above their discomfort of passing beyond the gates in the first place.

Catrina turned, looking back down at the open gates in the stone wall far below in the valley. She passed a look back at Brit who let her have room to confront this monster that had held her and her father prisoner for so long. Looking up at the blue sky of Earth, she could see the sunlight that shafted part way down, only to be swallowed up by the storm wall on the opposite side.

For a moment she felt the overwhelming urge to go home, anyway she could. The thought of Brit's vehicles only yards away from where they were standing and the cable they had secured into the snow covered rock at her feet, seemed to provide her the means to do so. She knew it had to be connected on the other end to Brit's vehicles.

Tinkering in her reasoning, she actually considered trying to jump through to reach the safety of the heavy vehicle that Brit had spoken of. Then the thoughts of her people and what they had come to mean to her, stepped back into her forethoughts, not to mention what had happened to the two crewmen that had already tried. This all caused her to think better of it. She thought of her mother, watching and waiting at home, alone in Montana, and longed to be with her.

She raised a hand to the swirling wall, letting her fingers glide across the surface tension. Energy sparks danced about her fingers, feeling it tingle like her fingers would after being really cold and starting to warm back up again. Its cold sent shivers up and down the back of her neck, even in the warmth of her hooded coat. Letting her hand slide into the wall, she could feel the wind tearing at it and the stinging, pelting snow.

Brit finally stepped up next to her and putting his arm around her waist, pulled her hand back out. It was wet and freezing. It seemed impossible to her, for them to get back through that raging torrent, back to Brit's time and world. She turned and let Brit hold her for a moment, then headed back down the ridge.

*　*　*　*　*

For several hours, Catrina and Brit worked alongside her people, digging around the large pieces and finding other smaller pieces, such as antennas, pitot tubes and such. For the most part, the pieces were relatively unharmed. It was almost like the airplane had been disassembled instead of torn apart. Considering the condition that Brit usually found most wrecks, it could be said that they could just about shove everything back together and if a runway was available, fly it out of here.

This whole project required quite a bit of engineering, as there were no powered machines here, only what they were able to produce locally with their hands. The platforms they had built were all fitted out with block and tackle sets. These were quickly erected to help not only raise the right wing and engine out of its resting place in the snow and onto a platform, but then used to move all of the pieces from one point to another by way of wide snow skids they had cleverly designed supporting each platform.

The rope they used was amazing stuff, unlike anything Brit had ever seen. It looked like braided leather, but ten times stronger and the clan had made several different sizes in varying lengths. Once Brit had gotten the whole run down from Catrina on what it was able to handle, he ordered it used to make harnesses to be rigged around each of the large pieces being staged. This way when it came time for the Sky Cranes to come in and remove them, they were already harnessed and ready to go. They would hover into position and hook up. He had done plenty of rigging before on a countless number of salvages. This rigging would be a piece of cake. The left wing and tail would be in one load, the right wing and miscellaneous parts in another load, then the fuselage in the last load.

Once a piece was raised from the ground, they would then have a crew of men pull or push that piece over into the pickup zone, platform and all, then unload it in the spot Brit had directed. Working with the right wing took only a moment to figure out why it had been snapped off.   The left wing had been taken off by several trees that had since been cut down to supply wood for the machines they were using to raise the airplane structures up. Buried deep, close to where the right wing was found was a huge boulder that the craft had apparently struck just inside the right engine nacelle. The huge radial engine was still attached to its mountings, but pitched sharply outward and the cowlings were bashed up pretty bad. All three blades on both propellers were bent over, but not as bad as it could have been if they had actually touched down on a hard surface. Thankfully, neither propeller had struck anything solid on impact; the weight of the airplane causing them to bend backwards.

The right forward fuel tank had been crushed when the wing was severed and this was where the avgas had leaked out and into the surrounding snowfield. The other tanks in both wings seemed to be just fine and still partially full of fuel. The avgas permeated snow could present a real problem. They would have to dig all day and through the night. Torches would have to be used and that could ignite the fuel, if there was enough of it congregated in one place. That would be a sight, burning snow.

Even more of a problem was getting, and keeping the workers on task. It was spooky enough for Brit to work under the storm; he could only imagine what this primitive thinking culture must be going through. Above their heads energy bolts constantly popped, though none of them ever hit the ground, always striking on the opposing walls of the cylindrical eye of the storm.

None of the Thulsian workers even had a clue that they were working in a time/space flux zone, the storm being the doorway to one reality and the great wall with its huge wooden gate to their own. In the middle was a world that constantly fluxed between the two. They couldn't possibly comprehend what was happening above or around them and that, in and of itself, was enough to make even the bravest of warriors nervous. It took a lot of reassurance from their Queen, but they continued.

All the men had volunteered for several reasons. The only entrance, at the moment, to this outside place was through the Winner's Spoil, a place that very few had ever laid eyes on. Just a chance to see it was worth the danger of the adventure. Then there was the whole adventure thing itself. A chance to do something new and uncommon, even potentially dangerous, was too inviting for most of them to resist.

Perhaps the most compelling reason was that their Queen had asked it of them. She did not command them, but asked for volunteers, as she often did. Moreover, they knew that she wouldn't ask them to do anything she wasn't willing to do herself. Indeed, she was right there with them, working alongside. Yes, there were times when, as their leader, she recognized that she had to make unpopular decisions and assignments, but it was always for the betterment of the clan. She had always let them choose their own destinies and helped them make it happen. They respected her every decision, although this one was about as far out there as any she had ever proposed to them. Nevertheless, they loved her and would do anything for her. By the word of her people, she was a great Queen.

*   *   *   *   *

With the surface pieces of the aircraft situated in the surveyed pickup zone, Sargon and his Thulsa engineers moved to digging out the fuselage. This required Brit and Cat to escort them down to the cave where The Amanda waited silently to be freed of her dark imprisonment. As Catrina moved about the back side of the aircraft at the avalanche wall with Sargon and his men, Brit quickly leaned against the airplane and spoke to her, reassuring Amanda that they were working on a solution to get her out and that she just needed to be patient a little longer. Above all, Brit had to impress on her to remain silent at all costs. She would be handled quite extensively by the workers of the Thulsa clan laboring to free her of her icy prison, and if she were to say hello or make noises in their heads, they would likely haul off and freak out, maybe start doing something rash.

Brit gave Cat the thumbs up, the group stepping carefully around the fuselage to the other side while she conversed with them in their native clan language. Brit was no linguist, but he imagined the language sounded something like Gallic, Swedish or Finnish. He had no idea; just that it used a lot of tongue and lip to make it audible.

The group continued their tour of the other side, Brit crawling inside and checking to make sure all the guns were secure and the safety levers were on. There was bound to be somebody trying to get inside, even though they would be instructed not to, and he wanted to make sure that there was no chance of them causing a problem. As Brit climbed up and out of the nose of the airplane, the whole group had reassembled just outside the plane and everything appeared to be in order. Moving to leave, Sargon turned back to Brit and spoke to him in broken English, with a very heavy accent.

"We will move her to your place on top?" Sargon was well respected in Thulsa as having the keenest engineering mind, yet remaining true to the ways of the Thulsa forefathers clear back to ancient times. He was well versed in the old ways, and how they could be adapted to the new ways. He was considered a very religious man and tried to be a good example in his living. There was nothing wrong with how he chose to live his life, on the contrary, he led a very benevolent life, which is what drew so many others to him, trying to emulate the way he lived and gain his knowledge of the old ways and beliefs. However, his beliefs did create a rift with conservatism and what others would consider progress in the clan.

"Yes," Brit answered, trying to look appreciative and sound respectful.

Catrina turned back to hear the conversation. She wanted to make sure it was appropriate and if not, she could be there to save the day so to speak. Sargon and his men had already been fully appraised of the task at hand before any of it had ever started and like all the other workers, their Queen had asked them, giving them the option to help. This exchange indicated that there was something else that was bothering Sargon.

"Then you will take her away, and the storm will never come again?" Sargon asked carefully.

"That's our hope," Brit answered, not really knowing where this was all going. Everyone had already been apprised of the plan and the basic reasoning for it.

"How will you take her away from your place on top?"

Brit drew in a deep breath. He wasn't exactly sure how to answer Sargon in such a way that he would understand. He would have to know, all of them would, as they all would probably be present and helping him with the hoisting hardware when the Sky Cranes flew in to hover, pick the pieces up and fly them out. He passed Cat a quick glance, who waited to see how he would answer the question.

"In my world, this great machine and many like it fly all over the land, carrying people quickly from one place to another. We have flying machines that will come in from above, pick up the pieces of this one and carry it away. When they do this, the storm should go away." Brit waited for the engineer to respond.

Sargon turned to his men and spoke to them in his language. They all looked over at Britten oddly, their leader continuing to speak. The expression on their faces indicating that there was still something troubling them. Several of them turned back to The Amanda, and then faced Brit again.

"Does she wish to leave?" Sargon asked.

"Does who wish to leave?" Catrina cut in quickly. Both she and Brit were a little shocked at the question. "Who do you speak of?"

"Amanda," came the simple reply.

Brit was speechless, but relieved. Catrina shared his relief and turned her focus to the matter of how in the world Sargon knew about the soul of the aircraft.

"My friend," she addressed them softly. "Why would you ask such a question?"

This conversation would have been much better spoken in their native language, but since it was originally directed at Brit and he was a big part of the subject matter, they did their best to speak so that he could understand.

"My Queen, you know that all things have life within them." Following Sargon's lead, they all bowed their heads slightly, showing the proper respect for their Queen. "The ground, the sky, the wind, the rocks and the animals, everything, even this great machine has life. She lays silent now because you have told her to do so, fearing that she might frighten us were we to touch her and she would speak."

"You've spoken to her?" Cat asked surprised. When did they have time to touch her and speak to her? She was with them the entire time they had been down here. There was no way any of them could have had time to touch her, let alone communicate with The Amanda.

"No my queen, but we have felt her. As we have worked with her other pieces up on top, we could not help but hear her whispers."

"Ah nuts!" Brit exclaimed, a little fearful that the cat might be out of the bag here. They hadn't counted on the other pieces being a part of this as well, though it made perfect sense now. Her soul was in all of the aircraft, not just the fuselage. They didn't have any time for this. It was going to take a great deal of effort on everyone's part to get The Amanda out of the cave, back to the surface and prepped for extraction. They needed all the effort and forward movement they could muster to make this happen. Catrina passed Brit a quick glance, but kept her focus on Sargon.

"What would you have me say?" she asked carefully. Queen or not, he could really cause a big kink in the works if he decided that what they were trying to do was wrong.

"Yes," Brit jumped back in.

"Yes what?" Catrina asked, turning her attention to Brit.

"Yes, we have spoken to her and she speaks back to us."

Cat passed him a steely glare. *What in the world was he up to?*

"She knows that the storm comes for her and she wishes to be free from this prison. If we can free her, I can take her home with me and the storms will stop coming. It's what she wants."

This wasn't exactly the approach that Catrina was going for in this situation, but she was sort of at a loss for words.

"Will you speak to her?" Brit asked.

Sargon fidgeted a bit. His men behind him would be quite wary of the idea, but something told him that it was all right. He would have still finished the task without this experience, but he thought it might be well with his men, though he knew they would never participate in such an act. Too close to unconventional wisdom and possible witchcraft, even in their culture. Sargon bravely nodded and stepped back to the airplane, followed by his men.

Catrina grabbed Brit's arm firmly and leaned into him, following the others. He sort of liked the closeness, but wasn't as sure about her tone as she whispered close to his ear.

"Are you out of your ever lovin' mind?" she whispered. "Sargon is a deeply religious man of reputation. If he thinks there's anything even remotely screwed up or out of this world, he'll shut down this entire project or at the very least, slow it down."

"We need him totally onboard with all of this," Brit fired back, leaning his head right into hers. Touching her in any manner was pleasant and while she wasn't actually angry, she was quite perplexed at what he was trying to do.

"Yeah, we need him, but I don't think that scaring him off with spooky voices in his head is going to win friends and influence enemies here," she whispered, catching up with the rest of the group.

Brit "shushed" her and stepped up to the airplane with Sargon. Catrina stood right behind both of them. He turned to Sargon and put his own hand on the fuselage. He could instantly feel The Amanda's presence, but he remained focused on the engineer.

"Clear your mind sir and do not be afraid. She will speak to you. Ask her anything you would like to know."

Sargon practiced communion with the nature around him. He well knew and had felt the energy forces of many different things. He couldn't move rocks or talk to animals with his mind, but he was keenly aware of their life force and found much solace and peace in his communion. This interaction with nature had helped him reach a certain state of humility that served to open his mind to so many new things in his life time.

As Sargon lifted his hand to touch the surface, Brit pulled his away and let them connect. Catrina sort of held her breath. She really didn't like this idea at all. One wrong word from anyone, for whatever reason and this could be the Salem Witch Hunts all over again. It took only a moment for Sargon to make contact with The Amanda, the exchange lasting only a couple of minutes.

Turning to the others, Sargon's expression was changed. A person can have faith in many things in life, but until some things are actually experienced, one never really knows for sure. He now did. He had never spoken to a rock, a bird or other animals, but he sure got an education here at the side of an alien flying machine. His men were anxious to hear of his experience and what they must do by his word. He only turned to Brit and Catrina, bowing his head a bit.

"Forgive me for my nonbelief," he said quietly. Turning to his men, he spoke sharply in their own language and they started back up the passage for the surface to start their work. Brit watched them go for a moment, then turned back to The Amanda and smiled.

"You sure have a way with people," he commented smiling.

"As do you," Catrina said with an admiring smile.

She took his hand in hers and intertwined her fingers with his, then gently squeezed. It felt like free flowing energy to Brit and he couldn't help but smile at her. *What was the magical power she had over him? In truth, the same feelings and questions were racing through Catrina's mind. How was it that they felt so at ease when they were together? Almost like, they were each becoming a part of the other.* He had dated many girls, held their hands, hugged and even kissed a couple of them. There was nothing more exciting, but none of them had ever made him feel like Catrina did now. Responding gladly, he squeezed her hand, passing the same energy back. He could see that it was doing similar things to her, making him feel even more a part of her.

Taking her other hand, Brit faced her, feeling himself once again melting into her big, soft brown eyes. His thoughts flashed to the first time he saw the picture of her mother on the boat off the eastern shores of Brazil. He just couldn't understand why his brother and friends didn't have the same reaction to Catrina that he did. It just didn't make any sense to him. Actually, he was very glad they didn't have the same reaction. Less he had to worry about and the more focus he could direct towards her and that focus was pretty intense right at the moment.

Their eyes searching, they moved slowly closer, drawn by an invisible string or forced by some kind of unseen press, each looking at facial features up close until they zeroed in on the lips. Their eyes instinctively melting closed, their heads tilting in opposing directions as they came together.

Before they could complete the anticipated embrace, the shuffle of feet and the clamor of armor interrupted them. It was her guards, come to find her, and she instantly pulled back. The guards hesitated a moment wondering if they had blundered into something they shouldn't have, then addressed their queen in their language. She nodded silently, and then turned back to Brit.

"It will be several hours," she said slowly, still entranced by what almost was, "before Sargon and his men will reach The Amanda. The training room has been made ready for your training. We need to go." Her voice had the sound of heavy reluctance.

Both were disappointed, and the tone of her voice said it all. Brit once again became aware of the swords strapped under each arm and slowly let go of her hands, nodding in agreement.

"Nuts," he mumbled, raising a hand to one of the hilts and letting it rest there as he followed her and the guards back up the passage.

Sticks

Once back up in the Manor training room, a couple of servants assisted Brit in getting the Twins and his outside winter gear off, then helped him don training gear. He felt really stupid trying to move around in the ungainly garb. As the training foe stepped to the center of the room, Brit turned and reached for the Twins, but was stopped by Catrina.

"You won't need those right now."

"Uhm, why not?" he asked, a bit confused. He thought that he really needed to train with the swords if he was to have any chance of defending himself in the arena, should the time come.

"Until you learn to fight, you're liable to not only hurt yourself, but my training foe as well. Better to use something that isn't going to cause any permanent damage," she explained, dropping a set of sticks down on the table next to the Twins.

"Sticks? I get to use sticks?"

"Put the gloves on. They will keep you from getting bloody knuckles or broken fingers."

"Is this really necessary?" he asked, a little frustrated. He would much rather be holding onto the swords. They felt so natural in his hands and he even felt like he could wield them the same way Catrina had when she had tested them earlier.

"Oh, it's necessary, believe me."

"But sticks? Really?" he said, picking one up.

It was a little larger in diameter than one would normally think of a stick. Apparently these were specially designed and made with combat training in mind. They were straight and round and only about two feet long. Brit remembered seeing one attached to Catrina's side armor when they had first met in the Spoil, only hers was much more ornate. These sticks were just boned smooth so they wouldn't chip under the rigors of training lessons.

"Keep the helmet on tight and the face shield down in place," she instructed, trying to help him get everything in order.

"Can you at least give me a couple of sticks that are cut and shaped like real swords? These are just sticks." Brit was being a little bit ridiculous, and getting on Cat's nerves.

She gave him an impatient look, then grabbed one of the sticks and stepped out onto the training room floor, addressing the training foe. The foe donned two sticks, whereas Catrina had only one. All of the sticks had been crafted to be about the same size as the Twins and their diameter was the same as the hilts. The whole thing seemed too simple for just a couple of sticks until the two began to spar.

Right away, it became quite clear to Brit that Catrina was a master. She didn't need two sticks to defend herself from the foe. She was aggressively taking the offensive. He watched her, amazed as the two sparred around the room, the foe using both his stick to swing and jab at the Queen of Thulsa, while she used her single weapon to not only ward off his advances, but drive him back. She used a variety of slick moves that looked more like a cheerleader's baton twirling exhibition than a training sword fight. There was a lot of spinning and whirling from both participants, blows deflected from the side and the back. Very few blows ever landed and none landed on Cat. She finally figured that she had gotten her point across, landing several blows, disarming the training foe. She quickly passed the stick back over to Brit, who barely caught it, then turned and picked up the other one. She stepped up to him puffing somewhat, but with a glisten in her eye.

"Just sticks," she said, stepping to one side and gesturing for him to give it a try.

Brit wasn't one to be outdone by a woman, but even he had figured out that Cat was no ordinary woman. Still, he had an ego just like the next guy and was anxious to prove himself and impress her in some way, so he stepped towards the training foe and raised his sticks like he was going to try and pummel the guy to death.

"Address him," Catrina spoke up, watching him closely.

"Hi, how are ya?" he said, feeling a little stupid. He was about to feel even more so.

"No, don't talk to him," she said impatiently. "You must indicate that you are ready to fight by bowing, or at least nodding your head."

"Can't someone just say go or something?"

"No, now address him!"

Brit held up a stick in front of his face like a foil and nodded sternly, feeling exceptionally awkward. He was startled by the instant change in the foe's stance. Cat could see what Brit's next move was going to be, and he didn't disappoint. He was standing all wrong and he was holding his weapons all wrong. Brit thought back on his mock fighting at the Knight's Expo down in Ririe, Idaho. This is what he had to draw on, so he did only what he knew and started swinging at the foe's sticks.

At first, everything went off swimmingly. He was doing a great job hitting his opponent's sticks, but after about a minute of this, he could see that the foe was almost holding out one stick for him to hit while he scratched his back with the other one and looked around the room, yawning. Ok, so it was obvious he had no idea how to repeat Catrina's skill sets, so he did what he thought was the next best thing. He started to move forward on the foe and instead of aiming to hit just the sticks; he moved his blows a little closer to where the foe was holding onto them. The foe responded in kind and shifted the position of where he held them to counter the blows, but Brit was still just aiming to hit the sticks. This went on for another couple of minutes until Catrina barked out a command in clan language and all of a sudden, the foe changed his positioning and started to hit Brit's sticks.

Brit quickly found himself not hitting, but defending hits. He flinched with every strike and tensed up, pulling his arms close into his body. Cat barked another string of instructions in clan language and suddenly, the foe was nipping his fingers, but then started to outright bang on them until it became too painful for Brit to hang onto the sticks and he dropped them.

A bit angry, embarrassed and fingers smarting, Brit spun away from the foe waving his hands trying to fling off the pain. He was quick to pick them back up and start over again, but this process went on again and again, until Brit started to lose his cool. In frustration, he started swinging wildly, trying to get a hit somewhere and yet keep from getting his own hands thumped.

This time, the foe hit both hands at the same time and as Brit turned away again, he got hit from behind, kicked off balance and sent sprawling to the floor. Now the pupil was madder than a wet hen and coming back to his feet, he swirled around only to find Catrina standing in front of him with both his sticks in her hands. He grabbed for his weapons and attempted to pull them from her, but she held them fast in her own grip. When he found that she would not let go, he caught himself in his own anger, checked it and turned away.

"You would be dead and in several pieces right now had these been real swords," she said, trying to remain unemotional and focused on the training.

"He's just having fun with me," Brit spit angrily, looking around Cat at the foe.

"Of course he is," she responded quickly. "You're not fighting him, you're hitting his sticks."

"I thought this was a training lesson?"

"It is and we've just had our first look at how much work we need to do in order to keep you alive in the arena. You said you had fought before, where?"

"At a Knight's Expo."

There were several comments that Catrina wanted to make, but held her tongue. It would only serve to humiliate and embarrass him further. She had no idea what an Expo was and it really didn't matter. She was trying to look at this as a glass half full kind of thing, rather than the other way around. This wasn't entirely hopeless, but certainly was going to be a challenge. Her problem was time. They had much training to do, but a lot of time needed to be spent out in the snow helping get The Amanda raised to the surface and readied for transport home.

It was probably best if they just started with the basics. There are a multitude of techniques or methods of teaching someone the art of sword fighting. However, there was no time available to them to teach him everything he needed to know to make it all happen.

She turned and signaled something to the foe, letting out an exasperated sigh. The foe instantly handed her his sticks and stepped back out of the way. Turning back around, she handed the sticks back to Brit, who had quite the look of befuddlement pasted across his face.

"What are you doing?" he asked, a little apprehensive.

"Teaching," she said, holding her sticks up. "I'm going to lunge at you gently and you are going to ward off the attack with your weapons, and we're going to do this until you have it down. It's not that tough. Just takes practice."

"Well, don't you need a training suit, some pads or guards or something?"

Cat grinned from ear to ear.

"I'll be fine," she said, swaying back and forth a couple of times, starting towards him. She knew there was no chance of him being able to land his weapons anywhere on her, intentional or accidental. She had to do something here to get him started to at least be able to defend himself.

"I will attack, and you defend, like this," she said, showing him how to ward off a blow. "You must learn to be able to do this automatically. Don't worry about doing anything fancy. Fancy doesn't generally defend, basic defends."

She continued to jab at him with one stick and he warded off the jab as instructed. She then started jabbing at him with both sticks alternately. He in turn deflected the advances in kind until it became almost mechanical. Jabbing faster, she maneuvered him all around the room in different directions, and then started jabbing across at his opposing hands. At first he missed a time or two, but then figured it out and soon it became mechanical. She began to throw the pattern at him alternately, but this time he made the transition flawlessly.

Finally she barked out some orders in clan and the training foe stepped back up, took her sticks and started jabbing at Brit, who instantly followed the mechanics of what he had just learned. Cat stepped back, leaning against the table, watching intently as the two moved around the room, their sticks clacking together in rhythm. After five or ten minutes, she called out to change roles and Brit took on the role of attacker. Not to try and hit the foe really, but to get use to the feel of jabbing and being deflected. Once he got use to that, she called to the foe in clan and he started to turn and twist with every strike. It didn't take Brit very long to figure out what the strategy here was. At first he thought the twisting and turning was to show off and try to be fancy or something, but then he remembered Catrina's words that fancy doesn't generally defend. It didn't take him very long to figure out that these defensive moves were quite distracting, and that was the whole idea. Distract your opponent as much as possible and it will be easier to defend yourself. These distractions required him to focus on his own offensive maneuvers.

Before long, he was able to maintain his mechanics, no matter what the foe did to try and distract him. Without breaking his rhythm, the foe swirled around at lightning speed to deflect a jab and fire one of his own off at the trainee. Brit was now able to maintain his focus on cross deflection and a random mix of both cross and side on side deflections and a series of attacks. Finally, Catrina stopped them and motioned for Brit to rest a moment over by the table.

"Very nice," she complimented him, as he pulled his helmet and gloves off. "Now you have the basics understood, you need lots of practice. Something we have no time for, so we'll move you right into a staff."

Brit looked at the long rod lying on the table in front of him. He was a little confused about what the staff was going to teach him. At least he understood what the sticks were all about. They were fashioned to emulate the short swords. How could a staff help him with handling the Twins?

"Ok," he said, picking it up and gripping it firmly. "I understand the sticks now. Still wished we were using the swords, but I get it. Don't want to cut anyone's fingers off."

"Yes, that would be bad," she agreed. "Sorta need those for this and other important things. The staff will teach you agility. It's fairly easy to master and can be quite formidable should you be disarmed for any reason. Therefore, you must learn two things quickly here. To use it as a weapon and use it with much speed and accuracy."

"Makes perfect sense," he said, starting to twirl it in front of him. "Now this I can do."

He then started moves that he knew. Having learned to use the staff at the expo, he had become quite good with it and executing a series of quick maneuvers, his short exhibition gave Cat a little bit of hope. When he had finished showing off what he knew, she taught him some other maneuvers that he either didn't quite have down or didn't know at all. These he caught quickly, much to Catrina's delight. So much so, that she had the foe step back so that she could spar with Brit.

It was a fun exchange for both of them, because he was so much more at ease with the staff and she could challenge him in such a way as to make him feel good about how well he was doing. While she wasn't going all out with him, she was giving him a good work out and she caught him only a couple of times, but the training gloves and helmet kept him from anything serious. He finally pulled the helmet off and puffing, turned a circle around her with a big grin on his face. He appeared to really be enjoying himself now.

"Let's try this again," he said, letting the helmet roll away.

Cat stood still watching him circle her. He kept his staff spinning slowly in his gloved hands as she lowered her chin toward her chest and watched him from the side.

"What, not confident enough to lose the gloves to?" she asked, a smile streaking across her lips.

"Do I have moron written across my forehead?" Brit asked with glee, coming full circle in front of her.

"You do have something written up there, we'll have to see what it says." She lunged sharply at him in a whirl of stick he was barely able to defend against.

Somehow he got his stick in front of every lighting jab and swing she threw at him. It took him only a couple of moments to recover from her blitz assault and he quickly spun, bringing his own staff in for a set of lighting swings, followed by several jabs that went perfectly checked. Both combatants sparred all around the room in a carefully choreographed ballet, both alternately taking the offensive and then defending splendidly. They each twirled their staffs in front of the other almost hand on hand for a moment then came together on the same move designed to push the other one back and off balance. Instead, they locked staffs together and found themselves face to face looking at one another between the staffs.

"Close enough to read what it says now?" he puffed with a big grin, keeping his eyes locked on her expression.

He knew that she would shift her expression the moment before she tried an escape maneuver and if he held her there long enough, she would flinch and then he could counter her move and turn away without her making any contact on him.

"I can read it now," she said unmoving.

They were both exerting a fair amount of energy to hold the other one back. He could see that she was close to doing something. Then a radical idea entered his thought process that just might get him the upper hand. He had only a split second to act before he was sure she would.

He tightened up his lip as if he were going to push harder with one end of his staff to try and maneuver her into a different position, but instead, he relaxed and she was set forward off balance, sending her reeling towards the weapons table. Passing by him and trying to catch her balance somehow, he let his own staff slap her on the behind real good, then sprang back and stood ready. Stopping herself at the table, she turned with a grand smile, holding up her finger and waving it at him.

"Oh, you did not just do that," she hissed with glee. Cat was both surprised and proud of him and his advancements.

"Your hand rubbing your hind end there suggests otherwise," he said flippantly. Now he was just being down right cocky. And why not? He had just spanked the Queen of Thulsa.

Catrina realized that he was right. Without knowing it, she found herself rubbing the spot where he had landed his staff. She smiled and looked over at the training foe who had just watched the little encounter and was trying to remain straight faced. It was a little humorous. It wasn't often that the Queen ever got hit in training. She was a master in all her disciplines and if she did make a mistake, she would practice and practice until she got it right. Cat reaffirmed her grip on the staff and stepped back into the training area, shaking her head and chuckling at the same time. Brit knew what was coming next.

"Ok, smarty pants," she said, resetting herself in front of him, staff ready. "Let's see if that was skill or skunk."

The smile disappeared from her lips, watching carefully for him to throw the first attack swing. Both remained frozen for several seconds, then he noticed her start to relax a little bit, coming alive like a lightning bolt in a flurry of jabs and swings that were poetry in motion. However, this was a poem he understood. His staff almost had a mind of its own, defending every blow and countering with equal speed and force. Again, they found themselves staring each other down through crossed staffs, but this time Cat took the first maneuver out by suddenly sliding the end of her staff down his towards his hand in an effort to knock it loose and land the blow or even knock him down.

It would have worked had Brit not read it as it happened and countered. He released his lower hand, spinning completely around and bringing his weapon back up to bare against her, but she was waiting for him and they started again through a quick barrage of jabs and swings that were all met with a defensive maneuver. Then Brit found another freak opening that neither could have anticipated. It all happened at once and the timing was just right for him to slide right past her, back to back with staff ends clacking together, passing out of her circle, his staff end came back up and once again struck her on the back side. She wasn't even off balance this time. It was just a blow that had the right timing, but Brit was going to take all the credit. Cat turned away and looked back at him with a smile.

"That kind of thing is going to stop right here, right now," she puffed good-naturedly.

He had this staff stuff down pretty good, but she wasn't about to let him land another hit, especially where he seemed to be aiming, if he was aiming at all. Brit chuckled in his overconfidence knowing that he was frustrating her, maybe even handing her a little piece of humble pie. It was clear to him that he had proven both himself and his point. Now, the trick was to get out of any further engagements

with her. He knew that his credit limit had probably been reached.
Trouble was, he wasn't sure that she would let him off the hook
without a good butt whoopin'. He abruptly stepped out of defensive
mode and into address mode, holding his staff out in front of him and
engaging her head on, standing up straight, then bowing his head
carefully to her.

"I am only as good as the teacher," he said, making it sound very
convincing.

He knew that she had to save face in front of the foe. Wouldn't
want it to get out that a pupil got the best of her. Cat really wanted to
knock his butt into next week, and she might have done it anyway, but
since the foe was still standing there and Brit was bowing out of the
fight, protocol dictated that she, too, bow and retire from the combat.
They were finished with this portion of the training anyway and it was
time for rest, refreshment and diversion.

She toned her expression down, dampening her lightly bruised
pride and bowed, then both disarmed and stepped back over to the
table. Brit removed his gloves with a smile still pasted across his face.
Catrina, on the other hand, while not fuming, was still trying to
process how in the heck he had done so well and landed both hits. He
was an amateur for heck sake! How did he do that? The first move
was just stupid on her part. She had used that move many times
before. It was basic in nature and was generally easily anticipated and
countered.   Had she become so taken with him, that she was letting it
affect her focus on the fight?

One thing was for sure, while she was fairly confident in his
abilities with the staff, that didn't necessarily translate to what he
could do with the sword, especially the Twins. Fighting with two
weapons at the same time took uncommon abilities. She had taken
years to learn to do it effectively. She used a specially made broad
style sword that fit her in both weight and design. It was considerably
smaller than traditional broad swords. For her it didn't need to be big
and wouldn't do her any good if it were. The smaller sword was
perfect for her and the broad style worked well. Her other weapon of
choice was a single fighting stick, about the size of the ones they had
been training with earlier. She found a single to be more effective
when used in conjunction with her battle sword. Of course you
wouldn't really use such a weapon against steel, but it was quite
formidable when used to disarm and maneuver about other weaponry
because of its relatively light weight. Used properly, it could easily
snap bones and cause painful bruising where a blade couldn't reach
because of defense.

Catrina motioned for the foe to leave, removing her own gloves,
then turning and facing Brit. She wasn't even sure how she felt now.
She wanted to chew him up one side and down the other, but at the

same time wanted to compliment him with the same vigor for his progress. Brit could read the confused look and offered an out.

"Thank you," he said with a casual smile, trying to look as though he was so proud of himself because of her. Actually, this wasn't too far from the truth, but he couldn't help feeling like he was tough stuff all on his own. "I could never have learned any of that all on my own."

"Thank you," she replied softly, accepting his gratitude and his attempt at helping her save face. "You have natural talent with the staff. Why have you not pursued it?"

"I have always liked the staff," he responded carefully. "I just don't get too many opportunities to practice, let alone compete with one."

"Please tell me you have the same problem with the sword," she said, realizing she may have just insulted him.

"The sword is more popular at an Expo for the obvious reasons," he said, letting out a half smirk. "I've used it, even competed with one. They make great chick magnets."

"Well, let's hope we can make the sword feel as natural as you do the staff." Cat started for the door. "We need to get cleaned up and fed, then check on the progress outside." Brit stepped slightly behind her, exiting the room and starting down the hall towards a large door. As Cat opened it and stepped through, she turned and stopped Brit short of entering.

"Uhm," she said, holding him back and the door close to her, "my chambers. You can't come in. Yours are over there. Wash up and change and I'll meet you out here shortly."

"What's so secret about your room?" he asked, trying to look past her inside.

"Nothing," she responded with her face set against the edge while she slowly inched it closed. "It's just my room and you aren't allowed inside."

"Why not?" he asked, not getting it at all.

"Because I'm a girl and you're a boy, that's why."

That did the trick. Brit suddenly figured out the basics and he instantly felt a rush of extreme embarrassment like being out of sync in a crowd call out.   He sheepishly turned to his own door, but looked after her, slowly pulling her head inside, keeping her eyes on him. Finally, the door closed and he turned to his own room, but he couldn't get the door open. He pulled and tugged on the handle, he even twisted on the key a couple of times thinking it was locked or something, but nothing. Try as he might he could not pull it open. Then he heard Catrina's voice from behind her door giving him instructions.

"Try pushing on the door."

"Yeah right," he smirked. "That's what I was doing," he lied, bald faced. He felt really stupid now as he reversed his efforts on the door and it swung effortlessly open.

"Good man," came the faint voice from Catrina's chambers as he stepped inside his own room.

"Smooth Garrett," he said, closing the door behind him and stepping over to get cleaned up. "Real smooth."

The Texture of Reality

Once cleaned up and fed, the two walked together through the Spoil towards the open gates to the outside. Brit stopped Catrina at the altar, examining it more closely before proceeding. It seemed rather ordinary as ancient looking stone altars go with the exception of all the writing and glyphs everywhere on it.

"You really can't read any of this?" he asked, looking closely at it.

"No idea what any of it is. I always assumed that it came from another planet. We have never found anything on our world here that has anything even remotely similar to this kind of writing, and with so many different beings brought here by the storm, we figured that it came with them somehow."

"Ever thought that it might not have come through the storm?"

"If not through the storm, then how?" she asked, looking around thinking there might be some other clue nearby that would give them the answers they were seeking.

Brit looked up at the twin suns and three moons that painted the sky with various shades of light and color. Catrina passed him a glance, then looked up to see what he might be looking at.

"What?"

He glanced back down at her, then back up at the sky.

"Wait, you're not suggesting that men in flying saucers brought it from outer space?" she asked disbelieving.

"You think that's too far from reality? Why would that be so hard to imagine? I mean, look out the gate," Brit said, stepping over to the gate and pointing at the swirling storm outside. "It's a space portal for heck sakes. I'd say that's pretty extraordinary, even in my time. You come here and you have two suns and three moons. I think that's pretty far off the chart. Why not think that someone dropped it off here from another world?"

He made a very good point and it seemed to really open her mind to so many other possibilities. Cat looked back up at the moons in differing orbits around Argyle. She hadn't even thought of things in that manner. Terry had plotted the orbits of the moons circling the planet, just to make sure that they were indeed moons. One thing they had not been able to reproduce was a means for making a telescope for looking closer at the other moons. They had binoculars from the bomber, but that can only get you so far. Manufacturing magnification glass here would be quite difficult and not a priority. For all she knew, there were other life forms on one or all the moons. It all really got her thinking and she quickly realized that he could very well be right. It actually made much more sense than someone trying to carry this thing through the hurricane force winds of the storm.

Brit let his hands glide across the top surface of the altar.

"Careful," Catrina warned him. "Remember the nice jolt you got from it the other day?"

"I don't think the field is active without the Twins in place."

"How did you know how to pull them out without getting knocked on your can again?' she asked, stepping back next to him and letting her hand come to rest on his shoulder.

It still amazed him how such a simple act of touching could create such a furor with his senses. Every sensation possible raced through his being in response to just her simple touch. He had to really fight to remain focused, looking closely at the writing on the top surface. Brit couldn't help but smile gently while pointing down at one of the glyphs.

"Says right here."

The glyph was a pictorial of a figure removing the swords while not touching the ground.

"All you had to do was not be touching the ground," she said, looking closely at it. "That never even occurred to any of us. But then again, there was really no need for any of us to remove them." The two were interrupted by one of Sargon's men.

"My Queen," he said, stopping in front of them and bowing. Catrina turned to the man and acknowledged his respect.

"We have breached the avalanche to the cave. Sargon urgently calls for you both."

Cat looked over at Brit. Sargon didn't need any help. He was far better equipped to handle this work than either of them. Something must be really wrong.

"We'll come straight away, thank you." She said, dismissing him.

"Wonder what that's all about?" Brit asked, looking after the messenger.

Cat looked back down at the altar and ran her hands along the two long rectangular slots on either side of the altar top.

"What do you suppose these are for?"

"Not sure, but we better get out there and find out what's up." With that they turned back to the gate and out into the snow covered valley floor where several men were still working with the ropes surrounding the airplane wings and tail. Once secured, they would be moved farther out towards the middle of the valley for pickup. Examining them carefully, Brit worked to ensure that there would be enough rigging supporting the parts that they would hold when the Sky Cranes arrived.

Then they made their way over to where the cave was being excavated, noticing a large contingent of workers standing far back away from the angled hole, many of them muttering something in clan. Catrina and Brit made their way through the crowd, Cat finding it hard make any sense of all the commotion.

Finally, they were able to make their way down into the deep channel in the snow that the men had carved out clear through to the cave. Indeed, Brit could see the jagged edges of the torn fuselage as they carefully stepped closer. Two workers were speaking a little louder and Catrina stopped to listen to them, while Brit continued to the back side of the airplane.

Inside, Sargon was crouched down against the fuselage wall, weeping bitterly.   Brit stooped down next to him, an odd feeling developing across his chest where the twins were strapped. A moment later Catrina appeared next to them.

"The workers said while they were digging out around the plane, several of them touched the metal and could hear mad screams in their heads. Sargon pulled them clear and stepped inside. When he touched the plane, he called to us and began to weep."

Cat tried to pull Sargon free of his hold of the airplane, but he seemed almost glued to it. Brit reached around him and pried his fingers free of the part he was holding onto and he instantly seemed to relax, but continued to sob uncontrollably. After they had pulled him out of the plane, a couple of his men came to his aid and he quickly began to regain his composure. Catrina tried her best to comfort him from whatever it was that had overcome him, while Brit turned back to the plane.

He could feel the hum of the Twins; even hear them in their sheaths. He grasped them both and held them by their scabbards. It was not a pleasant feeling or sound; similar to when he had pulled one out earlier in the airplane with Bryan. He motioned for Cat to come back inside the fuselage. After she had felt the vibration of the sheathed swords, they each carefully pulled a sword a little ways out of its scabbard. To their shock and amazement, the once pleasant blue glow had been replaced with a spitting red color. Pushing the blades back down into place, they looked around at the inside of the fuselage.

"Better have a little talk with her," Brit said quietly, stepping over to the wall.

Sargon had composed himself by now and scrambled to get to his feet in order to stop them from touching the plane, but it was too late. The moment Brit touched the metal his head was filled with an ear piercing scream that fired through his whole body. The sound was almost deafening and the pain associated with it was worse. It seemed as though every nerve ending in his body was on fire. He found his thoughts rolling wildly through a horrible red/black storm, powerless to control anything. It took an immense amount of concentration, but after some fighting, he was able to gain enough control of what was happening in his head to be able to block out the noise. He called out to The Amanda several times while struggling to concentrate and finally found himself crawling through angry black, red, and blue colors.

In his mind's eye, it appeared that he was within the angry walls of the storm itself. Even with the concentration and control he was struggling to maintain, he could feel it tearing at him, threatening to rip him to pieces and blow him away. After some navigation through the darkness of ugly color and noise, he thought he could see someone ahead of him, sitting on the ground, hands covering their face. Drawing closer, he recognized a woman, sobbing.

Maneuvering closer to her, there was something familiar about her. He could see that she had short brown hair and was wearing a pretty yellow dress, extending to just below the knee, a scabbard with the hilt of a sword strapped around her waist. Finally able to crawl to the spot where she sat crying, Brit knelt in front of her.

It was perfectly calm where she was, though they were both completely enveloped in the horrible scene around them. He recognized her, putting both his hands on her wrists and gently pulling her hands from her tear filled eyes. Her big brown pools sparkled, looking up at him. He smiled at her and carefully wiped away her tears, then held both her hands in his. Her expression was that of pain, mixed with intense fear, almost terror.

"Amanda," he said, quite happy to actually meet her, or at least the manifestation of her. It felt like they were meeting in a dream. She nodded through her tears, but was unable to smile back at him.

"Tell me, what is it?"

"Please," she sobbed almost uncontrollably. "Make it stop!" She tried to bury her face back into her hands, but Brit held them back.

"What? Make what stop?"

"It hurts!" she sobbed. "The storm, it's found me and it's tearing at me, trying to pull me back."

The only thing Brit could figure was that when the engineers had breached the avalanche of ice and snow, the storm had discovered her exact location and was focusing in on her, trying to pull the energy back that had been transferred when she came through the first time.

He settled next to her and held her in his arms while she wept. Rocking her gently, he let her cry and as he tried to comfort her, he noticed another figure in the dimness approaching them. Their surroundings began to calm somewhat, the figure starting towards them and a second later, he recognized Catrina, stopping in front of them, looking around.

"What is this place?" she asked, looking around then down at them.

"I assume it's Amanda's consciousness," Brit answered, continuing to rock the sobbing woman.

"This is not a very happy place at all," she said, somewhat bewildered. "What is happening here? Why is this woman crying? Who is she?"

The woman in Brit's arms had calmed down somewhat at the sound of both Brit and Catrina's voices and she turned her face up to the Queen of Thulsa. Cat froze in place and just stared down in shock and disbelief, then slowly sank to her knees, leaning in closer to look at her own reflection.

Amanda tried to smile a little while Catrina examined every part of her. Brit was getting a bit of a kick out of the expressions on both women's faces. They were fascinated by their nearly identical features. Amanda had stopped crying and seemed to not even notice the turmoil surrounding all three of them. She reached out and touched Catrina's soft brown hair, letting her hand slide down her left cheek to her chin. Cat performed the same gesture, smiling gently at Amanda.

"I had no idea how beautiful you had become," Amanda remarked quietly, smiling and holding her hand back up against Cat's cheek.

Catrina was starting to become somewhat emotional herself. She realized that this manifestation was a carbon copy of what her father saw in her mother, Amanda. In essence, she was looking right at her mother and holding her hand against her face.   Mother and daughter were together again.

"Mother," Catrina whispered, embracing Amanda, taking her from Brit and wrapping her arms around her.

Cat began to weep openly as years of pent up emotion began to flow. Oh how she missed being with her mother, doing things and spending time with her. They had been so much a part of each other growing up, having done so many things together. She had bottled up the pain of the separation from her mother for so long and now she was able to let some of it go. However, her release was tempered somewhat by knowing that, while this apparition looked just like her mother, it was indeed only that, an apparition.

It was not really her mother. While this Amanda looked and sounded like her, even had some shared memories, she was indeed distinctly different. This Amanda had been born in an aircraft factory in Kansas and had fought in a brutal war with her comrades living and dying all around her. This Amanda held the memories of her crew that occupied her frame. How she had grown to love them, especially Tony. This Amanda had been willing to do anything to protect them.

Her feelings for Catrina were also very real. She had fallen in love with this little girl at East Base AFB when Tony had come home. Then, to have the ten year old girl ride with them on their last tour of duty and the adventures they had gone through together before all this mess with the Storm. Her spirit was the same as her name sake, for

Tony had created her in that image, so in this instance, the flow of emotional support worked and was appropriate.

"Cat," Brit spoke up quietly.

She looked up at him, tears streaming down her cheeks. In that moment, he could not help but have compassion for what she must be feeling. For an instant, his mind was transported across time and space to a little house in the suburbs of Helena, Montana, where a lonely old woman watched and waited for her husband and daughter to return home to her. So long she had hoped and waited. He knew of the love that she had for her lost family and understood how and why that kind of emotion should be exchanged here and now. He also realized, as Catrina looked up at him, that he loved her. He felt an overwhelming feeling within him begin to boil up, that he could not live without her and had to be with her always, but more to the point right now.

"We have to get her out of here," he said, looking around at the angry space all about them. "She can't stay here."

"What would you have me do?" Catrina replied through her own emotion, holding Amanda close to her.

Brit stepped in a couple of different directions nervously. He had no idea. He only knew that they had to change these conditions. This was a hold up that they didn't have time for, no matter how dire Amanda's circumstances were. They had to somehow figure out a way to keep her attention off and away from the furry of the storm trying to tear at her to reclaim its energy and essence.

Brit looked around, taking note that their surroundings had started to lighten and the colors began to brighten until it was almost like day all around them. They could hear the distinct sound of music starting to fill the space all about them. Catrina and Amanda pulled apart, looking around as well.

"It's a Thulsa lullaby." Cat got to her feet recognizing the tune.

The feeling of hate, anger and fear, seemed to flee as light filled in all around them, the chorus of men's voices growing stronger. As it did so, both Catrina and Brit's spirits began to lift and Amanda soon got to her feet. Her mind now free of the fear and pain she had been held hostage by. Now, her very being was being filled with compassion and hope from all those around her. A moment later, Sargon appeared in front of them. He too, looked around them, then at Amanda.

"Are you all right now?" he asked, stepping towards her.

"Yes, how did you know?" Amanda asked, smiling and basking in the comfort of the light and the feelings of warmth and wellbeing. Sargon looked back at his Queen and Brit.

"The Storm reaches directly for your energy and you have fear of it. It's an angry swirl of consuming madness that demands your attention. If you are able to focus your attention elsewhere, it has very little power over you. Our people will see to it that you are attended to until your departure. With your permission my Queen, I recommend having the people sing and attend her until she leaves this place."

"Thank you." Amanda stepped to Sargon and embraced him, then stepped back. "I was so thrilled to finally see the light of day that I did not realize what would happen when the storm gained direct access to me."

Brit smiled and nodded as Catrina bowed to Sargon in gratitude. It was a very wise and well thought out tactic.

"Forgive my boldness my Queen," he said, bowing before her. "I tried to stop both of you before you touched her. I knew what had to be done, but was trapped myself. I will attend to Amanda more closely until she leaves this place."

"I can think of no one better suited for the role," Catrina agreed, giving the chief engineer the reassurance he needed. Knowing that he still had her full confidence in getting this monumental task completed was of the utmost importance and she was certain that she had given him that confidence. She turned back to Amanda as Brit gave her a hug and stepped back.

"And thank you," Amanda said, with a contagious grin.

"Well, don't thank me just yet. It's a long way to Driggs. But if I have anything to do with it, you'll get there, I promise."

"I was supposed to fly right over it a long time ago. It will be good to finally get there."

Cat stepped up and hugged her again, then held both her hands. While she knew this was not her mother, she knew that Amanda loved her like her real mother and for now, that was enough.

"Thank you," Catrina finally said to Amanda.

"For what? You three have saved me.   It is I who am thankful." Amanda pointed out happily. Cat stepped back next to Brit who instinctively took her hand in his.

"Thank you for being what and," she paused just a moment, then went ahead and said it, "who you are." She finished, confirming her belief that Amanda was indeed, real. With that, the three of them disappeared leaving Amanda in a wonderful, bright and cheery place.

Tug of War

When Brit and Catrina let go of the airplane, they were still holding hands. Looking at each other for a moment, they listened to the song of the workers, who had started digging again around the fuselage. While they were somewhat confident that no one would touch the airplane with the intent of disturbing The Amanda, they weren't worried about her creating any panic among them either.

Stepping out of the fuselage hand in hand, they made their way back out to the surface where they found Sargon directing the work. He had already sent messengers into town to fetch other people willing to come out to attend The Amanda. It might prove difficult, but he was sure enough of them would come to help. Even with their cheery song, the Storm still raged above them, but the song of the working men appeared to subdue even the noise of the storm. After surveying all the work going on around them, Sargon turned to them.

"We still have hours before we can pull her to the surface," he said, looking back at the men working and singing, carving a suitable ramp through the deep avalanche field from the cave to the surface. Because the fuselage was estimated to weigh more than their lifting machines could lift, the idea was to slide it back up and out the same way it went in, and then transport it across the snow to the pickup zone.

"That will give us plenty of time for more training," Catrina announced, still grasping Brit's hand. "You have a lot to learn yet."

"I keep hearing that all the time," Brit responded, both irritated and grateful for her dedication to his wellbeing.

"You must train as much as possible," she reaffirmed.

"Nag, Nag, Nag," he responded good-naturedly, tipping his head gently into hers.

She smiled and leaned her head down onto his shoulder for a moment, until one of the clans women walked by and smiled at them. She seemed genuinely pleased to see her Queen actually enjoying the company of a man. She had not afforded this kind of affection with any previous relationship she had tried to have. Now they had completely forgotten themselves and that they were openly showing affection towards the other. Brit didn't mind at all, but Cat became a little bit worried. Had this man been from Thulsa, she wouldn't have given it a second thought, although the woman probably would have reacted the same way.   Brit was supposed to be in her custody, but it appeared that she was falling into his and while the decree had gone out that he would help direct the rescue operation, he was still essentially a stranger to everyone else and they had no idea about him. For all they knew, he had put some kind of a hex on her and was going to do something similar to what Ivan had in mind when he first tried to take over Thulsa. The excavation she had them doing out here beyond the Spoil with all this snow and airplane pieces, was certainly quite out of the norm, but she had never steered them wrong before, even when Ivan tried to make the moves on her and Thulsa.

As they stood holding hands, she once again began tracking a myriad of thoughts running through her mind. She looked up at the swirling storm above them and tried to sort some of them out. She so wanted to go home to her own world, to her mother. Earlier, standing up on the ridge and being only feet away from it was almost unbearable, but the thoughts of leaving Thulsa were equally as heart wrenching. The pros and cons seemed to cancel each other completely out. She understood that she was experiencing some very strong feelings towards Brit. She really wanted to go where he was going, but at the same time, Thulsa was now the only world she really knew and she loved it and its people. She loved being their queen, and while there were some perks that naturally came with the office, she liked it more because it offered her a chance to give back to her people.

She looked over at Brit with an adoring, impassioned gaze. He did not notice her looking at him, but kept his attention focused on the work going on in front of them. She felt strange, trying to imagine herself with him on earth. However, the only things that came to mind were this world and her people. Perhaps there was a life together with him here in Thulsa? If you love someone enough, you'll find a way to make it work. She asked herself if she could just walk away from Thulsa, just leave it and never come back. Did she have the right to ask Britten if he would stay here with her in Thulsa and rule by her side? Did he have the right to ask her to leave? She loved her people so much. She loved being a part of their culture and a part of their process for creating their own destinies, guiding them in figuring out what was ultimately best for them as a whole instead of self.

She looked back over at Brit again and watched him for a moment. Major league attractions aside, was this the kind of guy that she could build any kind of life with? Britten was certainly a nice person. She liked his demeanor and his personality, but she had to ask herself if this was what he was really like or was he just putting his best foot forward? What would married life be like with him? What would he have her doing with all this salvage business if she were to follow him to his world? What would she have him doing if he were to stay?

While she still didn't fully understand what it was he did for a living, her insatiable curiosity gave her cause to really want to find out. The experiences etched in face and demeanor sparked her imagination and she could only imagine the grand adventures they could have together. How would she be able to reintegrate into a society that she hadn't been in since she was a 10 year old? To counter that question, how did she integrate into this society? The two cultures were very different in just about every aspect. How would she be viewed in his world? What was entailed with salvaging wrecks from all over the world? All over the world! Goodness, that seemed like an impossibility. She hadn't even scratched the surface of the extent of Argyle's vastness as a planet. She had no idea how large it really was, even in relationship to earth. She hadn't even considered what he might think of the notion of remaining behind, although that may have already been decided when he and his friends stepped into the Argyle world.

Realistically, what would she have him do? What would he want to do?   Aircraft and ship salvage weren't too much in demand here in Thulsa and while she had never ventured very far beyond their own borders, she was sure there wasn't much call for services like this in realms closer to the sea shores of Argyle. One thing was for sure, there were a lot of questions spinning around in her head and very few answers to any of them. Answers were what she desperately needed right now. She was becoming increasingly conflicted as to what to do and where to go with all of this.

"What?"

Cat was suddenly brought back to reality, Brit noticing her looking straight at him and asking what she was looking at. She hadn't realized that she had completely zoned out, trying to process all the information and questions forming in her mind.

"We need to go," she finally said, snapping back to full operational status.

"Lead the way," he gestured with a smile and his free hand.

He held firmly to her hand, even though she was now feeling a little uncomfortable with it and was hoping for a reason to let go. Requiring a bit of a balancing act, she was able to let go in a more strategic way than just trying to shake loose from him.

Making their way back to the gate and the Winner's Spoil, her operational status again shifted and she started walking on autopilot. She continued to try and work through all the questions now percolating around in her head.

Stepping along the path through the Winner's Spoil, Cat didn't even realize that Brit was carrying on a conversation from behind. It wasn't until she got to the top of the pathway between the two boulders that she sensed he was no longer behind her. She popped back into reality, turning to find him standing in the middle of the Spoil looking silently at her. She was hoping that he would either continue or at least ask the question again, whatever it was, but he only looked at her in silence.

"Really?" Brit stated plainly.

"Really what?"

"You didn't even hear a word that I said."

Catrina was speechless. She certainly had not and wasn't even sure how to admit to it. If she did, she would have to explain why she didn't hear him and she wasn't so sure she was ready to open up that conversation. How was she going to slide around this one? It was obvious that she had hurt his feelings by not paying attention to him. She fumbled a moment, trying to put some words together, but nothing came. Apparently, there was no way around it now. She had to think quickly to avoid something worse than where she thought this whole thing might be heading.

"No," she finally admitted humbly, lowering her eyes and looking away.

"What's wrong?"

"I'm sorry. My mind is somewhere else."

"I'd say so," he said, stepping towards her, sounding a little less offended at her inattentiveness.

"I could have just named off all eleven of our kids and you wouldn't have even known it."

Perhaps he was being too hard on her. She was a queen after all and there were many things that she was responsible for.

"Who said anything about having kids?" she asked abruptly. Even in jest, his last suggestion of their imagined children hit her in the absolutely worst way. She suddenly found herself quite upset and she was going to lash out right at Brit if she wasn't careful. Brit instantly shifted to a serious defensive mode. He sort of figured that she had a lot on her mind through all of this. In her position, how do you not?

"Sorry," he held his hands up in defense. "I wasn't trying to start anything, really."

"I'm sorry. I'm having a hard time with this whole business of going home." She finally admitted, stepping back down the path towards him.

She wondered if there would ever be an end to all this new territory she was treading. Right now it wasn't about what was happening around them, but what was happening between them that Catrina was having issues with. She was falling in love with Brit and a great tug of war had begun between going home to Earth and staying here on Argyle. She dearly loved her people and the thought of leaving them was breaking her heart. Conversely, the thought of staying behind was doing similar things to her. Her mother was on Earth, not here. She knew what her father wanted. Though he had never voiced it directly, it was painfully obvious that given the opportunity, he would do whatever he could to get back to his beloved Amanda. However, Brit had said that she was 90, considerably older physically, than Tony was now. What kind of life would that leave them?

"What's to worry about?" Brit asked unthinkingly. It all seemed fairly simple to him. "When you're dad gets back with my brother and friends, we'll use the Signet and then climb back out the same way we came in. Kind of a no brainer here." He finished, as she stopped in front of him.

"Really?" she asked, a little bit irritated at his apparent insensitivity to the feelings she was wrestling with. There were decisions that were forthcoming and drastic consequences associated with them. She would have to deal with them, and consider all the other people that those decisions affected. She could feel anger trying to boil up, but before she got really frustrated, it occurred to her that she hadn't even expressed to him what she was going through. She also had to consider his maturity, not just his age. While she was physiologically the same age as he was, she had lived several life times longer than he had and had gained so much more maturity from her expanse of time.

"What about all of this?" She asked, looking around them. "What about these men?" she asked, referring to the stationed guards in the Spoil.

"Yeah, what about them? Do they want to come too?" Brit stood his ground and raised his hands to his hips.

"I mean this place, these people," she said, folding her arms and focusing on his face.

Catrina remained silent for a moment. She was about to start tapping her foot, but then heard footsteps from behind and turned. A large warrior came tromping along the path between the entryway boulders to the Spoil, leading a small contingent of children accompanied by several mothers and a few other warriors, probably fathers. They had obviously been dispatched by Sargon, to provide music for The Amanda.

Brit and Cat stepped aside, allowing them to make their way past them towards the open gates. Each child was looking all around at all the pretty treasures situated in the Spoil. Cat watched smiling as they approached the gates, but then one of the smaller children, probably about four years old, broke ranks and came running back to her. Brit watched the Queen of Thulsa kneel to greet her. The little girl was a bit shy, but thrilled to be able to greet her queen.

"I'm pleased to meet you my queen," she said in a little voice.

Cat's expression broadened to instant glee. A moment later, all the children broke ranks and came trotting back to greet their queen. They knew they could because she spent so much time out among her people, greeting them and working alongside them. Cat wasn't afraid to get her hands dirty nor did she look down on anyone who did. She was instantly surrounded by excited children. She returned each and every greeting, individually, giving them hugs and a kiss on the cheek.

"And where are you kids off to?" she asked, scanning their little faces.

She was so thrilled to be able to chat with them. Brit stepped back out of the way and watched her with them closely, the adults from their escort trickling back to observe the exchange. He watched how she focused in on each one of them, making them feel like they were her only concern.

"We were asked to come sing songs," one child finally piped up to her.

"Oh really? That sounds so wonderful!   And what songs will you be singing?" She asked, her arms around one of them.

"We have ten songs," one of the smaller boys announced, holding up seven fingers.

Another boy leaned next to him, cupped his hand and whispered loudly into his ear.

"You're only showing 7 fingers. It's 10 songs, but that was a really good try." It was obvious that the older one was his brother. The younger brother was all good about the correction though.

"Thanks, yes, 10 songs," he said, looking at his fingers and counting, sticking them all out into her face.

Brit chuckled at the innocence of youth. What gems they all were!

"We're gonna sing my mom's sleeping songs and the pine tree song you taught us."

"You are?" Cat responded with delight. "Oh, I love that song. It's my favorite. Can I hear you sing it right now?" She looked up at their escorts, who were smiling happily.

They too were so impressed by their queen's demeanor and that she truly cared for and loved her people, especially the children. They all nodded and one of the mothers leaned down to get them started. They sang a wonderful song about the love of pine trees that Catrina had taught all the children from the time she had begun to be their monarch.

Brit watched the children sing; alternately gazing at the delighted look on Catrina's beaming face. Even the escort warriors, these big gruffy men, had pleasant looks on their faces, as they too were touched by the children's voices.

After the children finished their song, they each took turns giving their queen a hug and a kiss and then returned to their place in line to continue with their assignment to sing. As the last little one strung off, the whole group of adults got a good laugh out of the first little boy who had held up his fingers indicating how many songs they were going to sing. Once again he was holding up seven fingers and repeating that they were going to sing ten songs. Then his older brother corrected him again and he held up all ten fingers and corrected himself, then fell into line and marched off through the gates with the rest.

Brit stepped quickly forward, helping Catrina back to her feet. She gently brushed her clothes, making sure everything was in order, then finally looked up at Brit who stood back away from her with his arms folded. He slowly stepped back over to her, looking over at the gates as the entourage disappeared, then back at her.

"That's what's bothering you. That's what this is all about, isn't it?" He said with a mixed smile.

Catrina looked back down at the ground for a moment and then voiced her greatest fear. Her voice had an emotional shake in it as she looked back up into his eyes.

"How can I leave my people?"

Brit was somewhat embarrassed to admit to his own insensitivity, coming to a full realization of what she was going through. Up until now, he really had no idea. He had been completely clueless, paid no attention to it at all. He was so focused on finding the airplane and getting through everything that had anything to do with himself, including Catrina, that he hadn't even stopped to think what she might be going through. Now, he found himself looking at everything from a whole new angle and what he was seeing caused him to want to crawl under a rock.

"Why in the heck is Catrina having anything to do with me?" He cringed internally, thinking about how much of a knucklehead he had been since he had first met her. He had thought of almost nothing but himself through everything they had gone through since he had gotten here. He had thought about how wonderful he would feel when he brought Catrina and her father back through the gate. Back to Earth in his time and showed everyone what he had done and how cool he was for doing it. He thought about how awesome he would be if he could bring Tony back to Amanda and reunite them. Not once had he even considered what they might be feeling about this entire thing. That thought hadn't even entered into his mind, only how he would feel about it.

"What a complete and utter jerk!" he thought. The thoughts of how he had behaved, were hitting him like a ton of bricks now. Catrina watched the shift happen before her eyes, reading the change transforming him.

Speechless at first, he stepped over to her and took her by the hands. This was his defining moment for her, so she let him struggle through it. He looked down at her hands, caressing them gently with his thumbs. They were strong hands, but so soft and feminine. How he loved to touch them and hold them. He fumbled for the words while trying to get the courage up to look her in the eye.

"Big dummy," he thought to himself. *"If you'd just look and get it over with, you'd feel so much better, once you were looking into her wonderful brown eyes."*

She knew exactly what he was thinking and feeling, somehow she just knew.

"Come on, you can do it, I know you can," she thought, watching him opened his mouth to speak. One thing that this whole adventure had taught him so far was emotion and lots of it. The Amanda had tapped into a direct vein and now that seemed to rule just about everything else he did.

"I....." he fumbled. "I am truly sorry Catrina. I did not see to understand."

Cat looked around at the Spoil guards. This wasn't exactly the place to be having this discussion. She could order her Royal Guard to fall back out of hearing distance, but the Spoil guards couldn't be ordered away from their duties. She turned, taking one of Brit's hands, leading him up and out of the Spoil with her royal guard in tow. Once outside and on the path towards the city, she ordered her guards to give them a little distance, then put her arm around his, walking with him, practically gluing herself to his side.

"I can't fully understand what you're going through here," Brit said to her, feeling her warmth as they walked. "But I want to try." He stopped her and looked in to her wonderful ebony eyes. "I love you and I want you to come back to Earth with me, but I know that there has to be more to it than just how I feel towards you. I really want to understand your feelings about these people. If you would be willing, I would love to listen and try to understand what you're going through."

Catrina smiled broadly, a warm dart piercing her deeply when he vocalized his love for her, and that warmth swelled within her. Again, another new sensation to deal with that was even more powerful than the others. She thought she had recognized it as profound satisfaction for a great accomplishment, but this had more of an intense, heartfelt warmth to it. While Brit hadn't said it, she felt like if she asked him to, he would seriously consider staying here in Thulsa with her. She realized in that moment that she loved him and wanted to be with him always. The feeling filled her entire being and she was finding that her smile would not go away.

The Jabbaway

The Torres forest that lay inside the borders of the Kenlar had a well-used road. It had actually been carved out of the forest centuries previous by the Omar clan, who at that time, had their boundaries divided quite differently than they were currently. Indeed, they used to own parts of the Thulsa and Kenlar territories, but as happens over time with societies such as the clans, wars are fought, won and lost, and lands move from hand to hand. The Torres wasn't particularly deep, dank or dark, but it was a rough way to travel if you were not on the road. There were few pathways through this forest other than the main road, mostly because of the rough terrain that it covered and the ground cover on the forest floor. Foliage much like ivy snaked and twisted everywhere, covering obstacles that might prove difficult for the traveler on foot to navigate. Even if the ground were completely flat, the twisting vines wrapping themselves around any and everything, made it very slow going through a place that you would just as soon not be in during the dark hours. Even so, there were many places where the ivy-like vines didn't permeate the lower layer several feet above the forest floor. Here a fern type layer kept anything else from growing, forming a lower canopy where you could hide from the forest from within the forest. Even the daylight hours could be somewhat treacherous. While there was wildlife of all kinds that populated this vast forest, many animals refused to stay long because several predators called this place home. The Torres was a cornucopia of bountiful food sources for all kinds of critters that lived in this part of Argyle. Unless a critter got caught up in what it was feasting on, most of them avoided the Torres at certain times, most notably, when the Jabbaway were moving from the forest tree tops out to the plains and meadow areas, then back again to roost for the night.

As Tony and Terry had indicated to Bryan earlier in the morning, it was more of a larger cross between a wolverine and a badger with wings. Most of them were as small as badgers, but many were the size of Earth dogs with some being as large as a Newfoundland. They fed mostly on fruit, bugs and smaller rodents, but were not opposed to taking down larger game when the opportunity presented itself. It steered clear of the human population as best it could, but encounters were inevitable as the population grew and smaller settlements encroached on their habitat. All the encounters the clans had with the Jabba ended badly, mostly for the Jabba. The Jabba did not purposely look for a fight and usually did its best to avoid any contact, but when cornered or wounded, it could be quite ferocious.

Even so, Tony and his band had come prepared for any encounter with the Jabba. Each man was issued a set of long daggers and a set of bolas. These bolas were made of three ropes, fashioned of rawhide flaxen all attached together at one end. A hard ball or rock was attached to the free end of each rope. You would sling these weapons at an enemy or animal and entangle or ensnare them, knocking them down thus disabling them while the kill was made.

Neither Bryan nor his two friends had ever used these before and had no idea how to make them work. Making their way through the forest, Terry instructed them to practice on trees standing along the road ahead of them. Ideally, you wanted the three balls to spin evenly separated as you slung it. This took a great deal of practice according to Terry and Tony, who had no trouble twirling theirs above their heads and flinging them. The other three had a go at it a couple of times. Bryan nearly clubbing himself and his horse, trying to get the Bolas to twirl above his head. Jerry couldn't even get them to twirl at all and they kept getting wrapped around his neck. Danny kept trying and ultimately just threw them as hard as he could. At least they landed in a tree, but that was about it. There was no wrapping or mock disabling, they just hung there. Finally, Terry instructed them to try twirling them from the side instead of over their heads. This seemed to work better. While this method wasn't nearly as accurate and you couldn't get it to go quite as far, at least you weren't going to bash in your own head.

Terry moved the small group along at a quick pace while Tony and his men kept a wary eye out in the treetops as they went. Danny and Jerry were comparing their slinging techniques as Bryan trodded along after the two warriors behind Tony, thinking of little Anna. Terry suddenly halted the whole group. He stood up in the saddle, looking around. Danny and Jerry were still goofing off and Terry had to silence them as he listened. Bryan couldn't detect a thing. Not a sound could be heard; even the trees seemed to be holding still. Suddenly, Terry spurred his horse, motioning for everyone to do the same. They rode hard down the road, moving along a steep ridge that fell a thousand feet into a ravine and a river below. As they ran their horses along the road, Bryan became aware of several shadowy objects streaking over the road at treetop level. The objects increased in number as they rode on, passing right over the top of the riders and then in front of them.

Terry glanced back at his group and yelled to drive the horses as hard as they would go. Bryan could hear the sound of fast air movement all around him, kicking at his horse to get it to run harder. That wasn't too difficult. The horses were already sensing the danger and were at a full run down the road. Then he could see shadowy objects coming out of the upper portion of the trees right above the road in front of them. Large winged animals bent on crossing the road right here, on their way to somewhere else. The further along the road they rode, the thicker they became and the lower they flew until they were at head height. Whatever they were, they began to make a funny chirping sound similar to what a locust might make.

Bryan leaned down close to his horse's neck, trying to avoid getting hit or knocked off as they raced along the road. To his right he could see the edge of the road, dropping sharply down into the deep ravine. To his left the terrain started to rise upwards deeper into the forest. Ahead, it appeared that the road veered away from the ravine, starting up towards higher ground. The creatures didn't seem to want to cross the road at that point, so the group made that their goal, hoping that might be a good place to stop and wait out this frenzied migration. With wings actually striking them as they approached the turn, the riders finally reached a point where the creatures weren't flying. Reining the horses to a stop, Terry turned his horse around, counting heads. All present, very good. Bryan looked over at Tony, who was eyeing the mass of wings and bodies.

"Jabbaway?"

"Jabbaway," Tony confirmed, steadying his nervous horse.

"What has them so spooked?" Danny asked, pulling closer to one of the warriors. He was having a hard time trying to steady his horse and being next to one that was holding still seemed to calm it.

"It's their time of day to flock and feed," Terry affirmed, "but I've not seen them in these numbers before. It's a good guess that they are riled up about something."

At that moment, two Jabba landed, feet running, just ahead of them, coming straight for the group. Several others dropped to the road behind them, looking rather angrily in their direction.

"Not good!" Tony yelled, pulling his bolas and twirling them over his head. His warriors pulled their swords and formed a defensive circle around Bryan and his two friends. Danny stupidly tried to twirl his bolas, but when he couldn't get them to quit hitting the side of his head, he moved them to his side and started revving them up to speed. Bryan and Jerry instinctively pulled their daggers, not that they could have done anything with them. A close in fight with a Jabbaway was not a good idea for even a seasoned warrior. They found out why real fast.

Tony and Terry were accurate in their description of these snarling masses of hair and wings. Bryan was naively more concerned about his horse getting hurt by the oncoming attack than he was about his own welfare. The dagger in his hand gave him a nice sense of false security. Terry let his bolas go on the first oncoming Jabba and it was sent tumbling off into the brush with a horrible whine. A much larger one with sliver stripes running the length of its back lit down onto the ground right where the other one had tumbled off. It looked over at the disabled whining mass of hair, then turned back to the group, howled like a wolf and charged. Several of the warriors let their bolas go on the closest animals attacking, and then started swinging their swords to keep the others at bay. Terry checked the road behind them. There were more starting to land to join in the fight. This was not good. He turned and looked back up the road. It was clear, beyond the bend and slope.

"Ride on! Let's go! Let's go!" Turning and spurring his horse he breezed past the large Jabba that swung at him with razor sharp claws. Having missed Terry and a couple of the other warriors following him, the Jabba turned and took aim right at Bryan. Rocketing full speed, the Jabba thrust itself right at Bryan and his frightened horse. In midair, its legs, wings and claws became entangled, the rocky balls of Tony's bolas spinning tightly around it with lightning precision, rendering it nearly immobile, but sailing onto Bryan and his frightened horse. The hairy beast stank horribly and its breath was worse. It growled viciously at a completely startled Bryan. Sensing the danger, his horse reared back and started to bolt back down the road. He felt fiery stings in one of his arms and his leg as the creature sank its claws into his flesh and flexed. Bryan tried to hang onto the horse as he fired past the other two warriors and his friends, who were helpless to do anything to help, having trouble enough of their own trying to fight off their attackers.

Seeing Bryan's bad fortune, Tony and the other warriors turned back around, spurring their horses to pursue. Terry jumped from his horse, pulling his sword and running to the disabled Jabba in the brush. He quickly dispatched its head and pulled his bolas loose, suddenly turning and swinging once, cut another Jabba in half as it darted past him. He started twirling his bolas again in the direction of two smaller Jabba heading towards Tony and his warriors, pursuing Bryan's runaway fury. Letting his weapon go, he turned; slicing two more attacking Jabba in half with opposing swings.

Terry had been self-taught to use a sword. There was no real finesse, but what he was doing was certainly effective. The Jabba steered clear of him from that point on. His bolas found their mark, taking both attacking animals down with one set. He jumped back onto his horse and headed back down into the fury of the fight, swinging his sword and sending winged Jabba in every direction.

Danny turned in Bryan's direction just in time to see his horse rear up again, this time spilling Bryan and the attacking Jabba to the ground. Then they were gone, rolling over the edge of the ravine. The horse bolted, and disappeared back down the road where they had come with a bunch of Jabba taking wing to pursue. The group continued to fight off the remaining beasts while Danny jumped from his horse as it came to a halt where Bryan had disappeared. Jerry followed quickly, the others finishing off the remaining animals that were flapping or scampering off.

"I can't see him!" Danny yelled, shifting and stretching to see where they had landed. Seeing disturbed brush and a cloud of dust, they could hear the sound of falling rocks and what not, but nothing distinguishable. The Jabba were still within the groups hearing distance and making plenty of noise.

"That's a long way down," Terry puffed, wiping blood spatter from his face and arms. "Good thousand feet. If he survived the fall, he's Jabba bait for sure."

"We've got to get down there!" Jerry said, going for his horse and the rope tied to the saddle.

"And do what? Clean up the rocks?" Terry asked, wiping his sword off and putting it back into its sheath. Tony stepped over to his friend and gave him a look of concern.

"Terry?"

Terry froze, looking at his friend. He finally understood the need to render whatever aid they could, no matter the cost in time. He knew all too well what the results of an encounter such as this were. It rarely came out with a happy ending for the human involved. In this instance, it would be a textbook example of what happens when the Jabba gets a hold of you. It isn't fair or even glorious. Bryan wasn't overwhelmed by a huge mass and went down fighting. His attacker was disabled and they had both fallen. It was likely that even if both man and beast had survived the fall, they would be disemboweled by the hungry flock or devoured by the carnivorous creatures that inhabited the river far below. The Jabba didn't care, it was food, regardless of whether it was one of their kind or something else, it was food.

Terry ordered the men to combine their ropes and secure one end to a nearby tree. While Danny and Jerry looked on anxiously, Terry fastened the rope around his waist and started down the steep face of the ravine. Tony and the warriors kept a wary look out all around them for signs of more Jabba activity.

As Terry descended, the rock face got steeper and less covered. There was a lot of noise going on below him and he had a good idea of what it was. Getting closer to a hedge of bushes that appeared to be a last barrier to anything coming down the face, his fears were confirmed. Below was a sheer rock drop off that fell a thousand feet to the river below. He could hear the river and a mass of Jabba chatter below him. It was certain that the flock below was making good on their reputation as cannibals and meat eaters. Peering over the brush, he watched masses of the creatures below him, flapping and beating at the air in two huge groups heading back down the river. He was certain that they were carrying off the remains to devour in a more secure location. There was nothing to be done here; Bryan Garrett was gone.

Danny and Jerry continued to ask a string of questions to which they received no answers as Terry made his way back up to the road. *What do you do or say in a case like this*? Reaching the top, he looked into the searching, anxious eyes of Bryan's two friends, but could only sadly shake his head, and then turn to his own horse. He stood and leaned his head into his saddle as Tony stepped up to him. He thought of his little Anna and how she loved this newcomer from Earth. She would be heart broken when they returned without him.

"They were carrying off what was left," was all Terry could choke out. Tony tried to comfort his friend with a hand to the shoulder. He too, was overcome with grief at the loss of Bryan. He had helped to make the case to bring them on this journey to retrieve the Signet. This wasn't a part of the plan to get back to Earth.

"What was left?" Danny exclaimed disbelieving. "What was left?" he repeated, becoming angry. "You couldn't see what was left! You have no idea of what was left!" Jerry threw his arms around his friend to hold him back from any physical outbursts and to gain comfort from the sting of losing his friend.

"Danny, he's gone," Jerry cried, his eyes filling with tears.

"No!" Danny yelled, trying to break Jerry's hold on him. "No! He's not gone! He's down there and he needs our help!"

"Dan!" Jerry bawled. "He's gone! Let it go! You have to let it go!" He held him tighter as his friend fought to get free, then settled as the pain of acceptance finally pierced him and grief flooded into his soul. "No!" he cried, breaking down in Jerry's arms, weeping together for several minutes.

Tony approached, putting his arms around them and trying to give comfort as best he could. The harsh realities of the situation still pressed the little band of men. They had a mission to complete and they were deep inside enemy territory fighting for their lives and they hadn't even met the enemy they had come to fight. Now they were down one of their key players. Time was very much against them and they had to move on.

Terry motioned for the warriors to remount and check the road ahead for any other Jabba or signs of flocks, then beckoned the other three to remount. After some reassurance and work to put their grief aside for now, the others got back onto their horses. Danny gave the ravine one last look, hoping somehow that Bryan would come crawling back up onto the road and they could get on with things, get the heck out of here and home. Finally, he turned and spurred his horse after the rest of the group.

Crosslake

Directly after their encounter with the Jabbaway, the band from Thulsa had to share the Torres road with long caravans of men and wooden machines of war moving in the opposite direction. The line was endless, stretching on for an hour of hard riding, before they came upon a crossroads where caravans took their turns taking to the main road. It was obvious to the group that this was the Kenlar and Omar armies marching on Thulsa.

The timing couldn't be any worse than it was right now. These armies could easily reach the walls of Thulsa by tomorrow and have their assault running at full force within hours of setting up positions and while Thulsa would be fully prepared for the upcoming assault, Brit's fight was scheduled the morning of the third day. Judging from the size of the armament pouring onto the road and towards Thulsa, there would be such a battle, the likes of which had never been seen before. Terry became a bit concerned as this processional of men and equipment would be passing within close proximity of Vespa Cull. Men and war machines were an unpredictable bunch, from any clan. There was no telling what they might have been ordered to do if given the opportunity to practice pillaging.

There was no worry for them, at least not yet. Terry had given them all a change of clothing and gear that resembled Kenlar fashion. Because of this, they were able to pass among all of the war caravans and warriors with little to no notice to themselves. Terry recognized all of them as being either Kenlar or Omar clansmen.   What was curious to him was the absence of any Gaylen clansman, a fact he pointed out to Tony, who was also a bit puzzled. The intelligence they had gotten was that the Kenlar and Omar clans were massing in the Kenlar regions, then meeting with the Gaylens on the plain where the Torres road emptied onto the plain of Thulsa. The spoils would be divided up among all the clans equally, including the lands of Thulsa. Their logic led them to believe there would have been at least a few garrisons or scouting parties mingled with the other clans here. Perhaps the Gaylens were having second thoughts?

They were impressed by what they were seeing the closer they got to Crosslake. They passed by several camps that were put together with specific purposes in mind. Some for making different hand weapons, others for making larger machines of war, all of them were heavily manned and turning out a surprising amount of product. If this is what they were seeing, just from the road, they were sure that there must be masses of warrior camps away from the road, off somewhere unseen.

Indeed, they were mobilizing in a big way to move down the road, headed in the direction of Thulsa. How in the world did the Kenlars manage to produce so much and with such efficiency? Both Tony and Terry knew that Ivan didn't have the mental intellect for this kind of logistic efficiency. To have gathered all of their manpower and assets in just this one place and combined them with the Omars was quite the feat in and of itself.

While impressed with their military buildup, that was indeed, quite massive, Tony couldn't help but wonder about command and control. You could have the biggest and baddest army on the planet, but if you couldn't get it to the fight or control it once it was there, it wasn't much good to you. He knew that Ivan of the Kenlars was street smart, but he had no gift for detailed strategy. He was always one for grand ideas, but liked to lead with brute force. It was always up to someone else to take care of the details.

Danny could smell the aroma of food and took special notice of the mess camps. These places were designed for feeding large groups. It takes a lot of food of all kinds to keep the human component of a war machine operating, and most warriors were not timid eaters. There was a good reason most warriors were large in stature. Part of it was breeding and part of it was lifestyle, but much of it was diet. These big men ate a lot, the Kenlars being mostly meat eaters, as it was the easiest form of food to harvest. The Omars were a bit more sophisticated, growing plants that expanded their diet. There must be something in the food itself that promoted such growth. Their size appeared to be universal among all the clans.

Danny looked carefully at the meat they were eating. He was hungry and the meager rations they had brought with them, wasn't doing his stomach much good. He hadn't noticed any livestock close by that might be used for such a purpose. He noticed at one of the camps, a butcher carving up a carcass. There was no mistaking what it was; freshly chopped wings dropping to the ground beside the table being used as a chopping block. The horrible sting of the loss of his friend came to mind as he watched the man chop up a Jabba, prepping it for cooking. A profound feeling of hatred for such an animal came to Danny's mind. If it hadn't been for this animal, Bryan would still be alive and riding alongside him and Jerry. He took a bit of satisfaction knowing that at least some of those filthy killing animals were getting what they deserved.

They were now crossing into new territory, making their way into Crosslake. Terry had no idea where the Kenlar spoil was from here. Crosslake was built on a high mountainous plateau area with alpine trees and some larger patches of Aspen looking trees strewn throughout. There were many cliffs and steeply rising mountains close by. A lake, for which the town was named, was a central geographical point of the area. It was feed by many mountain streams, but had only one river outlet flowing out of the city into a rocky abutment and cave, eventually falling a thousand feet from an opening in the cliff wall to join with a larger river far below. This river snaked through the more rugged parts of the Tera Mountain range, a natural barrier between Kenlar and Thulsa.

As the crow flies, Crosslake and Thulsa were not very far apart. It might take you only a couple of hours to walk it if you had a straight path, but the Tera trail through the Tera Mountain Range was steep, jagged and considered impassable for all except the most intrepid and most experienced travelers. The trail was treacherous and the region filled with hostile flocks of Jabbaway and Griffles. The Griffle, a bearlike animal, moved about on strong haunches, long stout forearms and articulating fingers on both hands and feet. They too, were veracious eaters, competing directly with the Jabbaway for food. Not a good combination for heavy travel.

Crosslake was not a complex city. Basic homes were built next to and on top of each other and from what the group could see, there was no real architecture at work here. It was nothing like the beauty of Thulsa. Both Danny and Jerry thought it looked something like mobile home parks squeezed so tightly together that there was no room for grass to grow. It might have more closely resembled the look of Pueblo Indian construction found in Arizona and New Mexico, or even that found in Egypt.

The lake in the center of the city was used for just about everything the clan folk needed. They really weren't too worried about pollution. That was for industrialized planets. Any refuse or pollution created here was channeled down the river and let flow out of Crosslake. Where it went from there, no one really cared, as long as it was not where they were. There were no obvious community buildings or a town square, no dedicated government buildings or places to hold public forums or gatherings for information or discussion. After some searching through the streets, it became apparent that this was more of a grouped housing complex than a city. Sort of like what you would find in a recreational area, except these people were actually living here, most of them anyway. It was big enough to be considered a city, but there just didn't seem to be any real infrastructure or services that could provide a better quality of life.

Continuing their search, they came upon a very large house, built into the side of a rocky hill near the river's exit from the city area. Terry kept the band moving as Tony gave it a careful look. Passing over a bridge crossing the river, they were able to look back towards the hill where the river disappeared into a cave. There was a path along the river and a couple of foot bridges downstream towards the hill. Continuing to ride, Tony leaned over to Terry in a casual manner.

It didn't appear that they were really being watched, but surely they had been noticed.

"I'd say it's a good bet that our buddy Ivan has the biggest house in Crosslake, wouldn't you say?"

"Are you kidding? I hear that in the side of a rock hill is all the rage these days," Terry sauntered back casually. "And I think it's a good bet that you would keep all your money in a cave right next to your own house."

"If this is Ivan's lair," Jerry piped, up hearing the conversation ahead of him, "shouldn't there be guards and warriors all over the place?" Tony and Terry stopped their mounts and looked back at the house.

"Oh, they are most certainly there, and I'm sure they've seen us," Tony said carefully. "The fact that we're not surrounded right now is a good thing. We might actually be able to pull this off."

"You don't seriously think we're going to be able to just walk into his spoil and check the book out like we're at the public library do you?" Danny piped in seriously. He had been rather whimsical and comedic up until this morning when they had lost Bryan, now his whole demeanor and attitude had shifted. He was filled with a lot of pain and anger, especially towards anything that had anything to do with this expedition. The fun was over for him and he wanted to get this business done, get the heck out of Argyle and never come back.

"Gonna need to speak with the librarian first," Tony responded carefully, trying to ignore Danny's issues. He knew his pain all too well. He had watched it happen repeatedly as good friends died. He could cite time after time when he knew he was sending men to their deaths and there was nothing to be done about it but accept it. They moved on for a bit until they reached what would have been termed a tavern, several hundred yards down the street, and dismounted. Terry was quick to purchase a couple of large mugs of ale and handed them to Jerry while he pulled his weapons off, grabbed a ragged blanket from his saddle and draped it over his head.

"Little early to be hitting the sauce isn't it?" Jerry asked, trying to figure out what the heck the lodge keeper was doing.

"A little recon my boy," he said, grabbing one of the mugs. Walking like he was quite drunk, he circled around the back side of the tavern reemerging in an open field next to the building and started back down the road towards Ivan's house. Jerry and Danny watched him as the others stepped inside. They were a little taken back at how intrepid this man of small stature was. His size certainly didn't match his boldness or prowess. Without really realizing what he was doing, Jerry took a sip of the ale from the mug Terry had left him. Neither of the Garrett boys drank; Danny and Jerry didn't either. He pulled a twisted grimace, suddenly realizing what he was doing and nearly spit it out, but a passerby kept him from drawing attention to himself or their group. He could only put on a happy face, raise the mug to them as they went by and hold the liquid in his mouth, trying not to spew it all over the place.

"What's wrong?" Danny asked straight faced, looking at his friend's odd expression.

Jerry's mouth and chin were dripping with ale, his cheeks puffed up like a Blowfish and his face appearing to change color. Ale tasted like what horse piss might taste, had either of them ever tasted it. It was a good description for an imagined flavor. Whatever the imagined taste, it was making him sick and he really needed to get it out of his mouth. Handing Danny the mug, he bent down near the hind end of one of the horses and let it go. At least this way, it looked authentic. The horse was likely going to pee right there anyway. With that taken care of, he quickly grabbed one of the animal skin flasks of water and started gulping it down in an effort to try and purge the taste from his mouth. Finally getting his color back, he turned to his friend who seemed quite disgusted with the whole event he had just had the pleasure of witnessing. Jerry had expected to get a good ribbing or at least a chuckle from his friend, but all he got was a hard stare, so he just grabbed the mug again and headed into the tavern to join Tony and the others.

Sitting with mugs in front of them, Jerry passed his to one of the warriors who swallowed it down quickly and ordered another. The barkeep gave Jerry and Danny a particularly odd look when Tony asked for a couple of cups of water for them. He spoke in the Kenlar language, which sounded every bit as weird as the Thulsa language, it sounding more like Scottish Gaelic than the Irish Gaelic of Thulsa. There was no sign of English being spoken here, so all communication would go through Tony and his men.

Jerry happily sipped on his mug of water, even though it was a little suspect as to where the water might have come from. He was sure that he had felt several floaters of some kind as he drank. It was probably dipped from the horse trough or a rain barrel.

Danny was not so interested in what was in front of him. The scene of Bryan and the Jabba falling was forever replaying in his mind. He kept running the scene over and over in his head, trying to figure out what could have been done differently that would have avoided the situation altogether, or trying figure out if there had been some way that Bryan could have survived the attack and the subsequent fall.

Tony had been keenly aware of Danny's condition from the time Bryan had fallen and knew what his young friend was going through, but up until now, there wasn't much, if anything, he could do to give comfort to the young man. This was a deeply personal thing for anyone and everyone dealt with grief and loss in infinitely different ways. Unfortunately for Danny, he had to get over it without the soothing compassion that would soften the pain or the scarring.

"Danny," Tony leaned in closely so he wouldn't be heard by anyone else in the tavern. Speaking a strange foreign language could be a really bad thing were anyone to overhear it. Spies were everywhere and suspicions ran high, but since they were away from the others in the room, keeping their voices low would be enough. "There was nothing anyone could do to save him."

"There's always something," Danny replied a bit despondent.

"You've had hours to figure it out," Tony came back, knowing all too well the whole process that an individual will take to place the blame. "What could have been done?" Danny only stared at his cup and picked at a spot on the table.

"I just can't believe he's gone," he finally choked, letting some of his pent up pain seep out.

"These things are never easy," Tony indicated, feeling his pain and trying to help. Danny could only see himself in the reflection of his drink. He could only feel himself suffering under the sting of the death of his friend. He could see and feel nothing else right now and he knew that no one had any idea of how he was feeling. No one could possibly know of his pain and he found Tony's platitudes and offerings of comfort, shallow and trivial. He could not even comprehend that the others were hurting as well; he could only see himself.

"What do you know about any of this?" he finally spoke up, in a bit of a trance. "That wasn't your friend that was killed. You can't possibly know what I'm going through. No one can," he finished, sinking further to the table in grief and depression.

"Hey, Danny, buddy," Jerry cut in quietly, trying to mitigate any real emotional outbursts that would draw attention to their group. "Bryan was my friend too. I was right there too. There was nothing either one of us could have done." Jerry was hurting to, who wouldn't be? He was just dealing with it in an entirely different way.

Tony was undeterred in his compassion for his new young friends, but he wasn't about to be brushed aside after all the years of death and pain he had endured. It would be good for Danny to get a little help out of the pity hole he was digging for himself and to know he had good friends here that cared for him and wanted to help however they could.

"I do know Danny, I do," Tony reaffirmed quietly. "I have seen it happen over and over again. Flying mission after mission over Germany and feeling The Amanda getting holed by flack bursts or machine gun fire. I'd be sitting in the pilot's seat wondering whether one of those hot pieces of metal was going to blow a hole through her skin and into me. I know what it's like to see your friends and crew get shot up by 80mm cannon fragments, getting their arms and legs blown off. I flew a mission with a B-17 crew where I had to land the airplane because a flack shell drove right up into the cockpit and

exploded. It blew both pilots to pieces." Tony held his hands in front
of Danny with them cupped together.

"I had to scoop their body parts out of the seat so I could sit down,
then wipe away all the blood and brains from the instruments and
windshield so I could see to fly. I've watched the life drain away from
some of my own gunners who were hit and I could do nothing about it.
By the time we got back on the ground, it was too late. I've watched
three sister ships take direct hits, right next to me and either go down
in flames or explode in mid-air. Here, I've seen great men die
standing right next to me, having taken an arrow to the chest or
fighting in hand to hand combat watching your comrades take a sword
jab through the neck or a mace to the head. There is NOTHING you
can tell me about death that I haven't seen or experienced. Believe
me when I say there wasn't anything that any of us could have done
for Bryan. I am truly sorry for what happened to him." Tony said
getting up and slipping outside the front door, still holding his drink.
He didn't want to say any more for fear of becoming indignant or loud.
None of them needed that right now.

Danny just stared down at the table trying to hold back his own
tears. He not only felt his own pain now, but also the images of death
that Tony had just painted came into sharp focus. While his friend's
demise was very real for him, what Tony had just described to him
started to put things into a little better perspective. He knew he had
to get over this or he might as well step up to Ivan's front door and
offer himself up.

He slowly turned and looked after Tony. He didn't know nearly as
much about this man as Britten or Bryan did. It had been their
business to know. He and Jerry were just along for the adventure and
it had certainly lived up to that so far. He still had only one real desire
and that was to get himself and his friends back home. Right now, he
was about as far away from home as he could get and the only way he
and Jerry were going to get back was to help Terry and Tony find that
book and get it back to Thulsa before the storm was gone. Hopefully
Terry would return soon with good news about Ivan's lair. They didn't
have long to wait.

Ten minutes later found the group reassembled at the table quietly
talking when a short drunken man came in with a blanket draped over
his head and an empty mug in his hand, singing something foul
sounding. He stumbled around the room waving the empty mug at
the barkeep and finally crashed into their table, plopping down and
dropping his head to the table top as if in a drunken stupor mumbling
and half unconscious. His head was practically in Danny's drink as he
turned an eye up to the bewildered young man.

Danny wasn't sure what to make of all this. He had dealt with
drunks before when he and Jerry would take people on excursions up
Darby Canyon to the Wind Caves, but he didn't think that one mug of

ale could produce these kinds of results. That must be some strong stuff. It certainly smelled like it anyway. Danny looked at him for a moment, almost disgusted that he was in such a state, and then Terry winked at him and smiled.

"Think we hit pay dirt," Terry whispered, as Tony leaned down to hear the report. "That's definitely Ivan's place, complete with internal and external Spoil entrances."

"He's got his own four car garage huh?" Jerry whispered, glad that they had found it.

"So how do we get in?" Danny asked, quietly scanning the room. It did not appear that Terry's drunken entrance had created much of a stir. "Are we just going to make a delivery or something?"

Tony looked up at the open back door beyond the bar keep's preparation table towards the back of the room. A wagon had just pulled up loaded with large kegs of ale and wines, the driver jumping down greeting the bar keep.

"That's a capital idea," he said, getting up slowly. "I think he and his men are probably quite thirsty." He motioned for a couple of his men to go out the front door and meet him around the back where the delivery had just taken place. Jerry looked down at Terry who didn't move, then up at Danny. What the heck were they supposed to do? Get up and walk out? They had no idea.

"Carry me out," a whispered voice from the table top rasped quietly. Danny looked back down at Terry who was cracking one eye. "Get me out of here, throw me up on my horse and head to the back of the building." Everyone finally got up while Danny and Jerry started to help him up, but the remaining warriors of Tony's stepped in and easily carried the smaller man out to the front of the tavern where their horses still waited. Terry was rather unceremoniously thrown up on his horse, more like a sack of potatoes rather than something human, but that was sort of the whole idea. He was supposed to appear completely soused and just thrown up for transport, and with that, they all mounted back up and carefully moved around to the back of building.

Upon their arrival, they found Tony and his other men, opening several of the barrels of ale and wine, dumping their contents onto the ground near the unconscious forms of the driver and the bar keep. Once they were all out of sight behind the building, Terry came alive again and helped with the operation.

Rearranging the load of barrels in the wagon, Tony and several of his men climbed inside the barrels and closed the lids. Terry hopped into the driver's seat and reined the horse team out from behind the building and down a side street to an alleyway that took them closer to the river and the cave. Before he could cross the river, he was stopped and searched then allowed to continue. Once the outer guard was satisfied that nothing was amiss, Terry coaxed the horse team across the fast moving river.

Danny, Jerry and the rest of the warriors watched silently, hidden in some trees close to the main road. There were several anxious minutes of waiting before they could see Tony wave at them to come over. Making their way across one of the foot bridges, they confronted the river crossing guard, quickly dispatching him and dumping the body in the river allowing the rest of the group access into the relative safety of the Spoil cave. At least here they were mostly out of plain view. From here, there were only a few different angles that they could be seen or attacked from.

The inside of the cave was lit by many torches that were kept burning all the time. These were not plumbed gas torches like the cavern The Amanda had been entombed in, but just oil soaked fabric wrapped sticks in holders on the walls wherever it was convenient to hang one.

Tony and his men had disposed of the inner guard's bodies in the same fashion his warriors had disposed of the outer river guardian. Their bodies would float downstream through the cave and make the long fall to the river far below.

The cave was rather unremarkable as caves go. It had a rocky floor with a crushed rock path winging its way deeper into the rocky hillside. It was more of a tunnel than a cave. The river ran through it and out a large opening in the side of the cliff behind Crosslake. It was very wide with tall ceilings throughout.

Making their way along the path, the group came upon several large chests, about five feet long with rounded tops. Making their way between them, they were confronted with a big stack of them situated in a large square formation. Indeed, if these were all filled with the same kind of treasure that Thulsa had in her Spoil, the Kenlars were far richer and had no need to try and plunder anyone else. Stepping carefully around the structure, they found that it was not just a stack of treasure chests, but a make shift house of some kind. There was a doorway on one side, covered with animal skins.

Tony motioned his warriors forward to investigate while he and Terry circled the structure for other openings. The wall of boxes seemed to be wedged tightly against the cavern wall, which helped to hold them firmly in place. Making a half circle around to the far side and seeing no other exits, they detected a scuffle and angry voices of objection from within. Terry and Tony stepped back around to the front of the make shift structure in time to see his men exiting the house holding a struggling man and woman.

Both looked remarkably well kept considering their living quarters. The woman was quite pretty with long blonde hair and a nice figure, even in the simple dress she was wearing. She angrily struggled against the large warriors who had a very firm grip on her. The man was about Tony's size and stature, having a lot of grey running through his well-kept hair. What in the world had they uncovered here in the Kenlar Spoil? Danny looked at them in a bit of a shock. So far, everyone they had come across on this planet was wearing stuff you would find in a Viking village, even Tony, Catrina and Terry. While their attire did still fit the description, how well they kept themselves didn't, especially considering they must be living here in the Spoil. The man was spitting mad, continuing to spout out expletives in Kenlar while struggling to gain his release.

Once Tony got a good look at him, a smile streaked across his face and he found a good place to sit down. Planting his sword in the rocks in front of him, he leaned his chin down on his hands and the hilt. He said something to the warriors holding the two tussling Kenlars and they were released. Somewhat indignant about the whole matter, the man saw to the woman's condition first and then turned to his captors to demand some kind of satisfaction. He started spouting Kenlar language towards the warriors first and then at Jerry. It all sounded like complete gibberish to him as he watched the man rant on at the speed that someone would rattle off Spanish back home. He paused slightly, seeing that neither Jerry nor Danny appeared to be in charge of whatever this intrusion was on their privacy. It wasn't until he turned; facing Tony and Terry, that the man suddenly stopped short and looked at the two of them for a moment, then started ranting again.

He continued to address the whole group, but then stopped again and turned back to Tony and Terry. There was a look of recognition on his face now, but he still wasn't so sure, not sure enough to acknowledge it in front of everyone. Terry swung his sword up onto the shoulders behind his head and let both his arms rest on the flat part of the blade, looking at the man with that, *"Come on, you know who I am,"* look. Tony still had a look of delight plastered all over his face.

"Come on Tim, you know it's me," he finally said with his chin still resting on his sword.

Tim Hansen blinked wide eyed several times, and then looked around at the others standing there, then back at Tony, then over at Terry.

"Yep," Terry said, smiling. "It's you're good buddy Terry."

Tim muttered something in Kenlar again, then stopped himself and rubbed his eyes.

"I think I've been in this cave too long," he muttered, and then looked back at Tony with a hard look. "Somehow, I always thought that Cat would be the one that came in here to break me out of this forsaken place."

Tony passed Terry a funny look and got up.

"We risk our necks to find you, bring you home, and you think my daughter was supposed to be the one to do it? Now I like that!"

"She is far better with the sword. I have no doubt that she could kick you know who's butt." Tim said, smiling as Tony stepped to him and gave him a big hug. "You have no idea how good it is to see you my friend."

Terry stepped over and took his turn giving welcomes and affection.

"It's so good to see you my friends," Tim repeated, giving them a good bear hug. He held onto Terry a little longer as his emotions for his friends began to bubble up. He had been here in Crosslake, cut off and isolated from the rest of this world and his friends for so long.

This was not what he had planned on when they had all gone their separate ways so long ago, looking to make their own lives on this planet. He had become a virtual prisoner here in Crosslake. Searching and searching for a way out and having tried many times to escape the control of Ivan Rubella, leader of the Kenlar clan. It was because he knew the contents of the Signet that Ivan kept him here close, right where he could find him at all times.   In most ways, that meant manipulation of those close to him, mostly at the expense of Tim's beloved wife, Kawti. She had been made to endure unspeakable punishments for their attempts at escape. Several times, whole families had been butchered on Ivan's order because they had harbored or helped Tim and Kawti in their attempts at freedom. Many of these butchering's had been carried out by Ivan personally. All of these horrific atrocities being committed while Tim and Kawti were forced to watch. Husbands, fathers, wives, mothers, children, brothers and sisters butchered right before their eyes. Now, perhaps, there was a glimmer of hope. Tony and Terry were standing right here and they had men with them. Wait a second! Reality suddenly slapped Tim in the face and he stepped back looking at everyone.

"You're here and you have no army with you?"

"Nope," Tony replied quickly.

"Then you're on a covert operation of some kind." The woman with Tim started muttering something in Kenlar that stopped him from going any further. The waist gunner turned and jumped up onto a large rock, looking up the cave to the entrance, then motioning everyone into the box structure.

"Where did the guards go? There were guards there at the mouth weren't there?" he inquired, almost in a panic.

"We took care of them toot sweet," Terry boasted, a matter a factly.

"Uhuh," Tim responded, very worried now. "That will look all wrong." He counted warrior heads quickly, stopping at Danny and Jerry and sizing them up. They obviously didn't fit the warrior profile. "You must be mental muscle or something." He turned back to his

Captain. "You'll need to set your guards in place of the ones you killed." He paused a moment looking around. "You did kill them didn't you?" Tony had a look of dismay blast across his face.

"Oh, they're dead all right. We let them have a ride down the river," he said, gesturing to the river and the direction it was flowing.

"Right," Tim responded quickly. "Get them replaced and we'll talk."

Tony motioned for his warriors to replace the positions they had taken out at the mouth of the cave and the river crossing while Tim talked with the woman. They jabbered back and forth for several minutes, and then she turned and headed towards the front part of the cave, while the rest went inside.

All things considered

The structure was deceivingly spacious inside. More of a façade than structure, it became apparent that the dwelling went back into another smaller cavern which provided quite a bit of spacious living for its occupants. Furniture of all kinds, some of it rivaling even modern day Earth standards, were situated neatly all around the interior. The floor was even covered in thickly woven rugs. The décor was actually quite nice, for being in a cave. There was a stone fireplace constructed of wonderful large river stones that had been carefully carved and fitted together to form tight joints and the chimney of mortared stone cleverly drafted the smoke up and out of the dwelling. Tim beckoned them to make themselves comfortable and the group was happy to have a seat in seemingly comfortable accommodations.

"Can I get you guys something?" Tim asked, pouring him a cup of wine from a jug on a small table situated against the cave wall. Everyone refused graciously. It occurred to Tim then that they refused because of the nature of their business here.

"Tim, who's the girl?" Terry asked. Tim looked over at the navigator/bombardier and held up his left hand. He was sporting a silver wedding band.

"My wife, Kawti Moft. I met her shortly after I got here. Seemed like a good reason to stick around. Things were good until Ivan showed up. No matter," he said, still reeling from the overwhelming relief that he was finally going to get out of this place. "Oh, yeah, well, some things never change," he said, downing the entire cup, then sat down and looked across at the two young men that looked out of place.

"Tim, where's Ivan?" Tony asked, feeling very uncomfortable knowing they were in such close proximity to his place of residence.

"Nah," Tim scoffed. "Don't worry about him. He's off to the training camps with Broc of the Omars setting up the last of their battle plans. He left Falcon in charge here and he's more interested in having sex with as many women as he can, than worrying about what's happening down here. Just relax, you're safe while you're in here."

"So why don't you just leave then?" Terry asked. Tim looked like he lived in good conditions here.

"I've tried many times, but Ivan is paranoid and has spies and people watching the entrance all the time. He doesn't want to let me out of his sight for very long. I'm how he gets his knowledge fix. Can't get it on his own, so he gets it from me."

"So you're providing him with superior knowledge and intel?" Terry asked, in a bit of an accusatory tone.

"Knowledge, yes, superior? I wouldn't go that far, and Intel? Please! What do you think I am? Yes, I know just about everything going on in most of the regions because the Jabbaway are my eyes and ears, but I'm not about to let Ivan know about any of that. Gotta say, I'm a little insulted here, but your assumptions are understandable so I guess I can't get too mad. No, I give only enough to satisfy his simple mind. I mean, you rode through Crosslake. Look around you here; do you see a Thulsa or a Mandell here? Do you see any of the technology that Thulsa has? I could have shown them everything you guys helped create in Thulsa and much more, but he doesn't have the intellect or good sense to use it wisely for the good of the people here. He only wants what he can see and what he thinks he can get his hands on. The guy has nothing! This is the Kenlar spoil for heck sakes and there's nothing here. He's flat broke," Tim gestured to the boxes that made up the facade of the front of his house. "There's nothing in any of these boxes. It's all gone. He's spent every last dime he has. The Kenlar economy is in ruin. He has to take Thulsa or everything here falls apart. Quite frankly, I'm surprised he's been patient long enough to build up his armies. He's like a spoiled child who wants everything when he wants it."

"So what's his plan for Thulsa?" Tony asked, settling down in a chair.

"You saw all the gear he has moving down through the Torres. He plans on taking the city from the east Thulsa plains by breaching the outer walls and overwhelming Thulsa's defenses. He certainly has more than enough manpower to do it, but the guy has no eye for strategy. He wants to ram against everything with full strength. I've tried to explain it to him, but he only wants to hear what he wants to hear. Says I have no idea about war."

"He has the Omars and the Gaylens with him, doesn't he? Are they all right here or moving down the Torres?" Tony came back.

"He has the Omars with him, but Broc is every bit as much a knothead as Ivan is. He tried to convince the Gaylens to join them. He had Condor eating out of his hand, but an internal coup got him beheaded and now Thulsa has an ace in the hole with the Gaylens."

"How so?"

"Their leader," Tim chuckled softly. He looked at both Tony and Terry. "It's Tom! Tom leads the Gaylens now! He reorganized Condor's military right out from under him and took him out. He's not about to join up with idiot Ivan. In fact, Ivan doesn't know it, but Tom has mobilized his armies to meet Ivan and Broc on the northern flank of the Thulsa plain when they arrive to make their attack. Even with that, it's going to be one heck of a fight for Thulsa to defend herself against a direct attack from Ivan and Broc, even with the Gaylens on her side."

"How did you come by all this information if you've never been able to get out of here?" Terry asked, not able to figure out his spy network, which was obviously quite extensive.

"Oh, don't worry about that," Tim boasted confidently. "I have the finest spies on this planet and plenty of them. I don't have to go anywhere to know what's going on around this whole area. So who are the new recruits?" He asked, finally getting to the two he didn't recognize. Tony drew in a deep breath and hedged at Terry who sat back a little further in his chair.

"This is Danny Niker and Jerry Gunn." He said, carefully letting his lungs exhale.

"Please to meet you gentlemen," Tim said, stepping over to them and shaking their hands. He greeted them rather oddly, as if already knowing where they had come from. "And what brings you men on a deep dark adventure into regions of the Kenlar with these two knuckleheads?" Jerry started to say something, but Tony spoke up first.

"They're from Earth Tim. They came through the Storm."

Tim froze, not wanting to believe what he had already suspected. A look of disbelief streaked across his face, while he tried to work everything out like it was some kind of a math problem. He passed a glance over at Terry, looked Jerry and Danny over real good, then back at Tony. His face was expressionless. It was as if he hadn't even heard what had been said.

After a couple of long, silent moments, he stepped over to a closed armoire on the other side of the room. Pulling a key from a chain that hung from his neck, he unlocked the double doors and carefully opened them. Inside, propped more for display than storage, was a large aluminum shaded book. It had several scuff marks on it and upon closer examination, had intricate scroll work and symbols much like the ones that Catrina and Britten had found on the sword altar. Danny and Jerry could see a clasp that held the book closed as Tim carefully removed it from its resting place and stepped back over to his own chair.

"No doubt you are here for this then," he said, setting both hands on the book in his lap. "So many things have I waited for since I was made a prisoner here. I never imagined that they would come all at once and all right in this time frame." He looked at the two younger men for a moment. "What era have you come from?" Danny and Jerry looked a little confused. "What time frame did you come from?" Tim repeated.

"Early 21st century," Danny spoke up.

"Ah, no doubt much has changed of the world since we've been gone," Tim said quietly, thinking back to when life was more real than it had become now, in this place, in this time. 21st century Earth would be something wonderful to behold. Many times over the years, he and Kawti had talked about what he remembered of his life back on Earth and how wonderful it had been back then, even with a world at war. She too, had become every bit as excited to see it and experience it as he had described it. She would be riveted to his every word about its description and the many wonderful things that were there. She longed to see it, to leave this place and go back to Earth with him, to be together in such a wonderful place. Even though it had changed, he was sure that it was for the better. He looked back over at his two friends for a bit.

"Tell me how this all happened, everything. Don't leave anything out. The slightest detail could be important." Tony gestured to Danny and Jerry and they proceeded to tell it as best they could. There was some detail missing because they weren't in the places that Britten and Bryan had been. Once they reached the Winner Spoil, Tony sort of took over and relayed the story of Brit pulling the Twins. Tim seemed to be extra interested in this part and asked many questions that seemed silly to everyone else.

Their story starting to wind down a bit, Danny and Jerry relayed the story of talking to The Amanda and the story she had told all four of them. Tony, Terry and Tim were riveted to their every word about her. Somehow, Tony and Terry had missed this part of it when Bryan had given his version last night at Vespa Cull. All three airmen became a bit misty eyed, coming to the realization that The Amanda did indeed have a soul and that she had loved them every bit as much as they had come to revere her. Every pilot and crew somehow comes to a knowledge of their airplanes own consciousness and their own mortality, struggling for life together.

Danny finally came to the part in their story where they lost Bryan several hours ago. Tim sat forward anxiously as the young man told his version, and then Jerry took his turn. Tim then turned to his two friends for their versions of what had happened.

"Described the Jabba to me," he said as they finished their description of the events on the Torres road.

"What do you mean, describe it?" Tony asked, a little surprised. "Lots of hair, teeth, claws, wings and a bunch of stink. What else is there to describe?

"Color?" Tim asked anxiously. "Color, what color was he?" Tony looked over at Terry who thought for a moment.

"It was much larger than the others, flew right past me," Terry finally said. "I remember it was lighter in color, almost silver, especially on its back."

"Skunk stripes down its back?"

"Yes, come to think of it. Yes, it did have a double stripe down its back, just like a skunk," Terry confirming, coming a little more alive with the description.

"The filthy thing had a patch of black fur around its left eye as well," Danny announced disdainfully.

"Jocko," Tim stated coolly, standing up and giving a short whistle towards the door.

"What about the book?" Tony asked, looking at Tim who held onto it tightly. A moment later Kawti reentered the room.

"Call Digi in here, quickly." Kawti looked at him for a moment then at the others in the room.

"But Tobor might hear the call as well," she objected in a low voice.

"We'll have to risk it, off you go, hurry."

With that, she exited the house and turned for the cliff side of the cave. Tim turned back to his friends and sat down.

"Tim," Tony repeated, tugging at his attention. "The book, what about the book?" Tim leaned forward in his chair, making sure he had everyone's attention.

"Everything that you have ever heard about this book and the knowledge contained within is all true. I figured out the language long ago and was able to translate everything in these pages. Aside from a few very close, trusted friends, it has all been committed to memory."

"How did you figure it out, let alone memorize an entire book?" Jerry asked, looking at the size of it.

"I have had plenty of time on my hands," Tim admitted with a smile. He did have lots of time as he and Kawti remained in this place with not much else to do.

"Even mid-20th century radio training provides you with skills, and before I took my turn as an airman, I took some linguist training."

"There's so much information of monumental proportions in this book. Much of it, I can't even begin to tell you what it is. This book has knowledge that spans the known universe and makes the fact that there's a portal to another place in the universe seem like little fish. More to the point here though, it tells how to use the altar and the Twins to control time and space through that portal.

"I don't understand about the whole storm and the three days thing. Does the book say anything about that?" Tony asked.

"Certainly, but it would take a day or so to explain it all to you."

"So just give us the kindergarten version for the slow class," Terry said with a smirk. Tim chuckled. He was just delighted to have new pupils to teach all this information he had running around in his head.

"The storm is only a storm. There's nothing great, grand or glorious about it. It's just an intense electromagnetic weather phenomenon spun up to super strength by way of a temporal rift."

"What's a temporal rift?" Jerry asked.

Tim thought a moment then reached over and picked up the cup he had just drank from. He held it up and looked it over.

"This isn't perfectly cylindrical, but it'll have to do. Think of it as this perfectly round spinning tube. It's sort of a spinning distortion in the fabric of space and time. It's a byproduct of creation, much like asteroids and comets. This rift moves around the galaxy in a set path or pattern. It always has, and it always will. What is not exactly predictable is how long it will take to complete its pattern."

"Wait," Danny interrupted. "You're telling us that this cup shape moves all around the galaxy always landing in the same place, but you don't know when it will land? How the freak does that work?"

"The cup represents the cylindrical shaped rift. Sort of looks like it actually, just in miniature."

"Whatever," Danny shot back. He still wasn't in the mood for much of anything.

"This rift has always been in the galaxy. It has always traveled the same path. Long after you and I are gone, it will travel, but it makes stops in various places around the universe and the movement of solar systems and celestial bodies creates it's time variable. In our case, Earth and Argyle are places on its path.   They just happen to occupy similar positions on opposite sides of the universe and are therefore connected in a way. It's too complicated to help you understand exactly how. You're just going to have to take some things on a little faith here. For Earth, this rift's trajectory passes across the mountain top where we crashed and conversely, it passes along a similar type valley beyond the stone wall of the Thulsa Spoil. Normally, it would just whip up a storm and pass right by and continue on its merry way."

"But?" Tony asked, waiting for the answer that none of them really understood, none of them but Tim.

"You have to understand that ALL things are living and therefore they all have a life force. Rocks, trees, water, metal, animals, humans, we all have a life force. The elements that make up the metal and fabric of The Amanda, all have energy right down to the subatomic level. It's those subatomic particles that reacted with the rift, transferring a portion of its energy, to those particles and creating a higher form of consciousness.   Upper forms of life have a consciousness, but when we flew The Amanda through the storm, she reacted with the electromagnetic characteristics in the storm and it produced alpha energy, effectively bringing her to a state of pseudo consciousness. It's a little more complicated than that, but you get the general idea.   You boys got to experience her first hand," he said, gesturing towards Jerry and Danny.

"So why does the storm stop over the valley for three days and then fizzle out?"

"It's actually three and a half days in earth time, that's the time variable," Tim explained, getting even more excited. "There are places all over the galaxy where this thing has either passed through something that it has reacted with or vice versa, a metal alloy on another planet or moon or some debris floating in space or whatever. In the case of Earth, it was The Amanda. The Rift never stopped here before; it just passed through. However, with The Amanda stuck in the valley outside the Thulsa Spoil, it stops there every time it passes because it's attracted to her energy and attempts to regain what it lost when she flew through it. It fizzles after three and a half days because in order for it to maintain its own consciousness, it must remain on the move."

"Wait," Danny stopped the top turret gunner. "You're trying to tell us that thing has a mind? A soul? That storm, is alive?"

"Exactly!" Tim was almost bursting with excitement about the implications. "But, to stay alive it must pull energy from many different sources throughout the galaxy. Other suns, Nova, dwarf stars, nebula, comets, cosmic storms in space, stuff like that. The fizzling out is just the rift moving along its path again and the storm is left behind. Without the Rift, the storm is nothing. So here's the really neat thing about this guy," Tim said, sitting forward looking at his cup.

"It doesn't make any difference which planet it's passing through, Earth or Argyle; you can enter its flux vortex from any location, above or beneath. Kind of hard to do above because of the physical heights involved, but you could. The whole interior of the rift becomes a flux field during the time the storm is there and while we can exist in the flux field of two worlds, it's two places trying to exist in the same place at the same time. When this thing leaves, it leaves behind a sort of vortex reflection that can remain in place for hours, the Signet really doesn't specify." Tim became almost hypnotic at this point and it was obvious that he had everything all figured out and running exponentially in his mind even as he spoke.

"Light passes for a time, but matter cannot. It would be like looking through a window at another place. You could see it, but you couldn't touch it. It would be almost transparent. Sort of like the residual heat of a fire. The fire goes out, but the heat distortion is still there until it can dissipate. The longer and the hotter the fire, the longer it should take to dissipate. The Ancients put the altar there as a means for controlling the portal that the rift creates."

"The Ancients?" Danny piped up, just as engrossed in Tim's dissertation on the whole Storm subject as everyone else was.

"A race of travelers that came here long ago. Ages before the clans developed. They traveled the galaxy on a mission of discovery, seeking to find and see all the mysteries of existence. They had tracked this Rift from one side of the galaxy to the other."

"So where are they now?" Jerry asked. "What happened to them?"

"They left," Tim stated plainly. "There's nothing in this book that indicates why they left or where they went, nothing."

"So the altar," Tony inquired, very interested in its workings. "What can and can't it control?"

"My understanding is that it cannot control the rift's trajectory or hold it in place, it can only control the time frame of the portal and where the portal opens to. I got the distinct impression that there's still a lot about the Rift that the Ancients didn't include in the Signet." Tim said, opening the book up and thumbing through its pages. He looked back and forth a couple of times until he found the right illustration and then turned the book pages so everyone could see. It was a diagram of the Altar's top surface, its control surfaces and instrument orifices. The diagram showed how you would insert the Twin blades into the slots on the altar and move them in such a way as to control its function.

"The Twins are the key to making this thing work and controlling the Rift's characteristics. They power the altar, providing the means to make coarse adjustments to the Rift. So you would use both the Twins to activate the altar, then using one to shift where you want to go and then the other sword to shift what time in that world you would want to go to, otherwise, the portal and it's time event remains constant to the last place and time it was set to."

"Wait a second," Terry was a little confused. "Shift the portal to another place? I thought you said that it was a portal between Argyle and Earth. You're talking about shifting that portal door to another place aren't you? Doesn't the Rift have to settle in a common place in the galaxy for the door to open to anywhere?"

"Not at all," Tim replied patiently, shaking his head with a smile. "Without the altar activated, the portal exists in the Rift between Argyle and Earth on its own because that's the last place they were activated to. With the altar activated, now it can control the Rift's portal and bend it in any direction you care to go and conversely, any time within that portal."

Tony got a very odd look that didn't go unnoticed by Tim, who paused a moment. He could tell that Captain Dallas had some wheels turning madly in his head just by the expression on his face, so he remained silent a while longer to let him try and work it out.

"You're telling me that we can use the Twin swords to take us back in time?" Tony finally asked, not really believing the conclusions he was coming up with. It couldn't possibly be this simple or this real!

"Anywhere, to any time," Tim said, knowing where Tony was going with his thinking. The Thulsa Captain looked over at Danny and Jerry, then back at Tim, who had a bit of a smile forming across his face.

"Keep in mind here that right now, without the altar activated, the portal or doorway remains the same. Where the storm is here, it is on Earth as well. You will emerge at the edge of the valley that we crashed in, but at whatever time frame you set the altar to." A grand expression of hope suddenly streaked across Tony's face as all the pieces suddenly dropped into place and the thoughts of his beloved Amanda came into sharp focus. Was it really possible that he could get back and still live a wonderful life with her? He had held himself for her after all this time. He almost couldn't believe that it was even possible.

"I know what you're thinking Tony," Tim remarked carefully. "Please understand that time travel is not for the faint of heart or the idiot. I can't stress this enough so let me make it crystal clear," he said, becoming steely serious. "There is a terrible risk inherent in manipulating history if you step back in time. The only thing Earth knows is that we crashed in the Teton Mountains back in 1945 and were lost. If you were to reappear anytime in their past now, you could risk interrupting the timeline that led these guys here. Any interruption to that timeline would create a spacial paradox that could either blow the universe apart or at the very least, change history and we could cease to exist instantaneously. You must think things all the way through or carefully limit your exposure to history so as to not affect it. You wouldn't be free of this limitation until you caught up with the time line our friends here came from." This subject required a much deeper explanation, but there just wasn't time for it. They were all pushing their luck here as it was.

"I know how you feel here Tony and normally I wouldn't even suggest it. Kawti and I have been waiting for this opportunity and are content to go back to Earth with your young friends here. You are the one that has the most to gain and we have the most to lose if something goes wrong should you do this. You must carry the responsibility for that decision."

"You're saying I couldn't interact with anyone?" Tony asked, just starting to grab the just of all the ramifications of going back in time.

"You would have to avoid all contact with everyone and everything just to get yourself home to Montana. You could ask no one for help or affect anything to get there. Once you reached Amanda, you would have to remain hidden with her and never interact with anyone without fear of altering the timeline."

"Wouldn't I be altering the timeline with Amanda?"

"Not exactly," Tim responded. "We have a limited historical account of her timeline from Danny and Jerry. I suspect that their friend Brit could add a bit more perspective to it because he interviewed her before he came here. Only after these boys cross over into this world would you be free of your limitations."

Tony thought deeply for a long moment. In his mind, the risk was worth the possible outcome. He would do anything to get back to his beloved Amanda. Even if that meant a life with her, cut off from the rest of the world, it was worth the risk to him. Time and distance couldn't keep them apart nor cause their love to fade. He knew he had to do whatever it took to get back to her.

"I understand," he finally stated resolutely. Tim gazed at his friend and former Captain for a long moment. He and Terry had an idea of what he was going through. Both had found love and a companion here on Argyle. They could not help but remember the relationship that Tony and Amanda had from the instant they had come together. Something like it only comes along once in a very great while. While they truly loved their respective wives, each could only hope that they could have the magic that Tony and Amanda had once shared and still did, even a galaxy apart.

Just then, Tim was interrupted by Kawti, who jabbered something from the front door, then stepped to one side as a creature entered the room. Tony and Terry were instantly to their feet with their swords drawn. Danny became enraged and pulled his long dagger as a Newfoundland sized Jabbaway swanked into the room, its wings folded tightly against its upper body and breathing heavily. It showed no fear of the drawn blades pointed at it or the angry faces behind them. Jerry instinctively held Danny back.

This was an awesome display of the armament of the Jabbaway, up close and personal. It had incisor hooks on its forewings, about where a bat would have its claws. Its front and hind paws were set with two rows of razor sharp hook claws that could extend and retract. Its head and body did indeed look like a large wolverine, but this one was even bigger. It sneered a little at Danny who was still trying to pry himself free from Jerry. As it did so, you could see large rows of shark like teeth. These weren't yellow and dank looking either. Maybe the Jabba brush their teeth after they eat, because this one's were gleaming white against a bright red gum line. Its brown and grey fur shimmered as it moved across the floor towards Tim.

This animal was well aware of the feelings between humans and the Jabbaway. Long had the humans hunted the Jabba. What it boiled down to was killing from fear. Both feared the other, the human more so because of the look and the actions of the Jabba. The Jabba fought to defend itself and because it did not understand the human fear. Now, there was something different going on in this room. This Jabba did not fear these humans, least of all Tim. Terry and Tony reaffirmed the grip on their swords, holding them at the ready as the animal stopped, sitting back on its haunches. To everyone's complete surprise, except for Tim, the Jabba spoke plainly.

"I came as quickly as I dared my friend. How may I serve?"

Danny instantly stopped struggling; Jerry dropping his arms in shock. You would think that after everything that they had experienced in these last two days that they wouldn't be surprised by anything now. Nevertheless, here it was, plain as day, a big wolverine with wings, sitting in front of them speaking proper English and in a very pleasant voice to boot. Tony and Terry were equally flabbergasted and slowly lowered their swords. The Jabba glanced at the two of them, raising an eyebrow.

"Gentlemen," Tim said smugly. "I'd like to introduce you to my good friend Digi," he continued, gesturing towards the animal. Digi looked at Tony and Terry as they lowered their swords and moved them towards their sheaths. He turned his head towards Jerry, who bowed slightly, not sure just how you were supposed to greet a Jabbaway, a tame one anyway. The Jabba then turned and faced Danny, who still held his long dagger up in front of him.

"Digi, I suspect you know Tony and Terry from the descriptions I have given over the years."

"Yes," the Jabba said quietly, turning his head back towards them to nod. He turned back to Danny and kept his eyes right on the angry young man.

"These other two are Jerry and Danny," Tim gestured towards the two younger men, but Digi was still facing Danny. "The one still holding onto the knife like an idiot is Danny and he better put it down before he gets himself into trouble." Tim hoped that Danny would get the idea and lower the weapon, but he remained unmoved, battling something from within. Danny wanted revenge. All he could see was his friend Bryan falling to his death from the Jabba attack. This was one of the filthy beasts almost offering himself up to him to atone for the senseless killing.

"Because he has no chance of getting out of it if he starts it," Tim asserted. "So, if he knows what's good for him, he'll put the knife away." Tim put most of the emphasis on the last part of his purposely elongated sentence. He was trying to get Danny's attention without coming right out and yelling at him point blank. The situation required defusing immediately.   A tame Jabba was still just as deadly as a wild one. Digi stepped over to Danny, his eyes growing large as the animal approached. While hate burned in his eyes and revenge boiled within his heart, he was suddenly scared to death to try and act on such feelings.

"Did your mother not instruct you about the rudeness of pointing at people?" Digi remained quite calm and well mannered.

"You aren't people," Danny finally said nervously.

"Very true," Digi agreed. "But I sure sound like one, don't I?" The Jabba asked with a grin. This isn't exactly what Danny had expected from a Jabba and the tone of Digi's voice and mannerisms disarmed him enough that he backed down, lowering his weapon and nodding. Digi turned back to Tim.

"You might have told them before you brought me in here," he said, sitting back down.

"Sorry ol' man," Tim apologized. "No time. Barely have any as it is. My friends were attacked on the Torres road this morning during a flocking. Have you heard anything about it?"

"Well, the way they are dressed, it's no wonder," Digi said, gesturing to Terry and Tony.

"What's wrong with what we're wearing?" Terry objected. He had picked these clothes out for everyone on purpose. They needed to blend in with the Kenlars to get here.

"You look like a band of Kenlars, but you smell entirely different. Something very strange about your smell," he said, motioning in the direction of Danny and Jerry. Normally, the two would be pointing at the other and saying it was him, but Danny was still quite frazzled. "You're lucky any of you survived the attack at all," Digi countered carefully. Terry opened his mouth to object, but the ensuing argument wasn't worth the time it would waste.

"Yes, I have heard about it," Digi came back finally.

"Ah, news travels fast with the Jabbaway," Tim responded delighted.

"A band of Kenlars on the Torres road, I can only assume that it was you," Digi said, looking around at everyone. "Riding fast from the Thulsa frontier, came through the Binion flock. A fight ensued-."

"You started it!" Danny came to life angrily.

"Steady young Niker," Tim interjected. "The Binion flock has been hit very hard by the Kenlar and Omar clans. They have standing orders to kill as many Jabba as they can. Ivan and Broc are using them as meat factories to feed their armies because he's decimated most of the other livestock. The Jabba are understandably a little irritated and on edge."

"But we aren't Kenlar or Omar!" Danny shot back, letting his anger get him all riled up again. "We aren't even from Thulsa! We're from Earth!" he started throttling up. "All we want to do is get this book and get back home. We didn't ask for any of this. Bryan didn't ask to get himself killed!" Jerry tried to calm his still grieving friend, but Danny remained undeterred. He could only see what Terry had told them earlier when they had left Vespa Cull. The only good Jabba was a dead one.

"Jocko of the Binions joined the attack, but was caught off guard by an entangler and landed on one of the warriors. The two fell from the road and into the Basks ravine. They were both caught by the flock, but their condition is unknown. The flock was headed back out of the Torres to the east plain of Thulsa. I have not heard of their actual whereabouts as of yet, but I will depart immediately to find out." Digi started for the door and Tim took his place in the center of the room.

Ivan Rubella

"Now for the escape plan," Tim said, excitedly hanging onto the book. "Are your horses still secured?"

"Yes," Tony responded, feeling a little nervous all of a sudden. "What do we need to get going?"

Just then there was a loud ruckus outside, the sounds of vicious growling, yelling and men fighting. Everyone was instantly to their feet as several large warriors came charging into the dwelling with swords drawn. There was no time for anyone to draw their weapons again as the room was full of big men and steel in an instant. Tim quickly stepped back to his chair and dropped the book behind him, kicking it under the chair. From any angle, it was hidden from view now. He knew these men very well but hadn't counted on them being here so soon. They were supposed to be at the training camps with Ivan. Then a slightly smaller warrior lumbered into the dwelling and looked around menacingly.

"Talon Thalar," Tim sighed, frustrated at the sight of Ivan's right hand man. This brawny man sported dual swords strapped about his hips like a gun slinger would wear his weapons for a gun fight. He sported two daggers slung over his shoulders in much the same fashion. His garb was quite a bit flashier than the warriors that had preceded him. His pants and shirt were of the same fashion, but made of a brighter and more colorful material. His helmet had no horns on it like many of the others, but was a sleeker design coming down tightly around the back of his head and forward, just covering the ears. Forward was a metal brim shaped much like a baseball player would wear while at bat. He was clean shaven with the exception of a dark goatee and short mustache. His hair was cut much shorter than the other men and was almost jet black. His eyes were quite stark and wolf like. Stepping into the middle of the room, he pulled a chair with him, bidding Tim and his group to sit.

"Mr. Hansen," he finally said, sitting down. "You're in a bit of a situation here."

"How so?" Tim asked, knowing full well that he was forbidden from having any visitors without one of Ivan's escorts with them at all times.

"Ivan isn't going to be very happy at all," Talon said, shaking his head.

"Ivan is never very happy unless he's raping and pillaging," Tim shot back angrily.

"What else is there to life that's worth while?" Talon chuckled. It
was obvious to everyone in the room that this man had something
more about him that set him apart from the other warriors. While he
was a bit gruff, he had an air of arrogance about him. Not brash like
Ivan, but he held it somewhere underneath.

"I can rattle off a whole list," Tim countered back.

"Blah, blah, blah. Yes Mr. Hansen. Preach your crap of goodness
and hard work to those peasants who would serve instead of rule."

Talon had higher aspirations than just being a right hand man to
Ivan. He was just biding his time, waiting for his chance to take
command. He knew that sooner or later, Ivan would make a mistake
somewhere and get himself killed. Talon had only to stay out of the
way, do Ivan's dirty work for a while and wait for his moment to step
in. From his point of view, why not enjoy his rise as much as possible.
He had no problem with killing. In fact, he loved it, but he did not
have the ardent lust for it like Ivan and his other warriors did, rather
he loved, "The Kill". He had mastered the art of fighting and relished
the hunt for the kill. He went to great pains to evaluate his quarry,
find their weakness and exploit it, then use his superior fighting and
killing skills to claim his victories, and he had many.

He loved to explore the different ways he could take a life. Slow
and painful, or quick and silent, using whatever manner he could
devise. He did hold himself to a kind of standard though, he refused
to assist in the senseless slaughter of innocent women and children,
something Ivan and Broc had no trouble with, and he had gotten into
trouble many times for his refusal to do so.   There was no challenge
or sport in it. It was something that anyone could do. He relished
only the difficult and loved to hone his skill at inspection, dissection
and finally disposal. Ivan kept him as his second because he had a
good mind for strategy, so he let Talon deal with the details of waging
a war and he and Broc would deal with most of the killing.

"My time will come and then all of you will be under my boot," he
informed them in a rather casual manner, leaning back and removing
his helmet.   Tony looked over at Terry who rolled his eyes and looked
the other direction to hide the amused look on his face.

"You don't believe me Captain Dallas?" Talon asked, reading the
looks on their faces.

"Truly it doesn't matter what any of us believe right now," Tony
responded, holding onto the grip of his sheathed sword. Talon held up
a finger and froze, listening to what was happening outside.

"Ah, sounds like we're about ready for the big man himself." He
then leaned forward to the three in front of him. "Good luck with this
one," he said with a grin, got up, then turned and left the room along
with several warriors, the noise outside beginning to escalate. They
recognized the growling and hissing sounds the Jabba had made on
the Torres road when they were attacked earlier. Tony looked over at

Terry trying to figure out what was going on. Was Digi fighting with more of these men? Tim knew and slowly sat back motioning for the others to do the same.

Settling back in their chairs, the outer door opened again and another large warrior stepped inside. He was covered with a lot of reddish colored facial hair that merged with his head hair. Most of it was quite unkempt and ratted. Didn't this guy believe in grooming? He lumbered into the room looking around at the occupants, and then sat down in the chair with a bit of a clamor. He was wearing a sword, but it seemed somewhat small for a man of his stature. Tony noticed fresh blood on the hilt and spatter on his arms and hands. Ivan eyed the five of them, leaning his elbow down on one knee and twirling his beard with one of his fingers. He looked straight at Tony and carefully leaned back to relax. He certainly had the air of total confidence in his command of the situation.

"Ah, my good friend Captain Dallas," he finally said in a deep Scottish sounding voice. There were, of course, no Scotsman here, but it was obvious that he had been taught English and this was his Kenlar accent. "How wonderful to see you once again."

There was a lot of sarcasm in his voice that everyone found to be quite irritating. He leaned hard to one side and forced a very long, loud fart, then let out a loud sigh of relief in a rather crude manner. Danny and Jerry looked at each other surprised. Had the circumstances been a little different and they weren't both under a huge amount of stress, they might have busted up laughing, as bathroom humor was their specialty. It didn't take long for the stench to permeate the whole room and Jerry worried that any kind of an ignition source might prove fatal to everyone. Tony closed his eyes, the smell filling his nostrils. He counted himself an eternal optimist, but this man continually proved himself an animal, making it hard to find anything endearing about him.

"Always a pleasure Ivan," he finally blurted out, trying not to cough. He wasn't sure what this man's diet was like, but it was certain that his bowels didn't agree with it. Tony and Terry started to pull their swords out to surrender them to their captor, but Ivan stopped them, holding his hand up and waving them off.

"Please keep them. It'll make it more sporting. And how's my little lassie, Cat?" he asked flippantly.

"She's even more beautiful than the last time you were with us. Says you need a bath, a shave, and a haircut. Although, let's see, sort of got yourself in a little bit of a pickle with that last encounter, didn't ya?"

"Yeah, well, that was a misunderstanding."

"Yes, it was. It was yours."

"And how is her personal guard then, Master Carl? He was a good man." Ivan was purposely trying to rile Tony up, and the Thulsa Captain knew it.

"I think we all know how he is and how it all went down."

"Tsk, tsk, tsk," Ivan chided, still prodding him. "Heard he got himself killed in a hunting accident. It's a tragic thing," he lied in a most insulting way, shaking his head and looking at the floor.

"What do you want Ivan?" Tony asked, not letting his taunting get to him.

"What do I want?" He repeated, looking up instantly. "What do I want? You barge into my place and mess with my men and then have the gall to ask what I want?" He asked raising his voice, quickly becoming irritated. You could still hear the noise of the fight going on outside. He leaned forward in his chair and pulled his scruffy hair back.

"The better question is, what do you want?" Ivan asked, pointing his big finger right at Tony who fought the urge to look over at Terry or Tim but held his eyes on Ivan, remaining silent. The Kenlar warlord continued to stare at the Thulsa Captain in hopes that he would at least make something up and speak, but got nothing. He shifted his eyes to Tim, who was sitting fairly relaxed. A moment as tense as this ought to be making him squirm nervously. He finally looked over at Terry, who was showing some signs of tension. Ivan counted himself a fair judge of body language and could tell that they were hiding something.

"How's the little wife and that big herd of brats Terry?" he finally asked, toning back down again and shifting his attention over to the tavern keeper. Terry held his eyes focused on Ivan as well. All three of them knew that Ivan was looking for an opening and shifting eye contact away from him to another member, might provide him with something.

"They're doing quite well," Terry responded unemotional, "thanks for asking."

"Hope you have them off on vacation somewhere. I would feel just awful if my men came through that place of yours and things got a little torn up. Sometimes they get a little anxious or overzealous in their work and forget where the battle is. Not a good thing at all," he finished, shaking his head slowly.

"I'm quite certain they will be just fine." Actually, Terry was quite concerned, but at the same time, he knew that Caroline could take care of herself and would be able to see the problem as it approached and take the correct action. Still, you couldn't help but be worried about it.

"I hope you're right," Ivan lied. The fight outside was starting to wind down, or so it sounded, and this was enough to shift a little attention away from this polite conversation.

"Sounds like we're just about done outside," he said getting up. "Shall we go out and have look see as to how things are progressing?" He looked around at everyone, then motioned for them to follow him, but the group remained unmoved. Tony was just waiting for Ivan to explode and show his true nature. He'd feel a whole lot more comfortable if he would. This polite chit-chat crap was just that and it had them all a bit unnerved to say the least. Usually, Ivan was a ranter and threw a fit at the drop of a hat, having some violent tantrums.

"Well, come on then!" he beckoned in a more demanding tone. Everyone finally got up and followed Ivan out of Tim's house, back into the open cave. To Tony's horror he found Ivan's men tossing the beheaded bodies of his warriors into the river, along with the severed heads. There was only one of his men left and he was being held by two of Ivan's warriors near where the carnage had already taken place. Ivan stepped out to where they were doing their dirty work, motioning for his men to bring the last of the Thulsa warriors with them.

"Maybe this one knows what happened to all my men," he announced, turning to his men who forced the beaten warrior to his knees. "What do you think man? Can you tell me where my men are?" he asked loudly, almost yelling it in the man's ear. Ivan tried speaking Kenlar, but got only silence. The war lord didn't speak Thulsian, so there could be no response.

Tony saw his warrior raise defiant eyes to him, but there was nothing Captain Dallas could do. His men had been purposely left in the dark about their mission here, so that it couldn't be tortured out of them. The look on his man's face told him that he was prepared to die. Captain Dallas fought the turmoil within, remaining silent. There was a certain hate that he had for executions. A different kind of torture and death pulled hard at his soul.

Ivan gave Tony a disgusted growl, grabbing the man by the hair and pulling his head back.

"Do you cut your warriors tongues out or something?" he asked, frustratedly trying to look into the man mouth. He finally pulled his big dagger out and slit the man's throat from ear to ear. Holding onto the man's hair, he let him drown in his own blood, it gushing freely from the razor incision. Ivan then pulled his own sword out and easily lopped off the head, still holding onto the hair. The beheaded body slumped to the ground while Ivan held the head up by the hair.

"My, my, my," he said, walking back to everyone. "Nasty business going on out here. Did you know these men?" He asked, holding the head up by the hair. It was a grotesque sight. Danny and Jerry had to look away, while Tim and Terry grimaced silently. "Well come on then!" He said, thrusting the head at the Thulsa Captain, blood still streaming from the severed neck. "Speak up man! These aren't any of my men. I can't seem to find the ones I left here. Maybe you know what happened to them," Ivan taunted, stepping right up to Captain Dallas with the head held right up to his face. Tony could see Ivan losing his patience. Now he was feeling a little more comfortable. An angry Ivan was a predictable Ivan. Danny glanced over at where all the noise was happening. There was a group of Ivan's men gathered around a snarling growling brawl happening further down along the river bank. He could see blood spattered around on the rocks nearby. It was apparent that this blood was not part of the blood bath that had just taken place. He watched as the last body was shoved into the river.

Tony and Ivan stared the other down for several more seconds, and then Ivan came unhinged, roaring angrily, throwing the head as hard as he could into the river, then drawing his own sword and pointing it right at Tony's throat. Of course this was an idle threat and it would take Ivan some time to figure it out. Tony knew Ivan wasn't going to kill him, at least not yet. He hadn't found any of the answers to the many predictable questions that were no doubt still forming in his simple mind, but Tony had command of Ivan for now. Of course Tony wasn't going to be phased by any of Ivan threats to kill him. He had just butchered six of his best warriors, one of them right in front of him. All of them had been good friends. He was naturally upset, but at the same time, he had become hardened to these kinds of things. Such was the nature of war and you had to turn a deaf ear and a blind eye to death and not let it bother you or you wouldn't survive very long.

"What exactly do you want me to say Ivan?" Tony finally spoke, looking down the blade of the small sword, quite unphased by Ivan's threatening looks.

"A couple of things," a now angry Ivan hissed. "Where are my men, and speak carefully because I'm in no mood. Why are you here? Why would you risk everything to be in this place, right here, right now?"

"You already know the answers to those questions?" Tony responded, sounding a little annoyed.

"But I want to hear you say it," he said, poking the tip of his sword against Captain Dallas' throat. Tony had to swallow, but tried to do so with as little movement as possible.

"Very well," Tony finally agreed, holding his poker face on Ivan's wild eyes. "A little less steel will go a long way here," he said, making sure that he had Ivan's complete attention and a level of upper control. Ivan stared blankly at Tony, who sort of changed his facial expression to indicate that he was waiting for an answer. Ivan shifted his eyes to one side and then the other, looking at the others standing around him.

"Less steel?" he asked, not getting the gist of Tony's request.

"Yeah," Tony gestured with his eyes towards the steel blade pointed at his throat. "Less steel."

Ivan finally got the hint and lowered his weapon while stepping back. He reached over to one of his men who were with the group just finishing up with the mess they had created and pulled a device from the side of his leg. He turned and pointing a crossbow pistol right at Tim's leg, fired it without any warning. The small, but sharp steel arrow pierced into Tim's left leg and stuck there. Tim let out an agonizing yell and dropped to the ground in intense pain.

"There," Ivan said in a very matter a fact tone. "Less steel."

"What did you do that for?" Danny leaped towards the big Kenlar man to attack him. It was a stupid move on his part and he was met almost instantly with the back of Ivan's broad and powerful fist, sending him flying flat on his back, next to a squirming Tim. Talon burst into laughter, leaning against the outside wall of Tim's dwelling, away from everyone else. The blow, and the subsequent fall, completely knocked the wind out of Danny. Jerry rushed to his side to help him as Terry bent down to help Tim. The little steel arrow had black guiding feathers on it and the shaft had buried into Tim's leg almost to the feathers. The steel tip was twin barbed, so trying to back it out the same way it entered was out of the question. Ivan bent down in front of a still moaning Tim and held up the pistol sized crossbow.

"Fine little invention you have provided. It has proved quite useful now and will in the future," he said admiring the weapon, not caring whether Tim was going to bleed to death or not. Tim gritted his teeth in agony, trying to squeeze his own leg hoping to ease the pain. His eyes were not just squinting in pain, but utter hatred for this animal of a person.

"You shot me! What are you doing shooting me?" he asked, a bit surprised. Ivan had never really harmed him. He was considered too valuable because of his ability to translate things out of the book.

"They obviously came here after you. Now you can't leave, at least not very quickly and without me knowing it. Ok," Ivan stood back up and glancing over at Danny and Jerry who were still on the ground, Danny still trying to catch his breath. The left side of his face was throbbing where Ivan had walloped him. He then turned back to Tony, who was still standing unmoved. "Let's see, where were we? Ah yes, you were about to lay out your best laid plans for what you're doing here and what you did with my men. Please, proceed," Ivan said, confident that he still had command of the situation. He folded his huge arms across his broad chest and focused in on Tony with a gesture that he was leaning in with a listening ear. The Thulsian Captain looked over at the ruckus still going on over by the river's edge. Whatever the fight was, it was moving in their direction.

"Oh don't worry about that. It's my pet Jabba, Tobor, playing around with Tim's little pet doggie. What's that stupid name you gave him, Digit or something?"

"Digi," Tim corrected him through his pain. He could hear the Jabba fighting, but also a high pitched chirping coming from Digi, perhaps a call for help? Terry whispered something in his ear and Tim nodded. Terry peeled the feathers off the shaft and shoved as hard as he could on the butt end of the black arrow. Tim let out a howl as the shaft was shoved the rest of the way through his flesh sending the barbed end out the other side. Once the barb was clear of the flesh, Terry reached around the back side where it had exited his trousers and pulled it the rest of the way through. He set it down in Tim's lap and worked to make some kind of bandages from his own clothing. Tim, regaining some of his composure, whispered something back to Terry, then lay back so Terry could render first aid.

"Whatever," Ivan said, looking over at the brawl. The Jabba battled savagely with no apparent victor as of yet. Ivan seemed to be taking particular delight in the battle. It didn't seem to matter to him if his Jabba got beat up or not. The carnage seemed to be what was feeding him. "Anyway, let's hear it," he said, turning back to Tony.

"You're right Ivan, my good man," Tony spoke up finally, trying to sound unaffected by everything going on around him. "You have it all figured out." The best way to control him now was to give him what he already knew, so he saw no reason not to tell the truth, or at least parts of it. Ivan was taken off guard with both his tone and his agreement with him.

"Right? About what? What have I got all figured out?" He asked stupidly.

"Everything." Tony said quickly. "My men and I came in here, slaughtered yours and dumped their bodies in the river. Probably Jabba meat by now. It was actually quite easy. You should have better men guarding all the riches of your spoil or guys like me can just walk in here like we own the place and take whatever we want, whenever we want." Tony stepped up next to Ivan and watched the two Jabba fighting with their razor claws and fangs.

"We knew your armies were coming, so we had to come and scope out what we're up against and when."

"That's what spies are for," Ivan pointed out gruffly, looking over at him.

"They have been a little untrustworthy as of late. The information on you was that you had Broc of the Omars and Condor of the Gaylens with you now. I had to come and see for myself."

"Bah," Ivan spat angrily. "Condor went and got himself killed. Some other buffoon is in charge there now. Said their armies were too weak to be of any use. I think he just didn't have the stomach for the fight."

"Could be," Tony agreed carefully. "Didn't know that there was a change up over there, wonder who the new man of the house is?" Ivan shook his head while shaking his fist at the fight in front of them. Both Jabba were evenly matched.

"Don't know, never met the man before. I just know he's some kind of a coward and afraid to fight. Had I had the time, I would have taken over the Gaylen clan myself and then gone for Thulsa. I'll just have to do it without them for now."

Behind the conversing Tony and Ivan, Terry leaned over to Jerry and Danny to check on them.

"We're about to make a break for it boys." Terry informed them in a whisper, making sure neither Ivan, nor his men could not hear him speak. "Dive for the river when you get the signal."

"What's the signal?" Jerry asked, helping Danny to his feet.

"You'll know it when you see it," Terry responded, pulling a strip of material off Danny's shirt for Tim's leg.

"I'd like to take this opportunity to point out that the river empties out over a waterfall about 50 yards from where we are right now," Danny said hoarsely. He had no choice but to utter his words almost inaudibly. He was still trying to regain the use of his stunned lungs. "And you said earlier the drop is quite lengthy."

"Tim has it all figured out. Just go with it or you'll end up like Tony's men."

Tim continued to wince as Terry worked with his leg, but managed to sit up long enough to call to his wife in a completely different language from Thulsa or Kenlar. Ivan instantly twisted around from the Jabba fight and a couple of his men placed themselves in front of Kawti approaching from the shadows. Tim read the distrust on Ivan's face and tried to reassure him.

"Since I'm bleeding to death here, thank you very much," Tim said sarcastically, while gesturing at his wound. "I'd like to get it dressed properly so I don't get gangrene or some other ungodly disease." Ivan eyed the blonde woman carefully, motioned for his men to stand aside and let her pass, then turned back to the fight that was now on the other side of the river, against the cave wall. The two animals were fighting half in the water and half out.

Tim rattled off some more foreign language and Kawti turned quietly to the door of the house and stepped inside. A moment later, Ivan gestured towards several of his men to surround Tony and his group. To Tim's horror, he motioned for Talon to move away from the dwelling as Ivan stepped inside the front door after Tim's wife. A moment later, everyone outside could hear her screaming and fighting as Ivan assaulted her. Tony started for the door, but Ivan's warriors held him back with the sharp tips of their swords. Terry held onto his friend, listening to the Kenlar animal savagely assaulting his wife. It was more than Tim could take as he struggled to get away from Terry and get to his feet. Jerry and Danny had to help hold him to the ground to keep Ivan's men from taking action against them.

Tony was powerless as well. If he moved to do anything, he would risk a bloody fight that couldn't be won under any of these circumstances. Talon started laughing, walking off towards the far end of the cave where it opened out to the cliff side. The scuffle inside went on for several minutes, everyone listening to Ivan having his way with her. Tim finally relaxed, weeping bitterly as the noise died off and was replaced by the Jabba battle. A couple of moments later, Ivan reappeared outside. Working his pants back into position and sporting a couple of bloody scratches across his face where Kawti had obviously gotten a few good licks of her own on him, he stepped back over to the river's edge next to Captain Dallas.

"Ah yeah," he drew in a deep breath. "That's just what I needed." He adjusted his britches again and glanced back at Tim, then at the door to the dwelling. "She's a good whore Master Tim. Lots of fight in her."

Tim could only sit sobbing softly in Terry's arms. Danny was incensed and stared at Ivan with daggers firing from his eyes. He remembered when he became so angry before about the nature of Ivan. That, coupled with what had brought them here and the price they had paid so far, had him boiling to the point where all good sense was pushed aside. He was ready to strike at this animal of a human with his bare hands and squeeze the life of out him if he could.

"I suppose that makes you feel more like a man?" Tony asked infuriated, but holding himself calm. Ivan looked over at him, then back at the Jabba fight still going on.

"She enjoyed it," he said callously. "So, what did I miss?"

Tony had to fight the urge to swing his sword right out of its scabbard and lop off Ivan's head. They had to wait for just the right moment or none of them would make it out of here in one piece. It was going to be tricky getting any of them out of there alive as it was.

Tim and Terry had it all worked out. He had observed them whispering and passing him looks and knew what to do when the time came. There was a lull in the Jabba fight, the two creatures appearing to rest. Both were dripping wet, patches of fur missing, a few broken claws, some cuts and gashes covering their bodies. They puffed heavily, carefully circling each other. One of them began to chirp loudly, irritating the other one.

"Knock it off Digg," Tobor snarled.

"Does that hurt your little ears?" Digi fired right back, chirping even louder.

"What are you doing? Calling for help? Can't fight your own fights? Gotta have help?"

"Like you Tobor, I take every advantage I can get," Digi snarled, passing Tim a glance and then lunging at the Kenlar Jabba.

A moment later the two were brawling in the river again. This time they were caught in the deep part and the swiftness of the current began to carry them down stream towards the falls. Ivan began to yell fiercely for Tobor to finish him off as the two battled in the water. Everyone shifted their attention to the two fighting Jabba, being swept closer to the falls. Terry helped Tim to his feet and the two moved closer to the river for a better view. Jerry and Danny stepped right next to them. Both men watching nervously for the signal.

Then it came, out of nowhere. There was a sudden rushing of the air around them and the light changed from behind. Ivan's men turned around to face a black wall of flapping, chirping Jabbaway completely blotting out the light coming from the other end of the cavern. There was no time for the warriors to pull their swords and mount any kind of a defense. The Jabba blitzed through the cave in mass with razor claws swinging and slicing into man flesh.

Terry shoved Jerry and Danny at the river, yelling for them to dive for it as the flock enveloped the whole area. Tim stepped up behind a startled Ivan, wrapping his left arm around his massive chest and taking the crossbow arrow that he had been shot with in his right hand, shoved it into Ivan's lower back as hard as he could. His face twisting, teeth gritting with hate for this heartless tyrant, he shoved and twisted it, sinking the barbed end deep between the ribs of Ivan's back.

"There," he hissed in his ear, flexing the steel arrow now buried in Ivan's flesh as he arched back in agony. "Less steel!"

Ivan had his sword out in an instant, trying to cut Tim in half, but was knocked down by several Jabba, allowing Tim to make a labored dive for the water, followed by Tony. The flock continued to harass Ivan's warriors as the river current quickly took the five towards the falls.

"Not too excited about this," Danny gasped for air, struggling to keep from going too fast. Terry tried to calm him a little, watching Tim enter the water.

"You'll be fine! Just relax and let the water take you over."

Danny had no concept of how that was going to make everything just fine. He had been in rough water before with white water tours he and Jerry would take all summer, but a thousand foot drop was a bit of a stretch for anyone to manage.

Tony looked back to see Ivan struggling to his feet with the crossbow arrow sunk deep in his lower back. Beyond him, at the door to the dwelling, he watched Kawti stumble from the open door and move carefully for the wall of the cavern to follow them downstream. She was ragged and bloody from the vicious sexual assault that Ivan had delivered on her, but she was still quite alive and in her arms she held firmly to the book that Tim had hidden under his chair. She knew that above all else, Ivan must never gain personal control of the book.

Tim had been able to fend him off all these years by making all the interpretations from it, but it was always possible that Ivan could find another interpreter who would give up all its secrets.

Tobor was the first to go over the falls. He immediately became airborne and flew off with a swarm of Jabbaway in hot pursuit. Digi was next and let himself fall quite a ways before he unfurled his wings and sailed carefully back up close to the falls to make sure everyone else went over all right. By now there was a large swarm of Jabba hovering below the falls ready to catch the Thulsa band. Tony continued to follow Kawti's progress, carefully making her way to the cliff's edge. She knew what had to be done. All she had to do was jump and Digi's flock of Jabba would catch her and the book.

Danny did his best to relax as the current took him and Jerry over the falls, out into the open Argyle air, and into a free fall. He couldn't help but let out a yell as he began to pick up speed. He liked log flumes, but this one was more like the ones you have in your dreams where you suddenly realize that things aren't going well. He closed his eyes, not wanting to see death reaching up at him from the jagged rocks below, but a moment later, he found himself in the grasp of several puffing, fury Jabbaway that quickly carried him and Jerry away. As Terry, Tim and Tony spilled over the edge, they too were whisked away by the Jabba flock to a safe distance. The cave finally began to empty of the flapping creatures as Tony and Tim turned back to the cavern.

Talon had stepped out of the cavern and was casually leaning against the cliff wall cleaning his finger nails when the Jabba attack had started. He didn't see any sense in him getting all beat up with all this. This was Ivan's party, not his.

Kawti, still holding the book firmly under her arm, was almost to the edge, walking right by Talon, who didn't even finch. Tim yelled out commands to the Jabba to help get them back into position the catch her, but to his horror, Ivan's men charged and surrounded her, cutting off any escape. The warriors were all bloodied from the flock attack, but still able to carry out commands from their leader, who was still battling with several Jabba.

Kawti held tightly to the book in one arm, sporting a long dagger in the other, turning continually trying to keep any of them from getting too close to her. Ivan roared an order to Talon in Kenlar, who responded by giving the warlord a look, then slowly made his way towards the circle as if he had just been given an assignment he thought completely beneath him. Tim yelled a warning to her, but the noise from the Jabba drowned his cries as Talon stepped to the circle. She needed to jump to save herself and the book, but it was too late for her to do so. There was no way for her to get past the ring of warriors. She would be stopped, easily disarmed and the book taken and if the warriors couldn't do it, Talon certainly would. The book was of paramount importance, far more than self-preservation.

She finally flipped the blade in her hand and threw it at Talon who had reached the circle. This diverted everyone's attention for just a moment, Talon deflecting it with his arm gauntlets, but it gave her just enough time to make a quick spin, launching the book well over their heads and out into the open air. Still clasped closed, the book spun as it sailed over the edge of the cliff and started its downward trek into the waiting Jabbaway.

Notably angry now, Talon grabbed her by the back of the neck and thrust one of his swords all the way through her from the back. Tim screamed helplessly, but it was too late, Talon's sword piercing her abdomen and out the front. She froze, staring at the blade as if it were surreal, not believing that it was actually piercing through her. A moment later, Talon put his boot on her back and yanked the blade out the same way it had entered. She stumbled forward, but caught herself as Talon and the Kenlar warriors were again besieged and battered by a squadron Jabba, Talon jumping quickly back against the cliff wall, staying out of the fray.

Kawti staggered sideways, the sensation of the massive piercing searing into her mind. She looked helplessly out at her husband, in tears again. Tim kicked and screamed for his flotilla to move closer to the cliff so he could save her, but she waved him back, shaking her head. They must not come so close that they would endanger themselves any further. She knew that the Jabba were having great difficulty holding them up this long.

She yelled something in Kenlar, staggering past several battling warriors and Jabba, then toppled over the edge of the cliff. She was almost instantly caught by several Jabba that had moved in beneath her. Ivan battled savagely with several Jabba trying to pull him and his men over to the edge of the cliff, somehow managing to fight them off, though many of his men did not fare so well. Digi's flock of Jabbaway turned, leaving Ivan down on one knee, yelling at them as they were carried off to safety.

No Time

Once safely away, the group was set down a short distance down river in the deep ravine on a small meadow along the river. Tim quickly ran to where the Jabba had set Kawti gently to the ground and carefully held her. She was a bloody mess, but somehow, she was still alive. Distraught, Tim looked her over bewildered. His mind couldn't think, he was completely numb from the whole experience and almost didn't even notice that Terry had scrambled to her side to render aid.

A quick overview of her condition looked quite bleak, but he wasn't about to tell Tim that. She opened her eyes and looked over at Digi as he set the book down next to her and gave him a weak thank you in Kenlar. It was a beautiful language and with her sweet voice, even in her condition, it sounded wonderful. She turned back and looked up into the tormented face of her husband. There had been no other way. If she hadn't done what she had done, Ivan would still have the book, she would probably still be dead and Tony's mission to rescue Tim and the book would have failed.

Moving was painful for her and considering what she had endured in the last fifteen minutes, it's a wonder she could move at all. She raised her hand to Tim's wet face and smiled. For many years she had listened to the stories of the wonders of Earth from her husband and longed to go there with him. She knew that he had always wanted to return someday and this was to be their ticket home. However, now she knew that she wasn't going to be able to go with him. Although her love for him had assured that he would have a fighting chance of making it back to that Earth, she knew her time had expired, but she needed to tell them all how she felt about him. She wanted everyone to hear what she was going to say so she spoke in broken English.

"He took only this body my husband, not the spirit within. I am forever yours." She spoke shakily, looking around at the others, especially Danny and Jerry. "My husband, you must go home now." Tim nodded through his tears, holding her hand, trying to give comfort.

"Your dear friends have found you and they will take you back to Earth with them now."

"Yes," Tim choked out, fighting back the fits of grief boiling freely from his soul.

"I always wished to live in such a wonderful place as what you have described to me all these years."

"Together has been our wonderful place," Tim smiled through his tears. Kawti smiled contentedly, rasping her final breath and slipping away. Terry pulled back to let Tim grieve. It would take some time before he could regain his composure.

Digi and his fellow Jabbaway quickly went to work digging in the rich soil that had been deposited in the small meadow by high run off, while others took off and returned a short time later with several strange corkscrew shaped tree trunks. These were about six feet long and looked like tree logs that had grown naturally in a spiral fashion. After working with the timbers for several hours and then some careful preparation, Tim placed Kawti gently into one of the spiral shaped logs, then watched with sadden eyes as Terry and Tony twisted the other spiral log into the first, effectively entombing her inside the two logs.

The four men from Thulsa then carried her casket to where the Jabba had prepared the grave site and carefully placed her coffin inside. Digi and several of the other attending Jabba then sang a wonderful Kenlar folk song that they knew Kawti loved. The Kenlar people were not a bad clan; truly they were a delightfully cultured folk with many deeply seeded and wonderful traditions. It was their tyrannical madman of a leader that had taken them into places of darkness and evil. Tony and Terry stepped back and sat down on a couple of stumps next to the ravine wall, watching the Jabba fill in the gravesite.

"Got an even bigger problem on our hands now," Tony stated, surveying their surroundings. "The Torres road was the only sure way back."

"It will take us forever to get back to it and they'll be watching it like a hawk now," Terry pointed out, turning to survey the steep ravine walls.

"Can't Digi and his flock fly us there?" Jerry asked, sitting down on a mossy spot nearby. Terry slowly shook his head looking over at the Jabba as they continued to fill in Kawti's grave.

"I've gotten just about everything I have ever known about them completely wrong, but the fact that they can't carry a human for long distances is still very true," he said, almost hypnotically, continuing to watch them. "How many other things in my life have I gotten so totally wrong?"

Tony looked over and watched them as well. Tim stood next to his friend Digi with an arm resting on his folded wing, watching the other Jabba finished their tasks. Kawti had always been such a good friend to the Jabba. She had introduced Tim to them as friends, not the savage animals they had been painted to be. Tim had learned Kenlar from Kawti and he in turn had taught her English and then taught English to the Jabba. They were delightfully intelligent creatures who were fiercely loyal to family and friends, gladly fighting to the death for all things they held dear. They had lost many Jabba on this attack, but everyone was in severe stress over losing Kawti. She had been

like a mother to all she had touched. Burial in this manner was one of
the highest honors a fallen Jabba could ever hope for. She had been
one of them. Tim and Digi embraced each another, then slowly turned
and approached the other four.

"Now things must happen quickly or all hope of success will be lost.
You might have me and the book, but we are still a very long ways
from Thulsa." Tim said slowly, heavy emotion still prevailed in his
voice. Expending an enormous amount of emotional energy to hold it
together, he picked up a stick trying it as a walking staff. While Tim
was bent over, Digi stretched to where Tim's injury was and thrust his
tongue deeply into the rear wound. Tim launched himself nearly into
Danny and Jerry and turned cursing, a surprised look on his face.

"What in the heck are trying to do, tear my leg off? Isn't it enough
that butt wipe of an idiot shot me, you have to make it sting with your
slimy snot?" Tim was still very raw both physically and emotionally
and not thinking clearly. He should have known right away what Digi
was trying to do. He reached back, feeling the wet saliva soaked spot
where the arrow had exited the back of his leg; it actually felt better.
In fact, he could hardly feel any pain in that part of the leg at all now.

"What did you do?" he asked, trying to look at it, but it was too far
behind for him to get a good look at it.

"You're so smart, but you have forgotten the simplest things," Digi
said, slowly nodding his head.

"Jabba spit," Terry trailed off, remembering something he had
learned a long time ago but had never really had an opportunity to try
out. "It's antiseptic qualities."

"That's why our teeth are so white and clean all the time," Digi
informed them, grinning broadly.

"But it has done nothing for your minty fresh breath," Danny
interjected. While he was no longer angry with this Jabba, he was still
reminded that it was a Jabba that had been the cause of his friend's
death. This one had just saved his life. Several of his kin had given
their lives so they could escape. He had to afford him some
consideration.

"It's the stomach that produces the foul breath, not the teeth," Digi
informed him. "Now drop your pants and I'll do this a little more
proper," he said, turning back to Tim who worked his pants open in
front of everyone. No one was exactly sure what they should be
looking at here.

"There's a proper way?" Tony winced at all the blood running
down Tim's leg as his pants came off. Digi was about to proceed with
the application of his tongue and saliva on both sides of the wound,
but Tony stopped him.

"Ah, for the sakes of the human stomachs gathered here today for
this auspicious occasion, can you please go wash all the blood off first
and then go over there behind that tree to do that?" Tim looked at the

bunch of them for a moment trying to figure out what the problem was.

"Oh come on, you guys aren't squeamish of a little blood are you?"

"Squeamish, no," Terry piped up. "Repulsed, yes."

"Oh, for the love of Pete!" Tim exclaimed, picking up his shoes and pants and starting for the river. "You fly a crap load of missions, see your men get all shot to pieces, a decorated war hero, Captain of the Thulsa armies and you can't stand the sight of a little blood?"

"It's your blood, ya wanky man. Come on, we're supposed to be civilized," Tony came back quickly, amused at Tim's indignation.

"My apologies if I have offended you," Digi offered humbly. Humor with humans was a difficult concept for the Jabbaway. Digi had tried to learn it, but they were always shifting from humor to serious so quickly, it was hard to keep track or tell the difference.

"No Digi," Tony reassured the Jabba. "It's not your fault. Some of us are not used to the graphic nature of a wound and certainly not used to how your folk take care of such things."

"Besides," Terry cut in, "you don't really want to have to clean up all that blood do you?"

"We crave the salt," Digi said in a rather matter of fact fashion. "And I find it quite tasty". Terry and Tony passed each other a glance, then spoke at the same instant.

"Yeah, you would."

"There!" Tim hollered, limping back up from the river. His leg was clean now, but blood was still working its way out the open wound on the front.

"Sit down and let's get this taken care of," Digi said, turning his back to the rest of the group. Tim lay down on his stomach and Digi worked the back side carefully with his tongue, slathering the wound good and then having him turn over so he could repeat the process again on the front side. It all stung at first, but then quickly went numb. The saliva also possessed fantastic blood clotting properties that would keep the wound from reopening or becoming infected for some time, if at all.

"Ah," Tim sighed in relief, "so much better." He stood up and tested his leg. "Almost as good as new."

"Yes, as good as new," Terry agreed. "Who knew spit could do such wonderful things. Now can you please put your pants back on?"

"Ah, he really shouldn't," Digi cautioned, as Tim finished wringing them out good. "The moisture will wash the saliva away and he will start to bleed again and the numbness will wear off."

"So what do you suggest I do?" Tim asked, looking at his pants and boots.

"Tie your pant legs together and put them around your neck," Tony suggested half serious, half in jest.

"Just wear the boots," Terry said with a chuckle. Tim gave them both a look of complete indignation. Still an emotional wreck, he understood what his friends were trying to do. It was difficult to focus on anything but the loss of his Kawti, but their attempts at a little humor to soften the situation did help.

"If we're walking anywhere," Jerry piped up, realizing the scene that could play out here. "I want to take point." Danny snickered softly, trying to hold it back. This was the first bit of amusement for him since the flock attack on the Torres road this morning.

"Serious?" Tim asked, looking at himself. He had on boxer type under shorts.

"It's either that or cut off the pant legs and make shorts out of them. I wouldn't recommend that though. We could be in for some rough terrain," Tony smiled.

"Nuts," Tim grumbled, sitting down and putting his boots on, then tied the ends of the wet pants together, putting them around his neck and modeling for everyone.

"It's a foregone conclusion that we can't go back the same way we came. Even if we could get back up the ravine, it would take forever to get back to the Torres road and besides, Ivan would expect it," Tim said, testing his walking stick.

"While I'm sure the Jabba are willing," Terry said, nodding at Digi who nodded back. "There's no way they could carry the five of us over Tera Mountains."

"Indeed," Digi responded, pleased they were trying to be considerate to his kind.

"Our only hope here is to take the Tera Pass Trail," Tony said, standing up and looking around for a good direction to start.

"It's a rough and treacherous trail," Digi stated coolly, looking up the almost vertical ravine wall. "But if you know the way, it can certainly get you back to Thulsa in time to save your friend."

"Good deal," Danny said, getting to his feet. "We're burning daylight."

"Hold on there Tex," Tim said, as everyone got to their feet. Danny's enthusiasm was a little infectious and everyone was anxious to put this day far behind them. "We don't know where we're going for sure."

"You don't know?" Terry stated, more than asking a question.

"Hello!" Tim pointed back towards the water fall in the distance that they had just escaped from. "Held against my will for years and years?"

"Well, I would have thought with all the time, knowledge and the spy network you had at your disposal, you would have had plenty of time to figure it all out," Terry cut back, a little frustrated.

"I know the maps in my head, but I've never been on the trails," Tim admitted, trying to calm him down a little.

"I know the trail," Tony piped up. "I just don't know where it is from here."

"I don't know the trail," Digi said, still looking up the ravine wall. "But I know where it is from here."

"This is beginning to sound like a jigsaw puzzle and everyone has a different piece of it," Danny whispered over to Jerry. Jerry was equally as skeptical and leaned back to his friend with another whispered comment.

"If we have to separate, my vote is with staying with the flying badger." Danny chuckled at the humor from his friend. Underneath he wasn't too keen on that idea, but said nothing. This barrier of his was going to take a lot of effort on his part to overcome. Digi's articulating ears twisted in their direction, detecting the comment and recognizing it as human humor. As the Jabba didn't normally laugh in the traditional sense that humans laughed, he wasn't sure how to express himself other than to recognize that he was a part of their humor.

"I heard that."

Jerry gave Danny a quick glance and blurted out an overdone laugh.

"Can we please get moving?" Terry asked impatiently.

"Digi," Tim asked, looking up. "Please tell me the trail isn't directly above us."

"Ok, I won't," the Jabba agreed. He stepped over to the ravine wall and started yanking on some thick tangled vines and then started to climb.

"So where is it?"

"You told me not to tell you," Digi grunted, moving up the wall.

"It was a joke," Tim exclaimed, a little exasperated. Digi let out a frustrated growl. He just couldn't seem to get the hang of their humor. Jerry looked around at everyone else and started climbing, followed closely by Danny.

"It's above this ravine, straight up." Digi said, looking back sensing they were starting to follow.

"Some animals just can't be taught new tricks," Tim grumbled.

Starting his ascent, he looked back at Kawti's grave site. Broken hearted and still very raw, he knew he had to somehow bury it so he could function and be a part of the Thulsa mission to bring him and the book back in time to make the dash for home. It was how Kawti would have wanted it. He gave the grave one last look and then turned his focus upward.

Bolas anyone?

Falling from his horse and down the steep slope of the ravine, Bryan listened to the Jabba, growling and chirping loudly. Not necessarily at him, though at this point it wouldn't have mattered anyway. Both clawed at the loose dirt or anything they could get a hold of, sliding helplessly towards a line of shabby brush. The Jabba still had its claws sunk deeply in Bryan's thighs and one arm, but was clawing at the ground with the other one. That was about all it could do. The Bolas were still firmly wrapped around it, preventing it from flying away. Bryan figured that if the animal had wanted to kill him, he would have done it already. It had plenty of opportunity being in this close proximity. A quick bite to the throat or other vital part, maybe even a slash with its free claw would have been more than enough to do him in. Perhaps he wasn't out to kill him at all. Bryan certainly wasn't in the frame of mind to kill, even now, after all this. In fact, he seemed to have developed an attachment to the animal, in more ways than one. There had to be a way to save them both.

He tried to pull one of the claws out of his flesh, but that only served to increase his pain and took that hand away from trying to stop their descent towards the edge of a very high cliff. He could only imagine what was on the other side of the line of scrub they were sliding rapidly towards. Overhead, hoards of flapping Jabba were congregating, chirping loudly. As the incline steepened, they both started to roll. This was even more uncomfortable as it created more pressure on the entry points of the animal's claws as it tried to hang on. Every time they made a revolution, Bryan would land on one of the three bola rocks wrapped around the Jabba. It felt like he was breaking a rib every time they rolled. He tried to turn their roll uphill so they would at least stop rolling and start sliding again. They had a better chance at stopping their descent if he could have vertical control of his legs, feet or his hands. This rolling was doing nothing to slow their decent. If anything, it was speeding them up, beating the crap out of them.

Dirt and rocks flying in all directions, he finally managed to get his feet pointed downhill again just in time for them to hit the berm of scrub brush, but they were moving so fast, they blew right through it, blowing plants right out of the dirt and rock. To his horror, there was nothing else to slide on. The berm was the last place for anything to grow before plunging straight down a sheer rock cliff to a wild river far below.

Bryan quickly rolled partially onto his stomach, taking the Jabba with him. The animal's claws flexing sharply as they hit the rock ledge. Starting over the edge, he tried desperately to grab hold of any of the surrounding brush, but what he grabbed pulled right out and he let it fly. Curiously, slipping over the side and out into free air, all he could think about was a scripture in the Bible, talking about sowing seeds on rocky soil.

Tumbling into a free fall, Bryan struggled to get himself free of the animal, although he wasn't exactly sure why. His thinking led him to believe that if he could get free of the animal, he could somehow still save both himself and the animal. It was actually the other way around. The flock of chirping Jabba suddenly grew thick, some even knocking into them as they picked up speed. Their tumble slowing, he could look straight down now, the river and large rocks coming quickly up to meet them. At this point, they were pretty much dead, just waiting for the sudden stop at the bottom.

"Not good!" he yelled in a panic. This wasn't what he had envisioned his demise would be like. He was thinking more along the lines of saving a young child from drowning and being too exhausted to save himself, or running into a burning building to save an old woman and pushing her out a window right before the building collapsed on top of him. Oh, how about saving a family in a car crash only to get pinned beneath the car himself and dying in his girlfriend's arms, as she wept bitterly while he slipped away? Wait, that wasn't going to work, he didn't have a girlfriend. Well, the family being saved was good anyway.

How silly all these ideas were. What, was he writing a romance or adventure novel of some kind? No, he was falling from a cliff, holding on to a vicious animal, watching the jagged rocks below reach up at him.

"Let go of me," called a voice from nearby.

"What?" he responded, thinking he might already be dead. That wouldn't be so bad. You actually die before you hit the ground, perfect!

"Let go of me and push away, my friends will catch you," called the voice again.

Bryan looked at the Jabba who was looking right at him.

"That's right, I said that," the Jabba said. "Now turn me loose and push away!"

"I can't push, you have your meat hooks in me," he replied, not believing that he was now having a conversation with a wild animal while falling off a cliff to his death.

"Oh, yeah," the Jabba responded, retracting his claws from Bryan's flesh. Pushing away, the tangled up Jabba instantly let out short burst of loud chirps. By now, they had reached terminal velocity and the flock of Jabba following them down had to move in fast in order to catch them.

Moments later, he found himself in the firm clutches of about six of the beasts, flapping madly to slow their decent. Pulling away from the cliff wall and out over the river, several other Jabba came into help check the built up speed and trajectory. The water was still coming up rapidly, the Jabba straining harder to check the fall and start moving horizontally. They had him by the legs and one arm, his other arm and head hanging lower.

Several more Jabba joined in the rescue as they arched right at the water. Swooping closer to the water, he thought he could see several large fish beneath the white foam of the rapids, their dorsal fins surfacing, heading straight at them.

"Oh crap!" he yelled, as his lower arm started hitting the water. He thought he saw several long tentacles fire out at him from beneath the surface.

"Flap harder!" he screamed, his head hitting the boiling rapids. Two more tentacles went whizzing past his head while he tried to pull himself up higher. Being already injured, hitting the water at this speed would have just added to his discomfort. Not to mention whatever was in the water certainly seemed like it wanted to get a hold of him. He bounced several times off the surface, each time the Jabba above him were able to slow him down even more and regain a couple of feet of altitude.

Finally, there was one last skim across the rapids of the river, something big jumping at him from the waves but he couldn't really tell what it was. More Jabba joined in to assist the others, helping to lift them back up above the river. How they were able to flap their wings without hitting each other was quite beyond his reasoning and really, he was less worried about that and more worried about the trees on both sides of the river.

They weren't gaining altitude very fast, and were moving towards the trees. Water at high speed was bad enough. Getting flogged in the head by tree limbs wasn't going to do anything for his sense of wellbeing either. *Let's just find a nice sand bar or an open meadow somewhere and set me down gently.*

Wait, Terry had said that they roost in trees at night, whenever that was, then flew from tree top to tree top to open meadows and plains to feed. Ok, so the meadow is a bad idea. Maybe they could just set him down somewhere and leave him to go tend to their friend, wherever he ended up. However, none of that appeared to be happening.

They were gaining altitude faster now and starting to veer away from the river's path, though not quite high enough, as Bryan found himself occasionally being slammed by tree tops.

"A little higher please," he called out, spitting some leaf pieces out of his mouth.

"Sorry," a voice called back. "They're doing the best they can. You aren't exactly a light weight."

"You calling me fat?" he asked, looking up at the flock of fur and wings.

"I think it would be better put as, heavier than what we can normally carry," came the familiar voice from off to his right. He strained his head around to see another cluster of Jabba carrying the Jabba he had fallen with, still tangled up in the Bolas.

"Sounded like a fat joke to me," Bryan commented, feeling a little dizzy. "Where are they taking us?" Bryan asked, starting to feel a bit sick too. He was seriously injured with a good case of road rash and some very deep gashes where the Jabba had clawed him. Then to be held in such an awkward position while flying, well this was about as much roller coaster as he wanted for one day.

"Towards the Thulsa frontier. It's safer there."

"Uhm," Bryan said, starting to see sparkles develop in his vision. He was not feeling well at all now and he knew that he wasn't going to be able to remain conscious for very much longer. He realized that he was a bloody mess. "I'm not in very good shape here. I don't know if you know too much about humans, but when we get damaged severely, or lose too much of our blood, we don't stay conscious for very long."

"The alternative is to have them drop you where we are," the Jabba replied, as they swung out over the forest and continued north. Bryan noticed the sparkles becoming even more apparent and his vision starting to dim. A moment later he could see and hear nothing but darkness the fading sounds of the Jabba's wings, and then he slipped into unconsciousness. There were moments where he could still hear Jabba wings and chirping, then he thought he felt himself being set down and let go.

When he awoke, he carefully got to his feet. He found himself standing on the razor ridge of Spring Creek summit looking west over the Teton valley at his home of Driggs, Idaho. This ridge was on Earth, directly to the south of the Lake Valley ridges and bowl where this whole adventure had started. Something was very odd about what he was experiencing; now summer time on the mountain. The sky was as blue as it could be and the sun was warm on his face, a gentle breeze drifting across the ridge line.

He could see an eagle working a lazy circle along the ridge he was standing on. He was in his hiking pants and a short sleeved shirt with hiking boots and a day pack. He stood looking at the wonderful view, something that he thought he'd never see again. He was overjoyed to be standing right where he was.   He didn't even care how he had gotten home, just that he was. Reaching into his pocket, he pulled his

Smartphone out, looking at the display. The date was correct and the time seemed to be about the right time for the position of the sun. The signal bars on the phone showed he had full signal strength, so he pulled up all his contacts lists and checked that his network was operating the way it should.

He looked at his phone a moment and then looked around at his surroundings. Was it really possible for the last several days to have all been a dream? Not even possible, but then again, how was it possible for a doorway to another world to open up on a mountain top and they step through to a civilization with clans called the Omars, Gaylens, Kenlars and Thulsians? How do you reconcile the memories of having a hairy winged beast with lots of claws and teeth attack you and knock you over a cliff? Those things don't just come from nowhere! Standing there feeling quite warm and comfortable, he held his phone up and activated its voice recognition app.

"Call Brit," he spoke out loud to it. It responded instantly in its own familiar voice.

"Calling Britten Garrett."

Bryan watched the eagle work his way back and forth along the ridge as he put the phone to his ear and listened to it ring.

"It's going to voice mail," he muttered, counting the rings until the answering service came on and the familiar voice of Brit's greeting started talking. At first he was just going to hang up, but then decided that if this was a dream, wouldn't it be cool to leave a ridiculous message for his older brother? He listened all the way to the end of the greeting, but as Brit finished his normal greeting, he started an additional line.

"If this is Bryan and you're standing at the summit of Spring Creek on a nice warm summers day and there isn't a cloud in the sky, don't worry too much. You'll be waking up shortly and be right back in the same nightmare you thought you had just dropped out of. If I'm in a pickle, then so are you little brother. Be tough and keep it real, bye."

Bryan shut the phone off, squeezing it disgusted.

"Great! Just great!"

He could suddenly hear the roar of the storm, and swinging around facing the north ridge, there it was, a huge, snarling mass of swirling, grey/ black clouds, quickly expanding. He turned to the south and started running along the ridgeline across the saddle of the ridge between the Lake Valley ridge and the Spring Creek summit.

Looking back at the storm, it was obvious that it was growing so fast that it was easily going to overtake him and swallow him up. He remembered the stories Tony and Catrina had told them about Chuck and Dale's attempts at passing through the storm and how it had picked them up and either tore them to pieces or threw them out the top, to their deaths. He glanced up at the eagle still soaring above him as he ran. It suddenly banked at the approach of the storm and dove right down at him.

"Get ready for another wild ride there kiddo," the bird hollered. "You probably ought to wake up before that thing catches you and spits you out the top."

Overtaken by the swirling mass of madness, Bryan was picked up like a rag doll and tossed in every direction. He could see the ground passing quickly beneath him. One moment he was looking out at the Teton valley, the next he was looking at the Teton Mountains, and then he was seeing the city of Thulsa below him, then the Kenlar Mountains then the Tera mountain range.   He caught a glimpse of Vespa Cull and the Torres River and then the storm launched him up at a ferocious velocity, spitting him out the top into the free air of its calm eye. He stupidly tried flapping his arms to remain airborne or at the very least slow his rate of descent.

He had done this in a dream before, being able to run and jump, then flap his arms to fly over the treetops. It worked well in his dreams as long as he kept flapping his arms. If this was a dream, then it should work here, right? He looked down at the ground as it came up to meet him. He was falling into a mass of Jabba milling about on the ground around a motionless figure. Falling closer, he could see that it was himself laying there in a pool of blood.

"I am absolutely sick and tired of all this falling crap," he yelled, dropping faster and faster. One of the animals looked up at him as he drew closer, hearing him come.

"Then wake up," it said quietly, almost inaudible.

"Were it that easy," he thought to himself.

He suddenly opened his eyes right before he would have hit and looked around him. He was lying on his side, more or less in a heap, his legs twisted like a bread stick. One arm was pulled under him and the other arm was cocked back over his head in a most uncomfortable way. It was like he had been folded up into a pretzel or something. The body was not designed to be in this position.

He blinked a couple of times and tried to move but found himself completely unable. Being tied up like a pretzel would tend to impair a person's ability to move. He still felt a little woozy, but at least he wasn't nauseous like he had been while being carried from the cliff and over the river. He decided that trying to move all of his body parts at once probably hadn't been the best course of action, so he concentrated on just the arm folded back over the top of him.

How in the heck did I get into this position to begin with? What was this, some kind of Yoga? If it is, mental note, don't ever try it again. What the heck!

Finally, with a great amount of effort, he got his arm back where it belonged and was able to roll over onto his back. He felt like he was lying in a hog wallow or something. He turned his head to look at whatever it was that was caked all over the side of his face and the arm. It was a sticky, dark muddy substance and took him a moment to realize that it was his own blood. He looked himself over to see if he could find the source, checking his legs and abdomen. The deep claw incisions were still there, but they were no longer bleeding, none of his wounds were. He could feel no pain associated with any of the surface wounds on his body. That's not to say he wasn't in pain, certainly he was. He had bumps and bruises over every inch of his body. He felt like he had been through the wash cycle of an upright washing machine, without the water in it. He was sure he had at least one broken or cracked rib.

Rolling slowly onto his back his legs became mostly untangled. He decided that it was time to try and sit up. He rolled a little further onto his other side and brought himself slowly up into a sitting position. The pain in his ribs was off the chart excruciating, but he managed to remain in a sitting position. He blinked several times wincing painfully. Every part of him felt like it was on fire. A bottle of Ibuprofen would be his best friend right now.

He blinked again to clear his eyes of the dust and muck that had accumulated around them and looked around. He found himself completely surrounded by a very large flock of Jabbaway. Every one of them sat motionless on their haunches with their wings folded tightly on their backs. He blinked and tried to get up, but was still quite weak, besides it being painful, so he just sat there looking at them.

"Should I be selling tickets?" he finally asked tiredly. He had a thumper of a headache going on now as he tried to wipe off the mud and blood from his face with the torn sleeve of his shirt, which was pretty much in rags. He examined himself again seeing that every spot on him that had a cut or scratch on it was covered with some kind of a thick gooey substance. He noted that both of his daggers were gone. Those might have come in handy right about now.

"It would be best to not try and remove the saliva. It will keep your wounds from bleeding any more and it will continue to numb the pain until you can get proper medical attention," a voice came from his right. Bryan turned his head carefully in the direction of a Jabba that was stepping out from the rest. He was larger than the others and lighter in color with silver fur striping down his back in parallel lines, much like an earth skunk, and a patch of black around his left eye.

"Best to stay out of the water as well," the Jabba instructed, circling closer. "It will wash off and you'll have the same problem you did when we set you down."

Bryan looked down at the rather large dark spot of mud and blood beside him. He probably should have been close to death by now from blood loss, but somehow these animals had not only stopped the flow, but healed him.

"I don't understand," he said, closing his eyes and trying to think back to what happened. The only thing that was coming to mind was the wild dream he had right before he woke up. "How did you...?"

"Save you?" the Jabba cut in. "There are many things about the Jabba that humans have not bothered to figure out. Our body fluids have great healing properties and you are now seeing the benefits of such properties." Bryan opened his eyes again and nodded his head.

"I guess a better question then, would be why did you bother to save me? I'm a human."

The Jabba chirped loudly which brought the flock to a loud chorus of chirping. So much so that it hurt Bryan's head. He had a good headache going on and this wasn't doing anything to mitigate the pain. The chirping quickly fell silent when the Jabba made a quick motion with its head.

"What was your intent on the cliff as we were falling from your horse and sliding down the ravine?" The Jabba paced slowly back and forth in front of him. Bryan thought he was sizing him up for a meal.

"To keep from falling," Bryan responded, not understanding what the question was for or how it was even relevant.

The instructions that Terry and Tony had given him were that a Jabba was more or less a primitive animal capable of nothing more than killing any and everything it could to appease its voracious appetite. The only good Jabba was a dead Jabba. However, something wasn't adding up here. These Jabba acted like more than just a flock, almost more like a community or clan. And how in the heck could such a primitive animal speak? More importantly how did this animal from a planet that didn't appear to speak English, speak English?

"Why didn't you let go of me?"

"I don't know," Bryan shrugged, not sure what the Jabba was looking for. "I was scared. I didn't want you to fall either, I guess. Of course, your claws sunk into me made it rather difficult to let go of you."

"But you could have tried. You didn't want to let me fall. You were trying to save yourself, but also trying to save me from falling."

"I guess so. You were kind of tangled up in the Bolas there."

"Yes," the Jabba agreed, stopping in front of him and sitting. "And for that, you have my thanks and your life. My name is Jocko. I am the leader of the Binions." Bryan looked around and acknowledged the other Jabba by simply waving a hand in all directions.

"Hello, my name is Bryan Garrett, but you can just call me Bud," he said joking. He was talking to a bunch of winged wolverines for heck sakes! Why not joke about it? Many of the Jabba that appeared to understand him simply raised their eyebrows and pointed their ears straight up. It was odd to them to be called two different things. How would one keep track?

"Seriously, just call me Bryan," he said, reading the confused looks on their faces. He thought a moment and then looked back up at Jocko.

"Why haven't you killed me? Why did you save me?"

"Because you are not of the Kenlar or the Omar." Bryan was perplexed by Jocko's response.

"How can you tell? These are Kenlar clothes," he pointed out, looking at his tattered pants and shirt that was nearly in rags.

"It's not your clothes that define you," the Jabba explained. "It's' how you smell and hold yourself." Now Bryan was even more puzzled than before he had asked the question.

"Wait a minute, I smell?" he asked, completely baffled now. "What do you mean how I smell?"

"You humans are an odd bunch," Jocko said, tipping his head at an angle and trying to eye him differently. "You ask some of the strangest questions in the oddest of order." Now Bryan really had no idea where they were in this conversation.

"I'm very confused," Bryan said, closing his eyes to concentrate and follow along.

"You want to know how is it I can speak your language." Jocko announced, remaining unmoved.

"Tell me you're not reading my mind," Bryan said, working the conversation out in his head, or trying to. He became a little frustrated and held his hand up to stop the conversation and hopefully get on the same train this Jabba was traveling. "Never mind, let's just keep going the direction we were going and we'll get to that."

"Agreed."

"Ok," Bryan felt a little less stupid now. "Why did you save me from the fall?"

"You are not the enemy and you tried to save my life."

"Ok, got that point and a mental note made, moving on." Bryan nodded in approval. "Why am I still alive?"

"This question is tied to the first answer and the second statement. You are not an enemy. You are not Omar or Kenlar."

"Got it," Bryan said, making another mental check mark. "How do I smell any different from any other human? How do I hold myself differently?"

"Humans have a very poor sense of smell. By that I mean your range and sensitivity is quite limited. The Jabba is exactly opposite. While we have no heightened sense of smell, our ability to smell things from very long distances, and the range of what we can smell is far greater. You humans put off vastly different odors based on many things. The Kenlars all smell the same, as do the Omars; each clan has a distinct odor. On the road, I smelled Thulsian and something else that I have never smelled before. You and a couple of your friends are not of this world, are you?"

"No," Bryan answered simply. No sense hiding from an animal who could obviously tell you from your twin brother if you should happen to live in different parts of any world.

"You and your friends also ride differently than the Thulsians you were with."

"What? We're sitting in the saddle. Our feet are in the loop thingies, we were holding onto the reins." Bryan was no equestrian, but he was still a little insulted that he apparently wasn't riding correctly.

"Is this really necessary?" Jocko asked, letting his ears pull back just a little.

"No".

"Ask your last question."

"Doubt this will be my last," Bryan muttered under his breath. "Ok, the sixty four dollar question. How is it you can speak my language?" Bryan glanced around at the entire flock, figuring that if one could speak, they all could. "How is it you can speak at all?" he muttered.

"Oh good," Jocko said, lowering down onto his belly. This was more comfortable for the Jabba and Bryan found it more comfortable for him as well. "I like this question." The Jabba was almost excited about it. "Certainly English is not a native language of this planet. I am aware of at least 25 different human languages spoken on this hemisphere alone. There are many dialects of Jabba just in this area of Argyle."

"So you're not the only ones here," Bryan stated, stopping to confirm in his own mind what was obvious. This was a planet, probably about the size of earth and they were in just one tiny little patch of it. Like his planet, this one had life spread throughout the whole of it. It would be silly to assume that this was the only place that life existed.

"It would be presumptuous and arrogant of any species to assume so. Unfortunately for humans, they tend to think in those directions."

"No argument there," Bryan muttered.

"To my knowledge, there are at least twelve different species of Jabbaway that can speak your human language not to mention the indigenous languages of the surrounding clans. In the beginning there were five of us flock leaders who were taught to speak your English by a man such as yourself many, many years ago. He is a prisoner of the Kenlars now. He and his wife, Kawti Moft, are good friends of the Jabbaway, especially to the Binions and the Larks."

"You speak of Tim Hansen."

"I do."

"We were to rescue him from Ivan of the Kenlars."

"I apologize for the confusion. Not all of us Jabba can speak your language. Your smell and dress was confusing to us." Jocko's ears suddenly spiked and turned in all directions. Bryan could clearly see that he was sensing something external happening. His head rose like a shot and he flared his nostrils at almost the same instant the surrounding flock began to chirp softly, sounding nervous.

"What is it?" Bryan asked, looking around unable see or hear anything. Jocko sniffed the air carefully; looking in the direction they were all detecting the noise and the scent. He turned back to Bryan working his way up onto unsteady feet, the chirping becoming a little louder.

"Kenlar horseman coming this way through the northern Torres trail."

"Sure it's not more people wearing the wrong clothes?" Bryan asked, being sarcastic. "I thought the Torres road was the only way through the Torres forest?"

"Goodness no," Jocko responded, turning left and right, chirping quietly at the surrounding flock that went silent except for an occasional quiet random chirp. "There are several trails through the Torres and the Tera Mountains, the main road is just far easier and faster for humans to travel." Jocko went silent, turning his head back and forth, Bryan noticing his ears pivoting in all directions. "I can smell them close by, but cannot hear them," he said, scanning the perimeter of the large clearing they had been conversing in.

"Shouldn't your flock scatter?" Bryan asked in a hush. He was in no condition to be chasing off in the trees and it occurred to him that he was the one that was in the greatest of danger here. The Jabba could fly off into the trees and make good an escape, he couldn't. He could barely walk let alone run. This forest was very thick with heavy twisting underbrush. Traveling in any direction without a path would be tough going. He thought the river was directly in front of him. He could still hear it, but just wasn't sure. Jocko continued to scan their surroundings.

"Scattering right now would be unwise, even if this is a hunting or scouting party. Besides, I will not leave you here like this."

"So what do we do?" Bryan asked, as Jocko got to his feet. The Jabba leader began to chirp loudly which brought an instant volley of chirping from his flock, raising their wings in unison and waving them about as if fanning themselves.

"I cannot carry you, but I can get you to a safer location if you can hold onto me, we'll head down that path to the north."

"What about your flock?" Bryan asked, looking around at the hordes of them and stepping cautiously towards the large animal.

"Do they look like they need my help? They know what to do. They will be helping both of us."

"No," Bryan objected. "You should leave me and go with them. I'll be all right. I can use the path to head back to Vespa Cull. It's where I started this morning. I have good friends there that will help."

"You don't understand human," Jocko growled a little. "I can't leave with them. I can't fly yet."

"What? Why not?"

"Because I was damaged during our little wrestling match on the cliff and I have not yet had enough time to heal from within."

"You can heal that fast?"

"It's all in the salvia," Jocko said, becoming tenser with every passing moment.

"Spit," Bryan said.

"Whatever," the Jabba said, giving him a double take. "We move now and the flock will cover our escape into the forest, now go!" Jocko beckoned a little louder, the flock beginning to move along the ground in a northerly direction. Bryan carefully held onto the Jabba's fur and started down the path. At first, his legs did not want to work at all. There seemed to be absolutely no energy available in them and the Jabba leader practically had to drag him along. Even Jocko was still having a little bit of difficulty moving and having to assist his new human friend made it all the more difficult for him. Constantly twisting his head from side to side, Bryan could see the Jabba's pointed ears twisting in every direction, listening to the sounds all around them.

"Where is the river from here?" Bryan asked quietly, making their way down the narrow pathway.

"To your right," Jocko said, above the noise of the flock scampering through the thick forest all around them. Bryan was thinking that it was an option for an escape if they got cut off for any reason. Moving down the path, he caught movement out of the corner of his eye to his left, both behind him and in front. Besides the Jabba moving through the forest with their wings held up high, there appeared to be large figures moving in tandem with them, from tree to tree so as to remain as hidden as possible.

"Something very odd here," Jocko announced, stopping and poising resolutely, his head up high and his ears moving in every direction.

"What is it?" Bryan asked, pausing with him. He was grateful to be able to stop and rest. What he really wanted to do was to lie down in some nice tall, soft grass and take a nice long nap. Judging from the size of the blood spot he had left on the ground in the clearing, he had lost a considerable amount. What he needed to be doing was drinking lots of fluids and resting in bed, but here was neither a bed nor a meadow full of tall grass to lie in here.

"Two things happening at once now, very confusing," the Jabba said, with a hush as his flock moved right past them. He looked both ways again, his ears twitching, then raised his snout up and sniffed the air long and hard. "It's a Kenlar hunting party but," he paused again and sniffed. "Something else, more Kenlars moving fast in file along another path some distance from here to our left."

"Think I'd be more worried about the hunting party," Bryan said, the flock chirping louder and moving their wings more rapidly.

"Truly we are, but the other will pose a problem somewhere later on."

Jocko suddenly jumped into a response pose hearing a light whistling sound, and then the dull thud of a black arrow burying itself into a tree trunk right next to them. Two more immediately followed, whizzing right past Jocko's head and behind Bryan.

"Time to move!" Jocko snorted, bolting forward down the path with Bryan barely hanging on. Several nearby Jabba went down with a death shriek, being struck with the large arrows. To his horror, he saw a tangle of rocks and rope come sailing directly across their path in front of them. He looked left seeing several more Jabba fall in a tangle of wing, fur and bola. Hearing noise from the rear, he looked back. There was a band of Jabba on the path directly behind them following closely, but several of them went down with either arrows or bolas entangling them. Still surrounded on all sides by Jabba, it became apparent that they could not remain on this path.

Bolas streaked past Bryan from the rear, hitting Jocko hard behind his left temple but bouncing uselessly away. The flock leader staggered momentarily, so much so that Bryan thought he was going to have to keep him from falling over. After a quick reassurance that he was all right, they started down the path again, moving to try and stay ahead of the Kenlars. Bryan grimaced every time a Jabba went down. He knew that many of his new found friends were dying in order to save him and Jocko. Another set of bolas struck his friend, this time on the left rear haunch. Jocko let out a miserable wail and spun, knocking Bryan off balance sending him flying into the tangle of the forest next to the path.

"Get up!" Jocko beckoned him, staggering off into the forest in front of him. Bryan picked himself up only to be struck by a set of bolas that felt like they were breaking more ribs. Luckily for him, they had been thrown improperly and were not spinning. He would have loved to pick them up and throw them back as a little pay back, but the pain they had induced when they struck him was almost unbearable.

He stopped at a large tree and slid around its trunk to get cover so he could rest a moment. Settling back a bit, a black arrow pierced him through his left abdomen, grazing along the outer rib bones and passing back out the other side. The force of the strike nearly knocked him to the ground spinning him completely around and tripping in the tangle of vegetation, landing right on several Jabba. How were the Kenlar able to shoot so far with such accuracy? He hadn't known a bow to be able to produce these kinds of results. He couldn't even see them. There was too much forest, tangle and Jabba all around him.

"Where's Jocko?" he grimaced, checking his new wounds. His stomach was good and red where the Bolas had struck him and he had a really nice bleeder happening where the arrow had struck. Apparently none of these Jabba spoke his language because they just looked at him oddly and chattered loudly. One of them then leaned down to where he was bleeding profusely and gave it a good unceremonious lick of its broad tongue. Bryan was startled at first. He thought he was going to take a huge bite out of him, but when he looked down at the wound, it was clean and no longer bleeding. It still hurt like the dickens, but the pain was already starting to fade off.

"It's all in the spit eh?" he said good-naturedly. He gave the Jabba a good rub on the head like he would a good dog for a job well done. The Jabba seemed to settle somewhat and go into a purring mode of sorts as it closed its eyes and enjoyed the touch of the human. "Thank you," Bryan puffed, the pain dropping off.

He looked around for Jocko. There he was, several trees over to his left, moving deeper into the forest towards the river. Bryan got weakly to his feet and scrambled through the underbrush towards the silver backed Jabba as more arrows flew past. They seemed to be targeting him specifically. The Kenlars must have thought he was a spy or something. Which made perfect sense; why else would there be a human out here in the Torres alone? Being with a flock of Jabbaway would have been more of a puzzle but not likely being considered at the moment. He looked back at where he had been and saw the Jabba that had just helped him, lying in a heap with an arrow buried in its head. This was about as close to war as he wanted to get. The sick feeling in the pit of his stomach from the sight of death for animals such as these was really starting to get to him. He thought briefly of Tony and his air crew and what they had gone through in the skies above Germany. He wondered what it must have been like for those men to deal with the carnage of death on a daily basis. He could only imagine what it must have been like for any warrior, whether from this planet or his own.

He stumbled over several downed trees and a couple of rocks, landing in some bushes next to the tree Jocko was hunkered against. The animal wasn't moving very much, but was still alert and looking all around. Bryan ducked several bolas flying at him, crawling over next to the motionless Jabba. He caught sight of several of the Kenlar warriors trying to close in on them, but then they were again back out of sight as quickly as they had appeared. A couple of black arrows sank into the tree they were hidden behind as Bryan gave Jocko a once over. His feet had become completely entangled in a pair of bolas and Bryan could see his breathing was erratic and labored. He quickly pulled the ropes and rocks free from his legs and cradled him in his arms.

"I'd sure like to get my hands on one of those shooters they have. You ok?" he asked, looking around the trees for their pursuers. He saw and heard nothing.

"Just give me a moment to catch my breath," the Jabba gasped. "I'm afraid that while we can heal ourselves, we also damage much easier than others, including you humans."

"Can you move?" Bryan asked, keeping watch.

"Certainly can now. Once those abominable entanglers get around us, we have a hard time getting them off. Usually have to have someone help, DUCK!" he barked loudly. A sword came swinging at them from around the tree they were hiding behind.

Bryan dropped back and down, the steel blade burying itself into the tree trunk where his head had once rested. Jocko leaped at the Kenlar warrior who screamed in terror, the grey and silver ball of fur, fangs and claws coming at him, swinging and slicing. Bryan watched Jocko take the man by the throat, nearly biting his head off with his powerful jaws. Blood gushing freely, the Jabba looked up at his human friend's expression of shock and surprise, holding the Kenlar warrior by the throat like a wild lion that had just made a kill.

There was another sudden yell from behind the tree and another blade came at a frightened Bryan. Without thinking, he grabbed hold of the warrior's wrist and arm as he swung. Using the force of the swing, he flung the large man past him and into the ground. The warrior was a little slow to get up, and turned to face the bloodied Jocko who had just finished snapping the other warrior's neck, letting the head drop to the ground and roll off into the underbrush.

Infuriated, his companion charged the chirping Jabba. He only got halfway there before a large black arrow pierced through his chest under his left arm and came out the other side, sticking there. The warrior spun, eyes bulging and crashed to the ground next to his beheaded comrade. Jocko looked at the dead man for a moment, then looked over at Bryan who was still holding up the large dual crossbow the warrior had dropped when he had fallen the first time.

"This is how they are able to shoot from far distances with such accuracy," Bryan said, looking at the weapon. He knew how to shoot a crossbow. With his military training in sharp shooting, he was able to translate that talent to recreational shooting and that included the crossbow. "It's an amazing piece of weaponry and this one has some fancy advancements on it that I've never seen before. I bet the wood and the string are the key with this thing."

"Wooly bags for you," Jocko responded condescendingly. He was trying to resist his natural instinct to devour the warrior he had just beheaded. The Jabbaway loved all kinds of blood and flesh, even their own and this was a real temptation for him. However, he knew there was no time for such indulgences. Another arrow sank into a tree just beyond them; they had to keep moving.

He raised his head high and let out an ear piercing chattering that lasted only a few seconds. Moments later, they could hear and see a flutter of Jabba wings as the Binions took flight into the tree tops and away. The flock leader had surmised that they were of no more use trying to run a diversion for him and his human friend, so he had called them to scatter.

Bryan scrambled to grab both pouches of arrows from the dead men, reloaded both stocks and picked up one of the swords. It was too big for him to handle with any efficiency, so he dropped it in lieu of the big knife on one of their belts and then took off after his Jabba friend. He wished he knew how to handle the bolas, but the memory of his attempts up on the Torres road, combined with the attempts of his two friends came back quickly, surmising that they would just weight him down had he tried to bring them along.

"The river is not far," Jocko said, hopping up onto a big log as another arrow bounced off a tree trunk nearby. "I don't fancy going for a swim, but they are not likely to follow us across to the other side, unless there's something that you aren't telling me."

Bryan puffed hard, climbing up onto the tree trunk that seemed unnaturally large for a fallen tree. When this thing fell over, it was definitely heard and felt in Thulsa and Kenlar alike. He wasn't sure why they were being dogged so hard. Perhaps it was a combination of things. This was a hunting party for sure. They could see warriors in the distance carrying Jabba carcasses off to be dressed out. The only other thing he could think of was an advanced scout party passing by. If Bryan were to make it to Thulsa, he could spoil their perceived element of surprise.

"Nothing comes to mind," Bryan grunted, jumping down and under another large fallen tree with Jocko right on his heels. He was still incredibly tired, but their dogged pursuers were relentless and they had to keep moving to stay ahead of them.

"Tell you what," Jocko complained. "If I get hit with one more entangler I think I'm going to scream."

"You can do that?" Bryan asked, maneuvering through the thick forest.

"What, scream? Sure! I can if need be. But why would I?"

"Like a girl?" Bryan asked, trying to keep their situation as lite as possible.   At that moment, another set of Bolas flew at them and bounced harmlessly along a nearby log. "Never mind, don't answer that." He said, dodging another arrow. "Go, go, go!" he beckoned, trying to quicken their pace towards the river.

"Not looking forward to this," Jocko complained, scampering over several rocks and tree roots.

"Not looking forward to what?" Bryan puffed exhaustedly.

"The swim."

"Why, you can dog paddle can't you?"

"What is a dog?" Jocko asked, dodging a couple more arrows. He could see the river now. They were only yards from it.

"Animal from my planet," Bryan answered, smelling water now. "Four legs, smaller than you, no wings, barks real loud, hates cats."

"What's a cat?"

"Animal from my planet," Bryan said, stumbling through the twist of underbrush and tree roots. "Four legs, smaller than you, no wings, hates dogs, loves mice."

"What's a mice?"

"Never mind!" Bryan complained in hushed exasperation. "You'd think Tim would have told you guys about them."

"Get down!" Jocko growled loudly, showing his teeth and fangs. Bryan thought he was going to take a bite out of him as the Jabba dove right over him at a warrior, only feet away, raising his crossbow in their direction.

"Crap! How in the...." He didn't get to finish as another one appeared on the rock that Jocko had just jumped from. This one apparently hadn't seen Bryan, who was much lower than the top of the rock, and had his weapon poised to shoot the attacking Jabba. Bryan quickly grabbed a big stick and swung it as hard as he could around the back side of the warrior's lower legs causing his feet to come right out from under him. The big man landed flat on his back on top of the big rock. The force of the fall nearly knocked him unconscious. It certainly created intense pain directly to the spine.

Jocko was wrestling big time with his warrior, so it was up to Bryan to figure out what to do about this one. The warrior was about twice his size, so it wasn't like he could just climb up on the rock and beat the crap out of him. Well, he could, but the guy would probably laugh himself to death. A better idea came to mind as he climbed up and pushed the stunned man off the rock head first, falling between the rock and several fallen trees. He then pushed another log over the top of him. With the man now basically standing on his head with nowhere to go, there wasn't a whole lot he could do but make a bunch of noise.

Bryan grabbed his crossbow, but the warrior reached out and grabbed at his leg causing him to lose his balance. He slammed against the tall rock, popping off both arrows in secession. The first arrow went right through the warrior's leg and he went down in screaming pain. Jocko rolled off the other side of the trunk they had been fighting on. The second arrow pierced straight into the top of the man's shoulder next to his neck and disappeared. Jets of blood fountained up as the big man slid off the trunk and to the ground in a heap.

"What did you do that for?" Jocko complained loudly. "I had him!"

"Getting tired of saving your butt all the time," Bryan remarked, reloading his cross bow as Jocko sprang from under the tree trunk and started sniffing at the man that was trapped between the rock and the trees.

"My butt? Why you little…..." Jocko growled, figuring that the human was just ribbing him, which he was. They were only yards from the river now.   Bryan grabbed a small loaded crossbow pistol from the ground and quickly followed the Jabba over more rocks and downed trees towards the fast moving river.

"You starting a collection?" Jocko asked, looking back at the crossbow rifle and pistol Bryan was hauling with him towards the river.

"Never know when you might need a couple of these. There are dangers all about." He stopped on a large downed tree log that hung over the fast moving river. The water looked swift and cold.

"Like I said before," Jocko said, looking nervously at the water. "Not too excited about going for a swim."

"Jabba don't like the water?" Bryan asked, looking nervously behind them for more pursuers.

The Jabba looked up and down the bank of the river, looking for another means of crossing, a bridge or a big tree, anything but having to swim.

"It's not that. We're ok with it. I personally don't care for it too much. It's the Dungie and Farlaps that live in these waters."

Bryan mouthed the names Jocko had just blurted out.

"Dungies have long legs and poisonous spiked tongues. At least they are poisonous to Jabba. The Farlaps are flesh eaters. Like how clean this water looks? There's a good reason for it. They are big water mammals that have rotatable claws on their fins, all four of them." Bryan gave the water another look, clipping the crossbow pistol to his belt where his daggers had once been.

"I could have gone all day without hearing any of that. Should have just pushed me in and told me about it after the fact."

"You would have complained about it if I had."

"Tis the truth," he admitted, wishing that his older brother were with him right now. Britten always had a knack for figuring out tough situations and a flare for pulling off the impossible.

He wondered how he was faring just as a Kenlar warrior suddenly appeared with his sword swinging. Bryan had no time to react with any kind of a weapon. He still had a hold of the crossbow, but the blade was coming at him too quickly for him to do anything with it. He pulled back as far as he dared without losing his balance and falling into the river. It was only just barely enough.

He knew he wouldn't get a second chance to dodge another swing, and was able to bring his crossbow up, deflecting the following blow. The force of the swing smashed right through the wooden gun stock releasing both their draw strings, sending the arrows in different directions. Four of Bryan's left fingers were smashed by splintering wood and metal mechanics. It hurt like the dickens, but he somehow grabbed a hold of the metal bow stocks, swinging it at the warrior. His opponent dropped his sword trying to hold his balance on the same tree trunk Bryan was standing on.

Glancing over at Jocko sitting hunched on a rock some distance from him ready to strike, Bryan saw movement beyond him. Down the bank a bit, another warrior appeared, his bolas whirling above his head. Bryan opened his mouth to warn his friend, but ducked instead, avoiding his own Kenlar attacker's swinging bolas. The warrior swung a second time, Bryan watching Jocko launch himself a moment after the warrior behind him let his bolas fly. The entanglers hit precisely on their mark, instantly snaring Jocko, but he was already in missile mode, sailing right at Bryan who looked him eye to eye. He was in the act of pulling his bow pistol and raising it to fire at the warrior right before Jocko became air borne.

"Ah nuts!" he called out, a little frustrated and trying to laugh at the situation. Jocko landed squarely in his arms knocking him off the tree trunk. This whole thing seemed oddly familiar, falling towards the water. Bryan stretched out his pistol and fired, sending the little barbed arrow squarely through the chest of his assailant, and then the two were in the water. The shock of the cold wasn't as bad as Bryan had felt before. He and his brother were after all, divers and used to all kinds of water temperatures. They had gone skinny dipping in water that felt like it should have been solid instead of liquid. It was far colder than this, but this was cold enough to suck the air right out of his lungs. That and the fact that Jocko's dead weight thrown against him didn't help to mitigate the problem. He held onto Jocko as tight as he could and swam hard. He figured it was better to stay under the water for as long as possible. Work with the current to get down river as far away from their pursuers as possible. He was feeling pretty good about the distance they were able to travel under the waves until he realized that Jocko was struggling against him. He hadn't even thought about the Jabba not having the air capacity, so Bryan pulled him to the surface and they both sucked in a lung full of air, looking around.

"Get us to the other side," Jocko gasped, struggling against the entangler and the current sweeping them further down river. Bryan tried to pull the entangler from him, but the current and rapids were too much for him. It would be easier for him to just hang onto the Jabba by the scruff of the neck and pull him along, keeping his head above water as best he could.

Thankfully, neither was in the frame of mind or could see the spiked dorsal fins detecting their presence in the water, otherwise their struggle to keep themselves above the waves would have been even more difficult. Struggling in the swift water, arrows continued to rip into the waves all around them. It wasn't until Bryan had managed to get them into a calmer part of the river towards the other side that he could see the dorsal fins moving in their directions. Were these the Dungie or the Farlaps that Jocko had warned him about? Did it even matter which they were? Just that they were coming at them fast. Bryan was doing a decent job of keeping them both above water, though Jocko wasn't helping too much as he continued to struggle against his bonds.

"Will you hold still?" Bryan complained, moving them closer to the other shore.

"Not being in this water would be a very good idea right now," Jocko called out. Several more arrows went past them and into the water. Several more fell just short of them, all the while the low riding dorsals moving closer.

"Not getting shot by arrows is a good idea too," Bryan responded in between gasps of air, continuing towards the bank. His arms ached savagely, but that wasn't all. Every part of him was hurting again and he felt so tired. They were only a couple of yards from shore now and he knew if he could just get himself and Jocko up onto the dry bank that they could rest and feel a lot better. They were in a curl pool now, where the current was lazy and he didn't have to fight the river so much. He turned in time to see more arrows flying at them. It was amazing the distance, speed and accuracy they were able to shoot with their crossbows.

"Not getting chewed on by Dungies is even better," Jocko said, watching the dorsals coming right at them now.

"We'll make it," Bryan gasped, struggling harder to reach something solid. A Dungie surfaced some yards from them, its mouth opening and hissing. Jocko knew what was coming next. The rows of sharp teeth gleamed in the reflecting light of the river and sky and a ball of tongue appeared. It suddenly shot straight at the helpless Jabba like an earthly frog or toad, plunging into the water right in front of Jocko, wrapping around him. At the same moment, Bryan struck a submerged log and tree branches with his free arm. Feeling like they were being held in place, he reached for the tree and pulled, trying to speed up their progress to shore.

Grasping at the submerged log for a better grip, it felt like Jocko was struggling needlessly against him. When he turned to see what the problem was, he couldn't see the Jabba at all. He could still feel that he had a hold of him, but he was now submerged. A dorsal suddenly surfaced close to them, then a head with its mouth open and tongue stretching towards them.

"Whoa Nelly!" Bryan called out startled, pulling on his friend, bringing him back to the surface gasping and sputtering. Again he reached for the submerged log, finally getting a good firm grip on it. Pulling with his might and hoping that it would hold, it was now a tug of war between the Dungie and the human, for the Jabba.

Bryan could see that more were starting to move in from other directions as well. This wasn't good at all, not to mention that now he was starting to see blood in the water. Jocko must be getting injured by the attack and it was attracting more attention from other Dungie. The barbed tongue was supposed to be poisonous. He strained against the Dungie, but his arms were almost like Jell-O now. He looked back to see another volley of Kenlar arrows sailing at them. One ripped into the water right next to him and one off to his right, then three came out of nowhere and struck the Dungie in the back and the neck as it was giving a mighty pull that would surely have pulled Jocko out of Bryan's grip.

There was a loud wail from the creature as it reared back and up out of the water where two more arrows, intended for him and the Jabba, struck it again, this time in the head. One arrow pierced through its skull and out the other side. The other buried itself deep, protruding out the front of the face through the eye socket. The strikes caused the Dungie to release Jocko and he was sent sailing up nearly out of the water and onto the gravel bank. Bryan scrambled over the submerged log, using it to thrust himself up and out of the water as more Dungie turned from their attack to the wounded Dungie. Bryan and Jocko were completely out of breath, watching their water pursuers dismember and devour the wounded Dungie in a matter of minutes.

"You didn't get bit did you?" Bryan asked, checking the Jabba over for injuries.

"No, thankfully. Now get this infernal entangler off me and I think I can get away from the river," Jocko said, breathing hard and coughing.

"What about the screaming like a girl thing?" Bryan puffed heavily. "You said you would scream like a girl if you got hit with one of these again." Jocko was not amused at all, but Bryan gave out a loud chuckle. "I need to catch my breath," he said, trying to relax a little. "Let's rest right here a moment."

"There is no moment my friend," Jocko gasped. "As soon they are done feeding on their own kind, they will come for us, not to mention we still have Kenlar arrows coming at us. I suspect that there are Kenlar or Omar scouts on this side as well. We need to get to cover, and," he said looking his friend over good, "you require medical attention again." Bryan looked at himself. Besides being soaking wet, he was also bleeding.

"Not again," he said, looking for the source. "Now where am I hit?" He pulled his tattered rags aside to reveal that all of his previous wounds, that had been doctored by the Jabba, were once again, bleeding freely. Jocko had warned him that getting them wet would wash the Jabba saliva off and they would start to bleed and the pain would return.

"Not to worry," Jocko said, looking back as Bryan worked to free him of the entangler. "After such a journey through the water, I should have plenty of, what did you call it?"

"Spit," Bryan said, pulling the ropes away as a couple of arrows landed close to them. They both got up as best they could and stumbled into the forest, away from the river. The Dungie finished off their comrade and had turned to the intruders on the river bank, shooting their long tongues in their direction, only to miss and pull in tree limbs and rocks.

Once they were some distance away, Bryan dropped into an old tree stump hole, over grown with moss and thick foliage, while the Jocko made a quick scout of the area. When he returned to Bryan's side, the Jabba found him unconscious. Jocko was exhausted as well. Perhaps a rest was the best thing for the both of them. They seemed to be quite hidden for the time being. The forest all around them was very thick, but not as twisted as the other side of the river. There was plenty of growth, but it was more of a fern type plant that grew several feet high. The best thing to do would be to hunker down and wait for a couple of hours.

He started working to clean up Bryan's wounds, leaving a good slathering of his fluids on as many of the wounds as he could access. The rest would have to be left up to human biology to take care of. With that, he placed himself as close to Bryan as possible to help keep the human warm and then watched the forest for movement.

Hunt the Hunters

Several hours passed before Bryan began to stir. Jocko had moved to a perch on a lower hanging tree limb, but remained vigilant. The forest was quiet, yet very much alive as it normally would be. Jocko turned his head towards his stirring friend and sniffed the air. He had smelled Kenlar on the breeze the entire time they had been in this spot, but never anything close by.

The animal life here didn't seem too bothered by their presence or anything else that might be happening in the area around them. He knew where his flock was and for the time being, they were safe from any further hunting by the Kenlars. He knew where he and his human friend were and while it was safe for now, it posed a particular problem for getting his new human friend back to his own kind, specifically, his own friends.

Bryan opened his eyes and turned over onto his back, staring straight up into the dense trees. It was nice and quiet, well, as quiet as a normal forest would be. He could hear birds and some odd animal sounds that didn't seem to alarm him at all. There was a gentle breeze blowing through the tree tops high above. He wasn't sure if he wasn't back to that dreaming thing again as nice as this was.

He lay there wondering if he were to move, would he start to hurt again. Actually, the quiet was kind of loud. After all the action of the last little bit, it was almost too quiet. He thought about where his two friends might be right now. Were they still riding towards Crosslake or maybe they were still looking for him? Maybe they were trying to make a rescue or something? That wouldn't have been a very good idea considering how far he had come since he had fallen from his horse.

Let's see, he had been attacked by a flock of Jabbaway. Knocked off his horse and sliced up, slid down the side of a ravine and fell off a cliff. He figured he'd be picking rocks out of his skin for a while after that one. Carried off by the same flock of Jabba and tangled up like a pretzel, licked all over with Jabba spit, chased through the forest, shot at with arrows, hit with arrows, attacked with swords, nearly drowned in a raging river, attacked by some weird looking river fish frogs with long spiked tongues and shot at some more. So far, it's been a right busy day and he was just plain tuckered out. Oh, lest we forget how many times he was saved by his Jabba friends, who had first been his enemies and then his friends, and how many times had he saved his new friend?

Jocko! Where was he? Had he left Bryan alone to fend for himself, to try and find his own way back to Vespa Cull? That would certainly suck. Bryan looked carefully around without moving his head. He wasn't even sure he could still move. Maybe his body had absorbed too much of that Jabba spit and it had paralyzed him and now they were coming to eat him while he was still alive, fresh meat!

"That didn't make any sense! That's the stupidest thing ever," he thought to himself. *"Why would Jocko have gone to all that trouble, just so they could eat him? Dumb!"* He finally forced himself to move his head from one side to the other, looking at his surroundings. There were certainly no signs of a ravenous flock ready to pounce on his hapless battered body. He then caught sight of something, on a low hanging tree branch, perched above him, to his left.

"I was starting to worry a little bit about you," Jocko said unmoving. His chin rested on his two fore paws as he looked down at his human friend. "How do you feel my friend?" Bryan tried to sit up.

"Like I've been stuffed in a washing machine and run without any water in it."

"You humans, do you have a machine for everything? Can't you just use your own hands instead of relying on mechanical things to do your work for you?"

"It's called quality of life," Bryan responded tiredly, forcing himself to sit up. The back of his head ached savagely and there wasn't a spot on him that didn't either have a scratch, bruise, bump or laceration.

"You know," Bryan said, trying to stretch, but finding it painful to even get close to it, "I thought in my line of work I'd be exempt from this kind of abuse."

"And what line of work is that?" Jocko inquired. Bryan looked around some more, then back at the Jabba. He was suddenly struck with the notion that he could tell him what he did for a living, but he likely would have no concept of what he was talking about. How in the world would he ever explain it to him in a way that he could understand? What kind of a reference point could he use so his friend would comprehend what he was even trying to describe to him? He could just be out with it and see what kind of a reaction he got, or he could just give a very basic dumb man's explanation. Since this was an intelligent animal, he decided that somewhere in between might work the best. Actually, the reality that he was laying here in a thick forest talking to an animal was still a little tough to swallow. Terry and Tony hadn't said anything about the Jabba being intelligent creatures. Still, Jocko was an animal all the same and it took some getting used to. Bryan opened his mouth to speak, but hesitated, still trying to figure out how to word it so he would understand. The Jabba just drew in a deep breath and let it out, sensing his friend's quandary.

"Go ahead," he encouraged, knowing what Bryan was going through. He was fully aware that human's thought themselves the high link on the food chain and anything beneath them was just a dumb animal for their use and pleasure. He wasn't insulted, but amused at the expression on Bryan's face as he tried to spit it out.

"My brother and I find things," he finally stated. He felt like that was totally inadequate as an answer, but a good starting point anyway.

"We all find things," Jocko responded. "I once found a bug under a rock. What kind of things do you find?"

"Machines," Bryan blurted out, thinking he had found a common comparison point. The Jabba remained expressionless, waiting for further information from which to draw some kind of conclusion. Bryan finally decided it might be easier to just spill it out all at once and let him understand what he could understand, then work his way from there.

"We have many machines on our planet that do a variety of different things. There are great ships that can carry heavy loads across large oceans."

"An ocean, a large body of water, usually consisting of a cocktail of minerals, covering a vast portion of a planetary body, such as Argyle," Jocko rattled off, looking up as if reading it from an invisible book or something. Bryan tossed him with a surprised look. The Jabba smiled, reading the funny expression.

"Remember, we were taught to speak by Tim Hansen long ago. Do you think we just learned a couple of lines from Tom and Sally, then flittered off?" A light finally came on in the human's head and he just let it all rattle out.

"These great ships are made of heavy metal and sometimes they sink to the bottom of the ocean. If the cargo they carry is valuable enough, we go and find them and bring it back, likewise with flying machines. We have built metal airplanes that can carry many people and large loads. We search out these machines that have fallen from the sky."

"So why are you here?"

"We were searching for the airplane that brought Tim Hansen."

"Ah yes, I have seen it. Did you come to this world the same way that Tim Hansen and his friends came?"

"Though the same storm?" Bryan asked. "Yes, just not by the same method they did. They flew into the storm and crashed here, we crawled in from the west ridge face."

"I know the valley beyond the Thulsa gate well. It's called Valley of Honey among the Jabbaway. The humans call it Valley of the Lakes. It was once a very beautiful place to go when you wanted to be alone on warm days here on Argyle. Not many go there any more as it has been locked in snow and ice for a very long time, shortly before Tim Hansen arrived in Crosslake. Very angry storms hover over it twice a year for several days, as if searching, for something."

Bryan developed an odd look trying to understand the significance of the Jocko's description of the storms timing.

"Well, there's a doozy there right now and I have to get back to it soon or I'll be trapped here," Bryan said, getting to his feet. He was wobbly at first, but with a log to steady him, he was soon able to stand straight up.

"Why will you be trapped?"

"I came through the storm and it only stays for three or four days, then it leaves and with it, my way back home," Bryan explained, brushing himself off a little. He was still wet on his backside and he was still feeling quite poorly. Jocko's attention to his wounds could only go so far and last only so long. He needed human medical attention and something to eat.

"Why not just use the Twins?"

"How do you know about the Twins?" Bryan turned to the Jabba, passing him an odd look. Jocko gave his human friend a bit of a side glance, as if he should already know where he got all of his information.

"The Signet of course."

"You know of the Signet? Do you know where it is?" Bryan became quite excited with this information. Perhaps his misfortune wasn't as bad as he had originally thought.

"Tim has it," Jocko got to his feet and stretched.

"Tim told you about the Twins from the Signet?"

"Certainly, where else would one learn about them?" Jocko was a bit puzzled. If Bryan knew about the ancient book, then why was he acting so surprised about the Twins? Jocko jumped down from his perch and stood in front of his friend, gesturing to a small pile of dark colored berries.

"Here, eat these. They will give you strength for the journey."

Picking the berries from the ground, he sniffed them, popping one in his mouth. Bryan was even more puzzled than the Jabba. The Twins were just swords. Short glowing swords, but still, just swords. He had seen nothing on them or about them that would indicate they had any special powers, certainly nothing on a scale grand enough to control a spacial anomaly like this storm. They were after all, only swords, weren't they?

"What else did he tell you?" Bryan finally asked, feeling a little bit better with every berry he consumed. "How can using the Twins help in getting us back home to our world?"

Jocko had to catch himself in a half chuckle. He had supposed that Bryan had the full story behind the Twins, the Altar and the Storm. Then realized that the humans hadn't had time to learn about it and even if they had, they didn't have the Signet to study from to learn about what the Twins really were.

He was also very aware of the comings and goings of the Storm beyond the Thulsa Spoil gates. How it use to just pass by, but when Tim Hansen and his friends came to this world by way of the Storm and ever since then, it would stop over the valley beyond the gates and hover there for days before moving off or dissipating. Over the years as Tim had taught his Jabba friends to speak the English language, he had also taught them the secrets of the Signet. He would call a few of them into his home at Crosslake, including Jocko and his friend Digi, and together they would study not only its language, but also its contents until they all practically had it memorized.

The book had been compiled long ago by an ancient race of celestial travelers whose vast knowledge base spanned the universe. These travelers had encountered the spacial rift traveling the galaxy and had figured out its unique quantum dynamics, enabling them to not only be able to open portals to different places across the universe, but also shift time within that portal. Time and space were inexplicably connected; adjusting one affects the other.

So many other wonderful things were contained within the Signet. Jocko and the other Jabbaway also knew that in the wrong hands, the book could be a serious threat to the very existence of Argyle and the people that inhabited it. Tim had impressed on them on so many occasions how important it was that people like Ivan Rubella never get their hands on the book. Even though it had been written in the language of the Ancients, the knowledge contained within its pages was so powerful, that in the wrong hands, it could spell disaster to even the simplest of people, not to mention the universal ramifications that could be created.

Jocko would not get to answer any more of the long list of questions Bryan had yet to as ask. They suddenly became secondary and a topic of later discussion as Jocko's pointed ears instantly spiked and began to turn. He tensed and turned his head up and to one side sniffing the air. Bryan instinctively lowered himself back to the ground and he too turned his attention in the direction of the Jabba's alert. The forest had suddenly gone quiet. Even the rustling of the tree tops in the breeze had gone still.

"Talk to me buddy," Bryan edged, nervously downing the last of the berries.

"Omars this time," Jocko informed him quietly. "Moving this way. Four sets of them, moving fast, on foot. These warriors are heavily armed. It would be a good thing if we moved out of here as fast as we can, in this direction," the Jabba said turning the other way. "There's an older, hidden path not far from here that runs parallel with the Torres road. It will lead us all the way back to the Thulsa plain."

"Any chance of getting your flock to come in and run some more interference for us?" Bryan asked, moving as carefully as he could out of his little hollow spot and in the direction the Jocko had indicated.

"No," the Jabba whispered. "They are long out of harm's way and I want to keep it that way. As you indicated before, they have already done enough for us. It would be best to remain silent from here on out, until we can get clear of the Omar. They are far more fearsome warriors than the Kenlars. If there were more of them, Ivan would be a foot soldier and Broc would be the leader of the two clans."

"You're saying Broc is bigger and badder than Ivan? From what I heard, it's the other way around," Bryan whispered, in a hush, moving quickly through the undergrowth and trees.

"No, Ivan is definitely the biggest and the baddest. Broc is second best. However, the one you never want to get into an all-out fight with would be Ivan's right hand man, Talon."

"Why?"

"Because while the other two have all the brawn and size, Talon has the speed and skill the others don't have. I would fear him more than the other two together. At least those two I could either run or fly away from. Talon would pursue and be more than a match for anyone. He can outthink and out fight his opponent in just about every respect. He is a methodical killing machine."

"A real mean dude, huh?" Bryan said, bumping his shoulder on a tree.   The Jabba moved slightly ahead of his human friend, sniffing his way through the low tree limbs.

Bryan lost sight of him for a moment, then saw his head pop up through the foliage, looking around like some kind of a periscope, then dropping back down under the floor canopy. He could still see him moving through the under growth, the large broad leafy style plants jostling and swaying as the Jabba passed through them. Struggling to keep up with the Jabba, Bryan continued making his way through the forest towards some unknown landmark. While feeling a bit reenergized, every part of him was hurting now, but there just wasn't any time for Jocko to give him another slobber treatment, at least not right now. Thankfully, there were no twisting vines and heavy undergrowth here, just the fern type foliage.

"You must move faster my friend," Jocko whispered, suddenly appearing right in front of him out of the growth.

"Easy for you to say," Bryan puffed heavily. He looked down at some of his wounds that had previously been attended to. They were starting to weep blood again. The smaller ones had started to scab over, but he was sure the ones Jocko hadn't gotten to, had to be bleeding again. Looking ahead, he tried to catch his breath.

"How much further to the path?"

"A very short distance, but you must move faster. They are overtaking us," the Jabba whispered nervously still sniffing at the air.

Bryan nodded tiredly and Jocko disappeared again under the growth. He started forward again, pushing through the thick bush trying to shield his face from the whipping switches that slapped mercilessly at him. He heard motion behind him and turned to see if he could detect their pursuers, but saw nothing. Turning forward again, he looked up in time to see a bent back tree branch come loose from the underbrush and fling forward off at an angle. He could hear Jocko chirping in terror and then watched the Jabba sail through the air in a tangled up ball, landing in a rolling heap some distance away.

There were calls from warriors in all directions as Jocko landed. Bryan spun several times trying to spot them, but saw nothing. He assumed that this was a good thing, as he would have probably been filled with arrows by now had they been able to see him. It was a good bet that they knew where Jocko was. The sling snare was quite effective at entangling and trapping its victim, but it was designed to toss smaller prey. Had Bryan walked into it, it would have just tangled him up and left him dangling there.

Bryan finally caught site of several warriors quickly moving in his direction. Dropping to the forest floor beneath the fern growth, he started crawling as fast as he dared towards the last spot he had observed Jocko land. He felt like they should have been traveling in this manner to begin with. It was much clearer down on the ground. Trying to push through the foliage from above was tough going and painful, being scratched and slapped constantly by brush and tree limbs. There was almost nothing under the floor growth. It had been grazed clean by the ground critters and insects. There was a bit of a worn path in the direction he was going, so he scampered along as quickly as he could.

It wasn't long before he came upon some freshly broken branches and what looked like a strike mark in the moist dirt of the forest floor. Scanning the area carefully, he listened quietly for any signs of Jocko. While it was easier going down here, it was much darker. The thick upper canopy made the forest itself dark, add the lower canopy to the floor and the green and blue light filtering through and conditions weren't too conducive for seeing at a distance.

Starting to move in a direction based on Jocko's last known trajectory, he froze, hearing something very close. Slowly turning his head, he held his breath, watching two sets of legs and feet moving silently through the foliage just past him, on either side. Through the lower canopy he could look up and see both warriors looking around, a dual arrow crossbow poised in his raised hands.

It was incredibly quiet. Holding his breath, Bryan thought he could hear his own heart pounding. Amazing how you can be absolutely still and all of a sudden, you have an itch under your nose, or worse, in it. He wished he still had the crossbow he had taken from the Kenlar warrior on the other side of the river. He'd smoke these two now, grab Jocko and make a run for it. Problem was he didn't know for sure where the Jabba was. He was sure he was close by, lying silent to keep from being detected.

Bryan noticed two other sets of feet approach, stepping right next to him on the other side. He could look up through the lower canopy and see the warriors next to him, watching them communicate silently using hand signals. These odds were not very good. Four big warrior dudes against one medium sized scuba diver from Earth.

If he and Jocko were discovered, which was probably inevitable, they were surely to be killed. In this game, which he didn't like playing anyway, you either kill or *BE* killed.

These Omar warriors all had swords, large daggers, two sets of bolas, and a dual crossbow for armament. Additionally, each had crossbow pistols holstered to each calf. Besides the sword tips and hanging bola rocks, the pistols were the only things he could see or had any access to. There was a pistol within easy reach on both sides of him, but to try and pull them from their holsters right now would be suicide. He would have to wait until they started to move so that the pistol removal was masked by their own movement. A bold move to be sure, but something they certainly wouldn't expect.

He was turning red, still holding his breath, waiting for them to move or make a sound of their own. Finally, they started forward again and he carefully controlled his exhale, coming slowly up on his knees and reaching for each pistol. As each man stepped forward, he pulled them gently and naturally from their holsters. Taking a controlled inhale, he pushed the safety strap away from each trigger and gripped them firmly. His only hope here was the element of surprise and his accuracy. He would have to bring down the first two in silence, then grab for their crossbow rifles and take out the other two before they had a chance to get to him. Everything depended on timing, skill and a lot of luck.

He quietly crouched himself into position, reaffirmed his grip on both pistols with fingers on the triggers, and waited for them to take another step away from him. Both men stepped into his line of sight through the lower canopy, right where he needed them to. He took aim and let both little arrows go at the same time. Though not as powerful as the rifle version of the crossbow, the pistols and the point blank range did the trick. The barbed arrows found their mark right through the lower back portion of the skull and up into the brain cavity.

Both men went down with hardly a sound. Bryan knew that even at that, they would not have gone unnoticed. He carefully scrambled over to grab a crossbow from one of them only to find that it had gone off when the warrior had dropped and the arrows were now gone. He rolled over to the other warrior, watching another pair of legs moving quickly back in his direction. The other crossbow was still loaded and pulling it from the dead warrior's hands, swung it up in front of him and fired one arrow through the underbrush, right into the heart of the approaching warrior.

He could still see the other warrior's legs some distance off, the third falling with a clamor right in front of him. Bryan reached for the second crossbow, spotting something else off to his left. In the dull under light of the lower canopy he noticed a dark lump gently expanding and contracting. Grabbing a pouch of arrows and both crossbows, he crawled several yards over to the dark mass.

The smell told him right away that it was Jocko. The Jabba was thoroughly and tightly entangled in bola ropes and rocks. He was sure that not only had he been pummeled by the rocks when the snare went off, but then a second time when it had tossed him and he hit the ground, rolling and tumbling. He was certain that he was probably pretty busted up inside. The ropes were so tightly wound around the animal that he could barely breathe, not to mention the fact that they had wrapped around his snout, effectively clamping his mouth shut.

He looked for other signs of outside damage but found no blood. He had to get him out of here, but he wasn't sure where to get him to. The only thought in his head was to get him to Vespa Cull. He knew the direction, but had to find the path before he could just jump up and make a run for it.

He looked around carefully, noting that he could no longer see the legs of the fourth warrior. Probably in hiding, waiting for Bryan to show himself first. The hunters had become the hunted in a deadly game of cat and mouse and while Bryan had taken out three, he was still at a great disadvantage. He had no idea where the fourth was now.

He left the crossbow with the single arrow still loaded in it next to Jocko, took the other with two loads in it and crawled carefully through the underbrush. The path had to be right here close and it would probably be much easier for him to see it if he were to stand up, but to do so would give away his position. Presently he came to an opening in the lower canopy where he could see his surroundings a little better and looking around at the opening, realized that he had just found the trail Jocko had spoken of.

Carefully poking his head out, he surveyed his surroundings. No sooner did he have his head out in the open and looking around when an arrow landed right between his hands. Bryan looked up into the nook of a tree some distance away at the fourth warrior who had just fired his crossbow at him. He was just jumping down to come at him when Bryan let one of his arrows go. The shot flew to the warrior's far left, missing him completely. Spooked, the warrior jumped back behind a stump, giving Bryan enough time to pull back into the underbrush without being seen. He had one shot left and knew the warrior had at least three. He scrambled off in another direction away from Jocko, heading for a nearby tree trunk.

The forest was somewhat spread out in this area, lending itself to a lot of open space for maneuvering in this deadly game. He intentionally popped his head up out of the lower brush near the tree and sighted the warrior to his right, still moving through the thick under growth. The warrior instantly fired another arrow at him, just missing him. Bryan brought his crossbow up but held his fire. He didn't want to give the warrior time to reload his rifle, but to pull his pistols and discharge them somehow. The ploy worked, the Omar dropping the crossbow and diving for cover, pulling his pistols.

Bryan dropped again and maneuvered around to another tree, making a half circle to the warrior's last known position and coming carefully up out of the growth. He was met with a blur of two smaller arrows coming at him and dodging the shots, let his last arrow go, finding its mark in the left shoulder of the warrior. The strike blew through his leather armor, shoulder blade and almost all the way out the back side, throwing the man back into the bush. Dropping the spent crossbow, Bryan made his way back over to where Jocko was still laying.

Now to make good their escape. He scooped the helpless Jabba up and put him over his right shoulder, then grabbed the other crossbow, quiver of arrows and headed for the trail. Jocko had to weight around 30-35 pounds and Bryan was already in bad shape. He hoped that they weren't too far from Vespa Cull, because he didn't figure that he was going to last very long with this kind of stress and the blood loss.

Finding the only path close by, he started as fast as he could, noting several more Omar warriors coming out of the forest some distance behind. Starting to work his way down the trail away from the area, he heard a whirling noise and turned to see the wounded warrior twirling his bolas over his head, looking right at him. Bryan was very tired of the whole chase and rolled his eyes in disgust that he was still going to have to contend with this last man, right here, right now. Before the warrior could let his bolas go, Bryan raised his crossbow and let the last arrow go. It found its mark right through the center of the man's chest. The warrior staggered and dropped the bolas, which came straight down, wrapping around his neck and pummeling his head, then fell into the underbrush.

There was no way for Bryan to hold onto his weapons and still carry his friend as far and as fast as needed. He wasn't sure how far he would be able to go in his condition. The only thing he knew was he had to get himself and Jocko as far away as possible, so he dropped his weapons, turned and started running with a grunting unconscious Jabba on his shoulders. Running along the narrow trail, his intent was to put as much distance between him and the other warriors, who were making their way through the forest to where his little skirmish had taken place.

After quite a distance, he had to stop and catch his breath, but he didn't dare set Jocko down or tarry too long, he had to keep going. Mile after mile he would run then stop to rest and catch his breath. He sensed it getting harder to get going again each time and he was moving slower, his legs feeling hollow and his head becoming dizzy. Finally, the forest began to thin and occasionally he caught glimpses of the Boris peaks through the trees, but exhaustion was quickly taking hold now and he was to the point where he could barely walk. About to collapse into the brush and give up, he stumbled onto the Torres road. He could look down the lane and see the opening to the Thulsa plain. He made it!

Shuffling down the road for a bit, he heard noise on the road behind him, so he stumbled back off into the bush and carefully set Jocko down in the tall grass, then collapsed himself. Moments later, he heard a lone horse trot past them on the road and then he lost consciousness. Just up the road at the base of the Boris mountain range, was Vespa Cull.

A dash of Madness

The business of life on Argyle is no different than any other place, least of all Earth. On the cultural ladder, Argyle was much younger than Earth, though physically, the planets were about the same age. The underlying theme of life on either, whether basic in nature or technologically advanced, remains the same, survival is living. This is true whether you are human or animal. Animals generally followed a set path for their day to day survival, but the human population has upper cognitive functions that allow them to think and reason on a much higher plane than most animal life. The true point was that, for most of Argyle's inhabitants, there was no time for leisure and play, unless you were the very young. Even then, there were plenty of chores to be done.

You would think that with so many children at her feet Caroline would have her hands full. However, she was a strong willed woman and ran a tight ship at Vespa Cull. She would even have her little Anna helping with some of the dishes when there was time for it. If they were full up for the evening, usually speed was of the essence and she just had to deal with everything as it came at her. Only this morning she had said goodbye to her husband and the band from Thulsa. The last of her guests had already left or were just heading out.

Even as everything appeared to be as tranquil and normal as any other afternoon, there seemed to be something that just wasn't quite right. Trusting her own instincts, she asked her oldest son to ride the ridgeline part way up one of the razor backs of Mount Boris for a good look around. She knew that the Kenlar and Omar armies would empty onto the East Thulsa plain and their route would lead them right past Vespa Cull. No one needed to tell her what she had to do. She had already started preparing to leave for Thulsa last night when Tony and his men had arrived, but now, there seemed to be an even greater urgency to leave. She couldn't put her finger on it. An intuition that was universal with all women, told her that something just wasn't right!

Following their instructions to pack and hide everything of value in prepared places of security, she stepped out onto the forward deck above the main doorway and scanned the horizon towards the Torres. She had taken note of a lot of birds heading away from the Torres a little earlier, but assumed that it was the approach of the Kenlar advanced setup army. They would likely not bother Vespa Cull, being in too much of a hurry to get into position on the east plain to guard

the setups of the heavy machines of war and the making of the camps.
It was what came after the mechanized column that concerned her
more, the actual troops.

There was still time to finish up departure preparations. She
turned to her left and scanned the ridgeline, spotting her oldest son on
horseback, riding carefully towards the furthest point where he looked
out on a wider view of the expanse to the west. From this vantage
point, the Thulsa plains, the Torres forest and many of river ravines
that drained from that region of Kenlar could be observed. She
watched him carefully as he scanned the area around Vespa Cull.
Remaining in one position for a very long time, he finally turned his
mount around and started to make his way back the same way he had
come to report his findings. As Caroline turned back for the door, she
just about stepped on a little Anna who had stepped out on the huge
deck to find her mother.

"Honestly child," Caroline grumbled, a little irritated, scooping the
little one up and heading back inside. As she did so, Anna stretched
out her little arm and pointed to the forest, babbling madly about
something. They were almost around the corner of the main archway
of the door when Caroline looked at her child, noting how emphatically
she was trying to get her mother's attention. Caroline turned back to
the deck door opening and looked around the corner. Anna continued
to jabber madly, so much so that Caroline became even more
uncomfortable. She turned to the inside rail and yelled down to the
rest of her children to hurry up with their preparations and then turned
back to the deck door. Stepping back out with Anna still in her arms,
the toddler continued to carry on as if something ominous were about
to take place.

"What is it Anna?" she asked, looking at her concerned little face
and then trying to see what the little tot was obviously seeing. "What
do you see?" Suddenly, off in the distance, she could see the dust trail
of a lone horse rising as the animal galloped at high speed towards the
house. She could not see a rider though. A shot of panic fired
through her chest, stepping to the rail for a better look at the horse
drawing closer. A moment later, her oldest son spurred his horse to
intercept the galloping animal's path and catch it. The image of her
son sitting upright in his saddle confirmed the absence of the other
horse's rider. He pulled it to a halt for a closer examination, Anna
babbling even more excitedly and continuing to point in the direction
that the horse had come. Caroline was about to converse with her
approaching son when she had to do a double take at a word that
Anna muttered.

"What did you say baby?"

"Bryan," Anna repeated excitedly. Bolting from the deck with her
youngest still in her arms, Caroline was outside in an instant as her
son came galloping up with the riderless horse. To her horror, she

could see that the horse had been injured in several places, indicating it had gotten into a scrape or something. She recognized the injuries as having been made from a Jabba attack. The saddle was still intact, but part of the bridle and the cinch had been sliced away. Additionally, the day pack they had taken with them was only hanging by one strap and the bolas were gone from their place on the saddle. There were deep claw marks all over the soft fur seat of the saddle and blood spots everywhere. This had been Bryan's horse. Caroline rattled out several commands to her son in Thulsian and then stroked the horse on the rear as he led it off to the open stables. Anna continued to point behind her mother, jabbering madly.

"Bryan," she repeated every so often. She kept her attention in the direction the horse had come. Caroline finally turned back around in time to see more birds take to the air near the turn in the road that headed into the Torres forest. Something was coming and she needed to find out what it was. She called out to her son, who promptly returned with the two horses. Her oldest daughter showed up, along with several of the other kids, who had been drawn by the commotion. Caroline passed Anna over to the oldest daughter, while her son passed his mother a sheathed dagger. She excitedly barked orders out to her other children who instantly jumped into action. Departure preparations were being moved up considerably.

She bounded up onto the good horse and spurred it towards the Torres road inlet while her children went into action. She wished that she had grabbed a sword of some kind, but there was no time. She thought she could at least get close enough to see what it was. Most likely the approach of the Kenlar army and she would have plenty of time to high tail it back to Vespa Cull to finish gathering her family up and get out of harm's way before the real fighting started.

Approaching the turn off, she slowed her horse to an easy trot. She wished that Terry were here doing this. The fact that one of their horses had come back without its rider was very unnerving to say the least. It was obvious that they had been attacked by a Jabba flock, but she knew that Terry was an expert at handling the Jabba and could certainly take of himself. A flock attack could be an unnerving experience, but usually if you had several experienced warriors or even hunters in the group, there would be no real dangers as most Jabba were fearful of groups of humans anyway.

Caroline trotted around the bend, scanning the road ahead and the brush that lined both sides of the dirt road. She stood up in the stirrups, continuing up the road for a little ways. She could see nothing coming down the road from the Torres, but heard the faint sound of Jabba chatter scattered in every direction in the distance beyond the brush. She held her nervous horse steady, stopping to listen and scan the area. She waited for a moment as everything dropped to dead silence. This was usually right when things happened, when it was quiet and a person was sure there was no danger. With this in mind, she gently settled back into the saddle and carefully turned her mount back to Vespa Cull. As she did so, she detected movement in the brush to her right. She held her position, and waited with her hand on the dagger attached to the saddle. The movement persisted, but did not change location, so she jumped down off the horse, pulling the long dagger from its sheath and carefully made her way around to the backside of the thicket to find the source of the commotion.

Laying in the scrub, completely tangled up in a bola was a large Jabba. It could hardly move because it was so thoroughly tangled up in the rope weapon. Even its mouth was clamped shut with the ropes wrapped around its snout. It was apparent to her, that this Jabba had been involved in the flock attack on her husband's group. It must have had a part in knocking Bryan from the horse that had just come in. The Jabba was breathing heavily as it struggled for air in the restricting tangled bola ropes. She could see no apparent injuries other than a little fur missing from a couple of locations. This animal must have been one of the lucky ones, knowing her husband would not have left one alive in this manner. What didn't make any sense was how it had gotten here in this condition. The only good Jabba was a dead Jabba.

She stepped over to the entangled beast with her dagger drawn ready to dispatch it quickly and then continue her search for anything else that might be out here, perhaps a better clue as to what happened to the Thulsa band. However, there was precious little time for such a search. She knew there was only a short time before they needed to be on the road ahead of the Ivan's marching armies. Soon this road would be a dust cloud of moving men, animals and machines, pulverizing the dirt beneath rolling wheels, kicking it up into the Argyle air.

The animal opened its eyes and looked up at her bending down and placing the tip of her dagger behind its left ear. It hardly made a sound, struggling again against the entangled ropes. Grabbing some of the ropes for leverage, she was about to apply full pressure to her blade and end its life when a dirty hand reached from within the shrubs and stayed her hand. Completely startled, she yelped and jumped back. The Jabba struggled again as a figure crawled from the shrubs and dropped to the ground beside the animal.

"No," he rasped, seemingly exhausted. "Don't kill him. It's not his fault." Bryan Garrett winced painfully, rolling on his side, to face Caroline. She thought she was seeing a ghost. The surprise had nearly caused her to pee her pants, but getting past the initial shock, she was quick to his side to render aid.

"What in the world, Master Garrett?" she asked, looking him over from head to foot. He had cuts and bruises everywhere. There were a few rather large gashes in his thighs, arms, and sides, with road rash all over his body.

"What happened? Where are the others?" she asked, trying to help him sit up.

"I think they're fine," he winced, sitting up and looking over at her. He was indeed, very glad to see a friendly face. "I probably wouldn't be here right now if it hadn't been for this Jabba," he said, looking back over at the tied up animal that now lay quietly in the grass.

"Clearly," she indicated, blaming his condition on the Jabba and looking him over carefully. "You're hurt pretty bad here."

"I think I've got some busted ribs," he said, letting her have a closer look at the wounds beneath what was left of his shirt.

"Here," she said, passing him her dagger, getting back to her feet and starting for the horse.

"What do I need this for?" he asked, looking at it having no idea what to do with it.

Caroline turned and gestured towards the Jabba, but then remembered his mention that it had saved his life. She wasn't sure what that was all about, but considering his condition, she didn't have time right now to get the whole story.

"To defend yourself from…...whatever," she finally finished, jumping back onto the horse and galloping off.

Bryan felt dizzy and a little nauseated. He was sure he was still suffering from blood loss and shock, not to mention his nervous system was screaming at him for all the injuries he had acquired in the last hour. He felt the urge to just lie down and try and get comfortable, but when he tried, he felt just as uncomfortable and sick. He finally turned to the Jabba and looked at his pitiful state, then looked at the digger in his hand. It wasn't really meant for cutting, but for stabbing. However, there was a bit of an edge on the blade, so he carefully reached over and started working to free the animal from the ropes.

After some cutting and tugging, he pulled the ropes from its snout and away from its razor hooks on its wings and then finally dropped back to the ground exhausted and sick. The two lay motionless for several minutes just breathing and trying to recoup some energy. Finally, Bryan carefully rolled to one side and faced the Jabba that continued to lay motionless.

"There," he puffed tiredly. "Now you can scream like a girl."

"'Bout time you got those ropes off," the Jabba spoke up.

"Hey, it was your boys that did away with the knives I had," he said with effort, trying to get a little more comfortable, as best as you could lying on the ground covered in rocks and twisted brush roots.

"You would have lost them somewhere in the forest anyway. How did you know to bring me here?" The Jabba asked, remaining motionless in the grass.

"It's like I told you before," he said, keeping his head resting on the ground. It seemed to feel better that way. "These people are my friends. It's sorta where we started our little journey. Besides, it was the only trail in the forest."

"I have lost many of my family to Vespa Cull over time. You'll forgive me if I'm a little skeptical. She would have finished me off if you had not stopped her."

"I think that makes us fairly even now, don't it?" Bryan stated tiredly.

"I think you mean, doesn't it, and I've lost count," the Jabba corrected him.

"You talk the way you like and I'll talk the way I like," Bryan came back tiredly. He rolled in the other direction, still trying to get comfortable. "Just what I need, a grammar correcting Jabba named Jocko," he mumbled, hearing the approach of horses again. A female voice chattered Thulsian, then the careful approach of footsteps, Caroline reappearing flanked by several of her children. All the children stared at the Jabba while Caroline knelt at Bryan's side to render better first aid with the medical supplies they had brought.

"We've brought you a wagon Master Bryan," she said, looking at the worst of his wounds.

"That'll be nice not to have to walk," he winced as she moved him.

"Did you get no further than this? How long have you been here?"

"It's been an entertaining day so far," Bryan responded, finally sitting up and looking at Caroline's three oldest children. "You might as well get Jocko loaded up first," he said, referring to the animal in the grass next to him. The teenagers hesitated to do anything. This was a Jabba. They had been taught that this animal was to be feared, hunted and killed wherever and whenever possible. Caroline said something in Thulsian and the kids relaxed a moment.

"Why are we concerned about this animal Master Bryan?" she asked, working on cleaning the worst of his wounds. She was a little irritated, but focused on Bryan.

"Because he pretty much saved my life," he responded, gritting a bit as Caroline worked. "I think things about these creatures need to be reevaluated just a bit."

"How so?" she asked, working quickly to get to the other wounds that needed immediate attention.

"I suspect that another time and place would be better for discussing this," Jocko said from his spot in the grass. He remained unmoved, except to breath. Caroline stopped what she was doing and froze.

"It can speak," she stated unbelieving. Truly they did need to rethink what they knew about the Jabba. She suddenly turned her gaze towards the Torres forest up the road. Bryan picked up on her alert and looked at Caroline.

"What is it?'

"Kenlar advanced scout party coming this way," Jocko said.

"We best get you in the wagon," Caroline finally said, getting up to help Bryan to his feet. Her kids stepped forward to help, but Bryan resisted.

"No, Jocko first," he insisted. Caroline looked down at the animal with great hesitation. "He's not going to hurt you. If he was, he would have done it a long time ago."

She would have felt better about handling this animal if it were still tied up and immobilized, but there was little time to argue the point. The advanced scouts would turn west on the Thulsa plain and not bother with Vespa Cull, but only if there was no perceived activity in that direction. If they were caught here, there would definitely be trouble.

Caroline finally gave quiet instructions to her teenagers to handle the Jabba first and get it into the wagon while she helped Bryan get to his feet. Bryan gritted his teeth with the pain of his stiffness and injuries; Jocko remaining calm and quiet as the three kids carefully picked him up and loaded him into the wagon. Once loaded and Caroline was seeing to her patients, the oldest boy turned the wagon around and drove them quickly back up the road towards Vespa Cull a ways, then pulled off into the brush, out of sight of the turnout of the Torres road.

Indeed, it wasn't long before the sound of hooves and road dust filled the air and several riders emerged onto the open Thulsa plain, and they kept coming. Instead of there being just what should have been an advanced war party, the main column of men, animals and machines came flooding out onto the open plain.

Caroline strained to see through the tall bushes her son had pulled them into. The Torres road was not in clear view of Vespa Cull, but she knew it was only a matter of time before someone would either notice it or remember that it was there and come plundering for what it could offer, even if it were just a place for higher troop commanders to rest and do whatever. She motioned for her son to maneuver the wagon through the brush as best he could, so they could remain hidden from the Kenlar and Omar armies. She had to get back to Vespa Cull as quickly as possible, gather her family and make an end run to Thulsa on the far side of the plain ahead of the army.

"Can you run over all of the stumps?" Bryan complained painfully, the wagon jolting every foot or so as they made their way through the thick brush. It was rough going for everyone, but he seemed to be suffering the most from the movement.

"I suppose they could let you out and you could walk," Jocko said, lifting his head up a bit.

The other kids in the wagon with them seemed to almost hang onto the outside of the wagon to stay away from the Jabba. The smell of the animal was a little disconcerting to them. Caroline read their discomfort and jabbered something in Thulsian for which they instantly bailed out of the wagon and disappeared off into the bush in the direction of Vespa Cull. Bryan and Jocko watched them disappear, looked at each other then back at Caroline who was still trying to get Bryan bandaged up good.

"Was it something we said?" they said almost at once. Caroline smiled, but kept her focus on what she was doing. It was difficult because the wagon was bouncing so badly. They were moving quite slowly in order to keep the noise at a minimum and because of the rough terrain.

"No," she said quickly. "We're out of time to leave Vespa Cull. That's the main war column, not the advanced scouts. Don't know where they are. They must have taken a different route somewhere. The column will be on the lookout for anything they can use as support, and some of them are bound to know about Vespa Cull. I've sent the kids ahead to get the horses and the other wagon ready. It's gonna be a fast ride."

"Ride?" Bryan repeated. "To where?"

"Thulsa."

Jocko struggled to get up, but was quite unable. Bryan passed him a quick look and then turned back to Caroline.

"Why are we going back there? I would have thought that we would be safer hiding out at Vespa Cull."

"Heavens no," Caroline scoffed a bit. "The Kenlars know all about Vespa Cull, Terry and I. You've got an army full of raging male hormones, a woman and some teenage girls and you have a big problem on your hands. Add to that, men who have been sleeping on the ground and eating nasty food for weeks and Vespa Cull looks really good. We are far better off on the other side of the Thulsa walls until this battle is over. That's where Terry, Tony and your friends will be going and while we do have a really good hiding place up on the other side of the mountain range, I want to be in Thulsa."

"You're that confident in Thulsa?" Bryan asked, grimacing with every bump they hit.

"I know of the world you come from Master Bryan," she said, working carefully to try and finish the bandage operation. "Living with Terry for these many years and listening to him tell his tales of what your world can do and knowing what Tony and Catrina have done for the people of Thulsa gives me great confidence in the city's abilities to hold its own against the likes of Ivan and the Kenlars."

"For the sake of you and your family, I hope you are correct," Jocko said quietly. "I have seen Ivan and Broc's army. They have war machines that have never been seen before. They have weapons that can shoot further and cause more destruction than anything ever used and he has a lot of them." The ride began to smooth out considerably as the terrain opened up into pastureland Terry and Caroline used for their stock and the wagon was able to go a little faster.

"Were my husband and friends not going to be there, we would not, but they are, so Thulsa is where we shall go," Caroline said resolutely, finishing her work with Bryan, then turned to Jocko. "Now, what can I do to help you? I can treat a cow, horse, pig or whatever," she said, hesitating a little bit. "Never doctored a…..a bird, no, a wolverine before, not sure what you are." She said, trying to figure out how to even examine the motionless animal.

"Jabba," Jocko said, lifting his head in her direction. "I'm called a Jabba, from the Binion flock. My name is Jocko, third Jabba to my father, Fangor, leader of the Binions."

"Ok, Jocko, third son of Fangor. How can I help you? What ails you?" Caroline asked, looking him over. Bryan couldn't help but crack a smile. He had been through this already this morning.

"Oh, you're gonna loves this," Bryan said, trying not to chuckle. "I guarantee it."

Caroline had a silly look on her face, waiting for the explanation. How hard could it be? The Jabba was a living, breathing animal.

"Thank you for your concern, but I'm doing fairly well here. This is my second or third time doing this today and things usually go a little faster each time. I can actually lift my head already. What do you think, Master Bryan?"

"Very articulate," he said, grinning at his friends' humor. Caroline was positively puzzled. She had no idea what was going on. "It's ok Caroline," Bryan finally said, as they drew near to the animal barn that was a short ways away from the main lodge of Vespa Cull. "The Jabba can heal themselves from within, provided the damage isn't too extensive. Their body fluids have a really nice healing quality to them. Something that would have been nice for you to have used on me earlier," Bryan said, gesturing towards his friend.

"Hey, I didn't have any time," Jocko said defensively. "Besides, I couldn't move."

"What do you mean, healing qualities?" Caroline asked, as the wagon turned into the open barn doors and ground to a halt inside.

"The Jabba's body fluids have remarkable healing powers. Their spit can numb the pain of wounds, and stop bleeding for hours. Their internal body fluids constantly circulate throughout their bodies and can heal internal injuries, provided they are not too severe. Truly remarkable beings," Bryan finished with admiration for his new found friend.

"Humans can do this. What's the big deal?"

"Not anywhere close to as fast as a Jabba can. What would take us weeks or months to heal, would only take them hours."

"Stranger and stranger," Caroline muttered. "This just doesn't make sense," she said, almost angrily.

"What doesn't make sense?" Jocko asked.

"My whole life I've always known that the only good Jabba is a dead one. My father taught me that and his father before him. Every encounter Terry and I have ever had with the Jabba has been a bad one. I cannot understand how you can be here like this and can do all the things you do. It just doesn't make any sense," she said, trailing off to close the barn doors while motioning for her son to check on the progress of her other children. As he scurried away to the adjacent room of the big barn, Caroline turned back to her two passengers. Jocko was now able to sit part way up, but kept his wings closed tightly around him. Bryan sat carefully up then gently lowered himself to the ground and stood on unsteady legs.

"Sure you want to do this?" Caroline asked, holding her hands out to steady him.

"Give me a couple more minutes and I can give you some of my spit," Jocko grinned. Caroline was repulsed by the very idea. She didn't care whether he could heal himself or others with his body fluids or not, licking an open wound sounded quite disgusting.

"I'll be fine," Bryan said, a little uncertain. "I just need to walk around a little bit and try to loosen up." He hobbled over to the closed barn doors and peered through the gap between the two outside doors. He could clearly see the main lodge and a forest beyond, stretching back for as far as the eye could see. It would make excellent cover if there was a road that went through it. He couldn't see up towards the open plain, but he could hear the columns of men, machines and animals pouring out onto it.

Just then, there was a familiar little yelp and a cooing coming from the other end of the barn. Bryan turned and looked back at Caroline who had several of her children with her and attached to her leg was a little hand and a head of red hair. Little Anna peered around her mother at Bryan with sparkling eyes and a grin that could melt iron. His demeanor lit up at the sight of the little two year old who came running at him full speed with her little arms spread wide to catch all of him.

"Oh boy," he grimaced smiling, knowing that if she landed on him just right, her little body would cause more pain than when he had first arrived yesterday. He gladly scooped her up and held her as tight as he dared with his injuries. She babbled and muttered constantly, squeezing him, then sitting back in his arms, she proceeded to scold him using her finger.

"I guess you're getting told just how it is," Caroline chuckled, watching and listening to her daughter go on and on. Bryan grinned broadly, looking back at a very serious Anna and tried to carry on a conversation with her, only guessing as to what she might be saying.

"Oh really!" he responded, trying not to burst out laughing at her seriousness. "I am so glad to see you again too." Anna babbled on again for several moments. "Well, I tried to be careful, but this big mean Jabba knocked me off my horse and we went for a tumble over a cliff."

"You'd be dead right now if it weren't for this big mean Jabba," Jocko said, carefully sitting up and steadying himself against the inside of the wagon. Anna turned in Bryan's arms as he stepped carefully back over to the wagon. She looked at the animal in the wagon then squirmed in Bryan's arms to get down with the Jabba. Caroline hedged nervously, but Bryan reassured her that it was ok. Jocko suddenly became a bit uncomfortable looking at the child climbing down next to him and then back up at Bryan. He glanced over at Caroline who had a wary look on her face, then at Bryan and suddenly found Anna looking right into his eyes.

She raised her little hands up to his snout and gently stroked him on both sides all the way back to his checks, then his ears. She seemed to be checking him for injuries or something. She studied his features carefully and silently, looking at both sides. He kind of liked it when her little hands rubbed around the back side of his ears. She looked right into his eyes again and just gazed into them deeply for a moment. Jocko moved back a little as Anna gave him a good once over, then she suddenly leaped forward, throwing her arms around the Jabba and began to say something that only another two year old would understand.

"Looks like you're part of the family now," Bryan said with a big grin. He watched his friend sort of resist at first, but the warmth and charm of the little red headed child was irresistible, so he closed his eyes, enjoying the embrace.

"Wonderful, another pet in the house," Caroline said with a hush. She made her way over to the closed barn door and looked out through the gap between the doors. They needed to get from this side of the lodge over to the cover on the other side, which was easy enough to do logistically, but doing it without drawing unwanted attention to themselves was another matter altogether. She could only hear the column moving and see the dust cloud it created in the air. She turned and motioned to her children, whispering loudly in Thulsian. They all instantly dispersed, most exiting to the adjacent room to the other waiting wagon. A few stayed and climbed in the wagon with Jocko, Anna, now snuggling up close to the fury Jabba.

"Can you drive a wagon?" Caroline asked, as Bryan pulled himself up onto the wagon's driver's seat.

"You saw my prowess with a horse."

"Point made," she said, climbing up after him and taking hold of the reins. "Everyone," she whispered loudly, looking around her and into the next room of the barn to her son in the other wagon. "Remember to stay as quiet as possible. Don't draw attention to yourself. Let's go," she motioned for the rear doors of the barn to be opened and both wagons gently rolled out and started around the backside of Vespa Cull. They could use the cover of the stables and a couple of other out buildings, but they would be exposed reaching the backside of the main lodge and out the other side until they reached the relative safety of the wooded area on the north side of the plain.

Caroline nervously watched her children in the wagon ahead of them, weaving through the corrals and sheds. Her oldest son was a master at riding horses and driving a team pulling a wagon, so she had no worries about whether he could get the wagon where it needed to go. It was just the worry of a mother for her children, no matter how capable or grown up they were.

Bryan looked behind him at the occupants in their wagon. Anna was hunkered down next to Jocko who had her snuggled up close to him. The other children in the wagon were still a bit edgy about being in any proximity with a Jabba under any circumstance. While they knew their little sister had a certain something about her, she was, after all, only two and really didn't know any better. They figured that to her, this Jabba was just another fury animal like any of the animals they had there at Vespa Cull.

Passing through an open area between buildings, he checked out the corner of his eye towards the Torres road. There were indeed long columns of men, machines and animals moving out onto the plain in droves, heading west towards Thulsa. They were moving fast and furious, making good on their hopes for a surprise attack. Turning straight for the back side of the lodge, he was able to get a better view of what was pouring out onto the plain.

There appeared to be an entire garrison of men and horses stationed at the Torres opening, directing traffic and keeping the column moving. It was much faster to have the army spread out in a fan formation, entering the plain so that the column on the road could move faster. He tried to keep his eye on the garrison of warriors, moving about directing traffic. There were several warriors just sitting, watching the action happen. Fortunately, none of them seemed very interested in Vespa Cull, at least at the moment.

Finally behind the lodge, Caroline stopped both wagons for a moment and had her oldest daughter jump out and clear the other side of the lodge. After seeing that no one had been snooping about unseen, she motioned the all clear and jumped back into the lead wagon, Caroline motioning everyone forward again. Moving out into the open, they were more likely to be seen as their angle to the Kenlars was more direct now. Everyone just sort of froze in position and the two wagons steadily moved across the open flat between the lodge and cover.

The narrow trail that ran into the forest started almost immediately heading down into the thicker parts of the vegetation. Everyone held their breath as both wagons were silently swallowed up by the forest.

A moment after the wagons disappeared, one of the Kenlar warriors noticed something odd on the far side of the Thulsian plain, a fading cloud of dust in the trees toward the Vespa Cull lodge. He motioned for several of his companions to follow for a look. They had been ordered to leave the lodge alone, although, if they were to encounter anyone of Thulsa descent, they were to be dealt with in any way suitable to the warriors.

The four horsemen trotted up to the edge of the forest and looked around, but could not immediately see anything. The first rider worked his way up towards the lodge, keeping his eye on the ground, looking for any sign of tracks of some kind. It was difficult to tell anything. As this was a lodge and frequented by so many different travelers from so many different places, there was no way of telling what local lodge traffic was and who was someone just passing through. This was Kenlar territory right now and anyone else was suspect, but again, it would be next to impossible to know for sure. He looked over at the silent lodge, then around at all the out buildings and empty corrals. It didn't take a genius to figure out that the place had probably been abandoned in anticipation of the Kenlar army arrival. Who would be dumb enough to stick around for something like that? When the fighting starts, no matter how far away, things get crazy fast.

The Kenlar warrior turned to the beckoning of his fellow warriors, noticing wagon tracks leading to a narrow path into the wooded area to the north. He reined his horse in that direction for a closer look. These tracks hadn't been made that long ago. The crushed tuffs of vegetation growing on the road were recent. He held his horse still and listened for several moments. He could not have total silence because of all the movement coming from the Torres road. Wagons, machines, beasts of burden and men clamored and made plenty of noise to shield any faint sounds that might be coming from this road or wagons on it. His fellow warriors summoned him again and he finally abandoned his suspicions, turned his horse and rode back to his group, then back to the Torres to report to his superiors.

Caroline and her family had been watching silently from the deep underbrush in the forest some distance down the road and were quite relieved when the warriors retreated to the other side of the plain. She kept everyone hushed and motioned for both wagons to continue as quickly as possible down the path towards the city of Thulsa. It would take them many hours to reach the eastern wall. That was if they didn't get held up by anything.

Revelation

Britten Garrett puffed heavily, stepping back from Catrina's training foe. They both held short swords much like the Twins. Brit's idea here was to give the foe a chance to rest, not that he needed it, it just made a good excuse for him to rest. He would rather just drop the weapon and go sit down with a cool drink. Brit was tired, not exhausted, but he was well on his way to that. He glanced over at Catrina who was watching them closely from the side lines. She stood unmoved, but he could read the look on her face. He quickly judged his own progress based on the last two hours of sparring with the training foe. He thought he was doing pretty well, but the look on Cat's face was telling a different story. He nodded at the foe again and attacked, this time trying to make his motions as fluid and effortless as possible, trying to see the response and anticipate the next move. He tried hard to be aggressive, but at the same time keep his defenses well-guarded, all the while making his technique exaggerated.

For several minutes Brit spared with the foe, pushing him back all around the room. He felt like he was doing pretty good and for a while he enjoyed a certain level of confidence, even relaxing a bit and enjoying the engagement. Then Catrina barked out a command and he suddenly found himself almost fighting for his life. The foe wasn't actually trying to run him through, but was starting to do just about everything else. He found parts of his body guard suit coming apart as the foe would slash at him in every place possible. Brit was very much on the defensive and nearly running around the room to get away from his opponent. He finally turned, frantically swinging back at his advancing sparring partner. This worked for a moment until the foe adjusted and started advancing on him again. He tried to remember his stick training. *"Fancy doesn't generally defend, basic defends."*
He had been concentrating so heavily on trying to not only smooth his technique out, but also look good for Catrina. In truth, he realized that he was trying to impress her with his form rather than worrying about truly fighting. This training was to prepare him for the real thing man! There wasn't going to be a, *"fight really well, shake hands and then leave for home."* It doesn't work that way, not here. He was going to have to go into that ring and either come out as the victor or worm food.

"Basic defends," he puffed barely audible. Shifting his focus from Catrina, he started using what he had learned in basic form, not only defending, but attacking as well. As this happened, suit parts stopped coming off and the foe quit advancing on him. Even with this shift, he was barely able to hold his own, unable to make any progress at gaining the upper hand on the training foe. His frustration continued to build until he started to once again loose his focus and control.

Catrina slowly shook her head, watching Brit start to flounder again. Her riveted expression indicated that she was trying to direct him subconsciously, but it was in vain. You just can't teach a novice to be an expert in a matter of days. It takes long, endless hours of practice over time, for a person to understand and master the intricacies of sword play. Anyone can be quickly taught to use a sword to fight in battle, but to use one in the arena, one on one with any hope of coming out of alive, that's something entirely different. Catrina didn't expect him to be an expert, but she did expect him to be able to defend himself. She was bound and determined to see that he did just that. Brit's frustration rose higher than he was able to control and he began to lose it again. As he did, Catrina stepped forward to intervene. A short rest, while she conferred with the foe for a moment, would be just the ticket to allow Brit to calm down, rest a moment and refocus.

"Hold!" she shouted over the clamor of the engagement, stepping forward to stop the sparring. Brit swung again at empty space, the foe backing away and disarming. His empty swing spinning him off balance, nearly sending him crashing to the ground.

"Are you ok?" she asked, letting her hand come to rest on his shoulder. He bent over a bit, breathing hard, sweat dripping from his forehead. Still a bit blinded by his own frustration and somewhat disoriented, he looked up at her, unable to read her look of concern.

"I'll be fine," he nodded between gasps of air. Cat was not convinced, but let him make his way slowly back over to the armory table, pulling his helmet off and removing the gloves as he went. He let the sword drop to the table with a clang, giving the Twins that lay sheathed on the other side, a double take. He passed Catrina and the training foe a quick glance. They were conferring on the other side of the room. Cat had her fists perched on her hips with her back to him, speaking with the foe, who was explaining where he thought some of the problems with this pupil lay.

Britten reached for one of the Twins and pulled it from its scabbard. The moment he touched the hilt, he felt a buzzing enter his head, the blade glowing brightly as he raised it to his face. There was something very interesting happening that he couldn't quite put his finger on. He took special note of the odd feeling he was sensing in his hand. The sensation seemed to be coming from the inlay of metal scroll work on the handle. He gazed at the inscription at the top of the hilt. He couldn't read it, but he remembered Cat's translation earlier. "Knowledge is power." Yeah, he certainly needed that right now. He glanced back over his shoulder at the other two. He was getting beat pretty good here and he wasn't going to last very long in the ring if he didn't figure out how to use these swords and quick. He carefully removed the other sword from its sheath and held it up with its twin. The sensation now duplicated itself in this hand as well. The feeling of a mild electrical current pulsing through his hands accompanied by a buzzing in his head, piercing deep between his ears, down the back of his neck and then giving way to something else, something very odd. It was as if something were being downloaded directly into his very being.

A vision of how to fight with both swords materialized within his mind. It was like child's play now. He now knew information that hadn't even occurred to him, techniques that he hadn't even been introduced to here or back on Earth. He could see himself holding the Twins as Catrina had when she maneuvered with them the first day in the fort manor. The visions in his head and the flowing knowledge were somewhat scary, but exciting at the same time. He turned from the table with the Twins in hand and poised himself into a stance similar to what Cat had used that first day. It felt natural for him to do so. He began to maneuver and swing the swords in a gentle, careful motion, getting the feel for them. It was exciting to hold them and to actually know what to do with them. Everything made sense now. He didn't know how this was even possible; he just knew the information was there. It felt like the Twins had provided all the knowledge he needed to wield them like an expert. He carefully moved back and forth, swinging the swords with near perfect fluidity. Inner-swinging them now and moving them faster and faster. He almost started to laugh; he was so excited about what was happening. He had an absolute clear vision of how everything worked and how to make them follow his every wish and command.

The training foe noticed Brit on the other end of the room first, but was so astonished at what he was seeing that he just froze in place and watched the pupil maneuver. Catrina continued speaking to the training foe, but finally realized that she was being ignored and turned her head to see what had him so mesmerized. She relaxed for just a split second, and was in the act of turning back to the trainer when it registered what was going on behind her. She let her hands drop from her hips, pivoted on one foot with a completely astonished look on her face.

"What the-," she uttered barely audible. She watched him carefully maneuvering through several fighting motions with the swords. Thinking it was just a routine he might have learned on Earth at one of his mock tournaments, she eyed him carefully looking at every detail. He certainly had their attention now, becoming poetry in motion. Gracefully arching the swords over his head, he stepped carefully towards the two spectators in the room, and then started to swing the two swords together, occasionally spinning them with his wrists. He leaped forward in an aggressive attack stance, and then pulled back with both swords back behind his person. He pivoted on one heel with swords swinging in all directions. Catrina's eyes widened watching him spin them against each other, like propellers on an airplane, but never striking, just like Cat had done. These were moves only an expert swordsman could master! How was he able to do this? He was mediocre at best and it would have taken him years to learn these moves and reach such an expert level as this.

Stepping carefully towards the two, the blades continued whirling madly in front of him until he was standing right in front of Cat and the foe. Both had quite the impressed look on their faces. Catrina suddenly became aware that she was no longer watching his moves and the blades spinning in front of her, but gazing right through them, into Britten's eyes. She saw intensity and confidence as he stepped back away. He suddenly halted the swirling swords, one over his head and the other out in front of him, both pointed right at the other two. He stood frozen, poised for a couple of seconds, then lowered the Twins and turned back for the table leaving Catrina and the training foe flabbergasted at what they had just witnessed. Brit was rather casual about the whole thing, stopping at the armory table and putting the Twins back into their scabbards, then proceeded to remove his training armor. Working the straps that held the armor to his body, his gaze remained forward, as a stunned Catrina Dallas stepped slowly up beside him, watching him carefully. She wasn't even sure she was looking at the same man that they had been training as she watched him work the buckles. Cat was still speechless and was trying to figure out how she could phrase what she wasn't even sure she wanted to say. Brit was having some real difficulty trying to remove a couple of the buckles that held his chest armor on. The buckles had become somewhat bent and the leather straps were worn with time and lots of use. Cat finally reached over and started helping him with the hardware as he fumbled to get it loose. He was tired and just wanted to get out of all this and into something a little more comfortable so he could relax.

"Are you sure you're all right?" Cat finally inquired, having no idea what else to say or how to approach anything else.

"I'm good," Brit said with a smile, pulling the leather breast plate away from his chest and working on the rest of the armor covering his legs.

"Just a little tired I guess," he said, rubbing his eyes. They seemed to go quite fuzzy for a moment, even spotting like he was going to black out. He didn't feel dizzy at all, just something odd with his sight.

"A little tired," Cat repeated. "I would hate to see you when you're exhausted," she said with a smile.

"No," Brit sighed heavily while giving his head a slight shake and opening his eyes to try and clear the apparent fog. "I don't imagine it would be pretty." He tossed the leg guards up onto the table and then slid the arm guards off, tossing them as well.

"So," Catrina edged carefully. "Hans and I were just wondering,-"

"Is that his name?" Brit asked looking over his shoulder at the foe that remained some distance away. Brit nodded with a smile.

"Hey Hans, word to your mother." Brit turned back and looked at Cat. "You know you could have told me that a long time ago instead of just having me bow at the guy. All this time and we could have been biker dudes."

"Brit," Cat said, taking a firmer stance. "How did you do that?"

"Do what?"

"That whole sword display you just did?"

Brit looked back out into the room, then turned back and faced Catrina.

"Oh," he said playing dumb. "Yeah, about that. Been meaning to try that for a while now, but just haven't been given the chance." He was a little irritated about the whole thing because he had wanted to start with the Twins to begin with, but she would not allow it.

"Britten," Cat reaffirmed, still dumbfounded about the whole event, but a little frustrated that she wasn't getting a straight answer.

Brit turned to the table, picked up the Twins and looked them over, then looked up at Catrina. He glanced over at Hans, then back at Cat who waited for a response. He motioned for her to follow him further away from the trainer. They found themselves walking out of the training room and down the hall, Cat remaining patiently waiting for Brit to explain what had just happened to him with the Twins. Brit was racking his brain trying to figure out something witty to say or at the least have some kind of an intelligent answer, but nothing was coming to mind. He finally stopped in the middle of the hall and turned to her.

"Cat," he said, looking at the swords then looking right into her eyes. "I have no idea."

They were silent for a few moments as she waited for some kind of a follow up that might lead them in some direction for an answer.

"No idea," she finally repeated. Even more frustrated now, she finally blurted out the obvious. "Brit, you stink as a swordsman. There's no way that you should have been able to do what you just did without some kind of an explanation." Catrina turned and continued to walk. "Some kind of help." Brit was a little put off by her apparent lack of faith in his abilities.

"Thanks for that," he said under his breath. He started walking again to catch up to her as she lagged a bit to allow him to keep in step. Catrina heard it anyway and realized that she may very well have just hurt his feelings or at the very least, bruised his ego a bit.

"I'm just being realistic," she said, knowing what she must have sounded like. She had not lied to him or given him any false hope so far and she wasn't about to start now.

"You are actually very good with a staff and if I thought you could defeat an opponent in the arena with just the staff, we wouldn't be going through this right now, but that's just not the case. You're going up against someone who will be just as intent on killing you and being set free as you will have to be. If you're holding back, though I can't understand for the life of me why you would, but if you are, you need to let me in on the joke 'cause I gotta tell ya, I'm not laughing."

"No, I don't imagine that you would. Look, Cat," Brit responded, a little more serious than before. "I really don't know what is happening here. I'd love to say that I told you so. That you should have let me start practicing with the Twins to begin with and that I knew exactly what I was doing, but,-" he paused a moment, the thoughts of what happened to him as he had handled both swords at the same time came to mind.

"But what?" Cat asked, still a little irritated with the whole event. She stopped and turned to him. He stood frozen, looking at the floor, trying to recap everything he had just gone through. Brit finally looked back at her.

"I didn't know what I was doing until I picked up both swords." Cat just stared at him not quite understanding what he was trying to say. "I picked up the swords," he repeated more to himself, starting to work the puzzle in his head. "Knowledge is power."

"Are you trying to tell me that the swords had something to do with it?" Cat asked skeptically. A smile spread across Brit's face as the answers started to fall into place. Indeed, it had to be the Twins.

"Let's find out," he said, making an about face.

"Wait," Catrina called after him. He certainly was a bit impulsive. Neither of them had any idea what they were really dealing with here, least of all Brit who was heading back to the training room at a quick trot, Catrina having to run to keep up with him.

Brit nearly ran into Hans who was just leaving the practice room. He assumed that his job was done for the time being. He had a perplexed look on his face as Brit made a quick maneuver past him, motioning for him to come back. Catrina entered the room in time to see Brit set the Twins down and pick up the training sword. He tried to swing it back and forth like he had with the Twins, but the motions were more of a grade school attempt at sword play with his little friends. He motioned for Hans to pick up his sword and engage him. Hans hesitated nervously looking over at Catrina who had a worried look on her face. She looked at Brit's determined expression and then motioned for the trainer to engage. This was a little dangerous as neither one of them had any training armor on to protect them. Hans could easily disarm Brit, but not without taking a chance on injury. It was possible for Brit to injure Hans with a wild swing, though Hans was certainly skilled enough that he could deflect just about anything that Brit could possibly throw in his direction.

Brit engaged Hans quickly and it didn't take long for everyone in the room to figure out that he wasn't putting on a show. While Brit understood most of the basics of sword play, he had no skill or mastery of how to implement even the simplest of skill sets to gain ground on his opponent, no matter how good or bad he was. After several minutes of fumbling around trying to figure out how to get some kind of an upper hand on the trainer, Brit stopped the engagement and stepped back over to the table, tossing the sword and picking up the Twins. He motioned for Hans to arm himself with another sword while he pulled the Twins from their scabbards then slowly stepped out into the middle of the floor. He stood still for a moment with his eyes closed and tried to control his breathing. Catrina held her breath and waited, as Brit remained frozen for several more moments, then slowly opened his eyes and carefully raised the swords up in front of him, slightly motioning for Hans to engage him again. Hans glanced over at the Queen of Thulsa who was transfixed on Brit, then looked forward and advanced with both his swords at the ready.

This time, the response was swift and immediate and Hans was instantly on the defensive. After a short exchange, Hans broke off and reset himself. Had he not been a party to this whole event, he would have thought this was someone else that he was now fighting. It was unbelievable what Brit had thrown at him in just the short thirty second engagement that had just transpired. He stepped back to gather his thoughts, then reengaged with renewed fury. His fury was met with a lightning blitz of glowing swords that came at him from every direction. It was all he could do to hold his ground. Indeed, he found that he was quite out matched here. He glanced through their clanging metal at Britten. His expression was one of steel, yet there was a pleased whisp swirling around his face, almost amused confidence which didn't go unnoticed. Catrina watched Brit carefully, not just his techniques and moves, but also the look on his face. She was not only stunned, but also a bit shocked, mixed with concerned at his expression. The look in his eyes was not that of the Brit she had come to know, but something else, mechanical, artificial. There was some expression, that of arrogance for the skill being displayed.

The two sparred around the room, Hans madly deflecting every blow as best as he could, Brit throwing jabs and swings, almost without effort. It was quite clear that Hans was now out matched and what was even more startling was that Brit was not backing down. It wasn't long before Catrina realized that he was no longer in control of himself. As Hans continued in retreat, he began to stumble, but having to keep up his defense, was unable to regain his balance and quickly went down, but held both his swords up in defense as Brit continued his advance. Brit swung again and again, until one of Hans' swords was sent flying and the other finally dropped to the floor with a clamor. Brit did a victory spin, swinging the glowing Twins over his head and then turned to strike with no mercy. Hans held his arms up in an instinctive defensive move as Brit swung with one sword and jabbed with the other, but both strikes were immediately deflected and the Twins sent spinning out of his hands and across the floor.

Hans rolled several times as Catrina put herself between him and his attacker, with swords at the ready. Brit's eyes were ablaze and his expression was that of over confident arrogance, mixed with out of control fury. He puffed hard, his eyes piercing right through Catrina as she held her ground firmly in front of him. It was like he didn't even recognize her and frankly, she didn't recognize him either, only that it looked like Britten. He continued to look right through her, but then, suddenly, his whole countenance changed and he turned, looking at Hans who was just getting to his feet, quite shaken with the whole experience. He looked at his still outstretched hands that once held onto the Twins then looked over at the glowing swords lying on opposite sides of the room. He turned back to Catrina with a look of complete astonishment. At that point, his sight started to cloud. First with sparkles all through his vision, then clouds of blackness started boiling up in his eyes and everything started to fade out of sight. He wasn't feeling wobbly or faint, there was just blackness shrouding over his eyes.

"What happened?" he asked, his voice shaking. Catrina was shaking as well. She wasn't sure if she wasn't going to have to do something a little more drastic than just knock the Twins from his hands.

"What do you mean what happened?" she responded, a little angrily. "You nearly killed Hans!"

"I did?" Brit asked, looking over in the direction he had last seen Hans. He was hoping that moving his eyes and head would bring back his vision quicker. It had to have something to do with the information download that had happened with the Twins. He tried to look again at his own hands but saw only boiling black clouds in his vision. He was becoming quite alarmed that his vision wasn't clearing. He looked back up at Catrina with a mortified look.

"I don't remember, I…." he stuttered, feeling a wave of shame sweep over him. "I remember picking them up and then the flow of knowledge went through me, then there was a split second dream and then I'm standing here looking at you."

It was obvious to Cat that he really had no idea of what had just happened. His hands were shaking now and he seemed to cower away in fear of her and what she might have been prepared to do to protect Hans. Brit carefully turned back in the direction he remembered Hans being. Catrina watched him carefully. She could see that something else was wrong, terribly wrong.

"I am so sorry," Brit offered humbly, not knowing what else to say. He tried to bow as he began to back away from Catrina, towards the armory table. It was all very awkward and he finally turned in an odd careful manner, stepping to the table and facing the other direction so they couldn't see his face. Catrina watched him closely as he fidgeted. She turned to Hans, who nodded that he was ok. Stepping over to the Twins, she picked them up, carrying them over to the table and set them down in front of Britten. He only kind of looked at them and appeared to move away, as if he were afraid of them now. He held his hand up to his eyes, covering them from something.

"Pick them up Brit," Catrina told him quietly. Brit refused, shaking his head.

"Pick them up," she repeated, a little more forcefully now. Brit again refused, this time muttering his refusal.

"No, I won't."

"Pick them up," she beckoned. "You must pick them back up," she reaffirmed.

"No, I will not," he refused with the same conviction as she was exerting on him.

"Why not?"

"Because."

"Because why?"

"Because I can't….."

"Can't what?" Cat asked, seeing his struggle now. Brit finally looked up and blinked several times. His vision was slowly returning to him as he turned and faced her. It must just be the transfer. It would just take time to get used to it. For now, he decided to just keep this to himself.

"I can't kill," he finally choked out. She hadn't seen it until now, until it had come bubbling up to the surface. He honestly thought that he would be able to get through all of this without actually killing. He was sure this was all just a big mistake, a bad dream and he would wake up or just be dismissed with a hand slap for trespassing and sent on his way. Cat knew better of course, but when you have never been faced with death, never faced the prospect of one's own mortality, you have no concept of what it will really take to kill or be killed until you are forced to face it head on. While Brit wasn't quite there, he was an astute observer of reality and had a good understanding of what was about to happen long before others in his situation would have. The near deadly exchange with Hans was the wake up call to this reality and he didn't want any part of it.

"You can and you will," Catrina asserted firmly. "You must," she softened a bit, starting to remember what it was like the first time she had to take another life in the defense of her own.

"There is no other way home for you. I promised I'd be right here to help you and I'm not going anywhere," she reassured him.

"But how can you help me through using these?" Brit asked, gesturing towards the two glowing swords. Catrina picked one of them up and looked at it carefully. She felt nothing but the light buzzing coming from it. She thought a moment remembering the words Britten had said before and after the incident. She caught sight of the writing on the hand guards of the hilts. "Knowledge is Power." She had no knowledge of the origin of these swords or what their intended purpose really was. She had no idea why this statement was written on the hilts of both swords, but she was able to reason rather quickly that it was a direction of sorts. Catrina reached for the other sword and then thrust them towards Brit who took a step back.

"Come on Sonny Jim," she said angrily. "Take them and just hold them." Brit gave her a long, hard look. He was relieved that his vision had fully returned to normal now. She had never lied or tried to lead him astray once since he had arrived here and so she had his trust. She had given him no reason to start doubting her now. Something else sparked in him at that moment though. He did not like being called, "*Sonny Jim*", not by her anyway. Whether she called him that on purpose to get him to stiffen up or not, was immaterial. He realized that while it was good to feel genuine remorse for nearly doing harm to an innocent, feeling sorry for himself wasn't going to get him through what he had to do to get home.

He carefully reached out with both hands and took hold of the Twins by the blades. He was a little apprehensive about the whole thing. He didn't want to risk a repeat and take a chance of maybe turning the whole thing back on Catrina. Hans may not be able to stop him in time. Cat motioned for him to hold them by the hilts.

"Let's try this again, but a step at a time. You tell me exactly what you're going on at every step and when things start going wrong or you feel," she paused, knowing that he already felt uncomfortable, "the dream coming on, we'll hold it right there and figure things out before it gets out of hand." Brit nodded carefully, setting the blades down on the table in front of them, then picking them back up again by the hilts. He tried to reason in his head that he needed to get his brain used to the download of information so he could not only control the Twins, but also avoid the blindness that followed. At first he felt only the buzzing from the glow, which after about a minute was a relief. Nothing like being totally out of control with your girlfriend watching.

"I feel fine," Brit said, as Hans stepped up next to him to observe what was happening. He was just as interested in how this man had been able to make such a dramatic change in an instant.

"They are buzzing my hands like they always have, but there's nothing else," Brit informed them, stepping out into the room with the swords held out in front of him.

"Now take a pose," Catrina directed, as she and Hans watched him carefully. Brit carefully raised a sword up over his head and held the other out in front of him.

"How do you feel?" Cat asked, watching his every move.

"Stupid," Brit responded, not feeling anything out of the ordinary. He looked back over at the other two and gave a slight shrug. "Nothing," he continued, trying to be graceful and fluid while going through the motions of sword practice. He wasn't fluid or graceful at all. It was like he was holding onto the regular swords. Catrina continued to watch him with steely eyes. There had to be something that they were missing here. She stepped out next to him with Hans by her side and motioned for the training foe to help him with his movements. It was like helping someone with two left feet, to dance, rather comical. After a few minutes of awkwardness, Cat motioned for Hans to stop and back away as Brit continued to try and go through the motions.

"Are you sure you're not feeling anything weird, no odd ball thoughts or sensations in your head?" she asked, shaking her head slowly, watching him go through the motions.

"Nothing, other than feeling like a complete idiot," Brit admitted, feeling silly, turning in a circle. Then there was something odd happening as he made his turn back towards Catrina. He felt a tingling starting to streak up both his arms and shoulders to his neck. Completing his turn towards Cat, he felt both his swords suddenly come to life and engage her sword that came out of nowhere at him. It was as though they were aware and had anticipated her attack. There was a weird sensation of electricity spinning through the back of his head and down his spine as he was suddenly embroiled in a swift sword exchange with Catrina, who was throwing blows at him at an alarming rate. However, he could see them all coming at him and he knew exactly what to do to defend himself and after a moment, he knew what to do to counter her charge, taking the offensive.

"Something is happening now!" he yelled, as the two sparred at a swift pace. Hans jumped out of the way and grabbing a couple of swords from the table, turned to try and protect his Queen from the attack. He knew very well what was about to happen and wanted to be ready for it.

"What is it?" Catrina hollered back at him as they continued the fight.

"Electricity running up my arms into my head," he called out, as Cat took notice of his eyes starting to glaze and a smile forming across his lips. "I feel like, like..." He didn't finish, but didn't have to, pressing the fight home harder and harder at Catrina. Hans quickly joined in the fray to try and divert Brit's attention from the Queen.

"No!" Catrina yelled back through the clash of swords. "He needs to control them, not them him! He will hear me!" Hans disengaged and backed carefully away with his swords still at the ready.

"Brit!" she yelled through the clash of their swords. "Take command! You know how!" she puffed, battling him. Watching his eyes, she knew the best way to reach him now was to lock up with the Twins and hold him engaged as long as she could. It would take all the expert skill she could muster, aggressively continuing to attack and trying to hold him on the defensive. Whatever she was going to do, she had to do it quickly. Every move she used on him was never effective a second time. It was as though the Twins were learning how to counter and adapt to her fighting style. It took only a few minutes before they were standing toe to toe with swords clashing at such a fierce pace it was difficult to know who, if anyone, was gaining the upper hand. It appeared as though there was no way to lock the swords up, so she did the only thing that came to mind and just let her brown eyes burrow into his. For a moment, there seemed to be nothing coming back at her but steel and mechanics, but then something happened that gave her hope. She saw shades of hazel whisp through his wide, unflinching eyes and his swings began to slow.

"Fight it Brit! Take command!" she yelled, as they continued. He was starting to back up a bit now and Catrina saw her chance, lunging in and locking her swords with his. She held them low and brought her face right up in front of his so that she could let her eyes dive directly into his. Spell broken and the glaze clearing, he slowly eased back on the pressure of the sword lock, carefully releasing the lock and backing away. He looked down at the swords, then back into the relieved, yet smiling face of Catrina Dallas.

"You're ok," he stated, not believing what he had just gone through. Once again, he could see the sparkles start around the edges of his vision and work their way quickly through his entire line of sight. Then the blackness came billowing up faster this time and he soon found himself in the dark once again. It boiled madly in his vision like he had been buried in an ocean wave and was being tossed about like a tiny piece of drift wood.

"And so are you," she responded, dropping her sword with a clamor and going to him, throwing her arms around him. Brit instantly dropped the Twins and returned her affectionate embrace, relieved that he hadn't hurt her. Again, he didn't feel dizzy at all, just no vision and now he was afraid of losing his balance. Hanging onto Catrina was a good way to keep himself standing; besides it felt really good. Hans was a little perplexed with the whole thing. He did not understand how any of this had happened, but from what he was able to figure out, with the evidence he had witnessed, these swords had some kind of magical powers to them that could give the holder ultimate power to wield them in any fight.

He carefully stepped over to one of the Twins, picking it up to examine it closer. He looked over at Britten and Catrina, who were still embracing. Catrina pulled from Brit's arms and turned to the training foe that had now picked up the other glowing weapon as he spoke. She listened to him intently while the trainer examined both swords. While Hans understood and spoke English, he did not speak it often and preferred his own native Thulsian tongue. Brit could only guess at what he was saying. He kept the fact that he was completely blind to himself, reasoning that the more he used the Twins and got use to the download, the more the blindness would diminish. There was no sense in getting these two all worried about something that should correct itself. There was a slight laugh from Catrina as she responded to what Hans was saying and gestured to Brit, who was a bit irritated that he couldn't see or understand what they were saying.

"How about we all get in on this?"

Cat gave Brit a double take with the second having a smile associated with it.

"I'm sorry. He is a little baffled on how all this happened. He just forgot himself."

"My apologies Master Garrett," Hans spoke up. "I meant no disrespect."

"None taken," Brit quickly responded, still wondering what all the interest was about. He blinked several times trying to accelerate the return of his sight, turning in the direction of Han's voice.

"I was asking the Queen what had happened. How you were able to do what you just did. I also wanted to know if anyone could do the same thing."

A funny look streaked across Brit's face. He had no idea. He had sort of been the unwitting host to this whole mess. The more he had to learn to fight, the more he started to think he would have been better off going with his brother to find the Signet. He faked a look at Catrina for an answer. She didn't have all the answers either, but had formulated a theory based on what she did know and the legends she had heard told repeatedly by the council elders.

"I'm fairly sure the Signet contains all of the instructions and information about the Twins, but what I do know is that only the person who removes them from the altar can unlock their power. I know what you're thinking Hans, and no, you or I could not experience the same thing that Brit has with them. There's no need for us to, not really. It provides the knowledge to the bearer as needed. Even if you or I were the bearer, it wouldn't do us any good because we already have knowledge of sword play."

"So what is the whole out of control thing about?" Brit asked. He was hoping that Cat might have an explanation about what was happening with his vision. "Why can't I remember what is happening?"

"I suspect it comes from not being able to control the exchange of information," Cat replied, spilling out everything that made sense to her. "The Twins sense the need for knowledge in you and quickly provide it to you."

"Sorta like a download," Brit offered, agreeing with her theory. Catrina and Hans gave him an odd look. Cat made a face gesture indicating that she was waiting for him to explain the unknown term to them. It took him a moment to remember that he wasn't in Kansas here and even though Catrina was very intelligent, she wasn't acquainted with computers, let alone the terminology associated with them.

"It's a 21st century Earth term," he paused a moment, to make sure that he phrased it in good basic form so they would understand. "Used to move information from one level or medium to another, whether it's by human or machine." Catrina nodded, continuing with her explanation, giving Brit a second glance and a smile.

"Yeah, thanks for that."

"Anytime."

"I would think that you can learn to control it fairly quickly," she said, trying to reassure him.

"Yeah, kind of like the way I've learn to fight with a sword," Brit stated with a little sarcasm. Cat flattened her lips together at Brit's comment. He noted that his sight was starting to clear a little. The blackness boiling in his eyes was starting to turn lighter and he could see objects appearing in the corners of his vision.

"These could be very dangerous weapons were they to fall into the wrong hands," Hans said, stepping back and trying a couple of swings with them. Of course if they followed Catrina's thinking, they would be of little use in the hands of someone who was a master of the sword already.

"We'll just have to see that doesn't happen," Cat said, as Hans handed her one of the swords. She looked at it curiously.

"Kind of odd that you have to be holding both of them in order for the information to," she paused a moment, looking over at Brit with a smile, "download," she finished and handed it back to Brit, Hans doing the same.

He could barely see her movement, but enough so that he was able to take it from her. Catrina gave him an odd look as he reached out and fumbled for the hilt. It was like he wasn't paying attention or something. Brit felt its buzzing and held it up close to his face. He still couldn't see clearly, but enough to detect the glow of its blade and he was just now coming to realize just how special they actually were. He wondered what other secrets they held and what was yet in store for all of them in the next day. Right now, he was tired and hungry and just wanted to relax for a while. His eyes ached, but at least his sight was clearing and he could now see Catrina and Hans, almost in full detail and focus.

"Is there a chance we can take a break from all this? My stomach feels like my throat's been cut."

Cat burst out laughing as his description of hunger just hit her kind of funny. Hans couldn't help but chuckle at it as well. Thulsa culture certainly had humor, but nothing like this. It was sort of like the humor shared between the British and the Americans back home on Earth.

"Yes of course, Hans, will you excuse us?" she asked, bowing to the foe and taking Brit by the arm. Hans bowed respectfully and watched them leave the room walking very close together. He wasn't stupid or blind to the affections that they obviously shared. He was only a training partner to the Queen, but had come to know her well over the many years she had been with the Thulsians. He had started teaching her swordsmanship several Argylian years after she had arrived. He had grown to love and respect her as queen, as had all the people of Thulsa. He always wanted to see her happy in some kind of a relationship, but it seemed that there was never the right combination for that to happen. Ivan certainly wasn't it. What he had noted here was that Catrina and Brit seemed to have the right combination. He had also observed that there was something holding her back, somewhat distant from him still. Whether it was coming from Britten or from her was unknown. Of course, it wasn't his place to intrude or to ask questions. He was just the royal trainer, not her confidant.

Mount Tera

The small band from Thulsa made their way along the narrow trail that was somehow cut right into the high mountain rock of the Tera Mountain range. Jerry Gunn stumbled tiredly and muttered angrily under his breath, nearly falling yet again. He was dead tired and very hungry. Their run in with Ivan and his men had stripped them almost entirely of any kind of provisions and there was little to no vegetation growing this high up. He reasoned that they weren't even half way up the mountain range. There appeared to be no pass of any kind that one would normally find in the mountains. The ledge trail seemed like it went on endlessly along facing high cliffs and jagged peaks. He was hoping that they would turn one of these corners and see a friendly mountain cottage, a lodge or at the very least a nice valley. Something like Vespa Cull would be nice to see right now. Alas, every time he was sure they would see something that would give them hope of nearing their journey's end; they would round the corner only to find more grey-violet rock. To make matters worse, it was starting to drizzle lightly. The only thing that could make it worse would be wind, heavy driving rain and snow. Well, maybe a little hail mixed in with it, but you get the idea.

They weren't soaked to the skin yet, but if they didn't change their tactics, Jerry was sure that wasn't too far away. He checked behind him as Danny struggled to keep up. Behind his friend, Terry and Tony were keeping them on the move. He turned forward where Digi stepped carefully behind his friend Tim, then looked up into the darkening skies. This was more fun than a guy ought to have. How in the heck were they going to make it over these jagged cliffs and rising peaks, through this weather, in time to make it to Thulsa before second sunup? They were all very tired and moving slower and slower the further they went and this weather wasn't going to help any of that along at all.

"I'm starving," Jerry grumbled, stopping for a moment to look out over the endless tracks of mountain and rocky peaks. "Does anyone have anything to eat? I could go a whole lot faster if I had some food."

"Gotta go with Jerr on this one," Danny puffed exhaustedly, "If we don't get something to eat here pretty quick, we aren't going to be going anywhere very fast."

"I could get you something," Digi said, holding his wings firmly around his body. The oils on his fury wings helped to keep the water out, but if it started to rain any harder, even he would start to feel its effects.

"You wouldn't like what he brought you, I guarantee it," Tim piped up from the front, continuing to trudge forward. He had the Signet strapped firmly to his back as he made his way along the jagged trail.

"Anything is better than starving. I mean my stomach feels like my throat's been cut," Danny complained.

"Haven't heard that expression used for quite some time," Tony piped up, trying to remain upbeat.

"What could be so awful up here that we wouldn't want it?" Jerry asked, thinking the same thing his friend had just voiced. "Doesn't look like there's anything to eat let alone be so terrible you couldn't eat it?"

"There are many unseen creatures that make these mountains their home," Digi explained, continuing behind his friend. "Some very small crawly things, others that are bigger than any of you."

"Well pick something in between and bring it on over," Danny puffed, struggling to keep up with Jerry.

"And how would you eat it?" Terry called from the rear. He was a bit uneasy. He felt like they were being watched, but there was next to no cover anywhere for anyone or anything to be hiding behind.

"A bite at a time," Danny came back quickly.

"Raw?" Terry snapped back.

"If need be," Danny said, getting a little riled up.

"Boys, Boys," Tony interjected, putting an end to a rising squabble. Everyone was a little on edge right now. The only one that didn't seem to be fazed by what was going on around him was Tim. He continued to soldier on in silence, remaining focused on the mission to get back to Thulsa as quickly as possible.

"I think silence is one of our better friends right now. We need to attract as little attention to ourselves as we can," Tony said, moving along behind Danny.

"Attract attention from what, the rocks?" Jerry asked loudly, looking around for anything else that wasn't stone. There was a breeze starting to come up now and it was growing darker and colder. If it started to storm with purpose, they would be in a bit of trouble.

"While it's true that there's next to nothing up here to listen to all the complaining coming from this train," Tim finally complained from the forward position. "I for one would appreciate a little less talking. I'm every bit as tired as all of you, and I'm the one that's injured."

"How is it that you humans always have to boast about who is having the roughest go of it?" Digi asked, waiting behind his friend. He too was tired and hungry, but it was too dark to hunt and he reasoned that they were too high up for there to be anything to hunt anyway. He could have eaten grass or some other foliage, if there were any.

"Not boasting really," Tim responded, as he continuing forward along the narrow trail. "Though I have to say, it is starting to hurt again."

"Well I should hope so," Digi said, nearly running into him as Tim shuffled along making sure of his footing. "You've been at it for hours here. My fluids weren't meant as a cure all. They work for us just fine, but it's only temporary for humans. You need human medical attention."

"Yes, yes, yes," Tim griped sarcastically.

"Quiet!" Terry yelled, freezing in place. The whole group instantly stopped and went silent, listening for any sound other than the light rain and the wind that continued to rise. Tony carefully turned, looking at Terry. He went to speak softly, but Terry stopped him with a raised finger, turning his head closer to the cliff wall to try and sense something, perhaps a distant rumble. Tony tried to lean down closer to Terry to try and pick up on what he was trying to hear, but there was nothing but the rain and the wind. Digi snorted impatiently, but this only brought Terry to an instant wave off, trying to maintain silence in order to hear. Tony finally had to ask for more information about what they were trying to hear.

"Terry, what is it?" he asked in a whisper.

"Something on the rock or," he paused, straining to hear, "something in it," he finished, looking back up at his Captain. Tony gave him a strange look.

"I know it sounds ridiculous Tony, but it seems like," he didn't get to finish his sentence.

"Like we're being watched," Tony finished quietly, looking all around them. "Yeah, I felt like that to, but I haven't seen a thing in any direction."

"That's just it," Terry said, still trying to listen. "I'm not seeing anything around us either, but I keep catching glimpses of things on the trail and the cliff walls, and I keep hearing a creaking or grinding noise from somewhere." Tony turned forward to Digi.

"Digi, you have better hearing than, us humans," he said, placing emphasis on his own species. "Have you heard anything out of the ordinary?"

"Only human complaining," the Jabba admitted. He was a little insulted that Terry was claiming to hear something as soft and faint as it appeared. Jabba hearing was much like that of the owls of Earth. Their ears were specifically designed to detect and zero in on even the faintest of sounds, useful for hunting purposes. Tony turned to move the group along, but then even he detected movement on the cliff wall out of the corner of his eye. A slight scraping sound seemed to be associated with the movement. In the fading light, Tony leaned a little closer to the cliff wall where he had detected the movement, but there was nothing there but cracks and rock. Perhaps it was just the movement of water running down the rock, or the groaning of the mountain. Terry huddled a little closer to Tony, hearing it as well. Tim and Digi had turned to watch what was going on as Jerry and Danny stepped back down the trail to see what Tony and Terry were looking at. Trying to see something that just wasn't there, Jerry finally turned and leaned back against the cliff wall to rest and wait for the group to continue. He felt like they really didn't have the time for this. They were all exhausted and still had an extremely long way to go. Truth be told, he wasn't even sure Tim had any idea where they were going. He said that he had studied the maps that detailed the trail through these mountains, but admitted that neither he nor Digi had ever actually been on the trail. Tim was going only by his memory of what the map said. He wasn't even sure it was accurate.

Jerry leaned his head back and closed his eyes, letting the rain drops freely speckle across his already damp skin. He almost wished that it were raining harder. They were very low on water and if there were enough rain falling, he could simply open his mouth and let it fill. He reasoned that it would take quite a downpour for that to be effective and then he'd be complaining about being too wet and cold. He saw no comfortable way to continue the journey home.

As he stood resting, he slowly turned his head towards the other three that were still trying to figure out where the noise was coming from. There was something in the wall right next to him. He shifted his head a little more, letting his left eye turn to the wall. He thought he might be looking at a mirror or something. There was another eye looking right back at him. He froze, holding his gaze on the eye. It wasn't a human eye, but a two dimensional eye looking out from the rock itself. Stone with an eye? That had to be just an optical illusion brought on by the fading light, the rain and their exhaustion. He slowly turned his head a little further so he wasn't straining his eye to see what it really was. Turning a little further and bringing his right eye into view, he could see that it was not one, but two eyes looking right back at him. He shifted a look at his friends without moving his head and instantly brought them back to the cliff wall. The eyes were still there. Ok, so this was quite unique. He carefully turned his shoulders in the direction of the wall so he could face it for a more direct look. There were more than just eyes there. A whole face, the texture and color of the rock itself.

He studied it closely, giving every feature a thorough looking over, taking note that it looked like it was studying him too. Holding his head frozen, he glanced up at his friends who were still busy trying to hear the sounds they were searching for. Shifting his eyes back to the face in the rock, Jerry raised an eyebrow and found the image doing the same. He straightened his eyebrow and the face did the same. He winked and to his surprise, the face winked back. He made a big cheesy grin, showing all his teeth and remarkably, the face responded likewise using small bits of rock and sand to form and give detailed resolution to its mouth and teeth. Jerry knew how to lift his eyebrows independently and gave it a try to see if the image in the rock could follow all of his moves. To his surprise, it matched his every move. He lifted an eyebrow with a slightly surprised look.

"Fascinating," he spoke quietly. The imagine mouthed his lip actions, but made no sound.

"SSSHHHH," Danny, Terry and Tony responded collectively. The three of them were still trying to determine what they had been hearing. Tim and Digi were resting against the cliff walls and looking out over the deep rocky gorge below them.

"Hey guys," Jerry piped up, his eyes glued to the image in the rock that was still mimicking his facial expressions.

"Come on Jerry," Tony called out. "We can't hear if you're going to keep making noise."

"Yeah," Danny echoed. "Let's have a little more quiet here, shall we?"

Jerry flattened his lips out and looked back at the image that was doing the same. He carefully raise his hands to the stone wall, all the while the image watching his hand approach its face. Before he touched the stone, the image of a hand appeared beside the face. Jerry smiled slightly and touched the stone where the hand was. The face looked at Jerry and then at their touching fingertips. There came a pleasant look rolling across the face and the whole hand image flattened out as Jerry pressed his entire hand onto the rock. He could feel nothing but the cold stone of the wet cliff wall, but somehow, that didn't seem to matter to the image. It was like it had never touched anything biological. There came a look of wonder on the face as Jerry raised his other hand in a gesture to touch the other hand. As his hand came close to the rock, another hand in the stone appeared, seeming anxious to have even more interaction.

As Jerry touched the rock and the hands touched palm to palm, Danny finally became tired of listening to nothing but the soft patter of rain and wind. He stood up stiffly, stretching while turning around to his friend who appeared to be leaning against the cliff wall working his calves or something.

"Are you assuming the position? What? You got a cramp or something?" He asked, as Terry and Tony finally gave up the search for whatever it was that they had heard or thought they had seen.

"Hey Tim, Digi," Danny called forward, ignoring anything else his friend was doing. He was stretching his tired legs. Runners do that sort of thing. "Can you see anything up ahead that might indicate that we're close to getting down off this rock?"

Tim and Digi turned and looked back at the others as Tony turned forward and looked at Jerry who looked like he was pushing against the wall, or maybe he was assuming the position one might when a body search is being conducted in an arrest. He glanced away to look behind him, but did a double take at the wall in front of Jerry.

"What the-," he said, gazing at the face looking back at him through Jerry's arm. Terry scrambled forward trying to have a look and not knock his Captain off the narrow trail. But there just wasn't any room for two people to look, so he raised one of Tony's arms and poked his head under his armpit.

"Holy buckets!" He exclaimed, bringing Danny's attention back down to his friend.

"What are you doing?" He asked, looking at the face in the rock. He thought that Jerry had just drawn a picture on the cliff wall, but when the face turned its eyes up at him and smiled, Danny jumped back into Tony's arms nearly knocking both Captain Dallas and Terry off balance.

"Whoa!" he exclaimed loudly. Danny watched the face mimicking his own surprised look then looking at his friend. It appeared to him that he seemed to be playing with it.

"Are you doing that?"

"Nope," Jerry responded, with a smirk. "This is the real deal here. Is this what you guys were looking for?"

"Don't know," Terry said, carefully gazing at the face. "Has it made any noise? Like a grinding sound or something?"

"Not a sound," Jerry said, smiling. The face smiled back at him again and then looked at everyone else that had surrounded the area of the cliff wall.

"Amazing," Terry said, reaching out to touch its face. It looked a little apprehensive about anyone but Jerry touching it and its hands disappeared as Jerry stepped back a little to allow the other three to have a look. Tony picked up a rock from the trail and carefully rubbed it on the side of the cliff close to where the image was looking at everyone. The slight rubbing sound of the two stone surfaces moving against the other brought the face to instant interest in both the noise and the action as it moved down next to where Tony was rubbing stone on stone. It moved all around the point where the two surfaces were making contact and looking back up at Tony as if astonished that he could make such a noise. By this time, Digi and Tim had made their way back to where the other four were watching the image closely.

"What's all the hubbub?" Tim asked, straining to see around everyone in the fading light. Digi sniffed curiously at the cliff wall, near where everyone was looking. When Tim finally got a good look at what all the interest was about, he turned back up the trail.

"It's only a Mynite, for heaven sakes! Let's get going. We've got a lot of ground to cover," he said disdainfully. He was hoping that it might have been something useful, like maybe something to eat. Instead it was a useless stone sprite, a mischievous and bothersome fairy of sorts. There wasn't a whole lot known about them other than just an interesting curiosity. He had encounters with them off and on over the years, sometimes right in his own home in the Kenlar spoil. Even the Ancients had referenced them in the Signet, but not much had been documented about them. They were generally very shy and elusive and communication with them was almost nonexistent. After all, talking to a rock is one thing. Man seemed to like to do that kind of thing for eons of time, worshipping idols and statues, but listening to one speak is something altogether different. Tim had figured that the Ancients didn't have or take the time to figure them out. More likely they just couldn't get close enough to do so. At any rate, there wasn't time to stop and play with something that served no practical purpose.

"Come on," Tim pressed everyone. "We need to get going. I don't expect this weather to get any better this high up and we're pressing our luck as it is." He turned and started back up the trail, followed by Digi and Danny. Jerry squatted back down next to the rock and looked back at the face in the rock. It suddenly looked a little dismayed as Tony and Terry slipped past him and headed up the trail after the others. Jerry turned to leave as well. He knew they couldn't linger long because of the hurry they were in. Not knowing what the trail was like through these mountains really slowed them down, much more than they had anticipated, so they were having to try and make up for the lost time. The Mynite glided along after him on the rock as they continued. Jerry watching it out of the corner of his eye, he could see its mouth open like it were trying to speak and its hands reaching across the rock surface, trying to hold him back. He took several more steps and looked back at the rock wall. The Mynite was still right there beside him trying to signal him to stay, or at least that's how it appeared to him. He looked around him in the fading light. There wasn't a whole lot to see but the steep mountain side, stark and grey, almost austere. The shrouding of misting, low flying clouds obscuring the darkening cliffs all around him and the associated rain and wind sent a chill through him. While it wasn't cold, it gave him the sensation of a chill. Back home in the mountains above Driggs, when it was like this, you could bet that it was going to be cold and probably have some lightning coming along shortly. A least a light jacket would be nice right now. He gave the beckoning Mynite another glance and then tiredly headed off to catch up with the others.

*   *   *   *   *

Winding along the high cliffs, the trail continued to narrow the higher into the mist they went. Tim had made way for Digi, who could not only see far better in the dark, but could also smell better. Having been traveling for several hours now, they had to do so without light.

While there was a constant drizzle with them, there was enough light from the three Argyle moons penetrating the clouds to provide some lumination. Practically holding onto the person directly ahead to keep from wandering too close to the edge or slipping on something unseen, they moved as quickly as possible despite the conditions getting worse the higher they went. Digi finally led them through a very cramped overhang of rock, almost a tunnel. Through here it was at least dry, albeit a bit breezy. Still it wasn't cold enough to really cause problems for the wet exhausted band, so they stopped just inside to rest a moment.

"I think we've reached the summit of the trail," Tim puffed tiredly, looking back at the others. Digi stepped towards the down side of the opening and sniffed the air. For the humans, there was nothing ahead of them but more clouds, rain, wind and walking, lots more walking.

"How far do you think we have to go?" Tim asked, as Tony plopped down next to Danny and Jerry who were trying to get some kind of rest.

"Well, unfortunately, the Tera summit is only about a third of the way to the southern borders of Thulsa. Then it's another hour or two from there," Tony finished grimly. They were still a very long way from home and there was no hope of making it there before the second sunrise. Tim looked over at his two friends with a look of helplessness. He couldn't think of any way to get the book to Thulsa before the allotted time had expired.

"What about strapping that thing to Digi and have him deliver it right to Catrina at the arena?" Terry piped tiredly.

"That would be all well and good," Digi said, turning from his watch. "And you know that I would do it if I thought there was hope for success, but there are a couple of problems with this plan." Tim let his eyes drop to the ground and hang there while Digi made his explanation.

"First off, I can't navigate in the dark. That's why we roost at night. Even this hiking you have me doing here in the middle of the night is quite taxing to my physiological disposition. I'm expending a tremendous amount of energy just to keep from have a psychotic episode. Second, I can't navigate through weather such as this." The Jabba began to growl as he continued to rattle off the problems associated with the suggestion. "And, if by some miracle I did make it through all this to Thulsa, I wouldn't even get on the ground before someone had me skinned and on a spit. Gentlemen, I respect and honor you all, but I will not throw my life away after foolishness."

"Yeah, yeah," Terry agreed contritely. "Didn't really think that one through very well, sorry," he finished almost under his breath.

"What about taking someone with you?" Danny asked tiredly, with his eyes still closed and his head resting on the rock behind him.

"They could explain that you are a friend to us." He didn't even realize what he had just openly stated.

"Thought you hated all Jabba?" Jerry asked, leaning close to his friend while keeping his eyes closed to rest. Danny nudged him good, shoulder to shoulder.

"This one ain't so bad," he muttered. His better sense had finally overruled his stubbornness and he had reached a state of humility enough to admit that all Jabba were not the same, but as individual as any human and likewise deserved to be treated accordingly.

"I'll refer you to line items one and two of my aforementioned list," Digi pointed out, trying to sniff the air blowing through their sheltered area. "And add to that, the reality that I cannot carry any human that far. Remember how many of my flock it took to hold each one of you up at the waterfall? Even then we could not remain aloft for very long. No, I'm afraid if we are to get to Thulsa by second sunup, it's going to have to be on foot somehow." Danny let out a short disgusted sigh.

"HHHMMM, yeah, didn't think that one through very good either, my bad."

Digi continued to sniff the air, Tim taking special note of his ears turning every which way, trying to hone in on something. Usually, a Jabba could sense something through their sense of smell before they could hear it, but with the weather being as it was, it was very difficult for him to pick up things on the air, as it was full of so many different smells kicked up by the weather.

"What have you got goin' on there Digg?" Tim asked, looking out into the grey black hoping to see what his friend could see, or smell.

"There is much on the wind in both sounds and smells," the Jabba replied carefully, still scanning with both nose and ears. "The rain and the wind pick up so many things; it's difficult to distinguish past from present."

"I would think that this high up there wouldn't be anything," Terry commented, resting against the outcrop wall next to Tony.

"One would think," Tony responded, thinking the same thing. Digi continued to scan and listen.

"I smell many indigenous creatures to these mountains, but it's difficult to distinguish any of them separately or tell where they might be. I smell Jabbaway as well, not my flock to be sure, but Jabbaway all the same. Again, it's unknown where or how many. I can also smell Thulsa."

"From this distance?" Tony asked, looking in the direction the Jabba was facing.

"Indeed," Digi responded twisting his ears.

"So how are we doing?" Tim asked, running his hands through his wet hair. Tony didn't know the trail very well, having traveled it but twice, once in each direction. Even at that, it was some time ago, but he remembered enough about it to know they were still quite a distance from the southern walls of the city. With the dense overcast, seeing anything by moonlight was out of the question.

"Not very good I'm afraid," Tony answered grimly. "I just don't see how we can possibly cover this kind of distance in the condition we are in. The only thing we can do is continue on the best we can and hope that something will avail itself. Let's hope your friend Britten has learned how to fight," Tony said, turning his last comment to Danny and Jerry.

"Cat teaching him?" Tim asked.

"Who better?" Tony replied with a half chuckle. "She would be the reason he has half a chance."

"Provided they can keep their hands off each other," Danny piped up, good-naturedly. Jerry gave him a nudge, but Tony knew all too well what was happening. It hadn't taken a genius to see it starting before they had left. The same thing had happened to him and his beloved Amanda. Catrina was a very strong woman and could maintain control when it was needed, although love can sometimes supersede even the most serious of situations. As her father, he couldn't help but wonder about how they were getting along with the seriousness of their situation and their blossoming relationship. Would they be able to navigate their way through the difficult situations that were no doubt confronting them now? He was sure that they would figure it all out one way or the other.

"If those two had any idea what Brit has possession of," Tim said, standing back up as Digi turned to the rest of the group.

"What do you mean?" Tony asked. "The Twins are the key to making the Altar operate, right?"

"Certainly," Tim reaffirmed. "It's what happens if Britten were to try and use them for actual fighting."

"Whoa, wait a second," Jerry piped up. "You haven't said anything about what happens if Brit uses the Twins for anything other than starting up the Altar. So what does happen? He has to take them into the arena to fight if we don't get back in time." Tim hesitated a moment realizing that he had overlooked the side effects of humans using the swords for anything other than Altar manipulation.

"The Twins were forged by the Ancients. It's unclear if they were actually made here on Argyle or brought here from somewhere else. I recall nothing in the Signet that suggests one way or the other," he explained, looking to Digi for confirmation. "They were designed for use by the Ancients, transferring the holder information on something as needed. Together, the swords can sense the need in the holder and can transfer that needed information, but the human physiology wasn't designed to handle that kind of a power transfer and we were never supposed to wield them in battle."

"So what happens when he starts trying to fight with them?" Terry spoke up from the back of the group. Tim glanced again at Digi who remained unmoved.

"The Twins will sense the needs of the situation he is in and transfer not only the information required for that task, but also take over command of his mental functions as sort of an automated guidance system."

"Sounds like he would be able to kick some serious hinny then," Danny said sleepily, from next to Jerry.

"Yes, he could," Digi finally spoke up. "But at a terrible cost to himself. The energy transfer will damage the neuro pathways in his brain. He will temporarily lose his sight at first. If he keeps using them, he will probably lose the use of his arms and other extremities. Eventually he will end up with permanent sight loss, paralysis and brain damage."

"You must understand that the human brain and nervous system, just wasn't designed to take this kind of information that fast." Tim finished, feeling a certain helplessness about the urgency of their situation. Danny and Jerry both looked back up at Tony who had a very grim look etched across his face.

"This would have been nice to know before we left him there with them," Jerry stated, looking back down at the dark rock they were sitting on. He also understood how helpless they were to try and do something about it. They were still so far away from Thulsa. Surely Britten had already started practicing with the Twins.

"If only the book had still been there to begin with," Danny responded sullenly.

"There would be no need for any of us to be here," the Jabba said, indicating he was ready to proceed.

"Well, I for one am glad that you guys came for me," Tim said, rubbing his leg wound. The moisture from the rain had worn off the Jabba saliva long ago and it hurt like the dickens now, especially after sitting for just a couple of minutes. At least it wasn't bleeding.

"I'm just glad we found you," Tony said, getting to his feet and stepping over Danny and Jerry. "I'm just very sorry about Kawti."

"Thanks my friend," Tim said, putting his hand on Tony's shoulder. The two gave each other a long look, and then Tim glanced back at the others. "We really need to get going." Tony looked back at the other three and nodded.

"We all need sleep, but that just isn't going to happen. Terry," Tony said, speaking up loudly now, "get them up, we have to move on as quickly as we can." Terry nodded tiredly, getting to his feet and starting to work on the other two, neither of which were happy about it, but reluctantly struggled to their feet. Though exhausted, they somehow managed to force themselves up and forward. Tony brought up the rear now, heading down the north side of the pass into the night wind and rain.

An intimate conversation

Britten ate like he hadn't seen food for days. He wasn't sure what he was eating, but it sure tasted good. Might be just as well not to know what it was as in a culture like this, there was no telling what strange pet he might be chewing on. Several different meats seemed similar to chicken and beef. The sauces used to enhance the flavor of the meats tasted incredible. Better than barbeque and he was quite the meat eater back home. Several other things there looked kind of familiar, but not quite. He barely noticed that they were back in the same room they had eaten their first meal in the day they were first brought to Stronghold Manor. He was just relieved that there was food and it smelled so good. Catrina had joined him, but was using her manners, holding to proper etiquette, even if they were the only two in the room. It's how she had always been, even as a little girl back on Earth, so long ago.

Brit didn't have bad manners nor was he a slob, but he certainly wasn't being delicate with eating. Part of that was because he was so hungry. Slinging metal around most of the day can cause a guy to work up a bit of an appetite. Catrina had to admit that she felt a bit starved herself and was very glad for the meal, but even happier to share it with Brit. At first he wasn't much for company. He was quite focused on eating, but after a bit, he realized that he had a spectator in Catrina and slowed himself down, not only to avoid the appearance of being an uncouth slob, but also to enjoy her company as much as possible. He realized that there was a napkin folded neatly beside his plate and could see Cat's draped across her lap. Having traveled the world and learning a bit of etiquette himself, he understood how it was all supposed to work. He had just completely forgotten his manners because of his appetite.

Trying to be as inconspicuous as possible, Brit stopped a moment, took the linen folded beside his plate and wiped his mouth before taking a drink. He then placed the linen in his lap and kept eating, looking up at Catrina several times and smiling. This was nice to be here, just the two of them. They had been so busy since coming back from the Spoil, there had been no time for them to be alone or have any conversation other than training. Perhaps now, at least for a little while, they could concentrate on just each other. Now, neither had a clue as to what to say to take them in the direction they wanted to go, until Brit noticed that all his gear stored in the corner of the room for safe keeping.

"I thought you had all that stuff stored down in the cave with The Amanda?"

Cat looked to her left in the corner of the room where their gear had been carefully placed.

"Sargon had them brought up when the workers broke through to the cave from the outside. He thought it better and safer here than having the curious get into something they ought not to."

"I can only imagine what some of them might think if they got a hold of some of that stuff," Brit commented taking another bite of food and washing it down with his drink. "They might think some of it was possessed or something," he said, chuckling slightly as an image came to mind.

Catrina realized that she hadn't really gotten a good look at much of what they had and was curious. She looked over at the gear in the corner again and then turned back to Brit.

"Maybe you could show me some of what you have? How far Earth has come since I was there?"

"You didn't see it all?" he asked, rubbing his eyes tiredly. They were doing much better, but still felt like he should be sleeping or at least lying down with his eyes closed. His neck and shoulders ached as well, but he just chalked it up to being sore from the workout.

"Well, I saw the moving picture plate *thing-a-ma-bob* your brother had when he was showing us all his time theories, but I never really got a good look at it. He had it most of the time, reading from it. I don't understand how he was able to read words from it without pages. The other gadgets, he either had in his hands doing something with them or they were stored away in his bag." Catrina took another bite and looked back across at Brit who now had a very distant look. She thought she must have said something wrong based on his expression. She felt a little embarrassed and wasn't quite sure where to go to get the conversation back on track.

"I am sorry if I've upset you," she quickly said, trying to make some kind of a recovery. Brit shifted slightly and popped out of his trance.

"Oh no," he said, setting his fork down and looking back across at her. "You've done nothing wrong. I am the one who should apologize. I was just thinking of Bryan, where he is and what he's doing right now." Catrina watched him as he spoke of his brother. She could see that they were very close. "I hope he's all right," Brit finished quietly.

He got up and stepped over to the gear situated in the corner. Fumbling around, he opened Bryan's pack and digging around inside, he pulled a few things out. Turning back around with his arms full, he carefully put the items down in a pile on the table. He took a couple of moments to spread everything out neatly, then pulled up a chair next to Catrina. Cat took one last bite of food, wiped her mouth and settled a little closer to Brit. She carefully scanned all the gadgets he had laid out in front of her, Brit watching her eyes sparkle with curiosity, as she looked them over. He could see that she was trying to work out in her head, what each one of them did and how to work it. A big smile floated across his face, watching her move from one thing to the next. He decided that this would be a fun game and a great way to interact with her on a much closer level. So far, it seemed as though their timing was so far off that there would never be a chance for them to really get inside the other's bubble. This appeared to be a good opportunity to do so, provided some silly servants didn't barge in on them and ruin everything, *again*. So here was a great opportunity for her to show just how smart she was. Let the guessing game begin.

"So, what do you see?" Brit asked, a little delighted with the game that neither had audibly agreed to, but both wanted to play. Catrina flashed Brit a wickedly delighted smile. There was a gleam in her eye that spoke volumes. She had them all figured out in her head and while she was delighted to be able to play the game, she was a little hesitant to start for fear of getting everything wrong. She decided to test his resolve and picked up one of the gadgets, twisting it in her hands trying to look at every surface for a clue.

"Looks like a bunch of junk to me," she said, knowing that she would get a reaction.

"Junk?" Brit cried loudly, but in a good-natured voice. "You're calling this stuff junk!"

Nailed it! She got exactly what she was hoping for.

"Well, I don't see how any of it can work. There's no place large enough to put any batteries in and how would you turn them on anyway, if they turn on at all?" she asked, looking over the array of equipment on the table. "If it doesn't have a blade on it, it's not much good in this world."

Brit grabbed a pouch from the table, pulled something out of a side pocket and started pulling on parts of it. A moment later he showed her not only a Swiss army knife, but a Leatherman tool, with everything extended. Catrina looked at the tools in his hands in awe.

"My dad used to have one of these," she said, taking the knife from him. "Only it didn't have this many things on it. Wow, this is amazing! Scissors, you have scissors on this! And a saw? Geez, could have used this about a million times here," she said, fascinated while studying every aspect of the knife.

"The Leatherman is actually more popular on Earth right now because of the pliers. Makes it handier," Brit said, giving the tool a good plug and working the pliers.

"Ok," Cat said, holding up the gadget that she had first picked up. "I think this one is for some kind of radioactivity detection or something." Brit gave her a stunned look. "Is that so you know if there's a radio station nearby or in what direction it would be?" She asked. Brit had to wonder where she had ever come up with that term, let alone her definitions.

Back in the mid to later parts of the 20th century they were called Geiger counters exclusively, but now there were smaller, more accurate devices that were far cheaper and did more things. That was exactly what that little box did. How did she know that? He continued to stare at her dumbfounded as she passed him a cheeky little grin and shrugged, looking the box over. Turning the box in her hand, Brit caught site of some writing on the side he hadn't noticed before. It was the label stating the maker of the device and what it did. "Radiation sensor, made by Pilmer, Inc." Catrina watched Brit's eyes drop to the gadget and noticing the label, knew the jig was up. She stopped rolling the device in her hand and instantly gave him an innocent look.

"Was I close?" she asked, giving him a cheesy, playful grin. Brit couldn't help but smile, snatching the detector from her hand.

"Give me that smarty pants."

"What?" she responded, trying to act all innocent. Brit turned the label back to her and pointed at it.

"You think you're so cute," he said in an accusatory tone. She certainly was. In this playful role she had assumed, he found her so adorable, that any resistance to her charm would prove quite difficult.

"I'm pretty sure you think I am," she said, still smiling with a half chuckle mixed in.

"That's entirely beside the point," he responded, putting the sensor aside. "Don't need you being a smart-alec here."

"Oh but why? Don't you think I play the part so well?"

"Too well," Brit shot back, turning all the devices with labels away from her line of sight.

"There," he said, looking up, a little more positive with his strategy now. "Let's see you cheat your way through the next one."

Catrina looked the instruments over good and picked up one shaped like a futuristic pistol or something. Brit watched her carefully to make sure she didn't look at the label on the bottom. There were no obvious holes where a projectile would exit, so she wasn't exactly sure what it could be used for. It had a display on the back side of it, a trigger, and on the square barrel side was a dark window of some kind with two little light bulbs on either side of the window.

"I'm not going to blow anything up if I pull the trigger, am I?" she asked, looking curiously at the end of what would be the barrel on a normal pistol. Brit laughed out loud and shook his head.

"No, no death rays or disintegrating laser beams."

Catrina gave him an odd glance then pointed the pistol at his plate of food, on the other side of the table, and pulled the trigger. Two little red specs appeared on his plate where the food was and a display lit up on the back side of the pistol. She casually released the trigger and looked the gun over some more, being careful that she didn't view the bottom of it where she knew it was identified, and then handed it back and thought for a moment. Brit slowly began to smile. She appeared to be stumped but was still trying to figure it all out. She looked back across at the plate of food on the other side of the table, then at the gun, then at Brit.

"I think it's used to measure the temperature of objects." The smile on Brit's face instantly dropped onto the table. She was spot on. An infrared heat sensor could measure the temperature of objects and air from a distance without having to actually touch something. Brit's shoulders dropped as well, looking down at the gun in his hand trying to figure out if she had somehow seen the label or something. He even tried looking at the object from her angle. He knew there was no way she could possibly know what it was. They didn't have this kind of technology back in 1945 when she had left Earth. How then was it possible? He puzzled about it a moment and then looked up at Catrina who was still grinning from ear to ear with glee.

"How did you-?" He pulled the trigger on the pistol letting the lasers shoot across the room at the wall and noticed the display on the back, light up. Right there in big bold letters was the temperature readings of the heat coming off the wall, measuring it in Fahrenheit and Celsius. He released the trigger and lowered it carefully back to the table. His eyes rolled in Catrina's direction and he turned his lips down in disdain.

"You know, this game ain't no fun if you're gonna cheat."

"What? It's fun for me!" Cat giggled, with a cheeky grin. "I like this game, pick another one!" Brit wasn't sure he wanted to continue now, although Catrina did seem to be having quite a lot of fun at his expense, her playfulness and humor quite contagious. This just wasn't exactly the route he was planning on for their time together this evening.

"Here," Cat said, picking up another object. "I'll guess on this one. I think it's a special alignment tool used on thermal heat detectors." It was a bottle cap opener. Brit snatched it from her fingers and stuffed it back into its place in one of the pouches. He was quite disgusted now and tried to act a little hurt. He wasn't hurt at all, but was doing everything in his power not to bust up laughing. He put on his bruised ego face and trying not to look at her, started rearranging the rest of the items on the table.

"It's not an alignment tool?" she asked innocently. Brit turned and gave her the disgusted look.

"Hardy, har, har," his voice heavy with sarcasm. "Very funny! You know it's a pop bottle opener."

"Oh, is that what it was? Looked much more complex than just a simple bottle opener," she lied unconvincingly.

"Tee, hee," he puffed, trying to sound even more irritated. "You are such a liar."

Catrina giggled again and leaned hard over into him, giving him a good-natured shove with her shoulder. The touch, even through the shoulders, instantly sent a spike of warmth through him. If there had been any anger at all in him, it was certainly gone now. She raised her hand, letting it come to rest on his shoulder and leaning into him just a bit, scanned the objects on the table before them.

"Can we look at this?" She pointed at Bryan's tablet. Brit gave her a glance and handed it to her. "This thing is amazing!" her eyes gleamed, looking it over. "A book with no pages. Now this I don't understand. Can you splain it to me?" she said, purposely slanging the word.

"It would take too long to explain how it works," Brit said, turning it on and bringing up the main page. "It will display anything that it has in its memory at just a touch of the finger."

"It must have a big memory," she said, the glow of the display lighting up her face.

"I think Bryan has a bunch of things stored in here. Couple of books, a bucket load of Apps, a couple of movies, all of his MP3 audio files and a bunch of his favorite music videos." Brit started to move his finger around the display, working the different icons around the screen and opening up a few different applications. He had his own device set up differently than Bryan's, so finding some stuff took a little doing, but it wasn't too hard. Catrina watched him maneuvering around the screen with his finger, her eyes fascinated with the technology unfolding in front of her.

"May I?" she asked, poking her finger towards the screen. She wanted to try and make things happen on it. Of course Brit was more than excited to let her give it a try. Cat moved her finger across the screen watching as a page moved out of the way to reveal more information under it.

"What does this do?" she asked, tapping different things all around the virtual reality window. It took her only a moment or two to figure out on her own how to make things work, opening up a whole new world. This was only a fraction of what the Earth had become in her absence and she realized rather quickly that she had really missed out on the century of technology. It seemed to be something that she was born for. The insatiable curiosity that once drove her so hard as a little girl back in 1945, came rushing back to her. Her mind shifting gears, she asked about everything. Brit could hardly keep up with answering the questions that were starting to come at him.

"So how do I see these music, "videos", you said he has stored on here?" she asked, swiping her fingers across the screen looking for what might be a clue. She had no idea what one was, but it sounded intriguing to her. Brit pointed to an icon and then directed her to scroll down the short list with a swipe of her finger. Letting the list spin down, she stopped it at a couple of the titles and started reading through a few of them.

"These are the names of the songs and the singers?" she asked, looking at some of the album art or photo covers that came with the song titles. Brit thought a moment. He was trying to put himself in her shoes, having been absent from the musical progression of Earth for a very long time. What was considered music back then would certainly have a much narrower audience now.

"Music is a bit different now and a video is a picture or short movie telling the story of what the song might be trying to say to you. Sometimes it's just a recording of the group of singers singing in front of a crowd of people. Other times it's an elaborate mystical production having absolutely nothing to do with the song, but an artistic point of view." Catrina suddenly slammed the cover over the screen with eyes wide.

"Oh my gosh!" she squealed, her face blushing. "I just saw a naked woman on a cover! Are you kidding me?" Brit was startled at first because of her sudden reaction, but then shifted over to 21st century thinking. He had overlooked the notion that proper modesty in the mid-20th century was far different than that of the early 21st century. He chuckled softly and took the device from her hands and opened it back up. He looked at the line she had seen and pulled it up.

"She's not naked," he said, looking at the cover of a very scantily clad female singer.

"Uhm, yeah, she certainly is!" Catrina maintained making sure she looked away from it. It was certainly improper to view things of that nature. She remembered all too well that airman in 1945 had pictures of women in bathing suits or less, painted on the sides of their airplanes.

"She's only mostly naked," Brit chuckled, bringing the cover up to full size. Catrina refused to even look at it.

"Mostly naked is naked and it shouldn't be looked at," she said, still quite embarrassed. She glanced over at Brit who was admiring the figure on the cover. "And you shouldn't be looking at it either," she said, clamping her hand over his eyes, grabbing the tablet with the other hand.

"Hey!" Brit objected only half-heartedly, trying to move her hand away, but Cat held her hand firmly over his eyes, spinning down the list some more. He finally managed to move her hand down from his face and just held onto it, which is what he was hoping for in the first place. Good opportunity to hold her hand. Cat stopped at a listing that looked interesting and examined it for a moment. While she browsed through the information being displayed before her eyes, Brit picked up his smart phone and turned it on. Cat only glanced up at it as it sang its tune while booting up. He was certain that there would be no signal, but he wasn't necessarily after a signal here. There are a myriad of things this phone would do without cell service. Once it came on line, he tapped through a few pages and then held it up in front of him, facing Catrina.

"Here, give us a big smile," he said, framing her in the view finder of the onboard camera function.

"What are you doing?" she asked, a little bewildered.

"Taking your picture," he said, focusing solely on her image in the view finder.

"That little thing takes pictures?" she asked, as he snapped a few pictures off.

"This little thing will do almost everything that the big thing you have in your hands will do. Now hold still and give me a smile." Catrina looked curiously at the phone he had held up in front of him, snapping pictures of her. She tried to reach out to take it, but Brit kept it out of her reach.

"Hey, I'm the doer here, keep your mitts off," he said, leaning back to stay out of her reach. In doing so, the chair he was sitting on leaned back too far and he nearly lost his balance. Catching himself at the last moment, arms flailing wildly to hold his balance, he brought the chair back to its normal resting position.

"Whoa," he said, wide eyed while resituating himself. "Nearly bought the farm on that one." Catrina laughed out loud, watching him nearly dump over backwards.

"You need to pay attention there Daffy. That thing really takes pictures?" she asked, examining the phone in his hands. It was still in camera mode and displaying the floor and the table.

"Sure, it will do a bunch of other things. Takes pictures," he said, raising it back up to snap off some more pictures, "makes movies and then plays them back. Also videos, like what you're looking at and it will act like a little radio, playing music that I can have sent to or stored on it. Come on! Hold still so I can take your picture properly. Pose like your mom," he said, trying to frame her image like that of her mother in the informational photo he had of Amanda. Catrina froze her curiosity for a moment and did her best pose of what she remembered of her mother's photo. He snapped off a few shots, and then looked through them quickly as Cat went back to exploring the music video listings on the viewer in front of her. A moment later Brit held up the phone again and pointed it at Catrina.

"Now what are you doing? Haven't you taken enough of my glorious self?"

"Don't get cocky," he responded, framing her back up. "Now you get to be in the movies."

"The movies?" she asked, looking up. "I get to be in the movies?"

"Sure," he said, framing her up. "I'll be your agent. Get you all kinds of gigs and you'll make millions and be famous."

Completely captivated, Catrina let her curiosity run free studying both the tablet and the phone taking moving pictures of her. Although she hadn't actually seen any of the pictures yet, the devices themselves and what they were doing was fascinating enough for her for the moment. As Brit continued to shoot the camera at her and the surrounding room, Catrina held up the tablet.

"How do you make the music play?" She asked, with a wonderfully child-like expression on her face, that of a ten year old girl opening her favorite gift on her birthday or Christmas morning. Brit tried to take the viewer from her but she resisted.

"Hey, I'm the doer here! Keep your mitts off," she said, laughing.

"You don't know what you're doing there," Brit said, playfully trying to get his hands on the tablet. "Let an expert do it."

"An expert is just a drip under pressure," Catrina responded with a giggle, tapping the line and bringing the cover up, and then tapping it again and the music began to play, all the while she was fighting Brit off from taking the viewer. As the video began to play, she gave him another playful shove as he tried again to retrieve the device. The shove sent him back off balance again and he toppled to the floor, chair and all. Catrina looked down at him horrified at first but soon discovered that he was laughing hysterically and that in turn brought her to laughter.

"Oh, the phone," she laughed. "Is it all right?"

"Don't mind me," he gasped between fits of laughter, still holding onto his phone. "I'm just down here checking for gum under the chairs," he snickered uncontrollably, trying to get back up.

"Are you all right?' she asked, trying to regain her composure. She turned in her chair to help him back up, but because he had up ended the chair as well, he sort of had to roll away from it in order to get himself right side up.

"No worries," he gasped, getting to his feet, still chuckling. "I saved the phone," he said, looking at the device in his hands. Actually it would have been just fine. In his line of work he found that he could go through a phone pretty fast. He had his encased in a high impact plastic casing bound in a tough rubber outer shell. It was very effective though it made the phone a bit bulky, but he had accepted it as a necessary element of his tools of the trade.

He finally got back up, righted the chair and sat back down next to Cat, now totally engrossed in watching the video playing in front of her. She was still chuckling softly as Brit scooted back up next to her and propped the phone up on the table with the camera pointed at them. He had reversed the image viewer on it so you could see to frame up the shot.

Catrina looked up from the music video playing in front of them when she noticed the smaller image on the phone's screen. Her focus instantly shifted to seeing her own image on the small screen. Brit was still smiling about the whole falling off the chair thing, but shifted the focus to what she was so fascinated with. He watched her move back and forth a few times and then wave at the camera.

"That's really me," she stated, completely amazed at what she was seeing. She had seen the movies before and remembered how it was all done. She remembered that day at East Base airfield when they had left and all the photo shoots and the military motion picture crew working their equipment. However, she also remembered that back in that era, when you took pictures or motion picture film, you had to have it sent away to get developed. Here now, it was instantaneous, she was actually watching it happen.

She carefully reached out, passing Brit a questioning look. He only urged her to go ahead, watching her pick up the phone and hold it. Cat was completely taken with the fact that you could not only take a picture or shoot movies, then instantly see it, but that it looked so sharp and life-like.

"It's like looking at a mirror," she commented with wonder. While she watched herself in the small phone display, Brit reached over and pulled the tablet over to him. Catrina went to stop him, but was more interested in the phone and the movie she was now shooting. Playing with the phone, she quickly figured out how it all worked. Brit shut off the music video, then started the onboard camera function of the viewer. Carefully pointing it at Cat, he watched her through the much larger screen.

"This is really a telephone?" She asked inquisitively.

"It allows me to talk to anyone at any place on Earth that's getting a signal." Brit stated, still holding the camera on her. She shook her head slowly. Her last memory of a telephone was the heavy corded hand set, rotary dial phone that sat on the end table in her parent's living room.

"I don't understand how it can. It's so small." Catrina was so focused on trying to work it all out in her head, she completely ignored the fact that he was shooting her with the tablet. Most would have given up on understanding the how and just focused on the doing, but not Catrina. She had to know all of the hows and the whys. Her inquisitive nature rushing to the surface, feeling as she did long ago. She wanted to know everything about what Earth had become, all the wonders it now held and what it had to offer.

"Please tell me," she asked, looking up at him, noticing that he was holding the viewer up and that he was looking so closely at it. "What are you looking at?" she asked, leaning over to him to see what it was. Brit smiled casually as she discovered that the tablet had a camera as well.

"Oh my," she said, setting the phone down and taking the tablet in hand. "Wow, it gets bigger!" She giggled, delighted at what she was experiencing. "Please tell me how it works, all of it," she said, looking at everything on the table. Brit picked up the phone, shutting it off as Catrina pointed the camera all around the room. How do you explain this level of technology to someone who hasn't got the knowledge base required to understand it? He spun for a moment in his thoughts, trying to figure out how he could help her. Watching her, there came a sudden thought to him that made the most sense, at least to him.

"I'm no teacher Cat, but I would like to show you how it all works and how you can understand it all." Cat continued to carefully move the camera pad slowly around the room until she stopped on Brit.

"Go on, I'm listening," she said grinning. "This is your big scene, don't blow it. And action!" She pointed a finger at him, just like a movie director would. Brit hesitated a moment. He knew what he was about to blurt out was a bit of a sensitive subject and he was almost certain that Catrina hadn't drawn any conclusions on it, but she was going to have to sooner or later and this seemed to be a good catalyst to move that along.

"Come back to Earth," he finally said, looking right at the camera lens. Catrina was gazing at the display with a pleased look and found herself looking right into Brit's eyes on the screen when he said it. The smile slowly melted from her lips as she just stared at his image. She finally lowered the tablet to the table, her eyes lowering with it.

"Come back home," Brit beckoned, trying to bring Catrina's eyes back up to his. He had brought it up; he might as well try a little more to make his case. If she couldn't decide to leave this people to just go back home, just to be going home, then maybe he could convince her to leave to discover all the wonders that their world now had to offer her. All the technology, the medical advances, the many cultures and how they had blended since Catrina and her father had disappeared from Earth. So many things that could be learned back on Earth, so many things to challenge the mind and spark the imagination. She had been here on Argyle a life time and yet, she could still spend another life time back on Earth learning so much more. Not to mention what she might be able to offer Earth itself. Life on another planet in a culture such as the clans had created over a millennia, could prove invaluable to science.

"We've talked about this already," Catrina finally responded in a quiet voice. She really didn't want to talk about this but at the same time knew that she had to decide what it was she really wanted to do. She knew that he was trying to help her, but it was a painful process that she only wanted to put off until the answer was clear.

"Yes, I know we've talked about it already and I suspect that you are still having a really hard time trying to figure it all out, I get that.

This," he said, holding up the tablet, "these things, are just another reason for you to come back," he explained, gesturing to everything in front of them and trying to be sensitive to her feelings. Catrina brought her eyes back up to his, searching for the reassurance he was trying to provide her.

"What about you?" she asked quietly. "What do you want?" She did not mean to skirt the issue or turn the question back around on him. It seemed as though she was looking for a better reason for something so monumental. Leaving Thulsa was not a materialist or intellectual question for her anymore. It had become an emotional one.

"I sorta of thought I made that pretty obvious the other day," Brit answered, throwing the issue right back into her lap. "But you have to be the one that decides. I have no right to dictate to you what your destiny is going to be. I'm just trying to provide you with information, tools that you can use to help you make that decision, to somehow make it easier for you." Cat glued her eyes to his, searching for the answers she so desperately needed, but it seemed the more she searched, the more she reached for those answers, the more fleeting they became bringing up more questions.

"It sounds like you're trying to convince me to just abandon my life with these people and come back with you. Is that fair to them?"

"I don't know what would be fair for them. Only you can answer that, but I'd be lying if I said I wasn't trying to convince you to come back with me," Brit admitted. "But again, you already know how I feel about it. And I think I have a pretty good handle on how you feel about leaving these people, but I will not make the decision for you or tell to you what you should do. It's for you to decide. If it bothers you, I'll quit bugging you about it."

Brit snapped his phone back into its protective belt case and set it aside, then reached for the tablet, but Catrina stopped him from taking it with her hand resting gently, but firmly on his. The warmth from the touch flowed freely and he could feel his heart start to beat faster. He wasn't alone in the exchange. Catrina was experiencing the same sensations, letting her fingers slide together with his until they had interlocked. They slowly raised their hands up so they could not only look at the embrace between them but also see into each other's eyes.

"Please," Catrina whispered. "Be patient with me." Brit smiled, squeezing her hand gently, then pulling the personal viewer over between them with the other hand and turning it back on.

He started going through everything he could think of that the device had to offer. From all the stored political news, to the celebrity news and current science achievements chronicled on the device. After what seemed like hours, the viewer started to indicate a low battery and it was shut off, put away along with the other stuff and they just sat together talking. Catrina was riveted to every word Brit was explaining about his view of Earth. Occasionally, he would pull his phone back out and show her pictures of things he had on it that could better illustrate the point he might be trying to make. She became especially interested when he started to talk about his own history, how he became so interested in salvage work, where it had taken him and the many things he had accomplished having such a career. She asked a million questions of how he did what he did and what all the equipment he had was. All of it completely fascinated her and she found herself wanting more. To actually do and see everything he was telling her about. Under water diving in lakes and the oceans, exploring ship wrecks and searching for things that people were interested in recovering. Knowing of the things that his own company, WACS, valued and why. Going through the history of his family's company, he got up and stepped back over to his gear in the corner of the room to put some of the things away that he had gotten out to show her. Catrina followed him and picked up one of the Hi-Tec parkas his group had been wearing when they came to Thulsa.

"These coats are amazing," she commented, looking them over. "What are they made of that they can protect you so well from the cold and the elements of the storm?"

Brit looked up from what he was doing and smiled. He recalled what airman in 1945 used to keep warm. He had even learned about their first attempts at installing heating elements into their flight suits. The early ones didn't work so well, but later attempts proved to be quite effective. Elements were still used even in his era, but the protection technology of fabrics and its insulating qualities had become quite advanced.

"Well, it's not just what they are made of, but how they are made," he said, pulling the Velcro tabs back to reveal the dual zipper and snaps that held the front closed. Catrina gasped at the sound of ripping as Brit opened the coat. He instantly froze and looked over at her.

"What?" he asked, looking back at her, searching for the problem.

"You've torn it somewhere. Is it ruined? Maybe I can have one of our seamstresses mend it." She said, examining the coat for the damage. Brit suddenly realized what had happened, and was quick to calm her fears.

"No, it's ok," he said, revealing the white colored hook and loop binding strips. "This is called Velcro. It interlocks with itself, holding the fabric together in certain places. It's really cool stuff." Brit pressed the two mating pairs together and had her pull them apart. It took a little exertion at first, but once she figured out that she wasn't actually tearing the material and that was just the sound it made, she became quite fascinated, running her fingers across both surfaces, seeing how the material interlocked together.

"It's like getting cockleburs in your hair," she exclaimed, very pleased with not only figuring out the science behind it but also that it worked so well.

"Just like it," Brit agreed, reinforcing her conclusion. "Here, give this a try and see what you think." He turned the coat around and opened it, indicating for her to try it on. Cat smiled, turning and putting her arms into the coat, letting Brit slip it up and over her shoulders.

"It's so lite," she said, pulling it closed around her. She admired it on her, looking down and pressing her hands smoothly to the bottom, then took hold of the zipper and worked it up. As she did so, a thought popped into her mind that she had wondered about almost since the first time she laid eyes on him and she just let it come out before she had a chance to second guess herself.

"Would you make a good husband?" Ok, there's a bombshell that just sort of got lobbed out there right at his feet! Brit was shocked for a moment, but held his composure nicely. He was neither qualified nor prepared to even try and answer a question like that and maybe that had been his and his friend's problem all along. Perhaps this was something that Bill Kyfie had been trying to get through to them the night before they came through the storm. Brit carefully checked his composure, trying to pretend that he was working with something on the back of the coat.

"I certainly hope so….yeah, I'm sure I would," he answered, trying to sound like he had put some real thought into it. In truth, without even realizing it, he had been prepared for such a question long ago. Even though he had been raised mostly by his father, he still remembered what it was like when his mother was still alive and how his father treated her. He had set a good example for how a husband should treat his wife and what it took to have a good close relationship with someone that you love and are committed to. He remembered that his parents didn't always agree with what the other believed or did, but they had decided early on in their marriage that it was good to agree to disagree and then respect the other for it, working to find some common ground. When one of them started to look inward instead of towards the other, conflicts invariably arose. It has always been when two people look to the others needs ahead of their own, that true marital bliss prevailed.

Brit expected a follow up question or discussion about the subject, but got nothing. It was as though she hadn't even asked the question. She finished zipping up the coat and snuggled in the fur lined collar. He watched her model it humbly, a smile of contentment on her face. With the contrast of her dark brown hair, deep brown eyes, and the white coat, she looked beautiful. Even so, he realized that she would look good in a gunny sack. The same was probably true of her wearing a hat. It didn't matter if it was a party cone hat or an elegant snood, she'd look good in it, and he would love her in it.

She unzipped the coat and Brit put it back on the pile of gear, then they both sat back down. Brit was still kind of hungry and pulled his plate back over in front of him. Catrina watched him eat for a moment as he spooned some red sauce onto the meat he was eating.

"This is good stuff. Tastes like ketchup."

"What about the rest of it?" she asked, looking over what he had left. Cat knew he was hungry and probably would have eaten just about anything anyway, but she did pride herself on the food that was being served. While she didn't actually cook this, she and her father brought this cuisine to Thulsa and taught the people how to grow and prepare it.

"Couldn't tell you what it is, but it eats pretty good," he said, downing the last of what there and downing the last of his drink.

"How many children do you want to have?" Cat asked, lobbing another gem out there. Brit spit his drink out, unable to hold it with the shock of the question. *What the heck was she going with here?* He had made a bit of a joke about children earlier in the Spoil and she wasn't amused. Now here she was, bringing it up again. Talk about awkward! As soon as he figured out what a woman wants from a man, he was going to patent, print and publish it. Then get rich selling it, because every man on either planet could use it and gladly pay through the nose for it.

Catrina giggled a bit under her breath. She knew that she was being rather forward. She was certain that she had him hopping all over the place trying to figure out what she was thinking. Truth be told, she really had no real direction she was trying to go with the question, other than to keep the conversation going. This question just kind of popped into her head and out her mouth. She remembered him teasing her a bit in the Spoil about naming all their children. A bit of erratic logic just let go and here we are.

Brit wiped his mouth and chin off, the liquid dripping to the table, then turned and gave her a look of surprise mixed with confusion. He couldn't believe that she had just asked that question. Now he was going to have to answer it. Actually, he had considered this question a few times in his late teens when a couple of his other friends had gotten married and had their first kids. Most of them didn't seem to want to be bothered with more than one or two and they named their kids with such stupid sounding names. It was like they wanted to be different from the generations before them by taking traditional names and twisting them with extra vowels, taking two names and jamming them together or even purposely spelling it wrong. Yeah, he had considered it, but only for a moment and stuck with what sounded good to him.

"Well?" she asked, still smiling. "Surely you've thought of it before."

"Well, yeah, I think everyone has at one point in their life," he said, in a rather matter a fact tone. Brit moved his cup away from him now. The thought of drinking what was left, after he had pretty much spewed everything back into it and all over the table, had no appeal.

"So?"

"Weren't you a little sore at me earlier for bringing up a similar question?" he asked, making sure she wanted a serious answer. Catrina shrugged being a little coy and glanced down to scratch at something on the table.

"Yes, I was," she admitted, looking right back at Brit, a slight hint of a smile still playing on her lips. "But you understand why I was."

"Certainly," Brit said, trying not to rehash something they had already worked through. It didn't make any sense to beat a dead horse. He gazed into her eyes for a moment. He had to be careful here though. He loved her more with every passing moment and looking into those eyes could get him lost in a place that could get him into trouble quickly. He smiled and looked away.

"Not really sure how many I would want to have actually," he said, thinking about it carefully. "I always assumed that was something that you had to decide with the girl you're gonna marry. Five or six sounds like a pretty good number to me."

"Do you have any names picked out for them?" she asked inquisitively.

"Always wanted a son named Robert and a daughter named Cathy."

"I like those names," Catrina responded, thinking about how they sounded to her. "Robert sounds so dashing and strong, and of course you'll spell Catherine with a C."

"Well duh," Brit laughed. "Wouldn't be able to call her CJ for short if I spelled it any other way."

"What's the "J" stand for?" Cat asked, resting her head on one of her propped up arms. Brit kind of got a little blush for a second, like he was embarrassed, but then let it out.

"I always thought Catherine Jennifer was a neat name."

"Seriously? That's about the most scrumptious name ever! Wouldn't have thought a guy could have come up with that all on his own."

Brit nodded wobbly and rolled his eyes.

"Ok, so what about you? What would you name your kids?"

"I never really wanted too many. Suppose that's because I was an only child, but I think I'd like to have a girl and name her Maria." Catrina seemed quite pleased with her choice and it was obvious to Brit that she had been thinking about this kind of thing for a very long time. When she had first brought up the whole, *"Would you make a good husband,"* thing and then how many children do you want, he was about as turned around as he could be. He wasn't sure she was serious about it or just messing with him. Now, the look on her face and the tone of her voice told a very different story

"How many brothers and sisters do you have?" she asked, after a moment of silence.

"Just me and Bryan," Brit came back quickly. His thoughts instantly shot across the distance in search of his brother and where he was. Sure wished he was back here now. Time was growing short.

"My mother passed away when Bryan was eight or nine," Brit said, almost hypnotically now. "Left my dad with a really rough problem of how to run a salvage business and raise a couple of little snot nosed boys."

"Well, I think he did a pretty good job," she said, smiling broadly at him, leaning down on her elbows.

"Sometimes I wonder." Brit sounded a little melancholy now. "It seems like I sort of rush into things a little too fast and about get my brother and me into trouble. Guess I'm kind of like my dad in that way. He was never one to think things through real good. Last one got him killed. My uncle had to take over after we lost dad until Bryan and I were old enough and took over dad's holdings in the business. He used to call me Skettles," Brit chuckled softly, thinking back to those times. "It was kind of a secret pet name he used for just me." Catrina turned solemn at the news of Brit's father. She was interested in knowing how he passed away, but wasn't sure how to ask in an appropriate manner.

"How long ago did that happen?" she finally asked, hoping she was making it sound correct. Brit finally broke out of his trace of deep thought and looked back over at Cat.

"I was 18 and just heading into the Air Force."

"Does it bother you to talk about it?" Cat asked, making sure she was on good ground.

It was good for Brit to talk about it. He always felt like holding things of this nature back inside him did nothing more than create a caustic poison within the soul that would, sooner or later, have to be purged anyway, so he had dealt with it at the time and moved on. This was not to say that he didn't think about it on occasion. He just resolved within himself that he wasn't going to let it drown him. There were days when it was tough, but if he thought about it and worked his way through it, he was fine.

"Oh no. My father loved flying jets. He had salvaged an old F4 Phantom from the Desert Rock test range in the Nevada desert way back when. Brought it home in pieces and tore it down to the rivets."

"Hold it," Catrina stopped him. "Just so I know what you're talking about. What is an F4 Phantom jet? I assume it's an airplane of some kind, but you have to remember that The Amanda is the last airplane from Earth I have ever known. There were no F4 Phantoms in 1945, were there?" she asked smiling. She really wanted to understand what he was talking about and was interested in hearing the story of his father. He sounded as though he liked talking about it, being a continuing form of therapy for him and she understood how he felt about it, for the most part any way. Brit got a slightly embarrassed look on his face, realizing his mistake and gave it a half chuckle.

"Sorry, my bad," he said, reaching for the tablet again. He knew it was low on power, but figured there was plenty for looking at a picture for a moment. Bringing up the image of the Jet, he passed it to Catrina who studied it, fascinated.

"Didn't your dad ever tell you that Germany came out with the first jets towards the end of the war?"

"No, he never said anything about a jet. Is this what they looked like?" she asked, looking over every detail of the old jet.

"Heavens no," Brit exclaimed. "Had they looked like this, they would have won the war hands down. The F4 came out 15 years after you guys disappeared. It was the fighter jet of the 1960s. Very fast, very mean. It could out fly and out fight anything anyone could throw at it. The Air Force used it for a long time. Clear up into the mid-1990s. Anyway, I'm sorry; I'm getting ahead of myself. A jet doesn't have a propeller."

"Clearly," Catrina agreed, looking at other pictures of the famous jet. "This thing looks bigger than the B-25." Brit smiled with a little glee.

"It was bigger, still had two engines, but that's about where the similarities end, other than they both flew.   A jet uses compressed fuel and air for its thrust. Sorta complicated, but that's a good basic definition. Air goes in those big scoops on the sides and mixes with a special fuel and ignites, sort of like a rocket only more controlled and variable. Anyway, dad put a lot of work and money into it putting this thing back together and getting it running again. Before he had it thoroughly checked out, he took it out to test the engines. Instead of just testing them out, he ran them a couple of minutes and then decided to take it for a flight. Once he got it airborne, it started having engine trouble. He wasn't going to be able to make it back for a landing. To keep it from crashing into any populated neighborhoods, he stayed with it all the way into the ground. That's just the way he was though. If he hadn't, a lot of people would have died." Brit went into a far off trance again, so Catrina set the tablet down and turned it off.

"I'm truly sorry," she said, setting both her hands down on his and squeezing. "Sounds like he was an incredible man."

"There are days when you really miss them and then there are other days when you don't even think about it. Almost like they were never there somehow, but then there's always a reminder somewhere in the little things that you're doing during the day," Brit said, turning to her and returning the gesture to her hands.

"I haven't asked you about my mother," Catrina stated carefully.

"I figured you would when you were ready," Brit said grinning. He had been dying to tell her everything he could remember about his meeting with her.

"My mother and father have this relationship that is so far and away above anything else that most couples can ever experience. I have never seen anything like it in all the time I've been here in Thulsa. I knew when you spoke of her how it would affect him. It was his moment and I didn't want to take anything from it. Truth be told, inside I was dying to know more. Will you tell me about her?"

Brit's smile continued. He had been hoping that she would come around to this. It's funny how a reluctant encounter with an old woman could have become so important. Now he wished that he had been able and willing to have spent more time with Amanda. Thinking back on it now, she seemed kind of lonely in that little house in Montana. He wished that he could have stuck around a little longer to visit more and keep her company. Had he known then what he and his brother were about to go through and what the events of the following week were going to present, he certainly would have. However, at the time, she was just another kind old lady with the same old story of lost loved ones. Everyone else on the planet had a similar story and had to endure the pain of their loss throughout their lives. Then he reminded himself that this kind old lady lost her loved ones in a celestial space rift to another planet. How many people on planet Earth can claim that one?

"I first laid eyes on your mother off the coast of Brazil on a recovery dive Bryan and I were just finishing up. It was her photo that I showed you and your dad. Absolutely fell in love with the woman when I first saw her. Oh my gosh, she is so pretty." Brit completely forgot himself, recalling his first viewing of her photo on the boat. It wasn't even dawning on him that while he was describing his feelings for what he saw in her mother, Amanda, he was describing Catrina too.

Cat felt a slight hint of embarrassment, mixed with flattery, as Brit continued to describe his feelings about her mother's image. She could very well have gotten jealous about it, but she knew how it all worked. Looking at her mother back then was like looking at herself now. She understood that; having experienced it first hand when they were confronted with the image of Amanda in the airplane earlier. Catrina listened in awe as Brit described her mother's picture to her and then proceeded to the day he knocked on her door and they met for the first time.

"I was expecting some little, old, white haired, frail looking thing," Brit explained with a chuckle. "You know the type I'm talking about.

But that's not who came to the door. Your mother still stands up tall, weighs a bit more," he said carefully. "Her hair is white, but short like it is in the photo. Her voice is very strong. She really doesn't seem like she's that old. I guess you'd say she has aged very gracefully."

"What did you talk about while you were there?" Cat asked quietly. Brit paused a moment as he had to think about it. It was only a couple of days ago, but so much had happened since that day in Montana that he had to recall his thoughts to make sure he had everything straight.

"Well, it started out as an interview to find out more detailed information about your dad's airplane, but it quickly changed over to more about your dad. I could tell that she has been terribly lonely for him, but she held herself in check pretty good. She talked about you a little bit too," Brit continued with a pleasant smile. "Not much, but before I left, she asked me to bring you and your dad home to her. I'm pretty sure she wanted closure as to what happened to you guys." He let out a slight chuckle. He was certain that she had meant for him to bring their remains or word of their demise home so she could lay them to rest once and for all.

Brit scanned Catrina's face, zeroing in on her lips. He really wanted to kiss her. He just hoped that she wanted the same thing. Nothing more embarrassing than going in for a kiss and having the girl pull back or be a little too playful and give you the jazz, ruining the moment.

"She wears glasses now, but her eyes are still a wonderful brown, just like yours," Brit said, looking right into hers now. He couldn't help it. Oh, how he loved her eyes! They were her most distinctive feature. Not that he didn't like the rest of her; it was just that her eyes were her focal point. He truly couldn't help but love her, but didn't realize how deeply until he felt his insides tumble and warm up like a clothes dryer tumbling sheets. It turned into the feeling you get when you curl up in those sheets right after they come out of the dryer. He was warm all over and starting to worry that he might be turning flush in the face.

Catrina was having similar feelings, and every bit as intense. She was nearly breathless now, their eyes locked, deep brown to crystal hazel. They gazed steadfast at one another, hand in hand, face to face, soaking in the moment. The urge to kiss was unmistakable and irresistible now and finally being alone, all the conditions were right for it. They could now express in action, what they had yet to say in words. He raised a hand to her cheek and let it slide around her neck under her wonderful dark brown hair. His fingers spread, allowing her silky hair to glide between them. The sensation went right off the charts for them as she let his hand melt into her hair and neck. Moving slowly closer, he sensed her edging towards him with equal caution. Finally, this was it! They could express how they felt and enjoy the other's affections. Brit took one last look at her as he drew close. He reveled in the look of anticipation on her face. She was completely committed to what they were both feeling. Catrina let her eyes melt closed, continuing to move towards him and wondering why it was taking so long to meet in the middle. She could feel his presence so close and yet, not close enough. They were only inches from touching, when a knock at the door startled them, instantly breaking them apart and turning. A servant entered, looking at them in a moment of hesitation, wondering if she had interrupted something. Catrina quickly composed herself before their embarrassment became evident and motioned for the servant to approach.

"For the love of Pete," Brit grumbled under his breath.

"Steady," Cat mumbled back, just as frustrated.   Were they ever going to catch a break? They looked beyond the servant to the door. They could see a figure just outside, but in the shadows.

The servant quickly stepped to the queen, whispering something in her ear. Catrina turned back to the door and nodded. Brit was a little frustrated with the bit of intrigue, as he didn't speak the native tongue and had no idea what was going on. The servant quickly made her way back to the door and another figure appeared. Brit recognized Sargon stepping carefully to their table.

"Please forgive this intrusion," he said, bowing respectfully. "I hope I'm not interrupting anything." Brit couldn't help but still be a little irritated that the moment had been lost. *Uhm, yeah! You are interrupting! Why couldn't he have come in about five minutes earlier,* **or better yet, five minutes later?**

"It's all right Sargon," Catrina said, nodding at him. Inside, she was a little frustrated too, but the spell had already been broken and there was obviously something very important at hand.

"My Queen, Master Garrett," he said, quickly coming to the point. His voice sounded excited and worried at the same time. "We have successfully brought the rest of The Amanda to the surface."

This seemed like good news, especially to Britten. With all the pieces in place, they had only to wait for Bryan and his two friends to return and they could call in the Sky Cranes for the pickup.

"Nice work Sargon," Brit responded excitedly, though he wondered why this couldn't have waited.

"You and your men have done so well," Catrina congratulated him for a job well done.

"As we have moved it towards the area Master Garrett has instructed us," Sargon continued, bowing in appreciation, "we have noticed that the storm has moved with it."

"What?" Brit asked, instantly shifting from jubilation to grave concern. "What do you mean it has moved? How can it move? Where did it move to?" The last question was probably better asked of his brother Bryan. He was the scientific mind in all of this, but he wasn't here, so they were left to try and figure it all out for themselves. Catrina dropped her eyes to the table top, trying to assemble all the pieces to the problem while Brit continued to try and grasp the situation vocally.

"I thought Amanda said it was here for her, for the energy it had lost?"

"I don't pretend to understand such things Master Garrett," Sargon responded carefully. "We noticed the storm shift when we started pulling The Amanda out of the cave and one of my men pointed at the west ridge."

"Strange, west ridge?" Brit repeated, trying to get a mental picture. Something suddenly popped into his head and he looked at Catrina, a very perplexed look etched across her face. He turned and grabbed two of the winter parkas.

"Sargon, will you show us?" he asked, as Catrina got to her feet and put the coat on that Brit had opened for her. Sargon nodded quietly as Brit shoved his arms into his own coat, grabbed a pair of binoculars out of one of the packs and turned to the Thulsa Engineer.

"What is it?" Catrina asked, still trying to figure out what was going on. It was apparent that Brit had something in mind, but the look on his face told her that he wanted verification first.

"I think we're in big trouble," Brit stated ominously. "Really big trouble," he reaffirmed grimly, moving quickly out of the room and down towards the cellars to the tunnel access, the queens royal guard following closely. Catrina had to trot quite fast to keep up with Britten who was just about running through the tunnel behind Sargon to the cave opening. Approaching the cavern that the aircraft fuselage had once occupied, Brit noticed the passageway getting much brighter and a lot more noise rumbling through the cold air, moving back up at them from the now open cave entrance.

Sacrifice for the Signet

Working their way down the mountain in the dark, Tim noticed Digi becoming even more agitated, trying several times to get around him and growling loudly when he couldn't because the trail was so narrow. To their left, there was nothing but darkness, the side of the mountain dropping away, a sheer drop down for who knows how far. The rain driving harder the further they went and the wind picking up dramatically. Tony indicated that he remembered the trail going on this way for quite some distance and they would have to remain vigilant to not misstep or slip and fall into what he recalled as a very deep chasm. Digi finally took the lead from Tim, making his way several steps ahead of the rest of the group, when Tim noticed him stop and shake his wings, then hold his head up erect, sniffing the wet night air. As the rest of the bunch caught up to the alerted Jabba, Tim figured it was the animals own exhaustion starting to get the better of him. A Jabba without sleep can be a much tougher customer than a tired human. The Jabba have been known to turn psychotic, while humans usually just fell asleep.

"What now?" Danny complained, coming to a halt in the driving rain. Like everyone else, he was soaked and tired; even their boots were wet clear through. Walking in wet boots turns the bottoms of your feet into a rubbery prune texture, making them feel quite uncomfortable.

"Digi has something," Tim whispered loudly, to be heard over the wind and the rain.

"Yeah, yeah, yeah," Jerry complained, heavily irritated. "He always has something. He's had something on the last four stops we've made and there was nothing. Come on, let's get moving." The rest of the band echoed Jerry's impatience with the Jabba, pressing themselves against the cliff wall to rest. At least it wasn't cold, but even so, wet was wet.

Tony leaned forward to glance up front when he caught site of the Jabba instantly stance and brace for something incoming from above. At that moment, the whole band was besieged in a furious attack of wet wings and razor sharp claws. A surprise Jabba attack! They were coming from everywhere, above and below. Terry and Tony had their swords out in an instant, swinging at the growling masses of fur and wing descending on them. Danny and Jerry dropped to the ground, rolling up tight against the cliff wall to keep out of the fray. Watching Terry and Tony through raised arms, Jerry and Danny could see them hacking and slashing at the winged animals attacking from multiple angles, chirping and growling loudly. Jerry turned his head up towards the front where Tim was fighting hand to hand with several Jabba and Digi was a complete mass of brawling fur rolling madly about on the narrow trail. Jerry couldn't tell which one was Digi and which his attackers were. In this darkness, they all seemed to look the same.

He remembered that he was carrying long daggers and that both he and Danny were lying on the ground cowering from a fight when they should be a part of it. What kind of friends were they, not to engage a fight after all they had been through together? Jerry felt something pulling at his legs and looked down to see a snarling Jabba tugging at him, trying to pull him toward the edge of the trail.

"Nope," he hollered. "Ain't gonna happen!" He started kicking it in the face, pulling both daggers, sitting up, and jabbing at the beast. Danny too, suddenly came alive with a similar realization, pulling his knives and jabbing at the same Jabba. Perhaps this would be Danny's revenge for what had happened to Bryan, but those thoughts were fleeting. Instinct took control of both men, repeatedly jabbing at the animal. Danny finally got himself into a good position to get at the animal still clawing its way up him to get to his friend. What was the big deal about getting at Jerry anyway? Did Jerry smell better than he did? He didn't care! The fact that it was going after his friend was enough.   He wasn't going to let another go. Taking both daggers, he wrapped one arm around the squirming beast and drove his left knife directly through its wrapped wings and into the animal's abdomen while shoving the right knife directly into its chest. The Jabba let out a miserable wail, dropping limp on Danny. Jerry pulled his legs out of the way and looked back at his friend.

"Oi," Danny puffed disgusted over the wind and the noise of the attack. "They stink even more after they've taken a shower!" He grimaced a bit, rolling the dead animal off and over the side of the trail edge. He looked down at the large gash and cuts in his pants and leg. It was hard to tell in the dark and the confusion of the attack, just how bad it really was, but it was enough to hurt.

"Shoot," Jerry said, checking his friend's leg.

"What?" Danny asked, looking at the injury wondering if it was a lot worse than what he had surmised it might be.

"Ya could have used that Jabba to heal this thing up."

"What?" Danny asked, a little irritated that his friend was worried about the dead animal he had just pushed over the edge.

"Spit brotha, spit," Jerry came back, as another Jabba landed behind a battling Tony and jumped at them.

"Too wet for that to do us any good. Look out!" Danny yelled, as the Jabba launched itself right at Jerry. Danny lunged forward with his daggers thrusting straight at the snarling animal. Both knives buried themselves to the hilts and the Jabba went down immediately, right on top of Jerry. Danny pulled the knives back out, crawling forward to push the dead carcass off his friend, who was already rolling to one side to get out from under it. Tony struck another Jabba dead with his sword and it fell directly onto the first one, half burying Jerry. It was a good thing that it was raining otherwise this would be a real big mess.

"Hey!" Jerry yelled, trying to keep a sense of humor about him. "The garbage chute is on your left!" He knew that Tony was in a heavy fight above him. Danny turned, getting to his knees in time to battle another Jabba that had landed behind him. He could see Tim ahead of them fighting with several of the angry flapping beasts, but still couldn't see Digi anywhere. Jerry finally got to his knees obstructing Danny's view of Tim, only to be set upon by two more growling Jabba. He swung his daggers wildly, trying to hit something solid, the two fury winged beast clawing and trying to bite with their razor sharp fangs. He and Danny were getting slashed up with every encounter, but adrenalin kept them fighting with even more ferocity. Another dead Jabba slumped into Jerry as he fought frantically with the two that had already engaged him. Danny no sooner had one finished off when another came from out of the darkness to attack. He didn't even flinch, the Jabba screeching, wings fully open and all claws extended to pounce. He sank his left dagger into its chest with a quick thrust and turning, drove the right dagger into the back of one of the Jabba that had beset his friend. He could feel its back bone cracking, the knife piercing through the spine and to vital organs. Getting to his feet, he maneuvered to help Tim with the mass of four or five growling animals all over him.

"Nuts," Danny mumbled, wiping the water from his face and charging into the fray, knocking off two and wrestling a third trying to pry the Signet from Tim's back. Fighting to pull the Jabba loose, he could see the other two were not only slashing at Tim, but also cutting through the straps holding the metal encased book to his back. He yanked and tugged at one of the snarling animals and suddenly pulled it free from Tim, but it had managed to bring the book with it. The straps had broken and they had the book, but Danny had a hold of the Jabba! He held onto its wings as it tried to flap away. Reaching down, he grabbed a hold of its hind legs with one hand and tried to wrap his arms around its wings with the other arm. The Jabba chirped, growling loudly and flapping as hard as it could. It was like holding onto a chicken by its legs. Danny dropped both daggers and held on for dear life, the animal frantic to escape. Perhaps it could pull the human right off the trail, out into the nothingness of the dark. No one really knew for sure what was over the edge. It looked very dark and foreboding.

Gritting his teeth, Danny strained against the flapping beast. His feet were starting to slide along the wet slippery rock of the trail, towards the edge and the dark drop off. Reaffirming his grip on the back legs, he held on, feeling the animal flexing its claws right into his hands. He knew he wouldn't be able to hold on much longer. The animal was either going to pull him over the edge or he was going to have to turn it loose. Danny started to let the Jabba sway back and forth a couple of times and then with a mighty turn, he swung the flapping animal right into the cliff wall. The collision stunned the beast enough that it dropped the book, sending it bouncing over next to the edge.   The animal sprang right back at him, fangs and claws extended.

Jerry wrestled frantically with the Jabba that had come at him, getting bitten hard a couple of times, enough to get really pissed off. Grabbing the animal by the jaws and trying to break its mouth wide open, but alas he was just a distance runner, born and bred to run and not built for massive strength in his arms and hands. He was growling about as loudly as the Jabba, fighting to get the upper hand. He took only a moment to glance off to see how his friend and Tim were faring, but had to concentrate on not getting torn to shreds by this smaller animal. You would think that he could kick the crap out of a small dog sized creature.

They seemed to come in all sizes. Some of them were the actual size of a wolverine and others, like Digi, were as big as a St. Bernard. He was becoming increasingly frustrated that he couldn't do away with the dumb thing. Jerry searched all around for the daggers he had dropped in the melee while still fighting with the creature, but all he could find were rocks. Desperate, he finally grabbed one and started beating the animal on the head. While this only served to anger the animal at first, it finally did the trick and the animal finally went limp. Jerry didn't know if he had killed it or just knocked it senseless. He didn't care and gave it a good shove over the edge of the trail into the darkness, wind and rain.

He turned in time to have another one come at him from above at the same moment he caught sight of the metal bound book tumbling across the trail to the edge. Both creature and human dove for the case, arriving at the same time and wrestling with it, the two rolling dangerously close to the edge. So much so, that Jerry could feel his legs hanging out over nothing. He didn't realize just how far over the edge he really was until he could feel the edge of the trail cutting into his mid thighs. The wet rock was slick and he could sense the Jabba trying to maneuver him off, but still hold onto the book. He glanced over at Danny who looked like he was pummeling a Jabba with his bare hands. Jerry held a death grip on the book handle with one hand and reached for the Jabba with the other. The animal was quick to try and bite his hand, Jerry grabbing at anything he could get a good pull on. He finally tricked the beast by switching sides of its head to get at him and he was able to grab a good hold of the scruff of its neck and with a mighty yank, pulled the Jabba right over the top of him and over the edge. Problem was, the Jabba still had a hold of the book and it pulled Jerry right over with it.

Starting to slide over, his friend Bryan came to mind and the last time they saw him falling from his horse to his death. Oh goodie, he was going to get to have the same adventure. As Jerry went over he felt something grab his other hand and stop his fall into the darkness. He looked up at Danny who had a hold of him with one hand and clawing at the bare rock surface of the trail with the other. This was not good in any circumstance. Neither were very strong men and the wind and rain compounded the issue. Their hands were already tired and sore from the battle and they were bloody and wet to boot, making for very slippery conditions. Trying to hold on to Jerry with one hand was hard enough, but to have a writhing jerking Jabba on the end of the line made it impossible and he could feel their hands slipping. Danny clawed at the bare rock, trying to pull Jerry back to safety, but it wasn't happening. Something else had to be done here or they were going to lose the book and his friend.

Danny had no decision to make. He would hold on no matter what. He squeezed harder trying to halt the relentless march of Jerry's hand sliding through his grip. Jerry, on the other hand, had a choice to make, but he had to make it quick or it would be made for him. There was no sense letting his friend in on his plan because he wouldn't agree with it and start arguing. There was only one thing he could see to be done. It was obvious that these Jabbaway were after the book. The Thulsa band had to see that they didn't get their claws on it, as it were. He pushed away from the wall with his feet, causing the Jabba to swing out with the book still tightly clamped in its claws. Danny grimaced with the added strain, wondering what Jerry was trying to do. They looked at each other, Danny trying to read what Jerry was thinking and Jerry trying to draw strength from his friend for what he knew had to be done. Jerry could feel his hand slipping further. There would only be one or two swings before he would lose his grip on his friend and slip away. He pushed off again and the Jabba swung away from the wall even further. Then, making one last big push and with a mighty heave, swung the Jabba and the book back up over his head. The whole maneuver took the Jabba completely off guard, tumbling right passed Danny, dropping the book and rolling into the cliff wall. No sooner had the animal hit the wall than Terry's blade came down, slicing it in half, but the deed was done and there was no way Danny could hang onto his friend, their grip slipping faster. Jerry looked silently up at his friend's craning face and grimaced, trying harder to hold on. He could see the figures of Terry and Tony moving to help Danny, but it was too late, their fingers slipping, coming apart. There would be no yelling or any death screams, just the rain and the wind as he disappeared into the darkness.

Danny lay completely stunned, unbelieving. What had just happened? There was no way that Jerry had just slipped away from him! There was just no way he had just lost another friend in nearly the same manner Bryan had lost his life! It simply wasn't possible! He went numb, lying there completely …...stunned, not believing his own senses. He could still feel a tingling in his fingers where he had gripped Jerry's hand so hard that it had cut off the circulation. The image of Jerry's face gazing up at Danny as he slid out of sight was still searing into his mind, finding a place of prominence in the forefront of his memory forever.

The attack was over, the book safe and the last Jabba were either killed or jumped from the trail, into the nothingness and flew away. Danny yelled into the darkness and listened carefully, but the only sound that came back at him was the wind and the rain. It just didn't make any sense that Jerry was gone. He continued to call his name for several minutes until Tony and Terry finally pulled him from the rock ledge. This time, Danny did not fight them to stay. He was too numb for defiance. Too stunned, filled with utter disbelief that now he was virtually alone on this alien planet. Alone to try and fight his way home.

The thoughts of Jerry being down there in need of help, just like he had thought of Bryan, raced through his head, but this time, the scars he had accumulated since then, had seared into him and he was forever changed. He was becoming hardened to the brutal realities of this world and the life and death struggle he was embroiled in. He sank back to the ground, leaning back against the cliff wall and let the rain wash freely over him while Tony saw to Tim's welfare and Terry searched ahead for Digi.

Danny leaned his head back against the rock and closed his eyes. He tried to cry, but nothing came to him. He felt no emotion at all, just emptiness. He had just lost his best friend and partner. Shouldn't he be hysterical and shedding tears over him? Something had to be wrong with him. He looked back at the spot where he had lost his grip on Jerry, half expecting to see his hands grasping the ledge, trying to get back up onto the safety of the trail, but all he could see was darkness. He just sat staring out into the dark for quite some time until Tim sat down next to him with the book held tightly to his chest. While it was probably quite dangerous to stay where they were, there was no place else to go. Besides, it was quite unlikely that the Jabba could navigate back for a return attack. They had probably made their way ahead of them somehow while it was still light and then lay in wait until they came along the trail.

Danny could see out of the corner of his eye that Tim kept trying to look at him every once in a while to gain his attention and maybe grant him some kind of comfort, but Danny felt nothing and searched his mind for some kind of emotion that would lead himself to somewhere, anywhere. Feeling nothing, left him frozen with no ambition to do anything, go forward or backward, only to just sit and look at the spot where he had let Jerry go. So they both just sat silent in the wind and the rain, waiting for Terry and Tony to come back. Tim noticed a faint noise coming from the cliff wall they were leaning against, but the rain and the wind made enough noise that he couldn't make out what it was. Sort of sounded like rock grinding against rock. Must just be the mountain groaning as it had earlier when they had encountered the Mynite.

Presently, Tim noticed two figures moving back up the trail towards them, one of them carrying something over his shoulder. Tim thrust the book at Danny as Tony carefully set Digi down in Tim's lap. Danny barely looked up to see his condition, but Tim was all about it. The Jabba was barely alive, breathing shallow and rapidly. His wings were torn up pretty bad and there was a lot of fur gone in places all over his body. Even in the dark they could see deep gashes in his thick coat.

"I know next to nothing about these guys," Terry said grimly. "But this don't look very good, even for a Jabba with healing spit."

Tim examined him as best he could in the darkness, feeling with his hands and fingers more than looking with his eyes. The cuts were indeed deep, but Digi's body fluids were doing their job. Given a chance to heal, he might just pull through. Trouble was, on a mountain side, in the dark, in the wind and the rain, wasn't conducive to healing of any kind. Finding good shelter and some heat was now paramount. There was a chill developing in the wind and with everything being wet; it was starting to draw away the heat from their tired battle weary bodies.

"He'll pull through, but we all need to get out of this weather or getting to Thulsa will be the least of our worries," Tim announced, getting to his knees to pick Digi up.   Tony squatted in front of Danny, who only stared right through him, still feeling only nothing.

"You ok?" Tony asked carefully. He remembered how distraught Danny had been when they had lost Bryan on the Torres road and how he had carried that all the way to Crosslake. No doubt he was in terrible turmoil now with the loss of yet another good friend. Danny slowly changed his focus to Tony and nodded his head, wiping the water from his face. He gripped the Signet firmly making sure that Jerry's loss wasn't in vain.

"Yeah," he finally rasped hoarsely. "We better get moving." He was about to make the effort to get to his feet, noting that Tim now had Digi perched across his shoulders, but placing his hands down to push off, both he and Tony froze, hearing a grinding sound coming from the cliff wall behind them. They turned their attention to the wall. Even in the dark, they could make out the outline of a Mynite face in the stone. It looked at all of them, even though Terry and Tim were busily engaged in preparing to start down the trail. They watched the face intensely as it tried to indicate something to them, but it was like trying to have a conversation with a mime. Usually you end up just wanting to punch them in the white painted face and get on with life. Tony leaned in closer, the grinding growing noticeably louder. The face looked like it was trying to speak as it opened and closed its mouth. Danny felt his hands starting to sink into the ground beneath him and figured it would be a lot more comfortable if he were to just twist to the left, right where he was so he didn't have to crane his neck to see what was going on. Attempting to turn, he noticed that his hands were stuck to the ground. The book still in his lap, he looked down at his hands to see what the problem was with all this mud, only to find his hands were completely immersed in the ground. He thought there was only rock here.

"Uhm," he said, trying to pull his hands free from the supposed mud. "A little help here." Tony glanced down at where Danny's hands should be. He reached down but felt only smooth stone. There was nothing but stone around the young man's wrists. He pulled the book from Danny's lap and examined what was happening.

"Ok, this is a new one," Tony called out, bringing the attention of the other two back to them. Terry dropped to his knees and started working to free Danny's other hand. Danny tugged frantically, but instead of coming out, they were sinking further up his arms, noticing that his rear end was being enveloped as well.

"Never heard of quick rock before," he exclaimed, quite alarmed at what was happening. He turned side to side, helping direct the effort to pull him free, then saw the face in the rock, still trying to indicate something to all of them. The grinding got louder until it was quite distinct over the wind and the rain. The others had become so intense with their efforts to free Danny from his stony bonds that they hadn't even noticed that it was happening to them as well. It wasn't until Terry had lost his grip on Danny's arm that he noticed that his feet had sunk in past the ankles, along with everyone else.

"This hasn't been a very good day," Tony called out, trying to make light of a very frightening situation.

"Yeah, just keeps getting better and better all the time! Remind me not to go on any more adventures with you guys," Danny exclaimed. His lap was enveloped in stone as he continued to steadily sink down and back into the cliff.

"How long can you hold your breath?" Tim called out, still holding tightly to Digi. Terry pulled his sword out and tried to pry himself lose, but that only served to gouge into his own flesh, so he put the sword and that idea away.

"This is going to give a whole new meaning to the term "rocks in your head," Terry joked, seeing no reason to get all upset. They were completely helpless to stop what was happening and while they were all terrified, there seemed to be something quite comical about the

whole scene. This might have proven useful before the Jabba attack.
They could have just disappeared into the rock. They would be dead
and buried, but at least the Jabba wouldn't have gotten to them or the
book.

Danny was soon up to his neck and the back of his head was
sinking into the rock behind him, but strangely, he wasn't finding it
hard to breathe at all, feeling quite warm and dry except where the
rain was still hitting his face. As the grinding got louder, he became
aware that it was not a grinding at all, but there were words forming in
the odd noise. He could distinctly hear low, growly words as the stone
started to envelope his ears then move around towards his cheeks and
mouth.

"Relax, carry you safe." He watched the stone covering his eyes,
then there was nothing but black.

*   *   *   *   *

Odd...............Danny blinked. That was an unusual sensation. The
mind would indicate to you that you were now buried in solid rock and
you should be frozen in place, but this was more like floating in
nothingness. If he were in rock, he shouldn't be able to blink. Wait a
minute. He held his hand up in front of his face. He couldn't see it,
but he could feel that he was moving it, along with other parts of his
body. He wished he could see so that he could have some sense of
reality. No sooner had he thought this than there was the same
growly voice all around him.

"Please be still, carry you safe."

"I can't see anything," Danny gulped nervously.

"Be still, soon see."

"Okie dokie," he responded, more baffled than terrified about
sinking into solid rock. Maybe they weren't in the rock at all. Maybe it
was something else. He didn't feel dead, so that couldn't be what was
happening. Danny was sure he'd know what it felt like if he were
dead. Wouldn't anyone know that feeling? He was breathing fine and
he could move freely though he had been asked not to. He knew that
if Bryan were in the situation he would be coming up with all sorts of
theories about what was going on and how this was all possible. Each
would be just as far-fetched as the next. He wondered if Tony and the
others were experiencing the same thing he was. Maybe they could
hear him. Whatever it was that was carrying them could obviously
hear him.

"Tony, Terry, can you hear me?" he called out loudly.

"Voice no hear. See soon, hear soon, be still," the voice spoke.
Even though it was quite growly and tough to make out the words, it
seemed to be very calm, so he just folded his arms and tried to relax.

After several minutes of holding as still as he could, the voice spoke again.

"See, hear now. Stand careful. Safe place."

Danny suddenly found himself stumbling out of a rock wall into a brightly lit cavern. Catching his balance, he looked immediately back for his host, but saw nothing. He stepped back to the wall and examined it carefully, putting his ear to it and listening for any sound at all. There was nothing but the silence of the rock and the trickle of water coming from somewhere inside the cavern where he had been deposited. He finally turned, looking carefully around in complete astonishment. The cavern was awash with glowing crystal structures reaching up from the floor, out from the walls, and hanging over head from the ceilings. These structures gave off a myriad of different colors and the combination made for quite the light show throughout the whole of the cathedral-like enclosure. He drew in a deep breath and stepped over to the nearest cluster. Each crystal about the size of a softball bat and as individually shaped as snowflakes. No two crystals emitted the same color light, or so it appeared to him. They were so curious to look at. Looking closely at them, he could feel a sense of warmth starting to envelope him and he discovered that he was no longer wet or chilled. He felt like he had been warming himself by a fireplace and was now dry and snuggly comfortable. It felt as though he had been gazing at the light for quite some time, when in reality it was only a couple of minutes and he became aware of something happening from the same direction he had entered the cave. He looked over just in time to see Terry and Tony suddenly appear from the solid rock wall, the book firmly locked in Tony's arms as they crashed to the floor. They appeared to be stunned, but unharmed as Danny stepped a little closer to make sure they were breathing.

"Well," Terry blinked, grunting a little and rolling over. "That was a completely new experience for me." Danny let out a forced half chuckle as the two looked up at him.

"Yea," Tony agreed with a yawn and a grunt. "Don't get to walk through walls very often. Especially stone ones." Danny stooped down to help them to their feet, Tony setting the book to one side and taking his hand for assistance.

"It's a heck of a lot nicer here than it is outside, that's for sure."

"Ok," Terry said, getting to his feet and looking around at the cavern. "So now we just need to figure out where here is." Tony looked around as well, but was instantly drawn to the crystals, their color and glow. He stepped over to a large cluster for a closer look as Danny stepped back to the wall they had all come from.

"I wonder where Tim ….." Speaking the words, Tim magically appeared from the wall and stepped into the cavern. He seemed to be a little more prepared for his entry than everyone else. Stepping in, he immediately turned back to wall and attacked, beating both fists against the cave.

"Bring him in!" he bellowed, beating on the wall.

"Whoa, settle down there," Tony said, trying to calm Tim down. "What's going on? Where's Digi?"

"He's still outside!" Tim yelled, backing away from the wall but still looking at it trying to get a response. "They wouldn't bring him in! Come on! He needs help! He needs to be with me!"

Tim ran at the wall again and pounded on it some more. However, there was only so much his fists could take and he had to back away. Still enraged that his friend had been left outside to die, he started picking up rocks and throwing them as hard as he could at the wall. Danny watched the anger displayed by their friend explode, but no one wanted to stop him. They had all had enough of those around them dying, Tim especially. Still suffering from the loss of his wife and now he would have to endure the demise of his best friend. Indeed, Danny had a pretty good sense of what he was going through right now. Maybe he should be right there with him, demanding that Jerry be brought back to him. How do you make demands of something you have no knowledge of? He had no clue of what had just happened to them or what it was that had made it happen, only that they were here and probably most importantly, the book was here, safe from anyone getting their hands on it.

The other three watched silently as Tim leaned against the wall and pounded, begging that Digi be brought in with the rest of them. Finally, he sank to the floor, sobbing softly, refusing to be consoled. Tony tried to render aide to his now bleeding hands, but Tim refused. He just wanted to be left alone, so Captain Dallas sank to the floor beside his friend and just sat with him. Danny continued to watch them, seeing them in a whole new light.

Since they had lost Bryan, he had been so focused on his own pain that he had no perception of how those around him were feeling and what they were going through, not only as a group, but as individuals. Tim had just lost his wife and now his best friend. That had to be unbearable for him. Looking at Tim in his sorrows, Danny glanced at Tony, who seemed to be feeling genuine sorrow for his friend. That appeared to be the prevailing attitude the Thulsian Captain had with everyone, seeing to their needs instead of looking to his own. How could that possibly work? How can you ignore your own turmoil, to try and sooth the sting of someone else's? Yet, Tony seemed to be so grounded and so loved by everyone with whom he had ever had dealings. Watching him now, Danny realized that inner peace came from the giving of one's own self to the aid of those around him. This didn't mean that one was immune from the pain and the hurt from within, but it did mean that it would hurt a little less and the healing process wouldn't take as long. It was all good medicine and the best that the human race had for such situations.

Terry quietly looked around at their new surroundings. They seemed to stretch beyond what the eye could easily see from their vantage point. He turned to a stack of crystals nearest him and examined them.

"Have you felt anything odd about these crystals?" he asked Danny in a hushed tone. They had just arrived here and Danny wasn't sure how he could possibly detect anything out of the ordinary, but yes, he did.

"Yeah," Danny replied, stepping closer to Terry, but keeping his gaze on Tim and Tony. "It feels like they are warming you from the inside out when you get close to them. You noticed it that fast?"

"Tired of picking up on something and not paying attention to it only to have it come back and bite me later on," Terry said, carefully touching the glowing crystals in front of him.

Danny knew he was referring to the Mynites. Maybe if they had been able to pick up on their presence while they were still on the Kenlar side of the Tera, they might not be in here minus two more of their ranks.

"Catch a load of this," Danny said, holding up his leg and showing him where the Jabba had clawed him and left several deep gashes. They were mostly healed up. Not even Jabba fluids could heal that fast. Terry examined Danny's leg very carefully and then checked his own wounds. Even though he and Tony had kept most of the attack away from themselves, several had made it through enough to claw and scratch. Now, it was like it had never happened.

"Geez," he whispered in astonishment. "Remind me to open up a spa down here." Terry looked around at all the crystals growing like clumps of grass everywhere. "I could have every warrior from here to the Mastell regions climbing this mountain and waiting in line for days for a chance to spend an hour down here."

"Your world and mine," Danny agreed, looking around again. He glanced back at Tim and Tony who were still sitting against the wall they had come in from.

"They brought us in here, we might as well have a look around," Terry said, thinking the same thing as Danny. They separated and started to explore the cave. Danny carefully made his way around to the far side of the cave that sloped downward. It looked as though there was no end to the cave or the glowing crystals that spiked out from everywhere. There was no real path here, but there were many flat spots and a kind of natural flow to them. Maybe they had been purposely put there, but never used. Occasionally he could hear the same grinding noise that they had all heard on the outside before the Mynite images would appear in the rock. However, whenever he would stop to have a listen or look in the direction it was coming from, he saw nothing. He stopped a couple of times for a drink at some clear cold pools of water that had collected around the rocks or in low areas of the cave. With each drink, he felt a renewed sense of energy surge within him and it wasn't long before he felt like he could take on the world again. Many of these pools had tiny trickles of water running into them from unseen cracks or even open chimneys to other places in the mountain.

The cave went on and on. He finally got tired of wondering when it was going to end or trying to find where it led to, so he turned around to make his way back to find the others. Working his way back up the cavern, it was filled with the grinding sounds that had accompanied the Mynites. Several times he caught sight of one out of the corner of his eye, but when he would look; there was nothing there on the walls or among the lighted crystals. At least now the Mynites were getting curious enough to be so close Danny could hear them distinctly and see them occasionally. By the time he had returned, Terry was waiting for him next to Tim and Tony. The grinding noises and the faces in the stone were no longer shy about showing themselves.

"Sorta feel like fish in a glass bowl," Terry commented, looking around at all the faces that seemed to be gawking at them.

"The cave just goes on and on down that way," Danny announced, leaning against one of the crystal formations.

"Same up the other way," Terry responded, starting to feel a little uncomfortable with all the noise and the faces. Everyone was on their feet now wondering what to do with all the attention they were getting.

"Do you know anything about these guys?" Tony asked, trying to get some kind of information of what or who they were dealing with, anything.

"Very little," Tim admitted, a little frustrated. He had thought that having learned the knowledge of the Ancients, he should have knowledge of the world around him. He was growing tired of the lessons in humility he was being taught through this adventure. He had hoped that when he had been rescued that it would be in a triumphant manner. He could ride back into Thulsa, being paraded all over in front of everyone. All the people would see how grand he was because he had survived Kenlar captivity under Ivan Rubella and had acquired the knowledge of the Ancients, committing it to memory. Right now, he felt about as dumb and worthless as a guy could get.

"I've never spoken with anyone who has had actual contact with them, only heard stories and overheard conversations. Suppose to be really hard to communicate with them. I don't think they can speak, only make noise."

"What about these crystals?" Tony stepped closer to the nearest cluster, looking them over good. Tim stepped up next to Captain Dallas and gave them a good look as well.

"I've seen some really small ones before, but nothing this big. Argylians call it Modavite. They are supposed to only exist deep underground and a single crystal at a time. Nothing like this," he said, looking at them from every angle.

"Sure makes you feel good to be around them," Terry announced, from behind the other two. "I felt like crap on the outside, but as soon as we got here," he hesitated a moment, "well, let's just say that even though things don't look so good, I feel pretty good about it," he finished with an upbeat tone in his voice.

"Yeah, they're rumored to have fantastic healing qualities. Even holding onto the very small ones will prolong your life, or so I've heard." Tim said, touching the crystals lightly. The stone glowed brighter whenever they were touched and this only fascinated the men even more.

"Ah, guys?" Danny said from behind. His eyes were fixed on something towards the wall from which they had entered. Terry and Tony turned to look, followed by Tim who was still fascinated by the glow coming from the crystals. They all lost interest in anything else, turning to see the outline of a human form on the wall of the cave. Watching carefully, it took on a three dimensional look, growing out of the rock. It was as if the rock itself had turned elastic and someone was trying to push through a thin membrane in order to enter the chamber. The grinding around them suddenly faded and concentrated itself where the image was forming in front of them. Under normal circumstances this would seem exceptionally remarkable to everyone standing there, especially Danny, but after everything they had all been through in the last three days, this seemed almost routine. After all they had just walked through walls so to speak, having a man made of rock, appear to them, was just an extension of the continuing stream of common remarkablisms they had all been witness to.

Finally, the figure stepped out into the chamber in front of them and stood frozen as it continued to form. It took on the form of a male, or so it appeared as definition filled in around all its body parts. As its eyes formed up, it turned its head and looked at each one of the ragged band from Thulsa carefully, then froze again and continued to form. Toes and fingers appeared, the finer detail materializing before them. Then the outline of clothing appeared and flesh color replaced the dull grey of stone. Finally, the facial features formed up in detail, complete with a full head of hair and a mustache, but otherwise clean shaven.

The Thulsa band gazed in awe at the figure before them, rubbing across their own facial hair at the same time. They all had some growth going on since they were last able to shave and groom back at Vespa Cull. The figure remained frozen with its eyes closed for some time giving the humans a chance to examine it more closely. It looked quite life like as Tim circled it carefully. He reached out and touched the bare arm, observing that it didn't feel anything like real flesh. He wasn't sure how to describe what it felt like, maybe a combination of rubber and course ocean sand. The figure did not respond to the touch, so Tim circled back around to the front and felt the other hand. The texture was the same.

"So is it real?" Tony inquired, as Tim looked right into its face.

"'Bout as real as rock can make itself," he answered, utterly fascinated by the finished product. "I thought I was pretty hot stuff for memorizing the Signet," he said, reaching a hand up to touch the hair on the head. "But this is far and away beyond anything I have read about of the Ancients."

"Do you suppose that this could be one of the Ancients?" Terry asked.

"Yeah, like I would know that," Tim responded sarcastically, looking back at his friends. "I'm assuming that they have constructed this in order to communicate with us somehow," he said, putting his hand on the head of the figure and patting the hair, testing it in comparison to the real thing. It looked very fine, but felt very course and didn't spring back like a normal head of hair would.

"You would be correct," a very low raspy voice said. Tim dropped his gaze down into the open grey eyes of the figure. He was not startled at all, freezing where he stood with his hand still resting on the head.

"Ah, Timothy," Captain Dallas said carefully. "Might want to remove your hand from the rock man there and step away." Tim looked over at Tony thinking he was fine right where he was until it dawned on him that he might be in this creature's personal space and it might not like it.

"Oh, yeah, sorry," he said, pulling his hand back and backing up, rejoining the ranks of the other three men. The figure looked at each of them, and then looked around the crystal chamber.

"It is our hope that we have not frightened you. It was not our intension to do so." Everyone in the group was a bit hesitant to respond until Terry nudged Tony. He was after all the ranking officer here, whether it would be on Earth or here on Argyle. Tony finally took a step forward and addressed the figure.

"Uhm, we're just not accustomed to traveling through stone, it's probably our biggest wow here."

"No, I would imagine that it is a very new experience for humans. Your molecular structure was not designed to do so."

"Then how were you able to bring us in here?" Tim inquired. His scientific mind now had a myriad of questions spinning up to speed and everything else that had happened to them became secondary. The figure turned its head to Tim. It was quite mechanical, and it was unclear if that was because it was still forming internally or if it was learning how normal human movement was accomplished.

"It is good that humans are so curious in nature. This speaks very highly of you as a species. You call us Mynites," the being stated coldly.

"Yes," Tony answered, a little nervous.

"This is an acceptable title for the purpose of our interaction."

"Is there something that we can call you?" Terry asked, trying to get in on the conversation. The being turned its head at Terry.

"My race is called something entirely different than Mynites, but it would be impossible for me to translate it into a human word as none exist that we are aware of. Because you require identification of individuals to keep order in your communications, you may call me Stone." There was silence for a moment, and then Terry edged forward.

"You want us to call you Stone?" he said, less as a question and more as a statement of disbelief.

"I thought it fitting. It is what this form is constructed of."

"Ok, Mr. Stone," Tim said, stepping up a bit. He had some business to attend to and he wasn't about to be bashful. "How did you get us in here and why wouldn't you bring my friend in with me?" Tim crossed his arms so as to not appear threatening, even though he was still fairly upset and mustering a bit of self-control to hold himself in check. He couldn't make demands on someone who held all the cards, especially if that someone, or thing, was made of rock. What was he going to do, beat him up? Stone turned his head at Tim. The movements were still mechanical and calculated, somewhat robotic.

"The creature was your friend, yet you were all fighting these creatures? Can you explain how this works?"

"We were crossing this mountain range to reach the city of Thulsa some distance from here. My friend Digi, a Jabbaway of the Binion flock, was helping us cross. We were ambushed by an aggressive enemy flock trying to take something and prevent us from reaching our destination. We killed many and fought them off. My friend Digi has saved my life many times. Several times on our journey over these mountains, but he has been badly injured and in need of assistance. Please bring him inside so I can help him," Tim pleaded carefully. Stone looked at him for several moments.

"What were these other Jabba trying to take from you and why?" Danny bent down and picked up the Signet.

"They were trying to take this," he said, showing him the metal bound book. There seemed to be something about these beings that told him they could be trusted with such things, besides, they really weren't in any kind of a position to refuse him. Being able to go through walls sort of qualified them to just take it if they wanted to. Stone gazed at it curiously.

"It's called the Signet," Tim informed him, trying to remain patient. "It holds all the knowledge of an ancient race of travelers. I have been the keeper of this book for a very long time. We were trying to get the book to a safe place to keep it from falling into the hands of those who would use its secrets for destruction and enslavement."

That should do it. The book was safe in here for now but Digi was not and so he wanted to try and change the focus of the conversation. Stone had other plans, leaning a little closer, but not moving his feet.

"Will you open it and show me?"

Tim was struggling to hold his patience, but motioned to Danny to hold it open for the being made of rock. Danny fumbled with the clasps for a moment, then pulled the pages back about in the middle and spread it open for Stone to examine. He studied the open pages before him for quite a while, making Tim even more impatient. Finally, he stood back up straight and tall turning his head back to Tim.

"You have carried a very heavy burden in keeping this knowledge safe from those who would abuse it. This book belongs in its rightful place."

"That's where we are trying to take it," Danny responded quickly.

"It belongs with the Gate Altar, where the Ancients meant it to stay," Stone commented abruptly. The four humans looked at each other completely bewildered. None were aware of anyone else knowing of the Ancients, especially beings that lived in rock.

"It's where we are taking it, to keep it safe," Tony said, looking at the open pages that Danny was scanning over.

"If this world on the surface has turned to warring as it would appear, then perhaps it is no longer safe on the surface," Stone pointed out, quietly freezing in position in front of them. Danny carefully closed the book and secured the clasps as Tim took a certain exception to Stone's choice of words.

"None the less," he spoke deliberately and with as much resolve as he could muster. "It belongs with the Gate Altar in the city of Thulsa and that's where we mean to take it. Now, will you please bring my friend inside with us, so we can help him?" Tim kept his eyes fixed on Stone who remained motionless for several more moments, then took a heavy step further from the wall.

"We are unable to locate your friend at this time. But we will search for him as best we can."

"As best you can?"

"Yes, even in the rock there are certain places that we cannot go, places we cannot reach. I am expending a great amount of effort to appear to you in this manner. We usually cannot leave the confines of the rock. We cannot cross over a crack in the rock. We must go around it and keep to the solid portions. If we encounter a crack, we have to find a way around it."

"I'm a little fuzzy on the whole rock thing," Danny said, cradling the book in his arms. "How does anything live in solid rock? Why is it so hard for you to appear to us this way?" Stone carefully stepped forward and the others watched him slowly walk around the cavern chamber.

"I take no offence to your question or wonder why you have no idea of how this is done. My race has always lived as we have. Humans are generally so self-absorbed and focused on themselves that they take little notice of other beings such as the Mynites or the different planes that others exist in, yet we are all tied together by a common bond." Stone turned towards one of the glowing crystal structures and gazed admiringly into its light emitting prisms. "Life exists in so many different realms, one as equally beautiful as the next," he said slowly, almost in a trance with the glow of the crystals before him. "We live and love the elements of the rock. We even enjoy some of the same things about Argyle that you humans do. We can see the same light that you do when we come to the exposed surface of the rock. We feel the wind and the water as you do, the very same way that animals of this planet's oceans experience it. Beneath us are beings we call Moltilans. They live in the very molten rock that is the core of this planet and they experience some of the same elements that we all do. The beings that inhabit the air, you call them birds or fowl. They too can touch and feel many of the same things that we do. Indeed, even off this world are beings that live in the very emptiness of space itself, making it not as empty as we would think, were we to ever think that deeply about it."

"Are you an Ancient?" Terry asked carefully. Stone glanced over at the four still standing in place watching him.

"The Mynites are very old, yes, even ancient. We do not keep records such as humans do, but," he said, standing back up straight, "no, we are not the Ancients that you speak of. We were placed here the same as the humans and everything else on this planet. But I know of the people who you speak of, these Ancients." Now Tim's interest was starting to peak.

"They wrote the Signet," Tim said, pointing at the book in Danny's arms. Stone looked at it knowing who the authors were.

"They were a delightful race," Stone finally said, letting his stone hands glide across one of the crystals that began to purr with his touch. "The Mynites inhabit the rock of the whole of Argyle and somehow the Ancients chose your city of Thulsa, close to these mountains to settle for a time."

"The Signet says that they were travelers of space," Tim asserted, trying to confirm his translations and findings within the book.

"Space and time, but that was only a small portion of the things they sought to discover and learn. They brought so much to this world, but took nothing from it. Only the enhancement of knowledge and the being of it. How infinite a race of beings can be that can do such."

"Sounds like you revered them as gods," Terry said, listening carefully. Stone looked right at Terry. Suddenly, Terry felt much smaller than his actual size.

"Such a statement is derived from human arrogance, but is also understandable considering where it came from. Yes, I suppose humans would consider them as such, as gods. But they would have been the first to say that they were far from it. As the question was asked of them before, they were quick to explain that they sought only the knowledge of the universe and its understanding, that it might make living in these dimensions more pleasant and meaningful. They were always quick to point out that true happiness in existence always came from giving from within to all those around them. Such beings are truly missed in any sphere," Stone said, letting his voice trail off to another place as it appeared he seemed to mourn the absence of the Ancients.

"What happened to them? Where did they go?" Danny asked.

"They left a millennia ago, leaving behind the Gate Altar and the Signet," Stone continued, looking back at the book. "It is such a wonderful and precious document." Stone looked down at Tim. "You understand what can happen were this knowledge used for unrighteous purposes. It has so much potential for greatness, yet that greatness is equaled by its potential for horror."

"Then you know the contents of this book and the importance of our mission," Tony spoke up. While he was no longer outside keeping track of time by what the sky might be doing, he had kept a mental note of the time since they had been brought inside and their conversation with Stone. The rock image seemed to be thinking about the past when the Ancients had been there and the associations they must have had. Surely, calculations about what these four humans were trying to accomplish were being factored.

"Yes, I think we understand what you are trying to do and where your hearts and true intensions lay." Stone looked directly at Tim. While the Mynite man had very little inflection in his facial features, Tim felt like he was pressing his attentions right at him. "But I sense that you know the secrets of the Signet human." Tim was a taken back just a bit. How did Stone know the knowledge he had stored in his head? Admitting to it was of little consequence, though it might be of some help.

"Yes," Tim admitted, thinking about it for a moment. "I have had opportunity to study and learn its secrets. I have studied it for so long that it's forever memorized."

"Then you know the dangers all too well of this knowledge falling into the wrong hands."

"Yes, I do. For this reason, it must be returned to the Gate Altar."

"I sense that it is not the only reason it is being returned." Tim let his eyes drop to the floor then edged over to Tony, who made a quick glance at the book still in Danny's arms.

"Yes," Tony spoke up. "There is another reason." Danny took a step back as Captain Dallas made the announcement. Stone shifted his attention from Tim to Tony, moving closer to him for the explanation.

"To help us stop the storms that come to the Valley of the Lakes beyond the western Thulsa gates." Stone froze again for a moment, giving the band of four cause to pass around uncertain looks. Tony stepped forward a little coming face to face with the stone man.

"A temporal Rift comes to this place and remains for days, bringing strangers from other places and taking people. We mean to use the knowledge of the book to stop it." Stone continued frozen, making everyone even more nervous. Tony looked back at Tim and shrugged while Danny stepped up next to Captain Dallas and looked closely at Stone's frozen face. It was fascinating how close to flesh it looked, yet didn't. He reached up and rapped on the side of the statue's head, trying to get any kind of a response, but nothing happened. He suddenly felt better about standing back behind the rest of the crowd and made a hasty retreat right before Stone suddenly stood back up erect and looked at all four of them.

"We know of this Rift and its travels. It is rumored that this is how the Ancients left Argyle, through the Rift. For eons of time it has moved mostly harmless, just passing by, but something has upset its natural balance and path. Do you have that information available to you?" Tony gave a glance back at Tim again, feeling that telling Stone everything was the right thing to do. It appeared that the Mynites knew all about the Ancients and the contents of the Signet.

"Yes, we know why it remains for so long. We do not come from this planet. We come from a place called Earth. It's on the other side of the known galaxy from Argyle. The vehicle we were traveling in encountered the Rift and was changed, transferring energy from the rift to the vehicle. We believe that the rift remains in place for extended periods of time to try and regain that which was lost to it."

"You passed through the Rift's portal from your world to this one then."

"Yes, it would seem so."

"When did this happen?" Tony thought a moment, glancing back at Tim and Terry.

"According to our young friend here," he said, motioning back at Danny. "We have been here for almost 70 years in Earth time." Stone looked them over really good, then focused back on Tony.

"This is a long time to be away from everything that you have ever known. What of this younger one?" he asked, looking over at Danny. "Did he come with you so long ago?"

"No, he and his friends came through the Rift several days ago."

"Why have you come young one?" Stone asked, directing his words at Danny.

"We came to recover the vehicle and the remains of those who were in it. We had no idea what this Rift was and if we don't get back to it soon, we'll be trapped here as these men have been."

"Then time is very valuable to you right now. You are still a very long way from the city of Thulsa and the sword altar. How will you prevent this Rift from stopping each time it comes by on its journey?"

"By removing the vehicle," Danny stated instantly. Stone froze again then looked at Tony and Tim, who only gazed back at the Mynite.

"You have a way of accomplishing this task as this vehicle assuredly is quite heavy and large in size?"

"Yes, we have heavy lifting vehicles that are waiting for our signal to come in, pick it up and carry it out."

"And you?"

"We came through at ground level on the far side of the valley. We intend to go back that way."

"That would be very unwise," Stone warned him quickly. Danny was instantly very concerned, as were the other three.

"I don't understand. We came through that way, why wouldn't we be able to leave that way?"

"The Rift is always consuming, never giving back. As it exhausts its ability to hold itself in place, its energy field will compress and it will spin faster. No doubt it has created some kind of a disturbance on both worlds where it has been spinning. As you are human and frail in comparison to Mynites, if you try to exit at the same place you entered, it will likely tear you apart. You would have to exit through the top or the bottom." Tony looked at the others, confirming how so many others had met their fates.

"How will your vehicles enter to pick up what is left of your first vehicle?" Stone asked, becoming more engaged with their problem. He appeared to know more about what was going on than Danny and the others did. Perhaps he knew the Signet at least as well as Tim did and was becoming quite concerned for the welfare of these intrepid men. Danny didn't have a whole lot of detail on the pickup operation. This would have been better addressed by Britten or Bryan, but he gave it his best shot.

"It's my understanding that our pickup vehicles will fly in through the top and lift them straight up the same way they came in." Stone thought a moment then nodded in agreement.

"This has a good chance for success, but be forewarned. There is still an element of danger associated with this method. It is understood that this is the only means for removing the cause of the

Rift's halt over the Valley of the Lakes, but the Rift will continue to try and regain what it lost when this vehicle flew through it the first time."

"How so?" Tim asked, stepping forward just behind Danny. Had he forgotten something or not remembered something in the Signet that told about the behavior of the Rift? It was certainly possible. He was human after all and subject to memory lapses. Indeed, the information was a lot to process and recall, but having been one who went through the Rift originally; he had studied these parts the most.

"By its very nature it will try and stop you from leaving and take back that which was taken by any means it has available. No doubt your damaged vehicle has taken on some interesting side effects from its encounter with this Rift."

"We mean to preserve her as she is now," Danny announced sternly. He remembered his encounter with The Amanda and the feelings that everyone had for her wellbeing. "She has become a wonderful life form of her own." Stone thought a moment, looking back at Danny's resolve, and then nodded.

"I sense that this life form is a being of compassion and true devotion. Perhaps a new life form created from the chaos of the Rift? How odd life is that something filled with love and well-being could have come from something so consuming. You humans are truly a step above so many others that we have observed. You have certainly evolved far beyond what we had expected of you. Will you allow the Mynites to assist you?" Danny turned to the others. They could certainly use all the help they could get. Problem was, they were in a cavern chamber in a mountain, still a considerable distance from Thulsa. What could these rock people do to help them? They all had equally confused looks having no idea how Stone could help them. Danny finally turned back around and spouted out the first thing that came to mind.

"We've lost two friends here on the mountain. The Jabba and another human who fell from the trail before you brought us inside. Can you find them?"

"We have been searching for the Jabba." Stone nodded. "There was talk of another human that fell from your location earlier, but I can't think that he could have survived a fall at that height. We will search for him as well, but thus far, none of the Mynites have reported anything about either. Certainly we will leave," The Mynite paused a moment, making sure everyone was looking at him, and then formed a big grin on his face. "We will leave no ...stone... unturned."

The Thulsa band froze, not quite understanding that a joke had just been made. Stone gave the humans an odd look. Maybe they didn't get it. Danny finally looked back up at Stone and slowly raised a finger at him, waving it slowly at first then grinning from ear to ear.

"You just pulled a funny one."

Stone grinned again. He had hoped that they would get his attempt at human humor. The entire group chuckled softly. "Yes, I thought it fitting."

"How are you able to know that you haven't found our friends?" Tim asked curiously. He sort of had an idea, but he wanted to be sure. Of course Stone was happy to converse with these humans, being so curious and intelligent.

"The Mynites are a collective of sorts. We move about the sphere of rock as you humans move about on the surface and through the air. Humans can speak freely to one another. I suspect that you can communicate at great distances as well. So too, it is true for the Mynites. I know it must be hard for your minds to comprehend that we move through the rock as easily as you move through the open air. We cannot survive in the open air for very long, just as you would be unable to survive in the confines of the rock for very long."

"But you brought us in here," Terry pointed out.

"Yes, as long as there are no cracks to cross, we can move quite rapidly and in the case of humans, we can provide an adequate air pocket for you to survive for a time."

"How do you know when you've encountered a crack?" Terry asked, shifting where he stood. Stone looked up at the ceiling of the chamber and thought a moment, then looked back down at his new friends and smiled again.

"You could say we bump our heads, much like you humans would if you were to walk into a wall." Tony was listening very intently to the information exchange, but at the same time, was watching Stone's body language. He seemed to be slowing down; his movements were becoming a bit labored. At the mention of not surviving for very long outside of the rock, he became quite concerned for the stone man's welfare. Their exchange had been going on for some time now and while he knew he didn't require air like they did, they must require something that prevented them from staying out of the rock for very long. He turned to a smiling Tim and Terry after the head bumping comment from the stone figure.

"I think we had better let Stone return to the rock," Tony said carefully.

"You perceive that I am holding my breath as you humans would?" Stone turned to Tony and looked at him for a moment.

"You did mention not being able to survive for very long outside of the rock," Tony reminded him cautiously. "You said that you're expending a considerable amount of energy outside of your element in this form."

"You are very astute human." Stone nodded in agreement. "If you will excuse me, I will return to the rock. We can continue to converse from there."

"Like you tried to do on the other side of the mountain?" Danny asked, as Stone lumbered slowly back over to the wall. He turned and gave the youngest Thulsa traveler an odd look.

"I recall no such encounter. Are you sure you saw one of us?"

"Pretty sure, there aren't very many rock people making faces in the side of a cliff."

Stone thought a moment, rubbing his chin.

"Like any life form, we have our young and intrepid as well and are not always in touch with them. It could have been one of them that you saw."

"Maybe one of them has found our other two friends?" Danny asked, sounding hopeful.

"That is entirely possible human." Stone leaned back against the wall and stood up straight. "The young ones are so impetuous. They don't ask before they do things. They just do."

Danny chuckled a little. It suddenly occurred to him that it didn't matter where he was in any plane of existence, any world or what you were, everyone belonged to a family somehow. They all interacted in similar fashion and they all appeared to have similar problems between the older and younger generations. He had certainly had his share of disagreements with his parents. He knew what he was doing with his life. Why did he have to tell them about it? They had enough trouble trying to figure theirs out. Yes, things certainly seemed universal in this matter and it sort of made him feel not so far away from all he had ever known.

Stone's body melted back into the rock until there was just a silhouetted outline of his face, much like it appeared in the cliff wall.

"How fast can you move through the rock?" Tim asked, sitting down next to one of the crystal structures.

Stone's voice was now different, rougher than before, but he seemed to be a little more at ease.

"I do not have a comparison number I can give you that you could understand. Do you have something in mind?"

Tim thought a moment and then looked over at Tony who was trying to figure out what he was thinking. About the time he figured it out, Terry leaned forward and asked the question.

"Could you take us to Thulsa?" he blurted out.

Stone thought a moment, his face disappearing a couple of times, but only for a moment.

"No," he finally said. The group kind of slumped a bit, Tony letting out a disappointed sigh.

"The rock of the mountain ends long before the city walls could be reached. However, there are several pillars within a short distance that we can get you to."

Tony stood up straighter with renewed hope.

"I calculate only a couple of hours to second sunup. Will you take us?"

"What is so important about second sunup?" Stone asked inquisitively.

"My friend has been held in the city until our return, contingent on the retrieval of the Signet. If we don't arrive at the arena by second sunup, he will have to fight to the death." Danny was quite emotional about his friend's plight. He had lost two friends already trying to save the third. His hope turned to finishing their mission.

"You humans, still so barbaric, still so much to learn," Stone said, shaking his head in disappointment. "How will your friend have to fight? Why was he chosen?"

"He was chosen because he pulled the Twins from the Gate Altar," Tony said stepping up, feeling a little responsible for the whole thing. "He will defend himself using the Twins."

"This he must absolutely not do," Stone replied, becoming very concerned. "Such wielding by a human will cause him severe damage. The Twins were not created for humans. They were designed to be used by the Ancients and them alone. The power they contain is too great for the course substances of your internal workings. We must get you there as soon as possible to stop him." The feeling in the cavern turned very somber now, shifting their concern to Britten Garrett.

"We're ready to leave whenever you are," Terry said, stepping up next to Captain Dallas.

"Then step to the wall and lean back. We will take you with as much speed as we can."

"What about our two friends?" Tim asked, stepping over to the wall with the rest of them.

"If they still live, we will find them and return them to you. Please remain still and do not speak or move. We can move faster and your air will last longer."

"What if we run out of air?" Tim asked, leaning back letting the rock start to melt around him.

"We will stop at the surface several times to refresh the air for you and continue on as quickly as we can." As the rock closed in around Danny, he held onto the book wondering if they were doing the right thing now by bringing it back to Thulsa. There was great goodness and great evil associated with this book. Maybe it would be better off in a place where no one could ever get to it. A place where it's keeper could never be reached. Even Tim could become a liability knowing its contents. Perhaps the human race wasn't quite evolved enough to have the wisdom to use such information in the right way.

"Stone?"

"Please young human, remain silent. We will move very fast now."
Stone was carrying Danny, something that made him feel a little more
comfort, but the young human had to ask him something.

"Please, I need to ask you something," he said quickly.

"Then be quick."

"Do you believe we should have this book?" Stone was silent for a
long moment.

"I believe there is great danger in the human possession of it, but I
can't think of anyone else who could keep it safe enough."

"I can," Danny finally muttered.   He went silent as they moved
through the darkness of solid rock. Stone didn't respond, but moved
the group through the bowels of the mountain range towards the
southern edge of the City of Thulsa.

Gaylens of the Modoc

Two horse drawn wagons creaked along the nearly nonexistent road through the southern forest boundary of the Modoc. Caroline was trying to keep as close to the Thulsa plain as possible without drawing any undue attention to her little group. Unlike the Torres, many roads ran through the Modoc. The road she chose for this trek was hardly ever used because it was so close to the wide open eastern plain of Thulsa. Normally, travelers would just ride out in the open on the roads made through all the farm land of the plain, but she wanted to make sure that they weren't detected. There weren't likely to be any warriors from Thulsa out this far. They were sure to be behind the great walls of the city preparing for the eminent battle that was fast approaching. Her only hope was to make for the wall and the main gates before the Kenlar battle emplacements had been made.

Riding along as fast as they dared without making too much noise, she checked her cargo in the wagon in front of her and the occupants of her own wagon. Most of her older kids were in the lead wagon driven by her oldest son, while the younger ones were hunkered down in the back of hers along with Bryan Garrett and the Jabba, Jocko. Her youngest, Anna snuggled up in Bryan's arms as he dozed in and out of sleep. He still needed all the rest he could get; including proper medical attention, something Caroline just didn't have available to her right now. Jocko's body fluid remedies could only go so far and she just didn't have the right materials to sew him up so he could heal properly. Not to mention that the last time she had checked on him, all of his ribs looked as though they had been used as a punching bag and painted with black and blue finger paints. She wasn't even sure he didn't have some internal injuries under all that color and pain.

Allowing the horses to continue to tread slowly along, she took notice of her son in the front, sitting up straight and looking off into the forest, not at anything particular, but all around, searching for something. She too joined in the search for something unseen, having no idea of what it was they were looking for. Certainly he had been aroused by something. Still night time, the triple moons did a great job of lightening the sky, casting a wonderful half-light across the Modoc. First sunup was coming on and to the south she could still make out the outline of the Tera Mountains in the far distance. Their tops obscured by storm clouds, but she saw no lighting associated with any storminess. She thought of Terry and hoped that he and the others had found what they had gone after and were on their way back to Thulsa. Nothing would calm her nerves more than to know he was either waiting for her and their family behind the safety of the Thulsa walls, or better yet, they would come riding out to find them and escort them in to safety.

They must be only half way from Vespa Cull to the city walls now, but at least they appeared to be ahead of the Kenlar war column. She was tempted to turn out onto the plain so they could move along faster, but thought better of it. No imagination was required to know what would happen if they were caught, especially with Bryan and Jocko onboard. She might feel a little better if they had armed themselves a little better. They had only a hand full of long daggers and two small swords hidden in a compartment under the seats of the wagons, which, by the way, had become quite uncomfortable with the long days travel. Her son settled back into his routine of wagon driving, only to perk back up and look into the forest again. She let her eyes scan all around them, even making a quick twist to look at the forest behind them. There was still nothing but the two wagons moving quietly through the soft mossy covered ground. Her son finally stopped and stood up, looking silently into the darker portions of the forest.

Caroline quickly dismounted and made her way carefully up next to her son, who remained silent while scanning the forest. She listened carefully for anything that might be making noise, but she could hear and see nothing. The forest was not only silent, but had completely stopped moving. There wasn't a bird in motion. Normally, there were firefly type insects buzzing all around them. They hadn't even noticed that things had gone quiet until now. She carefully reached into the compartment under the seat and pulled two swords from their hiding places and passed one up to her son. The rest of her children instinctively disappeared in the backs of the wagons when they saw the steel appear in their mother's hands. Coming down off the wagon, her son stepped up next to the horse to hold it steady, Caroline slowly drifted back to her own rig to hold the horse. Something was definitely wrong here. The hair on the back of her neck was nearly standing straight up. She held tightly to the bridle on her horse, holding her sword up and scanning the trees carefully.

Her heart skipped a couple of beats when she noticed an odd looking barb slowly extending from a thicket close to her position. Even in the half light of the triple moons and the impending first sunup, she could see several others appear all along the foliage line. Extending outward, they took on the appearance of arrowheads instead of just barbed twigs as she had originally thought. The grass right next to the road was thick and tall, but she suddenly realized that there were figures moving slowly towards her through it. She glanced back behind her and then down the road, noting many riders on horses standing quietly on the road. Quite shaken now, she watched eyes wide as warriors seem to just silently materialize into existence, coming from the forest, thickets and the tall grass. They were even surrounded on the plain side where the foliage was quite thin. Whoever these warriors were, they were masters of stealth and camouflage. Being up on a wagon would have given both her and her son a great advantage for seeing their surroundings. These people had them completely surrounded, and thinking of her children, she surmised the futility of any kind of resistance to capture.

Her son nervously glanced back at her as she tried to count how many there were, but finally gave up as more materialized from behind anything that could provide cover. She shifted her eyes carefully to her son and gave him a quick head shake. She wasn't about to just be taken like a helpless animal, but at the same time, she didn't want to start a blood bath with innocent children, especially her own. They both lowered their swords and carefully waited. To her relief, the arrows and spears pointed at them relaxed a bit as a couple of riders slowly moved toward them and came to a stop next to the first wagon.

The lead rider looked like someone straight out of an American West Indian tribe, wearing some kind of buckskin shirt and pants. Looking more closely at them, they were all wearing basically the same thing. It was furry buckskin, not short like deer or cow hide, but a shimmering velvet fur like the Jabbaway. Indeed, some of it bore a striking resemblance to many of the Jabba that Caroline and Terry had encountered over the years, only darker. The second rider dismounted and stepped over to the lead wagon, peering inside at the huddled children, and then turned to Caroline. A slender, taller woman, about her same age, gave Caroline a good looking over and then stepped past her to have a look in Caroline's wagon. Caroline tried to remain facing forward, but her youngest children were here and she naturally looked to their well-being. She was compelled by her motherly instincts to approach the woman and look at the occupants as well. To Caroline's surprise, everyone was huddled closely together on the mounds of straw except for Jocko. He was nowhere to be found. Perhaps he had healed enough during the last several hours and had taken off on his own. She scanned the whole wagon compartment for any signs that he had even been there, but all she saw were the faces of her young children and a sleeping Bryan Garrett on the straw. She passed a look back up at the woman who was eyeing Bryan carefully. The woman turned and looked Caroline in the eye for a moment, then skirted around her, heading back to the apparent leader of the group. She suddenly started to speak in a tongue that sounded familiar to Caroline. She hadn't heard it for a long time, and so she didn't know it very well, but she was able to put some words together.

It now dawned on her that they had driven right into a large Gaylen scouting party of some kind. The accent was very heavy and the dialect was difficult for her to follow, but there were words that she understood. She relaxed a little bit after putting together that they were not Kenlar or Omar and were no threat, but there still seemed to be something wrong. They weren't disarming, acting like they were looking for someone. Then they were saying something about searching the wagons. She wasn't quite sure. They spoke too fast for her to figure it out. She didn't know enough Gaylen to speak it at all, only enough to pick up a few words. She watched the lead warrior still on the horse. She thought he looked familiar to her, but she just blew it off as being an inn keeper's wife. You meet a lot of people over the years and all the faces seem to run together.

Several warriors stepped forward at the beckoning of the woman now barking out orders. A set of warriors went to the back of each wagon and began to beckon the occupants to get out. The frightened children looked to their mother and started to make some noise despite the attempts of the older children to keep the younger ones quiet. Caroline raised her finger to her lips to try and calm them but it would take more than a hushed finger to get them to relax. She finally called out to them in Thulsian instructing them to do what they were told and that it would be all right. This brought both the lead warrior and the woman to instant attention, halting the warriors ushering the kids from the wagon for a moment. The woman returned to Caroline with a knife drawn and the lead warrior right behind her, still mounted on his horse. Caroline looked down the blade of the knife now pointed right at her chest. She was still holding onto her short sword, but really hadn't even thought about using it to defend herself. There seemed to be little point so far, but now things didn't look so good. She looked up at the man on the horse, who was looking down at her carefully, then the woman holding the knife on her spoke in broken Thulsian.

As far as Caroline could make out, they were asking if she knew where a certain Jabbaway and a stranger could be found or if she had seen them. It was so hard for her to make it out because the accent was so heavy and the language, broken. At one point she thought they were asking if there were any horses in their upstairs bedroom, or something like that. Caroline tried to converse back with her to clarify the words, but there was too much difference in what was being meant and what was actually being said.

"This would be a whole lot easier if you spoke English," she finally muttered in desperation. This brought the woman to instant heighten attention and she stepped back, but held the dagger firmly, pointed right at Caroline. The man on the horse grinned a little bit, got off his horse and stepped over to the frightened Caroline. He stopped next to the woman and raised his hand to the knife, gently forcing her to lower it, while still looking at the short dark haired innkeeper.

"You're right, English is a lot·easier," he spoke calmly. At that moment, Bryan pulled himself up and looked out at everyone with bleary eyes.

"What am I right about?" He looked around wiping his eyes just as Anna stood up next to him, wrapping her arms around his neck and giving him a big hug that almost choked him. "Easy on the neck," Bryan choked bleary eyed, trying to loosen Anna's grip. The warrior looked around Caroline at Bryan, then back at Caroline.

"We are on the lookout for a Thulsian warrior traveling with a single Jabbaway. Have you seen such a pair?" he asked pleasantly. The Gaylen woman still had a skeptical look entrenched on her face, but remained just behind the shoulder of the warrior speaking. Caroline was a little nervous now. Truly they were seeking Bryan and Jocko, but since the Jabba wasn't in the wagon where she had last seen him several hours ago, it may be that they could just say no and be on their way. As far as they knew, Bryan was just a relative or a friend. There was really nothing to set him apart from anyone else, other than his injuries, but they were not apparent from within the wagon.

"Why are you looking for these two?" Caroline asked nervously. "Have they done something wrong?"

"It's rumored that they have stolen a book belonging to Ivan Rubella of the Kenlars and helped to kill many of his warriors."

"And you seek to return this stolen book and avenge the killings?" Caroline asked, trying to sound a little defiant. If what he had just said was true, then the Thulsa band's mission to retrieve the book from Ivan was successful and they were on their way home. There was a renewed hope flaring within her now, gripping her weapon a little harder in preparations to fight her way free if she had to. Suddenly, Jocko sprung from his hiding place under the straw in the back of the wagon and landed between Caroline and the two Gaylen warriors. Weapons were instantly raised; ready to dispatch the snarling Jabba that crouched growling, ready to strike. The leaders moved back and motioned for the rest of the warriors to back away as well. This seemed a little odd to Bryan who was still trying to recover from his near death fright of Jocko flying right over the top of him, landing on his paws in front of and equally startled Caroline.

"There will be no return of this book and if there's blood spilled now, then I will be the first to spill it," Jocko growled. "Who's first?"

"I am," a female voice from above called out. Jocko instantly stanced, looking up in time to see the wings of another Jabba fold up around its body and drop to the ground. The Jabba instantly struck a defensive pose between Jocko and the Gaylen warriors, a large circle forming around the two opposing battle ready Jabba.

"Very well," Jocko roared, both Jabba rearing back on their haunches at the same time Before he could charge, a little red headed child jumped in front of him and held both her hands up, yelling gibberish at him in a tone that told him that she meant business. A two year old? Really?

Caroline nearly had heart failure standing behind Jocko in complete shock. She hadn't even noticed her youngest climb from the wagon, make her way past her and in front of the angry Jabba. Bryan hadn't seen her until it was too late, not that he could have done anything about it anyway.

"Anna!" her mother cried, trying to move to grab her from behind Jocko, who was still poised to strike, but was holding back so as to not injure the toddler. The little red head continued to chastise the Jabba, almost yelling at the animal until she could no longer be ignored. Jocko retracted his claws and lowered his front paws, looking down at an emphatic Anna. The whole crowd watched in awe as the brazen little toddler proceeded to give the Jabba a tongue lashing that would have brought even Ivan Rubella to repentance. She jabbered endlessly, pointing back at the other Jabba that had relaxed as well and seemed to be smiling. Caroline finally gathered enough of herself together that she was able to side step past Jocko and quickly retrieve her little girl who continued to shake her little finger at the two animals. There was a bit of a chuckle that rolled through the crowd as Caroline retreated back to the wagon and handed the little youngster back over to Bryan, then turned back to face the standoff. Jocko now sat back on his haunches and looked curiously at the other Jabba sitting in front of him. There had been plenty of room made for the Jabba to fight, but that didn't appear to be the course this exchange was taking now. ***Thank you very much Anna!***

"I know you," Jocko finally said, looking at the other Jabba while twisting his head at her as if looking at her sideways would help in recognition.

"Well I should certainly hope so," the Jabba responded with a smile. "How can the years possibly erase me from your memory; after what we have shared?"

"Of course, I did not see or recognize you with the added color," Jocko replied quietly. "Please forgive me."

"There is nothing to forgive," the other Jabba said, stepping towards the middle of the empty circle where Jocko met her. "You have a little bit of, "added color" yourself my Jocko."

Bryan and Caroline were glued to the soft, almost emotional exchange, their mouths gapping open and eyes unflinching. Anna watched Bryan's dropped jaw, reaching up and pushing it closed with her little hands, giggling.

"I cannot express how happy I am to see you my Motta," Jocko said, nuzzling up to the female Jabbaway. Caroline glanced up at the warriors surrounding them who were equally as surprised to see this affectionate exchange. After a few moments of nuzzling, the two animals started to escalate things a little bit and it was becoming apparent that if something wasn't done quickly, there would be some National Geographic, of the wild type, activity going on right here in front of everyone. The lead Gaylen warrior stepped out into the circle and called to the female.

"Motta! I don't think this is the time or the place!" Motta broke off the embracing maneuvers and turned to the warrior.

"I have not seen my life mate for these many years. Would you not express in the same way with your wife Kingie?" The warrior looked back at the woman warrior and kind of tipped his head in agreement.

"Can't argue with you there," he said, smiling. "But I certainly wouldn't be doing this kind of show in front of everyone. Greater things are afoot, and yes, greater than the two of you."

"The book husband," Kingie reminded the warrior. The warrior turned slightly and raised his hand.

"Silence wife," he said softly. "I will know who they are first," he said, looking at Caroline and Bryan. Caroline still gripped her sword firmly. She still wasn't totally at ease here, but she was getting there.

"I am called Caroline of Vespa Cull. These are my children," she paused, looking back at her youngest, still in Bryan's arms. "The youngest you have already met, Anna." The warrior leader smiled and nodded. He seemed to be a lot more at ease now, though his wife was still a bit nervous.

"Ah yes, a true warrior in the making," he said with a big grin, looking at the little red head. "And who is the man in your wagon? Surely he is not yours." Bryan tried to sit up, but it was quite painful and Anna wasn't helping his comfort level, trying to hold tightly to him.

"I am Bryan Garrett," he paused a moment, "Of Driggs, Idaho."

"No, he is not mine," Caroline admitted. "Terry Lieder is my man." The expression on the warrior's face instantly changed. He carefully, but steadily stepped forward towards her until he was standing right in front of her looking down into her dark brown eyes. He looked at her carefully and then nodded.

"Of course, I've been deep in the Modoc for far too long. Forgive me." Caroline looked at him closely. He looked so familiar, but she couldn't place him. "I am Tom Walker. You might have heard of me as Tommy." Caroline thought hard trying to place him at the same time Bryan was looking at him oddly, running his name repeatedly in his head. He had heard of that name before as well. "I was one of the crew of The Amanda, the top turret gunner."

Bryan recalled a list of facts concerning the aircraft, its crew and the information that Catrina and Tony had given them several days ago at the Fort Manor in Thulsa. Caroline remembered him now as one who had not been to Vespa Cull in a very long time. She remembered him as being such good friends with Terry and Tony, but had vanished into the Modoc country long ago. She assumed that he had moved so far away as to never return or had perished in this harsh land.

Tony had indicated the night they had stayed at Vespa Cull that the Gaylens had joined with the Omars and Kenlars to rise up to battle against Thulsa and take the riches and bounty that were created there by hard work and good rule. Caroline gave him another look, still trying to figure out what was going on.

"I understood that Condor Durale leads the Gaylens," she stated coolly. Tommy smiled, looking around at his men.

"These warriors you see here are the core of those who would not be subjected to constant war and strife under the fist of Condor Durale. The people of the Gaylens have always looked to the Thulsian borders and their people as ones to be emulated, but Condor would rather take than work for his own keep. Now, we lead the people of the Gaylens and are on our way to help defend Thulsa from the designs of the Kenlar and Omar." Now Caroline and Bryan relaxed, well, mostly anyway. Kingie still had an angry look pasted on her face, even after everyone had pretty much disarmed.

"Is this the extent of your army?" Caroline asked, looking around at the fifty or so men and women.

"Certainly not," Kingie barked loudly. Tommy closed his eyes in controlled frustration and tried to hold his hand up to motion his hot headed wife to tone it down. "The Gaylen army is more than enough to match the might of the Kenlars!"

No bones about it, Kingie had taken an instant disliking to Caroline, being insulted with the question. Maybe Kingie felt threatened by her or thought Caroline was better looking than her. Frankly, any woman who could have this many children and still look as good as she did, couldn't help but be hated. Whatever it was, Kingie seemed to be determined to send a very clear message.

"The Gaylens stand ready to assist Thulsa, hidden just inside the Modoc forest near the city walls," Tom said, trying to remain in control of his wife without actually having to assert himself in front of everyone.

"Husband!" Kingie growled angrily from behind. Tom clamped down on his lower lip to try and hold his frustration in. "You would give away our positions to this Kenlar quisling?"

Caroline's blood instantly lathered into a froth. This term was about as insulting as it could get without calling her a whore or something as low. It meant that she somehow straddled both sides of the clan loyalties. It was true that Vespa Cull was open to all travelers. She made no distinctions between who was who, as long as they behaved themselves and paid their bill for lodging, she couldn't care less what clan you belonged to. Because they were still new to the Gaylens, and surrounded, it might be best if she held her tongue for now. But she had her limits and if Kingie wasn't careful, she might find herself in trouble with not only Tom, but Caroline as well. Tom made a quick turn to Kingie.

"You will take the point scouts and ride back towards the east to make sure they were not being pursued." Kingie angrily opened her mouth to object, but Tom's firm glare and raised hand shut her down. "I lead the Gaylens wife," he said, holding his anger back. "Please remember your place. Now go swiftly," he directed sternly, waiting for her to comply. Kingie glared at Tom for a moment, glanced at Caroline, then back at her husband. She finally lowered her eyes, carefully bowed to the clan leader, then quickly trotted back over to her waiting horse, jumped up and spurred the animal off at a trot with several warriors right behind her.

"Forgive her rudeness," Tom said with a sigh, looking after her in frustration. "She is a very high spirited woman and really a wonderful companion once you get to know her."

"I'm sure she is," Caroline lied nervously. What that woman needed was a good punch in the mouth and Caroline was sure she'd have to contend with Kingie again, sooner or later.

There arose a commotion from behind Tom, giving them both cause to forget the incident with Kingie. To their utter embarrassment, Jocko and Motta were mating with heightened energy right in the middle of the circle with everyone watching. Caroline looked over at the forward wagon and all her children gawking at the scene.

"Judas Motta! Get a room!" Tom yelled, stepping over to try and break up the exuberant animal embrace.

"Jocko!" Bryan called out, trying not to laugh. "You hound dog you!" Laughing would be quite painful, but it was sure humorous. Caroline put her hand to her face, turning away and trying not to laugh, covered her mouth. She needed to be parental here, but had to do it with control, something she didn't have at the moment.

"Be the adult Caroline," Bryan muttered quietly, holding his own glee in check.

"What about you?" Caroline came back under her breath.

"Hey, they aren't my kids," he said good-naturedly. Caroline finally composed herself, motioning for her children to sit back down in the back of the wagons. She turned to the forward wagon as Tom was engaged in trying to separate the two Jabbaway. He was only halfheartedly trying, being well aware of the mating activities of the Jabba and what it was like to spend a lot of time away from your mate, but all the same; they could have run off into the bushes or something.

It moved!

Britten came to a halt next to Sargon at the cave entrance and gazed up the shaft, made by the workers. The tale-tell signs of moving the fuselage were clearly visible through the snow and ice. Catrina stopped next to Brit and raised her hand to his shoulder, looking up the shaft at the storm still swirling outside. Brit followed Sargon quickly up to the surface with Catrina and her royal guards, right behind them. Once on top, they looked around. The storm had indeed moved its position, but how could that be?

They turned around, to the east, and looked out over the stone wall, noting that they could see the sides of the surrounding mountains of Earth over the wall now. The Rift wall had moved south as well. Brit turned back to the west ridge. Where there had been the west ridge of Lake Valley, the storm wall had now swallowed it, swirling much closer. He didn't have to use the binoculars to see that the whole stairway and emergency ice caves that Danny and Jerry had built were now on the other side of the storm wall. He turned and looked back down at the huge trench dug in the snow to the cave opening. Some things weren't exactly adding up here. Brit then turned back to Sargon who was watching him very closely.

The Thulsian engineer had only a basic understanding of what had happened, but he was a man of science and logic, wanting to understand. As Sargon had worked on this project, he had witnessed and felt things that defied his conventional Thulsian wisdom and religious beliefs, but he wanted to know the why, so he had force himself to open his mind to the unexplainable, trying to understand it. Had he not experienced the encounter with The Amanda, he would have no idea what Brit was trying to figure out. The group started walking the several hundred or so yards, towards the pickup zone.

"It appears to have happened when we pulled The Amanda from the cave," Sargon pointed out, hoping it would help put the puzzle together.

"How is she doing?" Brit asked, looking at the fuselage as they approached. It was now in position, next to the other aircraft parts, ready for pick up.

"She sleeps now," he answered, reaching the back end and peering inside. There was a mother and daughter curled up inside sleeping.

"We've found that we don't have to have choirs singing to her all the time," Sargon informed them, looking inside. "As long as someone is with her, keeping her company, anything to help hold her focus away from the storm, she is fine, for now anyway."

Brit looked back up at the mass of swirling clouds. He had a gnawing concern for The Amanda's welfare. Even if she were focused elsewhere, what was to keep the storm from trying to draw her energy back into its own collective? She was sitting right out in the open. Why wasn't it attacking her? There was nothing to stop it from trying to do so? Yet it only continued to swirl above her, an occasional plasma bolt streaking across to the opposite wall.   Was it possible that the positive energy created by the good people of Thulsa that stayed with The Amanda, somehow helped to shield her from the might of the storm? These were just theories in his mind, but whatever they were, he hoped they would hold up.

He shifted his gaze back over to where the west wall once was. While Bill Kyfie remained safe in the snowcoach on the ridge, their only means of communication with him was the walkie talkie that had been secured in the rocks where they had originally entered. It was now buried or swept away and without that means of communication, they were in a world of hurt.

"Oh boy," Brit sighed frustrated. Catrina slid her arm around his waist as he raised a pair of binoculars to his eyes for a closer look at where Spring Creek ridge was supposed to be. Even if he were able to breach the storm wall, there were no guarantees that the storm would remain in place long enough to get back to the snow cat to call in the helicopters.

"What is it?" Cat asked, trying to see what he was looking at. Brit handed her the binoculars and pointed to the spot where the ridge was supposed to be visible. He looked back at the assembled jumble of airplane hulks, then up at the storms new position. He examined the trench dug to the cave and the path left by the fuselage as it was moved across the snow to the loading zone. Two and two slowly came together as Catrina lowered the binoculars and looked back at Britten. Sargon was most interested in the magnification glasses and motioned to the Thulsa Queen to let him try them. He cautiously looked down into them, then raised them up to his face and looked around. As the engineer tried to figure out how they worked and the whole new world of magnification that had just opened up to him, Brit looked all around them to confirm his suspicions.

"The storm has moved because The Amanda has moved," he surmised, as it all finally made sense. He was sure that his brother would have come to the same conclusion, though much sooner.

"We can't reach the transmitter on the ridge now, if it's even still there. There's no way to talk to Bill up on the ridge."

Catrina knew that they couldn't just walk back through. That had been proven time and again in the past. She quickly determined that the situation had just gotten very serious.

"I'm not sure what to do. This really complicates matters. If we were all here right now, we might be able to make it back through, but

I'm not leaving without my brother and friends." Brit finished with resolve, glancing over at Sargon who still had the binoculars jammed to his eyes.

He was looking at everything and even putting his free hand out in front of him trying to touch all the things that were brought so close in his field of vision by the magnification power of the binoculars. It was comical watching him stagger about looking at things. Catrina finally reached over and took the binoculars from the engineer, who blinked and staggered even more, trying to adjust to his normal vision. He gave his queen a bewildered look that turned to embarrassment. He thought about saying something, stammering a moment, then awkwardly bowed and moved away. Brit continued to look around, as Catrina slowly dropped her arm and gently took his hand, looking over at him, her fingers interlocking with his. Brit turned and looked into her reassuring eyes. Things had just gotten a whole lot more complicated.

To the wall

Tom rode alongside the second wagon talking to Caroline and Bryan as they moved as quickly as possible down the road through the edge of the forest. Bryan did his best to sit up so he could better hear and be heard, but it was difficult to do so while hanging onto Anna and dealing with the bumpy road.

"You're hurt pretty bad there Mr. Garrett," Tom finally said, continuing to hold his horse in time with the wagon. Bryan thought he had been doing a fair job of keeping his pain under control and his wounds hidden. There was no time for voodoo medicine right now. They needed to get back to Thulsa quickly. Second sunup was only a few hours away and while Tom had agreed to help them make it to the walls of Thulsa, they would be cutting it close, provided there weren't any more delays.

"Yeah, Jocko and I had a pretty eventful day yesterday. Wish we could heal as fast as they do." Bryan said.

"They are truly remarkable creatures."

"In so many ways," Bryan agreed.

"You don't have the book, do you?" Tom asked straight way.

"Never even made it to Crosslake," Bryan replied. "Jocko mistook me for a Kenlar warrior and we went for a tumble."

"Well, you are wearing Kenlar clothes," Tom pointed out. "Or what's left of them. I know, I know. Terry and Tony wanted to try and blend in with the Kenlar, so he had you dressed in those clothes to keep from drawing attention to yourselves."

"You don't approve?" Caroline asked, thinking that he was mocking what her husband had tried to do.

"On the contrary. They did exactly what they should have done, but it's unfortunate that only the Gaylens have the knowledge of the Jabba. It could have saved you a lot of trouble."

"Ain't that the truth," Bryan mumbled, thinking of where his two friends were right now. "And how did you come to know the Jabba?"

"Motta is one of the original five taught to speak English by Tim. She is the matriarch of the Holtz flock, largest of all the flocks in this region."

"Does she also know the contents of the Signet?"

"No," Tom answered quickly. "She started with the others, but the Modoc is so far from Crosslake that she could not devote enough time to it with her position in the flock."

"What of the others? You said there were five that were taught to speak," Caroline asked tiredly from the front seat of the buckboard.

"Jocko and Motta you know," Tom said, looking around for the two Jabba. No doubt they were off somewhere private. "Digi is the eldest of the males and sticks fairly close to Tim Hansen in Crosslake. Digi has a younger brother, Tobor, who runs his flock with Ivan of the Kenlar. He is nearly a mindless animal anymore, killing indiscriminately, for no particular reason. Taunty, would be the fifth. She is a matriarch as well, leading the Nunes. But her flock inhabits the Brogan regions to the west of Thulsa beyond the Valley of the Lakes." Tom barely skipped a beat, changing subjects. "Tell me Mr. Garrett, in thirty words or less, how did you come through the storm?" Bryan thought a moment, thinking back fast trying to figure out when he had told Tom that he was from earth, but nothing was coming to mind. How did Tom know?

"Come on," Tom beckoned. "It's not that tough. Do you think I've been here for so long that I don't remember Earth? I remember where we were going and where we crashed. You said you were from Driggs, Idaho. That's in the basin valley to the west of the Teton mountain range where The Amanda went down. I assume the storm is still here and that's why you're in such a hurry to get back to Thulsa, so you can try and get back home."

"Is there anything you don't know?" Bryan responded, figuring there was no point in holding anything back. Tom got a smirk on his face. Seems like those of The Amanda crew that were left, all had a pretty good mechanism in place for keeping tabs on everything around them, despite their primitive means.

"Might be easier to tell you what I do know. I know that a band of Thulsa riders was sent out three days ago to find the Signet and that a human and a Jabba split off on their own.   They either stole the book while the rest ran interference or vice versa. I can only assume that it was you and Jocko. I know that Ivan doesn't have the book, but has several scout sized bands scouring everywhere to find it. I know that Tobor's flock searches for the Thulsa band with orders to kill them all and retrieve the book. I know that Ivan's and Broc's armies are massing and heading across the plain to the eastern walls of Thulsa if they aren't there already. Is this enough?"

"I don't know, is there more?"

"Not that you don't already know about," Tom said chuckling. "I know there's no way to get back home. Chuck and Dale tried it and were killed. Countless others have tried and failed. The storm wall cannot be breached."

"We got through to here," Bryan pointed out.

"As did we," Tom agreed. "But no one has ever been able to get back through. Believe me, if there had been a way, I would have; all of us would have, a long time ago." The three rode on quickly in silence for a while, then Bryan spoke up again.

"What if we have found a way, would you come back with us?" Tom remained silent for a couple of steps of his horse, then turned in his saddle and looked at Bryan.

"I would have no reason to return. As an only child of elderly parents who had no family on either side of the isle, there would be little point. Here, I feel like I am making a difference among this people, similar to what Tony and Catrina have accomplished with the people of Thulsa. Kingie really is a good woman. She can be a bit trying at times, but," he leaned a little closer and spoke in a hushed volume, "the sex is great!" Caroline acted aghast and Bryan restrained himself from laughing, trying to keep the pain at bay.

"No, if you have found a way home, I would say go and learn all the more from your adventures, but my place is here now." Tom stopped the horse and looked at them as Caroline halted the wagon. "But see that you get Tony home. Of all the people who need to be back on Earth, it's Tony. One of the greatest tragedies for either of our worlds is the separation of Amanda and Tony. As much as you and I love whom we are with, I have never known anything that can exceed the love those two have for one another and it just isn't fair that they should be separated. Life isn't fair sometimes, but this is one of those injustices that must be corrected. Get him back to her if you can." He then spurred his horse ahead, riding into a large encampment.

Caroline pulled her wagons to a stop in front of a large cluster of tents that were carefully situated in among the heavy foliage of the Modoc forest. This ancient forest was indeed deep and dark, or at least could be for the unwary traveler who did not know how to navigate through such a tangle. While the Torres forest was a lot of tangle, with few roads running through it, the Modoc was even deeper, having more tree growth.

Bryan carefully climbed down out of the back of the wagon with plenty of help, or hindrance, from Caroline's smaller children. Once he was firmly situated and stable, he turned back to a grinning Anna holding her arms held out wide for him to take her. The last thing he wanted to do was pick something up, but he was helpless to resist her, so he carefully held out his arms to take her from the wagon. Before he could reach her though, she giggled with glee, jumping into his waiting arms. Bryan thought he was going to fall over backwards as she landed squarely in his arms kicking and squealing joyfully with her arms wrapped around his neck. He was finally able to pry the little toddler away from him and set her down. She instantly went running off after her brothers and sisters, glad to be out of the wagons, if only for a few minutes. Tommy had come out of one of the large tents and had been audience to Bryan and Anna's exchange and he couldn't help but smile.

"Are you sure she's not yours?" he asked, looking after the little girl.

"Do you see any red hair?" Bryan asked, pointing to the mop of straight, dark brown hair on his head.

"I just don't get it," he eyed Caroline carefully. "Terry has no red hair either."

"Ok, ok," Caroline piped up, a little irritated. "We'll say it was the milk man if that will put an end to it. We appreciate the rest, but we have to get on to Thulsa."

"We're here," Tommy said, folding his arms and motioning with his head over his shoulder. Bryan and Caroline turned, looking through the thick trees towards the west. Sure enough, in the dim morning light of first sunup they could see the high walls of the city of Thulsa. Bryan tiredly stepped up next to Tommy to look at the great city walls he had left only a couple of days ago. He felt a glimmer of hope to not only get back to the city and then onto home, but also to be back in time to help spare his big brother from a deadly fight in the arena.

Caroline too, felt a ray of gladness begin to fill her. She thought of her husband who was, no doubt, within the walls waiting for her, or at least safe inside, preparing to help deliver the Signet to the Thulsian Council of Elders. It seemed kind of odd somehow. Terry had been away from Vespa Cull for days on hunting trips and she had not felt so glad to be so near to him as she did right now. She could hardly contain herself, turning and quietly calling to her children to gather. As she did so, Kingie and her scouts came riding in, quickly dismounting to report. She gave Caroline the expected evil eye as she approached her husband.

"Nothing on the road behind," she announced, puffing slightly.

"What did you see of the Kenlar?" Tom asked, looking towards the south east through the trees.

"They are assembled in the gullies and drainages on the plain, just out of sight of the city lookouts. They have many strange machines I have never seen before," she informed him quietly. "They have many companies of troops that are heavily armed. They carry much steel and strange crossbow weapons that have small arrows. The crossbows look too small to be effective against anything unless you're in very close quarters."

"Describe the weapons with the arrows," Bryan requested, stepping carefully backwards to Tommy. Kingie gave Bryan a hard look that was interpreted as a "none of your business" look and remained silent, trying to ignore him. Bryan wasn't feeling very well at all. While the blood had pretty much stopped coming from his wounds, he was sure that something internal was terribly wrong. He was feeling sick and becoming feverish. However, they couldn't stop now. The window of opportunity continued to swing closed. They had to make it back to the storm as soon as possible. Here, he was only trying to repay a little bit of kindness that Tom had showed them in helping them get back to Thulsa.

"These are matters of war," Kingie finally grunted, disdainful that she had to speak to these people. Caroline's children suddenly appeared all around the group and were excitedly bustling about, bumping into everyone. Some were playing tag, adding to the confusion of the moment. The game quickly got out of hand and kids, being oblivious of grown up talk, began to use the adults as shields for their play. Kingie's frustration boiled over as she was nearly tossed and knocked over by two of the younger kids play. She roughly grabbed them by the back of the necks, squeezing them until they started to cry and then tossed them to the side. No sooner had she let go of them than she was met with a fist squarely in the face. Taken completely off guard, she was sent sprawling backwards landing flat on her back. The blow was so hard that when she landed, it knock all the air out of her lungs and she could do nothing but lay flat waiting for her lungs to start working again. Blood trickled from a cut left in the corner of her mouth. Reaching up to stop the bleeding, she noticed the tip of a short blade pointed right at her chest with a very confident, very angry Caroline holding onto the hilt. The look in her eyes told Kingie that she had just crossed a line that should never, ever be crossed under any circumstance. This was a mother at her greatest, protecting her young. Kingie should have understood this all too well. While she didn't have any children herself, she knew it; all women knew it. Caroline was steely, controlled and ready to do whatever she had to do to ensure the safety of her offspring.

"Don't you ever lay a finger on any of my children again! Have I made myself perfectly clear?" Caroline sounded about as resolute as any mother could. She let the point of her sword rest directly on Kingie's chest. The weight of the steel weapon was applying just enough pressure to hurt and reinforce the point. Kingie finally nodded contritely, her lungs starting to work again. Caroline slowly backed away, holding the sword out with one hand and stretching her other arm out to back her children up behind her as she retreated. She finally lowered her weapon, turning to Tommy who still had his arms folded. Caroline expected to get a hard look from him for laying out his wife, but was surprised as she tried to apologize.

"Forgive me Tom," she offered humbly, starting to shake a little, the adrenalin rush beginning to crash.

"Forgive what?" he responded casually. "If you hadn't decked her, I would have. Saved me the trouble. She had it coming. Now I won't have to kiss and make up. Maybe now she'll respect you a little more. Kingie," he said, directing his attention to his wife, who was still struggling just to sit back up. "Please describe the crossbow weapons with the arrows to Mr. Garrett." Kingie sucked in a couple of breathes of air and then proceeded to describe the high tech crossbows that the

Kenlar and Omar armies were equipped with. After she was done, she got to her feet and stepped over to a water barrel to get a drink and wash the blood from her mouth, all the while, keeping her eyes on Caroline.

"Yes, we've seen those in action," a voice from above spoke up. Everyone looked up to see Jocko and Motta perched side by side in the tree, high above them. The male silver back winked at Bryan, purring softly.

"Yes," Bryan agreed, giving Jocko a double take and then looking directly at Tom. "These are some nasty crossbows." Tom seemed to be unconcerned with them.

"We've dealt with crossbows before. We use them as well, standard issue for our troops." Bryan nodded as he spoke, realizing that everyone had them, but not like this.

"I guarantee you've seen nothing like what these will do," Bryan insisted. "They can shoot farther, faster, straighter and cause much more damage than anything else you have."

"You're so sure of this?" Kingie spoke up, not quite believing what she was hearing. She had enough confidence in her troops and her people's abilities to produce the best weapons of any of the clans. The Gaylens were quite possibly the largest of the clans, and while spread out beyond the Modoc, they took in enough diversity, that they had many skilled disciplines at their disposal. Bryan's thoughts went back to the events in the Torres, he and Jocko fighting for their lives to escape the Kenlar and Omar scouting parties.

"Pretty sure," Bryan affirmed confidently, raising a hand to where he had been struck with the crossbow arrow. "I recommend that if the opportunity rises, you get as many as you can lay your hands on." Tommy looked up at Jocko to backup Bryan's word.

"He speaks the truth. These formidable weapons are a product of Ancient intelligence."

"From the Signet?" Tom inquired. Jocko nodded.

"Good for one, but not good for many," Bryan said, trying to be philosophical.

"Not sure humans have the wisdom to possess such a book as this Signet," Kingie remarked, quietly stepping up next to Tom.

"The hope is to use it to help us get back to Earth and stop the storms from coming," Bryan reiterated their cause. "From there, it's up to the people of Argyle to keep it however they feel right."

Caroline was more than ready to go, motioning for her children to climb back into the wagons. Bryan turned to climb in as well, but found he was so weak that his legs came out from under him before he reached the back. Caroline and Tom were quick to his aid, helping him back up and into the wagon. Tom motioned for Kingie to have a look at him as they prepared to leave. It took the warrior woman only a minute or so to confirm his broken ribs, numerous lacerations and something else in his abdomen below his broken ribs. She carefully probed the discolored lumpy area with her fingers, trying to be gentle, but it didn't seem to matter. It was like poking a hot iron in his side every time she even got near to it. She looked up at her husband and Caroline with a grim look.

"This is very serious," she admitted. "Something else is broken inside. He needs to have proper care very soon or he will not live."

"Not liking that prognosis much," Bryan admitted, tired and in pain. Kingie reached into one of the pouches on her belt, pulling out a handful of small seeds and giving them to Bryan.

"These will help ease the pain considerably," she said, handing him a water flask and motioning for him to swallow a few of the seeds. "You must see a healer very soon."

"What are they?" Caroline asked, pulling him up further into the wagon and the care of Anna and her older sisters.

"It's like morphine," Tom announced, as Jocko jumped down from his perch and hopped into the wagon. "He'll be feeling just fine here in about half an hour or so. You might think he's drunk."

"Great, just what we need. More noise. Girls, you will have to keep him quiet," Caroline said, looking after him as Jocko stepped up next to his friend.

"You will be fine now my friend," Jocko said, sitting down as Motta climbed in the wagon with him. "Seems like I'm always having to save your sorry human hide."

"Thanks to Jabba spit," Bryan said with a smile. Anna nestled down next to him for a moment, then got back up and walked over to Jocko and gave him a big hug.

"This is where we must part my friend," Jocko said, purring with the warmth of the embrace from Anna. Bryan kind of knew what Jocko had in mind.

"You mean to rally your flock to help in the fight?"

"As will Motta. With the exception of Tobor's Gangees flock, the other Jabbaway flocks will help the Gaylens defend Thulsa to the last Jabba if necessary."

Bryan smiled weakly. He wished he could sit up and give his friend a proper farewell, but all he could do was reach out and scratch behind his ears, then pull Anna from the Jabba.

"Somehow, I doubt it will come to that. I probably won't ever see you again," Bryan said quietly. "But I count myself so much the wiser for having known you my Jabba friend." Motta leaned down to Bryan and gently licked his face twice.

"Thank you for saving my Jocko," she said.

"No problem, seems like I was always having to save his sorry Jabba hide. By the way, if you ever want to hear him squeal like a little girl…..."

"I think we're done here," Jocko interrupted, moving to herd Motta out of the wagon. Bryan grinned from ear to ear.

"Squeal like a little girl?" Motta asked, getting ready to jump from the wagon. "What is this squealing like a little girl he speaks of?"

"Nothing, the human is delirious and needs a long rest. Come on, there is much to do," he said, looking back at Bryan one last time, winking and then taking to flight. Motta looked back at Tom who nodded and then she sprang into the air to flap off after the Binion leader. Tom then turned to Caroline and Kingie.

"Now that you two have come to an understanding, I think this is where I will bid you farewell and leave you in the very capable hands of Kingie. I have a surprise attack to plan and you need to get inside the walls. Kingie knows the way to the secret northern entrance. She can guide you," he said, directing his attention to Caroline. "From there, you will have to convince the guards to let you pass. They certainly aren't going to listen to a Gaylen." Tom turned to Bryan, who was resting comfortably with Anna next to him.

"What should I tell the others?" Bryan asked quietly. Tom thought a moment then grasped his hand firmly.

"Tell them, I'm where I'm supposed to be." With that, he smiled and backed away from the wagon. Caroline climbed back in giving the signal for the group to start again. Kingie jumped back up onto her horse, and led them out of the camp, towards the northern city walls. Bryan looked back at Tom, who waved at him for a few moments, then turned, disappearing into one of his tents.

*   *   *   *   *

Quietly approaching the outer walls, they came upon several small farm houses tucked back in the trees on the north side. In the growing light of the first sunup, Caroline could see several guards pacing the walls. On the upper deck of the northeast tower, she could see a lone figure standing, as if surveying the lay of the land to the east. It was still dark enough that she couldn't make any distinctions as to who it was, but this figure seemed to be dressed differently. She wasn't sure that it wasn't a woman. Drawing near to the northern walls she began to feel an anxiousness mixed with excitement for having made it to the relative safety of the great Thulsa embattlements.

Kingie slowed them down to a plod, working her way through the thickening forest growing right up to the northern walls. At length, the foliage became so thick that it looked as though the road would be swallowed up. The children had to stand up to hold bushes and tree branches out of the way in order to get the wagons through. Finally, the Gaylen warrior stopped them and motioned for Caroline to move on through the trees towards an overgrown old gate. Kingie stopped next to Caroline, leaning a little closer to her and spoke in a hushed voice.

"I am sorry for my rudeness.   I hope to see you again someday. Farewell Caroline of Vespa Cull," and with that she turned her horse and was gone.

Caroline looked after her for a moment, knowing that somewhere down the road, they would meet again, though maybe the next time, it would be under better circumstances and maybe she could get to know her the way that Tom knew her.

She moved her wagon into the front position and started to the old gate. It was shut tight and looked as though it had not been used very often. Indeed, if you didn't know where it was, it would be quite difficult to find. It was well over grown with many ivy type vines and bushes, heavily crowding the entryway. She stopped her wagon right in front of the door and got down, checking that the other wagon was right behind her position. She then pulled her sword from its resting place under the seat and turning to the gate, pounded on the heavy wooden door with the hilt.

Turn and face it

Catrina Dallas stood on the balcony of one of Thulsa's eastern most watch towers looking to the eastern horizon. She was here to inspect the eastern embattlements and the hosts of warriors that were in place to defend their beloved city of Thulsa. She had chosen not to make the inspections wearing her normal battle gear, having other matters to attend to. However, she wanted to take a moment after the inspections and spend a little time alone, pondering about the day to come. It was assured to be a busy one.

Catrina wore a simple, casual red gown that extended all the way to her ankles. The sleeves hugged her upper arms, but then flared out quite a bit starting at the elbow, giving the illusion of a flowing scarf or shawl. While the outfit was simple in nature, the red color had a deep, almost velvet look to it, and shimmered in varying light and angles as she moved. It had a high empire-waist that was trimmed in gold with a design in the center that connected down to an accent belt that rested on her hips. At the front of the skirt a V-slit revealed an under layer of ornate, golden fabric embellished with minuscule decorative designs. She had simple gold bracers on over the sleeves of her forearms and decorative cuffs on her upper arms. There were also gold accents on her shoulders. From this flowed more crimson material that draped down to knee length. A ruby and gold inlay adorned a simple choker band about her neck. In her hair was a gold barrette whose ruby stone and design matched her choker.

It was almost first dawn and the smaller sun was starting to make its presence known just beyond the horizon, ready to join the three moons in the lightening sky. She watched the Argyle satellites move in careful choreography overhead. The largest, called Alturas looked as though you could reach out and touch it. It appeared to move faster than the other two. The second, called Foris was very small and looked as though it were in orbit around Alturas. The smallest called Tolawa was the size of Earth's moon.

She searched the skies for stars, like she had done many nights as a younger woman. Catrina thought back to the time when she had first come to this world and she and her father would search the skies for anything that resembled their own star formations back home. There was nothing familiar about these skies. Furthermore, you couldn't see the stars here on Argyle like you could on Earth. There was so much reflective light coming from the three moons that most of the faint stars were blanked out, unlike Earth's skies at night. She remembered back to when her dad took her for overnight camping trips or they would camp next to his small airplane and there was no moon at all, only the light from the billions of stars. She remembered being able to identify all of the different constellations in the night sky of Earth, as they would lay out in the darkness and just talk about anything. That was such a long time ago. It seemed like a dream now. She continued to gaze up, wishing with all her heart that she could see the stars again like she once had. She didn't even care that she wasn't that little girl any more. She just wanted to see them again.

Catrina turned, stepping around the turret of the watch tower looking across the city of Thulsa. How wonderful it looked in the pre-dawn light. She could hear the sounds of children already up doing early morning chores and could still see fireflies moving about the homes below her. She remembered that Earth had them, but had never gotten to see them until she came here. Interesting that Argyle and Earth had so much in common, yet they were so different in many ways. She could see clear across the city towards the Spoil forest, and the indoor arena, from her location. Brit was due to begin his match sometime after second sun up. She had left him in the practice room with Hans, drilling with a set of swords identical to the Twins, instructing him not to use the two real swords until he had gotten used to using the duplicates. Catrina was quite concerned about Brit using the Twins. She hadn't been able to put her finger on what it was, but every time he had used them, he acted very strange afterwards. Much like he had lost some of his senses or wasn't in complete control of them for some reason. While they had identified the problems associated with using them, without careful supervision and control in training, they were very dangerous, and she had asked him not to pick them up unless she was present. He promised that he would follow her instructions, something that made her feel warm and valued.

She found herself smiling broadly, thinking of Brit. The toughest and most intrepid of the four men from Earth could also be humble and so attentive towards her. He treated her so differently from any other man and she found that and so many other things about him, incredibly attractive. She thought about all the things they had discussed in the last couple of days and the dilemma they faced. She thought about how he described life back on Earth and the work that he did. It sounded exciting and the more she thought about it, the more enticing it sounded to her. The whole of Earth and what it had become in their absence completely fascinated her. Scanning the city, she couldn't help but ask herself if this was all she was? Was this all she was ever going to be? Was there anything else for her here? Was there any need for more in her life or was this enough? She loved these people and they loved her, but was there really anything more that she, as their Queen, could do for them? Was it time for someone else to lead? Technically, she wasn't a Thulsian; she was from Earth.

Shouldn't it be a native Thulsian that led them? Perhaps they needed
to move in a direction that she had neither the knowledge base nor the
will to help them go. Maybe leaving them to someone else more
capable to take them in that direction was showing the ultimate gift of
love, whether she stayed among them or not.

Turning again to the east, a gentle early morning breeze blew
across her face, ruffling her dark brown hair slightly bringing a lock
partially down into her vision. She carefully pulled it back out of the
way with a quick stroke of her fingers. The city wall was right below
her and there were many homes and clustered neighborhoods strewn
without the walls and through the forest. She had been to most of
them, and even helped build some of them with her dad. They were
all beautiful homes that would rival any others known on Argyle. They
all looked so peaceful nestled in the wooded areas around the city
walls. She noticed a couple of wagons and a lone horseman plodding
slowly through the thick forest along the north walls, following their
progress until they disappeared. The homes and neighborhoods were
empty now, their inhabitants having been brought inside the city walls
for protection from the Kenlar attack that was sure to come from the
east. The time line for the invasion was still unknown, but she was
sure it would be before the coming day was over. The tree line
stretched out for only a couple hundred feet and then the rolling
Thulsa plain took over. It was covered with farmland almost all the
way to Mount Boris to the east. She was sure that this is where the
Kenlar attack would come. Directly to the south were the impassable
mountains of the Tera. To the north were the heavily forested regions
of the Modoc. To their own west, past the Winner's Spoil and their
western wall, was the Valley of the Lakes. Beyond that, the vast
expanse of the Brogan regions, completely unexplored, because to get
to it you either had to venture around the high mountains of the Tera
or go through Gaylen lands to reach a passable trail. No one ventured
into the Valley of the Lakes very often because of the storms. There
was no other direction that anyone could mount an attack, but from
the east.

Catrina turned to the south and looked out towards the high Tera
Mountains. She knew that on the other side of those rugged peaks lay
the regions of the Kenlar and more specifically, Crosslake. A worried
look streaked across her face now, staring at the mountain range.
Where was her father? Was he all right? He should have been back
by now. Was he able to retrieve the Signet from Tim? There wasn't
much time left. If he could get here before second sunup, Brit could
avoid having to fight at all.

Catrina thought about how far he had come in just the few days he
had been training. She figured he had a better than even chance of
getting through the fight alive. The big thing that would hold him back
was being able to take a life, to kill. In this game, you either kill or be

killed. There was no other way out of the arena. Arena fighting didn't happen very often, at least the fighting to the death kind didn't, but it did happen on occasion and the outcome was never pretty.

She turned for the tower stairs, but was approached by a familiar figure. Sargon bowed respectfully and then straightened to address his Queen.

"My Queen," his tone hushed. "May I speak with you privately for a few minutes?"

Catrina looked around. Her royal guards were stationed at the bottom of the stairs to the tower. Her and Sargon were the only two here, it couldn't get much more private than this. Still, she welcomed the diversion of conversation. There were so many thoughts and questions swirling around in her head that thinking of something else, if only for a couple of minutes, would be a welcome relief. She nodded and turned back to the tower rail to look out over the city.

"What's on your mind Sargon?" she asked, sounding more and more like she had just come from Earth. The moment she said it, she realized her tone and demeanor were out of place here and turned directly to the chief engineer.

"Forgive me. Sargon, how may I help you?"

Sargon gave her a strange look. This was exactly why he had come to converse with her. He had been watching her very carefully, since the new Earth people had arrived, especially the affect that Britten had on her. Not that it was unnatural, it was just that he had observed suitors come and go, but none of them had ever had such an effect on her as Britten did. He could see that she was struggling mightily with what to do about it.

"Master Garrett has a profound effect on you," he stated bluntly.

"Nothing like coming right out with it, eh?" she replied smiling. She leaned down on the rail and scanned the rooftops of Thulsa.

"You are troubled by this," Sargon continued carefully. Addressing the personal affairs of the Queen wasn't exactly in his job description, but in the absence of her father and considering what they had been through earlier with The Amanda, he felt like he had a bit of a personal connection with her now. Besides, he was fairly certain that if she didn't want him meddling in her love life, she'd tell him straight away. The Queen drew in a deep breath, letting it out with a heavy sigh.

"Yes," she finally said. "Yes, very troubled." She turned to the chief engineer. "What do you think I should do?"

Catrina was looking for opinions to help her answer all the questions she was battling. She was also conscious of the fact that Queens don't ask people for their opinions or ask them for help with questions of the heart. In the absence of her father, she was becoming a little desperate as to what to do and how to get answers.

"I would not presume to advise the Queen on such personal matters," Sargon said carefully. "However, if I may be so bold as to suggest, or rather reaffirm what you have no doubt already reasoned."

"What is that?" she asked, turning just her head and looking at the older gentleman.

"What does your heart tell you?" he asked quietly.

Catrina remained silent for a long moment, turning her gaze back out across the city. The gentle breeze continued to work its way around the wall turret as the early morning drove on and she considered her feelings.

"It's hard to tell," she finally responded quietly. "There's so much running through my head right now that I can hardly listen and if I think I am listening, I can't seem to understand the answer, if there even is one at all."

Sargon gave her a fatherly smile, thinking he might know what she was going through. Of course he would not presume to think that he was her parent in this situation and maybe even if he were, it might not be a good idea for a parent to get involved. But clearly she was looking for answers and he felt like he might be able to help.

"I didn't ask you about your head. I think you're making this far more complicated that it needs to be. I have found that a person usually has an argument when using their heads to solve a problem of the heart. Let me ask you this," he offered, settling against the rail some distance from her. "Do you love him?"

Catrina was shocked that he could perceive her feelings for Britten. She somehow managed to keep her gaze straight ahead, out across the city. Was it that obvious? She smiled softly as Brit's face instantly flashed into her head. She suddenly realized that he was all she could see. Nothing but him and the last three days they had been together. She chuckled out loud when the image of him pulling the Twins from the altar, came to mind, then demanding her name and calling her "Missy". She remembered watching him struggle to come to grips with his selfishness and pride in the face of her own struggles in considering leaving her beloved Thulsa and its people.

"Do I love him?" she repeated quietly. "Do I love him?" she asked herself again, her mind held his image squarely in focus. It suddenly occurred to her that she was taking entirely too long to state the obvious. *Of course she loved him! How could she not?*

"Yes, I do. I really do," she said, slightly apprehensive at first, then committed herself to her feelings. She stood up straight and faced Sargon who remained leaning against the rail looking up at her.

"I have loved him from the moment he stepped foot in Thulsa and I don't want to be without him."

"It is wise to find someone you cannot live without rather than someone you can live with. Does he know how you feel?"

"I think he does."

"You think he does?" Sargon asked in dismay. "You think? You do not know?"

"I'm pretty sure he knows," Catrina hedged, biting her lower lip, then her fingernail. "Or at least suspects," she said, thinking carefully but becoming excited at the same time. She realized that she was not acting very Queenly at the moment, but finding propriety being tossed aside. She was in love and was getting a certain thrill out of admitting to it and the emotions building within her were starting to make her a little giddy.

"Have you said the words to him?" Sargon asked, shaking his head and smiling slightly. He had no idea that some things humankind did were the same, no matter where you are in the universe? Why do we hide from our own feelings and hide them from those we should profess them to? It didn't take a genius to figure out what her problem was. She was in love with Britten Garrett, but she felt like her loyalties were here with the people of Thulsa. Sargon knew how she felt about them, long before Britten had come. There was no secret there. He had greatly admired her for her manner of rule among this delightful, yet primitive people. A people who had befriended strangers, long ago, found in a cave after yet another great storm in the Valley of the Lakes.

Catrina was suddenly so excited she could barely contain herself. Sargon could tell by the expression on her face that the flood gates had been thrown open. A wall of relief, along with emotional excitement, began flowing freely without thought for how she looked or what she wanted to do. She looked at the chief engineer with eyes wide and a smile that could hardly be contained. Sargon became aware that he was about to be the first recipient of her excitement. He came up from the railing bracing himself, trying to step away, as Catrina flung her arms around him, happily embracing him. How could she be so near to giggling and crying at the same time? She felt so happy and relieved as she held onto Sargon. She finally pulled away from him and looked him straight in the eye. He was a little embarrassed and not quite sure how to respond to her emotional outburst. However, she didn't wait for him to respond.

"Thank you," she whispered to him, and then she was gone, floating down the spiral stairs of the tower. Catrina didn't even wait for her royal guard, who, springing to their feet, had to run to catch up with her while they made their way back to the Fort Manor of Thulsa.

Doors on both sides

Tony and Terry found themselves stepping out of a huge granite monolith punching up through the ground several meters into the morning Argyle sky. Looking around they could see they were well out of the Tera mountains. Looking behind the stone obelisk, storm clouds still shrouded most of the Tera range far to their south. Where they were now was warm and pleasant with only partly cloudy skies. Two of the three Argylian moons were still mixing it up high in the skies, while the first sun had already dawned with the second starting to make its presence known. Soon, it too, would breach the horizon, signaling second sunup.

Tony knew exactly where they were. The Mynites had deposited them only a few miles from the southern walls of the City of Thulsa! He checked the sky at the same instant Tim emerged from the stone wall they had come out of only moments before. Terry checked their surroundings carefully, waiting for Danny to arrive. There was another stone outcrop of similar size about a hundred yards from where they had been deposited. Tim started scanning the area for Digi, hoping that the stone dwellers had been successful in locating him and that he was waiting for them somewhere close by.

"Wow!" Tony exclaimed with renewed hope.

"Wow what?" Terry responded, looking everywhere for Danny. He started walking around the side of the great rock obelisk that had been their conduit.

"Guys! We're only a couple of miles from the southern city walls," Tony exclaimed, excited enough that he started heading north towards more familiar surroundings.

"Wait up there, Jack wagon," Terry called, trotting around the far side of the rock looking for Danny. Tim was completely focused on trying to locate Digi. Perhaps he was in one of the many trees growing around the rock. Jabba liked trees, especially when they are healing themselves, providing a measure of protection. Terry came jogging back from the far side of the rock with a little bit of a panicked look on his face.

"We're missing a key player here," he announced, puffing a bit, coming to a stop in front of the other two. Tim only half acknowledged him, but Tony focused in fast. Without Danny, there was a real problem as he was carrying the Signet. Both men looked around, becoming a little bit frantic, until Tony witnessed Danny emerge from the second stone butte about a hundred yards to the east. Relieved, they both waved to him until he noticed them, waving back. Danny started to step in their direction, but then stopped and turned back to the stone, no doubt to thank the Mynites for their help. Tim started calling for Digi, walking all around the monolithic formation, while Tony and Terry started looking in Danny's direction. He remained facing the rock he had come from, as they worked their way to his location.

Drawing closer, they could hear Danny speaking, but couldn't make out the words. In the growing morning light they could see he was still holding onto the book but in an odd manner. It looked like he was holding it out in front of him. Quickening their pace, they took note of Danny dropping his hands into his pockets, then to his side, without the Signet!

"Danny!" Tony called out, almost running. Danny slowly turned to them as they came to a halt in front of him. A somber, yet confident look was engraven on his face now as he looked at his two friends who had come so far with him these last few days. Terry looked all around for the book while Tony gave the young man a very worried look.

"Danny, where's the Signet?" the Thulsa Captain asked not daring to guess what he might have just done. Danny remained silent for several moments until Terry joined Tony with the inquiry. Both men waited for an explanation. Had he buried it? If he had, he had done a superb job of hiding the place. The answer they got wasn't too far from the mark.

"I gave it to Stone. It's going back to the crystal cave in the Tera, to be kept safe."

"Wait, what?" Terry cried, not believing what he had just heard. Tony solidified in place, falling silent. "You gave it to Stone? What in the world possessed you to do that? Don't you remember that we have to have that in order to save your friend from fighting, to operate the gate to get you guys back home, to help stop the storms? Good laws boy! Are you mad? Do you know what you've done?" Terry continued incensed. "Do you see that man over there at the other rock?" He asked, pointing angrily at Tim who was still looking all over for Digi. "Tim has lost nearly everything that he has ever held dear for that book. He has put his life on the line to keep it safe! He has risked everything to help get it back to Thulsa to help save you and your friends. What about me? I left my wife and family risking my neck several times, to help get our hands on that thing and keep it from Ivan. What about your two friends? Was it worth Bryan getting himself killed before he even got to see it? And Jerry! Sakes man! He died keeping it from the Jabba! And Tony, of all the people, who has lost the most and has the most to...." Tony's hand came to rest on Terry's shoulder putting an instant halt to the tongue lashing being delivered.

Danny let his eyes drop to the ground, but held the same expression of somber confidence. Terry was flaming mad but still in control enough to respond to the firm hand of reason Tony always used in situations like these. He backed off a little bit, letting Tony shuffle forward to face Danny straight on. Captain Dallas was trying to figure out what was going on in the young man's reasoning to have given him the notion to hand the Signet over to Stone. He searched Danny's demeanor, waiting for the young man to respond with something logical.

"Danny?" Tony said quietly, noting that Tim was starting to make his way over to their location. "Tell us why you've done this?"

Danny kicked at the ground not wanting to speak because of Terry's anger. He knew that Tim would probably pitch a fit when he found out and he was feeling the pings of guilt for his decision starting to percolate into his resolve. He finally looked back up at Tony as Tim stepped up to them, still looking around for Digi.

"This adventure with the Garretts was supposed to be a joy ride for me and Jerr," he started out slowly. Tim looked a little bewildered not knowing what this was all about. His mind still held hostage from the loss of Kawti and now being so preoccupied with trying to find Digi he hadn't even noticed that Danny didn't have the book anymore. "We came along to help a couple friends find an old airplane wreck in an area in the mountains that we all grew up and played in. I didn't bargain for any of this! My idea of fun and adventure is riding dirt bikes, dune buggies or snowmachines, not planet hopping. It was a fun adventure until Bryan went and got himself killed. Then I get to hear all about how space travelers amass so much knowledge they can change time and travel to anywhere from that storm or rift or whatever it's called. Come to find out, the Ancients learned other things, apparently too horrible to mention to everyone, because we don't have the wisdom to use it wisely. I wonder if Jerry understood this when he was hanging off the ledge last night. That's probably why he didn't tell me what he was doing because he knew I would argue, he would still be gone and the Jabba would have the book. He knew how important it was that idiots like Ivan never get their hands on it. I don't know why it was ever taken from the altar or Thulsa to begin with, but I think the Ancients made a huge mistake by leaving it out for anyone to take. There's no way any human would be able to keep it safe indefinitely. Sooner or later, there would have been another Ivan or a Tim that comes along and is tempted by its knowledge. No, we're not smart enough, not wise enough to have possession of such a book and if that means that I lose all my friends and I never go home," Danny stood up resolute now, the three older men standing silent, listening to him as though he were their hero. "Then so be it. I have given the Signet to Stone. He promised to take it to the crystal chamber deep in the heart of the Tera and keep it there until the Ancients themselves come and ask for it."

Danny then waited for the hammer to come down. He was either going to get yelled at some more or busted in the jaw. Either would have felt the same and he half expected to get both, especially from Tim. He had lost everything, first his beloved Kawti and now his best friend Digi. Both had given their lives in the protection of the Signet.

Tony stepped closer to Danny and put a hand on his shoulder, looking straight into his eyes for a long moment, then smiling proudly, reaffirmed the grip on his shoulder.

"Well done, Dan, well done," he whispered, quietly stepping past him and starting for a small trail that led off in the direction of Thulsa.

Terry let out a big sigh, putting both hands on Danny's shoulders. He shook his head slowly with a look of humility stretching through his eyes.

"Forgive me Dan. I did not understand. You're quite a man. I'm finding out every day that I still have a lot to learn," he said, giving him a good shake and following Captain Dallas. Danny edged his eyes to Tim who stood looking at him with his arms folded leisurely across his ribs. He had a distant look in his eyes as he looked away, back towards the Tera. He looked back at Danny and stepped right up to him. So close that Danny felt like he was trying to get all up in his face.

"What you have done, none of the rest of us had the courage to do. I could not see because I was so close, but Kawti knew, as did Digi and your friends." Tim stepped back again and turned to the stone wall that had been the conduit for their arrival to this point. "I suspect the Mynites knew that too, but were waiting to see if we had grown wise enough to learn it for ourselves. Perhaps we've taken a step closer here; closer to having the wisdom to know of such things that are in the Signet." Tim put his hand on the stone wall as if feeling for the book. No doubt it was far away from here now, on its way to the crystal chamber. He turned back to Danny. "It's where it belongs for now, safe," he said, a half-smile materializing across his face. "Come on. We've got a fight to stop." He stepped past Danny, who turned and started after him.

"Tim? I never took the opportunity to express how badly I feel about Kawti. She must have been an amazing woman." Tim began scanning the trees for any signs of Digi.

"Thank you, yes, she was quite a woman and you would do well to find one just like her, but to find her, you have got to look. You aren't getting any younger. Just don't be looking in the same place I'm looking." With that he trotted on ahead to catch up with the other two. Danny grinned, feeling much better, now that everyone had accepted his decision to give the Signet to Stone. Now, to get Britten and get home.

He took a half skip and started jogging, easily catching up with the rest of the fast moving band. They were now on a little wider path, headed into a thickening forest, towards Thulsa. Tony led the way with Terry along-side looking all around them. While they had made it this close to the city walls, they were still in a great deal of danger. There was no telling where the Kenlar and Omar armies were stationed. They could be hidden in these very woods all around the city. Captain Dallas didn't put a whole lot of stock in Ivan's ability to think of spreading his warriors out in smaller bands. It would have been logical to do so in order to cover more ground, but not the Kenlar War Lord's style. It was entirely possible that Talon had a group of his men scouring the forest for them in case the band had made it over the Tera and through Tobor's flock. At this point in their long journey and with the time they had left, there was little they could do but be vigilant and move as quickly as possible.

The older three men moved slower than Danny, though he wasn't much better. He wasn't a runner, his friend Jerry had been the runner. They were all down to a slow jog as they made their way along the trail. Tim wished Digi were here, as he was always much better at taking note of his surroundings. He did the best he could to scan the surrounding forest for movement as they moved quickly along the twisting path. Tony felt like they were only inching towards the city walls. They couldn't go fast enough, the feeling of relief starting to permeate within all of them. They were ragged, tired and their jogging turned to plodding, with Tim finally having to stop and rest. They all stopped to catch their breath, but remained mainly on the trail.

"How far?" Terry puffed, trying to look down the trail for any signs of the high stone wall of the city. Tim backed up against a tree and sank to the ground trying to get off his aching legs and feet while Danny found a rock to rest on.

"Not much further," Tony responded, catching his breath, stooped over and resting his hands on his knees, "maybe half a mile or so." Terry passed his water pouch over to Tony, who took a couple of swallows and then tossed it over to Danny, who was grateful for the cold water. This water seemed to have something special about it. Drinking it had a similar effect to standing in the presence of the crystals in the chamber of the Tera. It completely removed their exhaustion, feeling reenergized within moments. Danny tossed the water container over to Tim who eagerly swallowed down as much as his stomach could take.

"Where'd you get this water?" Danny asked feeling refreshed and ready to go. Tony noticed it as well passing a look over to Terry, who only shrugged.

"I filled it in the crystal cave while Danny and I were searching the caves. Careful there Doolittle," Terry warned the radio operator, "you're gonna give yourself cramps and then we'll be held up even more." Terry looked oddly at the container Tim was drinking from, putting two and two together. "You don't suppose this water has some of the same properties those Tera crystals have, do you?"

"Those crystals are just like any other mineral deposit on this planet and would be dissolved in water with time," Tim remarked, matter of factly. He leaned back and closed his eyes for a moment; letting the warmth of energy the crystal water produced, flush through his system. Even his sore feet were starting to feel better. Reenergizing, he felt something wet land on his check. At first he thought it was just a drop of dew coming off the leaves from above, but there were several of them coming all at once and they felt odd. His skin seemed to go numb wherever the drops landed. He opened his eyes, looking up. Directly above him, hunched on a tree limb looking down at him, was a Jabba. At first he thought it was Digi, who had found them and was just having a bit of a lark, seeing which one would notice him first. However, looking up at the perched beast, he realized that it didn't have the right color to be Digi. This one was dark, almost black and kind of ugly looking. Indeed, as he gazed at the beast, he suddenly became aware that this was not the only drooling Jabba in the tree above him. He looked around at all the limbs. There were Jabbaway clustered all over in the branches. He turned his gaze over to the adjoining trees on both sides of the trail. These trees were laden with as many Jabba as they could possibly hold without posing a danger to the branches they were perched on.

Tim slowly sat forward, closing the water container and keeping his eyes glued to the animals in the trees on both sides of them. None of the Jabba made a sound; the only movement they made was following Tim's every move. It was like they were robots, mechanically taught to follow only his motion. He carefully got to his feet and gently tossed the water flask to Terry who gave him an odd look. Trying not to draw attention to the fact that he saw what was above them in the trees, he used his eyes to communicate with the bombardier. He kept trying to look at Terry and then shift his eyes up into the trees. It took several tries and about the time Terry figured out what he was trying to signal, Tony looked up. While most of the attentions seem to remain on Tim, Tony turned his head forward to the trail ahead of him. It was still clear, but he could see Jabba clumped in the trees ahead as well. He turned back to Danny, who was still slumped over watching at a bug crawling across the trail. While Tim slowly stepped closer to Terry, Tony hoped the movement of the other two would bring Danny's attention back up, but the young man remained oblivious to what was happening around them. Terry made it look like he was needing some help with the bundle strapped to his back and looked forward at Tony, who knew he was about to say something.

"I'll take the rear," he mumbled, trying to move his lips as little as possible, not making any more noise than humans would normally. Tony finally kicked a stone in front of him. It bounced several times and almost hit Danny on the knee. He quickly came up to attention, a little aggravated at first, but then read the look on Tony's face and the body language of the other two.

"Dan," Terry spoke up a little louder. "You're in front of Tim. Stay right behind Tony all the way to the wall." Tony shifted the small bundle on his back, making sure that his sword was ready to pull when the time came, and it was sure to come very soon. Danny's heart started to pound like it was going to jump from his chest and run down the trail ahead of them. This must be the Gangees, Tobor's flock, sent by Ivan to butcher the Thulsa band and retrieve the book. Tony had hoped that they had lost them on the tops of the Tera, especially since the Mynites had been so kind as to bring them so far in such a short time span. The city wall might as well be as far away as planet Earth now. This last half mile would be like starting all over again.

Danny was scared spitless. On the mountain trail, they didn't have time to think about the attack and then it didn't seem like there were as many animals to battle. Here it looked like the entire flock would be in on the attack. This would be like trying to run from a pack of Velociraptors or a herd of angry rhinos. There was no way they were going to make it without someone getting hurt. At least that's the way he was viewing their situation. He casually took his position behind Tony who milled about waiting for Terry to give him the signal. He thought his legs were going to buckle beneath him, waiting for the sprint to begin. He wished he had his daggers with him. Unfortunately he and Tim had lost their weapons during the first Jabba attack up on the Tera during the night. He sort of wished that Terry was in the lead and Tony was taking up the rear. Terry was amazing with the sword and he could keep the trail clear ahead of them as they ran for their lives. However, Tony was the only one who knew the way to the wall and once there, how to get in fast.

Keeping his gaze in the branches as much as possible, Tony prepared them to make a run for it. The Jabba remained still as the Thulsa band started slowly walking forward again. Why hadn't they attacked yet? What were they waiting for? The animals silently watched them move slowly through the forest. None made a noise or a move, except slowly moving their heads, following every step the four men took. Tony and Terry knew exactly what they were up to. Just because they had deeply underestimated and misunderstood these creatures from the start, didn't mean they didn't understand they were about to be attacked, gauntlet style.

"Gotta tell ya," Danny whispered quietly, starting to move a little faster down the trail. "I'm about to pee my pants right now."

"Well, pee them or poop them all you want, just make sure you're running as hard as you can when you do," Tim whispered back from behind as they made their way along the trail through the forest that became a little thicker with every step. Tony and Terry knew the Jabba would attack as soon as they had them surrounded equally from the front and the back. The trick for Tony was to start their run before the Jabba had a chance to try and swarm them.

"Look sharp," Tony ordered, reaching back and pulling his sword, alerting Terry to pull his out.

"Oh crap!" Danny whined loudly, absolutely petrified that they were about to be engulfed with razor claws and teeth. Tony brought the group to a fast trot, watching the Jabba unfurl their wings in preparation for attack.

"Time to go!" The Thulsa Captain yelled, instantly bolting forward. Danny felt like his legs were going to just crumple beneath him as Tony started throttling away and Tim's hand landed on his back, trying to push him forward. The youngest guy here and he felt like he was the slowest. There was a sudden blast of Jabba chirping as wings opened fully, but still nothing airborne. Tony held them at half speed in case he needed to sprint in a dire circumstance. He knew he was going to have to slow down in a moment anyway. Danny found his legs slowly coming alive as he started to overtake Tony. Running along the trail, Danny caught glimpses of what looked like a huge stone wall, but the trees were becoming so thick that he couldn't tell if it was their destination or not.

Then it came. The forest all around them turning black with flapping wings, the entire Gangees flock took to the wing, dropping out of the trees and swarming around them like locusts. At first it was just the rush of air and flapping that sounded like amplified bat wings. The chirping turned deafening as the flock moved in perfect choreography closer around the four running humans. Then the Jabba began to peel off one by one, making runs at the four, swiping at them with their claws as they flew past. Tony and Terry swung with lightning precision as one would sweep in from the front or the rear. Even as the winged attackers would try and take a jab at Tim or Danny, they somehow managed to make a quick turn and either smack them away or cause them to crash off in the surrounding woods. As more Jabba went down, many of the smaller animals pulled back to let the larger individuals get closer. It appeared that many of them were just afraid of getting injured or killed.

The four continued running along the trail towards the wall, having to slow down because of the swarm and the speed at which the Jabba were hitting them. For Tony, it was like hacking his way through a thick jungle to keep moving forward. No sooner would he have one cleared away either by slicing it length ways or just a fast smack with the side of his blade, then another one was right there. Danny and Tim kept squashing up tight against him, slowing to a fast walk.

Tim noticed three very large Jabba joining the fray from above, quickly circling in tight. He watched them wing around, taking notice of the one in front. It was Tobor himself, and he looked very angry. No doubt frustrated with his failed attempts at stopping the band from getting this far. He and his lieutenants weaved in and out of the circle, Tim watching and trying to warn Tony and Terry they were coming in, but the noise was too loud. They suddenly winged hard inward right at Tony. Tobor hit him broadside knocking him out of the line and nearly to the ground, the second one hitting Danny, knocking him off his feet. The third dipped right over the top of Tony and Danny, thrusting past Tim and into Terry's back, knocking him over as well. Tony was able to hold his balance enough to remain standing, but teetered to the side, into the bodies of Jabba winging around them, completely disrupting the flow of the air traffic. He spun sideways swinging and slashing at wings and claws as he went. The circle was suddenly a confused array of colliding animals as all their timing was interrupted. Danny remained on the ground for the moment since getting back up would put him into a sea of wings and black fur. He had gotten banged up pretty bad, still a bit stunned.

As Terry went down, he turned in mid fall, continuing to slash and swing making the maneuver just a part of the fall. Landing on his back, he used the momentum, letting it propel him into a somersault, springing right back onto his feet in the middle of the Jabba flow, or what was left of it. Tim stood still now, but to his complete surprise, none of the Jabba even attempted to come at him. It was as if he were invisible. After watching Terry complete his maneuver, he turned forward again, looking at Danny on the ground to the side, still a bit stunned. He watched Tony for a moment. His Captain bravely fighting anything that moved at him, completely overwhelmed but still standing. Tim knew Jabba behavior very well and could easily see that they were acting on strict orders from their hierarchy. It was quite apparent to him that they were after him and the others were to be disposed of. He quickly reasoned that if he were to remove himself from the situation, the other three would be left unharmed, being of no consequence.

Danny finally got his wits back, rolling over onto his stomach to get back up and looking ahead. Through the trees he could see the walls of Thulsa. They were almost there! If only he had something to fight with, he could help a completely overwhelmed Tony. He looked back at Terry, who was a snarling mass of bladed fury. There was quite a pile of Jabba parts building up around him and while he was taking some painful hits himself, he was definitely getting the better of the flock coming at him. As Danny turned back forward, a couple of Jabba parts, consisting of a set of front and rear paw claws, fell right in front of him. He tried to swipe them out of his way, starting to move forward on his belly but cut his hand on the claws, leaving bloody gashes. He moved again to toss them out of the way, but stopped. He had no weapons, but the Jabba did and they could be very effective. He picked up both sets of claws. One set was severed right at the paw joint and fit in his fist between his fingers very well. The other still had part of the leg bone attached and made for a good Kalinga axe.

Tony was close to being mauled to the ground, the Jabba starting to get the best of him. While there were only so many that could get at him at one time, these Jabba were a lot bigger than what they had fought before. Terry, on the other hand was doing just fine on his own. Tim started walking past Tony towards the high wall of the city, seemingly unaffected by the flying Jabba. Danny sprang to his feet and started working his will on the Jabba trying to overwhelm Tony. It didn't take long for him to make mincemeat out of the swarm all over the Thulsa Captain, clawing and slashing with his new found weapons. The Jabba were so taken aback by the boldness of this unanticipated warrior that they bolted from Tony, leaving him and trying to regroup out in the forest a short distance away.

Terry stepped over the mounds of carcasses, killing a couple of wounded Jabba that reached for him as he went by. While he was bruised and bleeding, none of the wounds were life threatening and he remained unencumbered, ready for more.

"Now these are the Jabba I'm used to dealing with," he said puffing, a little out of breath. Tony was ok as well. He had received several larger gashes to his forearms and a good sized cut over his right eye, but the rest were all minor in nature. There had been so many of the animals on him at once, few were able to really get at him. It had felt more like being mauled by a bunch of cats. Danny was yet, uninjured and ready to get back into it.

"I'm still in one piece, thanks to our new warrior man here," Tony said, breathing hard and looking at the young Niker.

"Nice work," Terry commented, stepping over the mess in front of Tony and looking around as the Jabba continued to swarm among the trees, regrouping. Their chirping was still quite loud, but was tuned out by the humans, starting forward again, toward the wall.

"Where's Tim?" Terry asked, looking everywhere for him, moving quickly. They didn't want to miss him hiding somewhere and leave him behind if he had gotten separated somehow.

"Ahead of us, near the wall," Danny announced, pointing at a figure with one of his Jabba claw weapons. Starting towards him, the Jabba began to swarm around them again. This time, the humans went into a full on sprint down the rest of the trail towards the wall. If they could get inside or at least close to the relative safety of the wall, the Thulsa guards would surely see what was happening and provide aid against the swarming mass.

Reaching Tim, the Gangees swarmed again, but this time their efforts weren't nearly as effective as before. There were three defenders now, and all of them were equally brazen and ferocious.

"What are you doing?" Danny asked Tim, who just stood nearly hypnotized, watching the attack and his friends trying to fight them off. The attack, while not well coordinated this time, was just as vicious and even with the extra help from Danny, they had their hands full trying to fight it back. Tony looked up at the wall as they drew near, expecting his men to appear due to all the commotion, but none could be seen anywhere on the wall. The main gate door remained shut and impassable and without someone at the wall to see that help was needed, there was no way to get it opened. While the Jabba could easily fly over, they normally didn't because the people of Thulsa would, as Digi had put it, *"have them down and skinned before they had a chance to land."* Tim turned back to Danny and shook his head.

"It's me they want. If I let them take me, they will leave you alone."

"Don't bet your life on it," Tony fired back, angrily fighting several smaller Jabba. "Ivan doesn't give a cart load of crap about any of us, especially me and Terry. Even if he did specifically order Tobor to bring you back and let us go, he has Tobor and the Gangees so engrained with hatred that they will kill us anyway, and once he finds out that you no longer have the book, you're going to be riding in the same crap cart with us. You did poke him pretty hard with that arrow. Now pick up a claw and give us a hand!"

"What now Captain?" Terry asked, slicing several smaller animals in half. There were so many that were falling, the men were becoming a bit of a mess with animal blood and flesh. "Where are the good guys? We have to get through that door!" Tony jumped to the wall with Danny right behind. Terry had to give Tim a good hard shove to get him there and even then, Danny had to help hold him up flat against the stone wall. At least here the Jabba were no longer able to encircle them and keep up their speed on the attack, but this caused the smaller ones to pull back again and allow the bigger ones an uncluttered pass at the Thulsa band.

Danny looked to the east. In the time they had fought their way to the southern wall, the second Argylian sun had breached the horizon and was working its way into the sky behind its smaller companion. Second sunup had arrived!

"We have to get in there now!" Danny exclaimed, pointing at the second sun. Terry and Tim turned towards the sunrises. Their view was partially blocked, the sky still full of Jabba, obstructing the view of the second sunrise. It was time for the arena fight to begin. Tony looked up again, hoping to see at least someone there. He knew that this side of the city was not as well guarded as the east wall was. There was no need. There was no way to get a large attacking force through these woods to mount such an attack. Every able bodied man would be towards the eastern wall, but there should have been at least a warning guard or a look out or someone here! Tony knew of a secret way in, but was hesitant to use it for fear of it being discovered by the Kenlar, but there seemed to be no other way in. They weren't going to last indefinitely, even against the wall. He'd have to risk it.

"Come on!" he hollered, moving along the wall, fighting off the bigger Jabba as he went. Tim was still a bit unwilling to follow. He had convinced himself that if he let them take him, they would spare his friends, but as they fought, being constantly battered and set upon by the Jabba, he realized that Tony was probably right. For Ivan and Tobor, this was personal now. He was almost sure that Digi had been finished off up on the mountain by Tobor and Ivan didn't care about having Tim. He just wanted the book back. He could always enslave someone else to learn its secrets. Ivan had always had an intense hatred for Tony. He felt a need to lay blame for his failure to win the heart of the Thulsa Queen, squarely on Tony's head. In his feeble reasoning, if he were to remove Tony, he could somehow show Catrina that he was the man that she could hold to and be loyal to. Never mind that it was all completely up to Catrina herself. She made her own choices and decided who was for her. Tony had never had anything to do with it.

After several minutes of battling along the wall, the group came to an area where the forest was so thick and the floor vegetation so heavy that it grew right up the wall. This worked both for and against them, making it so much harder to stay against the wall for protection and keep their weapons engaged on the swooping Jabba. But it also worked to hinder the Jabba; the thick forest made it more difficult for the Jabba to attack. Some had landed, working their way closer to the four men, since they could no longer attack from the air. Only feet away from them now, the Jabba snarled viciously, closing in on the struggling humans. Tony was looking for something, but with such thick vegetation and undergrowth, it was impossible to see anything of the wall.

"What exactly are you looking for?" Danny asked, taking several swings at a few Jabba coming closer, one of them was particularly large. Swinging his leg bone and claw, the beast caught it in mid swing with its powerful jaws giving it a mighty yank. The tug was hard enough that it pulled Danny off balance and forward towards the growling beast. Hitting the thick vines and growth he sank a little, then the Jabba rolled in on top of him. With the added weight, they suddenly broke through a hollow area below, both dropping out of sight. Tony and Terry looked a little surprised, as Tim leaned out, looking in the hole that had been created.

"This what you were looking for?" he asked, looking back at his two friends. Tony gave Tim a good shove forward. "Hey! A little dignity please!" Tim yelled, dropping out of sight head first. Terry and Tony fought the continued assault of the Jabbaway, back to back for several more moments until Terry finally beckoned Tony to go and he'd cover their escape.

"I guess he found it? Go! It's your hole!" Terry yelled, slashing several swooping Jabba. Nearly exhausted from the fight, there were far more of the angry animals than they would ever be able to take on. The Jabba could easily out last them by way of sheer numbers.

"The Captain always sees to the safety of his crew," Tony responded, continuing to fight the advancing beasts crawling towards them.

"This isn't The Amanda sir," Terry puffed, getting a spatter of blood across his chin, severing another flying Jabba in half. "Besides, it smells funny down there," Terry objected.

"Just get down there, I don't care what you smell," Tony commanded, pulling him off balance and steering his fall towards the hole. Terry dropped down the hole along with several Jabba, while Tony took a couple of swift swings at the animals advancing towards him and the hole, then made a quick step and jumped towards the hole.

Tony soft landed some ten or so feet below. Struggling to his feet, he realized that he had landed on the carcasses of most of the Jabba that had come in before him. He looked up at more Jabba that had come to the mouth of the hole but were hesitant to follow. There was definitely a foul odor down here and the Gangees flock didn't like it much at all. Tony turned towards the wall and a stairway the headed down to its base. Danny was doing away with the last of the Jabba that had made it down with them as Tim was trying to work the mechanism of an old metal door sunk deep into the base of the wall. Terry was holding his hand up to his nose trying to keep the smell out as Tony stepped to the door.

"What is that horrible stench?" Terry asked, as Tim moved aside to let Tony work the door.

"Ain't you ever been in a sewer before?" Tony asked, working the old door mechanism. It was old and rusty, reluctantly giving way to the twisting of the huge ring in the center of it.

"It's on my to-do list," Terry said, Tony pulling the old door back on creaking hinges.

"Smells like it's time to cross it off." Danny plugged his nose, getting a little over powered himself.

"This will take us under the wall and into the sewer system here on the southern end of the city. We'll have to come up through one of the vent shacks on a side street." Tony reached inside and struck the igniter on an old hanging lamp, giving Tim cause to come unglued, reaching to stop him.

"Are you off your noodle there Anton?" he asked, scared to death. "You'll blow us to kingdom come with all the methane down here."

"Too many vents all along the passage for that to happen," Tony reassured everyone as the lamp lite up.

"Well there sure is an accumulation right here," Tim came back, still very concerned.

"You'd rather take your chances up top with Tobor's group?" Tony came back, stepping through the door. Danny went in right after him and Tim finally followed with Terry hot on his heels. Closing the door behind him and making sure the mechanism was secure so the Jabba couldn't follow, he made his way along the passage behind, the others. After several minutes of traveling through foul water and smell, Tony led them up a set of rickety old stairs and out into the fresh air, inside the city walls. They made it in! As everyone exited the vent shack, Terry moved to secure the door behind him, but thought he heard a clamor back down the passage and stopped to listen. Stepping away from the rest of the group, Tony caught site of a single guard on the wall and called to him in Thulsian. Danny stepped closer to Terry and put his head through the door with him.

"What are we listening for?"

"I thought I heard something," Terry responded in a whisper. He was still trying to hear if there was any more noise coming from the tunnels they had just traveled. As Tony talked quickly to the warrior on the wall, Tim looked around for a street that looked like it might take them to the arena, but he had no clue where they were. He hadn't been in the city for many years and everything was completely unfamiliar to him. The streets were deserted, not even a dog was barking right now. This time of morning, he would have expected there to be children playing and people going about their day to day business, but it was like a ghost town here. Finally, Tony turned back to the group as Terry shut the door, having been unable to hear anything else coming from the passageway. It was probably just the Jabba making noise on the other end. Even if they could open the door on the outside, it wasn't likely that they would get very many of their numbers through. The Jabba had an aversion to confined spaces and they wouldn't come over the wall because of their fear of Thulsa warriors who would shoot them before they got very far. No, the Thulsa band was finally safe.

"The Queen had all of our people moved to a safer location to the west of the city and most of the warriors are at the east wall prepping for The Kenlar invasion. They expect them to attack before the day is out. I've ordered more men to guard the wall in case Tobor gets brave and tries to come over the top," Tony said, rounding up his group. "Stick very close to me. We're still kind of dressed like Kenlars, and we've got a little more running to do to make it to the arena. Let's move!" he commanded, leading the others quickly off in the direction of the arena as fast as they could make their tired legs go.

Brass Tacks

Britten checked the gear Hans was laying out in front of him. He was allowed only a shield and his weapons into the fighting arena. Neither opponent was allowed armor of any kind, only standard clothes provided by the council. If an opponent didn't have a weapon, one would be provided for them. Some basic weapons were provided on racks in the arena in the event a combatant lost or broke their weapon. They could use any weapon they brought in with them or whatever was in the arena.

The rules were fairly straight forward. Fight to the death by any means possible within the arena itself. If you tried to climb out, you would be killed. You were not allowed to spare a life. If you mortally wounded an opponent, but refused to finish them off, you would be killed. There was no time limit. Unfortunately for Brit, he did have a time limit. They had to get all this business taken care of and get back to the storm before it left or risk being stranded as the crew of The Amanda had been.

"I'm not allowed to know who your opponent is," Hans said from across the table. "I only know that they are chosen from prisoners of Thulsa. Thankfully, I am not aware of any of them being of our people. Most of them are either Kenlar or Omar, taken captive for one reason or another, mostly as spies. Seems there has been a lot of that as of late. You'll do fine my friend, good luck."

Brit looked around the mostly empty room. There was but one door to the wide corridor that led either out of the arena building or straight into the arena itself. It looked as though they used the arena for more than just fighting. He tried to keep things light in his mind, imagining that they held rodeos or even outdoor concerts.

"Have you seen Catri-," he stopped, giving Hans an intense look of apprehension. "Will the Queen be here before I go in?" Brit asked, trying to distance himself from his feelings and move himself into some kind of a fighting mentality. Hans smiled a little, perceiving what the young Master Garrett was doing. Trying to get into the zone for a fight seemed to come naturally to men. Call it a self-preservation mode, call it whatever you want, everyone that had to go into that ring seemed to go through it. Hans had grown attached to this Earth man since he had started training him just a couple of short days ago and although he still wasn't a very good swordsman, he had come a very long way. He could also see Brit's feelings for the Queen. No need for getting in any zone to figure that one out. Hans could also see that he needed a little bit more coaching, but this time, not in fighting.

"She had to attend to the eastern embattlements before the fight. If the Kenlar attack were to come now, your fight would have to be postponed until a more appropriate time."

"I can't imagine there being an appropriate time for this kind of thing."

"These are our ways Master Britten. It's how it has always been," Hans replied. "The Queen indicated that she would be back here before the start."

"Are you sure?' Brit asked, a little nervous.

"I can assure you that they will not start without her. She must be present to authorize the start of the fight."

"Wonderful," Brit responded in a low voice. He looked across the table at Hans with a mix of expressions that was confusing for the training foe to read.

"Have you told her highness how you feel?" Hans asked straight way. Britten sucked in a huge breath and held it for a couple of moments, then exhaled all at once. He figured that at this point, it wasn't going to matter if he revealed his true feelings to anyone else or not. No one had any reason to object to how he felt for her, even if she was their Queen.

"Sort of," Brit replied, shifting his eyes up to Hans to see his response. The training foe froze, then leaning over the table looking directly at Brit; he reached over and put one of his hands around the back on Brit's neck and firmly rocked him a little, then suddenly started rapping on his head with his fist.

"Hello! Is anyone in there?" he asked, a little irritated. Brit struggled to pull away, but Hans was a strong man and had a good hold on his neck. He finally managed to pull free, backing away from the table, not really sure what had happened.

"What was that all about?" Brit asked, rubbing his head.

"I know you aren't stupid," Hans replied quickly. "You've 'sort of' told her? Is this how it's 'sort of' done in the place that you come from?"

"Hey, I can't just come in here and sweep your Queen away from you and I can't expect her to just drop everything for a chance with me," Brit replied defensively.

"Chance? Chance?" Hans repeated becoming even more irritated. The people of Thulsa loved the Queen because she was such a good and wonderful person. Having her as their monarch was just a coincidence. They would have loved her no matter what role she played in their clan. She was just that kind of woman. While they loved her as their Queen, they always wanted her to have her own happiness and if that meant letting her go, they would be fine with it. Brit had stepped back away from the table and was a little taken back at Hans' boldness in speaking in this manner. Obviously there was a great deal of respect for this amazing woman.

"You think you take a chance with someone? Is that how you think where you are from?" Hans leaned a little further across the table at Brit, who shuffled back more. "You find that one that you can't live without and you love them like no other and you both work together to build something that cannot be broken by anything. You don't "CHANCE" anything! You grab a hold and hang on like something was trying to tear you apart, but you *NEVER* let go." Hans' demeanor toned down, stepping back and straightening up, hearing footsteps moving quickly down the outer corridor towards them.

"You tell her exactly how you feel. Tell her that you love her, because you do. Leave nothing to chance." He finished, stepping to the side of the door and waiting. The person in the corridor was either assigned to take him into the arena or it was someone else. It was someone else.

Catrina Dallas smiled, slowly stepping through the open door to find Britten standing on the other side of the table looking back at her with an expression full of mixed emotions. That was to be expected though. She had seen this expression many times before, lots of worry and confusion, mixed with a bunch of scared. What she didn't know, was the real cause of this expression. She acknowledged Hans just inside the door as he bowed. Brit glanced at him nervously as the training foe slipped out of the room, then looked back at Catrina, floating up to the table, letting her hands rest gently on it.

"I know you're nervous," she said in a clear, calm voice that was quite soothing to Brit's jumbled nerves. "You'll do just fine."

"Cat," he fumbled. "I need to tell you something."

"Ok," she agreed pleasantly. Brit stepped back to the table, trying to pull up his courage. He thought back to their time alone in the dining room in the Fort Manor, if only Sargon hadn't interrupted them, this might be a little easier if they would have already expressed unspoken emotions through the kiss.

"Cat, I," he paused a long moment, looking into her deep brown eyes. He couldn't live without them, without her. "I love you. I can't live without you. Catrina Amanda Dallas, will you marry me?" His heart was pounding, feeling like it was going to leap from his chest. Cat held her composure, letting a smile slip to her lips.

"Yes," she replied immediately, grinning calmly. She had made this decision on the east wall earlier; she was just waiting for him to ask. She turned and stepped around the table to face him up close. She reached out and took both his hands, holding them gently, gazing into his hazel eyes, moving closer to him. Brit realized she wasn't stopping. She continued in until it was obvious what she was after, what they were both after. Brit let go of her hands, encircling her in his arms and pressing his lips to hers. It was about as magical as it could get. Not a first kiss kind of feeling where you see stars and stuff. This kiss was like no other either had ever experienced before. Having kissed other would be lovers; neither had felt anything like this. Britten counted himself well-rehearsed in the art of kissing, feeling like he was an expert, but this was so far off the chart, there seemed like there was nothing else to compare it to. He didn't feel like she was teaching him anything. In truth, they were experiencing the same things. It was so enjoyable, feeling so natural that they didn't want it to stop. The entire Kenlar army couldn't come between them this time. They kissed passionately for several moments; then came up for air, but once wasn't even close to being enough. No sooner had they opened their eyes to look at each other, than they went right back in for more. The passion and emotion they had been feeling, came swelling out into the embrace. They weren't mauling, but there was a lot of heat and energy build up being released with the kiss. They pulled apart again to look and smile at the other. Relieved, they were finally able to exchange a wonderful expression of love and emotion. Brit could see only Cat and Catrina only Brit. Somehow, he had traveled across the galaxy and 60 years of time to find her and now, here she was, in his arms, right here, right now, and they couldn't be happier. They both wanted more and didn't want this to end, but knew it would have to and very soon, so they were determined to make the most of it, coming back together for another long warm kiss.

Catrina heard footsteps coming down the corridor and reluctantly pulled away from the kiss, but continued to hold him close.

"I don't want to let you go," she said quietly, suddenly feeling quite vulnerable. Here was another new sensation for her to figure out. She detected several guards stopping in the doorway, but they stepped back a little when they saw that the Queen was occupied.

"I love you," she whispered, leaning into him and resting her head on his shoulder. "You have to know that."

"Yes, I know. I have always known, just as I have always loved you. But I have to tell ya," he said, pushing her back and looking into her eyes. "You sure were a hard one to find." They both chuckled softly, letting their foreheads come carefully together. "Come back with me?" he asked, holding both her hands up between them, searching her features with endless hope. Cat gazed right back at him. She had figured out up on the east tower that her time here as the Queen of Thulsa had come to an end. It was time for her to go home, back to Earth, with this man that she couldn't live without. She knew that if she asked him, he would stay here with her, but she wanted to go home. She wanted to see and be with her mother again. She wanted to be with Brit and share his life on that wonderful planet called Earth.

"We can't," she sighed, relaxing a bit. Brit released her, feeling the moment starting to drop.

"Then I'll stay here with you," he said, still in a lower tone.

"No, it's not that," she said, taking a step back. Brit developed a confused look.

"I'll go anywhere with you," he reassured her.

"I know," she smiled. "But neither one of us is going anywhere until you get through the arena." Brit let out a small sigh, giving the guards who had been waiting patiently just outside the door a glance.

"Oh, yeah. Sorta forgot about that."

"Yeah, I did too," Catrina admitted, grinning.

Brit turned to the table and looked at the shield. It was very strong, but light weight. He picked it up and firmed his grip up on it. The shield felt good on his arm. He turned to Cat and grinned in an overly cheesy fashion while trying to flex and pose like a muscle man.

"How do I look?" he asked, trying to hold off the near paralyzing nervousness. Catrina held in a giggle with her fingers. She could well imagine what he was going through as the time for his event had arrived. The guards stepped inside to escort him out, so he picked up the Twins and hung them from his free arm.

"Just don't ding it up," Cat said, trying to keep the humor lighter than the situation was heavy. "It belongs to my Dad." Brit looked it over and admired how good its condition was.

"Didn't he ever use it?" It really was in pristine condition; there was hardly a mark on it.

"You're looking at the show overlay," she said, stepping over and pulling the holding clasps back then removing the round cover. Beneath the overlay, it was heavily marred with hack marks, gouges and endless chip marks. It was obvious that this shield had seen a lot of action. It wasn't very thick, which made Brit wonder how in the world it could possibly protect him from sword strikes.

"It's made from the wood of the Onark tree, found only in the Modoc forest. It's very strong and will serve you well."

"Thank you," he smiled, looking back at her. He let out another sigh of resignation, having run out of things to say or do to stall any more. He gave her a frightened look and Catrina stepped back to him and they embraced. Mouthing the words, "I love you", Cat pulled from him, stepped out and quickly headed back up the corridor to take her place in the royal box. Brit looked after her, then turned to his escort and tried to smile.

"Which way to the party boys?" He asked, gesturing in the other direction. He started down the hallway towards the large open gate at the other end with his guards on either side.

"Just got myself engaged," he said, looking at them, smiling. The guards didn't speak English and looked at him as though he was off his noodle. Who gets all excited about stepping into the fighting arena?

Usually, they had to drag the participants kicking and screaming. This one was acting kind of strange.

To the death

The arena was the size of a small Coliseum with seven or eight rows of steeply tiered seating built in the shape of a U around the outside. The far end of the arena was a stark, sheer rock wall that was the side of an abutment of high rocks forming a small butte. The walls immediately around the arena were high and smooth, making it impossible for anyone to scale them without the aid of a ladder or rope. There were two small wooden racks, one on each end of the arena. An axe, a couple of staffs and even a small sword in a scabbard, were hung on each rack.

As Britten entered the arena, he was joined by his opponent. He was an older man, but looked to be in fairly good shape. He wore heavy black trousers, no shirt and a pair of leather gauntlets around his wrists. He had a heavy beard that joined with his long bedraggled hair. He had no sword. It had likely been taken from him when he had been captured. He seemed to be confident, but scared at the same time, sort of what Britten was feeling.

Each man was escorted to opposite ends of the arena, turned to face each other and positioned next to the wooden rack displaying the extra weapons that had been supplied. Brit looked up into the stands to his right. Down at the edge of the ring was the royal box, but there was no sign of Catrina. Wasn't she supposed to be here to start the fight? Hans had been given only very basic instructions, which consisted of looking at the green flag and waiting for it to drop to begin the fight. There was no need for any other flags or signals. Once the fight began, only death could stop it. He waited nervously, looking across at his opponent who was trying to relax while examining the small sword that had been provided for him on the rack.

Looking all around, Brit could see that there weren't very many people here at all. He thought he should be feeling a little bit insulted. *"No top billing for a fight like this? Where was the promoter? Who was in charge of ticket sales? They weren't even selling peanuts in the stands".* Not that there was anyone in the stands to buy them. All of these were funny thoughts to try and take his mind off what was about to happen.

In truth, the people here were the council elders and a few cluster reps that had attended the original council meeting. These same had sent his brother and friends with Captain Dallas to the Kenlar to find the Signet. Speaking of which, he had hoped he would see them here in the stands, come to save the day at the last second. He looked around carefully, wishing Bryan would come strolling in, maybe lean against the royal box, flipping through the pages and motioning to the guards to lower a ladder for Brit to climb out. Then he could turn to the council. *Looking for this?"* he would ask. *"Yeah, that's right, we're here and we brought it back. Now if you'll excuse us, we have a storm to catch."* Yep, that's just what he'd say. Sure wished he was here to say it right now.

Finally, Brit caught site of Catrina walking along the top tier of the arena seating towards a set of stairs that descended down to the royal box. She was dressed in her full battle armor now. The same that she had worn the day he had met her in the Winners Spoil. Normally she would be wearing something a little more comfortable, but there was war close to their doorstep and she had to be ready should the Kenlars decide to move. She actually hoped that they would. It would postpone this fight and bring the possibility of a hasty release, there being no time for such things. However, if the people of Thulsa were consistent in one thing, it was sticking to procedures……………dang it.

Bowing to the council, Catrina stepped into her box. She acknowledged the guards in the arena, who turned and left by the only entrance, throwing the big wood slatted gate closed behind them. The Queen motioned for the two combatants to approach the royal box, noticing that Brit had left the Twins in their sheaths on the weapons rack and was carrying the short sword. The Kenlar prisoner scowled at her as she bowed to him. He arrogantly nodded and turned back to his end of the arena. He was ready to get on with it and was in no mood for pleasantries with the Thulsians. Catrina turned and bowed to Brit, who smiled a bit and bowed back.

"What are you doing?" she asked in a whisper, holding herself down. Brit looked a little embarrassed.

"What? What do you mean what am I doing? Bowing? Am I not supposed to bow?" he replied in a whisper as well.

"Why do you have that sword? Use the Twins and let's get this over with. You can do it," she beckoned to him. Brit was hesitant to say, but he was trying to hold off using them unless he absolutely had to. Cat's logic would suggest that this was absolutely necessary. Brit shook his head, but kept his eyes on Cat.

"I want to give this guy a fighting chance."

"He murdered a Thulsian farmer and his family to keep them from giving away his position as a spy. I think he's already had his fighting chance." This was certainly a good reason for capital punishment. Most of the time, the spy would have just been executed right when he was captured, but with looming war, information that he might have could have proven useful.

"I can't risk it unless it's absolutely necessary."

"Why? I think it's absolutely necessary." She was a little frustrated, looking around at the council members who were starting to eye her curiously.

"Because I go blind every time they download. My shoulders and arms go numb. They are hard to move and each time it gets worse." Catrina was stunned at the revelation.

"Wait, what? When did you discover this?" she asked, feeling a little panicked.

"Right after I used them."

"Why didn't you say something?"

"I didn't want to worry you and Hans if it was just me getting use to the download," Brit came back, noticing that his opponent was getting a little restless. Catrina could see that some of the council members were also getting restless at the delay.

"And you think I'm not worried now?" She cried in a whisper. "So you plan on fighting him with just that?" she asked, directing her attention to the small sword.

"That's what he's using," Brit responded, trying to sound confident in himself. "Let's get on with this." He said, backing away. Cat held herself down in the bent position, watching him head back to his starting point.

"Not good," she mumbled to herself, feeling an intense worry filling her soul. Catrina knew how well he could fight with a sword alone. "Not good at all," she repeated. She finally sat back in her chair as Brit signaled he was ready. She looked over at the Kenlar warrior and then released the green starting flag that was setting next to her seat in the royal box.

Brit instantly got into a defensive posture with shield and sword rocking back and forth to see what the Kenlar was going to do. At first, he just stood there passing his sword from hand to hand waiting for Brit to make a move. When it was apparent that Brit wasn't going to do anything, he stood up straight, looking at the Thulsa council and Queen, raising his sword over his head. Rattling something off defiantly in Kenlar, he turned and charged straight at Brit with an angry look.

"Oh boy," Brit mumbled to himself, trying to remember the basic defensive techniques Hans and Cat had tried to teach him. *"Remember, basic defends. Nothing fancy and you'll do fine,"* echoed in his mind. He was pretty nervous as the warrior came at him at a full charge, but he had a good idea as to what to do. Brit gave Cat one last look, then focused on the charge as the short sword came at him. He quickly brought his shield up, warding off the blow, returning the strike with a swing of his own. The sound the two small swords made was a sickening clatter. There was no elegant clang or after ring as the swords met again and again. Brit did his best to follow the Kenlar's sword at every turn. These swords were sharp in only one place, the tip, and that's all that mattered here. They skirmished around Brit's end of the arena for several minutes, taking turns backing the other up, first around the weapons rack, then up against the wall. They clashed in close, then further apart. Brit wasn't sure what was happening. He had kind of expected to get himself into trouble right away. Either this guy was just as bad as he was, or testing the Earth man to see what his strengths and weaknesses were.

Catrina carefully watched Brit sparred with the Kenlar man. She didn't even realize that she was digging out chunks of the wooden armrest with her fingernails while gently nipping at her lower lip with her teeth. What she saw worried her. He was fighting, or what would be termed fighting, just like he had in the training room with Hans. Somehow she had hoped that when confronted with the real thing, an aggressive nature would surface and give him a badly needed edge. This was all just defense. Brit didn't have time to just defend. He needed to get this done. She turned her gaze up at the sky, the first sun starting its rise over the top of the eastern wall of the arena. The second sun wouldn't be far behind. Watching him fight, she put herself right next to him, or even in his position, trying to coach him silently from her box. Many times she would groan or be frustrated at a lost opportunity or a missed shot, and then she'd cringe with a near miss.

Brit noticed the light changing ever so slowly, the first sun climbing higher in the sky with the ever moving moons. There came crawling into his head the nagging notion that he really needed to figure out how to finish this fight off as quickly as possible so they could get a move on. Up till now, he had been holding his own against the Kenlar, but that was all he was doing and it had remained pretty much a stalemate. He reasoned that while basic defends, it doesn't win and he needed to try and step out of the box to make something else happen, so he did. Brit waited till the warrior had made his swing patterns. It appeared that he was following the same theme with his swings. Swipe left, then right, then left and either lunge forward or back away, depending on whose turn it was to be aggressive. This time, as his opponent lunged forward, Brit dodged the thrust of the blade and made a quick swing inside. The tip of his blade made contact and ripped a gaping tear across the warrior's pants on his left thigh. Before Brit could pull away, the Kenlar made a fast swing as he withdrew and caught Brit on the left forearm, ripping the shirt and leaving a four inch cut that stung like the dickens.

Both combatants pulled back to nurse the sting of their wounds and reset themselves. Brit got back to it first, but let the other fighter have a moment to reset. He probably shouldn't have. Things weren't going to get done if he kept giving up his advantage and handing this guy a break. He finally went back to it, trading strikes and swipes. He tried again to get at him after following his predictable pattern, but this time he missed, and got struck with the flat side of the blade in the same place. A sudden streak of anger bolted through him and reaching forward with the back of his sword hand he struck the Kenlar as hard as he could squarely in the face. The blow was hard enough to knock the man backwards, but not off his feet. The warrior responded quickly and aggressively. He too, appeared to be getting a little frustrated that he hadn't been able to get the upper hand, so he was going to get it however he could. He lunged before Brit could bring his sword back up to defend. Brit tried to roll to one side using the shield to deflect the Kenlar, but the man caught him with his outstretched arm and brought him down in a tackle. When they both got back up, Brit got a fist full of dirt thrown in his face, the man diving at him with his sword straight out in front of him. The face full of dirt caused Brit to reel backward, landing on his back. He only just caught sight of his opponent diving at him and rolled to one side just in time. The strike missed, Brit struggling to get back to his feet, rubbing the dirt out of his eyes. He didn't have sight of the Kenlar now and that was a real problem. Regaining his feet, he found himself without his shield and sword, an even bigger problem. While still trying to clear his eyes, he turned to try and locate his opponent. He was met by a heavy blow to the side of his face that knocked him right back to the ground. Seeing stars now and his head spinning, at least now he could see, albeit only a cloud of dust kicked up when he landed. Getting back up to his knees, he was assaulted from the front with a foot to the face. Now that really hurt, and he was again, thrown back to the ground. He could taste blood now and felt his jaw, making sure it hadn't just been broken. Now it occurred to him that while he had dropped his sword, so had the Kenlar, otherwise, he would have used it on him while he was incapacitated.

Brit cleared his eyes again, looking at a figure standing by his feet. His opponent had found a sword and was moving to pick it up. Brit had what he thought was a great idea come to mind as the Kenlar moved towards him with his sword ready to strike. As the warrior stepped over his feet, Brit clamped his legs around the ankles of the warrior and rolled as hard as he could in the direction of his shield. This instantly brought the warrior down and Brit quickly came to his feet. Scooping up his shield and looking around for his sword, it was nowhere to be seen. It must have gotten buried in the deep dirt. He quickly backed up to the weapons rack while the Kenlar got to his feet. Brit fumbled with the rack, not wanting to take his eyes of his opponent, letting his hands do all the looking and watching the warrior start towards him.

Finally, Brit caught a hold of something familiar. With the warrior rushing, Brit let the shield drop and pulled a long rod from behind. Swinging hard, he knocked the sword from the Kenlars hand, then swung hard enough on the exposed shoulder to knock him away. The blow had to hurt from the feedback Britten was getting. He stepped away from the rack and spun the staff in his hands, taking a stance. Now he was cooking with the good stuff! The sword wasn't his cup of tea, the staff was. The maneuver only infuriated the Kenlar, quickly getting back to his feet and grabbing the axe on Brit's rack. It was a long handled axe, designed for a larger man. The business end was heavy and made wielding it all the more ungainly. This didn't seem to deter the Kenlar, who came at him swinging. Brit dodged and waited until the man's swing had cleared and then threw a couple of strikes at him with the staff. They must be hurting him as every hit caused him to cringe a bit and favor that part of his body. After some sparring in this fashion, his opponent getting angrier with each failure to get at Brit, the warrior finally found his sword again and dropped the axe in favor of the lighter weapon. Now the Kenlar felt like he had the upper hand as he had the sword and all Brit had, was a stick. Both combatants felt much more confident in their circumstances now and their attitudes shifted at the same time.

All together now

Captain Dallas worked his way through the streets of Thulsa, trying to keep close to the houses and trees as much as possible. While there was hardly anyone on the streets, it was still possible to be spotted and mistaken as Kenlar that had somehow gotten inside to open the gates or sabotage something. While the men were exhausted, they were relieved to be in the city and moving easily towards the city center. Finally, Danny recognized the opposite side of the town square. He really had come full circle and the thoughts of being hanged from the gallows only a few days ago, seemed like such a distant memory now.

On careful approach to the square, the four weary warriors spotted two wagons moving at a medium pace around the other side. They could get to the arena much faster if they could somehow convince the drivers that they weren't Kenlar and needed help. Their only hope was Tony's ability to speak fluent Thulsian and be recognized because of his distinctive features, but none of them could be sure that would work now. They had been gone long enough and had endured so much that they probably looked quite different from when they had left three days ago. Tim and Terry carefully checked their surroundings then motioned for Tony to make the attempt at contacting the drivers of the two wagons. The Thulsa Captain moved across the square in order to intercept and hopefully not be seen by someone the others hadn't noticed. He called out in Thulsian and the drivers reined their horses to a halt.

Caroline pulled back on her reins, looking back to see a ragged looking man plodding across the square towards their wagons. The voice sounded familiar, but the man wore clothes that didn't look Thulsian at all. They looked curiously Kenlar, but were so torn and beat up that it was difficult to tell. Still the voice kept her from whipping the horses and getting away as fast as they could to find help or warn the warriors that the enemy was within the walls. Coming closer and calling out again, they recognized each other at the same time.

"Tony?" she asked, not believing that it was even possible.

"Caroline?" Tony responded at the same time with the same surprised relief. He slowed to nearly a shuffled, feeling like his exhausted legs were going to give out now. They all had come so far on so little, doing it mostly on auto pilot.

"By the gods of Thulsa," she exclaimed, scrambling down from her seat and catching the bedraggled warrior Captain. "What happened?

Where have you been? We've been worried sick!" There was no time.
Both suns were climbing into the morning sky.

"We have to get to the arena now!" Tony puffed, slighting the
myriad of questions that were no doubt swirling around in her head.

"Can a stranger catch a ride too?" a voice called out from behind
Tony. Caroline knew that voice better than any of the others and
nearly burst into tears looking up at Tony, then side stepping the
Thulsa Captain to see her Terry strolling quickly up to them with Tim
and Danny in tow. That short little man, who was barely taller than
she, smiled with tired eyes. He appeared to be covered in dirt and
blood. Caroline's face exploded with excitement and tears, running
and jumping into his arms, hugging him like a baby monkey clinging to
its mother. There was a flurry of emotional hugging, kissing, more
hugging and then more kissing as Terry struggled to remain standing.
He was just as exhausted as the others. It was like there was a signal
to the body that said it was ok to give up and rest now that they had
reached the end of their long journey.

Danny and Tim stood a few feet away watching. They didn't want
to get too close to this, someone could get hurt and Terry and Caroline
probably wouldn't notice who it was or that it had even happened. As
wonderful as it was that they had found one another again, there was
still a big sense of urgency to make it to the arena as quickly as
possible.

"Caroline?" Tony beckoned, trying to get her attention. There was
a great deal of mauling going on right now and if they didn't get these
two apart quickly, Anna wasn't going to be their youngest.

"Caroline, we need to get to the arena fast," Tony said, with a little
more force. This brought them back to reality.

"We were headed in that direction," Caroline said, finally coming up
for air and sliding out of her husband's arms. "But we really have no
idea how to get there. It has been so long since Terry and I have
been here."

"How did you get this far?" Terry asked, letting go of his wife.

"Took a while to convince the north gate guards who we were.
Then the directions they gave us to get to the arena were a little less
than helpful. So we got lost a couple of times." By now all of Terry's
children were either lining the sides of the wagons or had gotten down
and were trying to get at him. Caroline had threatened the children
with their lives if they got out, but the happy reunion seemed to
countermand such threats as all the kids begged for a greeting and
love from their father. As Terry quickly made the rounds, putting the
wayward children back in their places in the wagons, he was about to
climb up into the seat of Caroline's lead wagon when he realized that
there was some added weight to his leg. He looked down to see
something with a head of red hair, clinging tightly to him. Anna
looked up with beaming eyes into her daddy's face.

"There's my little one!" he shouted, pulling her loose kicking and squealing with glee. "Have you been a good girl?" he asked, giving her a big zerbert kiss on her chubby little cheeks. Anna started doing the patented "Anna babble", pointing sharply at her mother, then at the wagons and the horses. Giving her daddy a glance, she was going to spout out more gibberish, but then just smiled and hugged him tightly.

"Ok, that settles it. You're riding up front with me," he said, hoisting her up onto the bench seat with him. Caroline moved quickly to climb up as well, but stopped, seeing Danny and Tim climbing in the wagon her oldest son was driving.

"Master Danny?" she called, out bringing his attention to her. She turned to Tony as Danny started towards her.

"The other wagon is the faster of the two," Caroline said, looking back at the other wagon as Tim climbed in. "Hurry and ride ahead of us." Tony gladly obliged and quickly jumped up onto the seat of the second wagon with the oldest Lieder boy. They bolted forward and around Caroline's wagon as Danny stepped up to the short woman.

"I think you need to be in this wagon, climb up." she ordered turning and climbing up next to her husband and a jabbering little red haired Anna, a smile forming on her face. Danny hopped up into the back of the wagon full of the younger of the kids. His body wanted to shut down and he was too tired to care which wagon he was in, so long as it was headed in the direction of home. All of the kids in the back just stared at him like he was from another planet or something. *Wait, he **was** from another planet. Ok, you can stare.* They were lined up in a bit of a huddle facing out from something else in the wagon. As Caroline whipped the horse and started moving through the streets after the lead wagon, Danny tried to get comfortable, but the wagon was small and the kids were taking up most of the available space. If they would just move a little further forward, it would be a heck of a lot more comfortable in here. He pushed his feet out in front of him, straightening and stretching them as far as he could. In doing so, he pushed right between one of the kids legs and hit something. It felt like another person was in the wagon with them.

"Hey," a voice called out in a very tired sickly tone. "This is my seat. Move to the back of the bus or I'll have my ruthless minions here lay waste to your face." There was a thought of recognition come to Danny's mind, but who it sounded like was impossible. He and Brit were the only two left and it was now a race against time to get home. Still, who else on this planet could sound so much like one of his best friends? It bore investigation and leaning forward, gently moved one of the kids to the side, revealing the other passenger in the wagon with him.

Danny nearly fell out of the back of the moving wagon with fright, as Bryan Garrett slowly turned his head in his direction. At first he thought he was looking at a ghost or at best, a corpse, a zombie or something. Bryan looked very sick; his face was pale and covered in sweat. There were dark circles around the bottoms of very tired looking eyes.

"What are you looking at knucklehead?" Bryan asked, trying to hold onto some humor. He could see that Danny did not believe what his eyes were seeing. He thought back to the last time they had seen each other. Danny and Jerry were riding ahead of him on the Torres road and he was being attacked by Jocko. It must have looked fairly grim to his friends. Neither had any idea what the other had been through for the past couple of days. Bryan was supposed to be dead and Danny should be toting a big book of some kind. Right now, the book was immaterial as Danny scooted up next to Bryan and touched him. *It just isn't possible for him to be here! He was dead!* He and Jerry saw Bryan fall with the Jabba. Tony had made Terry go down the cliff to make sure. Yet, here he was. He was in pretty bad shape from the look of him, but he was here all the same, and alive!

"You're alive," Danny choked emotionally, trying to fight back the tears. He had lost him to this world and now he was here, back from the dead. "You're here and you're alive." He repeated, putting his arm around his injured friend, holding him like a long lost relative. Bryan just let him rejoice in his own way. Didn't seem very manly to him, but he was too sick to object to anything.

"Yeah, I'm still with you guys. Afraid I got a little busted up inside though," Bryan said, as Anna knelt between them, giving each a hug. She seemed to know that Bryan was in even more trouble now than when he had first come back to them after his fall and subsequent escape from the Kenlar.

"Where's Jerry?" Bryan finally asked, looking around. It was possible he had gotten into the other wagon, but that seemed highly unlikely, as Danny and Jerry were generally inseparable. Even as young boys, they would be off together doing their own thing when Britten and Bryan weren't getting them into hot water with something else. Danny remained silent thinking of the events of last night. The scene of Jerry slipping from his grasp started to replay over again in his head; the look on Jerry's face disappearing into the darkness. The feelings of helplessness, watching him disappear. The past 24 hours had begun to numb him to the harsh realities of life and death.

"He didn't make it," Danny finally said, after a long moment of silence. "We lost him on the mountain."

"Lost him?" Bryan asked, not wanting to believe what he was hearing. While he knew they had all accepted a very real element of risk in having to go on this mission to rescue the Signet, he, like the other three had a warped concept of what a life and death adventure was really like. No one can possibly know unless they experience it for themselves. All of them were experts now and would be able to tell anyone what it was really like and no one had the right to say otherwise.

"We were attacked by Tobor's Jabba flock on the Tera high mountain pass last night. Jerry was protecting the Signet and fell from the trail."

"What about the Signet? Where is it?" Bryan asked, looking up through the trees spread throughout the whole city.

"The people of the Mynites have it safe now. Ivan can never reach it again." Bryan didn't understand, but he had figured out a little while ago that it was a moot point now anyway. Brit wouldn't have had to fight in the arena if they had gotten the Signet to the Council elders before second sunup on the third day. The fight would be well under way by now. He slowly nodded his head wondering what the whole story was, but knowing that it would have to wait for a better time.

"I'm sorry about Jerry," Bryan said tiredly, a different kind of sick feeling entering him. One of shock and disbelief for the reality of losing a good friend.

"He died saving the Signet," Danny responded slowly. Right now, there was no time for real mourning. It would have to wait and come when everyone could reflect and start the healing process. This wasn't the place for it now. There was only a moment for reflection and sadness for their fallen friend.

The two sat silent with little Anna between them listening to their conversation, basic as it was.

She pulled back, looking at Danny, leaned over and kissed Bryan on the cheek, then proceeded to ramble on about something that only a tot could possibly understand. It was gentle in nature and actually quite soothing. It may not have cured him of his injuries, but it couldn't hurt. Danny was just so overjoyed that he had at least one of his good friends back. His thoughts turned to Jerry now, wishing that he were still with them. He knew that he would have to make some explanations shortly, but right now, he was just glad to have Bryan here with him now.

Racing his wagon through the western streets of Thulsa, Terry had the feeling they were being watched. How strange. Everyone should be on the Eastern side defending the city wall. They didn't actually encounter anyone, but every now and again, when they would make a turn, he would catch a glimpse of movement behind them. It was of little consequence anyway, arriving at the arena, where everyone quickly piled out. When the second wagon finally pulled in behind the first, Danny and Terry helped Bryan out and up to the stairway leading into the grandstands. Working their way up, Bryan looked back to see Terry motioning Caroline to move the wagons into the large concourse on the front side of the structure. He watched Caroline and her oldest son, back the wagons into the large access corridor that ran under the grandstands to the gated entrance of the arena itself. Once secure in

the corridor, Caroline herded the kids into one of the side rooms with
instructions not to try to leave until she came for them, and then had
them lock the door behind her. She could hear the fight going on
through the locked slatted gate at the far end and was tempted to
watch from there, but she wanted to be at her husband's side, so she
ducked into one of the many side halls that would take her to the
stands. Once on top, she found Terry and Danny setting Bryan
carefully down behind the royal box where Tim had already settled. Of
course, Catrina was ecstatic that her father had arrived moments
before the others and quickly apprised his daughter of the situation,
giving her the condensed version of what had happened, the most
pressing information being the use of the Twins. He couldn't
emphasize enough that under no circumstances should they be used
or Brit would suffer serious side effects. The bomb that Brit had
dropped on her earlier before the fight started, just became much
larger and more ominous, as did the intensity of the fight happening in
the ring below.

Fry pan or fire?

The Kenlar warrior believed that with the sword, he would be able to just chop Brit's stick into kindling and then he'd have him. Aiming at the stick, the shorter he could make it, the closer he could get to the Earth man. That was proving very difficult; the more he tried to chop at the stick, the more he got struck by it. To make matters worse, this stick had two ends and he seemed to be getting struck by both ends of it. The Kenlar concentrated, throwing a flurry of jabs and swings that was sure to intimidate and draw Brit's focus away.

Brit's attention could not be diverted, in his element now and swinging confidently, almost without effort. He wasn't trying to be arrogant or over confident, only to do whatever it took to keep that blade away from his body. He kept telling himself that the moment he relaxed or got too cocky, that's when he'd slip up. At the same time, he was feeling more confident with his abilities to command the fight. There was still one problem here, killing.

First, the staff wasn't designed or meant to take a life. It was really only meant to defend and stun an opponent. Not that, in the hands of a master, it couldn't do the job. A well trained assassin could use their fingers to complete their task if need be. Brit was good with the staff but far from being a master of it. The biggest problem had been the same from the outset. Like most of the human race on planet Earth, he held to the basic belief of, *"Thou shalt not kill."* To kill in your own defense was certainly acceptable. It was just that he had never faced death before, never been in the situation of, kill or be killed. Sure he had served in the military, but only in peace time. He had been an avionics expert, working on Air Force aircraft. Even in his basic training, that all military conscripts had to complete, he had a hard time with "kill" training. He had a deep love for life and taking it just wasn't something that he had ever had to do, or wanted to. He knew how he could do it with the staff if he had to; it was just getting to that point.

Brit glanced up at Catrina while the Kenlar paused a moment to rest and reset. He was surprised to see someone sitting in the box with her now. She was also surrounded by several others. After giving everyone a double take, he thought he recognized Captain Dallas sitting next to the Queen! There were a couple of individuals he didn't recognize, but then caught site of two figures huddled together on the seats directly above the royal box. He squinted a bit at them, keeping an eye on his attacker who was preparing to make another assault. It was his brother Bryan and friend Danny! They made it! They were here! *This fight is over!* Brit relaxed a bit and started to back away in the direction of the box. The Kenlar relaxed a little, watching him carefully, thinking he was trying to position himself in another location for a better angle of attack or defense. Brit watched him, a little confused with the situation now. Why wasn't someone stopping the fight? Captain Dallas and Bryan had returned from Crosslake. Someone lower a ladder or open the exit gates up, we're done here! Shuffling closer to the wall where the box was, he looked up at the Queen.

"Uhm," he said carefully, trying to keep his eyes on the Kenlar. "Why haven't you stopped the fight?"

"I can't stop the fight," Catrina informed him, leaning over the rail. "Not until it's over."

"But it's over," Brit objected. "Your dad is back. Nice to see you Captain Dallas," he said, looking up at him quickly and then back at his opponent who was starting to move towards him again. Tony gave him a nod and a short smile, but remained serious. He looked quite the sight. Dirty, bloody with scrapes and cuts all over his bedraggled person. Brit glanced over at Terry Lieder, who equaled the Thulsa Captain in appearance.

"The conditions were that they return before second sunup. They missed the deadline," Cat informed him warily. "The rules of engagement will not allow me to stop the fight once it has started. You must finish this."

"Well, that sucks!" Brit became angry. How had he misunderstood that part? What started as a joyful glimmer of hope had quickly sunk back to the harsh reality he had faced to begin with. He reaffirmed his grip on the staff, stepping back towards a now charging Kenlar warrior, who was yelling to bolster his swing and give everyone the impression that he was now going for the kill. It took Brit a moment to refocus and get back into the groove of the fight as the two weapons met and the staff slapped the side of the blade to deflect it away.

Brit had to get this figured out, and fast. It was only a matter of time before the warrior discovered a way around the staff. A well placed jab could either disarm him or worse. Something always seemed to go wrong with Brit's best laid plans. The Kenlar came at him again and again, trying to get at him, each time Brit struck back with opposing ends of the staff. In some instances, Brit would strike his opponent's hands or forearms and the warrior would lose his grip, dropping the sword, only to pick it back up quickly and keep coming at him. Several times Brit had actually laid the Kenlar out by knocking his feet out from under him, but the warrior was always quick to either roll away and back up or spring right back to his feet.

The two sparred for several minutes in this fashion, moving towards the other end of the arena where the slatted entry/exit gate was located. Battling around the Kenlar's weapons rack, Brit caught movement out of the corner of his eye, in the darkness of the concourse beyond the gate. Turning to get a better look, the Kenlar made a dive at him, plowing into Brit's vertical staff. He could hear the staff snapping in half, the two going down in a tangled. The jagged edges of one of the staff pieces jabbed into his left ribs, lodging splinters deep in his flesh, pain spiking around the wound. Trying to pull them free, he had to keep moving to stay clear of the Kenlar, who was scrambling to not only get back to his feet, but bring his sword back up to bear.

Now Brit was back to sticks, well a stick anyway. The other broken piece was in the dirt at the feet of the Kenlar and he certainly wasn't about to afford any advantage to the Earth man. He wanted release just as much as Brit. Once the Kenlar realized that the odds had shifted considerably, the attack was pressed even harder. Now, with just a stick, it would be like fighting with a long, stale loaf of bread; it wasn't going to last very long. Brit had to somehow maneuver his way around to the Kenlar's weapons rack and at least get a hold of something better than this piece of staff. However, the warrior was well aware of the predicament Brit now faced. He also knew he held most of the cards now. All he had to do was prevent Brit from getting his hands on another weapon and keep hitting his stick until he had it whittled away to nothing. It was only be a matter of time now.

Fighting to hold his opponent back, Brit tried his best to maneuver around to the rack, but the Kenlar pressed him hard in the other direction, forcing him around towards the entry gate. As Brit retreated, his foot struck something and he nearly lost his balance. He passed a quick glance down at his feet; the other half of the broken staff had surfaced. The warrior threw another set of swings and jabs at him. Taking a chance, Brit grabbed the Kenlar's sword arm at the wrist and pulled him in close, both men straining, face to face, trying to overpower the other. While Brit was a strong man, the Argyle clans were born and bred for the hard life of this planet and war. This warrior, while not as big as most of the others, certainly had him in strength, bending Brit backwards. Seeing that he was going to reach a very uncomfortable position in a matter of moments, Brit suddenly pulled back as hard as he could, setting the Kenlar off balance and sending them both back to the ground. This time Brit kept pulling and using their combined momentum, tossed the Kenlar over the top of him and flat on his back. The warrior lost his sword in the maneuver; but was quick to his feet and searching for it again.

Grabbing the other half of his staff, Brit sprang back up with both jagged edges at the ready. This time, Brit didn't wait for the warrior to rearm. Instead he came at him with quick whipping type swings that drove the Kenlar back towards the gate. Now the warrior was unarmed and completely helpless, backing up with nowhere to go. No weapon and no way to get one now, there was only one thing left to do here. Brit had him against the gate and at his mercy, but he could show him none. He had to finish him in any way possible. Both staff halves were jagged and sharp. More than enough to finish him here and now, but he hesitated. He did not want to take the life of this man, but knew he had to. He was not only securing his own release, but exacting justice on a killer. He pulled his arm back to strike and jab, but saw a flash of light reflect off something metal behind the gate. A second later an arm reached through the slates of the gate, wrapping around the Kenlar's neck. There was the sickening sound of metal and flesh coming together and the expression on the warrior's face suddenly changed. His eyes throwing wide and his mouth dropping open, he looked down at a blade that was protruding out the front of his abdomen.

Brit jumped back, the man just standing there in a death stare. There was a clamor behind the gate as the locks were released and the gate swung open with the Kenlar still pinned against it. A figure stepping part way out into the light, put a foot against the gate behind the Kenlar and pulled the sword free. It wasn't a particularly large sword, but it was very pretty and highly effective. As the blade left the pinned warrior's body, he fell to the ground next to the concourse opening, dead. Everyone in the stands came to their feet as Talon Thalar stepped into the ring flanked by two large Kenlar warriors.

Brit carefully stepped backwards towards the middle of the ring, Talon continuing to walk out into the open arena looking like he owned the place. Brit glanced back at the dead warrior by the open gate. *Ah, the fight is over now, right?* That was his hope, but something told him that he was far from being on his way home. In fact, it looked as though things might have just gotten a lot more complicated.

*   *   *   *   *

Terry and Tony had their swords drawn in an instant. Terry spun around, looking in all directions, to see if any other Kenlar had somehow breached the city defenses and had made their way into the arena stands, but he saw nothing. Tony stepped in front of Catrina, who held her place for the moment, as Talon and his two warriors continued to walk out to the middle of the arena. Talon acted quite unconcerned that he was in a killing arena in the heart of the city of Thulsa. He brazenly flaunted his twin swords, holstered in their scabbards like a western gun slinger. He had one hand on the hilt of a sword and the other held onto one of the long daggers holstered across his chest. Nearing the center of the ring, he pulled his helmet off, revealing his jet black hair. Surprisingly, it was not long or matted, but clean cut and well groomed. He looked over at Britten, who stood off from the three of them, about half way between them and his weapons rack. Turning back and facing the royal box, Talon bowed very politely, holding himself down. He had to motion to his warriors to bow with him, as they didn't look like they wanted to do anything but make trouble, and lots of it. Finally bowing a bit, they came right back up as soon as Talon had come back to attention. The Kenlar lieutenant smiled at the Queen of Thulsa. Catrina motioned for Tony to step aside so she could address this Kenlar henchman properly, as she could detect no immediate threat from Talon. Tim fumed at the brazenness of this murderous assassin. If he had had the means, he would kill him where he stood. There was no remorse or feeling from this man or his boss, something Tim knew all too well.

Talon was a born and bred viscous killer. Taught from his youth to be a ruthless killing machine, he wasn't even Kenlar. He had come to Crosslake early in his youth, from a clan far beyond any borders in the area of the Kenlar or Thulsa. He had found some kindred spirits among the Kenlar, helping orchestrate the assassination of the previous Kenlar ruler, who had no aspirations to make war on the other clans. This made it easy for Ivan, who had the superior strength, to easily take command. Now, Talon was but one step away from rule of his own. Perhaps Thulsa was the prize he had been waiting to conqueror. If this was indeed the case, he would still have to contend with the man who had facilitated his rise to his current station in the clan of Kenlar.

Tim's soul remained quite raw from the murder of his beloved Kawti and here was her murderer. The scene of Talon running her through with one of his swords was forever seared in his mind. He was livid to think that this killer had the audacity to just walk right into Thulsa and challenge the clan leadership directly. Something else had to be afoot here. Looking quickly around, he spotted a narrow access stair behind the royal box. It was used by the clan leadership for entry and exit when the stands were full. Seeing that Talon had not noticed him, he slipped silently into the narrow passage and out of sight. Getting his bearings beneath the grandstands, he became aware that he wasn't alone. Danny was helping Bryan down the narrow stairs after him.

"What the heck do you think you're doing?" Tim asked, as Bryan steadied himself against Danny.

"We could be asking you the same thing," Bryan responded tiredly.

"You don't look like you're in any condition to do anything about what's going on here," Tim pointed out, looking Bryan over carefully.

"By the way," Danny said, putting a hand out towards Tim. "You two haven't met. Tim, Bryan, Bryan, Tim."

"I've got skills," Bryan said, giving Tim a quick smile while trying to stand up straight. He was in no condition to be doing anything but lying in a hospital bed.

"I understood that you were dead," Tim said looking him over good.

"Only mostly dead," Bryan smiled weakly.

"Yeah, I can see your skills. Something is about to go down here," Tim said, heading to the eastern end of the hallway.

"What do you mean?" Danny asked, helping Bryan along.

"Talon doesn't just run off half-cocked into the heart of another clan's territory all by his lonesome, unless he had more to back him up than just a couple of goons. My bet is he's grandstanding for Ivan, creating a diversion or something." Tim peered around a corner towards an outside wall, looking for an opening.

While Bryan was in no condition to be running around in the tunnels of the arena complex, he was feeling better. He had taken more of the pain killer seeds Kingie had given him before they had entered the city. With Danny's help, he was able to move around fairly well, but he knew that was only temporary. They stopped short when Tim suddenly put his hand up behind him while peeking around another corner. He then turned back to them as they caught up to him. It was as Tim had expected. There were Kenlar troops making their way up the concourses to every entry and exit point in the arena.

"Trust Ivan to make a production out of a war," he whispered quietly, huddling with them. "We need to have a little backup here," he said, looking to them for ideas. All he got from Danny was a blank stare. "Well?" Tim asked, knowing that they probably had no idea.

"Sorry, I'm fresh out of troops," Danny finally responded, patting down his imaginary pockets. Bryan got a funny look on his face, looking over his shoulder thinking of where to find the help they needed.

"I've got an idea," he said, starting back towards the other hall that would likely lead them to the main concourse. "We need to find the wagons. They should be in the main passageway on the east side."

"What? You have some weapons hidden in there?" Danny asked, moving to help his friend along.

"Nope, something better."

Let's make a deal

Talon took a couple of steps forward and addressed the Queen, in Kenlar. Tony rolled his eyes and sat forward.

"English Talon, in English!"

Talon paused a moment, cleared his throat and started over again.

"Your Highness," he addressed her, flippantly waving a hand in front of him. "I bring you greetings from Ivan of the Kenlar."

"Yeah, yeah, yeah," Tony piped up angrily. "We know all about the little war party you have going on outside the east walls. State your business and then get back to your men."

"It's good to see that you made it over the Tera, Captain Dallas." Talon chuckled softly. "Not many can make that trail and live to tell the tail. I understand that you have done this several times. This makes you a little more valued than the rest of these worthless parasites." Talon acknowledged Catrina still sitting patently and wanted to give her the same fake respect. "As it does you too, your highness." Catrina remained seated. To rise and address a mortal enemy in this way would be a sign of respect and signal weakness on her part.

"Talon Thalar," Catrina responded, holding back in her chair. The idea here was to remain as nonchalant as possible. "Can I assume that you are here to deliver a message for your leader?"

"You assume correctly," Talon replied, smiling broadly.

"Then, by all means," Catrina said, remaining unmoved. "Please deliver your message and then return to your armies without our gates."

Talon bowed slightly.

"He would ask you for an audience to ask your father for your hand in marriage, that the great clans of Kenlar and Thulsa may be joined and further bloodshed between us, averted."

Tony put a hand to his tired eyes, rubbing them in frustration.

"How many times do we have to go through this?" he muttered, in amazement. Catrina gave her father a humored look and then turned back to Talon.

"Is there anything else you would like to add?" she asked him, still smiling.

Talon kept his smile broad and confident.

"Why yes, your highness, there is, come to mention it. Captain Dallas and a few of his friends paid their respects in Crosslake. While there, they sort of tore the place up and stole a couple of things. In consideration of the marriage proposal, his Lordship is willing to let things slide if he will return his property, no questions asked."

"His Lordship," Catrina repeated, turning to her father who mused disgustedly. "Calls himself Lordship now. And what property would that be?" she asked, giving her father another glance.

"A book called the Signet and the translator, Tim Hansen." Tony dropped his hand to his sword and opened his mouth to shout him down but Catrina stopped him with a raised finger. She had not had enough time to get a full report from her father since his arrival, but she had a pretty good idea of what probably went down.

"Do you see this Tim Hansen here?" she asked. Talon looked around but could not locate the translator in the stands. Before he could make something up, Catrina continued. "Do you see this Signet you have asked for?"

"It would be easy enough for Captain Dallas to hide them," Talon remarked, starting to get tired of the exchange. He'd rather just come in and get what he was after rather than have to put on a play of sorts. Nevertheless, he always did have a flair for the dramatic. He liked it, but then liked to get right down to business.

"And how would you know if he had? He only arrived here before you," Catrina came back quickly, catching him in his words.

Talon dipped his head a little, but kept his eyes on the Queen.

"All too true," he agreed, trying to avoid further conversation. "Will you comply?"

Catrina paused a moment, as if she were actually considering what Talon was laying out.

"You can tell, his *Lordship*, that neither I, nor the good people of the Thulsa clan have any interest in making an alliance with the Kenlar as long as he rules. I will not accept any marriage proposal. I will not return the Signet and I will not hand over Tim Hansen." Catrina ended on a very defiant, authoritative note.

Talon chuckled a bit, shuffling his feet in the dirt, then looking back up.

"Yes, his Lordship said you would say that. Almost to the word. Well done, well done," he repeated with a smirk. "Very well then. You can deal with him personally." Catrina came to her feet as Talon clasped his hands behind his back and waited. Looking all around the arena, she watched several figures appeared in almost every upper concourse entry/exit in the arena. *Ivan was here!*

*   *   *   *   *

Warriors of the Kenlar, armed to the teeth with crossbow rifles, thigh pistols, swords and daggers, now stood guarding any way in or out of the arena, effectively trapping everyone inside. With Thulsa's entire troops deployed at the eastern walls, there was no one here to contest this infiltration. The Queen, Council of Elders, and everyone else in the arena were now captives of the Kenlar. There were approximately twelve warriors now stationed around the arena. Since there were so few here to watch the original fight, everyone was on one side of the arena and the other side was empty. Some of the Kenlar warriors stood at the openings of concourses which were pitch black behind them. Others were stationed around the top walkway so that no one could move without them knowing it. They also had an unobstructed view of the immediate surrounding areas of the arena so they could see any Thulsian warriors approaching.

When all the warriors had taken up their assigned positions around the council elders and the royal box, a large figure stepped up onto the top tier of the arena and made his way down the stairs. Catrina and Tony remained facing the arena as Ivan Rubella stepped triumphantly to the royal box. He seemed to be favoring his left side, where Tim had stabbed him with the arrow. Stopping next to the royal box, he removed his battle helmet and faced them. He was armed with only one sword, but it would be enough for him. This sword was far different than the one he had at the Kenlar spoil in Crosslake. It was considerably larger, having a construction style somewhere between a straight knight's broad sword and a curved Asian sword. The lavishly decorated hilt was enormous, but Ivan had very large hands and the sword had been custom forged for him. Surely it would take two hands from the normal human just to lift it, let alone swing it with any degree of efficiency.

Tony slowly turned to the Kenlar leader with his sword still held up in defense of his Queen, his daughter. To his utter surprise, he found that the Kenlar tyrant had changed his personal appearance. He was clean shaven, except for a mustache and goatee. His hair had been cut short and was well groomed. He had different clothes on, nice clothes, well-fitting clothes, clothes that were befitting a warrior ruler. All designed to be battle dress and functional, but made to impress royalty as well. While there was still nothing about this man that Tony or Catrina liked, right now, he did look good.

Ivan motioned that he would like to enter the box and sit down. Tony was so stunned at his appearance that he just stood there with his sword only half up. Ivan finally stepped into the box and carefully around Tony to face the Queen, who was still looking down at Talon. After he had gotten himself comfortably in a seat, he looked over at Tony, who turned and slowly lowered his sword. Ivan could see Terry on the other side of the isle beside them; Caroline behind her sword wielding husband. The Kenlar Warlord gave a controlled snort and waved for them to relax and sit down.

"Please, gentlemen," he said loudly in his heavy Kenlar accent. "I know you're both exhausted. Put those things away and sit down before you fall down." Catrina remained unmoved, refusing to sit or even look at Ivan. Tony finally put his sword away, slowly sinking to the other seat in the box. Terry followed suit, but kept his hand on the hilt of his sword. After they had settled back down, silence fell on the arena as everyone just waited for the next move, whatever it was going to be. Ivan was pretty much in command at the moment and the only hold out, was Catrina. But, everyone, even Ivan, understood that she was Queen, and was afforded certain, unwritten rights and privileges, if nothing else, because she was a woman.

Catrina was livid, but scared spitless at the same time. No good could possibly come of this encounter, but she could see no way out of it. Deciding that she had made her point known as loud and clear as possible without words, she finally settled back down in her chair, holding her eyes fixed on Talon and the two warriors in the ring. She shifted her gaze over at Brit who was leaning against his weapons rack, still holding the pieces of his broken staff. Their eyes sending silent messages that everything would be all right, even though nothing could be further from the truth now.

"There, that's better," Ivan said, letting out a big sigh. "So, no doubt my boy Talon there has given you the details of my proposal," he said, leaning in Catrina's direction. "I didn't get to hear the response because I was making an entrance. So are we agreeable with the terms lassie?" Catrina remained silent, still looking straight ahead, not at Talon or Brit anymore, but just out at the other side of the empty arena. Ivan was a little befuddled, glancing back over at Tony, then out at Talon, then back at the Queen. He tried to stretch over in front of her to look her in the eyes, but got no response.

"I don't get it," he said, turning back to Tony. "Have I done something wrong here?"

"What do you think?" Tony responded, irritated that Ivan was playing games here. He knew that the Kenlar Warlord was expending a lot of energy to remain calm and collected. It was in his nature to be loud, arrogant and generally demanding what he wanted, when he wanted it. Actually, between Ivan's change in appearance and mannerisms, Tony was quite impressed that he would go to such lengths to present himself in this manner.

"I shaved, cut and combed my hair, *AND*, took a bath. I only take those every so often," he said, turning back to Tony for that comment. "I had my clothes washed and look!" he said, pulling his big sword up so they could see part of it. "I'm sporting my big fighting sword."

"Do you plan on using it?" Catrina finally spoke up coolly.

Ivan gave her a puzzled look and shrugged.

"I really hadn't planned on it, but I suppose if I needed to I could. Did you have something in mind lass?"

"Every time you come here, you end up using it," Catrina responded in a stately manner. She was gaining more confidence with the situation as time pressed on. "I was just wondering if you had plans for it now, or later, out at the eastern wall." Ivan got out of his chair, picked it up and turned it around to face the Queen and the Captain of Thulsa.

"I thought we might come to some kind of an understanding here," he said, sitting back down and trying to draw them both into his conversation. "It would be much nicer to avoid a very messy, bloody war. Messy business with the new machines and weapons I have, thanks to Tim. By the way," he said, looking around again. "Where is the man? He is to be thanked for all the nice toys we have out in your front yard." Ivan couldn't find him readily and really, he wasn't much a part of his plan right now.

"Anyway, I thought it would be much nicer if I came to the city first, so we could have a heart to heart chat before any of this war stuff got started. I was trying really hard to figure out how I could do this when your father here provided me with a simple solution. I like simple, don't you? Makes things, so- simple. So your father and his friends sneak into my spoil; gave me the tips on hygiene that you suggested, but then they mess with my men and kidnap Tim; steal my book and then run off. Oh, by the way, did I mention that Tim's wife Kawti got herself killed in the whole process? Did he tell you all about that? Messy business for sure." Ivan was starting to get a little more excited as he continued with his best laid plans. "Thankfully, your father provided me with the means to get in here so we could have this little chat. So he's to be commended for a job well done in showing us where the secret entrance to the city is." Ivan leaned back over to Tony. "Might want to have that tunnel checked out, I think something has died in there. Smells really bad," Ivan twisted a repulsed face. "So, here we all are and I've made it quite simple. We avoid most of the bloodshed for today by you agreeing to my simple terms. We all go to the East wall and announce our wedding vows to your men and mine." He leaned closer to Catrina who tried to keep her focus away from him. "My men REALLY want to see and hear about that lassie. Otherwise they are likely to come in here looking for me and chances are they won't be too careful about what's in their way, if you get my meaning." Catrina shifted her eyes to Ivan. He really did look infinitely better than he had before. Well groomed became him, but a pretty exterior did not make up for what was inside.

"And if I don't agree to your terms?" She had a fair idea what he had in mind. Ivan shrugged and smiled broadly.

"Well, let's just say that in my clan, we don't need council people." Catrina got the message loud and clear. He meant to systematically butcher everyone in this arena until he got what he wanted. There was but one thing to be done here, but she in no way wanted to do it. If she didn't agree to his demands, not only would he kill everyone here, probably one at a time so that everyone else could see what was coming, but also open up war on the Thulsa's armies from within the city. The blood bath would be intense. Under normal conditions, the Thulsa army could out class and out fight the Kenlar and Omar from the relative safety of the city walls. Nevertheless, he and the contingent of men here could wreak havoc with the Thulsa army positions from behind and possibly get the gates open leaving the city open to the Kenlar and Omar armies. She had no idea what these "new machines" he had were capable of. She really didn't want to chance it, but at the same time, she would rather be the first one to fall instead of others. Her only recourse was to save her beloved people and accept.

"Tell you what," Ivan said, pushing his chair back into position between Catrina and Tony. "I have a little time to kill here." He paused a moment, then laughed out loud. "Get it? Time to kill," he repeated, looking at Catrina, then Tony. They were not amused. "Ah, come on! Where's your sense of humor?" He looked at them again, hoping they would join him in making things a little lighter. Nope, it wasn't going to happen. "Why don't you think on it real good lass? In the meantime, what have we got going on down here? You know, before Talon got here, some games or something?" Ivan looked around in the arena for some other warriors, but saw only his men and a smaller squire of some kind. Maybe this was an animal keeper or something.

"Talon," he called out loudly. "You oaf! What are you doing down there man? These people were having a bit of sport and you messed it up?" Ivan looked back at Catrina. "I'm really sorry lassie. He is a hard one to handle sometimes."

Talon straightened up to answer.

"This one over here," he said, pointing towards Britten, who came to attention. He would rather have remained invisible and forgotten. "He was fighting Otto over there. Otto lost."

"Otto? That's where he went. You guys had him the whole time? He was a pretty good, ah, ah, scout," Ivan stuttered, knowing that he had sent him in as a spy and gotten caught. "So what was this one's offense that you put him up against Otto?" he asked, looking back at Catrina.

"Our laws are our affair. I'm asking you to please stay out of it," she requested quietly, trying to protect Brit. The rules of engagement didn't really cover this kind of situation, but the outcome could be argued in Brit's behalf. His opponent was dead and Brit was still standing. By all rights, he was free to go.

"Ok, so I don't need to know, doesn't matter. He killed one of my guys so I have to demand some satisfaction." Catrina sat up a little bit. This was not good; in fact this was very bad.

"What? What do you mean satisfaction? What are you talking about?" Panic instantly filled her.

"I'm talking about some pay back for my man down there in the dirt," Ivan came back with a chuckle.

"But this man didn't kill your man, Talon did," she objected, coming more and more alive.

"Wait a minute," Ivan turned back to his lieutenant. "Talon, did you kill Otto?" he asked, pointing to the lifeless body by the open gate.

"He was losing. This man had him pinned against the gate, ready to finish him. I was just making a statement, getting everyone's attention for you." Ivan turned back to Catrina who now had a worried look on her face.

"I'm really sorry about all this lass. I just can't leave him alone for one minute." Ivan turned back to Talon. "Do you not have any respect for the laws of the lands here man?" He turned back to Catrina. "Make sure I get this right lassie," he instructed, turning back to Talon. "The rules of engagement in the arena state that an opponent must kill the other in order to be released. Your guy didn't kill Otto, Talon did."

"But he had him, Talon said it himself," Catrina argued. Ivan held his hand up to silence her.

"If the people cannot fear the law, how are they going to be expected to follow it?" Ivan was a little more serious now. "Let's have another opponent for this man," he called out, looking around at the council. No one moved or made a noise.

"There are no other prisoners available," Catrina said, hoping that would pacify him. Doing things by the book wasn't in Ivan's plan though. He looked back at the Queen for a moment and then stood up.

"Who here will fight this man?" There was only silence. "Oh come on, someone here has to have the stomach for it. How about you Terry? No? Maybe Captain Dallas? No one? Very well, then maybe I will do it," he said, reaching for his sword but Talon stopped him.

"I'll do it. I feel responsible for this whole trouble, so I will pay." Talon motioned for his two warriors to depart the arena.

"Ah, finally someone with some balls," Ivan said, sitting back down. Catrina went into a near panic, looking at Brit, whose face had just gone white.

"Ivan," she put her hand on the Kenlar's huge arm. Just the touch made her entire body shiver and her skin crawl, but she forced herself to hang onto him, even squeeze him in as feminine a manner as she could muster. "Please, this isn't necessary. This man has paid for his crime. Please, no more bloodshed here."

Ivan responded to her pleadings and turned to look upon her. She was a true beauty and he wanted her for his own. With a little time and a lot of force on his part, he was sure that he could tame her.

"So, you've considered my proposal then?" Catrina hesitated, thinking of Britten and then her people. She was trying to out think the situation, but was having a little difficulty because of her emotion for Britten. She knew how good Talon was. He was a killer, born and bred. His entire being was dedicated to the art of killing. He was excellent in all disciplines as that it was what he devoted most of his time to. If he weren't in a battle or on a job somewhere as an assassin, he was honing not only his own art, but also watching others fight, learning how to pick a fight apart. He had learned how to kill slowly and painfully and took great pleasure in it. If she didn't agree to Ivan's demands, she would not only put her people at great peril, but she would also be condemning Britten to death at the hands of Talon.

"Yes." She finally said, lowering her eyes to her lap. She would rather sacrifice herself than watch the man she loved killed at the hands of this murderous butcher. Her heart sank deep within her, feeling her emotions starting to well within. Somehow she had to hold them down, as Ivan reveled in the first of his many "perceived" victories of the day.

"It's a great day for sure!" Ivan yelled, standing up and turning to the council elders. "Today will bring our great clans together and we'll all become even more powerful than any of the other clans of Argyle." Tony leaned over to his sullen daughter.

"Are you sure you want to do this?" he asked, not believing what was happening. How could things turn out so horribly? Moreover, they were only going to get worse. There was no way that he was going to survive under the rule of Ivan. Catrina was sure to eventually be killed. She held her eyes downward into her lap and nodded. Ivan didn't care about her as a person or a wonderful woman; he only saw her outward beauty. He was incapable of seeing her inner beauty and appreciating her for who she really was. There was only one man, besides her father that was capable of this right now, and he wasn't about to let this happen. Britten stepped out towards Talon, still holding his staff pieces.

"Uhm, excuse me, Mr. Ivan Rhubarb whatever, sir," Brit said, swallowing his fear. He had been sitting against his weapons rack listening to this man's big plans and had concluded that he was an idiot. When it became apparent as to what his terms were and how laughable they were, he was feeling a little more at ease. Something this stupid, while being an irritation, couldn't possibly succeed for very long. While things might get ugly, in the end, the smarter ideas win out. Then when Ivan got to the part where Catrina would have to agree to be his wife in exchange for his own wellbeing, well that sort of tore it for him and his fear fled. He had already asked Catrina to marry him and she had accepted. He'd be danged if he was just going to let some dumb buffoon step in and take her away. Ivan looked around when he heard Britten's voice, trying to find the source of the possible descent. Brit raised his hand, stepping further out into the arena.

"Down here sir," he waved. Catrina instantly brought her gaze back up to Britten. What was he up to? She had saved him and he had a better than average chance of getting away, if he were to just remain quiet. No, that wasn't about to happen. Ivan raised his fists to his hips, looking down at the Earth man.

"Ah, the squire who would be warrior," Ivan bellowed flippantly, wondering what this little man was up to.

"Yes, I'd like to join in on your little negotiations here, if I may." Britten was purposely being a smart-alec. He knew Ivan's type, even if he was from another world, big, brawly, bullies were the same on this planet as they were on his. He had plenty of experience with them growing up and learned early the basic formula for dealing with them. This one just might require a little more effort.

"Am I the only one here that believes this is a really stupid idea?" Brit tossed his defiant expression directly at Ivan. "For the stupid, dumb and dumber present today, I'm lodging a formal complaint here."

Ivan stared at him blankly. He didn't even understand what Brit had just said. The Kenlar ruler looked at him, then back at Catrina and around at Tony for some kind of guidance. Cat had a hopeful sparkle in her eyes, her man stepping up to her defense and protection. Tony had a look of horror mixed with prideful admiration. He hadn't been here to watch their love blossom, but it was quite apparent that Brit loved his daughter enough that he was willing to take on the Kenlar in her defense.

"What does he even mean?" Ivan asked, feeling a little embarrassed now. He wasn't sure what it was all about. He couldn't even imagine that this man would possibly be considering challenging his word.

"It means, that's my girl pal, and I'm not going to let you or anyone else take her, that's what it means," Brit said defiantly.

Ivan was stunned. Was someone really talking to him like this? He swirled to Catrina, who had her eyes glued on Britten in the arena. Ivan instantly became enraged, realizing what was going on between the queen and this peasant boy.

"You mean to tell me that you are already betrothed to this, this….this boy?"

"That's what it means," Brit spoke up, bringing Ivan's attention right back to him. Catrina's eyes welled, feeling Brit's devotion for her, but also because he was giving himself up for no good reason. Ivan would have him killed and then she'd have to marry Ivan anyway. Ivan turned back to Brit and went to yell at him, but caught himself, thinking of a better idea. He slowly sat back down and began tapping his fingers on the armrest of the chair.

"So what do you have in mind little man?" Ivan asked, calming down.

"Britten, my name is Britten."

"Ok, Britten," Ivan agreed, a little disgusted that he was being made to show a little respect to get to the bottom of this. "What is it that you have in mind?"

"Surely the Kenlar have laws that govern this kind of thing, what do they have to say?" Tony leaned forward and tried to wave Britten off from going there. In point of fact, the Kenlar did have laws, although Ivan rarely followed them. He only did so when it suited him. Ivan formed a puzzled look for a moment then turned to Tony.

"Do I have laws that govern this?"

"In fact you do," Catrina responded, holding her composure. "And it's no surprise that you don't know what they are."

"I make the rules as needed. Wouldn't want to set any kind of an example or anything," Ivan chuckled.

"What happened to your statement, if the people cannot fear the law, how are they going to be expected to follow it?" Brit piped up. Ivan gave the Earth man a mean look while Tony gave the comment a smirk.

"A man can contest a dispute over a woman by means of a duel. Either player can duel for themselves or have a proxy stand in to fight for them. The fight is to the death." Catrina stated, rattling off the long forgotten law that Ivan knew nothing about.

"Is that really a Kenlar law? You just made that up," Ivan accused her. Catrina gave him a challenging look that meant she was telling the truth. Exasperated, Ivan turned back to Britten. The warlord had the feeling that he was being backed into a corner or something. "Are you challenging me or what?" Ivan asked, a little surprised at Brit's moxie.

"That's exactly what I'm doing," Brit replied without hesitation. Ivan rubbed his chin and gave Brit a smirk. This seemed too simple to be believable. He could have Brit butchered and skinned inside of two minutes, even with the big sword he was sporting. There had to be a downside he wasn't aware of.

"Ok lit-, Britten. I accept. I expect that you will be representing yourself then?"

"I was counting on it," Brit came back quickly.

"Well you won't begrudge me if I bow out and have my representative stand in for me. I can't be stepping down from the royal box here and getting myself all dirty. All that ruler stuff you know." Ivan said deceptively. "Talon, you won't mind will you?" Talon saluted with a nod and a finger to the brim of his helmet as he put it back on, then stepped over to the opponent rack. It didn't matter to him who or why. He was going to fight either way and enjoy doing it. Ivan sat back with a look of glee painted all over his face.

"Oh boy, this is gonna be good. So, just to be clear, whoever wins, gets the girl," he said, looking over at Catrina, who was watching Britten make his preparations. Brit dropped his broken staff pieces and picked up the short sword that had been half buried in the dirt a couple of feet away from his rack. Setting everything back up on the rack, he became aware that Talon was approaching him from behind. He instantly pulled the short sword out, swirling around to defend himself. Talon had Tony's shield, the other short sword and the axe in his hands as he stepped up in front of him, holding them out.

"Here, you're going to need these."

Brit looked at them puzzled, then at Talon.

"What about you?" he asked, wondering what this man was up to.

"I always come prepared," Talon said, putting his hands to his sword and dagger belts. He turned to go back to his rack, but stopped, turning back to Britten.

"I have to say, I admire your salt sir, but this can't turn out very good for you," Talon said, looking straight at Brit.

"You're so sure of that," Brit replied, trying to sound confident.

"I am Talon Thalar. Killing is what I do. It is all I have ever known. The man who takes me down cannot be of this world, or his skills. But let me make this perfectly clear and you can take peace in this. Unlike Ivan up there, I always fight fair. I have no reason to cheat. There is no sport or honor in cheating. But so long as you know as well, I will show you no mercy and I would hope that if the situation presents itself that you would do the same." With that, Talon turned back to his side of the arena and readied himself.

Out classed

Brit turned back to his rack, setting up the weapons that Talon had just left him, thinking not just about what he had said, but how he had said it. *"I always fight fair." Was he really that good that he had no reason to cheat? Would he really not fight fair if he were getting beaten?* With Talon's skill set, the thinking here might be that if he were getting beat, he deserved whatever he got and was not worthy to remain alive. Brit bumped the Twins and looked at them. Turning his gaze up to the royal box, he could see Catrina sitting forward in her chair, her hands to her mouth, trying to hold herself together. He could read the worried look waving through her expression. Looking back down at the swords, he could sense their light buzzing, but ignored them. The cost for their use was too great. Brit had a strategy all thought out though. He could occupy Talon the same way he had Otto. Wear him down with the staff, then work him into an impossible situation and then finish it. It was simple and made perfect sense to him, besides, it was the only thing he could come up with. It had worked at the Ririe tournaments back home on Earth, why not here?

Brit picked up the good staff, running his hands along the long stout rod. It was smooth, clean and felt good in his hands. This weapon had been a good friend to him through all his training and he felt the most confidence when using it. Now, more than ever, he would have to rely on it to lead him to his freedom. He dared not use the Twins unless it was absolutely necessary.

"Let's get on with it then!" Ivan bellowed from above, raising his hands up high. Catrina flinched a little, thinking that he might accidently strike her in his enthusiasm.

Brit turned to see Talon pulling one of his swords out and facing him. It was a medium length straight sword with a shiny, slender blade, kept honed to a razor sharp edge on both sides. Talon bowed slowly, and then started his advance towards Britten like he was casually walking over to have another conversation with him. But talking wasn't what he had in mind. Brit steadied himself. While he was still scared to death, he had a little better idea what to do with the advance of an opponent. He casually twirled his staff, standing sideways of Talon's approach, watching him come towards him. When he could see Talon start to flex back to strike, Brit came alive with the staff in front of him, knocking the swing away.

Brit swung with lightning precision at Talon, but the Kenlar Lieutenant spun away, bringing his blade around him and lopping off a small piece of Brit's staff. Unlike the short swords given each combatant earlier, this blade was razor sharp on both edges and could slice through just about anything. Brit evened up on the staff and kicked himself mentally for falling for that one. He had tried to get fancy, forgetting that these staffs were just wooden after all and couldn't withstand the force of a razor edge. He would have to use his attacks in such a way as to protect the staff as much as possible. He swung again, this time aiming at Talon's wrists. This actually worked pretty well for a while, using the rod to strike against the flat part of the blade, either right on the top of his hand or slapping at the hilt knocking off its trajectory. Several times, Talon recoiled back with the sting of the staff on his wrist.

For several minutes the two sparred nimbly all around the middle of the arena. While Brit's staff was starting to get gnarled up a bit by Talon's constant swipes, it was doing the job and so far, things were moving along about as well as Britten could have hoped for. Feeling more at ease in the fight, Brit found himself doing more expert moves to try and disarm his opponent, including body spins and reversals behind his back. The intent was to keep Talon off guard if he was trying to follow any kind of a pattern, but Brit discovered that his moves didn't work well more than a couple of times. It seemed as though Talon was able to analyze his style and technic, figuring out the best way to counteract them. It was all good anyway as Brit didn't have any set moves. He was just throwing at Talon, whatever came to mind and when the opportunity presented itself. For several more minutes they sparred around the arena, working their way back and forth. First Brit would be backing Talon up towards his own rack, and then Talon would be forcing Brit back towards the wall right below the royal box. Those on the first row in the stands had to stand up and look over the rail in order to watch the action. At length, Brit and Talon came together, locking up, eye to eye.

"You are excellent with the staff," Talon puffed. He had grossly underestimated his foe's abilities to fight. Brit smiled, feeling his own confidence and holding Talon in place. "I shall have to practice more with it." Talon continued.

"You mean you don't practice the staff art?" Brit asked, breathing hard himself.

"Certainly I do, but clearly not as much as I should have. There are very few that I deal with that use a staff. It is a wonderful weapon, but no one has the time to fight with it. But I have to say I grow tired of getting my hands slapped by it," he said, giving Brit a good shove backwards.

The move threw him straight to the ground, but turning it quickly into a somersault, he sprang back to his feet as if it were a part of an escape maneuver. Coming back up, Talon was right there swinging with a lightning move. Brit twisted hard letting the staff carry him around. Talon missed but took a hit to the shoulder as Brit's staff whirled in a blur. Talon spun away in pain, letting his sword swing around as well, the blade slicing through another larger section of staff. Feeling the piece let go as he spun, Brit let the rod slide through his hands till he was holding onto the end of it. Letting his hands clamp around the shorter stick, he allowed its momentum to build back up, finding its mark against the side of Talon's helmet. A loud clang and Talon staggered sideways, dropping his sword and falling back into the dirt. Brit saw him reaching for something on his chest as he went down knowing what was coming. Dropping to one knee, he let go of the staff, spinning back around with Tony's shield in front of him. Coming back up, Talon launched both of his daggers at Brit with pinpoint accuracy. Both blades buried themselves deep into the Onark wood. As the Onark wood was extremely hard, it would take quite a bit of effort to dislodge them.

Eyes wide, Brit looked over the shield at Talon.   The Kenlar was getting up, sword in hand, to come at him again. He slid his arm into the handles of the shield and picked his staff back up. Only now it was more like a long battle stick. It was better than nothing. He didn't have the time to turn and make a calculated selection from his armaments. He'd have to work Talon around his own rack in order to get something else. The axe would be useless, and probably get him into more trouble. There was the short sword, but that would put him in too close a proximity with a sword expert. He felt like he had done pretty well with the staff, considering who he was fighting. He still wasn't sure the Kenlar assassin wasn't just being easy on him. So far, the only one who had any strikes on him was Talon.

The two went at it again, only this time; Brit found himself using the shield more as Talon whittled down what was left of his staff. Finally, Brit had no choice but to grab the short sword. Talon could tell almost instantly that his opponent wasn't very good with the sword, so he slowed down a bit and relaxed more. Now he could pick this man apart and finish it. He started using fancier moves, some of them almost whimsical, while Brit struggled to defend. In his training he had not used a shield. Hans and Catrina had purposely done this so he could learn defending with the sword and not rely on the shield. Here now, he had an added tool that he could use with the sword. There really wasn't much skill required to use a shield effectively. Just hold it up in front of you when your opponent's weapon comes at you. The trick here was to not rely on it for your sole support. You might end up fighting all day. Of course Talon wasn't about to let that happen. While he seemed to be enjoying himself, almost mocking Brit, he used expert moves to chink into Brit's defenses. Starting to feel more frustrated at his situation, Brit began to come out from behind the shield to better strike at the Kenlar. He was tiring fast now and his forearm where Otto had struck him was hurting badly. The strategy to wear Talon down and finish him off had not worked like he had hoped. It seemed as though everything had worked in reverse, Brit quickly approaching exhaustion.

Catrina could see that Brit was in trouble now, Talon continually pushing him back using relatively basic moves. Brit was trying to come out from behind the shield, but every time he did so, he about got something chopped off. If it weren't for Tony's shield, he would have been dead by now. Cat found herself biting her nails, leaning anxiously forward with every strike that came at Britten. It quickly got to the point where he could hardly even hold the shield up, let alone return any kind of a jab or swing. At one point, they both came together, Talon holding onto Brit's shield so that he could talk to him.

"You're about out of options here Britten. You are tired and do not fight well with the sword. You are admirable with the staff, but not master enough to defeat me with it. Have you got nothing else but this shield to save you?" Talon was being a little smug, but at the same time, recognized a valiant effort when he saw it.

"Not really," Brit puffed heavily. "I only started training a couple of days ago."

"Hmmmm," Talon's expression changed to a little surprise mixed with frustration on his part. If this man had just started training only a couple of days ago and Talon was having this much trouble doing away with him, how did that reflect on his own abilities? He was up against a beginner and having this much of a problem with him? Maybe he ought to hand Brit his sword and he should take the shield.

"Let me show you how this can be done in five minutes or less," Talon growled lowly, pitching Britten backwards and spinning his sword in his hand to reset his grip. Brit went down again, but could only roll to his side, having no energy to somersault back to his feet. He somehow kept a hold of his sword and scrambled back up. He knew he was in trouble now, seeing the renewed look of determination in Talon's eyes. Even Tony's shield wouldn't be able to protect him much longer.

Talon came at him like a man possessed now, striking with blows that hurt even with the shield covering Brit's arm. There was almost no point to Brit holding onto the short sword. Occasionally he was able to strike out, but Talon no longer paid any swing he made any heed, as it usually never got anywhere even close. Britten sprawled backwards as Talon landed another blow. Trying to regain his balance, his arms began to flail, leaving himself exposed and Talon seized on the opportunity. He let his sword slash diagonally across the left side of Brit's chest. It wasn't a deep cut, but it stung instantly, as he was sweating and the perspiration seeped in quickly. Brit put his right hand to his chest, the pain enveloping him and before he could maneuver, Talon rammed the hilt side of his sword squarely in his face. The blow was so hard that it knocked Brit squarely onto his back, partially knocking the wind out of him. Somehow, he managed to roll away, but lost his sword. Just as well, it was more of a hindrance than anything else. He could sense Talon continuing his advance, feeling in the dirt for something he had struck when he went down. He let go of the shield and rolled over as Talon stepped to one side of him to deliver a fatal blow, but before he could, Brit brought two broken pieces of staff up out of the dirt landing savage hits, as hard as he could plant them, on the back of Talon's calves. Talon went down in a crash of excruciating pain, but somehow managed to hang on to his sword. Brit got to his knees and swung one of the pieces at Talon, striking him across the face with the jagged edge of the staff. He tried to land another blow with the other piece, but Talon was able to deflect the strike with his sword and bringing his leg up, kicked Brit in the temple, sending him rolling away.

Talon slowly got to his knees, his face bleeding from a large gash across his left cheek and upper lip. A bit dazed, it would take a little time to recover from the painful blows to his lower calves. He staggered to his feet, watching Brit crawling slowly towards the end of his weapons rack. He was completely defenseless now, bleeding from his nose and mouth. Exhausted, he struggled to reach the rack before Talon could start his unyielding advance on him. He had to get to his feet or he might as well roll over and let Talon finish him. Reaching the rack, he used it to steady himself, getting to his feet, watching Talon go mobile in his direction. He felt dizzy, sick and without any energy now. His legs shaking with exhaustion. Even if he could pick up a weapon, it couldn't rebut any of Talon's swings and Talon knew it. Brit tried to rest against the end of the rack, feeling a lite buzzing enter into his head as his hands came in contact with something metal. He looked down at the Twins dangling right where he had left them, on the end of the rack. If there was ever a time that these were absolutely necessary, this was it. He had time to pull one from its sheath as Talon came at him. The blue glow startled the Kenlar Lieutenant at first, but it did not stop him. There was no time for Brit to reach for the other twin as Talon let his blade fly at him. The two swords met at an angle, with a beautiful clang that resonated through the whole arena bringing everyone but Ivan to their feet.

Catrina didn't have any fingernails left. She knew what Brit must be going through down there. There were times when you fight so hard that suddenly you can barely stand. She could see that Brit was completely spent and there was only one thing left for him to do. It was just a matter of if he could make it happen now. Tony glanced over at Terry who returned a worried look to his Captain. The Twins were for the Ancients to use. Humans could not withstand their power.

Even the Kenlar warriors all around the arena had become engrossed in the action below. Many of them setting their crossbow rifles down but remained standing, occasionally looking back out at the outer grounds of the arena. A larger group of Kenlar warriors had taken up positions around the outside of the arena in case any Thulsian warriors were to happen by. All of them were oblivious to what was happening under their feet in the tunnels and concourses.

Even the odds

As Bryan led Danny and Tim to the main concourse, he suddenly slowed, then pressed himself against the wall, holding an arm out for the others to do that same. Danny became a little irritated, wanting to see what the sudden stealth mode was all about, but Bryan held him back flat against the dark walls.

"What's with all this James Bond crap?" he asked in a not so whispered voice. Bryan's hand was quick to clamp over his friend's mouth while he brought his finger up to his lips. All three pressed themselves against the wall and looked towards the hall opening into the main concourse as one of Talon's warriors slowly shuffled past. Once Bryan was sure he was gone, he dropped his hand from Danny's mouth, motioning for them to stay close. Peering carefully around the corner, he could see that there were two warriors now, standing inside the slatted gate of the arena, engrossed in watching Talon and Brit spar. Bryan turned back to Danny and Tim. He still wasn't feeling well. His ribs and something else inside still hurt like thunder, but there was a job to be done here. Unfortunately for the three of them, it didn't include these two warriors.

"Ok, this will be a piece of cake," Bryan said in a quiet whisper.

"Oh good, I like cake. What's gonna be a piece of cake?" Danny asked, trying to look around the corner. Tim gave the Garrett brother an apprehensive look. Bryan peered around the corner again, focusing on what they were carrying for armament. It was standard Kenlar issue. A large quiver of arrows for the crossbow rifle they each had strapped across their backs, and a small quiver with short black arrows for the pistols that were strapped around their legs, just below the knees. Also in view, was a sword sheathed on each hip. These two had helmets with various sized animal horns adorning them. This should be easier than disarming the Omar in the Torres. The whole trick was to not be heard, seen or felt.

"So how are you going to take those two out?" Tim asked, trying to size up the situation.

"I'm not going to take either of them out," Bryan announced, still whispering. "You two are." Tim and Danny looked at each other, perplexed looks flashing across their faces at the same time. Bryan was certainly in no condition to try and pull off his Omar maneuver. He needed a medical coma to give him time to properly recover from his injuries. No, these two would have to try and duplicate what he had done yesterday. Tim didn't like it but could see that Bryan was right. Danny just plain didn't like it and let his feelings be known.

"I'd like to point out here that my vote is to offer them food. Maybe some cake?"

"Food?" Bryan repeated, looking at his friend. "Really?"

"Yeah," Danny said, laying out his alternate plan. "We offer them cake. The way to a man's heart is with a good cake." In truth Danny had nothing. He just didn't want to get into another scrap. He was *SO* done with fighting for his life. He was all about just getting home.

"That's the dumbest thing I have ever heard," Bryan said, a little angry at his friend's light mindedness. This life and death struggle was serious business.

Just then they could hear the clang of a sword and looking back around the corner beyond the warriors and into the arena, they could see Brit fighting for his life against a superior Talon Thalar. Danny leaned back against the wall in the darkness and thought a moment. Think too long and he would talk himself out of it, maybe. He looked over at Tim who was mulling it over in his head as to how this was going to happen.

"Do we have to kill them?" Danny asked quietly.

"Kill them now or contend with them later on," Tim whispered back.

"This is war," Bryan cut in sharply. "You either kill or be killed. Those two aren't going to want to sit down and have tea and crumpets with you to discuss the matter. They will not hesitate to shoot first and ask questions later." Bryan was getting a little incensed at Danny's attitude. You would have thought that with all they had gone through in the last couple of days, he would have been hardened to the facts they all faced.

Danny was a little shocked, but realized that they were still on Argyle, in Thulsa, and still fighting for their lives. Just because they were together again didn't change their circumstance. Apparently Bryan had to kill to survive his adventure and Brit was out in the arena fighting for his life right now. He and Jerry had had to fight for their lives to make it back this far. Life isn't fair and sometimes you don't always make it, a testament to Jerry's absence now.

"You'll have to creep on your hands and knees," Bryan whispered, backing out of the way so they could look at what he was talking about. "Do you understand what I'm talking about when I say creep?"

"To creep," Danny said mechanically, looking at where they were going to have to go, "to move with your body close to the ground. To move slowly and stealthy."

"Thank you for that, Webster," Bryan nodded. Danny only saluted.

"Both of you together," Bryan continued. "You can't make a sound and you have to move together. Gently pull their outer pistols. Don't touch the inner ones. They come out just as easy, but they are in their line of vision and might attract attention to you. Then pull back to a safe distance and fire. You must aim at the base of the skull so they don't make any noise. You will have to catch them before they fall and pull them backwards."

"Would you like any sauce with that?" Danny complained, checking the list that Bryan had just rattled off. "What if the arrows don't fly straight? They are pistols after all."

"These won't miss," Tim reassured him. "They are as accurate as the bow rifles they have. Just make sure your aim is right on."

"Get to it boys," Bryan coaxed them out into the main passageway.

Danny was scared to death, feeling his heart pounding a million miles an hour. Crawling past the lead wagon and horse parked in the passage, he was sure that Tim had to be feeling the same thing. Even though there was a fight going on out in the arena and there was external noise coming from that direction, they still moved slowly, doing their best to remain right in stride with the other. Fortunately, the loose dirt was a couple of inches deep, muffling any sounds in the passage. Approaching silent, Danny could still see Brit out in the arena fighting Talon. It didn't appear that he was doing well. This seemed to help make the justification needed to do what had to be done here. He glanced over at Tim and nodded, both reaching for the outer pistols on each warrior standing above them.

While the pistols were held in place fairly well, it was surprising how easy it was to lift them out without making a sound or arousing the two men to their presence.   Danny glanced over at Tim, backing away together, making sure that they were in complete synchronization. Pulling back about six feet and coming up on their knees, then took aim. The warrior's helmets were bowl shaped and the bases of their skulls clearly visible. Danny muttered a silent prayer, making sure he asked for forgiveness for the life he was about to take, counted in sync with Tim and pulled the trigger. The small black arrows instantly found their marks, piercing deeply into their targets. No sooner had the arrows struck than Danny and Tim were on their feet catching the dead men. Danny collapsed under the weight of his, trying to pull him backwards. The warrior was even bigger than he had thought and quickly found himself pinned under dead weight.

"A little help here," he grunted, quietly trying to free himself from under the corpse. Tim shook his head; chuckling a little and helping Danny get free, then pulling the bodies back out of sight.

As Danny and Tim gathered up their new stash of weapons, Bryan glanced out into the arena through the slatted gate. Brit was having a real go of it. They would have to work fast if they were going to have any kind of a chance of saving everyone else from Ivan and his men.

"Ok, so we have some pretty good firepower here, but it isn't nearly enough," Tim said, examining the crossbow pistols and rifles. Danny was looking at the small quiver of pistol arrows and poking himself in the finger with one.

"Ouch!" he exclaimed. They turned out to be a lot sharper than he thought it would be.

"Yeah," Bryan said, turning for the door on the other side of the hallway. He had to step between the two wagons Caroline had parked here to get to the door. "Those things are used to kill. It's a pretty good bet they're sharp." Bryan could hear familiar voices coming from behind a locked door on the other side of the passage, realizing that Caroline's children were inside. This was exactly what he had been thinking of when they had first come down here. Overpowering the Kenlar warriors was just an added bonus. Tim looked after him, and then glanced out through the gate into the arena.

"We'll have to disarm every warrior up there if we're to gain the upper hand." He put a quiver of rifle arrows over his shoulder.

Danny worked on getting a quiver of pistol arrows around his hip as Bryan quietly knocked on the door. He was met with silence and had to knock several times before there was any indication that there was anyone in the room. After a little convincing of who he was, they unlocked the door and nearly mauled him as he came in. They were all very worried and very glad to see him, especially little Anna, who proceeded to scold him for something that he had or hadn't done. Once he got them all calmed down and reassured them that everything was just fine, he brought the four oldest out and told the rest to remain quiet until he or their parents came back for them. Instructing them to lock the door again, he pulled the door shut and listened to them work the lock. Tim stepped over to the small crowd with a perplexed look. He was hoping Bryan had something else in mind here.

"What are you doing?" He asked the Garrett brother handing the oldest a Kenlar long sword.

"Where there are two Kenlars with weapons, there are bunches more." Bryan responded, wishing he could just lie down in the back of one of the wagons they had come in on. "We'll have to work very fast and quiet."

"We?" Tim objected, more certain of what Bryan had in mind now. "Whose we?" Bryan stopped, looking back at Tim.

"If we don't get those weapons and stop what's going on out there," he said, pointing to the arena. "These kids are as good as dead anyway. This is the only way. Besides, I've seen these kids at work. If you had anything in your pockets, they would be handing it back to you right now." Bryan had a point. Tim watched them follow Bryan back up the side hallway.

"Now, we're not going to be able to completely disarm them," Bryan said, directing Tim and Danny to each take one of the youth with them to the different placements all around the arena, "but you should be able to get a hold of their pistols the same way you two did, without them knowing it."

"Are you sure?" Danny asked skeptically, looking at the Lieder kids. At Bryan's nod, he turned for a ramp to the back of the upper seating area with one of the kids in tow.

"Pretty sure," Bryan muttered, splitting off from Tim and heading in his own direction up a set of stairs towards the upper seating. He thought of his crazy skirmish against the Omar warriors in the Torres with Jocko. Yes, he was sure they could do it, even easier this time. In actuality, they were surprised at just how easy it was for the young teens to creep up from below the watching warriors, gently pull the pistols from their calf holsters, and then retreat into the darkness without being detected. In a few instances, they were even able to take a bow rifle as it was just leaning against the wall next to where the warriors were standing. Once their weapons cache had been added upon, they all met under the arena to ready their game plan.

A fair fight

Talon shoved Britten back, knocking him to the ground.

"That's a very pretty sword." Talon was still favoring his bruised calves and gazing at the glowing short sword's blade. "Where did you get it?" Brit slowly got back to his feet, leaning over a bit trying to catch his breath and get as much rest as he could. It didn't help that he was hurting something awful from the injuries Talon had inflicted.

"Picked them up in the Winner's Spoil," Brit wiped the blood away from his nose and mouth, looking up at Talon who now stood next to his rack. He hoped to keep the monolog going, providing more of an opportunity for rest. Talon looked down at the other sword hanging on the rack, then reached and pulled it from its scabbard, gazing at its blue glow.

"That's sort of how I got here," Brit continued, thinking back to several days ago. Seemed like forever ago now. If only he had known then what he knew now.

"Ah," Talon said, knowing the Thulsian law regarding trespassers of the spoil. The Kenlar had a similar law. "You got caught with your hand in the honey pot, eh?"

"We call them cookie jars where I come from," Brit commented, trying to be funny.

"You won't mind if I have these when we're through here then?" Talon asked confidently. "In fact," he said, flipping the sword in his hand so that he was holding the blade. "Why don't we make this a little more interesting? Maybe a little more of a challenge for me, if you think you're up to it?" Talon tossed the sword hilt first to Brit's feet. He then pulled his other sword out and proceeded to twirl them in his hands.

Brit looked at the other Twin in the dirt and then at the one in his hand. Yes, this would certainly be quite interesting. He looked up at Catrina, who stood silent with both fists under her chin. *This was it!* **It was absolutely necessary!**

"OK, we'll give it a shot," he finally said, reaching for the sword. Talon readied himself, a wicked smile slathered all across his face. He didn't get to use both swords at the same time very often. However, he was more than ready to use them for this. This is what he practiced and honed his skill for the most. Dual sword play was what he craved more than anything else. This is where he performed at his best. Alas, he knew this would be short lived.

As Brit picked up the sword, he could instantly feel the buzzing in his head and something energizing in his hands. Still feeling very weak, he managed to stand up straight, delighting Talon even more. Steadying himself, he felt the electricity tingling in his hands and starting to work its way up his arms towards his shoulders and the back of his head.

"By the way," Talon asked, twirling his blades again and stepping towards him, "where are you from?" Brit could feel the download starting and his exhausted limbs suddenly coming alive.

"A planet called Earth."

"Another planet?" Talon asked, a bit taken aback by the revelation. Brit twirled the Twins and firmed up his grip, sensing exactly what had to be done. It was all clear in his mind. It would be easier than breathing.

"Here it comes," he said, launching himself and the Twins at the Kenlar Lieutenant.

*　　*　　*　　*　　*

It took Talon several moments to figure out what had just hit him. The explosion of blades coming at him was astonishing. He was barely able to counter them as things grew to a blur. Yes, Talon was certainly capable of fighting like this, but he wasn't expecting this level of expertise from this opponent. It was inconceivable that Britten was able to do what he was doing with these blades. He had barely been able to defend himself in a basic manner with the single short sword. Now, here he was using two blades as a master would. On top of that, before Brit had picked up these glowing swords, he was nearly finished. Talon was able to read his exhausted body language. This Earth man had transformed into something completely opposite of what he was only a few moments ago. There were only two possibilities that could even be considered for an explanation. Either Talon had been played for the fool all along, tricked into believing that Britten could not fight, or there was something magical about these fantastic weapons he was clashing with.

There was little to no time to think about it now. Talon had to expend all his concentration on his own defense. The fury of blade against blade was mind boggling. They stood, swinging and jabbing, as if they were mechanical robots of some kind. Talon watched Brit's expression transform from that of fear and exhaustion, to power and confidence. The change was unnatural in a very spooky sort of way.

Brit could feel the energy pulsing through him now. His arms moving in perfect mechanics, swinging and deflecting with little effort. A great tingle of excitement raced through him that was almost impossible to contain. An uncontrollable urge to start laughing tried to envelop him. It felt like his senses were being amplified, racing through his very soul. Every emotion that he had ever experienced was recalled individually and intensified. There was so much

449

information running through his head right now that he could scarcely keep track of it. It was a wonder he was able to fight, but it all seemed to come automatically. He felt as if he was driving a super race car, only to discover that he wasn't actually driving it, merely experiencing the thrill of it.

His mind whirled and in only a moment, he was transported to other places. He looked up to the moons of Argyle, suddenly finding himself traveling through space at faster than the speed of light. The sensation of traveling at this speed was astounding to his very soul. He had the ability to go anywhere now and see anything he wanted. He could look out into the vastness of the universe and witness the glory of the fabric of existence. Take the brightest and most colorful images of the Aurora Borealis, combine it with color photos taken by the space telescopes of the infinite galaxies, Quasars and Nebula in the known universe and you might come to a fraction of the splendor and glory that could only be orchestrated and kept in its delicate balance by an omnipotent Being. So many things to see, to do, to experience. He knew that all he had to do was think of it and he could go there. He had no idea where all this information was coming from or where it could ultimately lead him. He just knew that it was amazing and that he didn't want it to stop. He wanted to go on forever and explore everywhere, see and do everything. Now he could see the people who had forged these swords. A delightful people, who existed on multiple planes of existence now, traveling the universe, constantly learning and imparting of their wisdom to cultures in need. He saw what the Twins had been created for and how they were used. Not as weapons, though they certainly worked as such, but as storage devices of the Ancient's knowledge and wisdom. The Twins could control the Rift through the altar, where it could open doors to other places and to any time frame in that place. He could see the internal workings of the gate altar and the virtual controls associated with using the Twins to operate it. Opening a portal through the Rift was only a fraction of the capabilities, no, possibilities, which were afforded the Twins. There was so much more that the Twins could do; things he could scarcely comprehend. However, he could also see that their power could be overwhelming, especially to beings as frail as humans. Without absolute command and control of their energy and the informational download, there is a terrible price the human body would have to pay.

He turned, looking all around him at the cosmos expanding before him, hearing a voice calling to him. Everything had become muted, being carried away in this vast sea of information. No sound of swords clashing, no cheering crowd, no shouts from Ivan, but this voice was still as clear as if she were standing right there next to him. He turned back to look at Argyle and her moons, but Catrina's image obscured everything. He turned again, looking back out at the molty array mixing before him, forming the grand cosmos to which there was no end. Surely this was where the Ancients had gone. The colors were intensely beautiful, calling to him, beckoning him to come and explore, but Catrina's voice called to him from the other direction. She called to him to take command. He gazed back at the infinite universe, realizing that he was not ready; mankind was not ready. If he were to go in the direction the information could take him, he would never come back and he would never be with or see Catrina ever again. He suddenly thought of Amanda and Tony. They were two that could not live without each other, somehow they had held onto their bond, a bond that could not be broken. What they had was timeless and the ultimate gift that two people can share, something that most couples struggle to achieve and hang on to. The cosmos would be just as empty as any void for Brit, without Catrina. Indeed, he had found the woman that he could not live without. He turned back to her image, and in an instant, he was once again back in the arena with Talon, swords clashing.

The look on Talon's face was that of frustration mixed with worry. He could not keep this up for very long; something had to change. Brit gave the royal box a glance. Ivan was on his feet now with both fists shaking at the two fighters, roaring his encouragement to his lieutenant. Beside him, Cat stood with her hands glued to the rail yelling at him. Tony, Terry and Caroline had also come to the rail and were yelling. He could feel his arms and hands now. He was in control! He was here now because he wanted to be here, not lost in the infinite knowledge of the universe, but right here, fighting for the right to be with the one he loved, the one he could not be without. Brit looked past his blades at Talon who was absolutely focused on the fight. He had no real beef with this man, but he also knew that his opponent would not hesitate to run Brit through given the chance now. He was also sure that Talon could not live with himself if Britten were to stop and disarm him. No, the only way forward, was ultimate defeat.

Brit spun suddenly, bringing his blades back up with lightning precision against Talon's, who shifted with his move. Talon seemed to be a bit relieved the toe to toe business had been broken and they were on the move again. There was nothing to analyze just standing there swinging and jabbing. Now he at least felt like he was doing something besides hitting a rock wall repeatedly. Using moves on Britten that should divert his attention and provide him a way to put the screws to the Earth man, Talon began to relax a little more. Brit could sense what he was trying to do, and instead of countering, let Talon move him about, little by little drawing the Kenlar into him, lulling him into a false sense of superiority.

"You are exquisite," Talon puffed, keeping his eyes on Brit's arms as he swung. "I have never seen or fought a more worthy opponent." Brit smiled, crossing both his blades with Talon's.

"You're not too bad yourself. It's too bad this has to end."

"Yes," Talon agreed, spinning, brining one sword back up and remaining low with the other one. Brit deflected the higher swing with both Twins and jumped in place, letting Talon's lower swing pass just under his feet. "You and I would have been undefeatable," he grunted, swinging up with both blades as Brit brought his down against them. "It would have been a beautiful thing indeed."

"Yes, it might have been, but you should know something before this is over."

"And what is that?" Talon asked, pushing Brit back towards the middle of the arena. Brit suddenly broke off the fight and backed up a few steps. Talon held his swords at the ready, watching him carefully. Brit held the Twins up together, looking at them one at a time, as individuals.

"These do not belong to me. They are not of this planet and the expertise they have provided me to fight you is not mine, but is of another world, another existence, another people. I have borrowed it so that I could beat you for the love of this woman," he gestured up at Catrina who smiled through worried eyes. "Even though I know that I will pay a terrible price for using them, I know it's worth anything to be with her. No human can wield these and live unscathed by their power. You have become one of the elite swordsmen of Argyle. If that's what you have aspired for all your life, then you have had success in your life. But now, it's over."

Brit lunged at Talon with another fury of sword swings, but Talon was ready for him, countering with a blitz of moves that nearly overpowered Britten. Talon fought for the upper hand and just when he felt he had it, he spun to land a death swipe across Britten's chest and neck. Bringing both his swords around for the finishing swipe, Britten lunged both the Twins forward and up in a lighting move. The strike sent both blades right through Talon's thin metal and leather armor piercing right up to the hilts. Talon's eyes went wide; the unanticipated death strike coming swiftly. Dropping his swords, he slumped towards Brit, who caught him and held him up. Talon looked down at both hilts that were stuck in his abdomen, just beneath his ribs. They did not pierce through to the other side. Rather, the strike had sent the blades up into his body cavity and beneath the ribs, into the vital areas of the liver, lungs and heart. Talon's legs buckled, darkness shrouding his eyes and holding onto Brit, looked back up into his face.

"Put them back where you found them," he whispered, starting to cough, choking on his own blood. Thankfully for him, he would pass out before he drowned in his own fluids. He became heavier as life quickly drained from his body. In his mind, he would die with honor. A coveted warrior's death, in an epic battle to the death, even if it was his own.

Britten held onto him for a moment as the assassin slumped in death, looking up at a still worried Catrina and Tony. Ivan was livid, clinching his fists and red faced. Brit felt a little shaky, laying Talon carefully down in the dirt and trying to pull the Twins from his body, but couldn't. His sight was already starting to cloud. First with sparkles all through his vision, then clouds of blackness boiling up in his view, everything starting to fade out of sight, just like before. He had still held out hope that somehow his body would have gotten used to the download, but it was apparent that it was not to be. In fact, it seemed worse this time as his body started to go limp. At first, it felt like heavy exhaustion with no energy available to remain standing, but as his legs began to buckle beneath him, he could not feel his arms or shoulders. The back of his neck and head were tingling heavily and it felt like the muscles there were going to snap. Collapsing, he saw the faint outline of Catrina dropping over the arena wall and running toward him.

Ivan roared with fury, still not believing that his champion was lying dead in the dirt in front of him. He looked as though he were going to burst a vein, watching Tony and Terry drop over the rail followed closely by Caroline and a few of the younger council members. He turned to his warriors stationed all around the arena, bellowing to them in Kenlar. They immediately responded, grabbing for their pistols and rifles, only to find that most of them were gone. In that instant, Tim popped up from behind the royal box, cocking a bow rifle stock behind his head to swing.

"Hello Ivan!" Ivan's face turned pomegranate red, looking as though he was going to bite through his own tongue. "Did you miss me?" Tim asked, swinging the butt of the bow rifle as hard as he could right into Ivan's face. The blow knocked him backwards, falling unceremoniously out of the royal box to the dirt arena below, unconscious. Tim turned and took aim. "NOW!" He yelled, letting his arrow fly at the nearest warrior. Several other heads popped up from the dark arena concourses with bow rifles and pistols firing. In the confusion of the moment, it was all over in a matter of a few seconds as Bryan, Danny and a few of the Lieder teens quickly dispatched all of Ivan's warriors. The whole plan to take them all out at the same time ran just like clockwork.

Catrina and her father were seeing to Britten while Terry and Caroline scrambled to get the gate open. Terry hastily brought the first wagon into the middle of the ring while Caroline went for her children. She about came unglued when she saw her older ones lowering a long ladder into the arena, helping the older council members down the wall. She had told them to remain in the safety of the room and when they told her that Bryan had them help take out Ivan's warriors, there was almost another fight. It wasn't until Tim and Tony explained to her that it had been the only way, did she calmed down. Getting her children loaded back into the wagons, she kept firing angry looks in Bryan's direction as he slowly stepped over to where Catrina and Tony were seeing to Britten. He too, had run out of energy; the medication Kingie had provided him, starting to wear off. He knelt down next to Catrina who was holding Britten in her arms.

"Hey big brother," he said, Brit opening his eyes, but staring straight up into the sky. "Sorry I'm late." Brit tried to see him, but there was nothing but blackness in his mind. He had no feeling in his arms or shoulders, though his neck and head still tingled.

"We put on a pretty good show for these people and we don't even get a cut of the profits," Brit responded exhausted. Catrina burst out laughing through her tears. She knew he was blind now and at least half paralyzed, as did her father, but it didn't matter to her. She knew he loved her for who she was, not for what she looked like.

"The day is young," Bryan replied with a labored chuckle, he and Tony looking into the sky watching the suns continue their relentless arc towards midday.

*　　*　　*　　*　　*

Tim stepped over to Talon's body and looked at him. While he held no love for this man and what he had become under Ivan's iron rule, looking at him now, he could not hate him, even though he had taken the life of his beloved Kawti. He knew that she would want him to forgive and not hold the cancer of hate inside, eventually consuming him. Tim reached down and carefully pulled the Twins from his body wiping them clean. He had never laid eyes on them until now. Holding them up together, he admired their glow, feeling the buzz they emitted. So much power and information right here in these two instruments. How would it be to see and feel what Britten had been privileged to experience? He knew he could never know, not in this plane of existence. He stepped over to Britten's weapon rack and grabbing the scabbards, sheathed the blades.

"We have to hurry," Tony said, as Terry hopped from the wagon to help with Brit. They quickly picked him up and gently laid him in. As Catrina climbed in with Bryan, she settled next to Britten and held him. Before they could get going, Caroline approached the wagon with a very angry little red head in her arms.

"She insists on riding with you, though right now I'm still so angry I could spit nails," she said, setting her tot down in the back of the wagon. These were her children and she felt like Bryan had carelessly put them in harm's way.

454

Little Anna stood up, faced her mother and proceeded to give her a tongue lashing that only a mother could understand. Somehow, Bryan got the essence of the scolding as Caroline's attitude shifted while she listened to her baby babble madly at her. He actually recognized many words as Thulsian. Caroline glanced back at Bryan a couple of times as Anna pointed back at him and then up in the seating of the arena. How can a little tot like this talk in such manner, speaking volumes but sounding like so much gibberish? Anna finally finished, just standing there on the tail of the wagon staring at her mother. Tony and Terry grinned gently, looking back at Caroline, her eyes filling with tears.

"I have no idea what she just said, but am I off the hook?" Bryan asked tiredly. He was starting to feel uneasy and sort of sick again. It was just too much being up and active for what was wrong with him.

"Shut up," Caroline rasped, turning and heading for the other wagon to help the rest of the council climb aboard. Some of them would not be coming, but would need to warn the Thulsa armies at the eastern gates that the walls had been compromised from the south.

"I don't fault you for what you thought you had to do," Terry said, leaning down to Bryan as the wagon began to move. "But watch out for a mother protecting her children." Bryan watched Caroline climb back into the second wagon as Anna squirmed onto his lap. He remembered what she had done to Kingie when she laid her out for roughing up her children earlier. No, best not get in the way of a mother and her offspring.

As the wagon headed for the gate, Danny jumped in the back with his two friends. He was relieved that they were together again and hopefully headed in the right direction, but that relief was tempered by their injuries. Britten had lost his sight and the use of his arms and shoulders, his legs still in question. Bryan was heading off in a bad way with busted up ribs and something else wrong internally. They had to get him proper medical attention and fast. Argyle did not have what was required, only on Earth could they find the proper knowledge to care for his injuries. Danny produced two small crystals, quickly stuffing them in the pockets of his friends. Stone had given them to him when they had parted. Being in the Crystal cave had healed them of their wounds; perhaps these would help his friends.

Danny still held out hope that somehow Jerry would show up somewhere along the way and they would all find their way back home. Maybe not so curiously now, he hoped the same thing for Digi. That somehow he and Jerry had survived the Tera, found each other and their way back to Thulsa. He wished they could all be together again, the same way they had started this adventure.

"What are those?" Catrina asked over the noise of the wagons. Danny pulled all his gear close to him, sitting back.

"Just a little something that a good friend of mine gave me. It might help them."

Exiting the arena and starting down the concourse passage to the outside, he noticed Ivan stirring where he had landed on his face. Danny quickly grabbed for a pistol arrow and shoved it into its slot on the small weapon, then worked the control to cock the mechanism back. Bryan watched him reach for another pistol and load it.

"Kind of like those don't ya? You expecting trouble?" He asked tiredly. After loading the second pistol, Danny reached for the two bow rifles and worked their mechanisms back into the cocked position. Picking up more speed, they blew through the concourse towards the square of bright sun light at the other end. He motioned to the men in the other wagon catching up to them, Tim waved back, turning in the seat while Caroline continued to drive.

"Wouldn't you be?" he responded, passing one of the pistols up to Terry, then passing one over to Catrina. Then it dawned on Bryan what was probably about to happen. Ivan wasn't stupid enough to haul all of his men into the arena without leaving some of them on the outside to protect against any Thulsian warriors that should happen by. Neither would he want anyone leaving the arena without him in the triumphant lead with Catrina on his arm, willing or not. It was a sure bet that they would have to run a gauntlet of warriors. They were about to find out.

Tony whipped at the horse, trying to get the beast to move as fast as possible. This was going to be a wild ride through stone-paved streets. He checked to make sure Tim and Caroline were right behind and gave the animal one final bit of encouragement, suddenly blowing out of the blackness of the concourse and into the bright sunlight of Argyle. Immediately turning the rig to the right towards the city square, the wagon fishtailed wildly, making the turn and coming face to face with a large band of Kenlar warriors, taken completely off guard by the two speeding wagons.

Tony and Terry fired their weapons. Warriors scrambling to pull bow rifles and pistols were laid out as arrows found their mark. As the first wagon plowed into the group of warriors, some were trampled under while others were either thrown to the side or dove out of the way. There was no time for the men to regain their composure as the second wagon sped by right behind the first. Terry traded pistols with Danny and took aim at another cluster of warriors that now blocked their way to the open streets of Thulsa. Catrina tossed her loaded pistol to her father, helping Danny reload the spent weapons. Bryan watched helplessly, becoming sicker with every passing moment. Being tossed about in the back of a wagon wasn't doing him any good either. He looked down at one of the loaded pistols that had gotten shoved to the side in the fury of the moving fire fight. Working their way through the last bunch of warriors, the wagons had to slow, bringing the second horse behind them, almost right up into the back of their wagon. Warriors were jumping to grab at the occupants of the wagons. He could see Tim in the rear wagon battling several warriors that had gotten hold of a council member, trying to pull them out.

Arrows started flying from several men on the outer edges, but because of the chaos, none found their marks. Bryan reached for the pistol, but could only hold onto it. He felt like he was going to vomit at any moment. He wished he had some more of that the pain seeds Kingie had given him earlier, but they were gone now. He watched helplessly, Cat and Danny madly reloading and passing weapons to Terry and Tony who fought to keep from being overwhelmed. At times, they would have to use their bare hands, or an elbow to the face battling the Kenlar trying to stop their advance to the open streets. Behind them, he could see several council members being pulled from the still moving wagon.

The council members in the wagon with him fought to keep the warriors from pulling them back out. The only thing Bryan could do was lay there holding the pistol. He could feel his heart racing and his left shoulder was sore along with every other part of his body that had been abused or beaten in the last two days. He looked over at his big brother lying next to him. Britten's eyes were open, his arm and shoulder bandaged in a make shift sling Catrina and Tony had fashioned for him. He was quite incapable of putting up any kind of a defense, the whole scene unfolding before Bryan turning into a surreal dreamlike encounter of action, slowing to slow motion. People in the wagons kicked and punched to keep from being pulled out or having the warriors climb in.

The children didn't seem to be noticed at all, keeping to themselves, huddled down as much as possible. Even Anna recognized the mortal danger all around them, snuggling in so close to Bryan that he hardly even knew she was there. His attention was drawn to Caroline, screaming as a warrior had managed to climb up onto the side of the still moving wagon, wrapping an arm around her to pull her down. Everyone else was occupied in a fight for their lives, unable to assist. Caroline held a death grip to the seat of the wagon with both hands, the warrior pulling with one arm and producing a dagger with the other. Summoning all his strength, Bryan raised the pistol and took aim, letting the arrow whistle pass the horse's head and striking the warrior in the ribs. Falling, the warrior caused a chain reaction, stripping the entire side of the wagon of attackers, toppling all of them. Caroline looked forward at Bryan who was still holding the spent pistol in her direction. She gave him a hard look, realizing that he had just saved her life. How do you stay angry at someone who just saved your bacon? She gave him a quick smile, and then focused on planting her little foot squarely in the face of another warrior.

Ivan had brought a lot more warriors through the secret entrance than any of them had anticipated. Tony kicked a face and slashed at another, then whipped the horse again, sending it bolting forward, braking free from the gauntlet and out into the open streets of Thulsa. Fighting like a lion, Terry stopped taking weapons from Catrina and Danny in favor of his own sword. He nearly fell backwards, as the wagon lunged forward again.

Danny and Catrina turned their attention to the wagon behind them now, firing their weapons as fast as they could reload them. In the distance, they could see Ivan coming out of the dark concourse of the arena they had exited only moments before. He was a big man, but with the injuries that Tim had managed to inflict on him, he wasn't moving very fast. Finally, the second wagon broke through and sped off after the first with only an occasional Kenlar arrow flying past.

Leaving the gauntlet behind, they raced towards the city square. It didn't take them long before they were speeding past the execution style apparatuses in the square and towards the Spoil forest. Once they reached the top of the Winners Spoil pathway, they reined the horses to a stop and started getting everyone out.

The Altar

As Danny and Tim helped to herd Caroline's family and the remaining council members down into the area where all of Thulsa's riches had been kept, they were met by Sargon. His expression suddenly turned to concern for their bedraggled appearance and frantic demeanor. Danny looked all around the Spoil; something was terribly wrong. Tim looked a little bewildered as well. Wasn't a Spoil supposed to have treasure and things of great worth stored in them? There was nothing here! Nothing but a large stone object in the far corner by the open gate doors.

"This place looks like the one at Crosslake," Tim commented, as people started moving down the path towards the wall and the gates. Tony and Catrina appeared at the top of the path helping to carry Britten down the path towards the open gate.

"What happened to all the loot?" Danny asked, stepping forward to help Terry and his oldest boy with Bryan, who now looked worse off than Britten. Caroline and her older girls took over herding the family close behind, with a few council members in tow. Sargon made his explanations as they walked. Catrina still sporting her battle armor, including the battle sword on her back.

"Forgive my boldness your highness," he said, directing his remarks to his Queen. She was in no mood for pleasantries, none of them were. They were in a hurry!

"Sargon!" she barked, heavy effort in her voice. Brit was still having a very hard time supporting any of his own weight and she was doing her best to help hold him up. "Out with it! What's going on?" The engineer was a bit taken back but then caught site of the arrow filled wagons behind them.

"I took the liberty of ordering the Winner's Spoil relocated to the cave The Amanda was removed from. We tried to move the sword altar, but were unable. I thought to make the riches of Thulsa more secure should there be a breach in our defenses. Apparently we've been compromised?"

"Yeah, you could say that," Tony responded, continuing towards the gate. "Have you got anyone else here with you?"

"Only a couple of my men Captain. I have dispatched every available man to the eastern walls."

"The breach is at the south wall," Tony informed him. "I sent guards to the east to warn them but I don't know if they got through."

The few council members that had made it to the Spoil, gathered in front of the altar, afraid to get too close to it. Most had never even seen it before, let alone gotten this close. As Tim stepped around towards the far side of the altar, he stopped and gazed out the open gate at the storm swirling madly overhead. Terry let Danny and Caroline's son take over helping Bryan, to join Tim watching the familiar phenomenon do its thing. The Argyle suns were not on the valley side of the wall, but they could see the shaft of sunlight from Earth piercing down towards the middle of the snow covered valley and the parts of The Amanda. They remembered it all too well, the morning Tony brought them through in one piece only to crash land and be buried in the cave. Such a long time ago, a lifetime ago.

"Just as scary now as it was when we came through," Terry commented, Tim gazing hypnotized by the massive rotation.

"It has its beautiful parts," Tim finally said, admiring the awesome power on display above them.

"Come on buddy," Terry beckoned, patting him on the back. "Let's see if we can get you guys home." He had to pull on his friend a bit to get him to break from his trance and turn back to the altar. Tim still had the Twins draped over his shoulder as he stepped around the back of the altar where the operator would stand. Bryan and Britten were carefully helped over next to the open gate, where they sank to the ground to rest while preparations were made for their departure. Catrina remained at Brit's side, attending to both him and his younger brother.

"When are your people scheduled to pick up The Amanda?" Tony asked Danny, as Tim examined the slot where the Signet would have been placed in the altar. Danny didn't know for sure. He thought that someone would have to go to the ridge and signal Bill in the snow cat to relay the go ahead down to operations in Driggs. He turned to Brit for answers, but he was still suffering the effects of the download. Catrina looked over at Sargon, who quickly stepped up with the needed information.

"When we removed The Amanda from the cave to the pickup area provided by Master Britten, the eye of the storm moved with her, remaining directly overhead. The communication device that was secured on the west ridge was lost."

"You mean there's no way for us to call out for a pickup?" Danny complained, looking over at Brit, in a near panic. "Now what?" he asked. Tony looked out at the storm thinking intensely

"I don't know Dano," Brit responded tiredly. "We only found out about this yesterday."

"Can't you just go through at a different location? Cat asked, trying to help figure out a solution. "Why does it have to be that same spot on the west ridge?"

"Because that's where Bill and the snow cat are located," Danny said, pointing out what was obvious to him.

"So go around to a place you can get out and just walk around the outside," she responded.

"Not enough time for that now," Brit replied, looking out at nothing. Being blind in a conversation was going to take some getting used to. "In our condition, it would take hours to make the walk around to where Bill is, *IF* we made it at all. If we're to have any hope of stopping the storms from coming, we have to get The Amanda out of here now. Gotta tell ya, the only way I can think of to get us out of here alive now, is to hitch a ride inside when they lift her out." Brit shook his head. "I have no idea how we're gonna get out of this one Dano." He could feel Catrina's warm hand touch his cheek and he did his best to squeeze it between his face and shoulder.

"What about sending in another helicopter to pick us up?" Danny inquired, remembering that Stone had told them that they would have to exit through either the top or the bottom of the Rift. The thoughts of dangling from a tether in the fuselage of the old wreck didn't sit well with him. This scenario, carried through to its proper conclusions, would have them riding a tilt a whirl at the carnival. The fuselage would surely to be spinning the entire time.

"No time and how would you call one in if there were?" Brit pointed out, trying to think it through. "I might just be stuck here with you," he said, turning in Catrina's direction. She looked up through the open gate at the storm outside. How odd that it seemed so easy to accidently blunder through that thing only to find out how complicated it was to get back out.

"It doesn't matter where," Cat whispered to him, squeezing his hands and kissing him on the cheek. Tony observed the exchange, standing at the open gate watching his daughter's affection for Britten. She was indeed a rare flower and he counted himself one of the most fortunate men in existence for having been privileged to be her father. He knew they could all stay here in Thulsa and be happy, but he remembered what it was like to come to grips with having to give up everything that you have ever held dear. He remembered how they tried so hard to get back through the storm to home, Chuck and Dale risking everything. They had climbed the western ridge and tried to walk through in a similar location that Britten and Bryan had crawled through. Now the ridge was engulfed by the storm and with it, no way to go back out the same way they came in. Maybe Brit had hit on something when he indicated that they would lift the wreckage out the top. Instead of going through the storm, perhaps going out the top in The Amanda was the only course for them. Someone still had to breach the storm to get a signal out for the pickup. Perhaps Catrina had mentioned the solution earlier. Instead of going through it, go under it at a different location entirely.

Tony looked back at an anxious Danny, then down at Bryan. He was in the worst condition. They had to get him to a hospital and fast.

Thulsa medicine did not have the expertise to deal with his type of injuries. He would die unless a way was found, and very soon. Tony looked back out at the storm, but this time, he caught sight of The Amanda laying in pieces, several hundred yards outside the gate. From his vantage point, he could clearly make out the painted nose art on her left side. An image suddenly popped into his mind. It was so distinct and clear that it took up nearly all his focus. It was his beloved Amanda smiling back at him with those big brown eyes. He looked back over at his daughter. They all deserved to be home, back where they belonged. He knew there was a different way home. He knew that he had all the time they needed. He knew what had to be done. However, he also knew the dangers associated with it.

"I'm not so sure about what you're thinking my friend," Terry commented, stepping next to Captain Dallas and looking at the storm. He had Anna in his arms. She peeked out at the noisy storm through little fingers pressed against her face. "I have come to know that my place is here now and I have no need to go back to Earth," he said, looking back at Caroline and his family. "I'm just not sure what you're considering can be done safely."

"Nothing is a sure thing," Tony replied. "I only know that I have to try." He turned to Tim, who was reading the inscriptions and scroll work on the altar. "Tim, let's get this thing fired up for time travel." Tim nodded and Tony stepped over in front of Britten, squatting. "You and Bryan know that valley better than any of us," he looked at a worried Catrina but addressed Brit. "What's going to be the best way out of there, on foot?"

It took Brit only a moment to understand what Captain Dallas had in mind. The concept of time travel through the Rift was clear in his own mind from the download of the Twins. If Tony could go back in time, on Earth, he could call the Sky Cranes to come in and pick up The Amanda with everyone else onboard. It might be a wild ride, but at least they would get out.

"The south ridge is the easiest. Do you remember how the bowl is shaped?"

"Don't think I can ever get that image out of my head." Tony nodded. Catrina puzzled, missing a vital piece of information in order to follow what her father intended to do.

"Dad?" she asked, putting her hand to his shoulder to get his attention. "What are you doing?"

Tony glanced behind him at the Altar and Tim who was examining the inscriptions carved all over it.

"It's a time portal Cat," he uttered excitedly. "I can go back in time and send in help. You guys can ride out in the fuselage." Cat was stunned by the revelation, quickly spinning her mind up to follow the logic of what he was purposing to do, but more than that, what he could do. She looked at the gleam in his eye as he turned his attention back to Britten.

"The south ridge slopes down much easier than the west ridges do. You could go through on the south where the snow is deep. Maybe you could tunnel in and wait for the Rift to pass over you, then work your way along the south west ridgeline. There are thick, tough trees that live along that ridge. They have survived winds like this for years. That will be your best bet; get into those trees and wait for the storm to pass. You should be able to find your way home after that."

"I need to know what time to set this thing to," Tim announced from the altar. Tony had had plenty of time to figure this all out. He gave Catrina a loving gaze, reaching out and putting his hand to her cheek.

"1960," he choked up a little bit. Catrina smiled, acknowledging the longing in her father's eyes. He intended to return to her mother as he was now, as she would be then. He would then be with her while they waited for time to catch up and he could send in help at the right time.

Tim pulled the Twins from their scabbards and held them over the altar, inserted them into the slots on either side of the altars top, between the arches, then stepped back a little and waited. Everyone looked closely to watch the wonder and the splendor that they supposed would come from the altar's activation, but nothing happened. Tim's expression shifted to confusion. He was sure this was how the altar was activated; it had to be. He knew the book forwards and backwards. The altar must be damaged or perhaps the Twins had gotten damaged in the duel. He tried to pull them out and reinsert them. He tried swapping the swords in the slots, thinking they must be inserted in a certain order.

"I don't understand," Tim mumbled frustrated. Terry and Danny stepped up next to him as some of the council members moved a little closer for a better look. "It should work, it has to work." He pulled them out, looking them over closely. There seemed to be nothing wrong, yet the altar remained dark and silent.

"Try reading the words on the altar," Terry said, pointing at the many glyphs engraven all over the sword altar. Tim looked it all over carefully, reading the inscriptions created by the Ancients, but slowly shook his head as he examined it.

"No, there's nothing here. It just gives reference to God for providing infinite learning and the opportunities available with the righteous use of his wisdom. It shows how to remove them after storage, and some other stuff." Tim continued to scan the glyphs mingled with the writing, not even noticing Brit shuffling up to the Altar with Catrina's help. Tim looked up at Brit with a surprised expression, and then at Catrina, who only shrugged.

"I know what's wrong," Brit informed him, trying to raise his hands, feeling for the top of the altar. Tim was a little indignant. He knew everything there was to know about the contents of the Signet and the instructions that had been provided within. How was this blind and half paralyzed man from Earth going to know more than him?

"I've been studying the Signet for most of my life here," Tim informed him, holding his place at the controls of the altar. "I think I have a little more of a handle on how this thing works than you do." Tim listened to himself and then felt a little ashamed at his tone and the way he had just spoken to Britten. There was a universal saying that he knew of on both planets. Doing the same thing repeatedly expecting different results is the definition of insanity.

"I have no doubt that you know the book better than anyone else on this planet," Brit responded hoarsely. "But I know something about this altar that wasn't put in the book." Tim suddenly became aware of his own arrogance. How could Brit even present such a statement? He had never laid eyes on the book. It then hit him like a ton of bricks; like a light switch turning on. Britten didn't need to see the book. He had just experienced the download of the Ancients. He had not only seen the contents of the Signet, but everything the Ancients had learned that wasn't contained in the Signet. It had been placed directly into Brit's mind. He was almost jealous of what Brit had experienced with the Twins, but was then reminded that what stood before him now was the terrible consequence of information that was not meant for human kind.

"The Twins," Brit gestured, trying to raise his arms to the deck of the altar. He had some mobility available to him through his shoulders, but it was quite limited and he required assistance just to raise his arms. Blackness still boiled heavily in his head, though occasionally he experienced tiny sparkles floating through the waves of blackness. Catrina helped him find the hilt closest to her and Tim did likewise on his side. Once Brit had a hand on both swords, he tried to pull them back out, but was quite unable.

"I'll hold them," he said, trying to do it on his own. "But you'll have to help me pull them out and reinsert them." Cat nodded at Tim and together they helped Brit raise the swords up out of the slots and then carefully let them lower back into place. As the hilts came to a rest at the bottom of their travel, a couple of tiny lights began to wink at the top of the arches. There was a sudden flash of light across the entire top of the altar and a soft buzzing floated through the air in the immediate area of the control device. The flash startled everyone, the council members stampeding way back. The control surfaces lit up like a video game console followed by a holographic image forming below the arches. Tim instantly recognized most of what he was seeing and understood how to work it.

There were two layers of holographic images overlaying a touch screen control that had materialized on top of the altar. The images looked as though they were three dimensional representations of spacial constellations of the universe. The upper portion was a representation of the star system that contained Argyle, while the bottom one contained that of Earth. The touch screen, or so it appeared to be, contained a myriad of displayed information and controls for different functions.

Sargon stepped around to the side of the altar for a closer look, but the council members maintained their distance. It was a little peculiar that they had asked for this information and now that it was here, they were afraid of it. In truth, they never really expected for any of this to get this far. They had assumed, in their primitive minds, that the book would be recovered and either an enchantment would be given or just the simple act of restoring the book to its rightful spot in the altar would be enough for the storms to cease. Sargon watched carefully as Tim began to touch controls, changing the displays before him. Catrina was absolutely fascinated by the beautiful colors and the floating arrays of lights in the small holographic images. Brit shuffled to one side to allow Tim full access. While he could still see it clearly in his mind, he could not see the real thing and therefore felt of little use except to clarify any questions that Tim might have. Cat held onto him tightly, knowing that he still couldn't stand on his own. It might be better if he was to sit back down to rest, but he was sure that Tim would have questions.

"You really need to rest," Cat whispered to him.

"Nag, Nag, Nag," he whispered back tiredly, but with a little humor pressed into his tone.

"Oh Brit," Cat spoke softly to him, gazing at the display before them. "It's so beautiful."

"Yes, I know it is," he responded, loving her so close. "Just wait, it gets even better."

"We have to be right on the money here," Tim announced, the controls responding to his every command. He was fortunate that he could read what he was seeing; otherwise, they'd be in a world of hurt. There was nothing simple about this. Traveling across the universe was complicated enough. Add time travel to that and it was almost too much for the human mind to take in at once.

"The right sword controls where the rift opens," Tim announced, calmly making checks and adjustments. "The left sword controls the time event horizon. It's sort of a matrix control with a million different combinations to a million different matrixes. They've built a gateway to the entire universe using this rift." Tim became a little emotional, realizing the vastness of knowledge required to make this whole thing work.

"So is it set to the right place?" Catrina asked. Tim checked the lower holograph at a speck of light glowing brighter than the others. He pointed at it with a big grin.

"This is Earth right here, the destination.   It's still open. No need to touch anything on the right side. The left side is the tricky part." Tim was like a little kid in a toy factory, having a little trouble focusing on what had to be done right now. There were so many things he wanted to explore, but he knew they were almost out of time.

Reaching across the altar to several touch controls, he carefully activated them, then let his fingers glide over to the left hilt. Holding it in place for a moment while he touched several more controls on the glowing altar deck, a low whir started to pulse from the base of the altar, then a noticeable change in pitch from beyond the gate and the storm outside as he carefully pulled back on the left hilt. Tony, Terry and Danny stepped to the gate and looked out. The storm walls grew black, energy bolts jumping across the cylindrical walls with even greater ferocity.

"Remember that part about pissing off the Rift?" Danny announced, looking back at Tim, who was now totally focused on what he was doing.

"Pretty angry, huh?" Tim smiled. "Kind of sucks when someone else is driving, eh?" Brit nudged Catrina to move him to the gate. Sargon took his place next to Tim to see how the altar worked. He had no idea what was going on, but the lights and the displays were very curious and delightful to look at.

"Captain Dallas." Brit said, as Catrina helped move him into position. "Just a couple of things real quick."

"Make it fast," Tony replied, pulling his sword off preparing for his departure.

"You have to know what time it is when you leave in order to send the choppers in a couple of minutes afterwards." Tony nodded, understanding what was at work here. "You also have to have the date right. Get yourself to Driggs in enough time after we pass through the storm, to convince Cal Schultz that you are the real deal and this is no joke. He's a tough nut, but make it real and he'll believe you."

"What would you suggest I tell him to make him believe me?" Tony asked, shedding everything but his shirt, pants and boots. Brit thought a moment thinking about something that only Cal would know. A smile slowly floated across Brit's face, thinking of the perfect idea.

"Tell him Skettles and the Boatman sent you. He'll believe you." Tony gave him an odd look, passing a glance over at his daughter who was grinning from ear to ear.

"Ok," he hedged a little bit. Tim was starting to get a little excited, as he was almost ready.

"You all need to get out to the plane," he announced, remaining focused.

"Anything else?" Tony asked, bending down to help Terry pick Bryan up.

"Yes, as a matter a fact, there is one more thing," he said, as Catrina carefully helped him towards the gate. "I'd like your permission to marry your daughter." Brit pushed it out as steady as he could make it sound. Catrina's heart stopped and she looked to her father who was laboring to get a half conscious Bryan to his feet. Tony looked back at the couple, smiled and then chuckled softly.

"My little Cat never needed my permission to do anything," he said, looking at her now. "But I defiantly approve and you certainly have my blessing. I'll have to check with her mother when I see her," he winked, "but I don't think there will be any issue. What you two have discovered is like a precious gem. It's something that only two people can share and others who have it can see. It's what your mother and I found a long time ago, in a place called Dubois, Idaho." Tony looked back at Britten, even though he knew he couldn't see him. Catrina let her head come to rest on Brit's shoulder.

"She is a rare rose, my boy. Take good care of her and she will do the same for you. Keep her in your heart," he said, looking back at Catrina now, who smiled broadly as he gave them his blessing. "And she will always be with you." It was how he had survived all these years without his beloved Amanda. She had always been kept forever burning in the forefront of his mind and heart. She was the one who made him the kind of man he had always strived to be, the man he was now.

*　　*　　*　　*　　*

Caroline and her family stepped forward, surrounding Bryan. He did his best to come to full attention and give this family who had saved him and given so much to see to his safety, a proper farewell. Caroline stood back and watched, with a tempered smile, as each of her girls stepped up and gently hugged him, then gave him a kiss on the cheek. Each boy in turn shook his hand. They had no real concept of how to greet or bid farewell with any degree of love or compassion, living their lives isolated from most civilization. In time, branching out and having adventures of their own would teach them how it was done. Then came a little tug at Bryan's pant leg. He fought off all the pain and nausea that continually tried to cloud his mind and pull him into unconscious. He looked down at a tiny little Anna smiling up at him with arms extended. Having no energy and in so much pain, he teetered on the threshold of passing out. Caroline could sense Bryan's condition as Terry did his best to steady him and help pick up the child. Anna carefully wrapped her little arms around him gently. She understood that his condition was grave and was doing her best not to make it any more uncomfortable for him. She laid her head on his shoulders and just held onto him, patting him on the back, and then started jabbering. All at once she pulled back in his arms, pulling the little Tera crystal from his shirt pocket. She played with it for a moment as Bryan tickled her cheek a little. She giggled, cocking her head to keep his fingers from getting too deep and dropped the crystal back where she had found it.

"Good bye my little one," Bryan finally said, fighting back the tears of parting from someone you have become attached to. Anna looked at him for a moment, then grinned from ear to ear and raised her little finger up like she was about to rattle off one of her long babbling speeches. What came out surprised everyone standing close by.

"Be more careful Bryan." She giggled, turning in his arms and reaching for her mother. Caroline and Terry looked astonished. They had only heard Anna ever speak in Thulsian and maybe one or two words of English, never a whole sentence. As Caroline took her in her arms, she wiped away a few tears herself.

"Got something caught in my eye," she lied, trying not to show her emotion for this young man with whom they had shared so much. She tried to straighten up, then stepped forward and gave Bryan a careful hug. Anna got in on the action again, not only wrapping an arm around her mother, but one around Bryan too.

"Take care of yourself Master Bryan," Caroline choked out. "We'll miss watching after you. I know Anna will miss you terribly."

"I already miss all you guys," he responded, wishing he could lie back down. Caroline finally pulled Anna free from the embrace and stepped back with the little red head waving with a coy little smile.

"Love you Master Bryan," she snickered, then turned and buried her face in her mother's shoulder. Nothing could have prepared Bryan for the wave of warmth that flooded through his being at that moment. It was then that he knew there was nothing greater in life than being a parent and raising children in righteousness. He made a mental note right then to try and find a red head with a dominant X chromosome. He hoped that they could make it like something he knew Tony, Amanda and his big brother and Catrina had found. Whoever it would be, he was sure he'd know. It would be someone he couldn't live without.

"Now, let's get everyone home," Tony said, stepping through the gate and into the snow.

Coalescing

There was a broad, well-packed trail leading directly to The Amanda and Bryan was able to summon enough strength to struggle along with the help of the others. Moving as quickly as possible towards the wreckage, the group could feel the cylindrical sides closing in around them, the storm above them howling.

Tim remained behind, continuing to work with the time dilation matrix at the altar. Probably a piece of cake for an Ancient, as it had to have been something that they did regularly. Even though he knew the instructions in the Signet, it still took an enormous amount of concentration on his part. He needed practice, but was only going to get to practice and take the final, all at the same time, as there was no room for error.

Finally, the display on the altar deck responded with information he recognized. Touching several more controls, he locked the time event horizon into the altar controls and activated them. The whir that had been emanating from the altar instantly changed to a loud low frequency pulse. Tim stepped away from the altar and stood at the gate, seeing the small group reaching the fuselage. The storm turned almost black now and it was becoming clear that it was starting to compress, as Stone said it would. The energy bolts now turned to continuous plasma traces, striking across to the other side and back on to itself. It was like being stuck in a plasma ball now. The energy fingers remaining intact, buzzing angrily in every direction. The shaft of Earth sunlight still pierced down through the center of the Rift's eye.

"1960!" Tim yelled to Tony, who was working on getting the WACS winter gear put on. As soon as Tony was under the Rift, Tim would turn the time event horizon back to Britten's time. Danny helped Bryan into the fuselage, sat him down, then removed the crystal he had given him and turned to Brit for the same. Catrina gave him an odd look, not understanding what he was up to. He had given them to his friends to help ease the pain of their wounds and now he was taking them back, why? Danny took the crystals and stepped over to Tony who was working to don the snowshoes that had been provided for him from the WACs gear.

"Here," Danny said, offering the crystals to Tony who reached for a pair of mittens. "You're going to need these?" Tony looked at them curiously, then recognized them as smaller versions of the crystals that were in the cave the Mynites had taken them to. He remembered how they had been healed when they were around them and how they replenished their energy for the long hike and ultimately racing through the Jabbaway gauntlet.

"Where did you get these?" Tony asked, taking them from him and looking at them carefully. He looked back at Britten and Bryan. They needed them worse than he did right now. His injuries were far less life threatening than theirs were, especially Bryan's.

"Stone gave them to me when I gave him the Signet. Somehow he knew we would need them. Captain, we'll need these back when I see you again," Danny said, smiling. Indeed, the Niker boy had grown up during their adventure, which was still far from over. He had done that which is hard for anyone to do, accept change. Not everyone arrives at each changing point together. What's important is how you got there and who you helped along the way.

Tony stepped out of the fuselage waving at Tim who turned back to the altar. Moving to leave, a firm hand tugged at him and he turned back to a very teary eyed daughter.

"Dad, I.…." she choked through the flood of tears gushing from her eyes. She tried to say more but couldn't. She had spent most of her life with him, longer than most people ever have a chance to. She feared for his life, but she also knew what was at stake and the tremendous responsibility he was about to shoulder. Getting through the Rift's wall would be hard enough. Traveling home to Montana without being detected would require everything that both worlds had ever taught him. At the same time, she knew that he had been waiting for this opportunity for most of a life time. He was willing to risk it all in order to get back to her mother, back to his Amanda. She was scared to death, but so happy for him at the same time, having a good idea of how he felt about her mother. What she had experienced in the last three and a half days with Britten was just the beginning of something so wonderful that words could hardly express.

Tony gazed back at his beautiful little girl. She wasn't so little any more. She was all grown up now. In a flash he reeled back through their lives together, from that little intellectual girl he and Amanda were constantly surprised by, to fighting side by side with her to defend the clan, Thulsa. He pulled his little girl to him and they held onto each other like they would never let go.

"I'll see you on the other side," he choked up a little himself. He had to let go. If he didn't, he never would. He reminded himself what was at stake and refocused on the task at hand. He turned and trotted past the front of The Amanda. Passing by the open pilot's window he caught site of a figure sitting in the left seat. It looked like Amanda as she appeared on the side of the airplane. He did a double take as he continued forward, but when he looked back, he saw only the empty cockpit of the old wreck. Perhaps it had been his mind playing tricks on him. The nose art of The Amanda was right there; perhaps it was just that. Whatever it was would have to remain a mystery or just a phantom that would be quickly forgotten as he pushed himself hard through the deepening snow towards the gentler slopes of the southern ridgeline of Lake Valley.

As Catrina watched her father go, she became distracted by a commotion back at the gate and turned to the rear of the broken fuselage for a better look. People were coming out through the gate in fear of something.

"Don't go anywhere without me," she said, looking in at Britten and then turning for a better look. Danny kept an eye on Catrina as she started walking back across the snow packed trail towards the gate to see what was happening. He started work on getting Brit into his winter gear while Terry struggled to help Bryan into his. During this vertical extraction, it was going to get a whole lot colder before it got warmer. They were going to need every bit of this winter clothing to keep from freezing to death at altitude when the copters came to lift them out. They were going to have to ride in The Amanda as the sky cranes were not really designed to take passengers. Usually manned by a crew of three, there just weren't any seats available, and without radio communications, there was no way for them to signal them.

Catrina was about halfway to the gate when she looked back to see her father's figure disappear under the black edge of the storm. The best thing he could have done was to burrow into the side of the hill and wait for the Rift wall to pass over him, and then crawl out on the other side. They should know in just a few minutes if he had been successful.

Turning back to the gate, she took notice of Caroline's children stampeding out onto the snow. They were followed in an instant by several winged blurs that banked sharply, one right after another, through the open gate, under the swirling blackness of the Rift's backdrop and the brilliant plasma bolts above. *Jabbaway!* What were they doing here? They never dared venture over the walls into the city. They would have been easy targets and brought down quickly. These Jabba were much larger than most of the ones she had encountered.

She pulled her battle sword from her back and started running for the gate and the panicked group still coming out. Drawing near, she called to everyone to move quickly down the other path in the direction of the cave The Amanda had been taken from.

Terry was also drawn to the commotion and bolted from the back of the airplane with his sword drawn. Sprinting, he watched his family being savagely harassed by the snarling animals. His oldest son had a short sword, taken from one of the wagons, fending off the flapping beasts, bravely protecting his brothers and sisters behind him. It was Tobor's flock, with the big angry beast himself leading the attack. Terry watched horrified, as Caroline was knocked to the ground by an attacking Jabba, sending little Anna sprawling across the hardened snow. Tobor saw the strike and banked long, out into the valley, then launched a screaming dive at the frightened little child, who was getting to her feet, looking around for her mother.

Catrina plowed into the Jabba, her sword swinging, knocking them off an overwhelmed Caroline who also toppled over. No sooner had Caroline gotten back to her feet than she was knocked down again by another Jabba that came firing through the open gate. Terry pushed his sprint harder, running faster than he had ever thought possible. Tobor was aiming to tear his little Anna to pieces with one pass. Terry meant to cut the Jabba in half before it reached her. Tightening his grip, all three were about to converged, but a fourth figure bolted from the open gate towards the redheaded toddler. Jerry Gunn dove across the snow and caught Anna, curling into a ball to protect her, both sliding out of harm's way. Terry jumped at the same moment Tobor twisted his razor claws, reaching for Jerry's rolling body. Terry swung twice, once on approach of Tobor in midair and again, passing right behind him. Tobor's right wing swung away first, sending the animal into a sharp right turning dive headlong into the snow. The left wing fluttering away, the Jabba piled into a heap of fur against the rock wall of the Thulsa Spoil. Terry curled and rolled as he landed, but was instantly back on his feet watching Tobor get up, his wings detached and laying useless across bloody snow. The Jabba let out a blood chilling howl, then charged at Terry as Jerry got to his feet with a screaming Anna in his arms and started running to the airplane. As Terry readied himself to do battle with this Newfoundland sized Jabbaway, another winged creature suddenly fired through the open gate, landing between the two combatants. Tobor instantly dug his paws into the snow, coming to a screeching halt. Terry was a little taken aback, but recognized the dark brown fur.

"No Terry," Digi said in a commanding voice. "See to your family, and I'll see to mine." Terry glanced back at Caroline and turned to her aide as Catrina fought two more Jabba that had beset the two women.

Tobor growled in pain, his wing stumps jetting blood. He moved carefully into a different position for his show down with Digi.

"So, now we will see which Jabbaway is the better," he snarled, chirping loudly.

"We are known by our acts Tobor. You chose the wrong master and now it's time for you to answer for it, including all the evil deeds that you have committed under his command," Digi said confidently, his wings still held wide open.

"Not much of a fair fight without wings," Tobor growled. Digi closed his wings, wrapping them tightly around his body.

"You might grow new ones back, but for now, this is the best I can do for you."

"It will be enough," Tobor said launching.

*　　*　　*　　*　　*

Danny watched in awe, the strangely familiar figure diving for Anna, grab her, roll and take off running in his direction. Once he was up on the packed path, he moved quite effortlessly towards the wreckage and drawing closer, Danny realized he was seeing another ghost. As Jerry reached the relative safety of the airplane, he set Anna down, the little tot instantly running to where Bryan lay drifting in and out of consciousness.

"You're alive!" Danny exclaimed, not believing what he was seeing.

"Well, yeah," Jerry said, looking himself over. "I think I'm all in one piece here." He looked back at his friend who was near to tears. Danny suddenly couldn't hold himself back, grabbing his friend and just holding onto him, crying. This overflow of emotion completely astonished him. He was never one for such things, but the tears just kept coming.

"I thought you were dead," Danny cried, doing his best to regain his composure.

"We all thought you were," came a very tired voice from further back in the plane. Bryan was still awake, but looking terrible. Anna sat firmly next to him, looking outside at what was happening. Jerry was ecstatic to see Bryan still alive as well and pulled away from a still sniffling Danny to kneel at his friend's side.

"Thought we had lost you on the Torres," Jerry said, quickly surveying his condition. He didn't look good at all. Jerry was no medic, but even he could see that his friend was in a bad way.

"You 'bout did," Bryan responded, looking outside. "But we make friends in some of the strangest places."

"I think we've all had enough of this adventure to last a life time," Britten commented, sitting across from his brother. Jerry turned to their expedition leader with a grin. Yes, they all had enough and were *MORE* than ready to go home. Jerry noticed something odd about the way Brit was looking at him, but said nothing. There was still too much commotion outside. He looked back down at the battle happening at the gate.

"We've got to do something to help them," Jerry commented, watching the events unfolding outside.

"What's happening out there?" Britten asked, thinking of Catrina. She needed to get back here to the wreckage soon.

"Jabba attack, the Gangees. That's Tobor's flock," Jerry answered, watching Catrina and Terry fight the harassing animals. He looked around for something they could use to mount some kind of a defense.

"Got something in mind?" Danny asked, watching as well. After the last three days, he and Jerry would be rushing head long into the fray, but they had no weapons here, or did they? They turned at the same instant and looked towards the front of the fuselage at the waist

473

gunner positions. Both fully loaded 50 caliber machines sat silently waiting for their operators to point and shoot.

"I've got an idea," they said simultaneously. Jerry looked outside while Danny made his way forward to check the gun.

"We're not pointing in the right direction," he announced. The back of the fuselage was facing the gate. They needed the side of the fuselage to have a full view of the gate. Danny checked the gun for movement. It was like it had just come out of the factory. "Gonna need your help out here buddy," Jerry called from outside.

Danny turned to make his way out to help Jerry, while Brit fumbled with the rest of his gear. As Danny stepped over him, Brit detected an odd noise or rather a feeling coming from above them. He could only listen and try to picture what it was. There was so much noise outside that it was impossible to clearly identify what it was, but it was getting louder and more distinct. The entire fuselage lurched, rocking several times. Her eyes wide, Anna held tightly to Bryan's motionless body, feeling the movement of Jerry and Danny pushing the back end of the airplane across the snow, positioning The Amanda broadside to the gate. The aircraft fuselage finally came to rest in its new position, tipping just a bit, and then stabilizing.

Moments later, Danny and Jerry were stumbling over the two Garrett boys to execute their plan. Moving past Brit, Bryan and Anna, they thought they heard something odd and stopped. It was a thumping noise of some kind, but there was so much noise that it was hard to tell. Danny reached the left waist gunners position and looked out at the skirmish. The Jabba were all over the council members and Lieder family alike. Jerry patted his friend on the back then climbed up and over the bomb bay towards the front of the old airplane as Danny took hold of the handles of the old machine gun, pulled back the bolt and took aim.

Lying helpless in the broken fuselage, Brit became aware of another figure moving towards them from behind Danny. At first he thought it could only be Jerry, but then heard him climbing over the metal bomb bay towards the front of the plane. In the dim light of the fuselage, he could see a yellow dress. *How could he see anything?* The download from the Twins had rendered him completely blind. Blackness still boiled madly in his vision, but he could see the outline of a dress none the less. *Was he dreaming?* He tried looking over at his brother as Amanda knelt down between them. She smiled, quietly looking at them, and then focusing her attention on Brit, placing one of her hands on his arms, the other over his eyes. He let his eye lids drop closed, instantly seeing her stepping into his mind through a thick mist of bellowing blackness. She smiled at him and took him by the hands.

"You've seen some pretty heavy action today," she stated calmly. Brit was a bit speechless here. The storm was worse now than before.

The last time he and Catrina had encounter her, she was experiencing great turmoil. *How was it that she was so calm now?*

"You have no idea," Brit replied, still surprised to see her again. "It's been a right busy day."

"I've seen worse," she came back quickly.

"I feel certain," he agreed readily. "How is that you are here, like this?" Amanda looked around them as if the storm were there inside.

"The storm's attention is diverted and my focus is here, for you and Bryan. Your friends have done something to control it. By doing so, they have weakened it and now I draw power from it. I saw Tony running past in the other direction. Where did he go?"

"We found a way to manipulate the storm and sent Tony back in time to go for help."

Amanda's eyes lit up, thinking of the possibility of finally getting out of the reach of the storm. She already felt some freedom just lying in the pickup zone awaiting extraction.

"Why are you here now?" Brit asked, sensing the stark, black cloud in his mind starting to dull and lighten a little bit.

"You have risked everything for me and now I want to give something back. The energy I am drawing from the storm can be used to help heal you." Britten instantly thought of his little brother. On death's doorstep, Bryan was in far worse shape. Brit could at least breathe and move, a little.

"No, please, go to Bryan first. He needs it more than I do," Brit pleaded, trying to push Amanda away. She was a little puzzled at first, but could sense his compassion for his brother. Still she lingered.

"I can heal only one of you," she informed him, holding his hands up with her arms extended.

"He will die before we can get help to him if you don't." Brit wondered if he was just unconscious, but the feelings he was experiencing now were so familiar that it had to be real, just like before. Amanda smiled, giving Brit a hug, then turning, disappeared into the blackness of his vision, leaving a trail of sparkles through the cloudiness. When he opened his eyes, he could now see boiling sparkles, dancing like fire flies through the blackness of his vision. He could still make out the outline of Amanda's yellow dress kneeling next to his brother.

*   *   *   *   *

Catrina's battle sword was a little big for such close quarters fighting, but she had the skill to deal with it, making short work of any Jabbaway within her range. She glanced over to see two very large Jabba fighting some distance from her, near the stone wall of the spoil. Caroline, who was still right next to her, was having a real time of it trying to keep from getting cut to ribbons by a couple of Jabba that had landed just beside her. She was already cut up in several locations.

To Catrina's dismay, she could also see more Jabba sailing through the open gate at an alarming rate. Dispatching her attackers, she turned to Caroline, drove her own sword into the snow, pulled both her daggers and launched them at the snarling beasts Caroline was struggling with, dropping them like loaded sacks of potatoes. Moments later, they both heard an odd popping noise. Airborne Jabba nearly exploded in flight, dropping dead to the ground, most of them mangled beyond recognition. The dull popping continued and more Jabba fell to the ground turning the white snow to crimson.

Cat pulled her daggers from the dead Jabba and turned to The Amanda, seeing muzzle flashes coming from the waist gunner's position as Danny did target practice on the Gangees. She could also see something else, high above them, directly over the wreckage. It was a gangly giant with flashing lights and spinning rotor blades, carefully navigating its way down towards the pickup zone. This must be one of the helicopters Britten had spoken of. *That meant that her father had made it!* There was no time to rejoice in his success, as she helped Caroline to her feet, handing her both daggers.   As Caroline dashed to where her son was battling several Jabba, Catrina grabbed her sword, heading for the open gate. The popping sound started again and nearly all the flying Jabba either disintegrated or fell to the ground in bloody pieces. The rest were dispatched with the sword or dagger.

*　*　*　*　*

The big .50 caliber machine gun bucked and vibrated with every squeeze of the trigger as Danny swung out a hose of tracers at the Gangees. He looked back at Brit and Bryan with a gleeful grin, clearing his gun of a jammed shell, pulling the bolt back and starting again. Now this was his idea of skeet shooting. The situation had gotten to the point where most of the Jabba had been obliterated from the air and only a few were left fighting on the ground. As more came through the open gate, they were easily dispatched.

Jerry fumbled around in the darkness of the cockpit, trying to find The Amanda's electrical panel. He had only been in this airplane once and had no idea where anything was. If he could get the electrical systems turned on, he could use the top turret to help Danny cover the gate. He sort of remembered where Brit had been working with it when they entered the aircraft for the first time in the cave.   He closed his eyes, trying to picture where it was, carefully feeling around in the dark. It took him a moment to see it in his mind, in front of the bomb bay. Finding the breakers on the electrical panel to the rear of

476

the flight deck, he started pushing them back into place and flipping switches. Finally, a few lights came on so he could read the labels.

"Stellar! Here they are!" he said finding the turret drive switches, turning them on. "Aren't I the awesome one?" Climbing up into the top turret gunner's position, Jerry could see Catrina reentering the spoil to help with the fight.

He was about to fire when he looked up to flashing lights above him. At first he thought he was looking up at some kind of a monster the Rift had created to take The Amanda away, but then recognized the loud thumping of rotor blades. The first of the Sky Cranes was here and hovering directly above them! Jerry could see a large hook lowering from the huge helicopter and knew it would be up to him to make the connection. He thought about just getting the main fuselage hooked up first, but that wouldn't work. Who would make the connections for the other parts of the airplane? The whole point here was to get The Amanda out and they would catch a ride with the last piece, the fuselage. He scrambled back down into the cockpit and worked the hatch door mechanism over the pilot and copilot's seats. Once he had carefully situated it out of the way, he climbed out and scampered over to the furthest wing. The aircraft sections had already been harnessed up by Britten previously. The only thing Jerry had to do was connect the giant hook and wait for them to take up the slack. He could see the crane operator clearly as he reached for the hook and guided it into place, then gave the "all ok", signal with thumbs up. He could smell the jet fuel exhaust as the pilot held his craft in place while the crane operator started the winch to pull the wing from the snow. Once it was airborne and somewhat stable, the pilot waved and gave his craft the throttle, rising almost straight up towards the shaft of sunlight beaming down through an ever constricting eye.

*　　*　　*　　*　　*

Upon reentering the Spoil, Catrina came face to face with two Kenlar warriors, both startled by the other.　 She had hoped that they could get out before the Kenlar had made the discovery as to where the group had stolen off to. She wished she had her daggers with her now as she could have dispatched at least one right off the bat and finished the other off with the sword. As it was, a quick jab to the face of one of them with the hilt of her sword and a kick to the groin of the other, sent them both sprawling far enough away for her to get the best of them. She spun effortlessly, letting her sword slash through the leather and flesh of both men, then turned to the open gates, pushing them closed to prevent any more of the Gangees from flying through and harassing the others. However, she did not secure them as Tim and Sargon were still inside with her.

477

Catrina turned to Tim and the altar, just catching sight of Ivan storming over the threshold of the spoil entrance. The Kenlar warlord's face was badly bruised from his ordeal at the arena, but more to the point, he was tired of being patient. He was down-right ticked-off now and ready to kill something. Catrina reached down, pulling the bow weapons from the two dead Kenlar warriors as more warriors appeared behind Ivan. She passed them over to Tim and Sargon who were crouching behind the still operating altar.

"Are Brit's helicopters coming in for the pickup yet?" Tim asked nervously, having already reset the time portal back to Britten's time. He and Sargon were a little more than anxious to leave the spoil, as there were only three of them to the Kenlar's building numbers at the top of the Spoil path.

"Yes, it would seem so," Catrina puffed softly, eyeing Ivan carefully. She knew what he was after now. **Her blood**, and he looked as though he was prepared to go through anyone or anything to satisfy his lust for it. The Kenlar warlord motioned his band of men to break into two groups and work their way down around the perimeter of the inner walls towards the gate. He was leaving nothing to chance this time. He had been outwitted at every turn in the last three days and he was tired of it. When he was finished here, he meant to deal with the Thulsa armies from within and take the spoils of war. Only one detail he hadn't counted on. *Where were the spoils of the mighty Thulsa?* He had been led to believe that Thulsa was the richest of the many clans in the surrounding areas. *So where were these riches?* He so hoped it wasn't one of those cheesy clichés about the true riches were in the people themselves and how delightful they were. He'd have to poop a big one and maybe vomit right along with it if that was indeed the case. If it were so, he would order the entire Thulsa people wiped from the face of the Argyle.

"Can you tell how much time is left?" Catrina inquired, motioning for Tim and Sargon to stay behind the altar.

"Time for what?" Tim asked, completely off his rhythm now. He was sure that Ivan had come for him this time and considering all the trouble he had caused the Kenlar warlord, he was sure he wasn't in for just a tongue lashing or a good spanking.

"The Rift!" Catrina stated impatiently. "How much time before the Rift collapses?" Tim suddenly came to life, feeling a little embarrassed about losing his train of thought. He popped up from behind the altar, looking down at the controls, scanning for the information and making the needed interpretations.

"Twenty minutes, maybe," he responded grimly. That wasn't very much time to resolve this situation and still make good their escape.

Catrina stepped out in front of the altar and stood posed with her battle sword resting on her right shoulder and her battle stick in her left hand resting near her hip. She had been waiting a long time for this opportunity to present itself. She knew she was much better than Ivan, but Ivan was much bigger and much stronger, though that didn't matter to her. She remembered hearing something when she was a little girl on Earth. *The bigger they are the harder they fall."* This gave her great confidence as she stood waiting for Ivan to make his move.

"Anything else you need to do to the altar to hold it to Britten's time event?" she asked, keeping her eyes glued on the big Kenlar warlord. Tim checked the readouts for the required information. It was too bad that this would be the only chance he would get to operate this thing. Their next trick would be to get themselves to The Amanda for pickup back to Earth.

"Nope, we're right on the money, we just need to get to The Amanda." Tim called out, glancing up at the warriors lining the inner Spoil walls and the Gangees taking roost on the tops of the surrounding walls. Sargon was becoming a little bit nervous. They had the weapons from the two dead warriors that Catrina had disposed of, but they were no match for all the other weapons that would no doubt be trained on just the three of them. This appeared to be a no win scenario. Even if Catrina was somehow victorious, there were too many warriors with orders to shoot whatever the outcome.

There would be very little chit chat this time as Ivan was delighted to be rid of her. If he couldn't have her, then no one could, least of all a puny stable boy named Britten Garrett. He slowly lumbered his big frame down the path towards her, pulling his sword. It was a giant among the swords of Argyle, long and slender, tapering out towards the end and curving up with sharp spikes on the top side. If he missed with a swipe, he could always back swing and tear flesh away from bone with the pointed row of teeth. The late morning sunlight reflected off his glistening arm muscles as he passed his sword back and forth between his hands several times approaching her, but Catrina remained focused and steely, letting his eyes blaze into her.

"Now Lassie," he thundered. "You've had your chance to make your choice..."

"And I have made it," Catrina cut him off boldly, holding her position steadfast. "I made that choice a long time ago."

Ivan bellowed enraged, letting his steel fly with all his might.

*　*　*　*　*

Digi and Tobor went at it hard and furious. In this fight, there were no rules. Only defeat and in this, it meant the death of one or the other. Dispatching the remaining Jabba harassing his family, Terry turned to the brawling leaders. He wanted to help, looking for an opening, but the two were too tightly balled together for him to get a clear swing. He was afraid of striking Digi. No, the best thing he could do right now was to stand watch and try to keep the others out of the way. He looked at the closed gate thinking about stepping over and pushing it back open, but then thought better of it as that would just invite more of the Gangees to attack.

The Jabba brawl was all over the place, with fur and blood flying everywhere they rolled. There was no way to know for sure who was who and who had the upper hand, until the two broke apart for a breather. Digi was missing fur in several places, bleeding behind his ears, with large gashes on his snout and rear paws. Tobor wasn't much better. His wing stumps and the surrounding areas were heavily matted with blood along with a few other places around his abdomen.

"Father would have been disappointed in you," Tobor gruffed between gasped of air.

"Our father chose the old ways," Digi pointed out, not letting Tobor get under his skin to taunt him. "Something you have never had any respect for," he finished, breathing heavily himself.

"The old ways are for mere animals," Tobor retorted angrily. "We have evolved to something higher, more powerful. You would have our kind serving the humans as beasts of burden."

"Had you taken the time to learn to read and discover the secrets of the Signet as Tim tried to get you to, you would know that humans and Jabba can easily live together as equals here on Argyle," Digi came back, preaching what had become a broken record to his brother.

"Speaking from personal experience brother," Tobor growled, "that will never happen."

"You made your choice to live under Ivan's boot."

"And what a glorious life it has been."

"So now it's time for it to end, my brother," Digi said, chirping and pressing his attack for the kill. Yes, Tobor was his brother, blood of his blood, flesh of his flesh. Nevertheless, he had followed a path that was against all the traditions and laws that governed the Jabbaway. He had taken a path of greed, a lust for blood and killing. For the Jabbaway, there was no return from this path. The animal instinct that flowed in their veins was simply too strong once they turned to this type of life. A Jabba taking this path would eventually self-destruct. Today was the day for Tobor to meet with his destiny at the hands of his own brother. Digi would take no pleasure in killing him, except in knowing that he would stop his destructive path and somehow find peace wherever a Jabbaway went after death.

The two Jabba battled viciously for several more moments until Digi was pinned to the ground by Tobor. Perhaps it would be the other way around for Digi, though whatever the outcome, he knew that Terry was standing by to make it all right. Tobor slashed ferociously at Digi's throat, slicing through his thick fur. Digi could feel the razor claws piercing through his flesh and as Tobor's paws sank through, he could only hope that it wasn't deep enough. As his brother carried through with his swing, Digi saw his opening and grabbed him by the snout and the back of the head. The neck bones instantly snapped with one quick twist and Tobor collapsed on top of Digi. He looked into the dark eyes of Tobor and said farewell to him. Terry carefully stepped up next to the two Jabba, Digi struggling to push Tobor's body off.

"Brothers?" Terry asked, looking at the large dark fur that was Tobor.

"Brothers," Digi reaffirmed, getting up and checking his throat. It was bleeding to be sure, but the strike had missed his vital arteries. He looked back at Tobor, then up at Terry. "And your daughter, is she all right?"

Terry suddenly became aware that he had no idea where she was or what had really happened to her. Everything had been such a blur when they had intercepted Tobor. Then afterwards he had become so preoccupied with protecting the others that he had completely forgotten about her. He looked frantically around the outside of the spoil and the snow covered valley.

"There she is!" Caroline yelled over the noise, pointing in the direction of The Amanda. Jerry had her back in his arms and walking in their direction. He kept looking back and up at the eye of the storm that continued to shrink. They also noticed the walls were getting closer. Indeed, the Rift was compressing, not only in thickness, but size as well. Navigating helicopters in and then back out with dangling cargo might prove to be harder than expected, especially with the light show going on all around them.

"So what happened to you guys?" Terry asked, relieved to see Jerry, while Caroline took a happy Anna from him. Digi stepped over next to him as Jerry looked down at the Jabba and chuckled softly. You couldn't hear it, but you could see it.

"Mynites have teenagers just like anyone else," he said, looking at the older Lieder kids. "They found us and took us into the Tera crystal caves."

"Wait, we were there too," Terry said, remembering that he and Danny had tried to explore to the ends of the caves, but turned back because it seemed as though they had no end. "We never saw you."

"They told us that the caves go on all through the heart of the Tera. Further than any of us could have walked it. Then they dropped us off south of the walls where we made our way here."

"Tobor had to be stopped," Digi said, licking his wounds. "He and the Gangees will trouble this world no more. Where is Tim?" Terry turned to the closed gate doors.

"I think he's still inside with Catrina working the altar. She closed the door to keep the other Gangees from coming out. I suspect that she could use our help." Jerry looked over his shoulder, detecting the thumping of rotor blades again. "Stand ready."

High above in the Earth sunlight, descending down towards the drop zone was the second Sky Crane. They needed to hurry. The Rift continued to compress and they were only ten to fifteen minutes from the last chopper making its run down through what was becoming a very narrow shaft. He knew there was nothing he could do here if there was to be another fight. Danny had the gate covered well enough with the .50 caliber machine gun, so he turned and jogged back up the trail to wait for the Sky Crane to pick up the second wing section and tail.

Terry put his ear against the thick wooden doors, trying to listen. It was very hard to hear anything, but he did detect the sound of clashing swords and decided that help would be appreciated. Pushing the doors open, a hail of large and small arrows came flying out at him. He spun out of the way just in time; letting the arrows sail harmlessly out into the snow. Caroline and the rest backed away to a safe distance, but were afraid to move too far back as the storm walls were gradually getting closer. To Terry's astonishment, none of the warriors tried to exit the Spoil to pursue anyone, but remained stationed around the inner perimeter. He peered around the corner through the open gate doors. Apparently it was just a warning shot not to interfere. He spotted Tim and Sargon standing at the altar with Kenlar warriors stationed behind them and extending all the way around the walls. All focus was on two combatants in the human made ring.

*　　*　　*　　*　　*

Catrina and Ivan were embroiled in a savage sword fight to the finish. This was not fencing, nor was it a knight's broad sword battle, though it would have suited Ivan better had it been so. He was a very big man and while his large sword was well suited for him, he lumbered about in comparison to Catrina's swift battle sword and stick fighting style. They were light and carefully tuned to her size and strength. In truth, Ivan's only advantage here was his strength. If he ever got a clear swing at the elegantly maneuvering Queen of Thulsa, he could easily cut her in half and be done with it. Catrina was certainly not willing to let that happen and was backing that notion up with her skill and mastery as a swordsman. As Ivan wasn't wearing nearly as much armor as Catrina, because he felt like he didn't need it, Catrina was able to land several strikes with her battle stick. Normally this would leave an attacker in extreme pain, usually with broken bones or even torn flesh, but Ivan had thick hair over heavy skin covered muscle, so it was like hitting a buffalo, having little to no effect. She was very good at avoiding the big sword Ivan was

482

swinging at her. A direct hit on her blade could not only be painful to her, but could severely damage her weapon.

Ivan was becoming more agitated at his failure to get past the Queen's defenses and the fact that she kept landing blows with her battle stick was starting to really grind on his nerves. He made note of the altar that Tim and Sargon seemed to be staying close to. It was obviously something of great worth to them. The pretty lights and three dimensional images hovering right over its top were something he had never seen before. Perhaps this was the riches of Thulsa? This machine created something for them and apparently Tim knew how it all worked. Seems his interpreter had been holding out on him. If Ivan had known just how much he had been holding back, Tim might not be alive right now.

Catrina held her focus, using Ivan's strength against him. Taking the energy he was expending on his swings to deflect and redirect it to either tire him or provide opportunities for a strike. She knew from the outset that she would not be able to just use a couple of fancy moves on him, dazzle his ego and then do away with him. She would have to use every technique in her arsenal to carefully pick him apart and even then, she would have to outlast him in the end. Ivan was such a large man and very powerful, she would have to remain solely in the zone in order to keep from getting hewn down by his big blade.

Catrina passed a glance at the gate as it reopen, a barrage of arrows sent flying through, but then the warriors turned back to the fight. It appeared that this exchange between her and Ivan was the dominant center piece for the Kenlar. The Gangees made no attempt at making the quick swoop from the spoil to the other side. The remaining flock were either perched on the wall watching the Kenlar warlord or milling about in the air. They were a bit wary of entering through the gate to the outside because of the noise and tumult emanating from the open doors. There seemed to be no leadership among them any longer as Tobor and his lieutenants were conspicuously missing.

She could feel the weight of time pressing hard on her mind. There just simply wasn't any available for this decisive exchange. She glanced over at Tim, who watched carefully, constantly looking around him at the warriors who seemed to largely ignore him and Sargon. She was going to have to maneuver Ivan into a different arena if she was going to make good her escape. Formulating a plan to do so, a thought came to mind about time itself. They had just sent her father back in time so that he could convince Cal Schultz to send in the rescue helicopters at a certain moment. *Why then, couldn't they do the same thing here? Why not finish this with Ivan, secure the safety of her people and then go back in time through the Rift at its next passing?"* Seemed logical enough to her at first, but then she reminded herself that it just wasn't that simple. The Rift was held in place by the presence of The Amanda. They were lifting her pieces out right now. The next time the Rift would pass by, it would not stop. Maybe the Ancients could still just walk through to wherever and whenever, but she was human and incapable of doing so. No, if she was going to escape, it had to be now, but there were about thirty warriors and Ivan standing in her way. How do you get past them? She needed to change the arena they were fighting in. Get Ivan and his men, out of the Spoil.

Catrina carefully and slowly worked Ivan around close to the altar, trying to hold as close to the perimeter of warriors as possible. Though Ivan could care less if he were to strike down one of his own men, just the presence of something standing there might divert his attention a little and keep him off balance. She also noted that he was becoming increasingly angry, expending even more energy to try and get at her. This could complicate things, as he would start to follow an irrational pattern. She continued to lead him down towards the altar, letting him push her back, but guiding him carefully. At one point, Ivan stopped advancing and she thought that he had discovered her ploy, but a couple of quick strikes to his legs and thighs from her battle stick and he was enraged enough to keep pushing her back. It was too bad she couldn't do the same with the sword. The battle stick was so light and maneuverable, that it was more than easy to just "flick" a quick swing in and out before Ivan could react.

Now Ivan was getting even more frustrated and took harder swings to get at her as she backed up right against the altar. She hadn't really wanted to get pushed back into this position, not against something solid anyway. She dodged several swings and deflected two, all to Ivan's enormous exasperation. She watched him wind up and throw the biggest swing at her yet and her only recourse on this one was to duck and roll. Ivan let out a loud bellow to help release his full energy on the swing. As Catrina rolled away and quickly got back to her feet, Ivan's big sword struck the left Twin, still inserted in the altar, squarely on its hilt. The blow was so powerful and the hit in just the right spot, that the Twin hilt snapped completely off and was sent spinning towards the open gate. There was a deafening howl associated with the strike, issuing from the open gate and the altar suddenly began to pulse even faster. The three dimensional images hovering over the altar interface faded in and out of sight a couple of times and the controls on the surface turned to distortion, then winked off.

Tim watched horrified as the hilt spun away to the ground. The left Twin controlled the time event horizon. Thankfully, it was already locked to Britten's time, but now there was no way to ever control the Rift. It was not likely that anyone could ever travel through it again after it left in just a few short minutes. *It was time to get out and get out now!* He watched Catrina being pushed back into the line of warriors near the gate as Ivan pressed his perceived advantage hard against her. As the warriors broke apart, making way for the fight heading out through the gate, Tim pushed Sargon through the bunched line of distracted Kenlar and out into the snow. Several warriors turned their reloaded weapons in Sargon's direction to fire, but Tim launched himself at them, knocking them to the ground. He quickly got to his feet trying to get free of the tangle and inadvertently stumbled too close to Ivan. Ivan was sent off balance by the interruption, and turned swinging blindly in a fit of furor. The huge sword sliced right through three warriors just getting to their feet and deeply across Tim's chest. All of the Kenlar flooded out into the valley beneath the storm as Tim was thrown back into the outer wall.

Terry held himself back after he had grabbed Sargon and quickly moved him some distance away with his family and the other council members. He too saw Tim fall with Ivan's anger blinded swing, but was powerless to render aide.   He watched him for signs of life, but Tim remained motionless. Terry fought the instinct to run to his friend and help him, but he knew if he were to try, he would be hewn down by Kenlar warriors or riddled to death with arrows. Terry finally sank back against Caroline and the crowd behind him to deal with his sorrow. Tim had endured so much since he had come here to Argyle. Held captive nearly the entire time; the loss of his beloved Kawti and thinking he had lost his best friend Digi. Now he was so close to going home, but wasn't going to make it. Terry watched as Digi swooped around the Kenlar and quietly landed unnoticed next to his friend.

The Jabba examined his inert friend carefully, nuzzling his face and then the deep splayed gash across his chest. Tim was only barely alive but fading fast.

"I'm here Tim," Digi said quietly in his ear so he could be heard. Tim could not raise his head to look, but recognized his friend. Though he was unable to show it, he was overjoyed that he was still alive and that he was here with him now, at the end.

"I saw the sun," Tim grunted, trying to breath. The massive incision had severely damaged his lungs and he was quickly suffocating. "I saw the Earth's sun. It's right there." Digi turned and looked up at the shrinking shaft of light high above. He could see the second helicopter starting to make its way back out, and it looked as though it was having quite a time doing so.

"I see it my friend," Digi responded, turning back to his dying friend.

"I told you it was real," Tim rasped. He paused a moment, still trying to look up at the Jabba.

"Yes, you were right. I never doubted you."

"Thank you for staying with me and believing in me." He forced his head up a little so he could look at Digi one last time. "Thanks for coming to say goodbye," he said, smiling weakly. Digi reached up and gently licked him on the cheek. When he looked at him again, he could see that he was gone. Digi looked back up at the sunlight, then back at Tim. He understood that Tim was with his Kawti now, and being together was their wonderful place.

"Goodbye my friend," he said in a whisper that only he could hear, then turned and flew back over to where Terry stood with his family.

*   *   *   *   *

Catrina watched Tim sink to the ground, mortally wounded. She instantly pressed her attack again, working Ivan around in a circle so she could get close to Tim. Ivan's entire garrison had emptied out into the valley, though now they were far more wary of what was going on above them than they were at what their warlord was doing. By the time Catrina had maneuvered around close to Tim, Digi had already left and she could see that Tim was dead. The slash across his chest was deep and looked like he had just under gone an autopsy in the wrong fashion. She could see no signs of life. How sad that he had come so far with her father and the others. Fought and suffered his way here, only to die at the hands of the monster that had held him hostage all these many Argylian years. She caught sight of the second helicopter lifting the second wing and tail section, struggling up and away from the ground. It was an awesome sight, but she had to hold her fascination for later. She had to concentrate on finishing this.

Ivan glanced down at Tim's inert body and frowned. *Idiot!* Now he would have to find another interpreter and force these others to tell him where Tim had hidden the book, even if he had to butcher every man, woman and child in Thulsa. He had to have those secrets, for they were the basis of his power and rule over a people who were naive, silly and superstitious. First, to finish off his would be bride.

The snow was somewhat uneven beneath their feet and trying to maneuver for the upper hand was difficult, some places there was slush, while other spots were hard as rock. This made balance a bit problematic and both combatants slowed their attacks to sure up their footing. Catrina found herself sliding with every maneuver she initiated, but Ivan was having the same traction issues. Then an opportunity presented itself. They both swung and slipped at the same time, going down hard. Ivan held onto his sword, though the fall had upended him more so than Catrina. She had lost her sword in the fall but retained her battle stick. Looking up at the shaft of light high above, she caught site of another helicopter dropping down out of the sky towards the main fuselage of The Amanda. *This was it! The last chopper was here!*

They both floundered, trying to get their feet back under them, Ivan because of his size and Catrina because of her armor. It was slippery in the snow and she actually went down two more times

486

before she was able to steady herself and get to her knees. As she did so, she felt a big hand grab a fist full of her hair and hold her right where she was. ***Ivan had her!*** The big warlord held her firmly in place and steadied his stance, bringing his sword up to her neck, pressing the spikes on the opposite side of her face right under her temple. Ivan puffed hard, waiting. He knew he had her right where he wanted her now and wanted to catch his breath to savor every moment of his blood lust and victory over the Queen of Thulsa.

"And now lassie, I'll take what is rightfully mine," he puffed victoriously.

Catrina fumbled in the snow, but could neither see nor feel her sword. The only thing she had in hand was her battle stick and it had proven less than effective against this big Kenlar. Ivan turned his blade slowly over so that the razor's edge was now against her smooth neck. The edge was still quite sharp despite the fight they had just had and it cut right through the hemp weave of the neck choker she was wearing. Looking up again, the descending chopper had nearly reached The Amanda. She had to do something now, or die!

Feeling Ivan flexing to start his cut, she swung her battle stick straight back and up as hard as she could; the butt end of the stick finding its mark directly in Ivan's groin. Not many men can take a direct hit to this area and remain upright. Ivan had always prided himself on the size of his man parts and libido. Today, they would be his undoing. He had no choice but to drop his sword, sinking to his knees and letting out a miserable wail while putting both hands to his enpained reproductive units. Catrina dropped her battle stick and still not being able to find her own sword, picked up Ivan's and got to her feet. Circling around behind him, she swung the huge sword as hard as she could without hesitating. The blade sank deep into the back and right side of the Kenlar Warlords' neck, but she didn't stop there. Knowing Ivan, he was still very dangerous, though at this point it seemed highly unlikely that he would be getting back to his feet again. She followed all the way through with her swing and then turned the other direction, swinging again. This time, the blow sank deep into the left side of his neck. His head cocked violently in the direction of the blow; a sudden gush of blood jetting from the right. Now she had to finish the job. Without total dominance here, the Kenlar would not believe that their leader had been conquered, whoever it was that claimed to be the victor. She continued her swing, rotating again, picking up speed, spinning and letting the blade strike again across the back of his neck. This time, the big heavy sword continued right through separating Ivan's head from the rest of him. Kneeling only for a moment longer, the warlord's body fell forward and crumpled into a heap on the now crimson snow.

Catrina wiped blood spatter from her face, looking up in time to see Jerry hooking the harness to the Sky Crane, then scrambling to climb back in through the top cockpit window of The Amanda. Catrina's arms ached from the fight and her legs felt weak, but she had to move. She could hear the whine of the engines starting to rev up and the rotor blades chopping at the air, the crane operator working the winch to pull up the slack.

Passing Terry a glance, she dropped Ivan's sword and started running. Breaking through the warrior circle, most of the Kenlar stood stunned at the site of their beheaded leader lying dead in the snow. Several warriors managed to bring themselves back to reality enough to carry out Ivan's orders. If for some reason he was defeated, they were to leave no one alive. Starting to turn their weapons in Catrina's direction, Terry detected muzzle flashes bellowing from the top of The Amanda and towards her rear. Jerry had climbed back into the top turret and was letting both fifties lose, with Danny at the waist position. The huge slugs, meant for tearing holes in aircraft, easily blew through Kenlar flesh, dropping to the ground behind a now racing Catrina.

She could feel the rotor wash blasting her face and the snow directly ahead of her went airborne as the harness went taut and the Sky Crane started to lift The Amanda from the frozen ground. She began to yell and wave her arms to get someone's attention, but the snow directly around the pickup zone went to a complete white-out, the helicopter's engines continuing to throttle up, lifting the fuselage higher. Catrina sprinted directly into the blizzard to reach the swaying cargo, the pilots holding their hover long enough for the load to stabilize under the rotor wash. She frantically reached for the back end of the fuselage as it began to lift up and away. No one could see her or knew she was there. Britten and Bryan were probably still lying incapacitated in the back of the plane while Danny and Jerry were covering her escape attempt from the forward machine guns. She was nearly out of gas, making one final attempt at grabbing the open back end, the chopping sound of the rotor blades growing in intensity. She jumped as hard as she could, reaching as far as she could. She hoped that somehow Britten would lean out the back and catch her, but there was no one there and nothing to grab a hold of. She touched nothing but swirling air filled with stinging snow, falling back to the ground.

Catrina rolled over, watching The Amanda rise higher up the collapsing Rift shaft towards the sunlight. As it did, the guns went silent, the fuselage gently swaying, slowly spinning as it rose. She turned her gaze back towards the gate to see all of the Kenlar warriors lying dead in the snow. Sargon was helping Caroline move her family and the council back towards the gate as Terry was running towards Catrina. Digi stepped over to the beheaded corpse of Ivan, picked up the head and holding it in his front paws flew through the open gate and disappeared.

Catrina was prepared to stay right where she was. Britten was leaving and she was supposed to be going with him. Everything they had done had led up to this point, but now she had missed her only chance to leave Argyle. She would be trapped here forever, never seeing Britten again. Numbness enveloped her as she watched The Amanda lifting away, being struck repeatedly by plasma bolts. How could this possibly be happening? This insidious monster had separated her and her parents and now it would continue to hold her captive from them, from Britten. She had fallen in love with him, discovering that she couldn't live without him, but just as importantly, she knew he felt the same way about her. She felt a wave of heartache suddenly slap her hard across the chest, tears welling in her eyes as the thoughts of life without Britten streaked through her mind. It was too much to bear. Now she just wanted to let the storm take her, as it had taken all the others. She didn't want to be in this world or any other world without Britten. Nothing mattered now. Then a defiant flame suddenly flickered within her, giving her cause for hope, and where there was hope, there was life. Is this what her father did when faced with the prospect of never being able to return to her mother? Is this what her parents would have her do? Is this how they had raised her? Just give up, because things seemed hopeless? Was this what Britten would have her do? Catrina rolled over and tried to get up, but found her strength gone.

The moment Terry reached Catrina; he was pulling her up, trying to drag her back down the path towards the safety of the gate. The light show above them grew in intensity, electric fingers combining into huge plasma balls, hurtling towards the rising fuselage of The Amanda. The shaft of light far above was almost obliterated by the wind and debris starting to cascade from the storm walls.

Even with Terry's help, Catrina could not continue, but he refused to give up on her. The little man finally turned to her, picked her up, and putting her over his shoulder, started running for the safety of the gate. Stumbling at the gate threshold, both Terry and Catrina went down. Caroline and Sargon quickly scrambled back out to help them inside, the collapsing Rift walls shaking the ground beneath them. All four looked up in time to see bolts of energy and plasma balls streaking towards and pummeling The Amanda in a shower of light and sparks as it rose towards the ever shrinking shaft of light high above. They could feel the wind start to blast at them as the collapsing Rift charged over the top of the wall and towards the gate. Everyone backed up and helped the children push the big doors shut behind them.

Loud silence

Britten could feel the movement of the fuselage as the helicopter began to rise and they became airborne. He could still make out the outline of Amanda's yellow dress feeling a quick flicker of excitement to be going home, but it was instantly quenched a moment later when he realized that Catrina hadn't gotten back onboard. Somehow, he had to hold the chopper for a moment longer to allow her to get on. He became frantic, but was helpless to do or say anything. He could hear the waist gun clanging as Danny popped off short bursts at the crowd of Kenlar warriors below them. Jerry was somewhere forward, but even at that, there was no way to communicate with the helicopter to ask them to wait for her. He tried to feel his way back to the open end of the torn fuselage, but what could he do? He was blind and half paralyzed.

He thought he could hear her calling to him, but the roar of the rotors above them and the storm all around them, completely obliterated just about everything else. He called to her as loud as he could, but he was so hoarse that even if there had been no noise, it would have been difficult to hear him from outside the airplane.

Rising higher, he became aware of faint flashes of light appearing in the boiling blackness of his mind, followed by the occasional spits of sparkles drifting across his vision. He began to sense something awful growing within him, right around his chest area. It was a horrible sinking pain, not a heart attack, but something even more devastating. *They had to wait! Catrina wasn't here! They had to wait for her to get onboard!* He noticed the guns go silent as they continued to rise and he turned back to where he had been sitting, trying to locate Amanda's dress in his field of vision. He looked in every direction, the flashing light in his mind becoming more intense and the noise rising to almost painful levels.

The fuselage was rocked by a massive pounding. It felt like it had been struck by something and he could feel energy surging through the entire frame of the plane. Then he heard a scream come from the forward section, just in front of the bomb bay. It was a woman's voice, perhaps Catrina had gotten onboard through the front hatch. He turned his head but could still see nothing but intense flashes of light. He leaned forward, feeling the floor on the other side until he found Bryan. Examining him with his hands, he could feel that he was still alive and seemed to be breathing fine, but unconscious.

"Danny!" he called out, thinking something must have happened to him. "Where are you?"

"I'm here," his friend called back, moving towards Brit. "We need to get you two as far forward as we can, away from the back. If this thing starts to spin hard, it could get as wild as the Tilt-a-Whirl at the fair."

"Did Catrina get onboard?" Brit called out frantically, trying to pull on his brother.

"I don't know," Danny answered, grunting as he pulled Bryan forward to one of the seats mounted directly behind the bomb bay bulkhead. "I saw her running towards us right before we lifted off, but I couldn't see her get on. It's possible she's up front with Jerry." There was another scream as another flash of bright light streaked across Britten's vision.

"What's going on?" Brit yelled, trying to help strap Bryan into his seat. In his condition, he wasn't much help, but did what he could. Danny glanced outside at the plasma fingers reaching out at them from the now pitch black walls of the spinning Rift.

"We're getting hammered by the Rift," he yelled back over the noise. The screams continued even louder and seemed to be coming from all around them now. With each strike, the screams would wail out to the point where they could hear almost nothing else. Danny helped Brit strap in, the fuselage bucking and swaying. He could see out the back as more plasma fingers reached at them. Some of them were getting so large that they formed giant balls. The array of colors was immense and there was a certain beauty in its madness, but there were no good feelings associated with this light show. Danny turned in his seat, yelling forward.

"Jerry! Are you ok?"

"Yeah," he yelled back above the noise. "What's going on? Who's doing all the screaming?" He was still in the top turret, firmly strapped in as things were starting to get turbulent. He had hoped to drop back down into the pilot's seat, but he found that he had a better view of everything right where he was. He just wished there was a little less noise.

"Is Catrina up there with you?" Danny yelled over the noise, as they continued their ascent. They almost couldn't tell that they were moving other than the feeling of just hanging from something being tossed about. Jerry didn't remember seeing her get in but he looked down into the empty cockpit anyway. It wasn't likely that she would have been able to crawl in through the bombardier's access tunnel to the nose position. He looked down at the hatch directly below him. It was still secured tightly. No, there was no one up front with him, yet someone was screaming in agony. He turned his head up at the Sky Crane steadily making its way to the narrowing shaft of light still quite high above them. Turning the turret around 360 degrees, all he could see was blackness and plasma energy streaking all along the Rift walls. He reasoned that the Rift was close to collapsing. The plasma

strikes and the size of the balls coming at them were increasing
exponentially. An uneasy feeling started building in his head watching
the plasma fingers streaking across the walls of the Rift, as if chasing
them and looking for a good place to launch at the rising fuselage.
They were going to have to move even faster if they were going to get
out before the portal closed.

"She's not up here, I thought she climbed in back there with you
guys," Jerry yelled back, a larger plasma ball striking the plane again.
The screams became even more frightful, if that was possible, as the
Sky Crane labored to pull the broken fuselage towards the shrinking
shaft of light above. Danny turned back to Britten with his report as
he worked his harness.

"He hasn't seen her," he said over the noise. A very sickening
feeling continued to take hold of Britten's heart. *She hadn't made it
onboard! That meant that she was still on the ground!* A sudden urge
to unbuckle and jump from the plane gripped him. He had to be with
her, but as he started to do so, a figure in yellow materialized right in
front of him.

"DON'T YOU DARE!" Amanda roared. Brit was stunned by her
sudden appearance, the tone of her voice, and the contorted look on
her face. He could see her plainly in his dark vision, which didn't make
any sense at all.

"She risked everything for you and you would throw your life away
in an attempt to rejoin her? No! I won't let you do it!" Amanda sank
to her knees in front of Britten with her hands holding her head, pain
twisting across her face. There was another plasma strike and she
screamed in agony.

"It's the Rift," Danny yelled. "It's trying to take her back." A
moment later he looked past the image of Amanda at a huge plasma
ball racing towards them. "INCOMING!" He yelled, bracing for the
impact. Brit saw a brilliant flash in his clouded vision as the ball
streaked right through the opening in the back of the plane and into
Amanda.

He could feel the heat from the burst exploding into her. Only her
image remaining in his vision, he watched electric fingers grab her and
pull her towards the open back of the broken fuselage. Her entire
being glowed from the energy strike. Energy tentacles enveloping her
image, light firing from her eyes and finger tips. She reached for
Britten, screaming in agony.

"Help me!"

Britten pulled at his harness, trying to work his way out of it, but
couldn't see the fasteners to undo them. He was able to get part way
out, just enough to reach out to Amanda and grab both her hands.

"Please, don't let it take me!" she pleaded, as it now became a tug
of war to hold her inside the plane. If the Rift got her outside, her

consciousness and energy would surely be reassimilated and lost forever.

"Hang on!" Brit yelled, straining against the plasmic pull. He tried to maintain his death grip on her, the plasma energy engulfing her. Streaks of electrical fingers charged down her arms, biting and nipping at him. It stung like nothing else he had ever felt before. He had never undergone a tasing demonstration, but he imagined that this is what it would have felt like had someone put the Taser to his hands and arms. Still suffering from the paralysis of the download, maintaining his hold on Amanda was impossible and he could feel his grip slipping.

Their eyes locked, straining to hang on. It was only a matter of moments before she would slip through his fingers and be pulled out, back to that thing that had given her life. He found it cruel and dastardly that he would lose Catrina and Amanda to this horrible spacial Rift. He could feel its power as it continued to snap and nip at his hands and slipping fingers.

Just as he could hold on no more, there came another set of hands that reached out and grabbed Amanda's. Britten reaffirmed his grip as Danny held onto her with firm strong hands. The plasma bolts spiked and nipped at his friend, both gritting their teeth under the strain and pain. Once they had a good hold on her, Brit thought he was seeing the light outside getting brighter and the walls turning a dark grey instead of the maddening black. He could make out different shapes of debris swirling along the Rift wall as it rotated closer.

"We're almost out!" Jerry called out from up front. The view of the Sky Crane above them was awesome as it struggled, even at full power, to make the needed altitude to break out over the top.   While these veteran pilots had seen their share of action, having been in worse weather than this, they were still filled with a strong sense of foreboding, mixed with quite a bit of apprehension for their surroundings. They imagined that this was what the inside of a tornado looked like up close. Aircraft of any type, least of all helicopters, don't mix with twisters in situations such as this. Indeed, Jerry imagined that the pilots had to be getting hammered and had thought more than once about dropping this load and getting the heck out of there. The fact that there were people in the fuselage was probably the only thing that kept them from doing so.

The pilot in command had the collective pulled up as high as he dared and the throttle up to maximum power to get the full amount of upward thrust out of the rotor blades. Under normal circumstances, this would not be standard operating procedures. They would be moving much slower to ensure the safety of their load, but there was nothing normal about this. They watched wide eyed, the walls continuing to close around them. It was going to be a real nail bitter yet.

Watching the bright circle of light growing closer above them, Jerry spun the top turret around, facing the rear of the plane. He could see the plasma hands and fingers holding onto the back of the broken fuselage. Several more bolts of energy joined with the many that were already forming the electrical appendages of the Rift, pulling at the whole fuselage now. Feeling quite unnerved by the sensation, Jerry look back up at the Sky Crane still rising at the same rate, but starting to strain with the added drag.

He felt helpless watching all the plasma energy flowing around the Rift walls finally converging into one massive arm and hand, fixing a firm hold on the plane. He could hear Amanda screaming from the back of the fuselage. It was obvious that the Rift was trying to reclaim her, but Jerry felt completely powerless to do anything about it. The only weapons he had were the twin fifties on either side of him in the turret. What good would bullets be against something like this?

He gave the guns a quick check anyway and pulled the triggers, carefully aiming through the rigging, trying to aim at the arm of plasma energy extending out from the Rift wall. He watched the tracers blow right through it only to disintegrate. He let a couple of bursts go at nothing in frustration knowing beforehand that what he had tried wasn't going to have any effect. As he let the last burst go, he watched them strike the Rifts spinning wall. Large ripples of bright purple plasma flowed outward from each strike point, just like a drop of water on the calm surface of a lake or throwing a stone in a still body of water. As it did so, he noticed that several bolts of energy separated from the main plasma arm and ran along with the ripples until they had faded away.

"Interesting," he mumbled to himself, spinning the turret ninety degrees of the fuselage and letting another burst go, moving it all around trying to make as much of a disturbance in the Rift wall as he could. More arms peeled off the main, following the ripples moving around the swirling wall. He fired again and again, each time striping more and more arms away from the back of the plane. He wished he could shoot downward, but he was on top and that just wasn't possible. There was no lower ball turret in this aircraft either, only the B-17 and B-24 carried those. However, the waist gunner could shoot downward. He paused a moment and yelled back over the bomb bay, hoping that everything was still ok back there.

"Hey guys! Point your guns down and shoot!" That was all he could do. That and hope they could hear and do something about it. He continued popping off short bursts into the Rift wall, the light above growing brighter. Spinning his turret around at various locations, his hope was to change where the burst came from in case the Rift figured out what he was doing. The energy fingers played like a kitten with a piece of yarn or a bug, following every ripple. A second set of machine guns began to chatter from the rear of the fuselage. Turning his turret, he could see muzzle flashes and feel the vibration of the waist guns spitting on both sides.

The ripples pulled more energy downward and soon the plasma arm that had once engulfed the rear of the plane disappeared. No sooner had it done so than the Sky Crane had cleared the rim at the top and was out of the thick of it. The pilots continued to hold their full power assent until the fuselage was well clear of the storm, and then started to relax a bit, applying forward movement to the west.

Danny watched out the back as they cleared the top of the storm. From his vantage point, he could see the hole close in a blaze of ionized energy and plasma balls shooting out directly above where it had been. Then, everything went quiet, or at least as quiet as it could be under a Sky Crane.

Amanda was gone. She had disappeared shortly after Jerry had started firing his guns at the Rift walls. It was a little disconcerting to both Britten and Danny, but they knew she had not gotten pulled out of the plane, so they held onto hope that she had retreated into the relative safety of the molecular makeup of the plane's airframe.

Brit placed a hand on the metal wall next to him and closing his eyes, tried to search for her. He could feel something, but calling to her repeatedly produced no results, only the faint twinge that she was there, somewhere. He pulled his hands back, coddling them in his lap. They were in excruciating pain now. He looked down at them, seeing second and even some third degree burns on them.

He looked over at Danny who was now sitting on the floor in front of Bryan, his eyes closed. His hands looked like they had burns on them as well. It was then that Brit realized that he was seeing what was around him. He held his enpained hands back up and looked at them. He could see sparkles still dancing wildly through his field of vision and trying to look straight at something still only resulted in boiling grey, but there was vision in both his peripherals.

"I can see," he muttered, choking up with the advent of the small miracle happening to him. He thought the download would render him permanently blind and paralyzed, but here was hope that perhaps he could recover.

Then, the rush of their escape faded, leaving him only the emptiness that had been lurking within, waiting for its turn to envelope him. It rolled over him in tidal wave after tidal wave; feeling like his heart was being pierced again and again. Each time it pierced, the pain became more intense, boiling harder and harder through him. What Talon had done to him was nothing compared to this. Yes, they had escaped and were on their way home. It would be only a couple of minutes before they would be over Driggs and landing, but he was without Catrina, without the woman he loved, the woman he could not live without. Heartbreak flooded his mind, his emotions taking him and he began to weep uncontrollably. He wished that he could bury his face in his hands, but they were too injured and raw to handle the touch or the saline in his tears. It would have stung like alcohol on an open wound, but nothing could hurt as bad as his breaking heart was now. For several minutes he wept bitterly, then noticed Bryan stirring next to him and did his best to clamp off the emotional flood to attend to his brother.

Looking out the window, slowly spinning under the Sky Crane, he could see they were descending over the Driggs airport and the landing zone that Cal had set up. The other pieces of the wreckage lay carefully cradled in some kind of a huge rack that had been built specifically for "The Amanda" a couple of days ago. The largest had been designed to cradle the fuselage.

He ached all over feeling physically sick. Certainly he was in turmoil emotionally, but somehow he would have to hold it back for another time. It was very difficult as just the act of descending closer to the airport and knowing that their ordeal was almost over was enough to cause him to lose it for a moment. Feeling "The Amanda" coming to rest in her cradle, he remained motionless, staring out the window at the afternoon sunlight and the deep snow that blanketed the entire region of eastern Idaho. He was home at last, glad for his brother and his friends, but all he wanted to do was go back. Go back to Argyle, back to Thulsa, back to her.

Men outside worked to disconnect the Sky Crane hook from the harness and finally, the huge helicopter moved off, the inside of the fuselage becoming calm. The quiet was loud and his ears rang with white noise. He could hear movement above him and looked up at a tired Jerry Gunn, who was grinning from ear to ear. His friend carefully maneuvered himself over the top of them and helped Danny to his feet, then they turned to Bryan to get him out of the harness. They could see a couple of ambulances pulling up next to the fuselage and several people running in their direction.

His uncle Cal was the first one to make it through the back of the fuselage to where Bryan and Brit were. He was followed closely by someone familiar, yet different looking. He thought it was Tony Dallas, but with his vision being as it was, it just didn't seem probable. His mind a jumble of confusion, he watched Tony pull something from his pocket and place it around his brother's neck, carefully tucking it inside his coat.

Everything started to move in slow motion now, turning surreal. Britten watched in stunned silence as his brother was carried out by several EMTs to an awaiting gurney. Jerry turned and helped Brit out of his harness, then putting his friend's arm over his shoulder for support, made their way out the back and into the stark cold sunlight of Earth. Looking around in a daze, the noise outside was muffled in Brit's ears. Upon exiting the plane, they came face to face with a woman. His vision was in such turmoil already and the brilliant sunlight made recognition next to impossible.

Leaning closer to him and putting something around his neck, he didn't have to see her to know who it was. Amanda Alice carefully tucked a Tera crystal, on a long golden necklace, down the front of his shirt, then wrapping a strong arm around him, helped Jerry walk him towards awaiting EMT personnel. He could see Bryan being evaluated closely and Danny was having his hands attended to at the door of another emergency vehicle. They helped Brit to a third ambulance where the EMTs started attending to the burns on his hands.

He just leaned back, looking up at the ceiling, listening to the muffled voices of Jerry talking to someone familiar. It was his uncle Cal, trying to get some kind of a report on what had happened. Jerry was trying to give him just the basics, but Cal was asking for details that made him sound a little more frantic than he should be. Finally, the older gentleman climbed up into Brit's vehicle, kneeling down on one knee in front of him.

"Brit, what happened?" Brit just stared at him. How do you explain the last three and a half days to someone so they could possibly believe it? It was almost like he didn't even hear his uncle. Jerry tried to pull the older man back to give the EMTs time to work on his hands, but Cal pressed his questions.

"What happened?" he asked, a little louder. Brit sat up, trying to see the look on his uncle's face. Out of his peripherals, he could see Tony and Amanda stepping away from the broken aircraft and approaching the back of the ambulance together. He knew what they were after and wished he could curl up and disappear. His eyes began to well, looking past Cal as Tony and Amanda carefully crowded behind Cal and Jerry to inquire of their daughter's whereabouts.

"She didn't make it," Britten choked out, shaking his head. Cal looked back at Jerry in shocked exasperation, then realized Brit wasn't talking to him and stepped aside to let Tony and Amanda in. Both parents lovingly took the sobbing Garrett brother in their arms and just held him as he cried.

After several moments of listening to Brit sob uncontrollably, Jerry had to step away from the scene. Brit was always the strongest of the four, but witnessing this kind of pain was a little more than Jerry was prepared to take. Heading back over to Danny's emergency vehicle, he watched Bryan's pulled away, sirens blaring.

Danny's hands were being wrapped, but other than that, he seemed to be in good spirits. He was joking with the medical team working on him, even flirting with one of the female EMTs he found to be quite cute.

"Working the scene already, eh?" Jerry asked, good-naturedly. Danny chuckled a bit, the EMT he was flirting with blushed and turned away. They were pretty much finished with his hands but wanted to give him a complete check out. All of them needed to be checked over thoroughly.

"Tell you what," Danny said, getting up to leave. "We'll all come on over to the hospital in a bit and then you can check me out all you want."

"Oh brother," Jerry complained grinning. "Like that line would ever work." Danny played the innocent, giving his friend a questioning look.

"What? We have to go get checked out, don't we?" He was trying hard to act like he was for real, but too many people knew these two all too well. "Well don't we?" he asked again, stepping away from the vehicle. "I suppose we could always check them out," he said in a silly sounding voice while he and Jerry started back over to the other ambulance.   Cal was just stepping away from the other vehicle and they stopped to see if they could get any further information on their friend's condition. The soft crying from inside the vehicle provided enough evidence that things were not going well. The Dallas's tried to console an anguished Britten while Jerry, Danny and Cal tried to listen.

"What happened?" Tony asked through his own tears. "Where's Cat?" Jerry bowed his head not wanting to be the bearer of bad news, but Danny didn't mind taking the lead here. He felt a renewed sense of confidence that, until now, he never realized he had. Somehow, there would be a change in him from here on out, a change in all of them.

"She didn't make it Tony. We saw her running for the plane as we were lifting off, but she never made it onboard. We couldn't even see her below us. There was just too much rotor wash from the helicopter and there was no way to signal the pilots. We barely got out as it was." Danny turned to Cal. "Your pilots should have dropped us and gotten out." Danny announced, stating his own opinions on their rescue from the storm.

"They didn't because Tony here told them that you guys would be inside, otherwise they would have never gone in there in the first place. This has all been pretty wild," Cal complained. The past three days had been no picnic for him either. He had been forced to take a lot of very strange things on faith. Tony and Amanda had just showed up out of the blue three days ago, claiming to know all kinds of things about the effort to salvage the wreck. Then they came up with this fantastic story about how Tony and his crew had flown "The Amanda" through the Rift and crash landed on Argyle. Then he traveled back in time to 1960, waiting for time to catch up and have the extraction helicopters go in to mount a rescue before the Rift departed. Cal was ready to have both of them committed to the mental facility in Blackfoot, until Tony called them by their nicknames, Skettles and Boatman. Only Cal knew those names. Tony could have only gotten them from his nephews. He had to be for real.

Mission's end

A pilot dressed in a green jumpsuit appeared from around the back side of the vehicle and tapped Cal on the shoulder.

"Cal, it looks like the storm has finally broken up. We're ready to drop your team in to extract Bill any time." Everyone turned and faced the mountain. Brit couldn't see it very well with his vision still impaired somewhat and full of tears. He wiped them clear as best he could, straining to see through the grey boil and sparkles still racing around in his vision. Indeed, the storm clouds were quickly dissipating and they could actually make out the ridgeline of Lake Valley. Cal turned and looked at the others, then directly at Britten. He still didn't have a clear view of what had happened up there, but he could see that his nephew's mind was still on the mountain.

"I'm sending Luke and Derek up to retrieve Bill and the snowcoach. Are you up to tagging along?" Cal asked, watching Brit wipe his face dry of moisture and nodding. "Better take Tony here with you," he said, as Britten leaned on his would be father-in-law.

"Thank you," Tony said, helping Brit away from the ambulance and towards a Jet Ranger helicopter that was starting up its engine. Minutes later, Cal and Brit's two friends watched with Amanda Alice as the small helicopter lifted gracefully into the cold Teton basin air, clawing for altitude towards the western slopes of the Tetons.

Brit remained silent, watching the snow covered terrain rising beneath them. It took them only a couple of minutes to reach the western slope of Lake Valley and by the time they had arrived, the skies had completely cleared. Everyone took note of the odd spacial apparition hanging over the entire bowl that was Lake Valley. It was as if it were producing a massive amount of heat, creating a huge spacial distortion rippling through the light. Tony described what he was seeing outside to Brit, both understanding what it meant. Tim had explained that this was the spacial distortion left by the Rift, after having expended all of its energy and moved on. It could last for hours, even days, depending on how much energy it would expend sitting in one place for extended periods. When this happened, it was possible to still see between the two worlds, but only light could pass, nothing else.

The pilot carefully set the chopper down, away from the ridge, behind the half buried snow cat and coach, and then shut down the engine. They all looked around at the eerie landscape floating before them, between two worlds. With the coach almost completely covered in snow and the backdrop of the spacial distortion rising from the hidden valley, it was as if there was a big bonfire there. It was quite the sight to see as Luke and Derek climbed out and put their snowshoes on. Tony leaned over closer to Brit as they looked out at the scene before them.

"You going to be ok?" he asked quietly, unbuckling his lap belt and helping Brit with his. Brit nodded silently, fumbling with the handle to open his door. Tony finished pushing on a pair of snow boots, climbed out and helped Brit do the same. As Luke and Derek approached the coach, a figure in a snowsuit appeared from around the front side. It was Bill working his way around the cat to see what its status was. He seemed to be perfectly fine and in good spirits considering his three and a half day ordeal in the jaws of the storm. The coach had provided sufficient protection for him and was none the worse for the wear, despite being buried clear over its roof in some places. He was very glad to see everyone, especially Britten.

"You sure know how to scare an old man out of ten years of life," he commented, while Tony helped Brit towards the rear of the coach and the open back door. Bill looked oddly at the man assisting Britten inside. Once they had all sat back down, Bill kicked the snow from his boots and got a better look at them.

"Son," he said, passing looks over at Tony, but focusing on his young friend. "You look terrible, what happened in there?" Brit tried to smile a little, thinking of the ordeal everyone had just endured for the last several days.

"It's a very long story Bill," Brit finally responded, not quite willing to recap it just yet. "There will be plenty of time later, after we get you down off this mountain."

"I could live in this thing indefinitely," Bill laughed, still stealing glances at Tony. "The only downside to this thing now," he said, referring to the snowcoach, "is the quiet." He finally turned to look right at Tony. "Sir, have we met?" Tony smiled and glanced over at Brit who gave him a distant nod.

"Well, not formally, but yes. A very long time ago, we met briefly."

Bill started to think back, trying to remember, shaking his finger at nothing.

"Don't tell me," Bill said, trying to figure it out on his own. "Don't tell me, I'll get it."

Brit turned to his brother's control center and the instruments that were still operating at the desk. He didn't know what half this stuff was or what it was telling him. He scanned everything in front of him, bewildered by the fact that they were actually here three days ago and had no clue what they were about to endure together. It was more reflective shock and a response to those past three days that seemed like an eternity ago now.

"So where's the rest of the crew?" Bill finally asked, still thinking hard about Tony. Brit turned back around as he detected Derek coming to the coach door.

"They are down at base camp in Driggs. We had to catch a ride out in the wreckage." Bill suddenly turned to Tony, pointing at him.

"You're that guy!" he exclaimed, excitedly waving his finger at Tony. "Yes! I remember you now! It was you! Back in 1960! You were the one that I met up here, wandering around looking like you had been half beaten to death. It was you!" Bill had a huge grin of recognition now as Tony smiled and nodded in agreement.

"Yes, that was me."

"Brit," Derek stated, pulling the door open. "Buddy you better come have a look at this."

"What's wrong?" Brit asked, feeling a chill instantly streak up his back, making the hairs on the back of his neck stand up. Derek had a pale look on his face, as though he had just seen a ghost.

"Better just come have a look," he said, shaking his head and backing away from the door. Tony assisted Brit up and back out of the vehicle, then followed Derek towards the front of the coach.

They had to maneuver around several giant snow drifts and the mostly buried snowmachines that Danny and Jerry had parked as the storm had hit, the last big drift trailing off from the front of the Sno-Cat. The entire ridge was nearly bare of snow; only grey broken rock was visible. Luke was standing several yards from the edge looking down at something. Tony and Brit could clearly see the spacial distortion, still rising from the valley below. Brit noticed that he was having a hard time remembering a lot of the information that had been downloaded into him by the Twins. He would need to sit down and document as much as he could remember soon. Luke turned to them with a facial expression equal to the one Derek had. It was like he too, had just seen a ghost.

As Brit struggled to take his steps, he seemed to be getting stronger with each passing minute, his eyesight improving as well. Tony stopped him just short of Luke and just stared down at the ridge edge some yards ahead of them. Brit's direct field of view was still a bit encumbered, as he looked up, observing that everyone seemed to be looking at the same thing. He felt Tony tighten the grip on his arm, trying to hold him back, but Brit finally pulled lose and pushed past Luke. He too froze in place for an instant. Sitting on the edge of the ridge, just inside the distortion was Catrina.

At first, Brit nearly burst into tears of relief, but somehow fought back the outburst and held onto his composure. He was so relieved to see her, but then he remembered the distortion field left by the Rift. It created the spatial distortion, allowing light to pass for a short period, but no matter could.

As he carefully shuffled to the edge, she looked up at him and watched through tear filled eyes as he sank to his knees beside her. He fought for control of his heartbreak but was slowly losing the battle as he gazed at her. He raised a bandaged hand to her face, knowing that he couldn't touch her, but the feeling was so overwhelming that he had to try. Brit struggled with the bandages, trying to get them off. Finally, the gauze was flung to the side and he raised his burned hand through the distortion. It passed right through her image, as though she weren't even there. He could feel nothing. This only worsened his battle to hold his composure, and the tears began to flow once again. He was raw now, watching her try to do the same with her hands.

Tony observed them trying to touch, but were unable. He couldn't help but feel their pain, seeing the same tragedy that had separated himself from his beloved Amanda Alice for all that time, now between his daughter and Britten. Two people so much in love, but now a galaxy apart. His empathy for their feelings and for the burden that they now had to bear for one another caught him in a very personal and hard way. He watched as Britten lost control, shaking his head and starting to sob.

"No," he sobbed, realizing the stark reality of their situation. Catrina held her hands up to him, but feeling the same heartbreak, there was little comfort that she could extend to him. She looked up past Britten at her father, who slowly knelt to the ground close to her. He found it difficult to look at his little girl now. The turmoil etched in her expression equaled that of the young man kneeling next to him, but there was nothing that anyone could do about it. This was the brutal truth of the hand that had been dealt them and there was no changing it. Here, only light could pass, but nothing else. They were separated now, unable to hear or touch the other, only to see the pain of that separation. Tony's eyes welled, knowing what they were feeling. It was nearly unbearable for him to watch. He tried to wipe his eyes as she opened her mouth to speak. At first he wasn't sure what she was trying to say, but after watching her lips instead of her eyes, he understood.

"Mother?" She repeated to him until he nodded with a happy grin, holding his hand to his heart. Actually, the look on his face spoke volumes to her. She grinned through her own emotion, the reality of her parent's reunion becoming apparent. Tony had made it home to her mother and they were together at last, something that she had longed for them the entire time they had been trapped on Argyle. Tony nudged Brit gently.

"Brit, we haven't got much time here. This distortion looks like it's starting to dissipate already." Brit looked over at Tony for a moment and then looked back out across the valley. Even with his limited vision he could see the distortion starting to collapse in places. He turned back to Catrina and held up his finger indicating that he had an idea. He needed to gather his wits and fast. Tony was right. No one really knew how long this distortion would last and it was apparent that it was starting to fade already. He turned around to Derek.

"In the coach, under the desk is a small white board and a couple of dry erase pens," Derek was already running back before Brit even finished the sentence. The moment he finished, Brit seemed to come alive. He pushed back his emotions, looking at Catrina with a smile of confidence. Yes, his heart still felt like it had been splayed open and left for the raven's to pick at, but he was feeling a bit of an attitude that said, *yes, you two have been dealt a really sucky hand, so figure it out. How are you going to work around it*? Derek was back in an instant puffing hard, handing Britten the small white board and pens. Brit scribbled something on the board and turned it to Catrina. She let out a half laugh, half sob, mouthing the words right back to him.

"I love you too."

Brit smiled and wiped his nose with his sleeve and turned the board back around, wiping it clean, then started writing some more and turned it back to her.

"We'll figure this out, I promise."

Cat nodded through her tears, trying to compose herself. She pointed to her eyes, then at Brit. He quickly scribbled more.

"Yes, I can see again, mostly. Amanda helped a little." Brit held up one of the crystals he had around his neck. "These did the rest." Catrina acknowledged with a relieved look. Brit wrote more.

"The distortion field is collapsing." Brit looked all around, noting the distortion edges slipping further away. Holding his focus, he quickly scribbled more.

"I will come for you."

Catrina looked at it then gave him a questioning gesture of how and when. Brit wrote faster, noticing that the edges all around them were already starting to fade in and out. He had no idea. Bryan was the expert when it came to this kind of thinking. However, he was sure that with all their combined knowledge of the Rift provided by Tim and the download, they would be able to come up with something.

"I don't know yet. Watch by Thulsa's gate for some kind of a signal and be ready."

Catrina nodded bravely, realizing that this might take some time to figure out. They were, after all, dealing with forces that were largely misunderstood and far above anything with which any human had ever had to deal with. There were absolutely no guarantees here, only the hope that somehow they could find a way, a way back to the other. As the distortion continued to dissipate, it occurred to them that this could be the last time that they ever saw each other. The moments were suddenly very precious as Tony watched the distortion fading

fast. Cat looked at her father as she too could see the distortion
starting to waiver.

"Tell mother I'm all right?" She held her hands to her heart, trying
to project her feelings for her parents. "I love you both." Tony
responded with a hand to the heart as well, returning parental
affection. Cat then looked back at Britten, their eyes finding each
other and locking tight so as to not let go.

"Don't forget me," she said, bringing her hands back up to the
distortion's edge. Britten raised his hands to hers, leaning closer. It
was impossible to touch, but he could still look deeply into her
wonderful ebony eyes, feeling them surround his aching heart.

"Not possible," he said, as she brought her face right up to his,
gazing into his hazel eyes. They held themselves together even after
the distortion field collapsed around them, their images disappearing.
Brit let his eyes sink closed as Catrina disappeared from view, trying to
hold her in his mind for as long as possible.

*　　*　　*　　*　　*

Tony sat with Britten, looking out across Lake Valley while the
others started working to dig out the snowmachines and the Sno-Cat.
The air was crisp and the skies completely void of any kind of clouds.
Most of the grey boiling had disappeared from Brit's vision, but
sparkles still danced around across his field of view. He could also see
the ghosting of his own heart beat in his peripherals. He looked down
into the valley at the place where Thulsa's gate would be located were
it still visible. Of course there was nothing there to see, only snowy
hills and pine trees. He scanned the area carefully, hoping to see
Catrina walking out into the open and start waving at them, but there
wasn't a sound and only the movement of ice crystals starting to
occupy the valley air. Now, she truly was gone.

Britten and Tony remained together on the ridge edge for quite
some time, just gazing out at the winter scene that lay before them,
letting Mother Nature's splendor soothe their troubled souls. One for
having lost a daughter, the other for having lost that one woman he
had been searching for. There was no need to say anything. They
knew what the other was feeling. Brit thought long and hard about
how they had gotten to and from Argyle and began to run things
repeatedly in his mind about how he would get back there. He
remained completely oblivious to everything until the quiet mountain
air was interrupted by the sound of a snowmachine motor and the
Sno-Cat coming to life.

Time to ponder

Spring in the Teton Basin always comes slowly and with a struggle. Just when all the snow is gone and you think it's about time for the grass to start turning green and spring bulbs to start trying to make their presence known, another good snow squall will come through and reblanket everything for a couple of days. It reminded everyone that this was high mountain terrain and despite it being a valley, Mother Nature was always in charge.

Spring does eventually come to the Basin and the snow lines on the surrounding mountains slowly start to retreat, back up to higher elevations. It isn't long before people are mowing their grass and watching the Aspen patches on the mountain sides start to come alive with green. Generally, it takes well into June before the snow disappears from the ridges of the western face of the Teton Range. Finally, the ardent hikers and off road vehicle enthusiasts can make their way back up the slopes to their favorite hiking and riding places, to the views that so few ever have a chance to enjoy.

Back in the 1980s, Driggs, Tetonia and Victor were simply sleepy little towns that tourists could pass through and still see what it was like to be in a quiet place, enjoy neighbors and the scenery of a place such as the Basin. All too often, the secret somehow gets out and everyone wants to come have a piece of paradise. Some are folks who were born and raised in the valley, only to move away, build their lives and fortunes elsewhere, then move back to retire, but bringing with them the comforts they had come to know in the big city. Heavy development and a lot of support housing inevitably follow in their wake. Driggs and Victor were not immune to these ravages of progress, turning quiet little towns into busy tourist traps with urban sprawl and all the problems naturally associated with it.

The Driggs airport becomes a hub of activity during the summer. High paying tourists converge from the four corners of the globe to take scenic flights in powered aircraft and sailplanes. On crisp mornings, even hot air balloons can be seen if people are willing to get up early enough and watch them rise majestically into the cool morning air, floating silently through the docile air currents all around the valley. Many of the large hangars at the airport have private biz jets stationed there for wealthy business people or even the occasional movie star. Some are owned by retired Air Force pilots who hangar old war birds permanently there for static display or as a base of operations for traveling around the country to air shows. Now, with all the new development of airport expansion and business parks, it could be considered its own township. One of the largest hangars had been there the longest. The WACs salvage company hangar was situated along the front row of all the aircraft structures built in the original airport annex.

WACs wasn't the biggest salvage company in business, in fact they would still be considered a mom and pop operation by the day's standards, but WACS did very well and was very good at their specialty. There were plenty of other companies, much larger, that specialized in huge government contracts for recovery or scrap. Many of these larger companies will take on monumental tasks of stripping entire naval war ships and then send them to the bottom of the ocean near coast lines to act as artificial reefs and important marine habitat.

Alongside the WACs hangar, lying in the weeds was what was left of the wood structures that had been used to cradle "The Amanda" when she was brought in from salvage several months ago. Inside the closed doors, there was a bustle of activity around all the equipment stationed here at its base of operations. A trailer with snowmachines was tucked neatly into a corner behind a Sno-Cat and attached coach, all covered up, waiting for the next winter when they could be pulled out and used again. A couple of pickup trucks and other vehicles were parked to the side of these stored vehicles, everything kept well out of the way of the main attraction that took up a good portion of the inside of the hangar. Bright lights burned all around the shiny fuselage of "The Amanda". Her tail, fuselage, and wings now reattached, she sat on her own wheels, undergoing a ridged inspection, reconstruction, and restoration process. Her propellers and engines were gone, having been removed and shipped out to subcontractors better equipped to accomplish a repair and rebuild of these aircraft components. The crew onsite doing this labor intensive project were sub contracted by WACs to do most of the work required to put the North American B-25J bomber back together to fully operational status.

From his inside second story office window, Cal looked out into the hangar at the work going on with the WWII Bomber. While he was quite pleased with the progress and how fast it was going, he was also very conscious of how much this was costing the company. This kind of specialized work was not cheap by any measure. Thank goodness it was what these guys did for a living. He had overseen several projects like this before, but none had ever gone this well. In watching and talking with all the craftsman and mechanics who worked tirelessly to complete their work, without fail, all of them expressed the same general theme with the project. It was almost as if the airframe itself were helping with the repair. Old damaged rivets and parts came off easily and went back together like the originals. When new parts had to be refabricated or strengthened, they went together so easily and fit in such a precise manner that it would have been difficult to tell the original from a rebuilt. Indeed, there were so many comments made to Cal that it felt like someone unseen was helping them, guiding them in the restoration. There just seemed to be too much of a coincidence that original parts were conveniently available and if they weren't, new ones could easily be manufactured and usually worked out better than the originals. The engines and propellers were due back within the month. Somehow, the rebuild facility on the other side of the state in Boise, Idaho, had hit a lull right as "The Amanda's" big Wright R-2600 radial engines were being shipped for inspection and rebuild. Therefore, they were able to get right to them for a fast turnaround.

Curiously, nearly all the subcontractors they had sent parts out to, commented that unless it was clear damage, everything appeared brand new. The team working here at WACs indicated that they were still months away from being able to roll "The Amanda" out to run engines for testing purposes. In the meantime, several updates, upgrades and improvements were being taken care of as the restoration project proceeded. One of the great challenges in accomplishing a mammoth project, such as this, is to incorporate these updates in such a way as to make the plane usable in the modern day environment, yet somehow preserve its original integrity as a WWII warbird. Some things had to be changed, such as radios upgraded to the latest and greatest and moved to a location a little more accessible to the pilots. Old outdated wiring had to be replaced with newer more robust cabling. Heating systems were vastly improved, especially for those people who rode in the back of the aircraft. While "The Amanda" had been retrofitted many times in wartime with several different test systems that never really made it to combat service, there were several systems that had and they all required close inspection. After all, this was an aircraft that had been through a traumatic crash landing, sustaining extensive damage. Best to make sure everything worked, as it should to prevent trouble later on.

Cal rubbed his bald head a little worried. WACs had the money available to complete this project and even sustain the bomber as an operational museum piece, but to what end? Was this salvage company to become a museum? Actually, they had recovered many artifacts and aircraft that would have served well in such a display. Nevertheless, this was a business and all about making money. They didn't get to where they were for as long as they had been in existence by not making money. Cal had no idea what it would take to keep "The Amanda" on operational status and market her as a viable money maker. He was hoping that his nephews, who had insisted that she be restored, had some great ideas as to how all this was going to be accomplished.

Since his nephew's return from the mountain with "The Amanda", they had provided him with precious little information about what had really happened for those three and a half anxious days. He felt like even Tony Dallas had held something back from him when he was first approached with the idea that he had traveled back in time to rescue his nephews from the storm. He had almost thought better of sending good pilots and expensive aircraft into very dangerous conditions to mount such an extraction. However, the looks on Tony and Amanda's faces somehow convinced him it was all true. The fact that Tony was standing in front of him at the time and looked as he did, had swayed him to act. While he still wished he had a better understanding of the facts, he was glad of the outcome. Still, he felt like he was just outside of a loop that continued to play itself out. There was more to this restoration project than just bringing an old bomber back to life, but none of them were prepared to say anything, yet.

Cal glanced back at Bryan Garrett, who sat poring over paper documents and comparing them to something on his computer. He had no idea what the younger Garrett was doing and Bryan refused to give him any details about it. It was frustrating, but Cal cut him some major slack. He was still recovering from his near death experience on the mountain. How he had survived to make it to the hospital was a miracle all by itself. The doctors had reported that he had suffered several broken ribs, a ruptured spleen and a punctured lung. Not to mention being terribly dehydrated, with lacerations and scars that he hadn't left here with when they had started out.

He looked back out at "The Amanda". In the cockpit, with his head buried deep under her control console, was Britten. He insisted that he perform the electronics upgrades and oversaw everything about this warbird's electrical system, from top to bottom. If he didn't like it, it was redone until he was satisfied. Since returning from his ordeal on the mountain, his vision had never been the same and he was forced to wear a pair of light weight glasses now. Cal had never gotten the full skinny on what all the emotional outbursts were all about either. Only that the Dallas' daughter had not returned with them. He could see why Tony and Amanda would be upset, but for the life of him, he couldn't figure out why Britten would be so broken up about it. Most of the questions he had asked had gone unanswered. The Dallas' hardly spoke a word after Tony had helped to retrieve Bill and the snow vehicles, then left shortly after the doctors had announced that Bryan was going to pull through. Truly, he was getting more than a little frustrated with the information blackout.

"You guys are letting Luke and Derek have all the fun you know," Cal finally said, drawing in a deep breath and letting it slowly out. Bryan looked up at the computer monitor screens in front of him. He had heard his uncle, but remained focused on what he was studying on the screens.

"It's good for them," he finally said slowly, his attention focused forward. "If we're to expand this company even further, we have to have good men who can do a great job. That can't happen if you've got them stuck doing all the little penny-ante jobs all the time."

"But our customers like the Garrett boys," Cal countered quickly. He understood what Bryan was getting at. They had had this discussion before, several times. You build up a rapport and a reputation with people and they come to expect certain things. "They know that things will get done right when the Garretts are on the job."

"We're only two people," Bryan responded almost hypnotically. He was so engrossed in what he was studying that he acted as though he could barely respond to his uncle. "We need to have more of us around here with great reputations." Bryan shifted back over to the paper documents he had been poring over, searching through the pages.

This only frustrated Cal even more. He respected a person's privacy, but these last several months were a little beyond what he was used to. He was used to knowing what was going on in his nephew's lives. Especially on the subject of what they were doing with company assets. All of the secrecy didn't sit well with him. He felt like the only way he was going to get any answers was to get all up in their faces and he just wasn't about any of that.

"What are you even doing over there?" Cal finally blurted out, turning towards Bryan's rather large desk. It was a sprawling mess. Paper, books, drawings and charts were strewn all over it. You couldn't see the desk top. The only evidence that it was actually there, were that the papers would have to levitate without it. Bryan remained silent, reading through several hand written papers. It might be easier for Cal to just wait until his nephew had left for the day and he could just look everything over himself, drawing his own conclusions. However, Bryan religiously took everything home with him every night and then brought it back the next day. He never left it unattended, even during the day. Even when he was at lunch, if he ever had lunch, he was right there, studying. *Studying what for heck sakes?*

Cal stepped over to have a good look see over Bryan's shoulder at what was displayed on the computer monitors. It looked like pictures of stars in space, like images taken from the Hubble or Spitzer telescopes. The rest of it had the appearance of weather charts and radar images. The documents and drawings were so intermixed and half buried that it was impossible to make heads or tails of it at a glance, which was about all he could ever get. Bryan quickly straightened papers up and shuffled things around when he detected his uncle hovering behind him. Cal was able to recognize a very lengthy document with many pages written in Britten's long hand, but like most of the youth of the day, you could hardly read it because writing and penmanship just weren't taught in most schools anymore.

"This is really boring stuff," Bryan commented, trying to divert the attention to something else. "What job did you send Derek and Luke out on anyway?"

"Boring huh?" Cal snapped disdainfully. "You don't seem very bored by it. What are you up to? What are you both up to?" Bryan wasn't exactly sure what his uncle was talking about other than to know what Bryan was doing. He wasn't doing anything with Brit. His brother had become obsessed with working on "The Amanda". They had hardly spoken since they had started the project shortly after Bryan had been released from the hospital. They both were adamant that she be restored, but then sort of went their separate ways once the project had begun. Odd behavior for either of them, but Cal suspected that there was some healing that was happening and that eventually they would come out and talk about it.

"Well I would have thought that what my brother was doing was pretty obvious," Bryan said, hitting the lock on his computer bringing the screen saver mode online. "As for me, I'm trying to figure out what caused all that hubbub up there on the mountain." With that he stuffed his papers in a briefcase, grabbed his rolled up charts and started for the door.

"Wait!" Cal called after him, as he rushed out the door. "With pictures of space?" Bryan didn't stop, making his way down the long flight of stairs and to the hangar door.

*　　*　　*　　*　　*

Britten was lying on his back tucked up under the instrument panel with both his hands deep in the back. He wore a head lamp so he could see in the dark places behind the instruments. His hands were full of wiring harnesses. To the untrained eye, this monumental mess had no chance of ever being straightened out. To Britten, and any other avionics installer, if you just take it a wire at a time or subsystem at a time, it wasn't complicated at all. Brit was just fitting the wiring harness for the new radios and navigational system back into place. Really the only thing left to do here was to dress the harness and mount them up into place, make a few connections to the aircraft's avionics power buss and he was finished. The actual radios and navigational stack had already been fitted, mounted and awaited final testing. "The Amanda's" batteries hadn't been installed yet, as there was still a bit of work to do on several other electrical subsystems throughout the aircraft.

Brit focused solely on his work, which seemed to be far less difficult than it had a right to be, but he kept hearing some kind of a buzzing in his head. Very faint and really, it could be a number of things.

510

Sometimes, your head just picks up a buzzing or a ring for no particular reason. It happens to everyone. It comes in and does its thing and then it's gone. It could be something one of the other technicians was doing on another part of the aircraft or in the shop. He had paid it no heed, being more focused on what was in front of him and what he had to get done overall, than a silly noise sporadically flowing in and out of his head.

Brit had removed the seats and yoke controls so that he could be a little more comfortable lying on the flight deck of "The Amanda". They weren't exactly built for working on in comfort; very few aircraft were. They were built to do a job and a service technician just had to figure out how to work around everything else. Continuing his work, his mind focused ardently on what he was doing, he became aware that the buzzing had been getting louder and flowing in and out more frequently. Was it possible there were lasting side effects from this download he hadn't been told about and they were just now starting to manifest themselves? Perhaps he was going to have a brain aneurism or an embolism or something. *That would certainly suck!* He wasn't even sure what those were, but they always sounded ominous. He didn't have a headache this time and with the exception of his vision being what it was, there didn't seem to be any problems otherwise, so he continued to work until he detected someone climbing up the access hatch behind the flight deck.

"Hey you wiring fiend you," a familiar voice called out, as a head appeared at his feet. Britten pressed his chin to his chest, looking past his feet at his brother scaling the ladder into the fuselage.

"Hey knucklehead," Brit called back from under the panel, shifting right back up to what he was doing. "And how are we feeling today?" referring to Bryan's recovery.

"I'm ok," Bryan responded quickly. "I'm still a tiny bit sore through the left lower ribs," he said, rubbing the spot where his broken bones had been. "I suspect that without these crystals the Dallas's gave us, that I'd still be in a world of hurt. What about you?"

"Just peachy," Brit said with a grunt, reaching for something way back that was hard to get to. "Been a while, what have you been up to?"

"Just studying those papers on the download that you wrote a couple of months ago, fascinating stuff really," Bryan said, looking around at the restoration job done on the flight deck. "Just wish you could have remembered more of it."

"I can hardly remember what the back side of my hand looks like two minutes after I've looked at it," Brit said, dressing up the harness he was working with. "You're lucky I was able to get what's there on paper. I can't even remember what I wrote, let alone anything else that happened. Only what you guys have told me. I don't even believe some of that." Bryan nodded thinking hard about some of the things that his brother had gone through.

"I've been documenting everything that happened to us in a journal," Bryan commented, pushing the turret seat up into position and climbing on. "I wish you could still remember everything. Actually, anything would be good. I think Danny and Jerry would just as soon forget it all ever happened. But they have been really good at letting me record everything they can remember." Brit looked back up under the panel to finish what he was doing. The buzzing in his head was really starting to annoy him as it got more pronounced with every passing moment.

"Well, I'm sorry I can't remember more. Some things might be better forgotten anyway," he said, thinking that somehow there was more that he should be remembering, but it was just a feeling. Britten had become far more irritable and sullen since the rescue and there always seemed to be something that was bothering him. He had even acknowledged it himself, but was never able to identify what it really was. He developed headaches frequently, something that almost never happened to him before the rescue. Tony and Bryan had tried several times to explain to Brit that he had a very strong relationship with Tony's daughter Catrina. Strong enough that Brit had asked Tony for Catrina's hand in marriage, but try as he might, he had absolutely no memory of this woman that they spoke so highly of. You would think they were describing a woman of exceptional beauty and a relationship that could endure anything, something quite unheard of in this day and age, a love at first sight. Someone like that would be pretty hard to forget. He could only take their word for it, for there were no feelings associated with what they had been describing, a brutal fact that nearly broke Tony's heart. The months following their rescue had been very hard on Britten. He had little to no memory of what had happened during those several days they had spent on the mountain. When the download began to deteriorate from his mind, it set up a block on the people and events of his time there, creating a situation of amnesia. Bryan and Tony would try to help him remember, but it only created a painful ache deep down. For him, the aching was painful enough that it was better not to try, just let any memories come whenever they were going to come, if they ever came at all. The buzzing in Brit's head was reaching an intolerable level and he finally climbed out from under the console and sat up.

"Can you hear something?" he asked angrily, dumping off his headlamp into the seat next to him and looking around outside.

"Yes," Bryan responded. "But I thought it was just in my head."

"It is in your head; mine too," Brit said angrily, trying to find the source of the noise. He leaned out the open copilot's window and the buzzing instantly stopped. Pulling his head back inside, the buzzing returned, but this time he noticed something warm against his chest.

He turned to Bryan as his brother pulled the crystal necklace out of his shirt and held it up. Brit remembered that he had one around his neck, but had no idea where it had come from. He fumbled in his shirt a moment, pulling on the gold chain until he was holding the attached crystal. Both crystals glowed with the same cold blue color.

Brit held his up, looking at its mesmerizing glow, but saw a flash of light coming from the instrument panel in front of him. It looked as though the radios, that he had just installed, were trying to come on. The displays flickered dimly and in a moment, they could both hear the crackle of static in the cabin speakers. Brit moved his crystal right up next to the top radio. It seemed to respond instantly to the crystal's proximity. It was as if someone was applying power to the aircraft systems. Bryan looked over at the electrical system's power buss panel and inspected all the breakers. All of them were turned off, even the main buss feed for the avionics power. Quite irritated now, Brit poked his head out the window again and called to the head mechanic working in an open wing root access panel.

"Have you guys installed the batteries in this thing?" Brit was spitting mad now because they were supposed to wait until everything was finished and the final check list had been gone through before the batteries were to even be put in their compartment. The mechanic shook his head and pointed to one of the many work benches lining the wall near the aircraft. The batteries were still in their boxes on the bench. They hadn't even been unpacked! Anger changing to confusion, Brit turned back to Bryan for some kind of an explanation, but his brother had none. The glow of the crystals and their radiating warmth continued to hold their attention, the radios in the avionics stack flickering brighter. Bryan jumped down off the turret seat, joining his brother in the cockpit with his crystal in hand. Watching the radios flicker, they could hear a voice in the static. It was very faint at first, but after a couple of moments, the static cleared and the voice became quite distinct.

"Britten, Bryan. Can you hear me? I am still here." It was The Amanda! Brit reached for the volume on the coms system, a chill streaking up his back, making the hairs on the back of his head stand straight up. He tried turning it up, but it had no effect. The radio displays continued to flicker and fade on and off. Brit looked at his brother, trying to process what he was hearing. Indeed, Brit had forgotten what had happened to them on Argyle. He didn't even remember being able to actually communicate with the consciousness of this airplane and was reluctant to even try. However, Bryan remembered and quickly pressed his hands to the bare bulkheads.

The buzzing in Bryan's head quickly faded away and in his mind, he found himself in a bare white room sitting on a white bench. On the other side of the room was a white bed where a woman in a white dress lay motionless. Stepping closer to the bed, he could see that she was wearing a white sword belt with the hilt of a white sword situated neatly at her side. Her hands were carefully crossed over her chest as if she were lying in state for her funeral viewing. Her eyes were closed, but her image was unmistakable. Bryan had never seen her the way that Catrina and his brother had seen her before. This was his first experience, having only voice contact with her before.

"Amanda," Bryan said, settling next to her on the bed. "I'm here." Reaching for one of her hands, Bryan felt a warmth coming from her. An instant rush of events fired through his mind as he touched her, remembering ghostly images of her holding him in her broken fuselage while they were being lifted out of the storm. He could see the fury of the Rift sending out fingers of energy, reaching for her, the huge surge of plasma balls and hands grabbing her, trying to pull her from the airframe and back into its own. But Brit and Danny would not let her go, hanging onto her even at the risk of their own lives, incurring severe burns to their hands and wrists. Then Jerry firing the top turret guns into the Rift's wall, providing enough of a distraction that she was able to retreat into the deep safety of herself long enough for the Sky Crane to pull her from the Rift's collapsing eye and to freedom.

Amanda slowly opened her eyes and looked up at Bryan, who gazed back at her with deep adoration. He felt so warm and confident in her presence now. She did indeed look just like the picture that had been included in the informational packet Cal had provided them before this whole salvage operation had begun. Strangely, she remained motionless, only moving her eyes around the room as if searching for something or someone. Her eyes finally came back to Bryan and a gentle smile formed on her lips.

"I am so happy to see that you are all right," she said, moving her head ever so slightly in his direction. "I was so afraid that I would be unable to sustain you long enough to get you home."

"If you hadn't, I would not have made it."

"You can thank Britten for that," she said, closing her eyes again.

"I don't understand." Bryan developed a strange look while searching her features for expression.

"I came to him first because of everything he has done for me, but he would not let me heal him. He said you were hurt far worse and told me to attend to you first." Bryan thought carefully.

"Hmmm, he did, did he? He never mentioned any of that." Bryan looked around at the stark white room. There was truly nothing in here but the bed and the bench.

"It is a cleansed mind," Amanda stated unmoving, watching him, sensing what he was wondering about.

"You can't move," Bryan said, coming back to her. "What's wrong?"

"I am yet incomplete."

"You were incomplete in Argyle."

"I was broken in Argyle. Here I am incomplete, but being restored," she said, with a broadening smile. "Big difference."

"You can thank Britten for that too," Bryan responded. Amanda looked about the room, and then closed her eyes.

"Why is he not here? I can feel him, but he is so distant."

"It has become a little complicated," Bryan said, thinking of his brother's condition.

"I don't understand," Amanda puzzled, searching for him. "I'm calling to him and I know he can hear me, but he isn't responding. Why?" She opened her eyes and looked back at Bryan, who hesitated to give the response.

"He's forgotten everything that happened on Argyle. The download with the Twins has somehow damaged or blocked his memory. I noticed as the knowledge of the Ancients left him; it took his ability to recall his own memories. I don't know how much more he will lose." Despite the warmth Bryan was feeling from Amanda, he had a very sad look. He hadn't been privy to everything that happened between his brother and Catrina Dallas, but he had a good idea just based on his observations at the time. Now, he knew that Brit had been suffering privately. Directly following their rescue, he commented that he could feel himself loosing so much of what had been downloaded to his mind from the Twins. Britten had raced to write everything down as quickly as he could, but Bryan had also observed his brother's memories of the events on Argyle disappear including the unthinkable, Catrina. In her place, only sadness and an unquenchable longing that could not be defined or pacified.

"He has forgotten about Catrina, hasn't he?" Amanda inquired, closing her eyes.

"Forgotten? No, I don't think he has forgotten her," Bryan finally said after thinking about it for a moment. "I think that the download has created a Rift, for lack of a better word, in his memory that has blocked everything about what happened on Argyle. I believe everything is still there, especially Catrina, but they are in there so deep down, he can't access any of those memories."

"I suspect that the human mind is a very complex mechanism," Amanda said carefully.

"I suspect you're right, but I have no idea how to help him," Bryan replied, grim faced. "Tony told me Brit was completely devastated when we left her behind on Argyle."

"Yes, I remember," Amanda agreed. "He tried to jump out, but I stopped him. The fall would have killed him."

"Of course you did the right thing," Bryan reassured her.

"Somehow you have to figure out how to help him remember," Amanda pleaded, becoming quite emphatic. "They have something that so few ever achieve. It is a beautiful thing."

"If only there was a way to bring her home," Bryan said, thinking hard about his brother and Catrina.

"You must find a way," Amanda said, opening her eyes and looking up at Bryan again. "Find a way to help him remember and bring her home to him." Bryan drew in a deep breath and held it. This was tall order to be sure. Something like this would certainly require more expertise than he had. He finally let the air slip out, realizing that she wasn't suggesting that he go this alone. Amanda could see the wheels turning in his head and the smirk that appeared on his face as he looked up at her.

"Come see me again when you have it all figured out," she said grinning. Bryan got up to leave but Amanda stopped him. "And Bryan, bring Britten with you next time." Bryan looked back at her and smiled.

"Next time, he will come to you." Then he was gone, leaving Amanda to sleep for a while longer.

Deep feelings

Britten seemed constantly irritated, always restless, but he couldn't figure out why. His headaches continued, something he found even more irritating, having more important things to deal with than a stupid headache. It seemed to Bryan and Cal that he got angry at the drop of a hat, over silly little things. It was now late July and the only things that brought him any peace was working on The Amanda, flying, and hiking. Neither he nor Bryan had been out on a WACs project since The Amanda salvage, but had consulted on several and helped to hire two more full time salvage specialists. With Bryan and Britten off doing other things and more jobs than ever coming in, Cal had no choice but to hire more people to help Luke and Derek. He was insistent that his two co-CEOs do the interviews and hiring. Afterwards, they seemed to disappear back into their own projects, Brit working hard on The Amanda and Bryan leaving for a two week vacation to who knew where, something about Central America and Hawaii. Even so, Cal felt like they had made some good choices in the people they had decided to hire. Luke and Derek had their hands full with all the larger jobs they were being sent out on, so these new crew members took over several smaller salvage projects, relieving a lot of pressure on Luke and Derek. They kept them young, but highly skilled, choosing a short blonde woman named Carman and a short African American, Stormy. Each had a specific skill set unique to them, but blended with Derek and Luke, they all made a good team.

This warm July morning found Britten flying the company Aviat Husky over the Teton's western mountain range. Flying from the south to north, he wasn't really looking for anything, just enjoying the breaking dawn and the smooth air. He had gotten up before the sunrise because he couldn't sleep and was looking for good ways to divert his attention away from his restlessness. Usually, thermal activity started by mid-morning, making flying along the ridgelines a bit of a challenge, but at this time of day, at 12,000 feet, the air was smooth as glass and created the perfect conditions for the diversion he sought. He had removed his headphones, listening to the air whistling around the aircraft. The engine noise was loud, but somehow it was soothing to him. Climbing to altitude, he flew south over Victor, turning over the southern mountain range to the east, intersecting with the Teton Range, and then turning north heading towards the Targhee Ski Resort.

The sunrise was off the charts amazing. A thin layer of clouds hovered around 14,000 feet, just higher than the highest peak of the

Tetons. The rising sun throwing its orange red rays against the stark jagged peaks, cast a shadow on the underside of the cloud layer. Not only was the sunrise a wonder to see, but the light painted on the bottom side of the clouds would be considered one of god's masterpieces of natural artwork.

Moving slowly, Brit let the Husky meander in lazy zig zags across the ridge lines, continuing north towards the ski resort area. Having trimmed the aircraft out so well, it did not require any elevator control to hold altitude and he could steer it without even touching the stick. He did everything with the rudder pedals. He turned his radios off, being about as alone and isolated as he could get now. Making his way along the Fox Creek Ridge lines towards the Darby area, he dropped his altitude to skim carefully over the ridges, watching the sunrise paint even more colors across the skies. Now he could see another, thinner cloud layer forming below him as the sun continued to rise. Not only was it illuminating the upper layer, but also across the top of the lower layer, refracting light through the suspended moisture particles, sending dancing darts of colors firing right into the cockpit.

Gazing at the site, he got what he came for. He felt calm, at peace within himself. There was no restlessness, nothing in the back of his mind trying to pry its way out, no headache. Just the rising sun and the painted colors associated with the morning rays. He smiled for a moment, feeling the relief of normalcy sweep across him as his little plane headed across the Darby Canyon Gap towards Spring Creek Ridge. Horseshoe Saddle and the south rim of Lake Valley lay directly ahead of him. Approaching Lake Valley, there came to him a gnawing feeling, deep down in his chest. It wasn't the feeling of restlessness that he had been suffering from these past many months, but something else, an ache or a longing. *Now what was this all about?* The conditions up here were perfect for him to just escape and enjoy. Why was he starting to feel like this? He checked his aircraft's instruments and systems. Everything was working perfectly. He clicked on his radios, listening to the local frequencies, then switched them back off. He was the only one up this time of morning. As the south rim of Lake Valley dropped behind him, the aching intensified. He banked to the east towards Pinnacle Peak. It felt like he was forgetting something, something very important. He turned back around to the west and flew back over Lake Valley, with the intensions of heading home to land.

Approaching the west ridge line, he thought he could hear a voice calling him. Pulling his headphones back over his ears, he listened carefully. There it was again! He reached for the radio to turn the volume up only to find that it was still switched off! The voice was female and sounded familiar to him, but there was a lot of other noise associated with it, as if she were calling to him from a wind storm or something. With the west ridge passing beneath him, the voice faded away and the image of a woman's face began to materialize in his head, but before he could identify it, it was gone. He looked all around, trying to see if someone was playing a trick on him, but there was nothing and he was left to the noise of the airplane and the view of the forest below as he headed out across the Basin valley towards the Driggs airport.

Once he landed and secured his aircraft, he quickly jumped into his Jeep and headed for the Chicken Hump access road and a hiking trail that would take him up the west slope to the ridge of Lake Valley. He really wasn't sure why he was going on a hike. While it wasn't his favorite thing to do, he did enjoy it, as it too, provided a certain level of isolation and solitude. He kept a day pack with him in the airplane and had brought it with him for the hike, thinking he would be gone most of the day. It took him several hours to make the hike, but he took his time, enjoying several stops to rest and look back out at the view of the valley from his vantage point. Making these stops, he had the feeling something was missing. Even after checking through his pack and then his new phone he had bought right after they had returned from salvaging The Amanda. His old one had gotten misplaced in all the confusion of the rescue's aftermath. He sat a while trying to figure out what was wrong, but the answers eluded him, so he continued, finally reaching the west ridge of Lake Valley.

On approach of the ridge line he stopped a little short of it. This was where the Sno-Cat sat in the snow for several days. He didn't remember it very clearly, but he did remember it. He recalled fragments of a conversation that he, his brother, and two friends had with Bill Kyfie the night before they went in to explore the wreckage. He looked carefully around, drinking from his canteen. There was a steady breeze blowing from the south, the sun rising high overhead in a now, completely clear sky. He stepped up to the edge of the ridge, looking out across Lake Valley at the west side of Pinnacle and the back side of Devils Staircase. He could see Table Rock from here and the Tetons were close enough he felt like he could reach out and touch them. He then turned his eyes down into the valley itself.

There was good reason it was called Lake Valley. A few stubborn patches of snow held on to the rocky slopes of the west ridge, some still touching the small ponds and lakes strewn throughout the entire landscape. Sinking to the edge to rest and eat some lunch, something came to his mind, like he had been here before. A strong feeling of déjà vu beset him and once again that aching feeling deep down in his chest started to swell. What was happening to him? Was this the start of a heart attack or something? What poor planning put him up here all alone, having a heart attack? A feeling of intense turmoil swirled madly around inside his very soul. Something was missing, as if he had lost something or someone very close to him, but didn't know what or who. What was happening to him? Then he heard the soft familiar voice of a woman on the wind, calling his name. It was faint and seemed to float away with the constant flow of the air moving across the ridge line. An image flashed into his head and then it was gone, but it was followed by another. It was of him sitting right where he was holding his hands up to touch someone, but he couldn't see who it was. There seemed to be even more heartache associated with the images fading in and out, all of them acting as ghostly phantoms, teasing his consciousness. He would reach for them, but they would flee at just the thought of any pursuit. There were so many of them, but none that were distinguishable. He put his head in his hands, trying to focus in on one of them, but they were all fleeting and left him with only an intense ache.

"Got a headache do ya?" Brit looked up at his younger brother who was sitting against a rock several yards up the ridge. He nodded, shifting in Bryan's direction. How did he not notice him up here when he arrived?

"Yeah, a pretty good one. I thought coming up here would take care of it, but it ain't happening." Bryan got up and stepped over to join him.

"Maybe you've got some stuff on your mind and just need to try and get it out."

"What are you doing up here? I thought you were on vacation?" Brit asked, as Bryan sat down, fumbling around in his own pack. He pulled out a bunch of stuff, making Britten wonder how he was ever able to pack it all up alone.

"Done with that," Bryan answered, pulling out a Smartphone and tablet. The phone looked familiar and Brit picked it up as Bryan took a couple of other things out, setting them down next to him.

"Hey," Brit said, recognizing his old phone. "Isn't this my-?"

"Yes, it's your old phone," Bryan said, concentrating on opening up the tablet. "And this would be MY tablet, emphasis on the "MY" part of that. Found these buried in a bunch of crap from our little adventure up here last winter."

"Yeah, so, what are you doing with all this stuff up here now?"

"Actually have an App for that," Bryan responded in a smart-aleck tone. "Haven't used this since we pulled The Amanda out of here. I was doing some research on some stuff while vacationing in the lands of the sun and beaches and opened up my tablet only to find that someone had run my battery down to the nothings. I realize these batteries don't stay charged indefinitely, but a bunch of my memory is all used up too. Thought I ought to check your phone to see if the same thing happened to you. Might shed some light on who the knucklehead was that got into our stuff." Brit turned his phone on and waited for it to boot up while Bryan cruised through his tablet.

"Ah ha!" Bryan bellowed loudly, opening a video file and started going through it. "I think we'll find out who the culprit is now." Brit opened his video applications as well and started going through his files. Many of them he remembered, but the last ones he didn't recognize.

"Voilà! Here we go," Bryan said, turning the screen towards his brother. "I think I recognize these two." Bryan turned up the volume so it could be heard clearly. Britten listened and watched closely as it played a video of a dimly lit room somewhere. He could hear his own voice and someone else, a woman. It was familiar to him. The same voice he heard calling to him in the airplane earlier this morning and then again on the wind here on the ridge. He was sitting very close to the source of the voice. She was a vision, so beautiful! They looked so happy together. The video on his phone played out similar scenes of him being videoed, and then the woman. He watched both devices alternately, showing them joking around and talking. She looked and sounded so familiar, but he couldn't recall who she was. Brit locked his eyes on the image of the woman, the deep aching intensifying as he watched her and the more he watched, the more he ached. It was becoming nearly unbearable and after a few minutes, he became aware that he had tears streaming from his eyes, some of them dripping onto his glasses. He looked up at his brother, about to ask him who she was and why he was feeling what he was feeling, but then heard her voice in the wind again, calling to him.

"Her father said you made her a promise," Bryan said reverently. He hadn't been there when this scene had played out, but he had formulated a pretty good image of what it was like based on what Tony had described to him. Brit tried to look away from the tablet, but the images on the screen in front of him held him in place. There was a sudden outburst of laughter in the video, causing the intense ach to ramp sharply. His heart feeling like it was going to burst wide open, an image of the woman in the video came at him from across time and space, focusing sharply in his mind. Catrina Amanda Dallas, *it was Cat!* A flood of memory suddenly gushed from the back of his consciousness. It had been locked up far back in the deepest reaches of his mind by an unspanable chasm created by the download. Now, the visions of Catrina had somehow spanned it and he remembered everything that happened, *EVERYTHING!* They both had been sitting right where he and his brother were now, before she had disappeared from view and he remembered every word he had spoken, like it had just happened.

"I will come for you," he repeated to his brother, a flood of emotion swelling over him like a tidal wave, adding to his tears. Bryan reached over, throwing his arms around his big brother and held him while he wept. The scene played out over and over again in Brit's mind.

"I made her a promise. I promised her I'd come for her, but there's no way I can keep that promise. I can't make it happen, she's gone." Brit cried, struggling to regain his composure. Bryan held him a while longer, looking down into the valley that was so much a part of this whole adventure.

"Yes, you made a promise," he pushed Brit back, looking into his wet eyes. "And there's no way that you can keep it all on your own." Bryan turned a confident smile. "But you haven't considered that your little brother might have a thing or two up his sleeve."

"I don't want to know what's up your nasty, smelly ol' sleeve," Brit smiled, wiping away his tears. Bryan chuckled, handing him a pair of binoculars and pointing down into Lake Valley.

"Trust me," he responded as Brit slowly turned to the beautiful mountain valley, barely a mile wide. "You're gonna be glad I use deodorant when I'm done with you." Brit looked in the direction his brother had pointed and started scanning the valley floor with the high powered binoculars. It wasn't long before he spotted something out of place. Bryan was busy doing something else in his bag as Brit focused in on what looked like a tube about four inches in diameter and about four or five feet long. It was propped up at an angle facing east. At its base was a small metal cylinder and a box with antenna wires branching out for several hundred feet in five or six different directions.

"What the freak? You gonna try and shell something?" Brit asked, trying to figure out what the contraption was. At first glance, he thought it was a mortar launcher used in the military to lob explosive shells towards an enemy at a distance. However, getting a hold of one of those for civilian use wasn't generally possible and to what end? In the direction the device was facing, a row of little flags were anchored deeply in the dirt. Brit looked over at Bryan who started pounding something into the solid rock of the ridge.

"What in the name of Sam Hill?" he asked, watching him pound the last stake into the ground and place a device in the middle of the small square of rock spikes he had just created. Bryan secured the device to all four spikes and tested it by yanking on it good and hard.

"What are you doing? What is that thing?" Bryan picked up his stuff, starting over to a two seat RZR sitting next to the tree line a short distance from the ridge.

"You're so smart big brother, you figure it out," he said, turning around after he had stowed his gear.

Brit raised the binoculars back to his eyes, looking at the device down in the valley. It looked like a launcher of some kind. What was he doing? How was this thing going to help him keep his promise to Cat? He looked down at the device Bryan had anchored to the rock of the ridge. A solid smooth looking device having only a warning sticker on it, "Please do not disturb." It was a sensing device of some kind. What was Bryan up to? Brit stood silent, looking out over the expanse of Lake Valley, the gentle afternoon breeze still blowing gently across the ridge. Now he could not only hear Catrina's voice in the wind, but see her image almost as plain as if she were standing right there. He let a smile form across his wet face, raising a hand to wipe his nose. He could almost picture her standing on the opposite side of the valley in the open gate to the Thulsa spoil.

"Come on, we've got a lot of work to do and not a whole lot of time to do it in." Bryan climbed into the vehicle and started it up. Brit finally grabbed his stuff and jumping into the vehicle with his brother, they headed back down the mountain.

Bryan knew that in order for his plan to succeed, their unspoken code of silence with the others would have to be broken. Cal would have to be made to understand and believe everything that had happened during their time on Argyle. Bryan also knew that he had to assemble every piece of information he had collected in the last couple of months, specifically, the last couple of weeks he was supposedly on vacation.

Meticulous planning

With the restoration of The Amanda as his back drop, Bryan had reassembled the same group that had started out on the first expedition, in the meeting room in the WACS hangar. This time, he would be the team leader. Nevertheless, he wasn't about to try and fool himself. He needed everyone in the room to understand what he had in mind. No one really knew what they had planned, except for Brit. Danny and Jerry had their suspicions and had dropped everything to come to the aide of their best friends, leaving their guide business to subs. Bill had nothing better to do and Cal had been itching to get all the details of what had happened. He was still a little irritated about being cut out of the loop, but after today, he would understand why.

After several hours of explanations of the events from everyone's perspectives, a lot of head and chin scratching on Cal's part, Bryan had everyone up to speed as to the details of what had happened during those four and a half days on the mountain. But neither Bryan nor Brit had voiced what they had in mind.

"Ok," Cal finally said, stepping to the glass window of the meeting room and looking out at the bomber under the bright hangar lights. "So what exactly do you have in mind here, Einstein? What's this all about?"

Bryan looked at the others. He had their full attention and he was ready for them. Turning to the wall plasma display, he brought up his tablet on the display.

"If you know all the pieces of the puzzle, the easier it is to put it all together. For the most part, we all understand the nature of the Rift as it travels the galaxy." A chart of the galaxy came up on the display. Cal really had no idea. The whole traveling to another planet idea still had his head spinning. He only knew that they went in to salvage an old World War II bomber, and there it was, sitting in the hangar being put back together. *So now what? Thanks for the explanation, now let's get on with life guys, we've got work to do.*

"Yes, but I've seen those computer generated videos of the nature of space and the planets and solar systems they contain," Brit said, looking at the multitude of light specs on the screen. "We all understand how insignificant we are in relationship to the size of the galaxy, not to mention the universe. Trying to find the Rift and knowing where it's going to be at any given time would be worse than looking for a preverbal needle in a hay stack." Bryan raised a finger in agreement.

"You are more right than you know big brother." He adjusted his screen and images changed, zooming in close on a cylindrical black spot in the star field. "Tell me what you see." Danny and Jerry got up for a closer look and Bryan stepped back so everyone could have a look see.

"This isn't-?" Jerry asked, gazing in disbelief at what he was seeing.

"Yes, it is." Bryan nodded slowly.

"But how could you possibly find it?" Brit asked, not believing it. Bryan changed the picture again. This time there were lines overlaid on the star field.

"Simple applied mathematics, a little luck and some really good friends at the Arecibo Radio Observatory in Puerto Rico and the Mauna Kea Telescope in Hawaii."

"Dude, you have friends?" Danny piped up, looking back at Bryan.

"Yes, I have lots of friends in strategic locations."

"No, I meant to ask, you have friends?' Danny grinned big. Just like old times.

"Ha, ha, ha, funny little man," Bryan said, taking the joke well.

"Seriously Bro, those places are hard to even get an appointment for a tour. How in the world did you get in to have a look at the skies?" Brit asked, studying the map carefully. He was really trying to follow his brother's logic to see the end result for making what they had in mind, a reality. No one wanted this to succeed more than him.

"Fa-rends," he enunciated loudly in Danny's direction, "in the right places. Look, you want the science? I'll give you the science, but the fact is, there it is, or was a couple of hours ago."

"You're tracking it?" Jerry asked, looking over his shoulder.

"Not in real time, but we were able to track it long enough to make good projections." There would be a little guess work here because they couldn't track the Rift directly, but they had enough information to make the proper calculations based on where it had been, it's arrival on the mountain and where it was now.

"So this thing travels the galaxy," Jerry stated, folding his arms, still looking at the map with Danny. "And we know it travels at least the speed of light, maybe faster according to Tim. What have you got in mind here? Are you trying to recreate the conditions or something, and why?"

Bryan was delighted with the question. It played right into the order of the discussion.

"What an intelligent lad," he chuckled delighted. "We know that the Rift can be manipulated by a number of things. Makes for placement forecasting a little bit of a challenge, but I think I've got that one covered too." Bryan touched a couple of buttons on his tablet and the picture changed to a video window. It was a recording of the approach of the storm into Lake Valley the day it arrived.

"We caught it all on video in high definition, popcorn anyone?" he asked, making the procedure sound common place. "Our instruments clocked this dude moving in on us at about 200 miles an hour. It was really cooking, obviously considerably slower than it moves through outer space. Of course when it reached The Amanda's location, it slowed and stopped."

"Yeah, but that's just it," Brit said, getting to his feet and pointing out the window into the hangar. "She ain't up there anymore, she's down here." Bryan held his hand up. Brit was getting ahead of his planned presentation.

"Patience my young apprentice, patience. We know it slows down as it passes through Earth's atmosphere, otherwise its speed would shear our atmosphere away or at the very least, create a pretty big ruckus that no one would be able to miss out on, and right now," Bryan touched his screen and the star chart appeared again. "Right now, the Rift is heading right here." Finishing his sentence, a circle appeared around a dim little spec among millions.

Brit stepped closer to the viewer, as did Danny and Jerry. Was this truly possible? On the other side of the galaxy, this tiny little dot. *Bryan had found Argyle!* Brit shot a glance over at Bryan, who nodded, smiling in his "know-it-all" face. Brit was completely fascinated with the ability to actually see it, to see Argyle. For a moment he almost felt like he had seen it before from this angle, only much closer. Every so often, he had shadows of information streak through the backside of his mind, but they were so dim and distant that he had difficulty holding them in place long enough to identify them. Brit's look of wonder changed to another question, turning back to his brother.

"Which way is the Rift traveling?" he asked, tracing the path back to what was indicated as Earth.

"Towards Argyle," Bryan responded quickly, hoping his brother was following a preconceived path of thinking.

"It's very close," Brit observed.

"Yes it is. It should pass by within a matter of days." Bryan waited for his brother to put two and two together. Jerry stepped back up, looking at the viewer.

"If the Rift goes by the same spot on Argyle, it does the same thing here."

"Wait, what?" Danny asked not following. Jerry remembered the operation of the doorway.

"Technically, the Rift exists in two places at once because of the space/time doorway. When it passes by the Valley of the Lakes on Argyle, its doorway passes by Lake Valley at the same time."

Bryan was really enjoying himself, watching and listening to his brother and friends figure things out. He touched a couple of controls on his pad, changing the graphic, and then pointed to the one closest to Earth.

"Here it is. It'll be here at the same time. There are two Rifts."

"Twins," Brit whispered, completely stunned by the revelation. Danny and Jerry exploded with astonishment.

"Holy Mother of Hanna!" Danny exclaimed excitedly, while Jerry examined the second Rift carefully.

"Tim didn't say anything about there being two Rifts," Jerry said, a little surprised himself.

"Neither did the Mynites," Danny responded with a look of wonder.

"Wait!" Brit yelled out to quiet everyone. He looked back over at Bryan. "How will we warn Catrina that the Rift is coming and how we're planning to bring her through?"

Cal instantly looked up when he heard the last part of that sentence, stepping back over to a chair and sitting down, remaining silent.

"Yeah, this doesn't give us much time at all," Jerry agreed.

Bryan shook his head and sat down in one of the chairs at the front, next to his calm and very quiet uncle Cal. He had been unusually quiet through all of this. While he was still trying to digest all the information about their adventures on Argyle, now he was racing to keep up with all this science and trying to figure out what they were planning to do next. Hard to wrap your head around such ambitious plans when you're still plain stunned that there was an Argyle in the first place.

"You overachievers," Bryan said, shaking his head. "First of all, you have to remember that we have to be patient here. I want to remind you all that we are dealing with cosmic forces that none of us even remotely understand and only one of us has ever seen before."

Everyone slowly turned to Britten, who nervously shook his head and sat down.

"Don't be looking at me. I can't remember a thing about all that stuff." It really wasn't important at this point, but it was still a bit amazing to think about the concept of what he must have observed when the download had occurred.

"Doesn't matter," Bryan said, getting back on track. "I have taken into account that there would be no time and really no possible way to try an extraction on this first pass. But there is time to get her a message letting her know all the whens, wheres and hows before the next pass." Uncle Cal finally spoke up; tired of being the casual observer. It was clear to him now that they planned to rescue Tony and Amanda's daughter.

"You're serious! That thing is moving across the mountain tops at 200 miles an hour. How do you expect to get her a message?"

"We're gonna toss it to her," Bryan responded confidently. Cal sat forward, looking at the display and slowly started to chuckle, that turned to a bit of a laugh. He was sure that his nephews were out of their minds, but he was going to let them lay out their plans and see how well they had thought this whole thing through.

"You're gonna walk right up to this thing and as it passes by, you'll hand off a letter or use a megaphone." The statement was a bit sarcastic, but expected. Bryan smiled as Brit turned to his uncle, remembering the device his brother had left up in Lake Valley.

"We're going to shoot it into Thulsa's gate," Brit spoke in a trance like tone as the pieces starting falling into place. Bryan continued with his confident grin as Brit explained. "He's set up a gas powered mortar launcher in Lake Valley, pointed at where the gate will appear. It will shoot a canister with instructions in it at the gate."

"How does it know when and where to shoot?" Jerry asked, sitting down next to Brit.

"He's set up a prox alarm on the west ridge tuned to the Rift's electromagnetic signature. When the eye passes by, it sends a signal to the cannon and it launches."

"But we couldn't use transmitters up there, remember?" Danny reminded them.

"We couldn't on our frequencies, but I've tuned the trigger to a lower sub frequency that will be strong enough to carry to the launch receiver." Bryan looked over at Brit. "She'll get the instructions." He leaned into his older brother and in a much lower tone gave him a reassuring nudge. "And a message from you." Bryan got back up, switched off the viewer and closed his tablet.

"And that concludes our lecture for today my loyal subjects. Please leave your generous donations in the jar at the door as you're leaving. Class dismissed."

"Hold the phone there whippersnapper," Bill piped up, after complete silence through the whole discussion. Everyone was starting to move in the direction of dispersment, but his old, yet commanding voice brought them back for a moment.

"And just what are her instructions? What is, "your plan"?" Bryan looked back at the old guide realizing that he had indeed forgotten a very important element of the whole operation. Bill continued.

"And I would like to point out that you said this thing slows down when it enters our atmosphere, but it's still moving at, what did you say, 200 miles per hour? I don't think I can run that fast, even on my best day."

"What about the Sky Cranes?" Jerry asked readily.

"Too slow aren't they?" Danny interjected. "What about a V-22 Osprey?"

"Yeah, I'm sure the Marines will be fine with loaning you one of those," Jerry came back quickly.

"We've kept the military out of this on purpose," Bryan said carefully. "If they were to catch wind of what this is all about, we'd have government people all over this like a chicken on a June Bug."

Bryan looked around the room as everything went silent. Everyone was looking at him for the answers. He sat back down and opened his tablet back up, scrolled through several pictures, then turned it around and set it on the table in front of Cal and Bill.

"There are a couple of A-stars on the field we could get a hold of," Cal said looking at the image. The A-star was a good choice, but Bryan was worried about the Rift's energy plasma and how to dissipate it from the aircraft going in.

"Know anyone that has one of these?" It was a picture of a Hughes MD 530F helicopter in flight, hovering next to a high tension, high voltage wire while an electrical technician in a special suit working on the insulators used to attach the wire to the tower. Cal looked at it for a moment and nodded.

"Yeah, got a friend with the power company that flies one, but that doesn't explain how you're gonna reach down and pluck up a person at 200 miles an hour, provided you can even get in there *AND* she's even there. The military has a system setup for rescues like that, but there ain't no way you're gonna be able to get one of their planes in there and you need considerable setup time." Bryan thought a moment, watching his brother step over to the hangar window and look out at The Amanda.

"We would have to find a way to slow it down even more, maybe even stop it," Bryan said quietly. "And we have to have that all worked out when the second Rift comes around again. I've got a couple of ideas kicking around but if anyone has anything brilliant, let me know so we can consider them."

* * * * *

As everyone began to disperse, Jerry and Danny stepped out into the hangar, looking back through the window at the Garrett brothers. They wanted to know if it was ok to have a closer look at The Amanda. Brit nodded and sat back down pulling something from his pocket, fumbling with it for a moment. He watched Bryan head upstairs while Cal stood frozen looking out into the hangar at The Amanda, Bill slowly shuffled out and back to his car.

There was silence in the room for several moments with only the sounds of work being done out in the hangar filtering through the glass window. Finally, Cal had a clear picture of what had happened for those four and a half days on the mountain and what his nephews now meant to do. This was risky business and dangerous for everyone, to say the least, but it appeared that his nephews and their friends thought it important enough to risk it. As principal CEO of

529

WACS, he could easily put the "kibosh" on their plans, but he knew if tried to stop it, they would just go around him and do it anyway. Finally, Brit's uncle spoke up, keeping his gaze out at the airplane.

"Is she worth it?" he asked, in a low, but firm tone.

Brit looked up from what he was doing and at the back of his uncle's head. He thought he was talking about the airplane out in the hangar, but they had discussed this a long time ago, in great detail. His uncle wasn't one to throw effort after foolishness, especially when it came to money. No, the tone and inflection in his voice was very different this time. At first Brit was a little angry that he would ask such a question and the tone he had used didn't sit well with him either. After what he and Bryan had gone through on Argyle, to ask that kind of a question? What part of this story did they miss telling him? Then he realized that his uncle was fishing for something greater than just the facts.

"Yes."

"Why? Why is she worth it?"

Wasn't it obvious? Cal had been witness to Britten's heart break in the ambulance after they had been rescued. They had recounted the scene on the ridge of Lake Valley. What more was there to say that would answer the question his uncle was asking? Cal twisted his upper body in his nephew's direction but remained where he stood.

"We've spent a great deal of money on this particular salvage, getting you guys in and out. You boys were nearly killed. Not to mention the people that died getting you back home, and now you want to go back and do it again? You want to fly an MD into that thing and pick up a girl? You want to put a pilot and his machine at risk, not to mention this girl? She's gonna take a huge risk stepping out into that thing to try and catch a ride back out. So nephew, you tell me why she's worth it and I'll go in there myself and get her."

Brit was a little shocked. His uncle Cal didn't like flying much anymore. Yes, he was a pilot and had a long illustrious career flying all kinds of helicopters and fixed winged aircraft, but the demands of being CEO of the business coupled with age, had started to slow him down. Brit looked down at the gadget he had pulled from his pocket. It was his old phone. He swiped through a couple of things and then pulled up his photos. There, in vivid HD color was the image of Catrina Dallas. He let himself sink into her eyes that looked back at him with a longing that spanned across the distance that separated them. He shifted his gaze out to the airplane in the hangar, noticing that Danny and Jerry had climbed up inside and were looking around. He looked back down at the image on his phone, then back up at his uncle.

"I can see only her and nothing else. I can't go anywhere or do anything without seeing her in my mind or seeing both of us together." Brit got out of his chair and stepped over to his uncle, handing him his phone. Cal turned it around and gazed at the image of Catrina Dallas looking back at him. She was certainly beautiful and he could see how anyone could get caught up in those eyes, but Cal was still waiting to hear something that would convince him.

"Without her," Brit stated, a little shaky now, "right now, I only exist, there's only a part of me here. I will do whatever it takes to bring her to me, or I'm going to go back to her. I love her, more than life itself."

Cal looked at the commitment and resolution in the face of his nephew. This is what he needed to see and hear. *'Bout time these boys stepped up and found someone to share their lives with. But why in the heck did he have to choose a girl that was on the other side of the galaxy? For heck sake!* He smiled slightly and handed the phone back to Britten, nodding once or twice and turning back to look at the big airplane in the hangar. Brit thought he detected a little bit of emotion in his uncles voice as he folded his arms across his chest again.

"Good enough," he said, his voice cracking slightly.

Brit looked back down at the picture of Catrina knowing that they still had some things to figure out, but he knew they were on the right track and his resolve was stronger than ever. He turned and started walking out of the briefing room, still looking at the picture of Cat.

"I'm coming for you," he whispered, barely audible.

*   *   *   *   *

A few days later Bryan returned to report that the launcher had gone off successfully and now they could only hope that their message was received. The canister had been fitted with a GPS tracker and it was nowhere to be found. He could only assume that it was now on Argyle. They had successfully tracked the Rift in and outbound and all their data showed that Bryan was right on with his calculations. In the following month, he made a couple more trips to Hawaii to confirm their tracking at Mauna Kea. After returning he closed himself up in his office at home and didn't emerge for a couple of days. When he did, he was as excited as he could be and couldn't wait to tell his brother and Cal. They sort of took a little of the wind out of his sail though.

"Ah, we sort of knew this already didn't we?" Brit said, helping one of the mechanics with some hydraulic lines in the main landing gear compartment of The Amanda. The next event would be in mid-March, exactly one year to the day the Rift had come through the first time.

"But this confirms it and narrows the time variable down to the minute it will arrive! Brit! This is it! We know where and when!" Bryan was thrilled with everything he had confirmed and while his brother shared his excitement, it was tempered with not having the last piece of the puzzle.

"Ok, so we're a couple of months away from that," Brit reminded his brother while wiping grease from his hands and checking a couple of things, their uncle coming through the outside door. "Have you tackled how you're going to slow it down so we can make the pickup?" Brit asked. The smile on Bryan's face instantly melted away as Cal stepped up to them and interrupted their conversation.

"Motors and props are sitting on a semi right outside boys. Shall we?" he gestured towards a forklift next to the big hangar bay doors. Everything else was pretty much finished on the old warbird. The Amanda sat nearly completed with only her newly rebuild radial engines and propellers to hang on empty motor mounts. It was mid-December now and Brit was not only getting anxious to get The Amanda finished, he was still racking his brain trying to figure out how they could slow the Rift down. He had watched his little brother pacing endlessly trying to figure it out, but as the days crawled by, he was becoming even more concerned that a solution could not be found. Time was running out.

Resurrection

Early January found the engines and propellers installed and ready for test trials. As the hangar doors were pulled open, The Amanda quietly slipped from her warm restoration home and into the crisp, cold air of the Idaho winter. With her engine cowlings removed she looked half naked, but it was a wise precaution as during testing, all engine fittings, connections and hoses would have to be properly inspected to make sure everything was as it should be. With auxiliary batteries connected and engine preheaters running, Britten climbed up into the B-25J and got ready to bring her back to life. The ground crew was busily engaged in pulling the propellers carefully through several revolutions to make sure there wasn't any oil cylinder lock occurring as Brit sat down in the pilot's seat and pulled the window open. Everyone had braved the cold for this occasion. Tony and Amanda Dallas had flown in from Helena. Danny and Jerry cleared their snow touring schedules so they could come and be with the Dallas family, lining up with Bryan and Cal to watch The Amanda's rebirth. Britten had tried to coax Tony into the cockpit to do the honors, she was after all, the plane he had gone to war and come home in. Nevertheless, Tony had emphatically refused, stating that this was Britten's honor alone and that it should be just him in there to enjoy it. The mechanics and ground crew gave the all clear signal as Brit read through the original pilot's operating hand book for startup procedures. Then came the time to actually energize her systems. He paused a moment before he flipped the master switches on, looking around inside. He felt like someone was inside the plane with him, but saw and heard no one.

"Time to wake up Amanda," he said, hitting the master switches. Gauges jumped and instruments responded to his every command. Sitting in the left seat, he looked out at the crew chief who gave him the thumbs up. Stepping through the start-up procedures on the left engine first, the starter began to whine and the big propeller started to turn. He counted six revolutions, turned on the mags and primed. A few cylinders instantly coughed, spinning the big blades faster and then several more came alive. Brit adjusted the throttle and mixture controls a little and the engine smoothed out and started running on its own. He let it run a little above idle for a minute, checking all the instruments for that engine and then throttled it back to idle. Repeating the procedure on the right engine, it responded in equal fashion. The blue white smoke billowing from behind each engine quickly disappeared, the radial motors warming up and running like the day they were new from the factory. After several minutes of running, the mechanics each had their turn inspecting the engines from behind and in other locations, getting only close enough to see what they were interested in. Once the all clear was given, Brit motioned with both hands in a circular fashion. The ground crew all nodded and Brit turned back to The Amanda's controls. He pressed down hard on the parking brake, took hold of the twin throttles and slowly pushed them forward. The powerful Wright Cyclone radial engines responded to his commands, steadily rising in pitch and volume. The Amanda felt like she could drag herself across the tarmac as the radial motors thundered at half throttle. Brit was gently jostled in his seat, the propeller blades slapping at the frigid morning air. His fingers tingled, holding the throttles at half and letting his vision glide over all the instruments, making sure everything was within their correct operating parameters. He made several checks of various systems that were operated at this engine speed, feeling a buzzing came to his head that was all too familiar to him. The longer he held The Amanda's engines at this RPM, the louder and more pronounced the buzzing became. A smile drifted across his face becoming broader the longer he held the throttles at half. He could feel her presence as strongly now as if she were sitting in the right seat. *This was such a thrill!* For him, there was nothing better than the feeling of the engines pulling on the airframe and the sense of the airplanes spirit coming back to life. He finally pulled the throttles smoothly back to idle. After a minute or two at idle, Brit went through the shutdown procedures.

Once the aircraft was quiet again and he had secured all the systems, he leaned back and closed his eyes. What an exhilarating feeling it was to actually be in the cockpit of this wonderful airplane, *especially this one*! He wished that Tony had been inside with him, but it was exciting all the same. Brit fiddled with the crystal still around his neck. He was thinking that he ought to return these.

He opened his eyes and prepared to disembark, but became aware that someone was sitting in the copilot's seat next to him. He turned and faced the radiant image of Amanda, in her yellow dress and sword belt, smiling back at him. Brit was a little startled at first, but then let the memories of their first meeting and subsequent encounters during his time on Argyle wash over him. She reached out and took his hand, cradling it in both hers. They were warm and soft, just like he remembered Catrina's.

"Thank you," Amanda whispered, reaching over and kissing him on the cheek. "I knew you could do it." A feeling of warmth surged through him as her lips touched his skin. There was a hint of what it was like to kiss Catrina. In that moment, he felt the intense ache of their separation and he pressed himself closer to Amanda, thinking that he would receive some kind of relief, but this was different. More of a feeling of what siblings might share one with another.

"Now bring Catrina home," she whispered.

At that moment, he could hear someone coming up the hatch towards the rear of the flight deck and turned to see Jerry poking his head up looking at him. When Brit turned back to Amanda, she was gone. A smile gently played across his face as he looked around at the inside of the airplane. She was still here and very much alive. Danny was quick to follow his friend up the ladder and into the airplane to congratulate Brit on the accomplishment of bringing the old airplane back to life.

"It was a group effort guys and if it wasn't for the Rift trying to retrieve its energy from her, it never would have been possible." Brit froze after he finished the sentence. Danny and Jerry watched him, wondering what had caught his attention. He ran a couple of things over in his head then gave them with one of those "Ah ha" expressions.

"I know how to slow the Rift down!" He exclaimed, scrambling out of the pilot's seat and past his friends to reach the lower hatch.

*   *   *   *   *

Tony was helping the ground crew push The Amanda back into the hangar for final inspections after the engine run up. Once her inspection panels and engine cowlings were reinstalled, she would be ready to undergo several hours of flight testing before she was considered airworthy. Helping to work the aircraft back into her parking spot in the hangar, Tony could hear a spirited discussion happening in the attached meeting room. Through the window, he could see Brit, Bryan and Cal talking, or arguing. The uncle didn't look very happy about what was being said. As Tony finished helping with the airplane, he stepped a little closer to the open door where Amanda met him.

"What's all the hubbub?" she whispered, as Tony tried to eavesdrop on the conversation inside. Tony shook his head as he hadn't been there long enough to know what the content was, but he continued to listen.

"I'm telling you that there's no way possible that I'm gonna let you fly that thing in there," Cal said, in a very commanding, adamant voice. "This company has invested way too many of its resources and money to put a plane like that in that kind of jeopardy. Find a different method."

"There is no other method," Brit retorted angrily. "It's the only way to slow the storm down enough to give the chopper pilot enough time to get in and out of there."

"We don't have an altar here on Earth to use to slow it down or stop it," Bryan pointed out, taking Britten's side on the matter. "If we do, it's hidden or lost."

"I'm sorry Brit," Cal spoke back up. "There's no way I'm going to let you fly that thing into the Rift. It just isn't going to happen. You want to take that airplane into hurricane force winds and known heavy icing conditions, on purpose, fly around inside the eye and expect to come back out in one piece? I think you're a great a pilot, I really do, but you just don't have the hours in a B-25 to raise my comfort level high enough to let that happen. I'm sorry, you just don't." Bryan went silent, thinking for a moment of what Cal had just said, while Brit continued to contend with his uncle.

"Come on, we've beefed up her deicing gear. It'll be a cinch. Fly in, put her in slow flight to really slow the Rift down and then fly back out when the MD clears the top. I can fly that thing blind folded!"

"I don't care if you can fly it with your bare toes," Cal came back. "Unless you know someone that has flown through something like that..."

"There's only one man alive I know of that has done that," Bryan said, stern faced. Brit and Cal turned to Bryan with a look of surprise. In their argumentative state, everyone had allowed their field of vision to narrow, not bothering to look beyond themselves, only at what they could do themselves.

"Who?" they both asked at the same time.

"That would be me," Tony announced, stepping through the door with Amanda right behind him. "What do you guys have in mind?"

Brit got one of those "Ah ha" looks again and Cal settled a bit, knowing what Tony's background was beyond just his service record in the Air Force. Any pilot who could bring his ship through a storm such as this thing could produce and then crash land it in such a way as to save everyone onboard certainly carried high marks. However, the fact that he had had to crash land didn't sit well with him. Now, if he had gone through it and was able to fly back out in one piece? Yeah, he'd be feeling a whole lot better about that. Trouble with that thinking was, if he had, they wouldn't be having this conversation right now.

Amanda followed Tony closely with a bit of a worried look. She wanted Tony to steer as far away from that thing as possible. Let the others take all the risks now. She didn't want to take a chance on losing her man to that thing again. However, the years had softened that tone a bit and the absence of her daughter pulled very hard on her heart strings. Here now was the chance they had been waiting for and it would come down to Tony having to once again, pilot The Amanda through that storm. Cal wasn't happy about the risk to both man and machine, but the looks he was getting from Brit, Tony and then Amanda, told him that he would have to live with the risk. If he had learned one thing from his nephews, it was that life was too short to sit cooped up in an office waiting for life to come to you. You had to take risks and get out and do things or what was the point? The business of life is to move forward and being scared of it wasn't going to give you any returns.

"All right," Cal relented. "Let's get this whole thing figured out right down to the last detail. I want to see it go off like clockwork and if I don't like something, I'm pulling the plug on it, understand?"

Brit and Bryan were kind of holding their breath until their uncle finally gave his ok; passing knuckle bumps and big grins. To Bryan, this was not only the best way he knew how to help his brother obtain that which was of the greatest importance to him, but also this would be one of the greatest personal triumphs of engineering for himself. Take a spacial entity and control it without the vast knowledge of the Ancients, now that's some genuine thinking right there. To Britten, the good old excitement of the great adventure was back, but also his number one focus since he had regained his memory.

Something important!

In the following weeks, the group met often to go over the details of the whole game plan. Cal had secured the use of a Hughes 500 and its pilot and to everyone's surprise, Cal demanded that he be the one to ride shotgun during the extraction. Tony and Brit would pilot The Amanda through the storm, slowing down to what would be considered slow flight, a condition where the aircraft is held in a nose up attitude, flaps extended and the power is pulled back to a lower setting. This would slow the airplane down to just above stall speed, any slower and the airplane would stop flying and start falling. This was an advanced maneuver taught to all student pilots, nearing completion of their training for a license. Doing it in a big World War II bomber was a little bit more of a challenge than a small civilian aircraft, but Tony had learned to do it in the service and with Brit's help, he felt confident that he could pull it off with no problem. They would approach in the opposite direction the Rift would be traveling, entering near the top of the rift, go into slow flight mode and circle until the chopper was clear, then pass out on the other side. There were a couple of unknowns that they would have to adjust for in real time. The Rift was likely to want to keep The Amanda in the center of its eye, causing the storm to wobble in a circular fashion. They would have to fly her in a tight circle to minimize that wobble. Then there was the problem of leaving. They would have to get back up to speed quickly and either fly out over the top or somehow break through the wall. The Rift was bound to be a little upset by the time they reached that point.

Listening to the discussions, a thought came to Amanda Dallas that no one here had considered. *How did the airplane itself feel about this mission?* Since she now had a tangible consciousness and a will to live, there had to be feelings there. They were essentially holding her out there as bait for this thing that had given her life. Was she prepared to put her life back on the line for the sake of this mission? As the meeting progressed, Amanda looked for a convenient opening to voice her concerns, but there seemed to be no good opportunity to do so. She finally got up, slipping silently out into the hangar bay towards the big war bird.

This was the first time that she had ever been totally alone with the airplane that had been through so much with her husband. She looked back at the window of the meeting room, then turned and made her way up the ladder, onto the flight deck. Not all the lights were on in the hangar as all the work on the airplane had been completed, but there was enough to illuminate the cockpit through the windshields and side windows. She carefully climbed into the copilot's seat and looked around. She had heard Britten and Bryan talking about how they were able to communicate with the airplane, but she had no idea how she would do it. It wasn't necessary for her to do anything special. The aircraft had sensed her approach and had hoped for an opportunity to actually meet and talk.

"I'm so glad that you have come," a voice said quietly from behind her. She turned to find a vision of herself as a young woman sitting in the engineer's chair. She recognized her yellow dress and sword belt situated around her waist. Amanda longed to have the figure and dark hair like that again, but the years had done their work and while they had had the aide of the Tera crystals for many years, age still finds a way to make things look overweight, grey and wrinkled.

"You won't mind if I call you Alice?" the younger version asked politely. Amanda could see the possibility of confusion here and agreed with the name choice. It was her middle name after all.

"You look amazing," Amanda Alice commented, admiring the younger woman. "Just as I remembered you….and I."

"It's all thanks to Britten and his friends. They have done so much for me. I can never repay them for risking everything for me." Amanda Alice hedged a bit, thoughts of what they were about to do flashing to the forefront of her mind. She opened her mouth to speak, but Amanda spoke first. She seemed to be so happy, perceiving her existence to be care-free now. The war was over for her and she had been rescued from the fury of the Rift. Her life back here on Earth was assured to be that of static displays, air shows and pleasure flights. Now she could focus on the safety of her passengers and the pleasures of carrying them, without having to worrying about her own welfare.

"Have Bryan and Britten found a way to rescue Catrina?" Amanda Alice looked at Amanda for a long moment and nodded.

"Yes," Amanda Alice said, almost hypnotically. "Their window of opportunity is the day after tomorrow."

Amanda gushed. She knew what Britten and Catrina had found together was the same thing that Tony and Amanda Alice shared. Something that was rare in the present day and age of Earth.

"They will make the attempt by slowing the Rift down as it passes through Lake Valley, flying a helicopter in and picking her up, then fly back out the top."

"Just like they rescued me!" Amanda was thrilled at the simplicity of the operation. "Helicopters are such wonderful machines and so versatile. They even have some now that can fly faster than I can. But heck, there are a lot of planes that can fly faster than me and carry a lot more." Amanda was starting to ramble, bubbling with the excitement of being in the world. Through her excitement, she noticed the somber look on Amanda Alice's face. Amanda stopped a moment, considering her own mood, giving Amanda Alice a long, hard look, trying to figure out what the problem was. She ran the information Amanda Alice had provided over again in her head.

"How do they plan to slow the Rift down?"

Amanda Alice opened her mouth to say something else, but stopped and looked out the side window of the airplane.

"The plan is to divert the Rift's attention from its course long enough to give Catrina a chance to get to the helicopter in the middle of the valley and then get out."

"What are they planning on using to slow the Rift down?" Amanda asked, becoming a bit more serious. She already knew the answer to the question.

"The only thing the Rift has ever shown any interest in," Amanda Alice replied, watching Britten and Bryan coming out of the office in their direction.

"They plan on flying me in to slow it down," Amanda said, her excited mood dropping away. She went from excited and happy, to scared and petrified in an instant.

"No, I can't go back there. I can't," she refused emphatically. There were sudden feelings of betrayal streaking through her being. About this time Britten started up the ladder into the flight deck, only to be met with the sounds of soft crying. He looked forward at Amanda, her face buried in her hands, then at Amanda Alice sitting turned in the copilot's seat. Brit looked back down at Bryan who was trying to follow him up, but the look on Brit's face told him to wait, something was wrong.

"Give me a couple of minutes. Have Danny and Jerry come up," he beckoned, as his brother backed down and slowly walked back to the office. "Amanda? What is it? What's wrong?" The young woman continued to weep softly and there seemed to be nothing that Brit could do to comfort her. He looked up at Amanda Alice for an explanation but she remained silent, looking out the window at nothing. Finally, as if hypnotized herself, she responded to his unspoken question.

"I told her that you were going to fly her back into the Rift."

Brit thought a moment. *OOPS!* It hadn't even occurred to any of them to ask The Amanda how she might feel about the possibility of sacrificing herself, again, to the fury of the Rift. The possibility of being destroyed in combat was one thing. The prospect of being held prisoner again or worse, reassimilated into the Rift was completely different. None of them were used to having to consider the feelings of a machine that had a living consciousness. This was a very big whoops, one that had to be handled delicately. They needed this airplane to perform at its absolute best. Amanda Alice was feeling kind of guilty about bringing it up as she watched Britten trying to console Amanda. Actually, she had done the whole team a great favor. Better to try and figure this all out right now, rather than when they are flying into bad weather and things start going wrong.

"Amanda," Brit said, taking her by the wrists and pulling her hands gently away from her face. "I should have told you about this when we discovered what had to be done. I was wrong and I'm sorry. Please, please listen to me," he pleaded, trying to get through to her. She tried to hold her emotion in check, but the mere thoughts of the Rift gave her cause for great fear.

"You promised," she sniffled, keeping her eyes down at the floor. "You promised that you would take me away from it and I would never be in harm's way again. You promised." Brit let her hands drop to the bench she was sitting on. He was a little lost as to what to say. She was certainly right. He had promised her early on that they would get her out and away from the fury of the Rift. Now, they were going to take her right back into it and it would start all over again. She just couldn't do it. It was too much to ask.

"Yes, I promised, but I also made a promise to Catrina. I promised that I would come for her and I need you to help me keep that promise. Without you, there's no way we can do it."

"I can't go back through, I just can't," she said, wiping the tears from her cheeks.

"You won't be alone Amanda," Brit fumbled. "You are stronger now than you ever were before. We have updated you and made your structure so much better. We've added some things to you that will help get you through it. I'm not going to let you go. I will be with you the entire way in and out. Do you hear me? We're not going in and leaving you in there. You're coming back out and this time, you're going to do it without the help of helicopters. You're flying out of there in one piece."

"We'll be right there with you too," Danny and Jerry said, poking their heads up the hatch.

"We're all going to be right here with you," Brit said, feeling her confidence coming back and the fear starting to slip away. "You needed us to save you. Now we need you to help save Catrina. I need your help to bring her home." Brit looked into her lovely, tear filled, brown eyes and smiled. She wiped her nose and nodded taking reassurance from everyone around her. She reached for Brit and hugged him.

"Promise you'll bring me back out?" She whispered from his shoulder.

Once again, Brit felt a twinge of what it was like to hold Catrina, but this was still different, but in a good way.

"I won't let you go, I promise," he said, holding her tight.

Danny and Jerry came back out from under the airplane and headed back to the office.

"Wait," Danny said, stopping his friend before they reached the door. "Where are we going to be?"

"You are such an idiot." Jerry rolled his eyes and stepped back into the conference room. He headed towards a seat but stopped, a flash back of their ride in the fuselage and the Rift's attack on The Amanda popped into his head. Tim and Stone had indicated that the Rift would stop at nothing to try and retrieve the energy it had lost to The Amanda. Indeed their escape had produced quite the violent encounter with the Rift as it shot plasma energy balls at the broken fuselage. All its energy coalescing into a giant hand of plasma energy bent on grabbing The Amanda's very consciousness and pulling her out of the plane, back into itself. The only thing that had stopped it from success was Brit and Danny hanging onto her while Jerry fired the turret guns. This had distracted the Rift long enough for his friends to pull her back in. He looked back at the airplane through the window. All of the guns had been removed from the aircraft and in their place, replicas. FAA and ATF had regulations against having operational firearms onboard experimental or "X" military aircraft. Jerry quickly turned to Bryan who was going over some of the details with Cal.

"We've forgotten something," he announced, seriously. This got their attention instantly. What detail had they missed? They had gone over this whole operation with a fine toothed comb!

"The guns!" Jerry blurted out. "We have to have the guns!" Bryan sat up while Cal scratched his head and rubbed his eyes.

"Mr. Gunn," Cal said, a little frustrated. "Pun intended." He knew they had covered everything and he could certainly see no need to have real guns onboard for this mission. "The replicas we have are just fine. Now please, I'm as tired as a cat nine miles from dirt."

"He's right!" Danny agreed, leaning down over the table. "We have to have the guns onboard. It's how we saved Amanda when they were hauling us out."

Bryan was deep in thought and started scrolling back through the incident log he had composed through all the interviews he had with everyone. He had been unconscious during the airlift out and could only go on what his brother and two friends had dictated to him.

"You tell me how shooting at the wind is going to help ensure the survival of that aircraft out there and I'll personally load them back in myself," Cal said, a bit angry. He was tired and more than ready to get on with this. He wasn't about to go against FAA regulations and run the chance of having them or ATF coming down on them. They were fortunate to still have the guns and ammo that was left in the aircraft when it was originally loaded up on the tour back in 1945. They were allowed to keep it because it was all part of the salvage; they just couldn't have it onboard the aircraft.

"It makes sense," Bryan mumbled, his eyes still glued to his notes.

"Hows that?" Cal asked, closing his eyes and leaning back.

"All the accounts indicate that the Rift was close to pulling Amanda's consciousness from the plane until Jerry started firing at the Rift wall. Jerry, you told me that there was no damage and yet the plasma energy followed the bullet strikes."

"Yes," Jerry agreed quickly. "I fired at the plasma hand that was reaching through the back of the fuselage, but it did nothing. It wasn't until I fired at the Rift wall that the energy bolts started to separate, following the ripples in the wall the strikes created."

"Brit and I fired the waist guns down as far as we could and that pulled more energy away, giving us time to get out," Danny informed him.

Cal could see he would eventually get overruled, even if he didn't believe what was being explained to him. It was easier to just believe it and go with it rather than ask for a dissertation on the science. It was whirling wind. How were bullets supposed to effect wind? Cal waved his hands over his head just so they could finish the last of the details.

"Doesn't matter, we'll load them up, but they come right back out as soon as that plane is back on the ground."

*　　*　　*　　*　　*

The following day was spent reloading the real machine guns back into their original positions and doing all the ground testing. Ammo belts were reloaded into the machine guns and made ready for test firing once they were airborne. Everyone worked tirelessly to make sure everything was ready. The Hughes MD530F pilot was thoroughly briefed on what to expect and what he might have to do if the Rift behaved the way it was predicted. Chances were, he might have to do a little hedge hoping just to stay ahead of the Rift as it followed The Amanda. Bryan would remain at the base command center he had setup in the hangar conference room and direct the whole operation via radio and online real time radar. He would have every app, program, and gadget imaginable, hooked up and running. He wanted to leave nothing to chance. Tomorrow was an even bigger day than the day they went into the Rift the first time.

As the day for the attempt dawned, everyone was up early to check everything one more time.

Brit was busy checking the brakes on the main landing gear of The Amanda as his brother stepped up behind him.

"Are you scared yet?" Bryan asked, watching Britten meticulously check every part of the wheel brakes. Brit passed his little brother a funny look and then continued with what he was doing.

"Scared? Nope, not scared. Why? Are you scared?" Bryan fidgeted a moment, trying to put how he was feeling into words.

543

"This isn't exact science here, so I try not to think about it," he finally said, watching his brother work his way up the main gear strut with his inspection. Brit let a chuckle pop out and gave Bryan a quick grin.

"I have to admit, I'm doing the same thing." Brit turned to his brother, looking at him with a curious expression. Bryan thought Brit was going to burst into tears at first. He could tell his brother was wrestling with something emotional. Brit stepped a little closer and put his hand on Bryan's shoulder, looking him squarely in the eye. Bryan had only seen this look once or twice before. Something heart felt was about to come out. Brit swallowed hard and shook his brother's shoulder gently.

"How is it every time I screw something up, you have to come along from behind and clean up the mess?"

"All part of my master plan to take over the galaxy," Bryan joked, putting his hand up on Brit's arm. His brother smiled a bit and looked over at one of the outer doorways as Tony and Amanda Dallas walked in, flanked by Danny and Jerry.

"Thanks for seeing this through," Brit said, still a little emotional, turning back to his inspections.

Have courage

Britten stepped quietly around The Amanda, performing his preflight inspections. Tony was doing the same preflight, only on opposite ends of the plane. There was nothing better than having two sets of eyes on the same thing to make sure everything was in its proper place and working the way it was supposed to. Finally, everyone loaded their gear into their places, the hangar doors were pulled back and an aircraft tug pulled the big bomber outside into the cold morning air. Once in position, the tug pulled away from the airplane and the ground crew took up positions all around the big aircraft. Britten looked back at the open hangar door where Bryan stood watching him as he was about to climb up into The Amanda. What a team they made. Was it possible that once again Britten had gotten everyone into this and now Bryan had to get everyone out of it? Seemed to be the way things went with these two. Brit watched Tony embracing Amanda Alice as Jerry pushed past him and up into the airplane. Cal appeared next to Bryan along with the Hughes helicopter pilot. They would time it to go about 30 minutes after The Amanda had gotten airborne. Amanda Alice followed Tony to the forward hatch and touched Britten on the shoulder before he made the ascent to the flight deck. She gave both her husband and Brit a careful look, then hugged them both, whispering between them.

"Be careful. Bring my baby home," she said, quickly turning before she became emotional and headed back to the hangar to join Bryan. Brit watched her go as Tony started up the ladder. He had made her a promise, some time ago when they had first met in Montana. Now, he meant to finish delivering on that promise.

"Right," he vocalized to himself, resolve heavy in his tone and ascended into the airplane. Once everyone was secure inside, the hatches were closed and startup procedures began. It wasn't long before the engines were rumbling loudly together and Brit was giving the ground crew the thumbs up. Tony sat in the left seat, pilot in command as he always had during those long days in the war. This was a feeling he never would, could or wanted to forget. The old plane felt as she always had and he quickly melted right back into being one with her.

He glanced out the window at a figure standing away from the plane in front of the hangar. Amanda stood tall and erect, with a brave chin, but a very worried expression. She had been here before, a very long time ago, watching him leave on his final tour. Yeah, that trip didn't end up very well. Tony smiled, blew Amanda a kiss and a reassuring wink. She let out a brave, but emotional laugh and waved to him, blowing a kiss back to her man in command of this wonderful machine. Tony finally turned back to the controls. Even though the pilot's handbook was forever etched into his mind, he still had Brit read through every pre take-off procedure. It was a rule he had never forgotten. Not once did he ever have a mishap from reading through every procedure line by line every time.

Finally it was go time, sitting at the end of the runway in position for take-off. Bryan gave the all clear over the radios and Brit gave Tony the thumbs up. Tony took hold of the throttles and gently pushed them forward. The Wright cyclone radials responded smoothly to the throttle commands, the big ship surging forward, rolling down the long runway. The propeller blades grabbed at the cold Basin air, the engine rpm continuing to climb until Tony had the throttle pushed all the way forward. Brit could feel The Amanda trying to lift into the morning air, but Tony held her down on her wheels until they reached the prescribed lift off speed. He relaxed his push on the yoke and the B-25 was suddenly airborne. The vibration from the wheels contacting the ground disappeared and Tony called for gear up. Britten reached for the control, feeling the hydraulics working while Tony established the proper climb rate. The old war bird lifted gracefully over the end of the runway reaching for altitude as it headed southwest out across the valley. Once the gear lights went out, indicating that they were flying clean, Brit went about checking the aircraft's systems while Tony made a couple of clearing turns and checked his aircraft's operational status. It didn't take them very long to reach the Big Holes mountain range on the west side of the Basin valley, where they flew south, still climbing. Turning over Victor and heading north again towards Driggs, they were heading for 14,000 feet. Somewhere over Driggs, they reached their intended altitude and leveled out, but went right to work in preparations for slow flight testing. It had been a considerable amount of time since Tony had performed this maneuver and he wanted to make sure he still knew how it was done. On this mission, on the job training wasn't the wisest of choices.

Tony slowed the airplane down to the prescribed speed, trimming it out so he had to work as little as possible to hold straight and level flight on the controls. Working carefully with resolution, he continued to pull the airplane back into a nose up position, pulling the throttles back at the same time. Brit added flaps as ordered by the veteran pilot and in no time at all, they were flying straight and level at a very slow speed, hovering just above the stall warning. Tony gently pushed the rudder pedal to the right and the airplane responded by sliding flatly to the right. He held the aircraft wings level staying right on top of the controls at all times. It was like he had never stopped flying. Once they had made their maneuver in a full circle, he pushed the left rudder pedal and they slowly turned in the other direction. Once he had completed the maneuver, he brought the aircraft back into normal flight configuration and ordered his copilot to replicate the maneuver.

Brit was a little apprehensive about this. Sure he had mastered this in his flight training and had even used the technique a time or two flying some search and rescue sorties in smaller aircraft, but he had never used it flying multi-engine aircraft and certainly didn't think it could be used on a World War II era bomber. When he tried it under Tony's direction, the aircraft responded much like any other aircraft he had flown. The exception here was instead of the slower 50-55 mph on a civil aircraft, he was dealing with speeds around 100-110 mph. Once he had duplicated the same maneuvers, he turned the controls back over to Tony. Bryan came on the radio and announced that Cal and the Hughes chopper had just departed and was on their way to the appointed way-point some distance from the Rift's trajectory. As time counted down, Tony made a couple of practice runs across Lake Valley running from north to south. The information Bryan had provided, based on what his instruments had been able to collect, indicated that the Rift would create a weather zone around it, between seven and ten miles. That would be a long time to fly through some wicked weather, but Brit was confident that the upgrades they had done to The Amanda's deicing system would be enough to keep them from becoming overcome by the ice that eventually brought her down the first time.

Acting as sort of an air traffic controller, Bryan directed the Hughes helicopter into position, the seconds ticking down. He was watching several displays from his vantage point in the hangar conference room. Amanda Alice sat nervously next to him trying to keep up with everything that was happening. This would take careful choreography to get everyone in the right place at the right time. As Bryan directed Tony to fly north for his setup run, Brit ordered Danny and Jerry to test fire their guns. Danny had taken up his position in the back of the plane and tested both waist positions first then crawled to the tail position and let out a short burst. This was his first time trying twin guns that were not directly controlled by hand. It was a fun experience and he sort of envied Jerry who got to be up in the top turret. He turned and looked forward after testing his guns. Over the bomb bay he could look up into the flight deck and see Jerry turning in his turret and hear his guns going off.

Once Jerry had fired a couple of short bursts from the top, he climbed down and crawled through the access tunnel to the front of the airplane where the navigator/bombardier sat. There were actually two guns here, a static straight forward mounted gun and another mounted in a ball and socket in the nose. He checked the movement of the front gun then let a couple of bursts go. He got a certain thrill out of hanging directly onto a bucking, chattering machine gun spewing lead. He almost envied Danny because he got to work the waist guns. Once he was finished up front, he crawled back through the aircraft to join Danny for the ride through the coming storm.

"I hope when my girlfriend needs rescuing that you guys will be willing to go to this much trouble," Danny said, shoving his headphones on and settling into his seat. Jerry smiled, working his seatbelt and pulling his mic boom a little closer to his mouth.

"Get a girlfriend first, then we'll talk about who needs to be rescued."

Danny gave his friend a double take and then grinned broadly. Brit and Tony looked at their watches at the same moment Bryan came on the radio.

"Time to rock and roll boys," he said, trying to remain calm and cool. He was sure that everyone in the air was nervous enough without him adding to it. Amanda certainly was and she was sitting right next to him. She was working on gnawing off the erasers of three pencils, had already broken two pens, and had lost the parts out of another by unscrewing it and letting the spring go flying across Bryan field of view. She finally put the pen parts down when Bryan gave her a good-natured, but exasperated look.

Tony checked his position in relation to where he thought he had last seen Lake Valley. He looked over at Britten who gave him a big sigh and a thumbs up.

"Let's do this," Brit said into his mic pickup.

Tony smiled and nodded, gently banked The Amanda to the right, holding a coordinated turn. They both watched the mountain range of the Tetons swing around through their view. Continuing through the turn, Brit looked to his right and up at the southern skyline. *There it was!* Coming in from the south, south/west! An angry black boiling cloud mass, moving fast as if born from a volcanic pyroclastic plume driven from a massive eruption. This was just as Brit had remembered it. Tony had never seen it coming directly, only the storm system associated with it, so this was a new experience for him. He was starting to wonder if they were going to have to blast through the cloud to reach the Rift, but just as he completed his turn, angry clouds materialized out of nowhere all around them, just as they had back in 1945. Completing the turn and heading south at the prescribed altitude, the air became choppy. Heavy turbulence buffeted The Amanda while they cut through the billowing storm clouds.

Brit checked their instruments and reported to Bryan what was happening. His brother coolly replied that they were still right on course and speed to intercept. Tony announced that things were going to get a whole lot worse from here on out and to just hang on. Moments later, they were slammed by massive sheets of rain and hail from every direction. The B-25 makes plenty of noise all on its own, without headphones the noise of the precipitation hitting the aircraft's nose and windshield was deafening. As Tony fought to hold their course, Brit noticed a figure appear just behind the pilot's seat. Amanda held tightly onto the backs of their chairs as lightning flashed all around them through pelting rain and hail. Brit passed her a quick glance. He could see controlled fear and a worried look in her eyes. He knew that she could hear him through his headset mic and tried to reassure her that it would be all right. She did not have as much fear for this part of the storm, even though it was the overwhelming ice that had brought her down the first time. She feared what lay at the center.

Tony had already called for carb heat and the deicing gear to be turned on right when the visible moisture appeared. Brit jammed his fingers a couple of times trying to set the controls, the turbulence was bouncing them about like a bobber in an angry sea. He had turned the defrosters and heaters up to full as the rain and hail turned to snow, the temperatures plummeting. Ice was already starting to build up on the engine cowlings and the windshields. Brit adjusted the radios and tried to focus on Bryan's voice as he directed them in. Static spit angrily through the transmission, obscuring his voice the further in they went. Despite feeling like they were being tossed everywhere except where they wanted to go, he sounded as though there was no trouble. Easy for him, he and Amanda were sitting safe and sound in the hangar at the airport. The aircraft crew was getting the crap kicked out of them in the air. Tony added a little more power trying to hold onto the indicated altitude and keep directional control. Not that he could see anything if the windshield wasn't iced up anyway. The clouds were almost completely black and the snow was a wall of solid flakes slamming the aircraft so hard it sounded like sand, but as they continued on, the noise got softer. Brit looked out at the leading edges of the wings and the engine cowls. There was heavy ice and snow building fast over every forward exposed surface. Brit gave Amanda and Tony a worried look. The deicing equipment was still working but the amount of ice buildup was completely overwhelming it. Tony announced that he was approaching full power now, trying to hold his altitude.

"This is worse than before," Amanda announced, holding onto Brit with one hand as heavy turbulence slammed the ship again.

In the back, Jerry and Danny were hanging on for dear life. Both held death grips on their seats and had cinched down their harnesses several times, almost to the point that it hurt just to sit still. Brit reported to Bryan that they were getting hammered by turbulence, ice was overwhelming the deicing system and the throttles were nearly at full power just to hold altitude. Heavy static spit in their ears as Bryan calmly, almost casually, came back telling them they were still on course and almost there. *Everything was going according to plan; just hold your course. Easy for him to say. He was probably sucking on a soda pop and munching caramel popcorn.*

Soldiering on, Brit noticed Amanda starting to slink further back behind the flight deck as if sensing something nearby. He looked back at the fear in her eyes. She was having difficulty holding her composure as they were tossed hard from side to side. Her eyes suddenly shifted to Brit.

"It's here," she whispered, terror etching at her voice. Brit turned back forward just in time for the aircraft to get slammed from the right, feeling it carrying them hard to the left. The light outside instantly turned grey, the snow slamming them from the right now. Tony fought to hold his course feeling his plane being driven madly to the left as if entering a swiftly moving current or whirlpool. The light continued to grow until suddenly they were punching out into the clear calm of the Rift's eye. Tony leveled the plane out and flew straight for a couple of moments, relieved that they were through. Brit glanced down at the radios. They had gone dead the moment they had punched through the Rift wall. So much for communications. Now they would have to rely solely on pre-planned choreography. The only way they could see, was to look out the side. Brit looked down at the valley below. He could see nothing from his angle. Tony couldn't see anything but the spinning wall of the Rift on his left, gently pushing on the right rudder pedal to steer away from the wall. The Amanda responded sluggishly, being weighed down by heavy snow and ice covering the leading edges and broad surfaces of the wings where lift was generated.

"I can't see jack crap back here!" Danny yelled into his intercom. "We're too high!"

"That's right where we want to be," Brit hollered back. Jerry had unbuckled from his seat in the back and had crawled forward over the bomb bay to energize the top turret drives.

"Wait for it," Brit exclaimed, knowing that it would be hard for anything to move right now because the plane was so thoroughly covered in ice. It was a wonder they were flying at all, indeed, once they had cleared the wall, they started losing altitude. As Tony guided the frozen bomber down along the Rift wall, he could see several fingers of energy starting to form and dance alongside them on the wall's surface.

"It senses me. It knows I'm here," Amanda said, starting to lose it. Brit turned to her, grabbing her hand.

"Pull yourself together missy, we're not going to let anything happen to you! You can do this Amanda; I know you can. Just hang in there."

Tony turned the sluggish aircraft along the south side of Lake Valley just as a white dragon fly shaped craft streaked right in front of them heading almost straight down.

"Holy pusbucket!" Brit yelled, getting the fright of his life. No one had noticed the Hughes helicopter coming and there were no communications with Bryan or the chopper pilot to let them in on what was happening. They had bigger worries right now as they fought to stay airborne. Even at full power and descending, Tony was having a tough time keeping the airplane flying. Several bolts of energy clapped across their path and behind their downward spiral. Brit strained to see out the side window, trying to follow the Hughes chopper all the way to the ground. At the speed and angle they were traveling, he could only imagine the panic and terror his uncle was going through. Military pilots used this maneuver often for strafing attacks. Enter the fire zone high to avoid ground fire, dive straight down on the target as hard and fast as possible, then pull back up and out as quickly as possible. Brit lost sight of the chopper's descent as they continued their circle. He glanced over at Tony who was struggling to maintain control of the aircraft. Slow flight maneuvers were simply out of the question now, having to hold as much speed as possible in order to keep from pancaking into a stall and just falling out of the sky. Something had to change quickly or they were going to be in the same situation he had been in back in 1945. There just wasn't enough heat outside to melt the ice off fast enough. The Amanda was losing altitude faster than Tony remembered the first time they had crashed, and they were carrying more weight back then. What none of them had counted on was the amount of ice they would encounter this time, causing them to lose altitude faster than anticipated.

Brit checked outside again noting only small amounts of ice coming lose and falling away, but at the rate they were dropping out of the air, it wasn't going to fall off fast enough for them to keep the airplane flying. He could see the lower edges of the swirling walls moving about like a wobbling top out of balance. The Rift was indeed trying to follow The Amanda just as Bryan had predicted it would. It seemed to be backing up as they flew south.   Energy flashes increased in front of them and some started streaking at them from across the opposite side of the swirling Rift walls. Pinnacle peak, on the east side of Lake Valley topped out at 9500 feet. They were sinking through 9000 feet, barely level with the west ridge of Lake Valley. A loud boom at the aircraft's mid-section that sounded like an explosion and Tony noticed a change in the airplanes flying characteristics. They were still losing altitude, only at a slower rate.

"We just took a direct hit at the waist position!" Danny came alive on the intercom. "I think I just wet myself. It blew off a bunch of ice! I thought it was going to take off the tail!"

Brit looked back at Amanda who was kneeling on the floor below Jerry with her hands covering her ears. She gazed back up at him in terror. The Rift sensed her presence and was trying to zero in on her, but it would have to go through the ice first. The ice! That's what had shielded her from the power of the Rift during her time on Argyle.

When they opened the cave and pulled her free, the Rift could see her. Now, here she was again, covered in ice! Brit looked up at Jerry who was still trying to get his turret to work. It was frozen fast all around the outer ring of its dome. He'd have to get out and chip it lose if he hoped to get it free again. Brit realized what had to happen, and unbuckling himself, climbed back to the engineer's position, grabbing Amanda by the hands and holding her close.

"Amanda, this is where we need you the most."

"No, it senses me! It has come for me!" Amanda refused, shaking her head in terror.

"It's just a spinning Rift that travels space," Brit gently squeezed her, trying to provide reassurance. *YEAH, just a spinning Rift! That's the understatement of the year!* "It has always come and it will always come, whether you are here or not, it will come. This is not your fault, it's no one's fault, but Amanda, we're going to crash again if you don't do something to help. You can beat this thing and be free of it forever, but you have to face it." Amanda gave Brit a puzzled look. What was he talking about? How much more could she do to help them now? She was iced up as she had been the first time. The Rift was here, it was searching for her and it was only a matter of moments before she was discovered.

"If you don't do something, we're gonna crash and you will be taken anyway. You are our only hope!" Brit watched her search herself for the strength to save them. She had no idea what he had in mind, but she realized that he was right. She could feel the sink rate of her airframe as they continued their unwilling descent.

"Brit, should we fire yet?" Jerry hollered from above.

"No! Wait for my signal!" He looked back at Amanda. "Amanda, I know you can do this!"

She thought back to when the Thulsa engineers had first opened the cave and she was exposed directly to the Storm. Britten and Catrina had come to give her comfort, but it was Sargon that had provided her a defense against the power of the Storm.

"If you are able to focus your attention elsewhere, it has very little power over you." She looked forward at Tony struggling with her controls, then back and Brit and nodded bravely.

"I think I know what to do," she finally responded, a little unsure.

Brit pulled her close, kissed her, and gave her a smile.

"I promise we'll protect you. Right now we need that thing to start throwing energy at us and lots of it."

Brit watched the expression on Amanda's face transform, looking out at the swirling Rift.

"Oh, it's going to be throwing energy all right. Just make sure you're ready to take advantage of it," she responded with firm resolve.

"I'm running out of room really fast here!" Tony called back. The throttles remained wide open and they were still dropping.

Amanda pulled free from Brit and stood up on the flight deck directly in front of the turret, looking at him as if saying goodbye.

"Remember me as I am," she stated pulling her sword, then rising straight up, right through the hull of the aircraft.

Outside, the Rift instantly went dark, almost black, energy strikes starting to pound the airplane as it circled. Brit quickly scrambled back into his seat and strapped back in, turning in his seat and looking up. Right behind the clear overhead hatch, he could see Amanda standing outside, directly in front of the top turret, with her sword drawn. Now she meant to face her demon head on, right here, right now.

"What am I doing?" Tony yelled, the ground drawing closer. Brit looked back up at Amanda, the energy bolts concentrating and striking out at the plane, many of them striking the aircraft, sending chunks of ice slinging off.

"Stay with it!"

"Into the ground?"

"Fly the plane!"

Tony adjusted the trim, the ship's behavior constantly changing. Brit finally got a good look out his right window. He could see the Hughes chopper hovering just above the ground in the middle of the valley. In the foreground he could see the long stone wall and the open doors of the gate, a figure running hard through the snow towards the waiting helicopter. Because the Rift walls were constantly moving to remain centered over The Amanda as she circled, the chopper pilot was a little concerned about setting down and getting stuck in the deep snow blanketing the valley floor. Brit couldn't get a good look at who it was at this distance. Only that they were wearing some kind of a white coat and brown pants. He only hoped that it was Cat; it had to be! Somehow, they had to keep the Rift centered over her as much as possible to buy her more time to reach the waiting helicopter. Danny was yelling at him in the com, wanting to start firing, the energy slivers merging, sending large angry plasma fingers streaking at The Amanda.

"If we can't get more lift, I'm only going to get one more pass," Tony informed Brit in a very worried voice, turning the bomber down the valley. Unless they could start climbing, their uphill turn would put them on the same level as the ground at the south end of the valley. The plasma bolts kept getting bigger and more frequent, but with every strike, the plane would fly differently. Tony noticed more control and a little more noise coming from the outside. At least the stall warning wasn't blaring in their ears anymore. Brit strained his neck trying to watch Cat running through the snow covered valley below as long as he could. Making their final turn up valley towards the south, he lost sight of her. Twisting the other direction, he glanced back up at Amanda who still stood on top of the fuselage, her arms stretched out as if inviting the Rift to come and get her, plasma fingers streaking at the low flying aircraft. Using her sword, she deflected the strikes, sending the bolts of energy blasting at the sheets of ice covering parts of the airplane. There was no need to hide anymore, so she used its energy to her advantage, enticing the Rift to come for her. It was a dangerous ploy, but she meant to protect her crew, even if it meant sacrificing herself, but Brit had something else in mind. He just hoped that there was enough time. The airframe shuddered, taking a plasma strike directly on the nose. The jolt shook the whole airplane, debris showering back from the front. Brit thought they were hitting the ground, but when he looked out to the side, he could see they were still moving, just above the snow covered surface. He looked forward, now able to see out the windshield. The strike had knocked a considerable amount of ice from the front end. He glanced over at the right wing just in time to see a huge piece of leading edge ice winging away. Tony struggled to hold the plane level as it tilted sharply to the left.

"I think this is it!" he yelled, watching the ground coming quickly up. A moment later another plasma strike hit the upper portion of the left engine nacelle, right behind the engine cowling. Tony and Brit shielded their eyes at the brilliant flash, energy fingering in every direction, away from the strike point and across the surface of the wing. A split second later, an entire sheet of ice lifted away from the wing and flew off. The plane instantly corrected its tilt, swaying back to the right. Brit looked right just as the right prop started spinning snow up, the wing tip licking the surface.

"I'd feel better if this was a runway and the wheels were down." Brit reached down and dropped in a notch of flaps as snow started pluming from the left side, the engines screaming and the props clawing at the air.

"Would it help if I got out and pushed?" Danny asked sarcastically from the rear. The ground looked so close that he could have just stepped out onto it. Jerry suddenly came alive again.

"My turret is free! The ice is gone up here!" Brit looked back out as another blast hit his side close to the wing root. As the strike dissipated, the ice that once covered the right nacelle was gone. This was like flying through flak, only they were so close to the ground that their propellers were skimming the snow covered surface. Tony had heard about B-17 pilots crossing the English Channel on one engine and getting so close to the water's surface that their propellers were kicking up water. He just wasn't sure which situation he would have chosen here. Just fly the plane! It still flies whether it's at 20,000 feet or two inches off the ground. He got his answer almost immediately. He glanced down at his vertical speed indicator. It was slowly rising, indicating a positive climb rate. Another strike on top near where Amanda was standing and the last of the heavy ice shattered, showering away from the aircraft as it arched triumphantly back into the air.

Brit strained to see behind them where the Hughes was still hovering. The Rift had been following them pretty close and he could see the north wall traveling up the valley towards the waiting helicopter, Catrina still struggling to reach it. They couldn't fly in an exact circle, so there would be only one more pass available to them before the Rift will have moved too far north. As The Amanda continued to climb, Brit turned and looked back, excepting to see Amanda drop back down inside the flight deck, but to his surprise, she was still standing on top of the fuselage with her arms still extended and sword in hand, plasma energy bolting at her from multiple directions. She held her sword out in front of her using it like a lightning rod of sorts. What was she doing? There was no need for her to be outside now. She should be back inside so they could protect her from the increasing strikes and the enlarging plasma fingers that reached out from the Rift walls at them. Amanda continually flung the energy blasts away, only to be set upon by several more, even bigger than before, some of them striking at her from behind. The moment a big finger of plasma would come at her, she would knock it away with her sword or deflect it back out into itself. In her mind, it was better for the Rift to be coming at her than blasting her airframe, putting its crew in greater peril.

Danny watched the last of the ice that had shrouded his tail gunner's dome slide away into the aircrafts slipstream. As it did so, several plasma fingers joined on the Rift walls and suddenly arched out towards the turning aircraft.

"IN-COMING!" he yelled, bracing himself for the impact. It was big and brilliant, streaking past the left twin tail section and striking right where Amanda was standing. The blast knocked her off the fuselage, sending her tumbling backwards over the top of Jerry's turret and towards the rear of the aircraft, her sword tumbling away in the slipstream. Amanda clawed at the smooth surface of the fuselage as she was pulled back towards the tail. A human would have been torn from this kind of a position and flung out into the open air, but Amanda was a part of the plane, her consciousness clung to the airframe, trying to hold onto life. She managed to stop herself on the right stabilizer section and hold on. Danny looked out his canopy at her, struggling to keep her grip. One more unprotected plasma blast from the Rift and it would grab her and take her back. There was only one thing he could do. He reached up and pulled the canopy emergency release, the plastic bubble instantly blowing away. He reached out and grabbed her by the waist, pulling as hard as he could. For a moment, he had a clear view of the ground, steadily dropping beneath them. He felt as though he was going to be sucked right out, the slipstream tearing at him, but with Amanda's help, he was able to pull her back inside. Breathing hard, he helped her forward to the waist gunner's position and sat her down.

"You sure know how to show a guy a good time, don't you?" Danny said, still breathing heavily.

"Where's Amanda?" Brit called out in a near panic.

"I've got her back here mid ship, Brit," Danny replied readily into the com system. "She's doing just fine. Can we get the heck out of here now?"

Amanda only closed her eyes and leaned back. She had thought the Rift had her on that last strike. Now she was tired of the fight to live as she was. She wished that she could go back to just having a love relationship with a flight crew, the way she had always been before this whole debacle happened, but these guys would not let her go. They wanted her to remain as she was now and had gone to great lengths, including putting their lives on the line, to see that she remained safe. She turned and looked out the right window as they continued to climb in a circle. Outside, on the ground, she could see Catrina reaching the open door of the hovering Hughes chopper. She could feel the power of her radial engines roaring at emergency full throttle trying to clear all the obstacles in the valley, but there was only so much they could do. Climbing out and maneuvering away would now take more than this airplane was designed to do. It was apparent now that there was more that she would have to give of herself, but she realized that there was only one way she could do it. She didn't have the strength to remain in her current form and still do what had to be done. If she was to exert what she had left to save them, she had to make a choice. Looking over at Danny she smiled, gently dropping her hands to the airframe, allowing them melt back into the aircraft, and then letting herself dematerialize.

* * * * *

"How we doing?" Tony asked circling back to the north.

"The Rift keeps sliding to the north. We'll be over Sheep Falls on the next pass and the south wall will have them. It's now or never!" Brit replied excitedly, scanning the ground for the Hughes. He could see the swirl marks it had left in the snow hovering close to the ground, but the helicopter was nowhere to be found.

"I can't see Cal! Has anyone got them?" There was silence on the coms for a couple of moments until Jerry started yelling in jubilation.

"To the left, right off your wing!" Tony instantly twisted in his seat to see out at what Jerry was looking at. Just off their wing and to the rear, the dragonfly shaped fuselage of the Hughes MD530F rose quickly into the turbulent air towards the top of the Rift.

Danny watched dozens of plasma fingers forming along the Rift wall as they continued to climb higher.

"Hey guys," he called out, watching the fingers converge, forming up even brighter and more powerful than ever. "I think we're in big trouble here!"

Jerry didn't have to spin his turret to see what was going on. Brit and Tony watched wide eyes, the Rift broiling darker, summoning everything it could to make a full on assault on The Amanda. The plasma fingers converged together forming great balls of intense energy slapping together and sent sailing out at them. Tony had hoped that they could just fly out over the top the way the Hughes was doing. They could still see it climbing for the hole at the top of the swirling Rift, occasionally being struck by energy bolts, but the special grounding rods that were mounted to the helicopter simply absorbed the electricity and it was dissipated harmlessly.

The B-25 Mitchell was pounded violently from every direct as the plasma balls exploded against The Amanda's hull. The noise was deafening and Jerry noticed ugly burn marks and peeling metal where the plasma balls struck.

"I don't know how many more of these things she can take." Tony stated, watching the balls coming at them. "I think I'd rather be flying through flak!"

"The plane is built to take it, but I don't think Amanda can take anymore," Brit yelled, shaking his head, taking note that they were flying north again along the wall. He glanced over at the altimeter, balls of plasma constantly streaming at them as they continued to climb. They were a long ways from climbing out the top and it was becoming clear that the Rift was about to summon everything it could to prevent the escape of The Amanda. A distraction was needed, right now.

"Jerry, can you see the Hughes?" he called back.

"It just cleared the top! They're out!"

"Ok guys, let's throw some lead" Brit ordered, climbing back to the flight deck and down under to the navigator's crawlway. Starting through the cramped crawl space towards the nose of the plane, he could hear Jerry guns popping. The plane was hailed violently by a gut pounding volley of plasma energy that shook the ship to its very frame. He thought he could hear Amanda's screams of agony over the noise as he scrambled to reach the bombardier position and the forward guns. They had not reloaded the cheek guns mounted on both side of the fuselage just under the pilot and copilots positions. There just hadn't been enough time. The airplane was slammed violently from side to side as more plasma balls streaked at them, hammering the side of the plane. Brit was only able to move a few inches before he was knocked about from all the plasma strikes being launched at them. Battered and bruised, he finally made it to the forward position, pulled back the bolt on the machine gun and took aim at the wall. He let his tracers go, making short striping bursts.

On top, Jerry varied his pattern while in the rear, Danny popped off short bursts as far away from the plane as possible. He watched the plasma fingers starting to break off, following the ripples made in the darkening walls.

"Jerry," Danny called up to him. "Turn to the opposite side and draw it off there." Jerry instantly swirled around and started popping off shots. It was working. The plasma balls vanished, the fingers dancing excitedly along the walls following the bullet strikes. Holding the firing triggers down on the twin fifties, they abruptly stopped. Panicked, he examined the loading magazines. EMPTY! They were running out of ammo! Danny left his tail position and started firing out the left waist. He didn't notice that Amanda was no longer sitting where he had left her. Outside, the Rift roared frustrated, compressing even faster, summoning everything it could channel to expend on the fight for The Amanda.

"We're not going to make it out with what ammo we have left," Jerry called out, expending the last of his rounds. Moments later, he came out of his turret, Britten crawling back up onto the flight deck and climbing back into the copilot's seat.

"See if Danny needs a hand," he said, strapping himself back in. Jerry was up and over the bomb bay in an instant.

"I need a plan of attack here," Tony commented, watching the fingers reforming, even more intense now.

Brit had a wild idea come to mind as they started their bank to the east, still climbing.

"Permission the take the controls?" he called out, grabbing the yoke. Tony instantly pulled his hands back, passing a glanced over at the intrepid young pilot. "Hang on!" Brit yelled into the headphone pickup, pushing hard left rudder and rolling in sharp aileron.

The Amanda instantly tilted hard on her left side, piercing through the Rift wall and out into the storm. They were immediately beset with blinding snow and a hail of lightning that lashed at them, twisting the airplane in every direction. Both men watched the artificial horizon tumble over as The Amanda rolled over on her back. The airspeed indicator started winding up higher indicating a massive speed buildup, the altimeter starting to wind downward. Brit could feel both engines starting to sputter knowing that carbureted engines don't run very well upside down. The vertical speed indicator pegged in the down position while Tony held on for dear life seeing that they were inverted and diving fast. He hoped his young copilot knew the terrain well, because they should be seeing ground just any moment. Brit pulled back on the throttles and yanked the yoke hard to the right then added a little rudder, the artificial horizon rolling back over. He twisted the wheel again, this time to the left, letting the craft continue to dive downwards. Tony glanced over at their altitude. They were below 9000 feet again, which meant they had ridges above their flight level somewhere, and they were still in the thick of the storm, heavy snow turning to pelting hail and sleet. Turbulence slamming them every which way, Brit held her in the dive for a few more seconds, trusting what the instruments were telling him. Out of the corner of his eye he noticed Sheep Falls flash by through the gloom and slowly eased the yoke back to try and level out. The sleet turned to rain and they could see with the occasional lightning flashes that the clouds were breaking up. Moments later, the ground appeared beneath them, still coming up at them. Brit started pulling back harder on the yoke, the other side of the Targhee Canyon looming ominously above their flight level, the nose still coming up with the ground and the airspeed dropping. The tree covered slope reached out at them, both pilots holding their breath, eyes wide open. Brit fully expected to hit something, they were that close! They could still see tree tops above them as the nose continued to pull up, their airspeed still falling off fast. Two very large, old pines on the canyon ridge now obstructed their flight path and that big old airplane wasn't going to fit between those old trees. There was no way to steer around them either! They needed power now!

"UHM, TREES!" Tony called out, bracing for impact.

"WORKING ON IT!" Brit called back, pushing the throttles all the way forward through the emergency full tabs. Amanda's engines thundered in response, her props clawing at the air. He pulled back hard on the yoke and twisted the wheel to the right, giving the G-meter a glance. The Amanda tilted hard up onto her right wing tip threading it between the two tree tops. Once the trees had passed behind them, he pushed forward, twisting the yoke. It felt like a roller coaster ride, their stomachs jumping to the roof. The horizon reappeared in front of them as Brit brought the wings horizontal again and the plane leveled out. Then they were over the Targhee ski resort just skimming along the tops of the trees, heading north. Both Britten and Tony were breathing hard, hearts pounding. Brit held a white knuckled grip on the yoke while Tony was holding onto the side of his seat and the visor edge of the instrument panel. Brit finally edged a look over at the older pilot, his eyes still wide.

"Your ship," he said in a shaky voice, indicating that he was ready to let Tony have control back. That was about the wildest ride, and he never wanted to experience it again for as long as he lived. He could only imagine what his friends had endured in the rear of the plane.

"My ship," Tony puffed wide eyed and breathless, finally dropping his hand to the yoke and letting his feet settled back on the rudder pedals. "You've got some balls."

He continued to let the bomber skim along the treetops under the over-cast. Brit pointed to a much darker area of the weather mass that appeared to be traveling faster than they were, accelerating away towards the upper atmosphere, rumbles of thunder and lightning flashes accompanying its departure. He pointed to his left at an opening between the clouds and the mountains as The Amanda glided smoothly down over the sloping mountainside, then Brit called back to his two friends.

"You boys still with us back there?" There was silence for a few moments and then the familiar voices of his two friends called back at him.

"We're in one piece if that's what you're asking? Like James Bond 007, shaken', not stirred." Jerry remarked quietly.

"Oh, and by the way," Danny said in just as somber a voice as his friend, "We are never speaking to you again!"

Brit smiled and leaned back. He looked out across the right wing; the deicers gently popped slushy wet ice lose and it whipped away in the passing air. Coming out from under the cloud cover and into the sunlight he recognized that they were flying out over Tetonia, several miles north of Driggs. He let his hands come to rest on the bare metal of the airplane as they gently banked to the west and slowly turned for home. Closing his eyes, he called to Amanda, concentrating hard to feel her, but there was nothing there. He called repeatedly, but only an odd silence came back to him. It was as though she was there, yet, not. Even when she had been upset, she would communicate with him, but now, only the rumble of the aircraft engines and the vibration of the old plane resonated through him.

"Danny, Jerry? Is Amanda back there with you guys?"

"No, we thought she was up there on the flight deck," they responded. Was it possible that the Rift had succeeded in taking her? Had she given everything she had to save them from crashing and was unable to fight off the power of the Rift? Brit pressed harder to the airframe and called to her in his mind. Finally, a whisper of sorts came back into his mind, accompanied by a warm feeling that filled him.

"I'm still with you," she finally responded distantly. "I'm very tired though. I need to rest." Her voice was somewhat ghostly and had a faraway tone that faded off into the drone of the engines. Brit picked up the pilot's handbook and started the pre landing procedures on approach to the Driggs airport. The plane was eerily quiet, everyone sitting quietly while Tony set the big B-25J gently down on its mains and then the nose wheel touched. As they taxied off the runway, Brit could see the Hughes helicopter flying in over the tops of the hangars, setting down next to the open WACs hangar doors. He reached down and pulled the cowl flaps lever and the winged radial doors around the engines instantly opened up, letting the excess heat out while Tony slowed the big bird to a stop next to the settling helicopter. He could see the door on the helicopter opening up and the occupants climbing out.

*   *   *   *   *

All her life, Amanda Alice had tried to hold her emotions in check. It just wasn't proper to show it in public and cause problems for the man that she supported. She had tried so hard to be strong for Tony when returning from the war on leave, otherwise it would make it all the more difficult for him. But this wasn't war; this was her daughter, so all that was tossed aside. She wasn't about to wait for rotor blades to slow down either. She ran to her daughter in a fit of tears as Cat stepped away from the Hughes on the far side.

As copilot, Brit tried to concentrate on helping Tony with the shutdown check list as the big engines sat rumbling at idle, but there was only one thing on his mind now. Tony made several calls for confirmed shut down of aircraft systems that went unanswered. He looked over at Brit who sat frozen, looking out at a vision of beauty that was just pulling away from her mother, turning to face the big idling airplane. Her boots still covered in snow, she wore a light white animal skin jacket with brown fabric pants wrapped in leather binding all the way up the leg and around the waist. She was as he remembered her, her face beaming with delight, seeing Brit looking back at her from the cockpit. A hand came up into Brit's line of vision and Tony leaned a grinning smile into his field of vision.

"Hello? Do you think I've never done this before? I think someone out there would like to have a word with you. Now get out there and show this old codger how it's done!"

Brit couldn't get his harness off fast enough. He kept getting caught and tangled up as he fumbled with it, then tripping several times trying to get out and to the lower hatch. Finally the hatch and ladder dropped open and he was sliding down it as fast as he could go without hurting himself. Tony cut the left engine and the big propeller blade ticked to a stop just in time for Britten to emerge from the bottom of the plane. This would be like something right out of a Hollywood movie as Tony watched Catrina and Britten run and meet between the two aircraft. She jumped into his arms, wrapping her legs around him as he twirled her around once holding onto her as if he couldn't get close enough. She passed a glance up at her father in the cockpit of The Amanda with a look of emotional relief that couldn't be contained. As Brit set her down, he buried his face against her neck and into her wonderful dark brown hair. He spread his fingers out across her back, letting her energy soak into him. The feel of her tears warm on his neck as she held onto him.

Catrina had thought it impossible for her to ever see him again. She had ached endlessly, watching and waiting for him to come for her. The time that had elapsed had been nearly unbearable. Now, here he was, here she was, holding each other close. Just the sensation of feeling his warmth pressed tight against her sent a tingle through her arms and back. She held him around the shoulders, letting her hands rest on the back of his head and neck. She felt so safe, so alive now that he was holding her. Brit pulled back so he could look into her eyes. He raised his hands to her face and let his fingers snake up into her wonderful silky hair, holding her gently, gazing into those wonderfully deep brown eyes. They completely captivated him, holding him focused. However, neither was content to just look into the other's eyes. Catrina tilted slightly in one direction while Britten followed suit in the other direction, pressing their lips together in a kiss that was even better than when he had proposed. Now it was unencumbered by the ominous realities of life or death in the arena. At this moment, it was just the reality of Britten and Catrina and nothing else but what they shared together.

As Tony watched them, it all looked strangely familiar, the scene having been played out before, an age ago, at a different airfield back in 1945. He watched them for a few moments, embracing endlessly. He could see his Amanda approaching them with a broad grin on her wet face. Bryan and Cal were right behind her while Danny and Jerry emerged from the back of the bomber. Tony completed the shutdown procedures and secured the aircraft. Finishing up some work on the flight deck, he thought he heard someone call his name. Ignoring it at first, he heard it again. It came from behind him in the cockpit. He slowly turned to see a young woman dressed in yellow sitting in the copilot's seat, smiling at him.

"Amanda?" he whispered, not believing his own senses. She smiled broadly at him and blew him a kiss.

"Thank you," she whispered and then faded from sight. Tony blinked a couple of times, wondering if what he had just seen was actually real or a byproduct of the wild ride out of the storm. He finally turned and dropped down the ladder to the ground and the bright cold sunlight. Moments later, he too was in the arms of his daughter and then his beloved wife, Amanda Alice. Brit and Catrina were again embracing. It seemed so surreal that they had succeeded and they were together, never to part again.

"Look, you have glasses now," she said through her tears, raising her hands to his cheeks and just touching the frames. Brit smiled, rolling his eyes a bit.

"Yeah, a present provided by the Twins. I'm afraid I'm stuck with them now. Just call me four eyes." Cat looked past them into his hazel eyes. She didn't care. Not in the least. She was almost shaking she was so excited and relieved to be in his arms.

"You came for me," Catrina glowed, kissing him and holding onto him, soaking into him. "Took you long enough," she giggled through a sniffle.

"Nag, nag, nag," he chuckled back at her, still holding her tight.

"I love you," she half laughed, half cried.

"I love you back," he replied, holding onto her with the same commitment.

"Hey you two love birds," Bryan said with folded arms. "Do I get any of this goo?"

"Ok," Brit said, pulling free from Catrina's arms to give his brother a hug and a slobbery kiss on his cheek.

"I meant from her," Bryan puffed, wiping off the slobber as his big brother squeezed him good.

"Here's the real brain child behind your rescue." Brit let him go and turned to Catrina. "We couldn't have done this without him."

She stepped over to Bryan, putting her arms around him and kissed him on the check.

"I can't thank you enough Bryan," she whispered, then leaned back into the encircling arms of Britten. Standing a few steps away from them, Cal was busy explaining to Danny and Jerry his wild ride down into the valley to pick Catrina up, while at the same time, the two young men were trying to outdo the older gentleman with their own death defying tales of the ride in the back of the B-25.

Finally, Tony stepped up to Britten and Catrina with an arm wrapped around his Amanda. He gave his little girl a loving smile as a tear of thankfulness ran down his check. He too was grateful and relieved that they were all here together now. He looked at Brit who was nearly attached to his daughter. A feeling of gratitude swelled within him for this young man who had made a promise to his wife to bring them home to her and he had done just that.

"We couldn't have done it without The Amanda," Brit said, everyone turning around and looking back at the proud war bird sitting majestically on the tarmac in front of them. So many adventures in this wonderful machine, a marvel of human engineering, borne from a world at war. Brit's happiness was a little tempered by thoughts of The Amanda. He hoped that she was all right. Somehow, he got the feeling that her spirit would always permeate the aircraft. He might never see her again, but to her, he would be eternally grateful.

As they all turned and headed for the open hangar doors, arm in arm, a figure dressed in yellow materialized in the pilot's seat looking out after them. Amanda smiled at the sacrifices that she had made for them and the promises and sacrifices they had kept and made on her behalf in order to preserve her being. Resting her chin on her hands in the open window, she looked out at the bright sunlight of the Teton Basin valley. What a wonderful day to be alive!

The End

Or is it?

Acknowledgments

It would be ungrateful of me if I didn't mention a couple of very key people who helped to make this a reality. Never mind that it was originally written over 30 years ago and sat in a box for most of that time. My two living sons, Kevin and David are to be thanked first, for showing interest in hearing the original read to them as teenagers. Special mention to my youngest son, David. It was his brilliant idea to have it typed up, from long hand and given to me for a Christmas present. You're totally awesome David! Honorable mention given to his two sisters, Cathy and Julie, for helping get it typed up. They stayed up pretty late Christmas Eve playing tag team to get it done. Then there are the reading editors. Derek Williams, Carman McKellar, Catlin Jeffs, Connie Barg, Tina Gardener Skaggs, and Katie Dalling. They were the ones that read through the first drafts and made many suggestions for logical flow and helped in straightening things out that didn't make much sense. They were also sounding boards for how well the plot was being executed. To Brian Davidson, for his critical editing on this project without even knowing what it was really about before he ever laid eyes on it, what a great friend to volunteer to do something as tough as editing, thank you! To Kathryn Stone for doing the cover Titling. Thanks, you're awesome! To Anina Laird Swallow, thank you so much for your patience and your talents as an artist. This cover was tough, but you stayed with it and how wonderful it does look. You are amazing and I know that your career as an artist will be a great one.

Finally, I am truly grateful to the one who has given me the most support through this entire endeavor, my wife Lola Hazel. She was the constant sounding board as I went through this journey, listening to my rants and frustrations with trying to make a scene work. Thank you Lola for doing the main editing, making Brian's job infinitely easier. Alone, I could not have woven the feelings into these characters, whom I love so much. Without Lola, it would have been impossible to know what it would have felt like to feel pain and happiness in a relationship that I could transpose into the characters. Because of Lola, they are alive and waiting for everyone to join them again and again in their adventures.

Robert James Schultz

Robert is a graduate of Ricks College, now called BYU-Idaho. He currently works for BYU-Idaho AV Productions as the Chief Video Engineer. Robert holds a private pilot's certificate and works on light general and experimental aircraft avionics at the Rexburg Airport in his spare time. Water sports and riding motorcycles on road trips with his brothers are just some of his many interests. He loves participating in Triathlons and is a 2013 Ironman. Robert has loved writing stories since his early teens, most dealing with the science fiction genre. Married to Lola Hazel VanLeishout in 1983, they are the parents of five children and reside in Sugar City, Idaho.